SPRING-HEELED JACK

THE TERROR OF LONDON
(1886)
BOOK I

The Spring-Heeled Jack Library: Volume 2

EDITED WITH A NEW INTRODUCTION BY

J.S. Mackley

The Spring-Heeled Jack Library

Spring Heel'd Jack: The Terror of London (1863)*

Spring Heeled Jack: The Terror of London (2 vols.) (1886)

Spring-Heeled Jack: Articles and Short fiction (1838–1897)
The Resident of Peckham letter (1838)
The Spring Jack (1838)
Springheel Jack: The Terror of London (The Origin Story) (1878)
From *Chums* by Harleigh Severne (1878)
Spring-Heeled Jack, from *All the Year Round* (9 August 1884)
Spring Heel Jack, *or* the Masked Mystery of the Tower (1885)
Spring-Heeled Jack (The Dialect Story) (1888)
The Mystery of Spring Heel Jack, *or* The Haunted Grange (1897)

Spring-Heeled Jack: The Human Bat
The Human Bat (1899–1901)
The Black Phantom (1901)

Dandy Dick, *or* The King's Highway**
Dandy Dick (1900)
Dandy Dick's Double (1900-1901)

Spring-Heeled Jack: Man or Fiend (1904)*

The Winged Man; *or* 'Twixt Midnight and Dawn (1913)***

* Complete for the first time
** A story featuring Spring-Heeled Jack as an ancillary character
*** A story influenced by The Human Bat series

Introduction Copyright © 2020 J.S. Mackley

First published in Great Britain in 2020

New Edition 2024 Published by Isengrin Publishing

ISBN: 978-1-917130-01-1

www.jonmackley.com

For Richard Canning

INTRODUCTION

This is the second volume of the Spring-Heeled Jack Library. This volume has itself been split into two books for this collection of Spring-Heeled Jack stories owing to its considerable length. The first volume contained the first "Penny Dreadful" serial featuring Spring-Heeled Jack published in 1863. This second serial was published in 48 weekly issues in 1886 and then reprinted in 1889. The story is completely independent of the 1863 story.

The historical basis for all the Spring-Heeled Jack stories goes back to 1838. In that year concerns were raised to the Lord Mayor of London about the appearances of an urban ghost who had terrified residents in the villages around London. The name of Spring-Heeled Jack was soon attached to these incidents, and while some publications likened the attacks to the wild antics of Henry de la Poer Beresford, the third Marquis of Waterford, there was no evidence to link him directly to the "pranks". In February of that year, there were violent assaults on two women, Jane Alsop and Lucy Scales. These attacks were investigated by the police and there were similarities in both cases: a masked or helmeted individual with the ability to spurt blue flame, who assaulted the women by tearing out their hair or ripping their clothes with what appeared to be claws. No one was ever convicted of these attacks, and fear spread through the country as others imitated Jack's behaviour. It was claimed that people were afraid to venture out after dark for fear of encountering Spring-Heeled Jack. He took on the mantle of an urban myth, the "bogeyman", although this was not just a story told to terrify children: the adults were frightened as well.

Perhaps as a foil to the terror created by the reports circulated about Jack and his imitators, he became the subject of numerous plays that maintained his notorious popularity. Then, in 1863, twenty-five years after the original sightings, while still holding the epithet of "The Terror of London" his character became that of a folk hero through the "Penny Dreadful" serial. Although he continued his mischievous antics in this story, he also became a defender of the vulnerable and punisher of the wicked. The popularity of this serial saw its republication in 1867.

In the decades that followed, more plays were performed around the country. On the other hand, parallels were seen between criminal activities and Jack's antics, and the perpetrators were sometimes labelled as "a Spring-Heeled Jack". Furthermore, sightings of "ghosts" were often attributed to him, not just in London but all round the country. Most notably, in 1877 and 1878, assaults were attributed to Jack: at the barracks in Aldershot in Hampshire, and Colchester in Essex, as well as a report in 1877 of a leaping man seen at the Roman Newport Arch in Lincoln. There was also a short serial published in 1878.[1]

In this present story, Jack's character differs greatly from the other serials, but despite his notoriety, through the serial stories, the plays and his mentions in society more generally, it is remarkable that he remained so prominent in the public consciousness.

Spring-Heeled Jack in the 1860s and 1870s

The Theatre

Following the publication of the first serial in 1863, a series of plays featuring Jack were produced taking advantage of the popularity of the novel: "Spring-heeled Jack, or The Mysteries of the Old Red Grange" was performed at the Royal Adelphi Theatre. Scripts of the plays no longer survive and while a review, published in *Aris's Birmingham Gazette* (27 February 1864), provides a summary of the play, it unfortunately does not explain how Jack features in it. Likewise, a play entitled "Spring-Heeled Jack" was performed in the Theatre in Northampton in 1865 (*Northampton Mercury*, 28 October 1865).

Of more interest is that in 1868, shortly after the first serial had been reprinted, there were a few plays featuring Spring-Heeled Jack being performed both in and outside London. These include a play by W. Travers, which was performed in the Mercury Theatre in London, described as being "with extraordinary mechanical and special effects" (*Marylebone Mercury*, 23 May 1868) and one entitled "The Terror of

---

[1] This is included in the third volume of this library.

London, or £500 reward for Spring-heeled Jack" which was performed at the Royal Colosseum in Liverpool (*Liverpool Daily Post* 21 November 1868). Most noteworthy is a play performed at the Britannia Theatre entitled "The Terror of London". This play features the characters from the 1863 serial although the reviewer describes it as having "no plot in particular" and instead it focuses on the exploits of Spring-heeled Jack (*North London News and Finsbury Gazette*, 5 September 1868).

Criminal Activities and Ghostly Sightings

Away from the theatres, Spring-Heeled Jack's name was often attached to criminal behaviour as well as antics to scare women and children. Examples come from all around the country: in 1869, the *Newcastle Courant* reported on the "Capture of a 'Spring-Heel Jack' at Sunderland". The article explains that a 22-year old man named George Gorman was brought before the magistrates charged with "burglariously" entering houses in Monkwearmouth, "in a mysterious manner and making his exit so rapidly as to earn for himself the soubriquet of 'spring-heel Jack'." Gorman's *modus operandi* was to break into a house and then make his way to women's bedrooms to take "indecent liberties", often being found with his hands under the bedclothes. He then fled the scene when the women (or their husbands) awoke. When he was finally caught, his defence, that he *had* been at the house, but had been so drunk he hadn't known *where* he was, was not accepted by the courts and the bench committed him to take his trial at the next assizes (5 November 1869). When brought to trial, his defence had been that he had not intended to commit burglary, but had thought "it was the house in which his sweetheart lived". He had not stolen anything, but was convicted *only* of burglary: there is no mention of indecent assault when he was sentenced to six months' hard labour (*Newcastle Journal* and *Shields Daily Gazette*, 14 December 1869).

The epithet was also given to a "dangerous lunatic" from Wolverhampton named Richard Higgin who demanded food from several small shopkeepers, and fled "on the wings of heels that outstrip all chasing" at the arrival of the police. Higgin was rumoured to have "a capability to climb houses by the aid of the water-spout only, added to Herculean strength and savage ferocity". The report concludes that he "created as much alarm in Blakenhall as 'Spring-heeled Jack' once did in London" (*Birmingham Daily Gazette*, 7 September 1870).

A medical student in Preston named Whitehead was assaulted by a man with a "swarthy complexion … with 'large black whiskers close cropped or recently shaved'", wearing a cloth cap and dark clothing, who rushed at him shouting "at last we have met". The assailant then attempted to stab Whitehead in the heart with a large knife. The report concludes that "it is a little too terrifying to find that … Spring-heeled Jack is in our midst again, and at his old tricks" (*The Morning Advertiser*, 7 October 1871).

In Scotland, the *North Briton* newspaper claims "we were perfectly inundated with stories, more or less authentic" when making enquiries about Spring-Heeled Jack, listing locations in the villages surrounding Edinburgh including Fountainhead, Dalkeith and Leith where "his antics have had an alarming effect on the mind of the rustic inhabitants", resulting in vigilante groups seeking "revenge for sisters and sweethearts frightened" (10 February 1872). A witness describes the "ghost" as "a very tall figure, draped from head to foot in white—the face clear as if covered with a phosphorescent substance, but the features undistinguishable". Rather than accepting that this was a ghostly visitation, *The Southern Reporter* more pragmatically suggests that it was "a man who has springs in his boots" carrying a length of white material as an overall to which a head was attached, which created the illusion of "a phantom of ten or twelve feet" (15 February 1872). Rumours that this individual "bounded over a canal in a single leap, and thinks nothing of vaulting over a cab or pretty high wall" are exaggerated, although police went to great efforts to apprehend him (*Glasgow Herald*, 5 February 1872).

Not all reports were so fanciful. The name of Spring-Heeled Jack was adopted by local gangs as they imitated Jack's antics. In her journal, Beatrix Potter, the well-known children's author, notes that in Manchester, over a period of two months "a gang of young men calling themselves Spring-heeled Jacks have been going about in the dusk and frightening people. They wore India-rubber dresses which would puff up at will to a great size, horns, a lantern and springs in their boots" (1 March 1877). Clearly, these men were trading on the notion that the name of Spring-Heeled Jack carried with it a legacy of fear.

The Aldershot Ghost (1877)

In the same month as Potter's journal entry came the first report of the sightings at Aldershot Barracks. Initially this was consigned to a small article, almost hidden in the corner of page 4 of *Sheldrake's Aldershot and Hampshire Military Gazette*, under the heading of "Questionable 'Larks'" (17 March 1877). This, and further encounters, were also reported six weeks later in *The Times* (28 April 1877). The reporter from the *Gazette* makes it clear "we do not vouch for the correctness of the story". The two newspaper articles detail how around midnight on 9 March, the sentry was a private in the 19th Regiment who was on duty in the North Camp. He challenged an unknown intruder who, later in the article, was termed Spring-heeled Jack. According to the *Gazette*, the intruder started "dodging around the sentry box in a fantastic fashion" before running off with astonishing swiftness, while *The Times* claims that the assailant, the "would-be ghost … slapped the sentry in the face". The sentry loaded his rifle and fired at the apparition, although to no avail. The intruder then appeared to a private from the 100th Regiment on guard by a powder magazine near the Military Cemetery who also fired without hitting his target. While admitting the identity of the culprit is unknown, the *Gazette* reporter concludes "such little bits of fun might be carried too far; and enjoyments of this kind had better be discontinued before one of the nocturnal pranks leads to unpleasant results".

A second sighting was reported in the *Gazette* by a correspondent writing to the Editor who names himself as "the 'COVE'". (The North Camp was situated near Cove Common.) This report is written in response to "a spicy little paragraph" in *The World* newspaper (reprinted in the *Illustrated Police News*, 28 April 1877). When the *Illustrated Police News* republished the article, it was accompanied by a picture on the first page.[2]

---

[2] The *Illustrated Police News* was a tabloid-style newspaper that had a front page of illustrations, followed by three pages of articles. The readers of the *Pall Mall Gazette* gave it the dubious accolade of voting it the "worst newspaper in England". In an interview with the editor, George Purkess, the reporter from the *Gazette* referred to it as a "sensationalist newspaper", and the illustrations contained "vivid representations of tragedies and horrors of all kinds, while the content of the articles were "descriptive of the leading murders, suicides, offences, and casualties of the week". Purkess claimed that the illustrations were not imaginative but that the newspaper was "constantly striving after accuracy of delineation" ensured a weekly circulation of up to 600,000

The article in *The World* includes some sensational details noting that there are "two spectral-looking figures … glowing with phosphorous" who "suddenly manifest themselves, making tremendous springs of ten or twelve yards at a time". These accounts parallel the attacks on the assaults on Jane Alsop and Lucy Scales in 1838. The correspondent takes a political stance using the article to suggest that the visitants might be "the ghosts of officers who have died in the service since the abolition of purchase," that is, the ability to purchase officer commissions in the British Army without the necessity of being promoted, a practise which was abolished in 1871. It continues to protest that these ghosts "take these means of manifesting their displeasure at the confiscation by Government of their commission-money". However, the *Gazette* concludes on a more serious note that "this affair is getting altogether beyond a joke, and it is sincerely to be hoped that his ghostship will soon be convinced of the error of his ways, by being captured."

The Times (28 April 1877) provides more realistic additional details: the private from the 3rd Battalion 60th rifles was on guard near a powder magazine near the Basingstoke canal, when he was attacked from behind and his assailant attempted to take away his rifle. In the ensuing struggle

---

copies (*Pall Mall Gazette*, 23 November 1886). In addition to this story, the *IPN* published a second report on the Aldershot ghost and Jack's later appearance leaping on Newport Arch; all three stories were accompanied with illustrations.).

the soldier received "a pair of black eyes" and lost his shako (or military hat) which was later found in the canal. This report also discusses a further sighting a few days later when a sentry was discovered "in a state of horror-stricken alarm" at his post near the Female Hospital at the South Camp. When approached by a file of the guards, he pointed to a retreating figure of a tall man dressed in a tightly fitting white coat. The soldiers gave chase, but the "ghost" evaded them.

There was another sighting around the start of April reported in *The Times* article: at the hospital, a sentry was accosted by a man wearing a mask who claimed his intention was "to show the nation how easily he could frighten the soldiers of the present day". This was also covered in the *Gazette* (21 April) in a short paragraph concerning "Our Aldershot ghost" which also notes that the ghost's intention was to "frighten the British Army" and the reporter suggests that "his ghostship" might "postpone that laudable intention" and if instead he might "have a go at the Russians … he would do some good, and deserve the thanks of the Turks." This article was published just days before the start of the Russo-Turkish war (1877–1878) so military tensions were beginning to rise in Britain as the soldiers had had their medical inspections and were on official stand-by, expecting to engage in active service (*Aldershot Military Gazette*, 12 May 1877).

Also reported in *The Times* was a comment that around midnight towards the end of April, a tall man carrying a carpet bag entered the camp and, when challenged by some provosts, he claimed to be an officer (and, as the *Illustrated Police News* adds in an article published on 5 May 1877, "not smelling of sulphur), he passed unhindered. The reporter argues that it is unlikely that an officer would have returned to camp at that hour, nor would he have been carrying a carpet bag and concludes it is "not unreasonable to suppose that had the provosts followed the person in question the Aldershott [*sic*] ghost mystery would have been solved".

In May, the *Gazette* included a short paragraph observing that the Aldershot Ghost had not been seen for a while "and timid persons are beginning to venture out at dusk without an armed escort"; however, the story is still presented in supernatural terms, describing how "the dread apparition was beheld on … the hills on the top of the camp" and continues that "it is now probably doing penance" to purge "the deeds done in the days of flesh" (19 May 1877).

There was a lull in the reported appearances of the Aldershot Ghost until September when the *Illustrated Police News* published a second article (again accompanied by a cover illustration). The article notes that suspicion of who was perpetrating these attacks had been localised to one corps as encounters with the "ghost" had only occurred where that regiment had been based. However, by this time the regiment had left Aldershot, and yet the article describes how the ghost slapped the face of one of the sentries with a hand that was "arranged to feel as cold and clammy as that of a corpse" before "hopping and bounding into the mist" (8 September 1877) This story was not covered by the regular press and was only reported in the *Illustrated Police News*. Mike Dash comments that the principal suspects had already left the barracks before the end of August. He concludes "There seems to have been no first hand evidence and no new suspects, and no indication that the scare persisted into the autumn".

Colchester (1878)

After the 3rd Battalion 60th rifles left Aldershot, the garrison was stationed at Colchester. In October 1878, an article in *Truth* newspaper remarked that "The 'Aldershot Ghost' has become worse in his nightly pranks", although presumably this means that the epithet continued, even though the garrison was now at Colchester (republished in the *Hampshire Telegraph*, 12 October 1878). The *Chelmsford Chronicle* reports that "Spring-heel Jack" appeared to "lonely sentries on the Abbey Field at night" frightening them to the extent that "two are at present under treatment in the garrison hospital for shock to the nervous system" (1 November 1878). He attacked the sentries at places where they are most distant from others to the extent that four men faced a court-martial for deserting their posts and that the sentries were to be doubled. The article from the *Truth* concludes that there is a suspicion that the perpetrator of these attacks is not a soldier, but an officer! (*Hampshire Telegraph*, 12 October 1878).

Two days later, the *Globe* newspaper ran an article about the Aldershot Ghost, proclaiming "At last the military authorities have taken action against the uncanny wanderer". This information was taken from a memorandum issued from the Adjutant-General's Office declared that "the sentries are on no account to fire their rifles" as they may be charged with manslaughter" but instead they should "use their utmost efforts to capture any one interfering with them on their posts, and in self-defence may use their bayonets". Despite this warning, the *Globe* reports continued sightings of the "mischievous joker" and there were further reports that he "bounds over tall palings like a deer" (14 October 1878).

It appears that Jack's antics were not confined to the military compound, appearing to the landlady of a public house "arrayed in a wondrous leopard skin, from his mouth and nostrils he emitted phosphorous, while glaring eyes and wagging tail constituted a make-up that might well frighten the nervous" (*Uxbridge and West Drayton Gazette*, 9 November 1878). It is also suggested that he terrified a school master in Colchester (*Essex Standard*, 9 November 1878). On the other hand, a paragraph from *The Whitehall Review* notes another sighting of the "ghost", which resulted in the "spectre" being fired upon, was a white goat and stones thrown at the sentry were thrown by the "fair—no, foul—hands of sundry female camp followers who frequent the copses after dark". The commentator concludes "'Spring-heeled Jack,' I fear, comes in for a large share of vicarious blame" (republished in the *East Anglian Daily Times*, 25 October 1878).

The reappearance of Spring-Heeled Jack at Colchester was emphatically denied. The *Essex Standard* initially published a report asserting that "there appears to be not the slightest foundation to these stories" (9 November 1878). Even so, maintaining the old adage that "there is no smoke without fire", *The Bury and Norwich Post* collated three possible scenarios from other publications which led to the end of the Colchester ghost's appearances, noting that if the military were "pursuing this ignoble sport … [it] would deserve the most condign punishment" (24 December 1878) The first report came from *Vanity Fair* "that the sentry raised his rifle, fired at the ghost and shot him stone dead; after which it was discovered that the dead man was an officer of the regiment". The second article came from the *Evening Standard* where it is reported that the perpetrator of these assaults made a mistake and was injured by a bayonet wound to the leg. The last article, however, also from the *Evening Standard*, is a statement from Colonel W. Leigh Pemberton, commander of the 3rd Battalion, 60th Rifles, contradicting the previous article, and the *Evening Standard* was forced to reprint a retraction stating "the journal from which we quoted is entirely in error, as no officer in his battalion has been so wounded." In an article on the "Responsibilities of Journalism", the *Evening Standard*'s retraction was described as a "grudging apology", and the complaint made by Pemberton that the newspaper had published erroneous information was "'regretted', not because it was false, but because it was 'contradicted by such an excellent authority'" (*Colchester Gazette*, 8 January 1879).

Ultimately, it appears that the individual responsible for these attacks was identified, but these details were never made public. The *Dorset Chronicle* noted that the "delinquent", who was court-martialled, "turns out to be a subaltern officer, wearing the sombre trappings of one of the most distinguished of Her Majesty's regiments" (cited in the *Lloyds Weekly Newspaper*, 29 December 1878). A rather more charitable correspondent writing in the *Southern Times and Dorset County Herald* comments that "Mr 'Spring-heel' is undoubtedly a scoundrel—no gentleman—nevertheless I would give him a chance to retrieve his character—*humanum est errare*"[3] (21 December 1878).

The offender was never named. The *Buckingham Advertiser* describes the "exclusiveness of the 60th, who associate with no one [which] does not improve his chance of capture" (9 November 1878). It appears that once the military had found their perpetrator, they were keen that no additional details were revealed, and they dealt with the matter internally. However, in a submission to *Notes and Queries* in 1907, Alfred C.E. Welby, notes that "The pranks were popularly attributed to a lively officer of the Rifles; he certainly was not convicted by them, and I do not know that he acknowledged himself to be spring-heeled Jack" (10: vii 496).

The appearances of Spring-Heeled Jack at Aldershot and Colchester became the focus of an article over 75 years later in a 1954 edition of *Everybody's* magazine, in the "Have you a theory?" section, written by actor Valentine Dyall. In this feature, he suggested that the Aldershot Ghost "was no ordinary mortal [and] … a high proportion of those who saw him were convinced that he was not of this world, but either a spirit or a visitor from some distant planet", and that the audience should accept this supposition unless a natural theory can be found to take its place (20 February 1954, pp. 12–13, 38–39). This same hypothesis was also the conclusion drawn in a booklet by Roman Golicz entitled *Spring-heeled Jack: A Victorian Visitation at Aldershot*. The explanation is probably less imaginative.

Leaping on Newport Arch (1877)

In between the attacks on the sentries at Aldershot and Colchester, there was a further report that appeared only in the *Illustrated Police News* that Jack was seen leaping on to Newport Arch in Lincoln (3 November 1877). The front page of the publication contains an image depicting Spring-Heeled Jack jumping on the Roman Arch. An angry mob are gathered beneath him, some of them throwing stones, while two men fire guns at him. The account and the illustration have been sent in by "a correspondent".

---

[3] To err is human.

The correspondent details how "For some time past, the neighbourhood of Newport, near Lincoln, has been disturbed each evening by a man dressed in a sheep skin … with a long white tail to it. The man who is playing this mischief has springs to his boots, and can jump a height of 15 or 20 feet." He continues that the man leapt up on to a college roof and accessed a room through one of the windows, terrifying the female residents. A mob gathered arms with sticks and stones to try to catch him without success, and when the mysterious visitant leapt on Newport Arch, two men shot at him "but so tough is the hide he wears, that the shot did not penetrate it". He escaped by running along the rooftops and was later seen running along the wall of the barracks where he was shot at again, but once more, without effect. The correspondent ends his account by suggesting that this event is one "which we think worthy of a picture in the POLICE NEWS".

This report is noteworthy for several reasons. Jack is not mentioned by the original correspondent: it is the editors who have supplied the headline and the pictorial description "Spring-Heeled Jack Jumping on Newport Arch". Even if the correspondent did not have Spring-Heeled Jack in mind when he submitted the article, the description of Jack "dressed in a sheep skin" is reminiscent of the very early sightings of Jack that were reported in

January 1838 where "the ghost" as he was then dubbed, appeared dressed as a large white bull, a bear and a baboon and had the ability to leap walls. However, as with the *Illustrated Police News*'s second article on the Aldershot Ghost, the incident at Newport Arch was uniquely reported in this publication. No other newspapers make a mention of it, nor of the "other tricks" that the correspondent claims Jack has performed without providing any other details. It can be inferred from this that the account written was suitably sensational to appeal to the *Illustrated Police News* but was not taken seriously enough by the authorities to warrant any further investigation. The editors may have connected the similarities of the Newport Arch incident with the antics of the Aldershot Ghost, most notably the reports of jumping great distances and being unharmed when he is shot at. The parallels in the details here are not coincidental, however, given the popular and sensationalist natures of these publications, it ensured that Jack continued to capture the public's imagination.

Newport Arch today

The 1886 Serial Novel

Eight years after the final appearance of the Colchester "ghost", Spring-Heeled Jack was once more projected into the public spotlight, this time through the publication of this lengthy serial novel, the longest of the Spring-Heeled Jack stories, originally published in 48 issues, and running to 578 pages. Each issue comprises 12 pages, the first of which is a cover illustration and the second is left blank. The text—around 10,000 words per issue—is then tightly printed in two columns.

COMPLETE IN FOUR VOLUMES.
PRICE 1s. EACH.
SPRING-HEELED JACK,
The Terror of London.
The history of this remarkable being has been specially compiled, for this work only, by one of the best authors of the day, and readers will find that he has undoubtedly succeeded in producing a wonderful and sensational story, every page of which is replete with details of absorbing and thrilling interest.

Advertisement in the *East London Observer*, 5 March 1887

On the cover page to each of the individual issues, the author is only identified as having also written a serial called 'TURNPIKE DICK, the Star of the Road', a 60-issue serial about Dick Turpin. The British Library Catalogue entry for the Spring-Heeled Jack serial suggests it was written "[By Charlton Lea?]", a pseudonym for Alfred Sherrington Burrage. An online article by John Adcock notes that Burrage was a staff writer for Charles Fox "sometime between 1880 and 1890", which puts him in the right place to be writing the 1886 serial; however, as Adcock notes, it was not until 1902, when Burrage was working for the Aldine Company, that he began using the Charlton Lea pseudonym. So, while we can say with some certainty that Burrage was the author of the 1904 serial, it is not so easy to identify him as the author of this volume. Karl Bell attributes authorship of this 48-part serial to George Augustus Sala, although he claims that this was published in *The Boy's Standard* in 1878-79, which suggests he may be referring to the Origin Story (in volume 3 of this Library), published a year after the alleged sightings at Aldershot and Lincoln rather than to this version (Bell 39).

The story follows the misdeeds of Sir Roland Ashton, the central antagonist of the story. It begins with the murder of Herbert Leigh. Leigh has documents that prove his claim that he is heir to the Ashton Estates. Daisy Leigh, Herbert's daughter, is witness to the murder but, although she flees in fear for her life, she is protected by a mysterious being. A second claimant on the Ashton Estates, Ralph Ashton, declares that he is the only son of Sir Guy Ashton and is therefore the rightful heir to the Ashton estates. Sir Roland asserts that the documents are a forgery by Ralph, who is forced to flee, and his escape is covered by Spring-Heeled Jack. In the meantime, Sir Roland finds that his ward, Constance Marfield is betrothed to Ralph, but in an act of pure spite, once Constance achieves her majority, Sir Roland blackmails her into marrying him; Jack manages to thwart these plans. Both Constance and Daisy are forced into hiding. However, Sir Roland is resourceful, and he goes to every effort to find the women and to prevent Ralph Ashton from claiming what he asserts is rightfully his. The story follows the women as they are abducted despite their attempts to hide from Sir Roland and his many henchmen and associates, while Ralph frequently confronts his relative attempting to reclaim what is rightfully his. Throughout, Spring-Heeled Jack remains on the periphery of the story, appearing to protect or save the women from their oppressors, or meting justice against the criminals.

One of the most striking differences between the 1886 serial contained in this volume and that from 1863, reproduced in volume 1, is in the illustrations. In 1863, Jack is seen wearing a mask, and, while Mephistophelian, Jack is always seen as a Victorian gentleman, often smiling in a benign manner. The covers of the present 1886 serial depict Jack as he is described in the text. He is bestial, almost demonic. The text describes Jack as having a 'hideous face which was not that of a mortal … with large eyes, with pointed eyebrows sticking out bristlingly, a peaky nose, and wide cavernous mouth" (I. 3), and with "long claw-like fingers" (I. 15). He has "a form as of Satan, a bat-like body, in red tight-fitting garments, with wide wings, and a devil's face, sulphurous flame and smoke issuing from his mouth" (I. 4). Sometimes described as having a "scarlet body" (I. 16), and elsewhere described as a "fiend in white, with wings, horns upon his head, and masses of tawny hair hanging about his shoulders" (II. 247). Despite this diabolical appearance, Ralph Ashton asserts "It is Spring-Heeled Jack's mission to punish the bad and reward the good (II. 138).

The 1886 serial bears no direct resemblance to the earlier 1863 story, and nor does it reference the historically attested assaults that Jack committed. That said, certain themes are repeated in the two serial novels, most particularly Jack protecting vulnerable women from their sadistic oppressors. Ralph Ashton is pursued by the authorities for allegedly forging a cheque in Sir Roland's name, just as James Slater forged a cheque in the name of his employer, Ralph Grasper, in the earlier story. For the most part, while not revealing Jack's *alter ego*, the narrator of the 1863 novel follows Jack. However, in the 1886 serial, Jack is mostly on the periphery of the story and only appears to protect or assist the main characters; we are never given his viewpoint. Although there are both hints and red herrings throughout the story, the identity of Spring-Heeled Jack, as well as his different appearances and ability to spring, are not directly revealed until the final chapters.

There are potentially some episodes that resonate with the historically documented incidents detailed above: there is a short scene that has echoes of the Aldershot incident: when a character, called Henry Palmer, is assisting Daisy Leigh's escape on one of the occasions she is abducted, he is challenged by a sentry who is then himself assaulted by Spring-Heeled Jack (II. 117). One might also find a parallel of the image of Jack standing on the stone arch of a little bridge with the leaping of the Newport Arch in Lincoln. However, these parallels may well be coincidental, and the author may not have known about these incidents.

When the Story is set

Although published in 1886, the events in the story take place earlier. The narrator claims "our story is a comparatively modern one" (I. 34). He observes that the "railways were then commencing to span the country" (I. 11); he also speaks of the railway not running from Barnet to London – this line opened in 1850. There were a handful of short, privately owned railways in the Eighteenth Century, but the first commercial railways date from 1825. There is also a mention that nursemaids used the name of Spring-Heeled Jack to frighten children in the same way that "nursemaids of thirty years before used the name of Napoleon, 'the Corsican ogre'" (I. 140). Napoleon was Emperor 1804–1814 and again, briefly in 1815, but even taking the earliest of these dates would place the story around 1834. At first sight, then, it appears that the story is set around, or just before, the time of the historically documented attacks by Spring-Heeled Jack, although these are never referenced.

However, a commentator in the *Quarterly Review* (July 1890) observes that the time of the story "is left in uncertainty but is presumably about the middle of the eighteenth century, noting that the constables of the story "are under the orders of a 'Commissioner'" (152). Within the text, there are also two references to Prince Charles Edward – more commonly known as Bonnie Prince Charlie, who was the Stuart clamant to the English throne from 1766 until his death in 1788. At one point in the story, Witchardson, the landlord of an inn, notes "Prince Charles Edward will establish his right to the throne of England yet" (I. 283), and on another, the villainous Bill Blarney threatens a gentleman by noting "Prince Charles Edward is not king yet" and further declaring the gentleman "an arch-traitor and a conspirator against the peace and throne of King George." (I. 349). George III was king of England from 1760 to 1820. These passing references, which admittedly add nothing to the story, contradict what has been suggested earlier and the references to Charles Edward Stuart place the story after 1766 but before 1788. It is likely that the author added these facts to set the story in a romanticised past as many of the encounters feature highwaymen. Bearing in mind that the principal audience for the Penny Fiction novels were working-class men, they would be unlikely to question the details in the story.

Responses to the "Penny Dreadful" Stories

The 1870 Elementary Education Act provided "free, compulsory, secular education" at the cost of the State, which resulted in a rise in literacy amongst the poorer classes. In an article headed "Penny Fiction" in 1890, a commentator in the *Quarterly Review* asks, contemplating on the progress two decades after the Act, "to what use they have put that painful training in the rudiments which has cost the country so much money?". He continues that the "literature of rascaldom … has done much to people our prisons, our reformatories, and our Colonies, with scapegraces and ne'er-do-wells" (*Quarterly Review* 150). He notes that "this foul and filthy trash circulates by thousands and tens of thousands week by week amongst lads who are at the most impressionable period of their lives, and whom the modern system of purely secular education has left without ballast or guidance" (154). The article refers directly to the reprinted publication of the 1886 serial, noting that the story is "a tale of highwaymen, murderers, burglars, wicked noblemen, and lovely and persecuted damsels, whose physical charms and voluptuous embraces are dilated upon with exceeding unction". It continues that "the highwaymen of the romance are not the sorry and sordid rogues we know them to have been in real life, but always 'dashing,' 'high-spirited,' and 'bold.' (152).

In a response to this article, other newspapers commentated that the "average taste for [Penny Fiction] literature is not a high one" and "do not give us a pleasing picture of the people who buy them". The stories themselves are described as "pernicious stuff … fitting literature for a community of youthful ghouls" (*The Walsall Advertiser*, 26 July 1890). The *Quarterly Review* observes that there are cheaper editions of more morally instructive authors, naming Dickens, Thackeray and Swift amongst them, but notes that "the ill-educated lads in our midst do not read them (151). This distaste for the Penny Fiction had been expressed years before the *Quarterly Review* article: in 1886 following the initial publication of the Spring-Heeled Jack story, one commentator complains that the protagonist of "'Spring-heeled Jack' or 'Tom Blueskin' lives happily ever afterwards with a fascinating heiress, whose relations he has murdered in cold blood – a circumstance which by no means mars the connubial bliss of the pair". It is the content of the story and its effect on the readers that distresses this critic, but he notes that more morally instructive novels are too expensive for this readership. "A shilling is far too large a portion of the slender weekly earnings – sixpence, even three pennies is too much to be spared. We must have penny books that shall not be 'dreadful', but which shall cast a ray of brightness into lives clouded with want and weariness". He further observes that this is not the content that this readership wants: "It is no use to offer caviare [*sic*] where cake would be preferable" (*Nottingham Daily Express* 29 April 1886). Certainly, in the 1886 serial, there is violence and murder committed by both the protagonist and principal antagonists, some of it presented in a very graphic form. In addition, both Constance Marfield and Daisy Leigh are described in detail as erotic beauties, so, for the time that the *Quarterly Review* article was published, it seemed their outrage was justified.

Serial stories such as *Spring-Heeled Jack* and the stories about highwaymen such as Dick Turpin, Jack Sheppard and Joe Blueskin were criticised for their lack of morality, but this was never their intention. As with the *Illustrated Police News*, such publications were not catering to a high-brow audience. Instead, the readers of Penny Fiction demanded sensational writing that would fuel their imagination. The re-publications of both the 1863 and 1886 versions of the Spring-Heeled Jack serial novels is a testament of the demand for stories in this genre, just as some readers of the newspapers wanted thrilling articles detailing crimes from around the country with imaginative and even provocative illustrations. The Editor of the *Illustrated Police News*, when it was voted the worst newspaper in the country, justified his publication by observing: "We can't all have *Timeses* and *Telegraphs*, and if we can't have the *Telegraph* or the *Times*, we must put up with the *Police News*" (quoted in *The Pall Mall Gazette*, 23 November 1886). And this was also where the market for the "Penny Dreadful" serial novels lay.

Editor's Note

This publication has been divided into two volumes because of the sheer length of the story – over 1000 pages or 500,000 words. The divide–the natural chapter break–comes almost exactly halfway through the story, a half-column before the end of issue 24.

J.S. Mackley
May 2020

Bibliography

"Penny Fiction" in *The Quarterly Review, July-October 1890*. (London: John Murray, 1890): 150–171.

Adcock, John. "Boys' Serials by Alfred Sherrington Burrage". Online article 31 January 2014. http://john-adcock.blogspot.com/2014/01/boys-serials-by-alfred-sherrington.html [accessed 3 May 2020].

Bell, Karl. *The Legend of Spring-Heeled Jack: Victorian Urban Folklore and Popular Cultures*. Woodbridge: The Boydell Press, 2012.

Dash, Mike. 'Spring-Heeled Jack: To Victorian Bugaboo from Suburban Ghost'.

https://d5abb186-3122-4344-bf7a-f35aa0561270.filesusr.com/ugd/7bb090_e0f718375aa54f789586c062f29dd204.pdf [accessed 16 May 2020].

Golicz, Roman. Spring-heeled Jack: A Victorian Visitation at Aldershot. 2nd Ed. Farnham: Don Namor Press, 2006.

Potter, Beatrix. *The Journal of Beatrix Potter from 1881–1897*. London: Frederick Warne and Co. Ltd, 1966.

SPRING-HEELED JACK,

THE TERROR OF LONDON.

By the Author of "TURNPIKE DICK, the Star of the Road."

SPRING-HEELED JACK FINDS THE MURDERED BODY OF HERBERT LEIGH.

No. 1.

CHAPTER I.
THE MURDER IN THE OLD MINT.

THE night was terrible, for a storm was raging over London. The wind was rushing with wild roars and shrieks along the streets, chimney pots were being hurled down upon the heads of the passers-by. On the river the shipping was being tossed and flung about, so that the vessels crashed against one another, and small boats were crushed into wreckage against the piers. The lightning flashed and the thunder boomed. But the roar of heaven's artillery did not drown the cries which rang out shrilly from a house in Wedge-street in the Mint.[4]

The ominous deadly cries—

"Help!—help! Murder!"

People heard it as they were retiring to rest, and paused and listened and rushed to their windows to open them in spite of the storm. Pedestrians heard it and quickened their pace to a run, the constables heard it and sprung their rattles and dashed off in the direction of the sound.

"Help! murder! Help!"

The landlord of the Three Mariners, what with the wind, and the lightning, and the thunder, and the terrible cry, dropped the shutter he was putting up, and nearly knocked over a tall man, wrapped in a long cloak, who had come upon him rapidly round the corner.

"The devil fly away with you for a clumsy brute!" cried the new-comer. "Ah! Simon Webster, is it you? You nearly smashed my toe."

The speaker was a man about forty, with a slouched hat and high riding boots, the rest of his attire being entirely concealed by his large cloak.

What could be seen of his face was dark and sinister, his eyes gleaming like coals of fire, and his black moustache hardly serving to conceal his wide and sensual mouth.

"Ah! is that you, Ned Wilmot?" said Simon. "I did not hear you coming. What with the rain, and the wind, and the thunder and lightning, and those terrible cries of murder, I was nigh dazed."

The man laughed hoarsely.

"Cries of murder in the Mint!" he said. "I should have thought that you'd got used to them. They're common enough here, I should have imagined. But let me enter. I'm wet to the skin, and shall be glad of something hot."

"You're welcome," said Simon, "though I'm not going to keep open long. Ah! there it is again. And see how the people are running—"

But before he could finish what he had to say the man whom he had addressed as Ned Wilmot had dived through the old-fashioned portae[5] of the Three Mariners and entered the public room.

Public or not it was private enough now.

Those who had been seated round the dying fire had deserted it to have a last drink at the bar, and so, unobserved by anyone, the man walked straight to the fire-place and glanced into the dingy glass above it.

---

[4] A district in Southwark, south London.
[5] Doors.

One glance and then all was forgotten; storm, and rushing crowds, and constables' rattles, and murder-cries.

All forgotten in the one stare he gave at a great splash on his face—the unmistakable splash of blood!

With a desperate oath he threw back his cloak so that one end resting on his left shoulder showed a well-fitting undercoat of a brownish-tinted cloth, and snatching a white handkerchief from his pocket he swiftly wiped from his features the hideous mark which the rain had kept damp upon them.

Then he flung the fine cambric[6] upon the fire, where the lazy flames licked round it, and, all too slowly for the eager-eyed watcher, devoured it with a rush and a splutter just as Simon Webster entered.

It was as this worthy made his way towards the fire that Ned Wilmot saw that the bundle of papers he had carried in his left hand were splashed with blood also, and he hastily concealed them under his cloak.

"A dismal fire to welcome a traveller in such weather as this, Simon," he said. "Pile on some fuel and let's have some grog.[7] I am frozen to the very marrow."

"It is too late to talk of making up the fire," said Simon, "I must close in a few moments."

"Nay, then, I need some supper and a bed," said Ned, "and what is more, I want a horse in the morning. I have to ride many miles before noon. Don't be surly, Simon, you know I always pay well."

With a kind of grumbling assent the landlord passed out.

Evidently he was in no good humour at the coming of his visitor.

And yet it seemed as if he dared not gainsay him.

Wilmot sat down and placed the tell-tale paper in his pocket.

"Confound that meddling fiend, whoever he may be," he muttered. "I was as nearly caught as a man could be. And that girl too. She saw my face. The Mint will be too warm for me now. What a clatter there is in the Street to be sure. One would think none of them had heard a cry of murder here before."

The rush of people was indeed great.

It seemed more than it would have done—mingled with the patter of rain and the roar of wind.

But it was enough, at any rate, to disconcert Ned Wilmot, and he rose from his seat again, pushed aside the red curtains, and peered out.

As he did so a vivid flash of lightning illumined the street, brightening up every dark and sullen-looking corner.

And for one instant he saw grinning at him a hideous face which was not that of a mortal.

A face with large eyes, with pointed eyebrows sticking out bristlingly, a peaky nose, and wide cavernous mouth.

This was all he could see now.

But he had seen the face and form too within the hour, and, with a cry of horror, he drew back.

Where he had seen it we shall know presently.

"That hideous fiend again," he said, shudderingly, as he drew back towards the fire.

---

[6] A lightweight, plain-weave cloth.
[7] Alcoholic drink.

"Surely he is not going to haunt me! Death would be preferable to that."

As he spoke Simon Webster re-entered with two steaming glasses of grog and some wood and coals to cheer up the fire.

He could not but observe how ghastly pale was the face of his guest.

But his thoughts were quickly diverted into a new channel.

Scarcely had Ned Wilmot drank off at a draught the contents of one of the glasses, when a thundering knock was heard at the door, and a loud, authoritative voice exclaiming—

"Open in the name of the law!"

Ned started up.

A wild, hunted look was upon his face.

"I mustn't be found here," he cried. "I know my way out by the back."

And without a word he rushed past the landlord and fled up the stairs.

In a moment Simon Webster had opened the door, and a number of constables entered.

"Let us come in and close your doors," said the leader of the body of constables. "We are in want of a murderer, and must search the house instantly."

"Come in at once, gentlemen," said Simon. "You may search wherever you please as long as you don't drag my wife out of bed."

He was like most of the inhabitants of the Mint—not very affectionately disposed towards the constables.

But he knew he must keep in favour with them for the sake of his living, and consequently he never placed any obstacles in their way.

The constables soon spread themselves over the house; cellars, bar parlour, bedrooms, all were searched; not excepting that of Mistress Webster, who treated them to some language far less polite than that of her husband; or that of the barmaid and servant, who cowered under the bedclothes to hide their fat little shoulders, but were inwardly laughing at the joke, as could be seen from the merry twinkle of their eyes.

At length, at the rear of the premises, they came upon an open window leading out to the leads.[8]

Running along these a man could easily leave the premises and drop into the street.

"This is where the villain has escaped," cried Joe Bonsor, the head constable. "Let us go out and see where he has dropped."

But as he spoke a terrific flash of lightning seemed to rend the heavens, and cast a lurid gleam over the dreary, time-stained buildings at the rear of the Three Mariners, and a clap of thunder boomed forth enough to shake the place to its foundation.

And as they stood awe-stricken in that interval of light they beheld a terrible thing.

Leaping high in the air, springing over the summit of a stack of chimneys, was a form as of Satan, a bat-like body, in red tight-fitting garments, with wide wings, and a devil's face, sulphurous flame and smoke issuing from his mouth.

He leaped almost into the window where they stood spellbound.

But the light was gone then—darkness had fallen heavily, and they could only see his shadow form for an instant, before, with a Satanic laugh and a fresh emission of flame, he disappeared with a bound, which took him clear across the leads into the street.

By the time that the constables regained sufficient courage to emerge upon the flat

---

[8] Flat roof covered with lead.

roof and continue their search, the murderer, if such he was, had had time to escape, and their efforts were useless.

But who had been murdered, and where had the crime been done?

CHAPTER II.

DAISY LEIGH—WAITING AND WATCHING—THE ASSASSIN— THE CRY FOR HELP—SPRING-HEELED JACK TO THE RESCUE.

IN order to explain the events in our first chapter we must ask our readers to accompany us to a house in a street not far from the Three Mariners.

This street was perhaps one of the worst in the Mint.

Over the whole place brooded the shadowy memory of Jack Sheppard[9] and his days of crime.

Not a really respectable house was in the whole thoroughfare; dingy beerhouses, greasy chandlers shops, nondescript places, with dingy bed curtains in parlour windows flush with the street; dark courts and alleys leading into gloomy passages.

Such was the kind of place whence the cry of murder had proceeded.

In an upper room in a house, the door of which—mostly open—led to a staircase, the woodwork of which was like tinder, a young girl had been watching for a long, weary time.

The apartment was terribly poor and desolate.

A broken piece of iron served as a fender;[10] the table had only three sound legs; there was only one chair and a stool.

In one corner lay a heap of straw covered with a few rags, and the window was patched with paper and other materials instead of glass.

Adjoining this place was a small ante-chamber—a cupboard—where a little bedstead made from rough pieces of wood had been constructed, or which was a paillasse[11] and a few ragged coverings.

In the grate in the larger room a fire was struggling for existence, and before this crouched a girl.

She was about seventeen, and anyone looking at her beauty would have said what shame it was that she should be habited in such rags.

Her hair was dark and glossy, and arranged round her head in short, crisp curls.

Her eyes—large, brown, and brilliant—wore a sad and melancholy look, and a shadow of scorn marked her ripe, red lips.

Her dress consisted of a short skirt, ragged boots and stockings, and a low underbody, a shawl being drawn over her to hide the white and rounded shoulders and bosom, which matched the rare beauty of her face and the exquisite form, whose contours were lavishly shown by the thin, clinging garment.

Her only dress hung up in the little ante-chamber; she dare not risk wearing that in the squalid room, lest the chances of her going out would be destroyed.

The young girl, shivering before the miserable apology of a fire, shuddered more as

---

[9] Highwayman (1702–1724), known for his escapes from prison, he became a folk hero like Dick Turpin. See Vol. 5 of the Spring-Heeled Jack Library, *Dandy Dick* or, *The King's Highway* where Sheppard features as a character in the story

[10] Fireplace hearth.

[11] Mattress filled with straw.

she looked back upon the past.

She had memories of an infancy spent in a handsome house, and of tender faces and gentle voices round her.

Then came school-time at a pretty place by the sea—holidays spent at home with her father, Herbert Leigh, in a comparatively generously-kept and appointed house, and pleasant visitors, and plenty of life and fun.

Then came a sudden fall.

She was hurried home from school to meet a haggard, hunted-looking man, who took her instantly from home, and straight from luxury and happiness, to the hateful squalor of a third-rate lodging-house.

He could explain nothing.

He only said that terrible misfortune had fallen upon him—that he was accused of a deadly crime, was powerless to prove his innocence, and dared not show his face in any neighbourhood where he was known.

From this moment they went from bad to worse, until at last we see Daisy Leigh— pretty, dainty Daisy Leigh—crouched, cold and shuddering, by a dying fire in a wretched garret, waiting for her father's coming.

Presently, when her heart had become weary with watching, she heard a heavy foot upon the stairs.

She listened intently; the step came nearer—the door opened.

Yes, it was, indeed, her father, and in a moment her warm young arms were about his neck.

Then, as she drew him to the fire, she observed that his eyes were brighter than usual and a smile was on his lips, in spite of the wet state of his habiliments.

"Put on your dress, little one," he said; "don't shiver in the cold any more. I've brought you a better one to go out in, and better luck too. One more night in this wretched place and we can go to comfortable quarters."

"Oh! never mind me," said Daisy, drawing her shawl tighter round her bare shoulders. "Take off that wet overcoat, and I'll put the rest of the coals on the fire. If you have had good luck perhaps we can buy some more presently next door."

Herbert Leigh did as he desired, and then, while she was busy making up the fire, he opened a large bundle he had brought with him.

In this were a dress, a jacket, gloves, boots, and so forth, and in a separate bundle some food and a bottle of port wine.

"Drink some of that, Daisy," he said; "it will warm your blood, and then I will explain a little of what has happened.

"In the first place I am no longer compelled to hide my face," he continued, as Daisy drank some wine out of a broken tea-cup, "and in the second place I have discovered my enemy."

Daisy shuddered.

"Then pray let him rest," she said. "You have gone through enough danger. You do not want to use your perilous knowledge to bring fresh disaster on yourself."

As she spoke she started.

What was that sound?

Was it a creak of a footstep upon the stairs?

"Hush, father," she added. "I think I heard someone coming."

"Maybe James Winter going up to his room."

Daisy blushed.

"You forget," she said, "he left this place yesterday. I will go to the door and listen."

She went at once, but the sounds she had heard had ceased, whatever they were.

A furious wind blew up the stairs, and swept over her with a strange, death-like chill, the lightning flashed and illumined the dark landing and the darker stairs.

But she saw nothing.

There was a sound as of heavy breathing, but she set that down to the drunken snoring of Gadge Foote, the dwarf bagsman,[12] who slept on the floor below, and closing the door she returned to her seat at her father's side.

"It was only fancy, I expect," she said; "the wind making the old stairs creep. Go on, father; I am all eagerness to know your story."

A shade crossed Herbert Leigh's brow.

"Ah! my child," he said, "I cannot tell you that now. It would be dangerous. But I have here, let me tell you, the papers which prove my right to wealth and name, usurped so long by the man who has been the cause of all my misery."

As he spoke, the door was flung open, the wind nearly extinguishing the candle, and a man's figure was seen standing—a dark shadow on a darker threshold.

"Whoever you are, enter," cried Herbert Leigh, rising and drawing back, with a strange, indefinable fear crawling to his heart. "I cannot talk to anyone whom I do not see, and the wind will put the light out if you do not close the door."

He had clutched the papers, which he had commenced opening on the table, and retreated behind the latter, pushing his daughter behind him as he spoke.

The newcomer uttered a low, guttural laugh, and entering, closed the door.

The flame of the candle became steady again, and, as he removed his hat, Herbert recognised him.

His face at first grew white and then swiftly flushed with anger.

"What do you want here, Ned Wilmot?" he cried. "Have I not had enough of misery and peril through you, that you need follow me here?"

"Don't talk like that, Mr. Leigh," returned Ned Wilmot, jeeringly. "You'll find it doesn't suit the situation at all. I'm here to demand from you the papers you have stolen."

"Stolen! What mean you, ruffian?" cried Leigh, indignantly. "The papers I have this night taken from Ashton Hall are my own; the papers which prove my birthright and my claims. It would be unpleasant if I called for aid, and had you arrested as the poacher, robber, and highway-man you are."

Ned Wilmot's evil face was distorted by an ominous scowl as these words were uttered.

"You'd better beware what you are saying," he said, savagely. "You'd find it difficult to get any aid here just now. I've taken special care that no one is in the house, and, as for anyone outside of it, you might shout and scream as loudly as you like. What with the wind, and the rain, and the thunder, you'd find no one to hear you."

Daisy trembled as she gazed at the man who spoke.

The expression of his face was truly awful.

---

[12] Somebody who collects or distributes the proceeds of criminal activities.

But Herbert Leigh knew no fear.

He had obtained, after long years of waiting, of privations, and danger, the papers which could alone prove his innocence and his claims as next heir to Ashton Hall.

"Leave this room at once!" he cried, threateningly.

"Not without those papers!" cried Wilmot, fiercely, advancing a step nearer.

There was murder in his eyes, and Daisy's heart turned faint.

Her white bosom rose and fell in tremulous pulsations, and Ned Wilmot observing it, leered hideously.

"You'd best ask him to give them to me, Miss Daisy," he added, quickly. "Since you laughed at my love I've never felt very kindly towards you and yours; but, if he will give them to me, I promise never again to trouble you or him. If he doesn't give them to me willingly I'll have them by force, and you, too, before long."

There was that in his eyes which would have made many a girl less brave lose heart altogether.

But Daisy Leigh had a brave spirit in her plump, lithe form.

"Don't threaten me," she said; "I laugh at your menaces. But as for the papers I would rather my father gave them up than incur any danger. My love for him is greater than all my desire for wealth or position."

Ned Wilmot was about to reply, but Herbert Leigh interrupted him.

"Enough!" he said; "you have insulted both me and my child, and I refuse to say more to you tonight. I leave this place to morrow, and—"

"Give me those papers," said Ned Wilmot, interrupting threateningly.

"I refuse."

"Then I will take them."

With the words he sprang forward.

Herbert Leigh had anticipated this, and was ready for him.

Quickly passing the papers to Daisy, who clutched them in a brave, though tremulous, hand, he was just in time to avoid a blow aimed at him by his enemy.

Ned Wilmot was a strong man, and had been used to a rough and hardy life; but Herbert Leigh was by no means a contemptible antagonist.

He was in the prime of life—not, perhaps, more than forty-three years of age, and had seen a good deal of roughing it in his time.

The struggle was a deadly one.

The first blow being stopped, the two adversaries closed.

Chairs and table were overturned in the furious struggle, and Daisy, crouching in a corner, felt that some terrible crisis had come in the life of herself and father.

She could have escaped into her own room, but she would not desert him; and so, crouching there, pale, with tremulous bosom and palpitating heart, she sent forth again and again that awful cry which had rung out over the Mint through gusty wind and roaring thunder—

"Help—help—murder!"

But no help came.

At first, as Ned Wilmot had jeeringly declared, the voices of Nature had drowned the shrill cries.

And, so at length, when her father was thrown suddenly, and dashed his head against the iron of the fender, the only chance of aid for him was that of his brave child.

With desperate courage she sprang at the murderous villain.

But of what avail was her tender muscles against a brawny ruffian of this type?

Seeing at once her design, he struck her a blow as she approached him, which sent her, stunned and helpless, into a corner.

Then, as she lay there, unable to move, only able to collect her scattered senses sufficiently to know what the terrible scene meant, she beheld the final struggle.

Her father seemed to rouse himself for a last effort.

He used superhuman strength.

But in vain.

Ned Wilmot was not content with hands.

Just as Daisy hoped that her father had succeeded in obtaining a position where he could renew the battle, she saw something bright flash in Wilmot's hand.

Then there was an awful groan of pain and despair, and Herbert Leigh fell back dead, stabbed through the heart.

The sight of this seemed to infuse fresh strength into Daisy.

She roused herself, and, springing up, faced the assassin as he staggered to his feet.

She clutched in her left hand behind her the papers which had cost her father his life, and again her piercing cry resounded through the storm.

"Villain!" she exclaimed, with white lips. "I swear, by Heaven's mercy, to avenge this night's work. Be mine the task to hunt you to your doom. Ned Wilmot—"

"Cease your prating, wench!" said the man, advancing towards her with his face splashed with the blood of his victim. "Give me those papers!"

"Never, while life lasts!"

In an instant he sprang upon her.

But he had misjudged the power of those rounded limbs, now that their owner was roused to fierce energy by the spirit of revenge, despair, and her natural clinging to life.

Again and again he tried to fling her violently against the wall.

In vain.

Her muscles appeared to have resolved themselves into iron.

"I'll pay you out for this, my beauty," he said, in a voice of gasping rage, as he paused for a moment, holding her by both wrists.

Beauty!

That was indeed the word to express her appearance.

Her face was pale, with one spot of red on each cheek. In the struggle her shawl had been torn off, revealing the heaving roundness of her bosom, and the exquisite contour of her bare white shoulders.

Her eyes gleamed brightly; her lips were parted, showing the pearly teeth beneath.

In her left hand she still clutched the fatal papers.

By a sudden jerk, after a moment, Ned Wilmot endeavoured to throw her again; but as he did so an awful thing happened.

A loud and discordant laugh was heard without, and, in the midst of a terrific flash of lightning, there was a crashing of wood and glass, and an awful figure sprang into the room.

It was the form of Satan.

His body was attired in a red tight-fitting garment; his face was strange and horrible; his mouth wide, with fang-like teeth; horns grew from his forehead, and one foot was that of an animal with a cloven hoof.

As he gazed at the assassin with eyes which glowed like living coals, sulphurous flame and smoke was vomited from his mouth.

One glance was enough for Daisy.

She fell fainting on the floor.

As she did so the papers dropped from her nerveless grasp, and Ned Wilmot, with a wild cry, seized them, despite the presence of the fiend.

In an instant the Terrible Thing made a dash forward at him, but, with a cry like that of a lost spirit, the assassin leaped over the table and was gone.

The fiendish being who had caused the catastrophe glanced round the room for a moment, and, seeing pen and ink and paper, raised the table to its proper level, and, sitting down, wrote a few words.

> *"Fear not, Daisy Leigh! He whom you saw this night is your friend. He arrived too late to save your father's life. But he will aid you to avenge his death. Use the gold he leaves and go to the address he gives, or you will hear no more of your friend*
>
> *SPRING-HEELED JACK."*

The address was, "Mistress Barton, River Cottage, Edmonton" and the purse was a silk one, through the meshes of which shone the gleam of many gold pieces.

Having left these on the table he securely fastened the door, and turned his attention to Daisy.

Raising her from the floor he gazed intently at her, and placed her on the bed of rags.

For a moment he feared that she, too, had sped away into the vast unknown—her lips were so pale and cold, her eyelids so blue, her face so cold, her form so rigid.

But when he placed his hand, or rather claw, under her left breast, he felt the heart beating feebly.

"She lives—she lives!" murmured the terrible-looking being. "She will yet avenge her father; and by this mark she will one day know who it was that befriended her."

Then with his sharp talons he scratched a double cross on her left shoulder, on the delicate white of which the blood quickly flowed.

Then he threw her shawl over her, poured a little wine between the lips which were already trembling with returning life, and, leaping through the shattered window through which he had come, disappeared ere she opened her eyes upon the scene of horror.

With bounds of wondrous and supernatural agility he sprang over the roofs of outhouses, over chimney pots and across leads; an awful form in the blue gleam of the lightning, until presently he reached the spot where Mr. Bonsor and the other constables were just preparing to emerge from the window.

Ned Wilmot's attempted capture is easily accounted for.

A man who had heard the shrill cries of "Help—help! Murder!" had seen him emerge from the door of the old house, and fly like one demented along the street and round the corners.

He had pursued him, seen him enter the Three Mariners, and had at once hastened to give information to the constables.

By the time that Bonsor and his men, recovering from their terror of Spring-Heeled

Jack, had crossed the leads and dropped into the street, Ned. Wilmot had made his way along the dark and narrow thoroughfare, dashed down a narrow court, and made his way towards the river's side.

Here he had no difficulty in finding a boat.

He was not one to care who was owner of anything he desired to possess, and, accordingly, he leaped in, slipped the painter,[13] and was soon rowing up stream.

At a little creek near Vauxhall Bridge he pulled the skiff ashore, jumped on the muddy, oozy pebbles, and, casting the boat adrift to follow the tide where it liked, he approached some steps, hastened up them, and, making his way along a narrow lane between dingy, lonely warehouses, reached presently a dirty-looking beershop.

It was long past the usual hours of closing, but three peculiar taps brought to the door a hangdog-looking harridan of about sixty years of age, who grinned in surprise as she saw him.

"What! you back again, Ned?" she cried, "come back like a bad shilling! You do look scared-like, too, just as if you'd seen a ghost."

"I've seen worse! I've seen the devil!" cried Ned Wilmot, with a forced laugh. "Let's have a bedroom, mother, and something to eat and drink. I think the nabs[14] are after me, so put me in a room near the river's side, and I'll stop there on the quiet till to-morrow night."

And, while the assassin was calmly partaking of a good supper, the fiendish shape which had tried to thwart his designs on Daisy Leigh was darting across London in the now decreasing storm, leaping over the heads of the passers-by, flying over the hackney coaches, and creating such a panic in the minds of all that no one who saw him could sleep a wink that night.

And he, never caring about the terror he created, was speeding away towards Barnet on the first stage of his errand of vengeance.

CHAPTER III.
ASHTON HALL—A STORMY INTERVIEW—
A STOLEN MEETING—A SECOND MURDER.

IT was on the evening after the horrible murder in the Mint and the appearance of Spring-Heeled Jack, the mysterious unknown, that a man rode out from a little bye-alley near the Falcon Inn at Southgate, and made his way in the direction of Barnet.

The weather had now changed entirely.

Instead of rain and rushing wind, and the warring of lightning and thunder, there was only a light breeze, and the moon was shining brightly while myriads of stars gemmed the sky.

The man was dressed in ordinary costume, looking as if he belonged to the farming class; but there was an air of satisfaction and smugness about him which seemed to tell that he had just had a slice of luck or was looking forward to the coming of some certain good fortune.

Though railways were then commencing to span the country they were only

---

[13] Rope attached to a boat.
[14] Police.

commencing, and had not yet done away with the footpad and the highwayman.

Consequently, the man carried in his holsters a goodly pair of pistols.

People had given up wearing swords, having been compelled to do so by a "paternal government;" but things had not yet reached such a pitch that a man would be fined, perhaps imprisoned, for carrying a pistol to protect himself.

Metropolitan extensions had not in those days succeeded in joining Barnet to London.

Accordingly, it was not long before the man left the houses behind him, and started off on a wide, lonely road.

It was just the place to suit a dashing highwayman, and just the hour and the weather.

A crisp, hard road; on either side thickly-wooded land or high hedges; above a cloudless sky, and the moon and stars making a merry light.

Enough to give excuse for a high-spirited, daring fellow to turn out on the highway, and cry—"Hurrah—hurrah! for the road!" Even though it were only for fun and devilment. So thought the man—Job Joskins, as he left the inhabited parts of the hamlet, and found himself alone on the silent highway.

Many a time, as he rode on, he turned to take a stealthy glance round him; and now and then he pulled up to listen, as if frightened at the echoes of his horse's footsteps.

But, at length, satisfied that his fears were groundless, he put spurs to his horse, anxious to reach as quickly as possible his destination, which was none other than Ashton Hall, the place mentioned by Herbert Leigh, the victim of the cold-blooded murder in the Mint.

This place was inhabited by, and supposed to belong to, Sir Roland Ashton, who had come into the property, it was said, in consequence of the failure of the other heirs.

Strange rumours, however, were spread in regard to him and his succession to the property.

Rumours that papers had been concealed or destroyed, and even that dark deeds had been done in order to secure him safe use of the golden revenues of the estate.

But as is always the case where people have command of money, Sir Roland Ashton was, if not liked, at any rate tolerated in the very best society.

In the neighbourhood he attended all the hunt meetings, balls, garden parties, and so forth, for he was only forty years of age, handsome, stalwart, with plenty of money, and was he not, therefore, lionised in such a manner that he knew himself to be regarded as one of the most eligible parties in the neighbourhood.

He was a well-looking man enough in his way, and could take a fence or a hedge with any man in England.

But there was a sinister gleam in his eyes at the best of times, and a cruel smile often hovered about his lips.

His household consisted of the usual servants necessary to a proper establishment, a middle-aged housekeeper, and a ward.

The former was a woman of no particular character showing outwardly. The latter was a tall, elegant girl, evidently well fed, and yet having a shade of melancholy always in her face, even at the merriest meetings.

She was twenty-one on the day following the murder in the Mint, and her guardian had on that day promised to disclose to her the story of her life.

Otherwise she was a mysterious being. She had entered Sir Roland's house some nine years before, and, coming straight from school, had been treated with uniform kindness by him, though his constant hints and innuendoes cast a painful shadow on her life.

In appearance she was of great beauty—tall, with long, sweeping limbs, broad, rounded shoulders, and an exquisitely-developed and voluptuous bust.

Her face corresponded with her form, and masses of golden hair crowned her well-formed head.

It was to the home of this girl—Constance Marfield and Sir Roland Ashton—that Job Joskins was hurrying along the Barnet-road, when, coming suddenly round a bend where the rest of the highway was hidden from view, he came upon a man whose appearance caused his heart to beat violently, and his brain to reel.

The man was riding a fine horse, and was attired in a guise which made him resemble almost in every particular, except the mask, those gentlemen of the road who used to frequent the lonely highways in the time of Tom King and his companions.

Job Joskins was almost abreast with the stranger ere he recognised what kind of traveller he had met.

"Stop, on your life!" cried the latter, "I want a word with you."

Job's hand made a slow and tremulous movement towards his holster.

"Hold!" cried the man again; "if you move I will shoot you through the head."

He presented a pistol ere he went on—

"You are Job Joskins, and you are going to Ashton Hall to tell Sir Roland Ashton how much money you will be able to collect for him at Rickworth to-morrow evening."

"You're the devil!" muttered Job, tremblingly.

"No, I'm not, though he is an acquaintance of mine," returned the highwayman; "but I happen to know that you have in your possession a goodly sum of money which you have already collected for your master."

Job Joskins did not reply.

In fact he was too terrified; but at this moment there happened something which took his thoughts in another direction with a vengeance.

There was a sudden loud peal of laughter—"Ha! ha! ha!"—then a whirring sound above the heads of both Job and the highwayman, and, glancing up, they saw the terrible apparition of Spring-Heeled Jack.

His cloak was spread out so as to resemble the wings of a bat, and sulphurous smoke and flame was issuing more than ever from his mouth.

Job Joskins was so terrified that he could not utter a sound, but his hair bristled on end so that his hat fell off; while the arm of the highwayman which held the pistol remained rigid and immovable.

The terrible being who had thus appeared—looming up between them and the moon—sped over their heads with the rapidity of a rocket, and disappeared behind the hedge on the side opposite to that where it had risen.

For a few seconds only the two men and their horses stood motionless—the riders seemed riveted to their saddles, the animals seemed turned to stone.

But after this momentary lull they broke away, one dashing in one direction, the other in the other—Job Joskins rushing away towards Barnet, and his quondam[15] enemy

---

[15] Erstwhile.

making in all haste towards London, leaving the choice of road, fin act,[16] to his horse's discretion.

They had scarcely gone when Spring-Heeled Jack made his appearance again, and, with a wild, unearthly laugh, glanced after the highwayman.

"Ha, ha! he cried. "I knew you at once, Ned Wilmot. But you are not going to Ashton Hall before me. I am bound there tonight, to prowl round and discover all. We want no prying assassins there.

"As for Job Joskins," he added, as he glanced in the other direction along the road, where the "receiver" had just disappeared, "I have learned this night a secret which will be of use to me. It strikes me that there will be three people instead of two interested in the collection of money at Rickworth to-morrow night."

With many a leap and bound, over hedges, ditches, streams, and tree-tops, went the awful apparition, until it neared the site of an old ruin—the dilapidated remains of a house, which, a year or two before, had been burnt down, and which had never been rebuilt or even repaired.

He paused a moment ere he entered it, standing Satan-like behind a tree to think.

"I can hardly believe," he murmured aloud, "that I shall see again the body of Herbert Leigh in this strange spot. No doubt it was part of Ned Wilmot's bargain to bring the murdered man to this place, in order that Sir Roland should look upon it, and know that his hideous order was fulfilled. But how did he convey it hither when I have been on the watch?"

Overcoming his repugnance the weird being left his concealment, and, with a leap and a bound, had passed round the angle of the first ruined wall.

The moon was her shining in on gleaming belt of radiance, and in an instant Spring-Heeled Jack (since such was the name he had adopted) saw that the horrible thing was true.

Lying on its back, just where the moonlight fell upon its face, was the body of a man, and the features were those of Herbert Leigh.

"This is a strange mystery," said Spring-Heeled Jack, to himself. "Those who help me must be strangely remiss, or the body of this unfortunate could not have found its way to this spot. Ha! who comes here, I wonder. I will remain and see."

With his arms raised so as, by the aid of his cloak, to form the bat-like wings, he remained still, standing on the body, when, after a moment, a man came creeping round the angle of the wall.

This was Job Joskins.

The very last man whom Spring-Heeled Jack expected to see.

In an instant Job had recognised the weird form.

For one moment he was rooted to the spot in uncontrollable terror.

Then, with a wild yell, he turned to fly.

But Spring-Heeled Jack was too much for him.

In an instant he had bounded forward and seized the fugitive by the throat with his claw-like hands, then, with a twirl, flung him on his face.

"Ha! ha! ha!"

---

[16] The final action.

The demon laughter of the weird being resounded over the countryside as, kneeling down, he turned out all the pockets of the "collector."

Not a penny piece or a piece of paper escaped his notice, and, having transferred everything into a huge pocket, contained under his arm in the wing-like cloak, he proceeded to disrobe his victim.

"Oh! pray, Mr. Devil," cried Job Joskins, "pray leave me my clothes!"

"Not a bit of it," said Spring-Heeled Jack "if you ride home naked your master will know you have not robbed him. Quick, or I shall put a bullet through your skull, or strangle you."

His long, claw-like fingers clasped and unclasped before the eyes of the horrified man, and without further hesitation he began divesting himself of his clothes.

At every pause a grip of the terrible fingers was upon his neck, and at length he stood up as naked as he was born.

It was not a cold night, but still a man suddenly stripped of his warm clothes would naturally feel chilled, and he shuddered and trembled accordingly.

But while the luminous eyes of Spring-Heeled Jack were upon him he was powerless to move.

"Remember," said the apparition, in a solemn voice, "I know all. I know this murdered man. I know who killed him, and who urged him on to the deed. I know you, Job Joskins, and your dealings. Go home now and tell your master, Sir Roland Ashton, that Spring-Heeled Jack is on his track. Go home swiftly, without stopping, or I will follow and throttle the life out of you!"

And with these words the speaker gave a terrific bound over Job's head, and disappeared in a vapour of flame and sulphur emitted from his cavernous mouth.

Job Joskins gave one glance round furtively to see if his clothes were there; but they were all gone, even to his boots.

For an instant the hideous idea occurred to him of denuding the murdered man of his habiliments, and dressing himself in them, but hardly had the idea formed itself in his brain when the loud "Ha, ha, ha!" of the fiendish unknown was heard, and he fled towards the spot where he had left his horse.

On this he leaped, and, naked as he was galloped down the road as hard as he could tear towards Ashton Hall.

Turning suddenly round a bend in the road leading towards the turnpike, he met a young girl coming from market, and, thinking he was the devil, she cowered down by the side of the road and shrieked loudly for help.

Her cries roused the attention of two constables on duty, and they hastened forward only to see Job on his horse pass like a flash, and the girl still sobbing and cowering by the roadside.

"Why, what is the matter, young woman?" cried one of them, in vain endeavouring to keep his voice steady.

"Oh! if you please, sir," said the girl, still afraid to move, "I saw the devil go by, naked, on a horse, and—"

"Ha! ha! ha!"

A demon yell of laughter resounded from behind a hedge, and, as the startled trio listened, horror-stricken at the awful tones, the unknown form of the mysterious leaper whizzed up from the ground into the air, and bounded over their heads.

The moon was still shining brightly in an unclouded sky, and all of them were able to note minutely his appearance—his scarlet body, his bat-wings, his sulphurous-breathing mouth; with a yell of horror the constables fled, leaving the unfortunate girl to shift for herself, which she did by rising, with a shuddering cry, and following them as best she could.

Spring-Heeled Jack, with many a bound and miraculous leap, followed, caught them up, and leaped over their heads, after which, with a loud laugh, he magically disappeared.

CHAPTER IV.
SIR ROLAND AT HOME—AN UNWELCOME VISITOR—A STOLEN MEETING.

SIR ROLAND ASHTON was in his library.

A queer old room, solidly and sombrely furnished, and full of dark, strange corners, but still a comfortable apartment.

Sir Roland had a puzzled, worried look upon his face, and yet not an expression that told of being absolutely displeased.

"To-morrow is the day when all must be divulged," he said to himself, as presently he paused in a troubled walk to and fro, and threw himself into a large armchair by the fire. "Tomorrow all will be decided. I somehow fear that everything will not be as well as I could wish it; but I do not think there is anything to dread."

As he spoke there came an odd tapping, scratching at his window, and he started up.

Crossing the room quickly, in some surprise and perturbation, he drew aside the curtain and looked out.

But there was nothing near the window on the outside; only the tendrils and leaves of the vine, which crept nestlingly up the wall and stole upon the verandah.

He was just about to turn away impatiently when he gave utterance to an exclamation of bewilderment as he saw a naked rider dash across the grounds on a steed, which he seemed to recognise, though, in his present want of garb, he failed to distinguish the horseman.

As the mysterious apparition went by a thing like a huge bat rose from the ground and passed between him and the moon, leaping clean over the head of the naked rider and disappearing.

Sir Roland drew the curtains with a shudder, and walked back to his seat.

"Well," he said, "I do not believe in diablerie,[17] or I should think that Satan and one of his attendant imps was paying me a visit. However, I suppose I shall know soon."

A quarter of an hour, however, passed before anyone knocked at the door.

Then, in answer to his summons, Job Joskins appeared, his face still pale with fear and excitement.

Sir Roland, who had now drank himself into a jocular humour by frequent potations of old port, laughed loudly.

"Come in, Job," he cried. "Why, you look as if you had seen Old Nick himself."

"That's exactly what I have done," said the man, glancing over his shoulder and at every dark corner of the room.

---

[17] Devils, Black Magic.

"Drink a glass of wine, man, and don't be a fool," said Sir Roland, with some show of irritation; "do you know who it was who was riding just now naked through the grounds?"

"That was me, sir," said Job, with a grim smile, as he drank off the glass of wine; "and if you'll listen, sir, I'll explain everything."

"Go on ahead, then, Job," returned Sir Roland, with a yawn. "I daresay it's only a cock-and-a-bull story."

"I don't think you'll say so when you hear it," said Job, and, commencing from his start from Southgate, he narrated his adventures.

Sir Roland listened listlessly at first, and then eagerly, never once interrupting him.

When he had finished, he said—

"Are you certain that the man you saw lying dead was Herbert Leigh?"

"Quite certain. The moon was full on his face."

"That is well," muttered the baronet; "but it is strange that Ned Wilmot has not been here!"

"Ned Wilmot!" cried Job. "Ah! now I remember. He was dressed so strangely that I knew him not; but, now I think of it, it was he who stopped me on the road."

"But this mountebank[18]—this dressed-up acrobat—what of him?"

Job shuddered.

"Nay, it was no acrobat—no mountebank!" he cried. "It was the devil himself, for he vomited forth sulphurous flames."

"Ha, ha, ha!" laughed a demoniacal voice outside.

Both started up, the baronet now as agitated as his man; but when they glanced out of the window all was still, save that a faint laugh seemed dying away in the distance.

"If these fellows come here playing their mountebank tricks," said the baronet, as he returned to the fire, "they will get more than they bargain for. I should think nothing of shooting them like dogs."

But though he talked in this strain he drank up greedily a tumblerful of wine.

"Don't get gabbling among my people, Job," said he, "about this. You don't know what mischief fools would make out of such a circumstance. But remember tomorrow night. I think it will be best for me to go with you to Rickworth."

"Very well, sir," said Job, much relieved.

"There is a coach which starts back at eleven from the White Posts," continued Sir Roland. "We can catch that, and be home at midnight. Go on, Job, and get yourself some supper; and tell the housekeeper to get mine ready in my bedroom, with a roaring fire. This place has a loneliness about it tonight that I cannot endure. Remember, Job, not a word; and if you should meet Ned Wilmot coming here tonight, let him not know that you recognised him!"

In another moment the baronet was alone.

Save for his awful thoughts.

But not for long was he suffered to be undisturbed.

This time there was a loud and decided knock at the window, and Sir Roland sprang up with an oath.

---

[18] A person who deceives others, especially to trick them out of money.

"Confound these mysterious visitors!" he cried. "Who, in the fiend's name, can it be who comes to the window instead of to the door?"

He hastened to the casement, and saw standing on the terrace outside a man so covered by a long cloak that it was quite impossible to scan his figure or his dress.

His features were entirely concealed by a broad-brimmed hat of felt.

"Who is it who comes like this to my window, instead of to my door, like a thief?" cried the baronet, furiously.

"No thief, Sir Roland; but one who has a right to enter, though he thinks it not safe to do so by the door."

The baronet staggered back.

"That voice!" he cried.

The newcomer laughed.

"Ah! no doubt you know me," he said, in a loud voice "I am Ralph Ashton. Admit me at once."

There was no hesitation on the part of the baronet now.

He instantly opened the French windows and admitted the intruder, who, with a grim smile, entered and passed to the fireplace.

The baronet stepped out, glanced round him to see that there were no intruders, and then, re-entering, joined his unwelcome guest.

"May I ask the reason of this intrusion?" he said, furiously.

"Almost an unnecessary question, as if matters were not in a peculiar stage tonight," replied the one named Ralph Ashton.

He threw off his hat and cloak as he spoke, displaying an elegant costume, and coolly seated himself in a chair opposite to the baronet.

"Be quick and tell me the object of your mission," said Sir Roland. "I am in no humour to be interfered with tonight."

"I don't care one fig for your humour," said Ralph Ashton; "even if I came as usual to demand my rights, I should require a patient hearing, in spite of the cruel power over me which you have obtained through your villainy and falsehood; but I come on no common errand. I come to speak of the death of Herbert Leigh."

"I know of it," cried Sir Roland, who was, nevertheless, deeply impressed by the unexpected knowledge of his visitor.

"No doubt, since you ordered it."

"Have a care!" cried Sir Roland, extending his hand towards the bell-rope.

"Bah! I don't fear you," exclaimed Ralph. "I have a weapon with which I would shoot you like a cur, as you are, if you dared to ring."

He drew a tiny pistol from his pocket as he spoke, at which the baronet glanced, but made no reply.

"Yes," continued Ralph. "Herbert Leigh was murdered in the old Mint. I saw his dead body; and I know his murderer—Ned Wilmot."

"This is pure madness. I—"

"Spare your denials," said Ralph. "I am not in a position to show myself, in order to drag you to justice, but I will do so quickly, and risk all danger to myself, if you do not at once perform some tardy act of reparation."

"What mean you?"

"I mean that Herbert Leigh, who has been murdered by your order, has left a daughter."

The baronet recoiled.

"Ah!" he cried, "I knew not of this."

"No doubt," said Ralph;." but it is nevertheless true. Daisy Leigh lives in spite of her brutal assailant, and saw the murder of her father and knows his assassin."

"And whom do you say that she accuses?" said Sir Roland.

"Ned Wilmot, that ruffian, half-poacher, half-gamekeeper, who used to be in your employment, and who seems to be so still, although he is a highwayman and an assassin."

"Do you dare impute to me the incitement of Ned Wilmot to the murder of Herbert Leigh?" cried the baronet, fiercely.

"I say to your face that you are the most interested in Herbert Leigh's death, that I believe you ordered this man to procure you those papers at any cost, and that the reason why the body of the murdered man is even now lying not far hence, instead of peacefully in London, is because it was brought down here for you to identify."

Sir Roland was livid with rage.

He sprang up and seized the bell-rope.

"I will have you thrust from the door," he said. "I will listen to none of this. You have invented this story to frighten me and to extort money. There is no such person as Herbert Leigh. He died years ago, after hiding away from the consequences of his misconduct. Anybody, alive or dead, whom you produce as Leigh, will be an impostor. You cannot prove his identity."

"Daisy Leigh lives, and can prove all."

"She cannot prove anything, except that she is called Leigh. She cannot prove that her father was Herbert Leigh, for she knows not anything, save from his own lips, and that would go for nothing."

Ralph Ashton saw the difficulty.

"You have worked your villainy well indeed," he said; "but you shall not work in the same way with me. I am here once more to demand my papers."

"I have no papers."

"You may not have them, but you know where they are," replied Ralph. "You are afraid to let me have them, because you know that I could then prove my innocence of the vile charges brought against me, and boldly assert my rights."

The baronet had by this time recovered his equanimity somewhat.

The very mention of papers by Ralph had reminded him of his power.

"I refuse to hold converse with you. When you can prove your innocence you can return here, and I will do what I can for you. But I refuse to harbour in my place, a man over whose head the cloud of suspicion hangs. A forger is not a valuable acquisition to a family."

"You lie!" cried Ralph, fiercely, as he sprang to his feet. "You know I am innocent; you know you hold your title and your property by a fraud. I don't believe there is a drop of Ashton blood in your veins. But, beware; though at present I am compelled to visit you thus in the dead of the night it will not be for long. I will haunt you and yours in some way or another. I will force you to disgorge your ill-gotten spoil, and I swear never to rest until I bring you to justice as a thief and an assassin."

Sir Roland rang the bell violently.

"This is too much," he cried, "I cannot endure such insults in my own house. A prison cell will soon alter your feelings."

But Ralph was not to be caught thus.

Raising suddenly a glass which was half full of wine, he dashed it into the face of the baronet, and, rushing across the room, passed out upon the terrace.

Foaming with rage at the insult and the pain, the baronet rang more furiously still.

In a few moments two menservants appeared.

"Quick!" he said; "let the grounds be searched everywhere. That forging thief, who calls himself Ralph Ashton has been here, and has tried to take my life!"

The men waited for nothing more.

They fled through the window, calling on their way at the gardener's cottage to procure further assistance.

But it was all in vain.

Seek where they would they could find no one in the grounds.

At length, dispirited and tired, they were returning, expecting to receive savage abuse from their master for their failure, when a hollow sepulchral laugh sounded beside them.

Then a whirring, whizzing noise was heard, and they saw, leaping over their heads, the awful form of Spring-Heeled Jack.

They noted well his diabolical attributes, his red body, his bat wings, his cloven foot, and saw the sulphurous smoke and flame issuing from his mouth.

For an instant they were paralysed with horror and dismay.

Then, as if unbound from the chain of fear, they fled with loud cries of alarm, nor stopped until they had all huddled into the baronet's room.

They expected a torrent of abuse.

They found him trembling and half-fainting in his chair.

He, too, had seen the awful visitation, which had stood at the French windows, and flapped its wings, and emitted its sulphurous smoke and flame, and uttered the words—

"Beware, Sir Roland Ashton, your time will soon come"

He listened in bewilderment but no disbelief to the story told by the men.

He gulped down two glasses of wine, and gave the alarmed men some also.

"This is, of course, some vile trick," he said; "but it might frighten the women from the house. Say nothing of it below. I should not like it to reach the ears of Miss Marfield."

The men promised accordingly, and within half an hour the footman had told Emily, the lady's maid, the gardener had told his wife, and the butler had confided the news to the cook.

All, of course, under strict secrecy!

Meanwhile, while Sir Roland slunk up into his bedroom and locked himself in, drawing the curtain closely, strange events were happening in another part of the house.

CHAPTER V.

CONSTANCE MARFIELD—A LOVE MEETING UNDER DIFFICULTIES.

CONSTANCE MARFIELD, full of thoughts of the morrow, when she was to hear the story of her life, and know her proper position in society, had retired to her room before Ralph Ashton's unexpected visit to Sir Roland.

She was not weary.

In fact, she had no desire for sleep; she only desired to be alone.

Her thoughts were anything but calm or pleasant ones.

For a long time she had been secretly betrothed to Ralph, whom she had met ere the hideous charge of forgery had been brought against him by Sir Roland.

They had been brought up together, in fact, and had loved at an earlier period than is generally the case.

Ralph was supposed, until the age of sixteen, to be the son of a poor relation of the baronet, whom he had adopted from charity. Constance was a ward left in his charge by a friend.

They were always together, and consequently the young girl became an adept in all kinds of boyish exercises, which in after years stood her in good stead.

Rowing, fishing, riding, cricket, birds' nesting, occupied the two, for they were very little interfered with by Sir Roland, and in those happy days of rough and ready play Ralph had abundant chances of observing the beauties of his sweet young companion.

Her face had already a womanly tenderness in it, her figure was well developed for a girl of fifteen, with firm shoulders, a budding bust, and lower limbs—displayed freely by her short skirts—which had been rounded and brought to perfection by constant exercise.

Ralph could not but feel the sweet influence of her presence, and, scarcely knowing what his feelings were, he was unhappy save in her presence.

It was an accident which proved to both their mental feelings.

They had been boating on the river, and, feeling flushed and tired, they drew their little skiff under the shadow of some trees, and, getting out, sat, or rather half reclined, on the soft green velvet of the bank.

Constance was then approaching sixteen, while Ralph was a little over that age.

The young girl was dressed in a white muslin dress, trimmed with blue, which set off her beauty to the best advantage, cut, as it was, square, so as to display a tempting view of the soft and delicately-rounded bosom.

With her head on his shoulder, and his arm clasping her lithe waist, they talked of the present and the future, and he saw how her eyes dimmed when he spoke of going abroad as a soldier in a marching regiment.

"Don't talk of going away," she said. "I should be so lonely without you."

He looked at her curiously.

"I am afraid I cannot idle my time away here very long," he said. "I am here, so I am told, merely on sufferance, and as I get older I must do something for my living."

The tears came into the girl's eyes, and she flung her arms round his neck.

"Don't talk about it any more," she said. "I can't bear the thought of it."

And then, with her troubled little form palpitating in his arms, he found himself raining kisses on her lips, while their hearts beat madly against each other.

This was first love, and both knew it.

"Darling—darling Constance!" said Ralph, "I may have to leave you, but it will not be for long. I must make a position, and get a good home, for you must be my wife, Constance."

And the girl, under the intoxicating influence of this first passion, shed tears of joy, and gave her promise.

After this unexpected episode the two were never happy apart.

They had been together nearly always before.

Now they were inseparable, but by a kind of tacit understanding Constance gave up most of her boyish enjoyments.

The young lovers mostly spent their time strolling through the woods, or lying side by side on the banks of the river, looking into each other's eyes, and, between their passionate kisses, planning sweet schemes for the future.

There was to be a cruel awakening, and it soon came.

One evening, Sir Roland had gone to London, and the young people were left entirely to their own devices.

"Constance," said Ralph, "you have often wanted to have a look at the old west wing, which is never used. Let's go tonight. Sir Roland will not be home until tomorrow; and if you meet me in the blue corridor after supper we can prowl all over the old place without being observed. I confess I am quite as curious as you are."

Directly after they had partaken of supper with the housekeeper they bade each other goodnight and separated.

But as soon as all was quiet Ralph crept up to the blue corridor, tapped at the door of Constance's bedroom, and was soon joined by the young girl.

She was dressed in dark velvet, which, while it showed up the soft tinting of her skin, made her a less conspicuous object, and less likely to attract notice if anyone was watching.

We need not describe their wanderings about the old house.

They made no sound, for neither wore boots; and they had exhausted the old place, as they imagined, when they came suddenly upon a little door which had been left ajar.

All the rest of the building was dark and gloomy, and cobwebby and uncanny; but the room into which this door led was furnished in modern style, and was evidently used by Sir Roland as a kind of study, or counting-house.

There were papers littered about everywhere; and, indeed, no care seemed to have been made to conceal anything.

Nevertheless it appeared strange to Ralph that Sir Roland should choose such a place—far away across the uninhabited west wing—for a repository for his papers.

They were both going to retire and leave the place as they found it, when suddenly Ralph caught sight of his own name on a slip of paper.

Curiosity naturally caused him to examine the paper, and as he read a flush suffused his cheeks, and a bright light came into his eyes.

"Well," he muttered, presently, with clenched teeth, "I have been unable to warm towards Sir Roland, in spite of all he has done for me; but now I know him to be a villain."

Constance glanced at him as if she thought for the moment that he had taken leave of his senses.

"A villain? Oh! Ralph," she said, "Sir Roland may be stern and morose, and strange at times, but he is not a villain."

"Read this and see for yourself," said Ralph, with a laugh which was far from being musical.

SPRING-HEELED JACK,
THE TERROR OF LONDON.

By the Author of "TURNPIKE DICK, the Star of the Road."

SPRING-HEELED JACK WHIZZED UP FROM THE GROUND AND BOUNDED OVER THEIR HEADS.

The young girl took the paper and read.

We need not waste time in recapitulating it here; let it suffice to say that if the papers and certificates were true Ralph was the only son of Sir Guy Ashton, instead of the child of some distant poor relation.

"Now what do you think?" said Ralph, as Constance finished reading. "If this is true (and there can be no reason to doubt it), I am Sir Ralph Ashton, and proprietor of this place. If I can prove all this it will not be long before I am proprietor of something else, and that is yourself, dear Constance; for though we are both so young we are all the world to each other, and there can be no need to wait."

Hardly had the words left his lips when a loud and furious voice cried—

"What is the meaning of this? How dare you bring Miss Constance into the master's private study?"

It was the voice of Caleb Masters, the secretary and general factotum of the baronet.

He was a man of most unscrupulous mind, and, being deeply in the secrets of his master, he had often warned the baronet of the danger of leaving his private papers about.

"I am not aware that I have ever been ordered not to come into this room," said Ralph; "but what I have discovered now I am here makes me very thankful that I did come."

"And pray what have you discovered?" asked the secretary, concealing his alarm beneath a sneer.

"That I am Sir Ralph Ashton, only son of Sir Guy Ashton, and, consequently, master of this house," replied the daring youth. "While I hold in my hands these papers who can gainsay me?"

These words were fatal to his chance.

Caleb was a tall, wiry man, of great strength, and in an instant, before Ralph was aware of his intention, the secretary had leaped upon him.

Constance, thinking that murder was contemplated, filled the air with her shrieks.

But, finding that no one responded to her cries in that uninhabited wing, she cast aside all maidenly fear, and exerted all the power of her lithe young limbs to aid her lover.

In vain.

A cruel blow stretched Ralph on the floor, after he had made a brave resistance, and then Caleb turned savagely to Constance.

"You had better keep quiet, my young spitfire!" he said. "If you attack me again I shall make no difference because you are a girl. I shall serve you just the same as I have served him."

The girl saw that further resistance was impossible, or, at any rate, useless.

Her eyes were full of tears, and her bosom was heaving with emotion.

"You are a brute and a coward, Caleb Masters," she said; "and I don't believe that even Sir Roland will approve of what you have done. Help me to carry Master Ralph to his room."

"I don't want any help," cried Caleb, seizing the boy's insensible form, and carrying him as easily as if he had been a baby; "I'll take him to his bedroom, and you had better go to yours, or I shall have to take you. Ah! it's no use trying to look for the papers; I've got them safe enough. So come quickly."

Mostly for Ralph's sake Constance made no further resistance, and in a few moments the unfortunate boy was in his room, where Caleb roughly roused him to his senses, and locked him in.

This being done, and Constance having been secured also, Caleb saddled a horse and galloped away to London.

Next morning Sir Roland returned, and sent at once for Ralph.

The latter was furious at the discovery he had made, at Caleb's brutal blow, at the confinement in his room which had followed.

He confronted Sir Roland with flashing eyes.

"I am glad you have returned, Sir Roland," he said; "for, setting aside what I have discovered since you have been gone, I have been subjected to gross ill-treatment. When you know all you will, no doubt, turn Caleb Masters out of the house."

Sir Roland listened to what he had to say, and then said, calmly—

"I have heard all that has transpired since I left home, and I can only praise Mr. Masters for his courage and devotion to my service. In the first place those papers which you tried to steal are some old forgeries, which I keep by me in order to use if any of the old set try to annoy me. Sir Guy never had a son. But as to that I have no more to say. What I wish you to know is that I have discovered your ungrateful forgery of my name."

Ralph reeled back in horror and astonishment.

"Forgery!" he cried. "I fail to understand what you mean."

"You remember that you bought a bracelet for Constance, my ward?"

"Yes."

"At the time I remarked upon its value, and expressed wonder at your being able to buy it."

"Well?" said Ralph, haughtily.

"I find now you told me a falsehood," said Sir Roland. "You said you had been saving up your pocket money, and I find that you forged a cheque upon my bank for twenty pounds, and sent Tom Smith, the blacksmith's son, to cash it for you."

Ralph pressed his hand to his brow.

What complicated piece of villainy was this?

"But this is all false," he said; "you know it is. I have never—"

"Spare your words," said Sir Roland. "I have quite made up my mind how to act. I am going to give you fifty pounds, and you must leave my house within the hour. If ever you show your face here again—"

"It will be as master," cried Ralph.

The baronet laughed dryly, though there was a certain nervousness in his manner.

"Don't worry your mind or other people's with that folly," he said. "Those forgeries are all destroyed. To make any such claim would only make things worse for you. So take this cheque and go."

"And if I refuse?"

"I will send for the constables, and they will take you to the lock-up."

Ralph was in a strange predicament.

If he dared the baronet to do his worst he might be convicted for the mere want of anyone to take his part, unless the necessary papers to prove his innocence and his identity were forthcoming.

"I will go," he said, "and I will take your money also, because it is mine; but I warn you that this is the worst day's work you have ever done. In a very short time I shall be able to prove the falsity of your words. You, in your black heart, know that they are false, and the day will come when you will regret that you so cruelly ill-treated and maligned one of your own kindred."

He turned on his heel as he spoke and quitted the room.

Sir Roland made no effort to call him back, and Ralph at once went in search of Constance.

But he could find no trace of her.

She had evidently been either spirited away or she had been confined in some secret room till he had departed.

At any rate, from the time that Ralph and Constance had entered the private room of Sir Roland they had never met.

They had corresponded by means of bribes to servants and so forth; and in their letters they had poured forth all the love which they could not explain by word of mouth.

Their hearts were still true.

But after the lapse of all these years Ralph was no nearer to proving his innocence.

He seemed, in fact, to be surrounded by such a network of villainy, that it was impossible to break through it.

On this evening—the eve of Constance's twenty-first birthday—she had received a letter which had caused her heart to leap with joy.

It was from Ralph, and said, merely—

"I am coming to see Sir Roland tonight. If all goes well, I shall demand to see you. I think that his villainy is overreaching itself."

But the hours had gone by, and he had not come; and Constance began to undress to go to bed.

She smiled sadly as she stood opposite the mirror when she had removed her dress.

"I am sorry that he has not come," she murmured. "I am sure that I should please him. He left me a raw, uncultured, immature girl, though with a true and faithful heart. He will find a woman, mature in judgment as in form, and still true. I am sure he will not think my looks have deteriorated."

Indeed, no.

She could not be insensible to her own beauty as she stood there gazing at the sweet, sad face, the masses of wavy hair, the large, round, creamy shoulders; the firm, voluptuous bust; the soft, enticing arms.

As she stood thus, admiring her beauty for his sake, a slight rustle startled her.

She listened eagerly.

Again the sound.

It seemed to come from outside the window.

A joyous feeling entered her bosom.

Could this be Ralph?

She went softly to the window, and peered through the glass.

At first she saw nothing, but after a moment she heard again the rustling sound among the ivy; and then a man's head appeared.

She could not recognise him in the strange, dim light; in fact, not having seen him for so many years, it was difficult for her to say how she would recognise him at all.

The stranger tapped at the window.

"Hist! Open, Constance," he whispered, with his mouth against the glass; "it is I— Ralph!"

She hastily threw a light shawl loosely over her gleaming shoulders to protect herself against the night-chill, and threw up the window.

"Is it you, really, Ralph?" she said, in low and tremulous accents.

"Yes, Constance. I am but little changed save in height and strength. May I enter?"

How could she hesitate? How, after five years of separation, could they allow a feeling of prudery to prevent their enjoying the delights of this stolen meeting?

"Yes, Ralph, come in," she said; "but you must speak low, for the house is full of spies; and if Sir Roland found you here, his fury would know no bounds."

There was very little said either low or loud for the next few minutes after Constance had closed the window, for Ralph had caught her to his heart and devoured her with hungry kisses.

Their lips met in long, passionate caresses, which seemed like an interchange of souls, and then, when they were a little calmer, he sat down in a large easy chair by the fire, and she, jumping on his lap, as in the happy days of old, nestled in his arms.

They were boy and girl again.

The lapse of years was forgotten.

"And you really believe that Sir Roland is a murderer?" she said.

"Yes. That is to say, the horrid crime was committed by his orders. No matter who did it, he was the murderer if he ordered it."

"And what do you propose to do?"

"I can do nothing in the way of punishing him yet," said Ralph. "I must wait and be patient. But for you, dearest Constance, I see no obstacle now to our speedy union. To-morrow you will be twenty-one, and your own mistress. No matter how, I am earning enough to offer you a good home, and, consequently, if you make delay it will be your own fault."

She nestled to him closely.

"Don't speak crossly, Ralph," she said. "I am sure I shall put no obstacle in the way of our marriage. I shall only be too glad to escape from this place, which is like a prison, where I am watched every hour. But how can it be carried out?"

"You must escape to me," said Ralph, "within a week from this time. I will be at this window with a rope ladder, and I will aid you to reach the grounds. I shall have horses ready, and we must fly at once to Baddington.[19] There we can be married by special license, and we can defy all the Sir Rolands in the world."

"Within a week," she said.

They little knew what would happen in a week; little knew that at that very moment stealthy steps were approaching their chamber.

For a moment Constance gave herself up to the delicious thoughts roused in her mind by the words of her lover, who kissed and caressed her with a daring fervour which would at another time have brought blushes to her cheeks.

---

19 A parish in the English county of Cheshire.

Then she roused herself.

"I fancy I hear sounds without," she said. "Let me go and listen."

She glided from his lap, and in a few moments was listening at the door.

As she did so Ralph also thought he could hear sounds as of creeping steps and whispering voices.

Of course it is easy to listen in the dark until you can fancy that you hear sounds.

And so at first they were not sure.

Both were loth to part so soon after such a long separation; but, as presently the noises came nearer, Constance glided across once more to her lover.

"Pray fly, Ralph!" she cried. "You will be seized and made a prisoner if they have suspected you and they find you here. Go, and if all goes well it shall be as you wish."

One more fervid kiss, and Ralph rapidly, but noiselessly, approached the window and threw it up. In a moment he was outside, rapidly descending, as he had ascended, by the ivy.

Scarcely had the casement been closed again than a loud knocking came at the door.

"Who is there?" cried Constance, in a sleepy voice.

"Sir Roland and Mrs. Levine."

This was the housekeeper.

"What is it you require at this hour?"

"Open the door! You have had that villain Ralph Ashton here, and we are seeking him."

"I refuse to open," said Constance; "there is no one here."

She did not for a moment suppose that Sir Roland would proceed to violence; but in an instant she found her mistake, for, with a rush of his powerful shoulders, he burst open the door.

He found Constance standing defiantly in the middle of the room in the beautiful dishabille in which Ralph had surprised her, and, furious as he was, Sir Roland's eyes could not avoid resting for a moment on the girl's superb form and gleaming shoulders.

"Where is Ralph?" he cried.

"I refuse to answer. Search the room," replied Constance, as she snatched up a shawl and drew it round her.

They did with no effect, as we know.

"He has escaped by the window, Mrs. Levine," said the baronet, presently. "You are certain you heard his voice?"

"Yes—certain," replied the housekeeper. "I heard them talking and kissing, and I heard something said about a speedy marriage."

Sir Roland laughed, though his eyes flashed vengefully.

"Ha, ha!" he cried, "there will, no doubt, be a speedy marriage—eh, Mrs. Levine? But of that tomorrow. Meanwhile, I am ashamed to find that you have received a lover in your bedroom. It is not wonderful, however, considering the stock you come from. In a few hours you will know all. And now to saddle my horse and capture that traitor and assassin."

If these words were intended to create any terror or despair in the mind of Constance they utterly failed.

She merely turned away with a contemptuous smile and walked to the window.

In a few moments the baronet had passed down the stairs and been met by Caleb

Masters, who, though older, still looked just as powerful and just as crafty.

"Sir Roland," he whispered, "Ned Wilmot is here."

The baronet uttered an exclamation of astonishment yet half-pleasure.

"How imprudent!" he muttered; "yet he comes in the nick of time. Lead me to him. Where is he?"

"He is in your study. He says he comes to you on a matter of life or death, and no one has seen him save me."

In a few moments the baronet was in the presence of the dastardly assassin of the Mint.

"Excuse my intrusion at this hour," he began.

But Sir Roland interrupted him.

"Nay, this is no time for apology," he cried. "What I want you to understand as you are here is that Ralph Ashton has only just escaped from this house. He cannot be gone far, follow him and kill him, for he knows our secret. Talk of nothing now, but follow on his track and never come back hither until you can tell me he is no longer living. Hasten—waste no time!"

Ned Wilmot made a wry face.

"You see, money—"

The baronet flung a purse well filled on the table.

"Take that for the present," he said, "and linger no longer."

The assassin pocketed the money with a grin, coolly lifted the wine bottle to his lips, and took a goodly draught, and then going to the French window, passed out.

"Fear not," said he as he went, "Master Ralph shall not trouble you long. I know his haunts, and it will be a puzzler to me if my knife doesn't divide his left ribs within a week!"

This settled, a few words were exchanged between Sir Roland and Caleb, and then the former once more sought his bedchamber.

"By Jove! I never knew that Constance was such a lovely girl," he murmured to himself, as he got into bed. "I never before had such a good view of her charms. I must have her for myself. I might make a worse choice, and if I make up my mind I'll have her by fair means or foul."

CHAPTER VI.

DAISY LEIGH ONCE MORE—GEDGE FOOTE, THE DWARF BAGSMAN, TRAPPED.

GEDGE FOOTE, whom we mentioned in our first chapter, was almost the first one to enter the murder-room in the Mint after Ned Wilmot had escaped, and Spring-Heeled Jack had leaped out of the window.

He was a strange-looking being.

About four feet and a-half in height, he had a large head of a bullet shape, covered with shock red hair, massive shoulders, with scarcely any neck, long unshapely arms and bandy legs.

His hands were large and claw-like, and gave one the idea that one grip from them could squeeze the life out of a man were he ever so strong.

His face was such as might be expected from such a body, with small, cunning eyes, an upward turning nose and a big gash of a mouth.

He was a strange being, not only in his appearance but in his habits.

He was known as a bagsman, or "commercial traveller," but he was, in reality, a pedlar, who sold trinkets and so forth, and did odd strokes of business which were not consistent with strict notions of honesty.

In fact, he was supposed to be a receiver of stolen goods, and to take long journeys into distant parts of England for the purpose of disposing of things which had been appropriated by the thieves of the Mint.

Whatever he was, his movements were very mysterious, and he never gave the police the chance of catching him.

Well, on that dreadful evening, after Ned Wilmot had fled and the hue and cry after him was going on, Gedge Foote entered the room where the body of Herbert Leigh lay, with Daisy still on the couch of rags in the corner.

Those who had raised the alarm at first, when the cries of "Help—help—murder!" had ceased, had only seen the dead body, and had not observed the form of the girl in the half darkness.

But Gedge, who knew her well, and had often cast longing looks at the trim little figure in its shabby garments, and the neat little foot and ankle, was sure that the girl must be somewhere about; and relighting the candle, which had been overturned in the struggle, he sought for her and found her.

She was just recovering consciousness, her eyes were opening and gleaming round her as if to realise her position; her lips were pale—pale almost as the white breast which rose and fell in spasmodic throbs under Gedge's admiring gaze.

He knelt down and half-raised her, at the same time pouring a little brandy from his flask between the pouting lips.

"This is a terribly bad business, Miss Daisy," he said; "but you must try and bear up under it, if it's only for the sake of having revenge."

She shuddered as she looked at him.

He was so terribly ugly—uglier than ever when he tried to act the consoler.

But his kindness had given her life for the moment.

"If you will help me up I will go into my room and put on my things, so that I can see the people who will be sure to come," she said.

And she blushed even in the middle of her sorrow to think that he had caught her in such dishabille.[20]

She had scarcely dressed when the heavy tramp of feet was heard, and presently two constables, an inspector, and a surgeon entered.

The girl gave her account of the affair as well as she could; but she was not pressed to say much.

The next day the enquiry would take place, and before then she would be able to collect her thoughts.

"But you can't stop here, my dear," said the surgeon, kindly. "This is no scene for you, and there really does not seem to be any accommodation for you."

"There's a person over the way—Mrs. Porter," said Gedge Foote, "who would gladly give the young lady a bed."

"Yes, Mrs. Porter, I know her," said the inspector, "very well. Come with me, and we

---

[20] State of partial undress.

will see that you are safe for the night at least."

All those three stout-hearted men felt compassion for poor little Daisy; she seemed so small and fragile a flower to blossom into life in such a terrible way as this.

On undressing that night in her strange room, she found the note which Spring-Heeled Jack had placed in her bosom, after he had felt her heart to see if she still lived.

She shuddered as she remembered the awful apparition which had saved her from Ned Wilmot, but yet she felt sure that he was a friend.

"Spirit or no spirit," she thought, "he saved my life, and, maybe, my honour, for I saw passions of every evil kind in that murderer's face. I know not the place he mentions, but I can find out. Gedge Foote, hideous as he is, seems kind, I will ask him."

Kind!

How little she knew of human nature when she could dream of trusting such a being.

But, then, how could she imagine that she had excited in the mind of this hideous dwarf a wild, mad passion, which could only be extinguished by death?

While Daisy was sleeping, in spite of her terrible trouble, and in consequence of a sly little something put in her warm drink by the worthy Mrs. Porter, strange things were going on over at the house where the murder had been committed.

The door of the room had been locked, everything had been left just as the police had found it; and a constable was located in the porch below to keep watch.

At first, of course, considerable excitement prevailed in the street; a motley crowd gathered round the door, and groups stood chatting at different points.

But people at last grew weary and went off to bed, the street regained its normal aspect, and the murder was left to be raked up again in the morning.

About an hour after the place had become quiet a strange thing happened.

A hackney coach came slowly and methodically round the corner.

It came from the direction of the Three Mariners, and on the box beside the driver was a man dressed in the garb of a policeman.

In swift whispers he told her of the events which had occurred in the time which had elapsed since they last met.

They drove down the street very quietly, and stopped at the door of the house of murder.

Then the door of the cab was opened, and two more men in the garb of policemen stepped out.

Their knock brought out the constable who had been left to watch in the parlour, and who, naturally imagining that the corpse would not be likely to run away, thought it no harm to doze awhile.

He looked at them in dubious amazement.

"Why, what's the matter?" he said.

"Hush! I can't talk outside," replied the one who seemed in command of the new arrivals; and the whole party, including the one who had sat on the box with the driver, entered the house.

The constable looked still more disconcerted when he saw the newcomers in the light of the lamp.

There was not one familiar face.

"What is your business?" he asked.

"The body has to be removed."

"Where to?"

"The mortuary."

The man stared in bewilderment.

The proceeding, as he was well aware, was most unusual.

"By whose orders?" he asked.

"By those of the Chief Commissioner," said the head constable. "See, here is his order. Read for yourself."

The man was quite dazed by the wonderful quickness of the whole affair, but, in obedience to orders, he bent over the blue official-looking paper which the man produced.

That was all that was wanted.

In an instant one of the pretended constables drew from his pocket a handkerchief and thrust it into the face of the reading constable.

The effect was almost instantaneous.

He gave one reproachful look at the man in front of him, then his arms dropped helplessly by his side, his eyes closed, and he was a mere tool in their hands.

In an instant he was searched and the keys taken from him.

"Now then," said one of the men, "we must do all this very quickly. He won't be insensible more than a few minutes. You, Clarkson, stop here, and if he wants another sniff, why give it to him."

Leaving one of the sham constables, whom they addressed as Clarkson, to watch the insensible man, they then ascended the stairs, and, without hesitation, entered the room where the tragedy had occurred.

They looked quite callously at the dead body, which already began to look awful in its pallor and rigidity, more especially when taken in conjunction with the horrible surroundings.

To them death was nothing.

In one way or another they had become careless of it.

Without a word they raised the body, and, dispensing with throwing anything over it, proceeded to carry it downstairs.

To cover it up would have disarranged their plans.

When they reached the basement story they did not pass out of the front door, but, opening a side one, which led out into a little court, they so held the murdered man that he looked as if he was incapably drunk, and was being assisted along by the policemen.

In this manner they helped him along until they reached the street.

No one was about.

The wonder-seekers were at rest for the moment.

So they had no difficulty in placing the body in the hackney-coach, and in doing everything unseen and unknown by anyone.

Then a light whistle brought out the man who had been left to mind the constable, and in a few moments all had quitted the neighbourhood.

This is how the body of Herbert Leigh had made its appearance in the vicinity of Ashton Hall.

The excitement at the disappearance of the body was very great—the "Mint" chuckled at the utter confusion of the police—the papers made a great thing of it.

But no clue was obtained.

Wherever Herbert Leigh's dead body had been spirited away there it remained, and poor Daisy felt doubly bereft.

Of what use were her unavailing declarations?

She knew who had murdered her father, she felt sure who had instigated the murder; but of what use would it be for her to make reckless and unsupported declarations?

It was best to bide her time.

Though she had been terrified out of all measure by the apparition of Spring-Heeled Jack, she felt that he was her friend.

She did not dare, as it were, to believe in the supernatural; but, of course, it was impossible to account in any other way for the strange appearance of the being who had rescued her.

She was content, therefore, to abide by what she had seen, and trust to the future to explain all.

She was without any protector now.

She could not look for protection to a being whom she knew not, and whom she could not call to her aid.

So in this predicament she turned to Gedge Foote.

She saw no wrong in this.

He had been kind to her; and, having lived in the same house as herself and her father, was comparatively acquainted with them.

She resolved to ask him, therefore, what best to do.

From all Gedge could derive from her words, Ned Wilmot, the man who had murdered her father, had made up his mind to possess her for himself, consequently anything which enabled her to keep out of the clutches of this fiend would be acceptable.

Loving her with an insane passion, which she had not the slightest conception of, he lost sight of the idea of his own repulsive ugliness, and only thought that incessant and patient waiting and never-ceasing attention would win her to himself.

If Daisy had had one notion of such a thing as this she would never have accepted his aid.

But, perfectly innocent of the fact that he could conceive such a mad idea, she confided to him the fact that she desired to quit the Mint, and proceed to the place mentioned by Spring-Heeled Jack, Mrs. Barton, of River Cottage, Edmonton.

She was perfectly ignorant of localities, and consequently she was quite unprepared to give Gedge any idea of the neighbourhood to which she desired to go.

However, Gedge knew.

"I could take you to the place blindfolded," he said, "but I don't think you'll like it."

"I must put up with it," replied Daisy, "since my father is dead, and his body has been spirited away. I have nothing to bind me to this spot, and I wish to quit it as quickly as possible. I fear every moment to see the hateful face of Ned Wilmot."

"You ought to wish that," said Gedge, "you could then give him into custody."

"No, no. It is useless. I could prove nothing," said the young girl. "Leave him to time and private vengeance. He will receive far greater punishment than he would at the hand of the law."

"It shall all be as you please," said Gedge; "but don't you think that your sudden disappearance, after the vanishing of your father's body, will give subject for suspicion by the police."

"I care not," said Daisy. "I will risk that and anything to get away from this place."

That evening Gedge Foote and his confiding companion quitted Mrs. Porter's, and taking a hackney coach in the next street, began riding quickly towards the vicinity of Battersea.

Although our story is a comparatively modern one, this neighbourhood had no resemblance to what it is at the present day.

It abounded in narrow dirty alleys and lanes, and long dreary stretches of swamp; at night it often happened that houses built on the edge of the water were entirely obscured by mist.

As the hackney coach rolled into one of these alleys, and then came out upon a dismal piece of marsh with not a house visible, and only here and there a bare looking tree, the girl's heart sank within her bosom.

What could her mysterious friend mean by asking her to immure herself in such a terrible spot of desolation?

Could it be possible that she was only escaping from one trap to fall into another?

However, it was too late now to retreat.

So she only made some commonplace remark about the dreariness of the surroundings.

"Yes, you're right," said Gedge Foote, "it's about the most dismal swamp that you can find round London. I expect your friend, however, had excellent reasons for advising this as a place of safety."

"No doubt!" said Daisy, as the horse drew up before a house, which looked only like a huge black barn in the lampless darkness. "I expect he thinks that no one will be likely to seek me here."

"Just so," said Gedge, "but even if he deserts you, remember, I know where you are, and that I will never betray your whereabouts."

And as he helped her to alight the dwarf bagsman squeezed her hand impressively.

The house, approached across a dismal garden, was apparently a small squarely-built one, and the door was soon opened by an elderly woman of nondescript appearance.

Of course Daisy was unaware of the fact that Gedge Foote had been there during the day, that instead of being Barton the woman's name was Foster, and that Spring-Heeled Jack (whatever that mysterious person might be) knew no more of this female and her place than the man in the moon.

But so it was.

Mrs. Foster was a friend of the dwarf, had assumed the name of Barton to oblige him, and Daisy Leigh was fairly trapped.

However, she made no enquiries. Young and simple as she was she had formed plans secretly.

She was told that her friend had paid in advance for her lodging and board for a month, and, thinking the woman meant the awful apparition who had so mysteriously befriended her, she accepted her position gratefully, and only wondered how long it would be before the mystery was explained.

It was late when they had had supper, and Gedge Foote was leaving.

They were alone as he rose to say good-bye.

"Good-bye, Daisy," he said. "I hope you will be comfortable here. But there's one thing I fancy your friend has forgotten."

"What is that?"

"I don't think you have any money."

The young girl flushed. She had never thought of this. The money left her by Spring-Heeled Jack had already been spent.

"Well, she stammered, "that is true; but I don't think I shall want any, at any rate, just yet. Everything has been paid for."

"Yes, yes," said Gedge; "but then you don't know what may happen, and you have no clothes with you."

They were in the little parlour alone, and he took her hand.

The light was very dim.

Only two candles were there to illuminate the room.

He felt her tremble, but she did not refuse.

He placed in her hand two sovereigns,[21] which she held, reluctantly.

"You are very kind to me, Mr. Foote," she said. "I shall never be able to repay you."

"Will you not?" he said.

And then the impulse upon him proved too great—his passion overcame him.

In an instant his arm was round her waist, his lips glued to hers—her lithe body was held close up to his breast, so that he could feel the palpitation of her bosom and the rapid beating of her heart.

Then he released her without a word and fled.

Daisy fell into a chair—aghast, amazed, ashamed.

In an instant the whole truth was upon her.

This hideous dwarf loved her!

Herself was the reward he was going to claim for his protection.

She cried for very vexation, and spitefully wiped his kisses from her lips.

"Poor wretch!" she murmured; "perhaps he is not aware of his own hideous ugliness. But his wife! Heavens! that would be too terrible. I, who have been brought up, even through abject poverty, to be a lady in thought, and hope for a lady's career. Well, well! he has quickly put me on my guard. If he attempts to make love to me I must fly, no matter whither."

Poor little Daisy!

It was all very well for her to plan like this, but she knew not half the terrible wickedness of Gedge Foote's nature.

She was on the brink of an awful precipice!

CHAPTER VII.

PURSUED BY AN ASSASSIN—CONSTANCE HEARS BAD NEWS—
SIR ROLAND'S AND CALEB'S JOURNEY—SPRING-HEELED JACK TERRIFIES THE
PEOPLE ON THE STAGE COACH, AND TAKES A RISE OUT OF THE BARONET.

NED WILMOT, although he had expected a far different reception by Sir Roland, and had hoped to be able at once to have explained his perilous position, lost no time in carrying out the murderous designs of his employer.

---

[21] A coin worth one pound.

His plan was to follow the road which Ralph Ashton would be most like to take to reach London that night.

If he missed him he would disguise himself and haunt the neighbourhood day and night.

One thing was certain—

Sir Roland had made up his mind that Ralph Ashton must die.

And die he must.

The baronet had Ned Wilmot far too much in his power to allow of any denial.

So the man, whose character resembled nothing so much as that of an Italian bravo, rode off, whistling a song lowly to himself, and thinking how he should best get "the job" over quick and have time to enjoy himself.

Everything seemed very quiet.

The moon had come out suddenly and bathed all things in her silver glory.

Over park, and grounds, and lake, and road, the calm of an exquisite night had fallen.

Not a sound, save the vague and gentle sighing of the wind, was to be heard, and as Ned Wilmot's horse leaped the hedge and began to clatter along the high road, the noise of the horse's footsteps resounded far over the countryside.

He had scarcely reached the bend in the road where the ruins stood, the spot where the dead body of Herbert Leigh had been found by Spring-Heeled Jack, when there was heard the loud and demoniacal laugh which had so terrified Ned Wilmot in the murder-room in the Mint and on the highway.

And then there came the ominous whirring as of wings, and, glancing up, the assassin saw the awful figure which had crashed through the window at the time of the murder.

There were the bat-like wings formed by his arms, and his great cloak, his red body, his terrible face, and the sulphurous smoke and flame rushing from his mouth.

Ned Wilmot had made many brave resolutions—the will of Sir Roland was to be carried out at all costs.

But his courage oozed out at his fingers' ends as he heard the well-known "Ha! ha! ha!" of the mysterious apparition, and saw his bat-like form hovering for that instant over his head between him and the moon.

With a yell of terror he put spurs to his horse and fled.

But of what use was it for him to fly?

What horse could keep up with the giant leaps, and rushes, and springs of Spring-Heeled Jack?

Over hedges, over the horseman's head, he leaped and gambolled.

Ned Wilmot, gasping with terror, lost him once, and with a feeling of relief he pushed on at a still greater speed to reach the bridge near the stream.

"He has disappeared for tonight," he muttered, "and so has my enterprise. I feel no nerve to attempt anything now. I must go to the Corner Pin and have a good draught of brandy. That accursed thing has driven all the life out of me."

But no!

He had not escaped.

There was Spring-Heeled Jack standing on the stone arch of the little bridge, and as Ned Wilmot came dashing up, at a rate which made it impossible to stop his horse, the strange being went leaping and laughing far ahead of him.

The blood seemed to curdle in Ned Wilmot's veins.

The apparition was certainly unaccountable.

But none the less was it terrible.

Little by little Ned Wilmot felt his nerves getting weaker, his head becoming dizzy, and his respiration difficult.

He felt certain that the end of it would be that he should fall from his horse, and then—

He scarcely dared think what the end of it would be with a being whose power and nature he could not fathom.

But, as if to save him, there came suddenly a burst of laughter, and a band of roysterers came rolling along from the Corner Pin.

This was a tavern standing some distance back from the high road, with a large pond in front, and green benches and tables round the open space.

These men had evidently been enjoying themselves to the top of their bent, and their voices rolled loudly and merrily over the countryside.

Nerved by the sound of companionship, Ned Wilmot struck his spurs into his horse's flanks, and, dashing round the corner, nearly plunging headlong into the pond, made for the door of the tavern.

With his usual diabolical "Ha, ha, ha!" Spring-Heeled Jack sprang high in the air, clean over the head of the rider, and alighted in front of the astonished merrymakers.

The latter were for a moment so horrified, so stupefied by the unaccountable apparition, that they could not utter a sound.

But as Spring-Heeled Jack, with a sudden bound, leaped clean over the pond, and disappeared among the trees in a cloud of sulphurous flame, they burst into a chorus of terrified yells and fled in all directions.

There was scarcely a cottage within ten miles that night where this terror was not discussed—a terror so new, so strange, so unaccountable.

Spring-Heeled Jack had only made his appearance a few days, but already his fame was spreading far and wide.

But, at any rate, he had stopped the pursuit after Ralph.

Sir Roland or no Sir Roland, nothing would have induced Ned Wilmot to move out of the Corner Pin that night.

He had escaped the awful apparition when he had feared that it would pursue him to his death, and so he passed into the public room and steeped his crime-stained soul in drink, to drive away the weird phantoms which were beginning to be his constant companions.

"I'll haunt the place tomorrow in the daylight," he muttered to himself, as he shuddered in his bed after supper, and drew the bedclothes over his head, "and look out for this Ralph Ashton, but, hang me! if I could do it tonight. That infernal thing has destroyed all my nerves. Man or devil, I'll have a shot at him the first time we meet again!"

A valiant resolve, truly!

But the assassin little knew what would be the result of the trial.

Meanwhile, leaving Ralph Ashton, and Spring-Heeled Jack, and the cowardly assassin of Herbert Leigh, we must return to Ashton Grange.

Constance Marfield, despite the scene in the bedroom on the night before, appeared in the breakfast-room at the usual hour in the morning.

Had she known the thoughts which occupied the mind of Sir Roland she would probably not have attired herself as she did.

But she had only noticed the coarseness and rudeness of his bursting into her chamber the night before, and had not observed his look of admiration when his eyes had fallen unexpectedly on the glories of those rounded shoulders and the bare, voluptuous bosom.

As it was, the admiration of the sensual baronet—the man who placed his pleasures before everything; who spilled blood like water rather than suffer opposition—was heightened doubly by the ravishing picture she made on her birthday morning.

She was dressed in white muslin and blue ribbons; as on that day, long ago, when she and Ralph had first awakened to love's delicious thrill; her dress being really as low as for a ball, but a gauzy net veiling her creamy shoulders and superb bust, her bare arms gleaming also through the same material.

A beautiful colour was on her cheeks, an unusual sparkle in her eyes, her mouth seemed to pout more deliciously and to be wreathed by tremulous smiles.

How natural was it all?

For was she not to know love's sweet consummation within a week? Was not her longing love at length to be satisfied? Was not the patience of years to be rewarded, and was she not to be released from thraldom as Ralph Ashton's wife?

Alas! for her delicious hopes.

"You are looking quite charming on this your birthday morning," said Sir Roland, as she entered, and he advanced to meet her. "I think that as your guardian all these years I must claim a kiss."

She could scarcely refuse him this; and, in fact, he had often pressed her brow. So she raised her head for him to kiss, carrying out Ralph's suggestion that she was to allow him to suspect nothing.

But the kiss he gave her was not as usual.

He stooped and pressed his lips to hers greedily; not once, but twice and thrice, gliding his arm round her, and drawing her to him, and looking down into her astonished and half-frightened eyes.

"Really, this is a birthday to be remembered," he cried, as she contrived at last to release herself, blushing and afraid. "You seem to be younger and more girlish this morning than I have known you before. Sit down, my darling Constance; near me—so. I have very much to tell you. First, your own story, and then a great secret!"

Constance was unable to restrain a shudder.

Her guardian's manner had told her as plainly as it could what this secret would be.

She made no reply whatever, but as calmly as possible poured herself out a cup of coffee.

This seemed to produce an irritating effect upon the baronet, in spite of his love-sick mood.

His manner changed.

"By the way," he said, "I think I will tell you my secret first. From what happened last night I feel sure that you look upon Ralph Ashton as your lover still. This was all very well years ago, but since he has disgraced himself it is out of all reason."

"Nevertheless," replied Constance, recovering her equanimity and her speech in defence of her absent one, "I am going to be his wife. I have promised him, and I shall perform my promise. I am twenty-one today, and I can do as I please."

"In spite of his forgeries—in spite of the awful crime of murder which has now stained his soul?"

"I don't believe that he is guilty of anything of which you accuse him," said Constance, indignantly. "He is a good and true gentleman, and if the whole world is against him I will be his wife."

Sir Roland smiled sarcastically.

"We shall see," he said. "For my part I doubt it much."

Constance made no reply.

The baronet also, without further remark, began to unfasten some blue papers and others, which he had before him, tied with a piece of red tape.

He noted with pleasure and evil triumph, as he stole a glance across the table, that Constance had observed what he was doing, though she kept her eyes resolutely on her breakfast, and that her white breast heaved under its gauzy black lace covering.

He knew her thoughts.

Knew that, in spite of her affected indifference, she was eagerly anxious to learn her history.

As I have before said, she was unaware of the real events of her youth.

But after what Sir Roland had done and said she was determined not to express any eagerness.

In fact, she would have rather remained in ignorance than ask him the slightest favour.

However, there was no need to indulge in these dogged fancies of hers.

Sir Roland drank off a cup of coffee nervously, cleared his throat, and said—

"Well, Constance, before we proceed to talk further of the matter we alluded to, and which is, I can tell you, so dear to my heart, I will explain your position here. You are my ward, as you know."

"Yes."

"I have been kind to you during my guardianship, have I not?"

"In your idea, perhaps. I consider I have been a prisoner."

"Only for your own good—only to protect you against the machinations of evil-doers."

She smiled ironically, but made no reply.

"Well," he said, "that may be your opinion, but it is not mine. In the first place, then, I must tell you that your name is not Marfield at all, but Harland."

"Why have I been here under false pretences?" she cried.

"For your father's sake."

"Does he live?"

"Yes."

The girl's colour heightened, and her bosom leaped joyfully.

"Oh! I am so glad," she cried. "How soon can I see him?"

"We will talk of that presently," he said, drily. "I must no longer beat about the bush, but tell you the whole story. Come closer to me, my dear—I don't want everyone to hear my words."

"Thank you!" said Constance, coldly. "I have excellent hearing, and would rather remain as I am."

She was in no humour to submit to any more of his daring caresses and rapturous kisses.

He pressed her no more, but continued—

"Your father was a man I met years and years ago on the Continent and took a fancy to, for he was about the same age as myself, and had apparently the same tastes.

"We had both plenty of money and spent it freely, and consequently you may imagine the hours flew by on golden wings.

"Tom Harland had a wife and daughter, much about your size, of charming appearance, and with her I very quickly fell in love.

"She was a being of passionate nature, and after a very few weeks of acquaintance, at a ball, where she had lain in my arms in many a dreamy waltz, we confessed our mutual wishes, and were married the very next morning by special license."

Constance did not like the style in which he told his story.

"Really, Sir Roland," she said, "your love affairs are far from interesting to me. I am anxious to hear my own story."

"I am telling it," said the baronet, in a voice of annoyance; "it is so bound up with my own that I cannot divide one from the other.

"Well, very soon after the marriage, an awful thing was discovered, which ruined three people's lives.

"It was found that Tom Harland, though received in and courted by society, was little better than a thief. He was a forger, a cardsharper[22]; and, at last, to save himself from discovery and arrest, he committed the crime for which he was tried and sentenced.

"He murdered in cold blood the man whom he had basely robbed, and who had nearly effected his capture.

"He was arrested and tried (I forgot to say we were in England then), and was by some quibble of the law found guilty only of manslaughter.

"The judge, however, was of a different opinion to the jury, and sentenced him to penal servitude for life."

"And after all these years of terrible suffering he still lives?" said Constance, in tears.

"Yes; and, what is more, is free."

Constance uttered a joyful cry. "Free? Oh! then I shall see him?"

"I am afraid," said the baronet, dryly, "that your ecstasy at the idea of clasping to your heart a thief and assassin, as you did last night, will be doomed to speedy disappointment. But listen patiently. The sorrow and excitement killed my wretched sister-in-law, and drove my wife mad. She was taken to a lunatic asylum, where she died not long after. You were about six months old at the time, and at Tom Harland's earnest entreaty, for the sake of our old friendship, I took you in my care, promising not to divulge your secret until you were twenty-one, when I was to tell you, and leave you to judge for yourself. But, unfortunately, something has happened to put a different complexion on matters entirely."

"What is that?" asked Constance, excitedly.

"Simply that your father has escaped from prison, and I know where he is."

"Well?"

Constance eyed him narrowly.

In her eagerness to hear all she had not observed that he had been gradually drawing his chair nearer and nearer to hers.

There was a malevolent look upon his face that somewhat alarmed her.

"It is far from well," he said. "I had not intended ever to tell you anything. I thought Tom Harland's idea of disclosing his shameful story to you the idea of a madman.

---

[22] A cheat at cards

"I had intended to let you marry after you had attained the age of twenty-one, under the name of Marfield, and never tell you anything of the affair.

"That was when you were a little girl; but when you ripened into such glorious womanhood, my thoughts changed.

"In fact, Constance, I want you for my own wife."

"Ha! ha! ha!"

The demoniacal laugh of Spring-Heeled Jack resounded through the room, and a dark shadow crossed the window.

The baronet, leaping up with an oath, rushed to the French casement, opened it and hastened out on the terrace.

But in vain.

There was no sign of any being, human or otherwise.

With a much more subdued manner he returned to the room, and with an almost perceptible shudder closed the casement.

"Some absurd prank," he said, glancing at Constance, who was very pale. "I only hope that whoever has been mountebanking[23] out there has not heard our conversation."

"No, indeed, for my father's sake."

"You would not like to see him recaptured, then?"

"You need not ask me the question."

"Well, then," said Sir Roland, resuming his seat, but keeping his eyes fixed upon the window, "I have made up my mind that I cannot do better than make you my wife. You understand my ways; we have lived so long together that we shall agree immensely well. I have grown to love you, and your charms of person are such that they have come upon me as a surprise now that I have noticed them more observantly. It is only for you to name the day, and you can sink your father's wretched story in the knowledge that you are Lady Ashton."

"I fancy," said Constance, smiling, "that I should have a better chance of being Lady Ashton if I married Ralph."

Sir Roland reddened with anger, but, suppressing. it, said—

"My dear Constance, this is scarcely a joking matter. I offer you my hand, my heart, and my future. What is your reply?"

"I refuse unconditionally," she said, firmly.

"Will nothing move you?"

"Nothing."

"In that I fancy you are wrong," said Sir Roland; "if you refuse I shall, without a moment's hesitation, deliver your father over into the hands of justice. What he has suffered hitherto will be nothing to what he will suffer in the future."

"I pity my father; I am anxious to see him, that after all his trials I may forgive him," said Constance, with a wonderful calmness. "But I do not believe he desires to commit another crime."

"What crime?"

"To doom his child to marriage with an assassin, because he has himself been guilty, perhaps by accident, of a similar crime."

---

[23] Playing the charlatan

And with these words Constance rose defiantly from her chair, with flashing eyes and heaving bosom.

Sir Roland strove to approach her.

The interview had turned out badly—very different indeed to what he had expected—and he resolved to endeavour to pacify her in a different way, by kind words and so forth.

But she guessed his intention, and thwarted him at once.

"Today your influence over me ends," she cried. "I am now my own mistress, and I will no longer suffer your dictation. I shall quit this house today, and within a week I shall become the wife of Ralph Ashton."

The baronet, in spite of his rage, burst into a loud and discordant laugh.

"Ha, ha!" he cried. "Very good—very good! And, doubtless, as you will have to marry him in prison, you will be able to have your father to give you away. Ha, ha! a good joke, truly. See here."

He took from his pocket a piece of paper, printed with large characters, and handed it to her. It ran as follows—

"£100 REWARD.—This reward will be given to anyone who will give such information as shall lead to the apprehension of Ralph Ashton, accused of forgery and murder. A Free Pardon will be given to any accomplice turning Queen's Evidence.—Apply to or address Mr. Superintendent Buggins, Police Station, Barnet."

A second paper ran as follows—

"£20 REWARD will be given to anyone giving satisfactory information as to whereabouts of Thomas Harland, an escaped convict, who was sentenced nearly twenty-one years ago to transportation for life for robbery and murder, and who is known to have escaped to England. Believed to be in the neighbourhood of Barnet.—Information to be given to Mr. Superintendent Buggins, Police Station, Barnet; the Commissioners of Police, Chief Office, London; or any Police Station in the United Kingdom."

"Poor Ralph!" murmured Constance, tearfully.

"And you would marry him in spite of this?" cried Sir Roland.

"Yes; for he is innocent," she cried; "and you, in spite of my father's public disgrace—a renewed disgrace—would marry me?"

"Yes; because I love you—because there need be no disgrace. Your real name need never be known, and as for your father, I will assist him to quit the country at once, and fly to some country where no one can find him."

"When can I see him?" said Constance.

"Tomorrow night."

"Why not tonight?"

"Because I am going to Rickworth tonight with Caleb Masters to receive a large sum of money. I prefer taking him to going with Job Joskins, who came home here naked last night, and otherwise behaved himself like an idiot," returned the baronet; "besides, it will be necessary to be cautious in giving your father information of the rendezvous."

"Very well, then," said Constance, with cold calmness; "I will see him tomorrow night, and that interview will decide me. Till then, adieu!" The baronet's face flushed and he advanced a step.

"You give me hope, then?" he cried. Constance glanced at him with a look of derisive contempt from top to toe.

"Hope!" she cried; "yes, if you call that hope—a faint chance that you may be able to mate yourself with a woman who despises and hates you, and will always throughout her life regard you as lower than the most loathsome thing that crawls upon the face of the earth."

And with these words she suddenly swept from the room.

In spite of Sir Roland's words and the humiliating story she had heard, she had made up her mind, and it was by no means according to the notions of her guardian.

As soon as she had quitted the apartment Sir Roland opened the door and glanced after her.

He feared instant flight.

But that would not have suited Constance, for the simple reason that she would not have been able to communicate with her lover.

She passed straight up to her own room, and he heard her lock herself in.

Then he rang for Mrs. Levine.

The housekeeper, who had managed this strange household for so many years, was still comely, and hoped even now to be Lady Ashton when Sir Roland had sown his wild oats, hastened up.

She knew nothing of his matrimonial designs in regard to Constance.

"Mrs. Levine," he said, "I cannot quite explain to you my reasons, but I very much fear that Miss Marfield proposes to celebrate her majority by running away from home."

"Indeed!"

"And I must depend upon you to prevent this. When Miss Marfield comes down to dinner there must be some excuse for changing her room. Place her in the square chamber at the end of the gallery."

Mrs. Levine shuddered.

"That room, Sir Roland?"

The baronet frowned.

"Why not?" he cried. "What foolish fancies are you allowing to creep into your head? Have you been preaching to Miss Marfield, and infecting her with your idiotic reminiscences?"

This was not a very pleasant address to the woman who had prospective notions of marriage.

But she understood Sir Roland's moods.

"Certainly not," she said. "I will manage everything."

And so it came to pass that when Constance was going up to her room again that evening she was informed that she could not retire to her own room that night as the window had by some mysterious means fallen in, and been shattered to atoms.

Constance made little remark, because she suspected nothing.

But when she was once ensconced in her new chamber, which the housekeeper had endeavoured to render cosy by a bright fire, she knew the reason of the removal.

The windows were barred, and the door no only locked but secured by heavy bolts.

One glance she gave through the bars of her prison, at the moonlit landscape without, and then she flung herself on her knees beside the bed and burst into a passion of despairing tears.

CHAPTER VIII.
SPRING-HEELED JACK AND THE STAGE COACH

SIR ROLAND had decided, as we have said, to take Caleb Masters with him instead of Job Joskins, and accordingly, at eight that night the two worthies mounted their horses, and with pistols in their girdles, rode off to the Corner Pin where the coach would take them to their destination.

"I can't think what Ned Wilmot can be doing," said the baronet to Caleb, as they went on; "he has had plenty of time and opportunity to communicate with me."

"It's no use being impatient, sir," replied Caleb; "I think Ned's a wonderful man, and does the strangest tasks in the most wonderful way. I don't think he has had time to do much yet."

"Well, perhaps you are right," said Sir Roland; "but things are gathering round so strangely that, upon my honour, I begin to feel nervous."

"It's time you did," muttered Caleb.

"Eh! what's that?"

"I said there was nothing to feel nervous about," said Caleb, quickly. "He has had scarcely time to do anything yet, and, remember, he is always in danger of the hue and cry."

By this time they had reached the Corner Pin, and the baronet, alighting with his companion, passed into the bar.

The landlord at once bowed obsequiously, and turning to a shelf at the back of the bar, took from it a letter, which he handed to his guest.

The baronet eyed it unconcernedly, and ordering some warm brandy, opened the missive carelessly, and read it.

It was, as he expected, from Ned Wilmot, although the handwriting was disguised, and the name also.

It ran as follows—

"The person whom you wished me to follow has evidently left the neighbourhood; but I will endeavour to trace him to London, and obtain the interview which you think so necessary. I was followed and impeded in my search again last night by that hideous apparition which has lately come into this neighbourhood. If he follows me everywhere I fear I shall have but a poor chance of doing as you wish. John Maynard."

Ned Wilmot dared not sign his own name, and trusted to chance to enable the baronet to understand what it meant.

Sir Roland was not slow to comprehend.

He simply placed the note in his pocket, asked how soon the coach would be round, and ordered another glass for the landlord.

"Have you heard or seen anything of this strange appearance that has been going the rounds of the neighbourhood so much, Sir Roland?" asked Boniface.

"Yes; I have caught a glimpse of him," said the baronet; "and if I get near enough to him, and he plays his pranks on me, I will put a bullet through his head."

"That bain't no good, Sir Roland," put in a labourer, who was sitting over in a corner having a pint of ale; "cos big Tom Norris, the game-keeper, saw 'un last night, and put the contents of his gun in 'un; and he only laughed 'Ha! Ha! ha!' and jumped clean over his head."

SPRING-HEELED JACK,
THE TERROR OF LONDON.

By the Author of "TURNPIKE DICK, the Star of the Road."

AS THE AWFUL APPARITION SAILED UP INTO THE AIR THEY FIRED POINT BLANK AT IT.

No. 3.

"Bah! he missed his aim," said the baronet, derisively, though he felt very uncomfortable.

"Not he. He saw the light through the hole in his forehead, and he knows he shot him."

At this moment the awkward conversation was put a stop to by the arrival of the coach, and the entry of the driver and the guard.

"Got some extra pistols aboard for Spring-Heeled Jack?" cried the landlord.

The guard laughed, though there was very little merriment in the sound.

"Aye! that we have," he said. "Joe here's got his pistols and so have I, and my gun's about loaded up to the muzzle."

A kind of nervous laugh, more like a giggle than anything else, went through the little band of travellers who were waiting to take their places in the coach—The Express—which still went its rumbling way, in spite of the innovating railway.

The "iron horse" had not yet come into common use, and there were an abundance of persons, as is well known, who clung to the old-fashioned style of conveyance long after the rails had made a network over all England.

Even in the present day there are plenty of people who delight in the Brighton or the St. Albans coach.

The night on the present occasion was an exceptionally fine one.

The moon was bright, and the air balmy, and everything seemed to promise a good run.

But somehow or another the party seemed ill at ease.

The mention of Spring-Heeled Jack had cast a damper on their spirits.

They might pretend to be brave.

But no one desired to see the portent.

However, they did not disclose their feelings to one another, and as no one liked to be more cowardly than his neighbour, they hastened to take their places.

All, however, including the baronet and Caleb Masters, were anxious—more so than they had ever been before—to reach their destination quickly.

They started at last, six outside and six in, two of the latter having come all the way from London, a widow and her daughter, who sat opposite one another, and were squeezed up in their corners by two male passengers of loud voice and large limbs, who professed to be quite at ease, but were, in reality, in a sad state of perturbation.

The road was hard and smooth, and the coach bowled on at a goodly pace.

But nothing happened.

As time went on and nothing appeared the travellers became more at ease, and even ventured to chaff[24] each other, and peer curiously at little clumps of trees, where the shadows seemed to linger more than in others.

And indeed all passed off well.

Spring-Heeled Jack seemed to have given the high road a rest, and Sir Roland and Caleb, when they descended at the door of the Three Jolly Wheelers, at Rickworth, were among the loudest of the scoffers.

As they passed into the hamlet, however, after booking their return places in the coach, which went back to Barnet at eleven, a horseman darted out from a bye-way suddenly, and passed them with lightning speed.

---

[24] Tease.

As he went by a demonaical "Ha! ha! ha!" burst from his lips, and a strange light glowed round his head.

The baronet staggered back, almost upsetting his company.

"Confound that demon!" he muttered; "I thought we had avoided him tonight."

"Fear not, good master," said his companion; "I do not think that was the being they call Spring-Heeled Jack. He never rides, but leaps about on his own account."

"Nevertheless, he emitted fire from his mouth, and what was his accursed laugh," said the baronet.

"One thing I am resolved upon, when we return if he begins to play his accursed tricks I will fire at him, be he man or devil, and you, Caleb, must do so, likewise."

"That I swear," said Caleb.

Their further walk towards their destination was a silent one.

Both knew, or at any rate were afraid, that they would meet the mysterious presence on their road home.

But they expressed no opinion about it, and went on moodily towards the house where they were to receive the gold.

The man from whom they expected it was one who sometimes made a difficulty in payment, and, consequently, Sir Roland made it a rule to go there for payment himself; otherwise he would not have ventured out of the precincts of his own place while such a being as Spring-Heeled Jack was supposed to be in the neighbourhood.

It so happened that on this occasion the debtor was most complacent.

He had had an unusually good run of luck, and the money was at once forthcoming.

So Sir Roland and Caleb were able to quit his house quickly, and return to the Three Jolly Wheelers.

Here they entered the public room.

There were not many people present, but all knew the baronet, and he was greeted respectfully.

"Strange doings down here lately, squire," said one of the labourers.

"What doings?" asked Sir Roland.

"These ere murders and such like."

"Indeed! I wasn't aware there had been any murders down here," said the baronet, ironically.

The yokel was indignant.

What did it matter to him whether one murder had been committed in the Mint, in London, and the other somewhere else twenty years ago, so that the supposed perpetrators were said to be in the neighbourhood.

"Why ain't you seen the police bills, Sir Roland?" he cried. "There's one bill as has got the name of someone same as yourn—Ashton. Hundred pounds! I wish I'd be the one to catch him!"

"I wish you could catch him," said the baronet, "I'd give you fifty pounds more. He's a distant relation of the family, and I tried to do the best for him; but he's a bad egg, and the sooner he's brought to justice the better."

"Funny he should hide about Barnet, then," said another of the men.

"Yes," said the aforesaid yokel; "and then there's another one—Tom Harland, a man that's escaped from prison in Australia, he's hanging about here for something or other."

The baronet smiled.

"We're likely to have plenty of excitement then down in our neighbourhood," he said, "what with escaped murderers and Spring-Heeled Jacks."

The men were silent at this for a moment, and a shudder was observed to pass through their frames.

"Have you seen him," asked Caleb Masters, "that you are so dumbfounded?"

The first speaker shook his head.

"Aye," he said, "you may well say that. I've seen him, and, in fact, most of us have seen him. He's been a-jumping and a-leaping about this 'ere place like mad tonight, and I'm blest if I shan't be glad when he takes it into his head to be off."

"Aye! I don't want my missus and my youngsters skeered[25] out o' their lives," said another; "and they do tell me that he was a-top o' the mission chapel tonight, a-sitting a-top of the little bell-tower, a-breathing out flame and smoke for all the world like a railway-engine."

Sir Roland laughed at this.

But nevertheless he looked askance at Caleb Masters to observe what effect the words had taken on him.

"Perhaps," said Caleb, "this diabolical apparition has something to do with the murders or the murderers."

A tall man who had been sitting in a corner rose up at this.

He had been sitting so far back in the shadow and was so surrounded by tobacco smoke that no one had been able to note his face much.

As he neared the door, the others could see that he was clad in rough garments, which did not seem to suit his style of figure.

His hair and beard were of grizzly hue, and his eyes were large and brilliant, with a hunted, frightened look in them.

"You're a meddlesome lot altogether," he said, as he looked savagely round at the assembled company, "and I expect this Spring-Heeled Jack that you talk about is the devil himself come to frighten out of ye the little wits you've got left."

And with this he went out, leaving the yokels sheepish and astonished, and Sir Roland white as death.

He leaned over towards Caleb, under pretence of taking a pipe-light to rekindle his cigar.

"That was Tom Harland!" he whispered.

Low as were the words, they reached the ears of one of the men, who whispered to one of his companions.

Then both rose and left the room.

Sir Roland turned the conversation into other channels, waiting impatiently for the Barnet coach to arrive.

But in a few minutes there was a hullabaloo outside, the rush of feet, and the two countrymen who had gone out came helter skelter into the room, one without his hat and blood all over his face.

"Why, what's the matter, Bob?" was the chorus.

"The Devil!" groaned he of the gory nose, as he sank all of a heap on a bench.

"What was it, Bill?" said another, addressing the second one.

---

[25] Scared.

"Spring-Heeled Jack!" he gasped.

"Have ye seen him?"

"Aye, and felt him, too," said Bill; "I thought I heard Sir Roland say 'that's Tom Harland,' and so I whispers to Bob, and we both goes out to watch him so as to get the reward. But when we gets just by the pump, where he'd disappeared like, up came the Devil, up—up, into the air, with such a whirr and a whizz, with great wings all spread out, for all the world like a bat and such a 'Ha—ha-ing,' enough to make yer head spin."

"And did he strike your companion?" asked Sir Roland.

"No; the Devil he comes plump down aside o' Bob, a breathing out smoke and flame, and Bob, he screams out and runs right ag'in the pump, and smashes his nose in, by the looks of it. When he picks himself up from the ground, where he fell, the Devil was gone."

It was a few minutes to eleven now.

Sir Roland rose.

"Well," he said, "if this mysterious personage, whoever he may be, sees that you always run away from him, why, you'll never get a chance of giving him a good leathering. For my part, if he comes near me tonight, I mean to put a bullet through him."

And with these words he took out his pistols and examined them in the light.

Then Caleb did the same, and with a goodnight to the scared countrymen they went out.

"Sir Roland means business," said one of the men; "I could see it in his eye."

"Aye, that may be," said Bill; "but it's a main rum thing that he should a' known Tom Harland."

Meanwhile the baronet and his secretary strolling out saw the coach rumbling swiftly on.

It drew up presently at the door, and it was seen at once that no untoward accident had occurred on the road.

Everyone was jolly, and the guard and driver were in their usual spirits.

"Caleb," whispered Sir Roland, "we had better make no remark about this matter to any of the travellers. I fancy these yokels have been misled by some shadows of their own fancy, or by some one of their own companions, who has been frightening them."

"But you will keep a good look out?"

"Aye! that I will," said the baronet; "and for that reason I shall ride on the box-seat, where I shall be able to fire at this masquerading lunatic, whoever he may be."

Caleb made no reply.

He had serious doubts as to there being any masquerading in the matter.

But he did not wish to explain his feelings to Sir Roland.

Although he served him faithfully through everything, he did not respect or like him, and these bantering jokes he simply detested.

It so happened that two travellers on the box seat descended at the Three Jolly Wheelers, and Sir Roland and his secretary were quickly accommodated.

In a few minutes the coach rolled off, and in the merry moonlight the horses trotted on swiftly towards Barnet.

For some little while all went well.

But presently, as they neared a part of the road where trees grew thickly on either side, loud shrill laughter resounded on all sides.

"Ha! ha! ha!"

It seemed to come from all points—behind, in front, on the left, and on the right; now loud and derisive, now shrill, now sonorous and defiant.

A dusky shadow of no particular shape seemed to flit from tree to tree, and mingle with the branches.

Then a strange form went leaping over the wide fields and gambolled in the moonlight.

An awe fell upon all.

Retreat it was useless to talk about.

They must go on, for, advance or retire, the fiendish unknown would follow.

Not a word was said.

The driver, alarmed as he was, nevertheless kept his team well in hand, so as to be ready if the horses took fright.

Sir Roland quickly drew a pistol from his breast pocket and waited.

Villain as he was he had abundant courage, and was resolved to put this matter to the test.

Presently, as the coach left the wooded part of the road behind, and came to a part where the hedges were high on either side, there was heard quite close at hand the demon laugh.

"Ha! ha! ha!"

And then, with a whirr and a whizz, Spring-Heeled Jack came leaping up towards the sky, clear above the heads of the terrified and astounded travellers, on the summit of the coach.

He looked an awful object, with his bat-like wings outspread, his mouth vomiting forth flame and smoke, his cloven foot showing plainly against the moonlit sky.

The horses, with discordant cries, huddled themselves together on their haunches. The guard, with a yell of terror, fell backwards from his seat, his blunderbuss[26] going off in the air as he fell.

Caleb cowered down affrightedly.

Not so Sir Roland.

As the awful apparition sailed up into the air, he rose from his seat, and, raising his pistol, fired point-blank at the figure.

An awful laugh broke from the lips of Spring-Heeled Jack.

Then, as he reached the ground again, he leaped once more over the coach, exclaiming, in his most sepulchral tones—

"Ha! ha! Sir Roland Ashton—murderer! You have failed."

This time he again alighted on the summit of the vehicle, where they could see his glaring eyes, his flaming mouth, his red, glossy body, his cloven hoof, and his long, talon-like hands.

Sir Roland, with a groan, fell fainting back upon the seat. The others, unable to look upon the awful being, cowered down and hid their faces.

"Caleb Masters," said the unknown, in a low voice, which sounded as if it were issuing from the tomb, "you have three hundred pounds in a bag in your pocket, belonging, as you think, to your master. Deliver that to me instantly or dread my vengeance. Refuse, and, at a word from me, the whole coach, with its occupants, will be consumed."

And, as he spoke, he breathed forth such a mass of flame and sulphurous smoke that his

---

[26] Musket.

body was enveloped in vapour, and a suffocating odour pervaded the whole atmosphere.

Caleb raised his head mechanically, and glanced at the terrible apparition.

That glance seemed to fascinate him, and, as if obeying some order that he could not gainsay, he drew from his pocket the bag containing the banknotes and gold, and handed it to Spring-Heeled Jack.

"Ha! ha! ha!" he laughed, as he placed it in a pocket in his wing-like cloak. "Tell Sir Roland I have come this time for some of his ill-gotten gains; next time I will come for his soul."

Then, in a cloud of vapour, which seemed suddenly to envelope him, he disappeared, no one seeing him quit the coach.

It was some minutes after his disappearance before anyone moved.

But as the demoniacal laugh sounded far away, as if it was gradually dying in the distance, the travellers and others roused themselves from their lethargy, and resumed their natural positions.

Sir Roland was with difficulty roused to life by the administration of some brandy. The guard, who had fallen so suddenly, was found to have seriously injured himself, having struck his head against a stone in the road.

However, all were able to proceed after a time, and Sir Roland was conveyed in a closed vehicle to the Hall, being unable to ride his horse from nervous weakness.

His evil heart, however, was by no means touched by the scene.

He recognised that some mysterious agency was at work against him, and that he had been robbed and threatened.

But he saw in all this nothing to cause him to amend his evil ways.

All the effect it had on him was to make him take additional vows of vengeance.

CHAPTER IX.

TWO FELLOW SUFFERERS—DAISY AND CONSTANCE—

DAISY'S PERIL—A STRUGGLE FOR LIBERTY AND HONOUR.

POOR Daisy Leigh and Constance Marfield were now fellow sufferers.

And both through the same man.

In the first instance, at any rate, for the immediate cause of Daisy's peril was Gedge Foote.

For two or three days after her arrival at the pretended Mrs. Barton's (the real Mrs. Foster) she lived an excessively quiet existence.

It was a melancholy one enough, what with the hideously dismal surroundings and the terrible reminiscences of her father's death.

Mrs. Foster was not the best of companions, and, consequently, Daisy spent most of her time in her own room, where the bright sun of August only showed her wastes of ground stretching down to the water's edge, and a few cultivated fields and dreary-looking shanties, while the night generally swallowed up everything in misty darkness.

Mrs. Foster's was a mysterious life altogether.

She had, in fact, no visible means of subsistence.

Apparently she had plenty of money; she rarely ever went out, but the tradesmen called, and she paid them.

But she did nothing for her living.

Occasionally carts would draw up of a night at the door, and loud, rough voices would be heard laughing in uproarious chorus in the side yard, where there were all manner of rough sheds.

She said that her husband was a sea captain, and she had lost sight of him for some years.

At any rate, she had plenty of time on hand, and would often come of her own accord to gossip.

"What a strange thing it is!" said Daisy one evening, when Mrs. Foster had invited her into her cosy kitchen. "What a strange thing it is that the mysterious person who sent me here has never turned up."

"Mysterious person!" laughed Mrs. Foster. "Why, what on earth do you mean?"

"The person who gave me your address, and told me to come here. I have never seen him since the day of my father's murder, and I long to see him, to thank him, and to hear what plans he proposes to hunt up the assassin."

The woman laughed at her, as if she thought that she was taking leave of her senses.

"Why, what do ye mean?" she cried. "Why, I never! Say you ain't seen him, when he came the other night, and brought you here, and stayed to supper, and kissed you when he went away, and all that. Well, I never did!"

Daisy flushed, but still she could not help smiling as she answered—

"Oh! I don't mean him, Mrs. Barton. He's nobody—that poor, ugly dwarf. He's very kind and lent me money, and showed me my way here and I think he did kiss me. But I forgave him, because, perhaps, he'd had a drop to drink and was excited."

"Well, look here, Miss Leigh," said Mrs. Foster, emphatically, "there's some very stupid mistake here. In the first place, my name ain't Barton. It's Foster. Poor Mr. Foote! he forgot my name when he told you, and when he came the afternoon afore you came he said, 'Bless me if I ain't told my sweetheart your name's so-and-so. Don't be surprised, then, if she calls ye so. If I tell her different, she's so timid, she'll get scared like.' And as for 'poor, ugly dwarf', wonder how you can talk like that about a chap you're going to marry, and the banns up and all."

This, considering the shuddering dread the words inspired, was a long speech for Daisy Leigh to listen to.

But she suffered Mrs. Foster to proceed and finish, and then broke into a loud, hysterical laugh.

"You are having a good joke at my expense Mrs. Foster," she said. "In the first place, have never had a sweetheart, as you call it, in my life. I never had a dozen words with Gedge Foote before the day after my poor father's death and as for banns, of course, that is your fun though banns can be nothing to me for many a long, long day. It was not Mr. Foote who bade me come here—it was a person whom I do not know (and she shuddered slightly). And so, since I am in the wrong place, I must get back to the Mint as quickly as I can, or I shall lose my best friend."

She rose as she spoke.

She was resolved to proceed to her own room at once, dress herself, and quit the house, using a few shillings to enable her to reach the Mint, and returning the rest to Gedge Foote at his own place.

Mrs. Foster's laugh alarmed her.

"What is there to laugh at?" she cried.

"Very much, I think."

"What do you mean?"

"You talk of quitting this house?"

"Yes."

"Don't you know you can't?"

"Why not?"

"There isn't a window or a door through which you could escape if you were flying for your life," said Mrs. Foster, with a bland smile. "Once upon a time, ye see, this 'ere place was a mad-house, leastways a private asylum, kept by a doctor and lor' bless ye, the bolts and bars are that strong it 'ud take half-a-dozen strong men all their time to get through."

"By what right can you detain me?" cried Daisy, drawing up her little body defiantly, her eyes flashing, and her bosom heaving.

"By the right given me by Mr. Foote," said Mrs. Foster, flushing and losing her temper. "He brought you here and paid me well, and said I was to take every care of you, and so on; and so you can't leave my house until Mr. Foote says you may."

Daisy had fallen into a trap.

She had suspected it before.

But now she was certain.

What was to be done?

Certainly nothing by being precipitate.

So she would be calm.

"When do you expect Mr. Foote?" she asked.

"Either to-night or to-morrow night," said Mrs. Foster, "and then he isn't going away until the wedding."

"Your talk is absurd, and it annoys me," said Daisy. "You must know that in England a forced marriage is impossible if the girl only has courage."

"Ah! but if you persist in refusing him," said Mrs. Foster, "there is something worse. He will remain under this roof with you until you will be glad to marry him."

Daisy, even without the horrid leer in the woman's eyes, would have known what she meant, and a shuddering thrill passed through her frame.

She passed towards the door.

"I will go to my room now," she said, "and if Mr. Foote makes his insane proposals to me, he will find how I appreciate his madness."

"You had better speak more civilly to him than you do of him," said Mrs. Foster, "or you may find him dangerous. He knows he can do as he likes here."

"And that you would help him in his iniquity," said Daisy.

"Just so."

"I fear you not," said Daisy, defiantly; "no harm will come to me. Heaven will protect the innocent, much as you scoff at my resistance."

And she quitted the room.

As she did so she was in the passage, and with a sudden impulse she flew to the front door.

It was barred and bolted, both bolts and bars being on the inside; but a formidable lock was on the door, in which the key had been turned and removed.

There at any rate there was no escape.

She hurried then into her own room, where she felt certain she had never seen any signs of bars at the windows.

As may be imagined, she dashed impatiently towards the casement.

But there she gave vent to a little cry of dismay.

No one would have suspected the presence of bars.

But there, nevertheless, they were; artfully concealed by creeping plants, which on more than one occasion she had complained of as making the room so dark.

"At any rate I am safe here for a time," she murmured, as she bolted and locked her door.

But as she did so another click told her that by some machinery the room had been locked on the outside as well.

Tears stood in Daisy's eyes.

But her good little heart beat high with brave determination.

"The battle has begun," she said, "but I will never yield with my life. I know not what love is; but whatever it is I could not feel it for such a being as Gedge Foote."

On one thing she was determined.

She would remain on the watch all night, and as far possible would refrain from food.

She had a suspicion that if she did not take this precaution something might be surreptitiously administered to make her insensible, or, at any rate, to dull her intellect.

She could contrive somewhat to neutralise the effect of anything by only taking the tiniest quantities at a time.

And another thing, she would not undress herself, so as to be ready for flight at any moment.

She had not been in her room long before Mrs. Foster's voice was heard outside, and then a kind of wicket in the wall at the side of the door was pushed open.

"Here is your supper," said the woman.

A savoury smell assailed the girl's nostrils,

But she was resolute.

"Thank you; I am not hungry," returned she.

The woman waited to hear no more, but slammed the little wicket to with a bang.

"All right," she muttered; "perhaps she won't be so cheeky when she's starved herself."

That night Daisy was undisturbed, and on the next likewise.

Loud voices and laughter were heard in the house.

But that was all.

She was used to strange noises in the place, and consequently this did not affect her.

She kept resolutely to her room all the time, and though Mrs. Foster unbolted the door, she never once took advantage of the permission.

Food she took in tiny quantities, just sufficient to keep body and soul together.

On the third night, however, just as she had removed her dress and her boots, to throw herself on her couch for a little rest, there was a knock at the front door, and presently someone entered.

Her room was not locked, and so springing noiselessly towards the door she opened it and listened.

"Quite a stranger," said Mrs. Foster to someone.

"Yes, quite. Couldn't get here before," said the familiar voice of Gedge Foote. "How's our young lady?"

"Hush! Don't speak loud. Don't speak here at all," said the woman. "She's turned rumbustious, and you'll have no end of trouble with her."

"I hope not," said Foote; "but let's go into the back parlour."

They were soon out of the passage, and, plucking up her courage, Daisy resolved to go down and listen.

Her bootless feet made little noise on the stairs, and it was not long before she stood in the front parlour, which was only divided from the back one by a folding door.

Here she cowered down, and, with eager ears, listened.

"I hope you've not been ill-using her," said Foote. "I didn't bring her here to be insulted, you know."

"Insulted! Who's insulted her I should like to know?" cried Mrs. Foster; "only I don't like these upstart wenches."

Gedge laughed.

"Well, you can't expect every girl to like to be treated in this way," he said; "and then I am not such a fool as to think I'm handsome."

"Oh! handsome is as handsome does," said Mrs. Foster. "Every girl can't expect to have her pick and choose, and she's as poor as poor can be—not got a farthing of her own, and you've been that generous to her."

"Well, never mind; tell us all that has happened."

The woman did so.

A brightly coloured story it was, too.

Evidently it did not increase Gedge Foote's good humour.

"It's no use her trying to escape me," he said. "I've had my eye on her ever since, a long time ago, I saw her trim little ankle tripping up the stairs on the Mint, and, hark ye, Mrs. Foster, it isn't only herself, though I'd be glad of her without a penny."

"What then?"

"Someday she'll be rich."

"How do you know?"

"That's my affair; but whoever marries her marries money. She won't be able to claim it yet, but she's bound to have it."

"Well, it's all easy enough if you only have pluck."

"How so?"

"Let me put a little sleeping stuff in her tea to-morrow evening; she'll go off into a fine slumber, and be as quiet as a lamb until morning. Then you can pay her a visit, and when she finds she can't help herself she'll go with you to church as ready as can be."

Daisy shuddered, and pressed her hands over her tremulous bosom.

Innocent of the world's ways as she was she had yet expected something of this kind; but she was not prepared for Gedge's answer.

"No, no! That won't do for me," he said; "it might do with some girls, but not for Daisy. She might marry me, but she'd hate me like poison ever after. And see how nice that would be when she got her money! No; I must tire her out, but I won't do as you say. Let's have a bit of supper now, and I'll think what's best to be done."

As Mrs. Foster kept her things in the front parlour Daisy thought it high time to go.

So she crept upstairs and into her room, where she locked herself in, and, throwing herself on the bed, indulged in a passion of tears.

This outburst and the quiet of the house, only disturbed by the dull murmur of voices, had their natural effect, and she fell presently into a heavy sleep.

How long she slept she knew not, but after a time she was awakened by a hot hand on her cold bare shoulder, shaking her to arouse her.

And, starting up, she saw Gedge Foote standing by the side of her bed.

His face wore a diabolical smile, and she could tell by the flush upon his hideous features that he had been drinking.

"I want to speak to you, Daisy," he said, in a thick voice.

"Why did you not send Mrs. Foster up, then, and I would have come down?" she said, striving to get away.

But this was not possible.

He had passed his arm round her waist, and was looking gloatingly upon her flushed face and her freely-displayed beauties—the white, dainty, girlish shoulders, and the budding bosom, now panting with angry excitement.

"Nay, I like you best thus, my pretty one," he said, bending down and kissing her pouting lips. "I shall not detain you long. Are you aware that your enemies are after you?"

"My enemies!" she cried. "Why should I have any?"

He laughed loudly.

"Why!" he cried. "You ask that? Was not your father murdered by your enemies because they feared he would prove his innocence and claim his property?"

"But my poor father is dead! Why should they persecute me?"

She was sitting quietly now, with her lovely head nearly resting on his chest, her white, dimpled shoulder touching his.

To resist him was, as she saw, utterly useless, and to cry out for help not only useless, but likely to bring upon her further disaster.

"Because you, as Herbert Leigh's daughter, are as dangerous as he was," said Gedge. "But I have sworn to protect you. You are poor and friendless. I will be your banker and your friend. I will make you my wife, and with my very life I will protect you against the world."

He could not but feel the shuddering thrill which invaded her form as he spoke, and it roused all his evil passions.

"Beware," he said, "how you insult me. I felt you tremble at my words."

"Can I help my feelings?" she said, meekly.

She thought it best to temporise.

"Nor can I help them," he said, and as if roused still more by her demure beauty he suddenly bent down and rained kisses on her lips, her neck, and her white, warm shoulders.

Strengthened by her shame she sprang up suddenly and wrenched herself from his clutches, with the exception of the grasp he had upon her arm with his left hand.

As she did so she gave vent to a long, piercing shriek.

This was followed by another and another, which rang through the old house, and went echoing out over the marshy land towards the river.

The effect upon Gedge was alarming.

His eyes glowed like coals of fire, his veins stood out like whipcord on his brow—his face was fairly distorted with passion.

"You've raised the devil in me now," he cried, as he rushed upon her and clasped her, once more round the waist, "and you must take the consequences."

Again and again she shrieked.

And as she did so she exerted all the strength of her lithe, round limbs to throw him off.

The struggle—the contact with her lovely active frame—only served to inflame him the more, and as they both breathed hard in their struggles Daisy felt her strength rapidly giving way.

"Release me and I will listen to you quietly," she gasped.

He only laughed loudly, and kissed her.

And then, like an echo, came a terrible laugh from without.

"Ha! ha! ha!"

The demon laugh of the mysterious apparition was new to Gedge Foote.

But it was hailed with joy by Daisy.

Poor, shrinking, ill-used Daisy! She seemed to recognise the fact that the awful being who was the terror of London was in some way or another her friend.

The sound gave her renewed strength, and the muscles of her strong arms stood out as she held Gedge for a moment away from her.

"Gedge, you're mad to-night," she cried, gaspingly, trying to smile. "Let me be quiet, and I'll listen to all you say. Perhaps even I'll give you a kiss if you're very good. There's a good Gedge: let's sit down and discuss the future."

But the demon himself seemed to have possessed the dwarf.

His eyes were red, his features were more than ever distorted, and he laughed again aloud as she uttered her words breathlessly, for her bosom was rising and falling in tumultuous panting after her exertions.

"A kiss? Bah! you've defied me, and that won't satisfy me now. I'll have a dozen!"

Again the loud demon laughter—"Ha! ha! ha!" and then a strange sound was heard in the wide chimney.

Gedge was so mad with rage and passion that he heard nothing.

But Daisy did, and the thought that her protector was near gave her superhuman strength.

Her limbs writhed like those of a wrestler as Gedge struggled with her; but, though she felt sure that the combat would end at last in her discomfiture if no help was near, she seemed to be full of hope that she would be able to hold out if this was really a champion coming to the rescue.

Almost at the instant that, with white, set face and panting breast, she felt that she could resist no more, there was a heavy fall down the chimney, something rolled out upon the floor, and with a wild and sepulchral laugh and a burst of sulphurous flame and smoke, Spring-Heeled Jack stood before them.

Daisy in her present dilemma felt not the slightest fear of him.

But on Gedge the effect was electrical.

His hair seemed fairly to bristle on his head, his eyes appeared to start from their sockets, and his features worked convulsively.

He appeared as if striving to speak for a moment.

Then a wild, piercing shriek rent the air, and he fell prone on his face, striking his head violently against the fender.

As these strange cries and noises resounded through the house, it seemed wonderful that Mrs. Foster did not hurry up the stairs.

But she thought, of course, that the cries came from Daisy in her desperate struggles with Gedge Foote, and she purposely took no notice.

Daisy, meanwhile, trembling from head to foot, awed by the terrible aspect of the whole scene, afraid to look in the face the awful apparition which had twice saved her, knelt at its feet, her eyes downcast, the long, silken waves of her hair veiling her bosom as she bent forward.

"How can I thank you, mysterious friend?" she said, in a low, gentle, quavering voice; "twice have you rescued me, first from the hands of an assassin, this time from a fate worse than death. I know not how, but some day I may be able to reward you."

There was no reply.

A strange stillness pervaded the room.

After a moment she looked up hurriedly, and a terrible faintness stole over her heart as she saw that the apparition had vanished.

A thick mist pervaded the room, a stifling sulphurous mist, which prevented her seeing much.

But, at any rate, she had heard and seen no movement, and she was alone with the senseless figure of Gedge Foote.

For a moment she stood leaning against the table in bewilderment.

The terrible scene which she had gone through, coupled with the apparition of Spring-Heeled Jack had for the time so shattered her nerves and bewildered her senses that she could not settle upon her course of action.

But with the first reawakening of her faculties she saw that unless something very miraculous occurred she was in no better position than before.

Gedge Foote would recover—he was only temporarily stunned—and after what had occurred he would be more desperate and furious than ever.

She could quit the room, but all the doors and, windows below were bolted, and barred, and locked, and how, then, was she to escape?

Her first impulse, however, as soon as her strength began to return, was to put on her dress, hat, jacket, and boots.

Then, as she turned to the toilet table, she saw something which made her heart leap with joy.

It was a large bunch of keys.

Her eyes shone with pleasure, her bosom palpitated; for an instant she almost feared to clutch the keys for fear they should disappear before her eyes.

But at last she plucked up courage and seized them.

Then, with trembling limbs—more trembling because she saw that Gedge Foote showed signs of recovering—she made her way across the room, glided out, closed the door after her, locked it, and descended the stairs.

Where was Mrs. Foster?

Not a sound could she hear at first.

Then a loud snoring assailed her ears, and in order to be sure and prepared for any contingency she approached the back parlour and peered in.

The sight within would at any other time have excited her merriment.

Mrs. Foster was reclining in an arm-chair in a drunken sleep, her arms hanging helplessly by her side, her eyes only half shut, her face flushed, her mouth wide open, her toes cocked up helplessly.

But Daisy did not remain a moment.

Creeping out again she approached the front, door, and as quickly as possible began to remove the bolts and bars.

Then she fitted a key to the lock, and, to her joy, opened it.

As she did so she heard a heavy stumbling noise upstairs, and Gedge Foote came heavily across the room, and began to try and force the lock.

He had recovered swiftly after she quitted the chamber; and now, finding himself in the dark and locked in, he began kicking and shouting to such an extent that he succeeded in awakening Mrs. Foster, who began to mumble vaguely and stumble about.

But by this time Daisy had succeeded in passing out.

Shutting the door as softly as she could she ran along the little garden, and without thinking which way she was going scaled the fence opposite, and hurried across the marsh land towards the river.

The only guide she had was a small trembling light, which she had often seen from her window, and which she therefore knew must be a fixture belonging to some riverside cottage or landing place.

The way she had come, however, was a rough and difficult one.

Fearful every moment of pursuit she endeavoured to rush quickly on, but the ground was full of holes and ruts, and every now and then she sank above her ankles in the cloddy soil.

As she toiled slowly on she became aware of sounds behind her, and, looking back, she saw someone pursuing her with a lantern.

It must be Gedge Foote.

The idea gave wings to Daisy's feet.

She had so lately escaped from desperate peril that her heart gave a great leap of annoyance and disgust at the very notion of being once more in his power, even for a moment.

Perilous and rugged as was the road, therefore, she hastened on.

Gedge, however, knew his way better than she did, and was able to make more rapid progress.

She soon saw this, and glanced round in every direction in search of some spot which would afford her temporary shelter.

But with the exception of a few stunted trees and so forth there was nothing.

She must go on trusting to her fleetness of foot and quickness of eye.

On, on she went, now falling on her hands, now going ankle deep in the slush and mud, cutting her palms and bruising her soft little knees against the hard stones.

But she was resolute.

Anything was better than falling again into the power of her pretended friend, the one who had so basely betrayed her.

She cared not for cuts and bruises as long as she was able to put a good distance between herself and pursuer.

The attempt, however, seemed vain.

Gedge Foote came on nearer and nearer.

As she was now not far from the river, she could see that the light she had before noticed was on a barge anchored close to the bank.

If she could but reach this!

Panting for breath, her heart beating rebelliously in her swelling bosom, she made one final effort.

The ground, however, became more rugged.

Gedge Foote was close behind her, she could hear his hard breathing; she seemed almost able to feel his clutching hands.

She knew now that wherever he caught her he would have no mercy.

And so, sick at heart at the prospect of losing home, and perhaps life itself, out on that desolate waste land, she gave one long shrill shriek for help, and made one more desperate struggle.

"Ha! ha! ha!"

What was that?

A loud demon laugh, a whirring sound of wings, a stump, stump, stump, as of some strange leaping animal.

And then a wild shriek from Gedge Foote, as the terrible apparition of Spring-Heeled Jack sprang between him and his victim.

To Daisy the awful sight was associated with safety.

And so, although she had no desire to pause in its presence, she made no exclamation of fear, but dashed away as quickly as possible towards the river.

Gedge Foote had fallen into a deep hole, and there for a few moments he remained crouching, with his hands over his eyes.

Then, as all seemed quiet, he ventured to remove his hands, and look up.

But Spring-Heeled Jack was not gone.

He was still near at hand, standing on a mound, a weird and spectral figure in the grey light, a strange vaporous cloud surrounding him, and smoke and flame issuing from his mouth.

"She has escaped me now by the devil's aid," he said; "but she shall not escape me always. Let her go now. I shall soon be on her track again."

The young girl meanwhile fled on towards the river bank, without once turning her head.

Now that Gedge Foote was not behind her, or rather was not pursuing her, she resolved not to trust herself on the barge.

She knew not what characters she might be trusting herself to.

Her late adventures had made her particularly careful.

And so she hastened along the towing-path, making her way naturally away from London.

Presently, arriving at a little rough-looking house, she saw several boats moored.

No one was near, and the idea occurred to her that she might pull herself across the river, and so make her way towards Barnet, where she might obtain some information in regard to Sir Roland Ashton, and learn perhaps the mystery which enveloped her father's death.

She was an imprudent little thing, but the thought occurred to her that if she was on the other side of the river she would at least have the broad Thames flowing between herself and her enemy.

So, without thinking of the peril to herself, she went down to the water's side, chose a light skiff, and entered it.

She had had very little experience with oars.

In fact, her trials had been confined to certain excursions she had taken with her father to places where she could pull a little boat over a still lake.

She had no conception of the force and current of the great river, and in a few moments, though exerting all her skill, she found herself being rapidly forced in the very direction she desired to avoid—towards London.

She had brought this peril on herself by her own act, and instead of screaming out, she tried all she could to make up for her rashness.

But it was a vain and weary struggle.

She still stuck to the oars, and contrived to keep the boat from coming broadside on to the current; but she could not properly guide it, and she saw that if she was not able soon to pause in her course she would be dashed against one of the stationary barges, or against some other obstacle, and flung headlong into the river.

Suddenly she saw on the left bank of the river a light which resembled the fire of a gipsy encampment, and as she neared it she observed with pleasure several figures gathered round it.

Instantly, without thinking who these people might be, feeling sure that Gedge Foote could not be there, or any of his crew, she uttered a loud cry for help.

As she did so, turning her head rashly towards the light, she did not see where she was going. The boat went with a crash against some black, ugly piles belonging to an old disused wharf or landing-stage, and in an instant the frail craft was upset.

There was one wild, despairing uplifting of her arms as she sprang up, a long shriek, one gleam of the white, dainty limbs, and the waters had closed over her!

CHAPTER X.
JOE DIMITY, THE SHOWMAN, AND HIS "MERRIE COMPANIE."

THE "GRAND IMPERIAL CIRCUS and Royal Theatre," proprietor, Mr. Joseph Dimity, was on tour.

They had just reached the outskirts of the metropolis from the south coast, where they had done more or less successful business, and were now about to proceed to the north of England.

Nothing was farther from the thoughts of any one of them than the occurrence of any unusual thing to break the monotonous routine of their existence.

They were a kind of family party, in fact, and had dawdled on an existence of weary, dreary sameness for years.

Joe Dimity was a man of about fifty, with grizzly hair, a florid complexion, rather protuberant though kindly eyes, a big, wide mouth, and a podgy body.

He took the heavy father in the sensation dramas (lasting a quarter of an hour), which were acted by the company—characters in which he had to roll out his "r's" and talk of his "chee-ild," and so forth, and spread out grimy hands in benediction.

Mrs. Dimity was a tragedy-queen off and on the stage—a tall, bony woman, with a set colour, and black hair and eyes.

But she was the very reverse of what her appearance denoted, for she was the kindest-hearted woman that ever walked a stage, and was appealed to by everyone in the company when in trouble.

Then there was Miss Maria Hoskins, who united singing, dancing, and acting, and who was really wife to the Signor Bellini (alias Tom Bell), who was the dark-browed villain of the company, and who, off the stage, was the mildest fellow who ever emptied a pot of four-half[27] in a village beer-house.

Maria was cruelly fair, with a roundish face, insipid blue eyes, and nose very much *retroussé*;[28] but then her arms were a marvel, her shoulders well rounded, her bust superb, and everyone who had seen her dance in those very flimsy and very short skirts of hers, and those excessively pinked and glossy tights, declared that she possessed the finest pair of legs on the travelling stage.

There was Harry Banks, the clown, and Audley Harcourt (alias John Mullins), the walking gentleman and general lover, and Bob Lightley, the comedian, and others, all more or less clever, all contented, all happy in their way, and all very badly paid.

In fact, "treasury" was sometimes a pure fiction.

They clubbed together to procure their food, and often Joe Dimity and his wife would partake with much dignity of a piece of bread and cheese offered by one of his "company:" "With great pleasure, my boy. Don't feel hungry to-day, and 'twill save the missus cooking this hot day."

Poor Joe! Everyone knew the "house" had been an empty one the night before, but no one ventured to say so.

They lived in a gipsy kind of way, in fact, and had been together now so long, with the exception of two or three younger members, that they constituted quite a happy family.

On the evening when Daisy made her escape from Gedge Foote, Joe Dimity and his company had reached a wide piece of waste ground on the river-bank, where they resolved to camp out for the night.

They never put up at any place where they had to pay unless they were compelled to do so.

The caravans, three in number, carried the materials for stage and "auditorium" on their tops outside, and the company contrived to squeeze into the inside.

It was not altogether a very reputable or comfortable arrangement, but it saved money, and a week's lodging saved by all meant roast beef for dinner on Sunday.

So the married couples had half-a-caravan each—just room to stretch their legs—the bachelors had one caravan between them, and the spinsters the same.

The company had taken a considerable sum of money that day, and were enjoying a goodly al-fresco supper when poor Daisy's shrill cry for help resounded over the waters of the Thames and echoed along the gloomy banks.

It was not an unusual thing to hear the loud cry of some unfortunate creature plunging away "out of life's misery."

But there was something in the ring of Daisy's voice which seemed to tell that it was

----

[27] Half ale, half porter – a dark beer.
[28] Turned up.

a young girl.

Harry Banks, the clown, and Bob Lightley, the comedian, both started to their feet.

"What's the matter?" cried Joe Dimity, almost dropping his spoon as he was devouring some fragrant pea-soup; for he was rather deaf.

"I heard a cry for help," said Lightley.

"Yes, and so did I," cried Harry Banks; "let's be off and see what it is."

Not to be outdone, the kindly showman and Audley Harcourt and the other male members of the company followed the clown and the comedian, who had already started off.

They were close to the river's bank, and in a few moments they were at the water's edge.

When they reached it, however, all was quiet.

But they remained perfectly still, listening.

Presently they heard another faint cry, and fancied they saw a white face drifting with the tide.

Harry Banks, the clown, was a powerful swimmer, as well as a brave man; and so he resolved to be the one to attempt the rescue.

"Look out for a boat, gentlemen," he said. "Now, then. Hullo! boys. Here we are again!"

And as he kicked off his boots (which were none too tight), he took a rush along one of the slippery beams which supported the piles, and plunged into the water.

The tide, as we have said, was running very strong, and Daisy, gradually becoming numbed in all her limbs, was being rapidly carried towards London.

She had only gone down once, and had come up without having swallowed much water, and so was able to cry out again for help.

Now, her clothes helping to keep her so, she was floating on top of the water but her legs were rapidly losing all feeling, and, little as was the power of thought left in her, she knew that she was in momentary danger of the cramping chill stealing upwards to her body.

There were other things to fear also; she might be dashed against barges, and sucked beneath by the eddying water; her head might come in contact with piles or floating objects; or she might be left to suffocate amongst the river mud.

None of which was a pleasant prospect, and no doubt the very fear, which set her little heart beating so wildly, was the means of sending the warm blood rushing more warmly through her rapidly chilling body.

She saw even in the uncertain light the forms of the players dashing down to the side of the water.

She knew, therefore, that there were those not far off who would try and save her.

This sent a thrill of pleasure through her frame, and kept her blood warm and her spirits up.

But she was drifting so rapidly!

Everything round her was so dark and gloomy.

Only far away the bright lights of the city.

All else black and sombre.

But what was that?

She heard a cheery voice; then a loud splash.

Some one had come to the rescue.

For an instant a wretched feeling came over her—a wretched question framed itself in her mind.

Could it be Gedge Foote?

But, no!

He could not have reached the spot in time.

"Oh! Heaven help me! she said, "and give me strength. Only a few minutes more, and I shall be safe!"

Just as this idea came into her head with a pleasurable shock, she saw ahead of her some black beams standing up threateningly high out of the water.

A moment before she would have feared.

Now she welcomed it, and with a sudden access of strength thrust out her grasping hand to seize the woodwork.

Life is sweet, even to those who are in pain and misery, and consequently to Daisy Leigh her young and beautiful existence was a treasure she did not care to lose, with all its promises of future joy and happiness.

So with eager haste and unexpected power she seized the beam, and held on.

Still the bitter cold in her legs numbed them and made them useless, but her heart was beating hopefully, and her blood was beginning to course so rapidly through her veins that her head began to swim.

Oh! she prayed that her unknown rescuer might succeed.

And as if her prayer was answered, a dark object suddenly swam alongside of her. She saw something white which she knew to be a human face, and she felt that she was about to be saved.

Then came a reaction which might have been fatal.

The strain upon her nerves had been so great that now, when she felt rescue near, her strength gave way and she fainted.

However, Harry Banks was there, brave, good-looking, strong Harry, with his stout heart and iron resolution; the young girl was caught to his breast like a young baby, with his left arm, and with his right he struck out for the shore.

His companions had ran full speed along the shore, while he was swimming rapidly with the current, and as they saw the young girl fall senseless into his arms they were close upon them.

"Here! Harry—this way! By Jove! he's over-weighted there," cried Audley Harcourt, and as there seemed some difficulty he too shook himself bootless, and plunged into the rushing stream.

Their united efforts soon brought the girl ashore.

"Now, then, for a good run," cried Harry Banks. "I don't wonder this poor little thing has frozen limbs. I'm like an icicle myself, and it's only autumn."

How much of this speech was heard by his friends we cannot say, for he had already started to run with his burden held to his breast like a baby.

He was immensely strong, as most men in his branch of the profession are, and Daisy Leigh was but a light weight.

More than this, he had caught a glimpse of her face before she had lost her senses, and he had recognised the fact that she was beautiful.

Harry Banks had need of a wife. At present there was not much accommodation for a fresh couple unless they slept on top of the caravans, but that he did not think of.

No one in the company pleased his fancy, except "Maria," and she was another person's property, and not for him. Thinking, therefore, he might have found a prize, "rescued from the deep," he hastened on with superhuman strength, towards the "camp."

Poor Harry Banks!

If he had only known to what peril he was bearing pretty Daisy Leigh, he would certainly have thought twice before he made such a rush with her to the caravan.

But it is not given to us to have fore-knowledge, and so on he went, followed by the rest of the company—the male members—until they reached the spot where the female strollers[29] were dawdling over their suppers, and exchanging notes as to the cause of the excitement which had caused the desertion of all the male members of the show.

On learning the true reason of the defection, every one was ready at once to offer help.

"The poor dear!" "The pretty child!" and all manner of endearing epithets were applied to Daisy; but the most practical and beneficial thing was the taking her into the principal caravan by Maria and Mrs. Dimity, who stripped her, gave her hot drink, and rubbed her numbed little body all over with rough towels.

"She's a beautiful little thing," said Mrs. Joe, as they at last rested from their labours, and Daisy was re-dressed in night-things, and tucked comfortably in bed; "and there's nothing about her to show that she had any reason to commit suicide. It's been an accident or something."

"So I think," said Maria; "but let's examine her clothes, and see if they throw any light on the subject."

In another moment Mrs. Dimity had searched the scanty garments, which were Daisy's only possessions.

But they told no tales.

All the searchers found was a purse containing Gedge Foote's two sovereigns.

Maria smiled at this.

"She did not try to kill herself from poverty, then," she said.

"No, indeed," cried the 'tragedy-queen.' "Who knows? We may be on the brink of some strange discovery. Who can tell what mystery hangs about the life of this pretty child?"

"Well, she isn't exactly a child," said Maria. "She's quite seventeen by all I can see of her. However, she seems a lady, and I don't believe there's anything mysterious about her being in the water, except an accident."

Daisy, when at last she woke from the semi-sleep which followed her insensibility, tried to speak.

But Mrs. Dimity, curious as she was to know all, would not allow it.

She was conscious of the fact that a doctor ought, in the natural order of things, to have been called in.

But she was not a particular friend of the medical profession, and objected to strangers "spying about," and so, knowing she had applied the best remedies, she would not let Daisy spoil her chance by over-exciting herself.

"No, no, my dear," she whispered, kindly, as she bent over her pretty patient; "you must not excite yourself now. There will be plenty of time to-morrow."

"Only one thing," said Daisy, with a half-sob.

---

[29] Actors or performers.

"Well, what is it?"

"You mustn't think I tried to commit suicide," said the poor girl. "I could not be so wicked. I was escaping from a cruel enemy, and I was upset from a boat."

"All right, my dear. We believe you," said Mrs. Joe; "but we won't listen to a word more until to-morrow."

And so Daisy was left to herself and her slumbers.

That night Maria slept with Daisy, and Signor Bellini—alias Tom Bell—had to accommodate himself with the comforts of the bachelors' caravan.

Next morning Daisy was delirious.

And she was still in the same condition, although a doctor had been called in, when the caravan once more set out towards Barnet, bearing the senseless girl towards the home of her deadliest foe—Sir Roland Ashton.

CHAPTER XI.

HOW CONSTANCE MARFIELD MET HER FATHER.

SIR ROLAND ASHTON'S terror at seeing Spring-Heeled Jack, and at the non-success of his attack upon that mysterious being, caused him a severe shock, and he was ill for several days.

But it had no effect on his malevolent spirit, except, in fact, to make him more brutal, and more eager for revenge.

During his illness he was attended by Caleb Masters.

The company of this vile parasite seemed to suit him.

They could plan over their evil schemes together, and this was just what kept the baronet pleased and amused.

At the end of the week he was quite recovered, and then his thoughts went back at once to the matters which, before his short illness, he had resolved upon performing.

And the principal matter was his marriage with Constance Marfield, or, as he now called her, Constance Harland.

She was still in her room; bolted and barred in, with barred windows, too, and seeing no one but the housekeeper, Mrs. Levine.

But her spirit was unbroken.

However much she might weep and mourn in secret, she was calm, bold, and defiant, when Mrs. Levine presented herself.

She expressed herself much delighted when she heard of Sir Roland's illness.

"It is a just punishment upon him," she said.

"And he loves you so," returned Mrs. Levine.

Now this sentiment was put on, and Constance knew it.

As we have said, the housekeeper had, in fact, been setting her cap for years at the master of the house, and was hoping that some day or another he would give up wooing elsewhere, and subside for comfort upon her very substantial bosom.

So she was in no way eager to aid him to the possession of Constance Marfield.

"He would make you a very good husband, Mrs. Levine," said Constance, somewhat contemptuously; "but he would not suit me. I know what a villain he is. I believe he is even worse than we really know."

SPRING-HEELED JACK,
THE TERROR OF LONDON.

By the Author of "TURNPIKE DICK, the Star of the Road."

SPRING-HEELED JACK SCENTS A HAWK IN THE DOVE'S NEST.

"I do not believe it."

Mrs. Levine spoke positively.

It did not suit her to give credence to reports.

She was content to know that Sir Roland was only forty, wealthy, and handsome, and rich.

What more did she require in exchange for her own robust and mature charms?

"That is well, then," said Constance; "you are just the one for him. As for myself, I love Ralph Ashton (Sir Ralph he will be some day, as he ought to be now), and between him and Sir Roland there is rather a vast difference."

Mrs. Levine had evidently been thinking over a plan of her own.

"Yes; you are right," she said, musingly. "Can you keep a secret?"

Constance eagerly caught at this.

Evidently this woman had some plan in view which would benefit her.

"Yes; I swear to keep it, unless it is in regard to some crime, and in that case I do not wish to hear it."

Mrs. Levine laughed.

"No," she said; "it is no crime. It is a piece of fun which may benefit both you and me. Listen! I must whisper it to you, for even walls have ears, you know."

The housekeeper bent forward, and began talking rapidly and eagerly.

As Constance listened a smile passed over her lips, though a crimson blush spread from her cheeks up to the roots of her hair, and crept down pink and beautiful over the lovely bosom.

"Well," said Mrs. Levine, laughing, when she had confided her secret, "what do you think of my plan?"

"It is very clever," said Constance, still blushing; "but I cannot see how it would succeed."

"Oh! leave that to me," said Mrs. Levine; "I have been married once, and I'm no fool. I'll carry it through, and be glad of it. But there's no hurry. If you have to give in at all in regard to the marriage, plead illness and have it put off. Then have all manner of scruples, and you'll see when the time comes I'll make it all right."

On the day after the scene on the mail-coach Sir Roland Ashton received a mysterious missive.

This was from Tom Harland.

But the escaped convict was obliged to put off the promised interview for ten days.

At the end of that time Constance, still a prisoner, received a message in writing from Sir Roland that the time was come to see her father.

The young girl's heart gave a great leap.

She knew what her father had done, or, at any rate, been accused of and suffered for in the past.

But, nevertheless, she was so utterly destitute of friends that there was a wonderful pleasure in the idea that she was about to see one of her parents, one who had a right to protect her.

Alas! poor Constance.

She little knew the truth, little guessed the real character of the man with whom she was about to be brought face to face.

It was evening when for the first time for so many days she was permitted to leave her room.

Sir Roland, who had now quite recovered from the shock, and was looking his very best, awaited her in the drawing-room.

He had purposely taken excessive pains with his toilet, and looked younger even than he was.

No one looking into his easy, careless face would have imagined it possible that behind the handsome mask there lurked a soul as black as Satan.

"Good evening, Constance," he said, as calmly as if nothing extraordinary had happened in the household. "I hope you have not confided to any one the secret of your father's presence in the neighbourhood?"

Constance smiled derisively.

"I should have found it difficult to confide in any one," she said, "considering that I have been bolted and barred in my room. I have seen no one but Mrs. Levine, and my conversation with her has related to a very different matter."

She said this rather significantly, but Sir Roland did not observe her manner.

"True; but lovers can talk through bars," he said, lightly.

Constance made no reply.

Seeing her mood, he thought it best not to irritate her further.

"I have to exact from you one promise," he said, "before you can see Mr. Harland."

"What is that?" she said. "I will not make you even a shadow of a promise unless I know beforehand what it is."

"Oh! it is very simple," said Sir Roland. "It is simply that you will promise to keep quiet while we go and see your father—that you will make not the slightest attempt at escape on this occasion, but return as you came."

"I promise," said Constance.

A short time before she would not have made this promise.

But since her conversation with Mrs. Levine affairs were altogether different.

"Very well," said Sir Roland; "pray go at once, and get ready for a walk. Do not delay, for your father is in great danger; he was seen at the inn the other night and recognised, in spite of his disguise, and the constables are after him everywhere."

Constance made no reply.

In a few minutes she and Sir Roland had set out.

Often afterwards she thought what an imprudent thing it was to have trusted herself alone on a dreary night with one possessing the desperate and villainous character of Sir Roland.

But, although such mystery and horror enveloped her father, her bosom was full of eagerness to see him; and, having given her promise to return quickly, she almost looked upon this as an implied assurance on the part of her companion that she was in no danger of being detained.

Passing across the grounds of the park, they made for a little gate which led out into a bye-lane.

At the other side of this lane was a kind of waste ground, with the ruins of some old buildings on it. People said that it had once been a training stable.

It was here that Tom Harland was to meet them.

Sir Roland did not at once cross the lane and enter the waste ground.

He passed up one way and Constance the other to see if they were watched, or if there were any one approaching either way who would be likely to notice where they were going.

No one was about.

"Let us lose no time now," said Sir Roland, "we are in luck's way. Come—quickly!"

He broke violently through the hedge.

As he did so a man's desperate voice said—

"Stop, or I fire!"

It was Harland who spoke.

"All right, Tom—it's a friend," said the baronet. "It is I—Roland Ashton, and I bring your daughter. Go into the ruin, and I will follow you."

The wretched man at once did as he was bid, and in a few moments Sir Roland and Constance had followed him into the ruined building.

An old crazy door closed the first portion of this, and having secured this, the escaped convict led the way in the dim light further into the stable.

Here he lit a lamp, and for the first time Constance Marfield, or Harland, stood face to face with her father.

Such a father!

He was a tall, broadly-built man, as we have already described him when we met him at the Three Jolly Wheelers, but his largeness was more the result of big bones than stoutness.

His clothes hung on him loosely, as if he had had all his flesh worn off him by hard labour and trouble.

His face was gaunt and coarse; it was white now with mingled dread and emotion, but you could see by the nose and the sensual mouth what manner of man he was when he had the chance of a debauch.

His eyes had an eager, hungry, hunted look, as of a wild beast.

Constance looked at him with a shudder.

But she tried as far as possible to disguise the appearance of disgust.

This man was, after all, her father, and it would scarcely do to betray to him at their first interview the feeling with which his first appearance had inspired her.

"This, then, is my father," she said.

"Yes," said Sir Roland. "Harland, this is your daughter."

The man had been quite surprised for a moment.

But he quickly recovered himself, and advancing, he put out his coarse hand to take her thin, slim one.

Constance, repressing the horror with which he inspired her, suffered him to grasp her palm.

"I am pleased to find you," said he, "more pleased than you can think. But I wish I could have met you under better and more pleasing circumstances."

"Yes, father. I wish we were not standing in the shadow of an old sorrow."

"That sorrow will always overshadow me while I am in England," said Harland, coming at once to the point. "What I want is to go away for ever from this country, and even from Europe, and when I can do that, you need not fear that any shame will ever fall upon your name or your father's. But while I am here, there is no limit to the disgrace which may overwhelm both you and me."

Constance, accustomed as she was to the trickeries of Sir Roland and all those round him, was not able to see through the shallow pretence of this man.

Father or no father, he was no gentleman, no man to be proud of, and, consequently, he would probably not be affected by any show of disrespect on her part.

But she felt that gentle sentiment towards him that she would never have dreamed of doing anything which would have made him seem little in his own eyes.

"Can I do anything to help you?" she said, softly.

"Yes," he said, "everything."

His manner was rudely eager.

But she ascribed this to her strange position, and, putting this together with his wild eyes and hunted look, she pitied him.

"Pray tell me how?" said Constance.

"In this way; in order to get away from England I must have money; in order to have money you must make me a promise. You are the only one who can—"

"Do not be evasive, dear father," said Constance. "Tell me plainly what you mean."

Tom Harland was incapable of understanding the bitter feelings of the young girl before him.

He came at once to the point.

"I mean this, then, Constance," he said. "I have no money, and there is only one man in England of whom I can get it. That man is Sir Roland Ashton."

"Well?"

"He is here, he will answer for himself," said Harland; "he is willing to advance me anything in reason to take me away to a foreign country, where I shall never be able to trouble anyone again."

"Yes."

"He makes one stipulation."

"Yes."

"And that is that you become his wife."

Constance turned deadly pale.

But she had the courage to speak out—

"And you—my father—surely you will not dream of such a sacrifice?"

"What am I to do?" he said; "this is my only chance. Do you know what is the terrible alternative?"

"No."

"Simply this—that, as my life is forfeited to the law, I shall be hanged!"

The girl shuddered.

But in a moment a thought occurred to her.

"You could only return to prison if they caught you," she said; "they could not take your life for a crime for which you were only sentenced to penal servitude."

Tom Harland laughed—a terrible, unmusical laugh.

"Ha! ha!" he cried, "you do not know all. For that old crime, which they chose to call murder, I was sentenced to transportation, but for the other crime I should swing."

"What crime?"

"The crime that gave me my freedom; for in order to obtain that I had to shoot one of the warders. That was, in my eyes, a necessary means of obtaining my freedom; but in the eyes of the law it is murder."

The girl, into whose bosom a ray of light had for a moment penetrated, shuddered with dread.

The toils were indeed closing round her.

How could she deliberately send this man to such a doom?

How could she consent to see this man hung—who, though a hardened criminal apparently, was yet her father?

"What am I to do?" she murmured.

The words were only addressed to herself, but Tom Harland replied to them.

"Your course is easy, my child," he said; "there is a handsome, rich man, in the prime of life, who wishes to make you his wife. What more easy than compliance? What hardship is there in that?"

"Every hardship," said Constance, melting into tears. "You do not understand; you cannot. Here, before the face of Sir Roland Ashton, I tell him plainly that I hate him. I shudder at his caresses, and were I to become his wife, my existence would be a living horror."

"Then you would prefer to devote me to a terrible and cruel death?"

He spoke bitterly.

But his manner was not quite that which was convincing to the young girl.

She wrung her hands.

"Oh!" she cried. "Oh! if I had only some one to advise me! Oh! Ralph, if only you were here to help me!"

As if in answer to her appeal for help a loud "Ha! ha! ha!" echoed in the night air.

Sir Roland started and turned pale, and seemed waiting for some horrid event.

But nothing came.

"You are not likely to obtain advice or help here," said he, after a pause; "you have simply to act upon your own responsibility."

"Let me speak to her alone," said Tom Harland; "retire a moment to the other end of the chamber. I may find an argument to change her stolid nature."

Sir Roland very reluctantly did as he was asked, and Tom Harland, coming close to Constance, passed his arm round her waist and pressed her to him.

As he did so he bent and kissed her, pressing his smoke-polluted lips to her tremulous ones.

Criminal as he was, she could hardly refuse to submit to this embrace, which was given in far from a fatherly manner; but when it was repeated again and again she repulsed him.

"Do not waste time, father," she said; "let me hear what you have to say. If you can find a way out of this terrible dilemma, pray help me!"

"I can, I think," said Harland, still keeping his arm round her lissom waist, and whispering in her ear. "Give your consent, so that I can get some money, and then, when I have made my escape, you can refuse to carry it out."

"I should be telling a lie."

"Nonsense! Only let me get the money and escape, and I shall write you a letter which will explain to you the means of evading the whole affair without uttering anything in the shape of a falsehood."

She could feel him breathing with eagerness as he pressed her to him.

It was an awful trial for him.

This, of course, she knew.

But what was her position—torn between parental duty and her loathing for the man who desired to force his love upon her?

"Tell me all, then," she said. "What am I to say to this man?"

"Say that to save me you will marry him in a month," replied Harland. "Say that, in order to prove all is right, he can give me half the money I want, and the rest after the ceremony. I will ask, twice as much as I intended, and if he never sends me the other I shall not be hurt. So if you don't marry him I shall be no worse off."

"How much shall you ask?"

"In all, five hundred pounds."

He felt a sudden thrill pass through her form.

The light in her eyes showed it was one of pleasure.

"Listen!" she said, in a very low voice. "I have two hundred pounds saved up."

"You?"

"Yes; I have never spent half the money which he gave me as my allowance. Why—"

"You are a long time consulting," said Sir Roland, in an impatient voice.

"Not longer than is necessary," said Harland. "Proceed, Constance."

"Why he gave me so large a one, I could never understand," she continued; "at any rate, I have that sum in the Imperial Bank in London. If you come to my window in an hour or two's time I will give you an order to draw it all. You need not trouble yourself, therefore, about the second payment."

"But how am I to reach the window?" asked Tom Harland.

"You must do the same as Ralph Ashton did," she answered.

"And what was that?"

"Climb up by the ivy."

"Very well," said Harland, eagerly. "I will note carefully all the windows of the Hall to-night, and I will make my way to the one where I see two lights shown."

"Very well."

Harland released her now with evident reluctance.

"Sir Roland," he said, "I think I have arranged everything satisfactorily."

"She consents?"

"Yes. Ask her?"

For an instant the baronet seemed too overjoyed to speak.

His eyes beamed with delight, and his lips wreathed themselves into a smile.

He advanced quickly. "You consent, then, my darling?" he said.

She looked at him contemptuously.

"Do not talk to me in that way," she said. "As I have told you, the word love as between us is worse than a farce. I loathe and detest you more than I should have thought it possible I could have done any human being; but I consent to yield to you simply to save my father from disgrace and death."

He took her hand.

"No matter; how I win you I care not!" he cried. "Were I to marry you by force I should be satisfied, because I know that you will love me afterwards. Loathing will turn to liking under my kindness and caresses."

She shuddered at this.

"Pray do not insult me," she said. "It is your caresses I dread. But, remember, I cannot be your wife for a month."

"Nay, I cannot agree to that," said Sir Roland. "All is ready. I have obtained a special license, and the ceremony will take place to-morrow night in the drawing-room."

Constance wrenched away her hand.

"Nay!" she said; "never will I consent to it. Not even to save my father's life could I agree to so swift a yielding up of all my hopes in life."

Harland here approached.

"Sir Roland," he said, "this is but fair. She has yielded solely to my persuasions. I have put everything before her in a straightforward way, and she has consented to become your wife. What more can you expect?"

"I do not expect shuffling."

"There is no shuffling, said Tom Harland. "You cannot expect Constance to be pleased at the prospect before her, or to wish to rush into matrimony against her will. In order that there shall be no doubt as to her intentions half the money I ask for can stand over until I reach America."

"What money is it you ask?"

"Five hundred pounds!"

"A cool demand," said the baronet; "but still dear Constance here is worth fifty times that amount. Be it so, then. I will give you three hundred pounds to-night, and the other shall be sent to you, wherever you are, the instant Constance becomes my wife."

"Which will be never," thought the young girl and Tom Harland as well.

"Very well; all is settled, then," said Constance. "Let us return to the house."

The baronet would fain have expressed his delight at her acquiescence.

But she drew away from him.

"There will be time enough for thanks another time," she said. "Let us return to the Hall."

"I will say good-bye, then, Constance," said Harland. "You have my eternal gratitude, if that is of any use to you, and gives you any satisfaction, and may you be more happy in the future than you now seem to hope."

She made no reply, and Tom Harland pressed her to his heart, and imprinted several kisses on her lips, much to the anger of Sir Roland, who throughout the interview had strangely resented the man's manner, and who now said—

"Come, Harland, you forget your danger. I and Constance will hasten back to the Hall now, and you had better remain here until we are out of reach. It will be safer for you not to remain with us too long."

"But the money? I wish to leave England to-morrow!"

"Very good. When all is quiet, make your way to the terrace beneath my study window, and knock three times. I will admit you then, and give you the money."

"How?"

"In gold or notes."

"That is well; I will be there," said Harland.

And then, as they prepared to go, he drew back into the shadow and concealed himself.

Sir Roland talked eagerly and freely to his companion as they made their way towards the Hall.

But he received no reply.

This dogged silence gave him a misgiving.

Constance and Harland had whispered together.

What if father and daughter had planned to deceive him?

He resolved at once to run no risks.

When, therefore, they reached the Hall, he called Mrs. Levine, and intimated that Constance was to be placed in the same bedroom as before.

The girl's heart sank at this.

She had hoped, either through Harland or Ralph, to escape before the forced marriage.

But now even that faint hope was taken from her.

As she entered her room after supper, being escorted to it by Sir Roland and Mrs. Levine, the former caught her in his arms and kissed her passionately.

"Ah!" he cried, as he held her resisting form tightly in his strong grasp. "Fate is, indeed, unkind to make you hate me, when my love for you is so great that the very touch of your lips thrills my whole form with ecstasy."

Her face was crimson with anger and shame.

But she made no reply.

Only when the door was closed, and she was once more alone, she flung herself on her knees in tears.

"Never can I be his," she cried; "never, never! I could not submit to the humiliation and shame. I will die first—I will die first."

For hours she waited and waited for Tom Harland.

But he came not.

"I am deserted by all, even by Ralph," she murmured, as presently she undressed and retired to her bed; "but I will still hope on. Death must be preferable to being in the ignominious position of a slave to a man one hates."

CHAPTER XII.

RALPH ASHTON ONCE MORE—IN THE OLD MILL—
LAURA'S TREACHERY—RALPH CAPTURED.

WHEN Ralph Ashton quitted Constance's bedroom on the night when Mrs. Levine had heard the two conversing, he made his way as swiftly as he could to the highway. After attending to a little business, and crossing over into a dense plantation, he found his horse, and leaping on its back, turned its head northwards and rode leisurely away.

He knew well that a reward had been offered for his capture.

He knew also that were he captured he would have great difficulty in proving his innocence.

But still he seemed quite careless of the necessity of disguise, and rode on as leisurely as if there was nothing to fear.

He had not proceeded very far, however, before he turned abruptly to the left and made his way in the direction of an old mill, which stood, deserted and weird-looking, on the margin of a stream.

Outside this he stood for a moment or so, and glanced round him to see if anyone might chance to be observing him.

Then he knelt down by the side of a tree, and groping about by the roots, got hold of a rope artfully concealed among the leaves and earth.

With this he gently pulled from the side of the mill a small ladder, which, it seemed, was the only means of entering the half-ruined edifice.

On reaching the little terrace, as it may be called, which ran round the mill, he opened a door which admitted him into the interior of the crazy old building.

He, of course, had first drawn up the ladder, and when he passed in he was in no hurry to strike a light.

Evidently he was well acquainted with the place.

He closed the door behind him, and then groping his way in the darkness, he grasped firmly the balustrade of the staircase, leading down to the basement.

Half way down this it was safe to light a lamp, and accordingly he carefully sought about for a niche where he had deposited some candles and an oil lamp.

They were gone!

He started in wonder and some fear.

Someone must have discovered his haunt.

For a long time he had made this spot one of his secret hiding places.

Who could have found him out?

Or was it only some other fugitive from justice, who had accidentally chosen the same place as himself?

The rats might have eaten the candles, but the disappearance of the lamp seemed to point with certainty to a human visitor.

The secret of the ladder had evidently not been discovered, but still it was with much doubt and trepidation that he struck a light and proceeded slowly down to the lower part of the casement.

As he went, he trod on something slippery, and looking down, he found it was a candle which someone had evidently dropped in his hurry.

He lit this as well as he could in its dilapidated state, and then, with a pistol in his right hand, he proceeded in his descent.

The days of which we write were, of course, comparatively modern.

Railways had commenced to spread their iron bands over England, and the old stage coach was beginning to retire before them.

But they were far from being extinct.

Years and years after the time when Spring-Heeled Jack began to frighten people in the suburbs of London the "Royal Mails" and "Expresses," and so forth, still ran over the dark highway road.

Very few were the cases, however, in which they were stopped by footpads.[30]

Now and then the robbers became bold and defiant as of old, and great was the consternation about this time, when it became known in London that highwaymen had once more made their appearance.

They were not attired in the gay and jaunty dress which distinguished Tom King and Blueskin and so forth.[31]

But the attire which they affected was sufficiently like the old style to cast terror and

---

[30] A highwayman who robs people on foot rather than riding a horse
[31] Highwaymen; King was an associate of Dick Turpin, Blueskin's real name was Joseph Blake. All these characters feature in Volume 5 of the Spring-Heeled Jack Library, *Dandy Dick* or, *The King's Highway.*

dismay into the hearts of any timid citizens who might come across them.

A tight-fitting, frogged frock-coat, a hat of a somewhat conical shape, a pair of high military boots, and a pair of pistols, recalled sufficiently well the memories of the days of Black Bess and Dick Turpin; and the blunderbuss, and so forth, were once more coming into fashion.

It was not, therefore, to be wondered at if Ralph Ashton, finding that his lamp was gone, suspected at once that his place of concealment had been discovered and utilised by some of the gentlemen of the road.

Cautiously he descended.

There was no light below—no sign, indeed, of life.

But he still clutched his pistol as he entered the vault, which on so many occasions lately had served as his resting-place.

For a few moments after he went in—the feeble light of his candle hardly serving to dispel the gloom—he could see nothing.

But presently he saw something lying in a corner.

He stood still and listened.

The silence was terrible.

Not a sound broke it, not even the breathing of a light sleeper.

What then was that "something" lying on the heap of straw, which until now had served him as a bed?

It certainly looked like a human form.

But could it be alive—so still, so breathless?

Summoning up all his courage, he approached, and bent down.

The form, whatever it was, was covered up with straw, and he drew some of it away.

There before him, sure enough, was a human body.

But it was dead.

The face was that of a man about forty years of age, dressed in a somewhat rough fashion, and with a somewhat rough-featured face.

His features were placid in death now, however, and pale as marble.

For a few moments Ralph Ashton could not discern how the unfortunate man had met his death.

But after a while he saw a dagger sticking in his breast with a piece of parchment attached to it.

He knelt down and detached it, and on it were the words, "A victim of the vengeance of the Black Brotherhood!"

Strange words these in modern times!

"The Black Brotherhood!" repeated Ralph. "What can the words mean? It brings me back to times long, long ago. But whatever it may signify, it will not be safe to leave him here. Where shall I place the body?"

To leave him where he was would be to bring certain suspicion upon himself.

He resolved to search the pockets of the dead man in order to see whether there was any clue whatever to his identity.

But search as he would he could find nothing.

Conquering as well as he could his natural repugnance, he raised the dead body in his arms and began to re-ascend the stairs.

The lamp he had discovered on a little shelf in the vault, and by leaving the door open he was enabled to drag the body up without any fear of falling.

When he reached at last the terrace, which as I have before said, ran round the old mill, he dragged his hideous burden to that part which overhung the water.

The stream was very deep at this point, and rushed on with impetuosity, swollen with the late rains.

It was a deep stream, which at one time had been used to turn the big wheel of the mill.

Glancing round to see that he was not observed, he raised the body with all his strength, poised it for a moment over the wooden parapet, and let it fall with a great splash into the water.

It disappeared for a moment amid spray and foam, but presently as he watched he saw a dark object rise to the surface and go whirling away.

Ralph Ashton heaved a sigh of relief.

"There was no danger now," he thought, "of being accused of a crime which he never committed."

He would not, however, have been so easy in his mind if he had observed that at the very moment when he threw the body into the stream a man was watching him.

A man dressed from head to foot in black, with a black mask concealing his features.

He was standing concealed in the shadow of some trees on the other side of the stream, and he never uttered a word as the victim of the Black Brotherhood was dropped into the stream.

But as soon as Ralph Ashton had passed into the mill and closed himself in once more, the mysterious figure hurried along the bank of the river towards a wooden bridge which spanned the water at some distance.

Crossing this he came stealthily along the bank on which the old mill stood, and approaching it he swung himself with wonderous agility to the terrace.

Here he endeavoured to enter by the door, but found it closed on the inside.

He paused for a moment to think; and then, muttering, "I will keep watch elsewhere," he let himself down once more, and in a few moments was safely ensconced among the trees.

Meanwhile, Ralph, having once more descended to the bottom of the old structure, proceeded to a door at the back which opened out upon the level ground, and unfastening the rusty old chains and bolts, once more peered cautiously forth.

He might have taken the body out this way, but he would have had great difficulty in carrying it over the piles of rubbish and so forth which lay between the building and the stream.

Now, however, he passed out, proceeded to the spot where he had left his horse, and bringing him in, stabled him in the lower passage, and once more re-bolted the door.

Then returning to his room, if so it could be called, he removed the straw on which the dead body had been laid and placed it in an adjoining cellar.

Returning, he locked himself securely in, and going to a cupboard took out the materials for a fire.

Having lit this he brought out some food and a bottle of wine.

"The Black Brotherhood weren't hungry or thirsty, at any rate," he thought, with a smile, as he sat down before the pleasant blaze; "but I must find myself some new quarters. I can't make a dead house of my lodgings for anyone; neither can I share it with the Black Avengers."

His attempt to be cheerful was a very poor one. He had enough, indeed, to disturb his mind—the danger of Constance, the reward for his own apprehension, and the deadly enmity of Sir Roland.

He saw no chance whatever, in case of arrest, of being able to prove his innocence, and it was necessary therefore to conceal himself until by some miraculous means he discovered, and was able publicly to denounce the guilty party.

It was a wretched existence.

But there were mysterious circumstances connected with his secret life that broke the monotony.

Of these we shall know more hereafter.

At present we cannot raise the veil. Little dreaming of the watcher so near—of the new peril hanging over him—Ralph, in spite of all, passed presently into a heavy slumber, wrapped in his large cloak before the fire.

The corner where the dead man lay he carefully eschewed.

Nothing occurred during the night.

Ralph slept as if he was reclining upon the downiest of feather beds, and dreamed soft dreams of success and happiness.

The enemy, or whoever he was who kept watch without, made no sign.

And accordingly when he awoke in the morning, and found himself refreshed and invigorated, and his lamp burning low, Ralph almost for a moment forgot the terrible danger which was threatening him.

He arose quickly, roused the fire into a healthy blaze, and proceeded at once to get himself some breakfast.

A dismal commencement to a day this, cooped up in a dark and noisome cellar, cooking by the aid of a single lamp, while outside the sun was revelling amid the woodlands and glinting on the voiceful stream.

But it meant safety.

And this to Ralph Ashton was everything now in his unfortunate position.

He had very little prospect of success or happiness at present.

All he hoped for and worked for was the discovery of the guilt of Sir Roland, and the papers which would prove the falseness and treachery of the villain who reigned at the Hall.

To do this he must remain in England, and near to his old home.

Otherwise he would most certainly have cast everything to the winds, and endeavoured with Constance to have quitted England never to return.

One thing was very certain.

The old mill must no longer be his resting-place; at any rate for some time to come.

He had imagined himself quite at home and free from all intrusion in this deserted spot; but the discovery of the dead body had convinced him that he was not alone in the selection of the mill as a place of concealment, and he resolved to abandon it.

But whither was he to go?

Suddenly he gave vent to a smothered exclamation as a wild and daring scheme entered his mind.

At first he almost laughed at the wild romance of the idea.

But the more he dwelt upon it, the more feasible it became, until at length his thoughts had so far fixed themselves upon it, that he resolved at all events to try it.

It was a wild and daring project, but what it was we must reserve at present.

Its precise nature, and the extraordinary adventures to which it led, must be explained as our story unfolds.

Once this idea had settled itself on his brain it seemed to give elasticity to his frame and spirits.

He ate his breakfast with relish, and as soon as he had done so, he made his way to the stables and saddled his horse.

He had intended to remain where he was until night had covered the earth.

But he altered his plan now.

He would be off and away as swiftly as he could, and having paid a visit to Edmonton, would return as quickly as possible to put his plan into execution.

No one seemed anywhere near as he led his steed out into the open air.

Leaping into the saddle, he at once threaded his way through the dense plantation, and was soon in the highway galloping along in the fresh crisp breeze of the morning.

He had not been gone many minutes before another horseman emerged from the wood and followed him.

This was the man who had been watching him all night; but since the time when Ralph had disposed of the body by flinging it into the river, he had altered his appearance, and was no longer masked or attired all in black.

A brown, light-fitting surtout[32] covered him, and his appearance now was very much like that of an ordinary traveller.

Edmonton was some distance from Barnet, and evening was already coming on when Ralph reached the town.

He made his way when he reached it to a little narrow thoroughfare leading from its centre to the open country.

Here he paused at the door of a small cottage and knocked.

The door was opened by an elderly female, who glanced at him in some astonishment, combined, however, with evident pleasure—

"Well, Mr. Ashton, she said, "this is, indeed, a surprise."

"I hope a pleasant one," he said, as he vaulted from the saddle.

"Indeed so, Mr. Ashton," she answered. "I thought it would be a long time before we should see you again, seeing what they're saying in those horrid police bills about you."

"Ah! well, they say a good many untruths," said Ashton, "and the worst of it is when the police get hold of anything there is no use in contradicting them. Once they get an idea in their heads it would take a regiment of drummers to beat it out again. But, come, I will take my horse round, and then—"

"No, no," she said, hurriedly, "you pop in. There have been a good many suspicious folks round here lately, and I don't think it's safe to show yourself too much."

"Perhaps you're right, Mrs. Barton," he said. "Is Laura at home?"

"Oh! yes."

"But where is the horse going?"

---

[32] Literally 'over-all', An overcoat similar to a frock coat.

"I shall just take him through our passage and out into the back yard. You won't be stopping long, may be, and no one will notice it there."

"Very well," said Ralph, and knowing that her advice was the best, he hastened into the front parlour of the cottage, where a young girl was sitting, apparently unconscious of all that was going on around her.

She was about eighteen years of age, and was attired in somewhat dark and sombre garments, but they fitted her to such perfection as to show to advantage her rounded shoulders and her firm, solid bust.

She was far from *petite*, and her form and limbs were of the substantial order, though delicately moulded.

Her face was not by any means beautiful, but there was a pleasant look upon her features, and her eyes had a *piquante*[33] expression in them which was very enticing.

She jumped up with an exclamation of pleasure as she saw Ralph.

"Oh! Mr. Ashton," she cried, "I am so pleased to see you again."

Ralph had lived in the house, and had been on friendly terms with mother and daughter.

But he was not prepared for the very enthusiastic nature of his reception, or for the way in which Laura's breast heaved and fell at greeting him.

"And so am I pleased to see you," said Ralph, as he took her hand. "I had not thought it possible to come and see you for many a long day."

"How was that?"

"Because I have been so hunted about for no fault of my own."

Laura turned slightly pale, and coming nearer to him placed her hand upon his arm and looked up into his face.

"Is it then really true?" she said.

"What?"

"That you are accused of murder."

"Yes. But accusation is neither guilt nor conviction," said Ralph, as he pressed her hand and sat down. "I know I am innocent, and feel sure that I shall prove it."

"Indeed, I hope so," said Laura, with what was to him unexpected and unnecessary fervour. "I should indeed be unhappy if I thought that you were in such peril."

Ralph began to feel uncomfortable. He had never imagined that he had roused in Laura's breast anything more than mere brotherly feelings; and this intense susceptibility on account of his danger was anything but pleasing.

His heart was still true to Constance, his first love.

And, if not, Laura's grand and ample charms were by no means those which appealed to him in her stead.

"I am most gratified by your words," he said, somewhat uncomfortably; "and I only hope, therefore, that you will congratulate me upon the escape which I hope I shall be able to make."

"Soon?" asked Laura, anxiously.

"Yes; within a month," he said.

"And where do you propose to go to?"

"To America. But before I go I shall be united to the dear one of my heart."

He gave her no encouragement by his look to dream that she was the chosen one.

---

[33] Intriguing.

But perhaps at the idea of being united to Constance his face lighted up with pleasure.

At any rate, she uttered what was apparently a cry of gladness, and with ready blushes threw herself upon his breast, twining her large round arms round his neck, so that he could feel the throbbing of her heart and the warmth of her bosom against his.

This was more than he bargained for. It put him in an awkward position. What was he to do?

"Laura," he said, "I fear you are making a great mistake."

"How so?"

"I swear that I never in my life gave you any right to believe that I was your lover."

The girl drew herself up proudly. He could feel a cold shudder pass through her frame as she withdrew herself from the position which she had taken up on his breast.

"You lie, Ralph Ashton," she said. "I have always looked upon you as my future husband. If was to me you told all your troubles, to me you explained everything, and spoke of the happy future; and now you think to fool me by talking of your love for another girl."

"I have never loved but one," said Ralph, calmly, though his heart misgave him as to the results of this interview—"Constance Marfield, who has been my betrothed almost from childhood."

"Then what meant all your kind words to me?" she cried, fiercely. "What all the whispered nothings with which you cowards deceive weak women? What meant you by your actions, by all your behaviour to me?"

"I meant nothing," cried Ralph, earnestly. "I swear I did not. You and your mother acted kindly to me; that was all, and I thought myself bound to be kind also to you. I try to act kindly to all, and yet I could not marry all those to whom I do so."

The girl's great brown eyes glared fiercely at him as he said this.

She seemed to imagine that he was jeering her, and this idea made her bosom swell with indignation.

One moment she sat still.

Then slowly she rose.

"I have made a mistake," she said.

And she quitted the room.

As she did so Mrs. Barton entered.

She was too hospitably eager to notice Laura.

The troubled look on Ralph's face she set down to general worry.

"I've seen to the horse," she said; "and I think I may say that only me and Laura know anything about your being here. It's safely housed now, however, and there needn't be any bother about hurrying off."

As she was speaking she was setting out on the table requisites for a good meal.

"You are very kind, Mrs. Barton," he said; "but I mustn't stop. In fact, I have only run down just to see you, and say good-bye, pay what I owe, and take away the few papers I left behind."

Mrs. Barton looked somewhat dubious at this.

"Ah! just so," she said.

Then, as if one thing was suggested by the other, she added, quickly—

"Why, where's Laura gone to?"

"I don't know," replied Ralph, as unconcernedly as possible. "I fancy Laura took offence at something I said."

"Ah! you young people," cried Mrs. Barton, "you're always a-quarrelling, and a-going on. Been making her jealous, I expect!"

"No, indeed," said Ralph, wishing sincerely that he was well out of the difficulty; "I have never led Laura to believe that I looked upon her as a sweetheart. I have been betrothed ever since I was a boy to Miss Constance Marfield, and I hope that in the course of a month I shall be her husband, and go with her to America."

Mrs. Barton looked sad.

But she was by no means of the same temperament as her daughter.

She was sorry for Laura.

Sorry, because she knew her wild, ungovernable spirit.

But she had never made up her mind as Laura had done.

Apart from his money, about which she had never as yet taken pains to enquire, she had regarded him as a very suitable husband for the girl, but she had never gone so far as to say that he had ever made love to her.

She would have looked more sad still if she had observed the figure crouching to listen outside the door—the figure of Laura, with wild, distended eyes, burning too much to admit of tears, her hands clenched, and her bosom heaving tumultuously.

"He means it, then," she muttered, "the cold-hearted villain! And he will go away to this other girl and leave me without even a sigh at my distress. But I will have my revenge. If I do not have him no one else shall."

Meanwhile, Ralph Ashton, rather relieved than otherwise by the absence of Laura Barton, ate his meal in peace, chatting meanwhile with Mrs. Barton.

"You quite make me forget my troubles," he said, after a while. "I shall begin to imagine my danger is over."

"I wish it could be so," said the woman; "but if I were in your shoes I should never feel myself safe until I was out of England. Murder is a very ticklish thing to be accused of."

"You are right," said Ralph, "and in this case I should find it very difficult to prove that I was in the right."

As if in answer to these words the door of the room was flung suddenly and violently open.

Two men in the garb of police officers entered and closed the door behind them.

Ralph sprang up, and naturally glanced towards the window.

But one of the officers, coming forward, said—

"Mr. Ashton, let me beg of you not to make a scene. The window is guarded outside by several constables. I knew you, Mr. Ralph, when you were a boy, and if I could do you a service I would; but in this case I can do nothing. It is my duty to arrest you on a charge of murder."

"May I ask the name of the supposed victim?" asked Ralph, trying hard to be calm.

"Herbert Leigh."

"Then I am not far wrong in saying that the informant is my kind and virtuous relative, Sir Roland Ashton?"

"In the first place, yes," replied the man; "in the present case, however, information as to your whereabouts was brought by Miss Barton."

Ralph staggered back in horror.

Mrs. Barton turned deadly pale and caught hold of a chair-back for support.

"Great Heavens!" she cried; "rash, head-strong girl! what has she done?"

"She has had her revenge," said a voice as the door opened, and Laura stood on the threshold, pale and ghastly, with blazing eyes.

"Fiend!" said Ralph, with a contemptuous smile. "Constables, I am ready."

Within half-an-hour Ralph Ashton was an inmate of a prison cell charged with the wilful murder of Herbert Leigh.

CHAPTER XIII.
JOE DIMITY'S CIRCUS ONCE MORE—DAISY IN CHARACTER— A HAWK IN THE DOVE'S NEST.

BARNET is by no means a lively place at any time.

But when we write about it, before the railway had roused it up a bit, it was a most barren looking spot.

However, a few days after the arrest of Ralph Ashton it seemed as if it had taken a new lease of life.

And no wonder.

There was a show.

Joe Dimity's Circus and Theatre Royal had arrived, and great was the excitement of all, young and old.

Daisy by this time had quite recovered from the effects of her impromptu bath.

And having nothing better to do, she had resolved to throw in her lot with the "strollers."

By doing so, she would escape all peril from Gedge Foote, at any rate, for a time.

And she would be able to earn her living honestly, if in what Banks the clown called "a rough and tumble fashion."

She was somewhat timid when for the first time she donned her theatrical dress and tights, exhibiting as it did, to a daring degree, her white shoulders and girlish breasts, and all the soft contours of her lower limbs.

Mrs. Dimity had been the one to suggest to her husband the propriety of retaining Daisy in the company.

She and "Maria" had had an excellent opportunity, when recovering her from the effects of her bath in the Thames, of observing the exquisite roundness of her form, and the softness and beauty of her limbs.

"Maria" was by no means jealous.

Her first thoughts were "professional."

"Wouldn't she look well in tights, Mrs. D.?" was her remark as she surveyed the half senseless girl critically.

"Yes; and perhaps she'll wear 'em the first time on the boards of the Theatre Royal," said the kind-hearted tragedy queen, suggestively.

"I daresay she'd be glad," said Maria; "I shouldn't fancy she's got many friends, although there's no doubt she's respectable."

And so when poor Daisy came to herself, after her long, delirious sleep, and found herself surrounded by kindly faces, and heard gentle voices speaking to her, she almost made up her mind to ask them to permit her to remain with them for a time, even before genial Maria suggested it.

When the latter first spoke of it she was attired ready for the performance of a court page—not of the usual type, but more of the character of a bayadeer,[34] with plumed hat, excessively low dress, and trunk hose not much larger or more covering than a pair of bathing drawers.

The display of charms, consequently, were excessively lavish, and little Daisy blushed at the possibility of having to appear in similar costume.

Maria laughed at her scruples.

"My dear," she said, "you mustn't be squeamish. You would look ever so much better than I do in this dress because you're younger and smaller. I should be glad to give over this *rôle* to you. You have a charming little figure, and will look quite dainty and tempting in trunk hose and tights."

"But where am I to get any to fit me?" she said.

The words were uttered so demurely that Maria went into an ecstasy of laughter.

"Well, I don't pretend that mine will do for you, my dear!" she cried, shaking all over as she put a last finishing touch to her face with the hare's-foot, and then powdering her fat shoulders. "You would look as if you had just put on the clothes of Dimity's giantess, lately deceased. I'll get you a good set of tights at the next town, and as for the trunk hose and velvet bodice, and all that, we can soon make something up for you that will send the audience into ecstasies."

Daisy—modest as she was—was not foolish enough to worry her newly-found friends by indulging in prudery.

So, after a very little persuasion, she consented to join the company and to take "pages' parts," and others which would display her figure to advantage, until she had got rid of her "stage fright," and was able to take talking *rôles*.

The first time she was arrayed in her new and unusual finery she was the admiration of all the company, and Harry Banks fell head over ears in love with her.

Even before the strollers it was bad enough for timid Daisy to stand in that daring state of undress.

But when she went on the boards, and heard the buzz of voices, and saw the sea of heads, she felt dizzy and confused, and was hardly able to stand.

Harry Banks's jolly, genial voice was there, however, to cheer and encourage her.

"Keep up, little 'un!" he cried, sotto voce; "I'm here. If you fall I'll catch you."

But apart from this there was another thing which gave her courage.

This was the undisguised admiration of the audience.

Loud clapping of hands resounded through the wood and canvas theatre, mingled with all kinds of exclamations.

"Isn't she a stunner?"

"What a lovely figure!"

"What a pretty, innocent face!"

And then, to crown all—

"If she only learns to act that figure will carry her on to the London boards."

This reception roused Daisy to do her best, and in a very short time she had learned to go off and on the stage without feeling as if she was weak in her knees, and her legs

---

[34] Hindu dancer.

trembling as if with ague.

Before the night was over Daisy Leigh (or Lottie Day as she was called in her new vocation) was the talk of the audience, though Maria's massive charms and really good idea of acting called forth the usual rounds of applause.

It was evident that Barnet was going to be a golden spot for Joe Dimity.

He absolutely kissed Daisy's forehead after the performance, which, far from making the "tragedy queen" jealous, caused her to laugh immodestly.

"My dear," he said, "you're a success. When you can learn to say a few words you'll get along famously."

"I'm glad you're pleased," she said, smiling round upon the genial company gathered on the stage after the audience had departed. "It is some little return for the kindness you have shown me. If it hadn't been for Mr. Banks I should have been drowned; and if it hadn't been for Mrs. Dimity and Maria I should have never got through my illness."

An explosion of merriment followed this speech, which somewhat disconcerted Daisy, who had so innocently called the leading actress "Maria," as if they had been bosom friends for years.

But that worthy lady soon put matters right.

"It's a shame to laugh," she cried, laughing herself all the time. "She's a dear, grateful, loving thing. There!"

And she threw her plump, warm arms round Daisy's white, rounded shoulders, and kissed her three times with such genuine vigour that Harry Banks, the clown, forgetting that for the nonce[35] he was attired as a "swell[36] of the period," threw a somersault, and came up before the two ladies with his toes together, and his forefinger in his mouth, crying—

"Here we are again![37] Holler boys! Oh! my, ain't it nice?"

Whereat Maria boxed his ears.

"Order in the gallery!" cried Joe Dimity. "To your dressing-rooms, ladies and gentlemen! and when you've made yourselves presentable, we'll have some supper at the Black Lion."

That night when Daisy went to rest in the little room at the inn, which was to be shared by Agnes Dymot, one of the strollers, about her own age, the latter, who had been detained on the stairs by Joe Dimity as she was hastening up, brought the orphan girl two packages.

The first she opened was from Joe Dimity.

It contained the fifteen shillings which she had paid for her tights and boots at a second-hand warehouse recommended by "Maria," and these words were written on a piece of paper in which they were enclosed.

"Thank you for buying necessaries out of the two pounds, which were your only property! I return it as a first mark of my esteem, and I will pay you every week all the salary I can possibly afford."

Poor Joe!

He dare not promise more.

––––––––––––––––––

[35] For the present

[36] Fashionable Man

[37] Catchphrase popular in the Music Halls, famously used by Dan Leno.

The second note was from Harry Banks, and in it was enclosed a rose.

He had bought this early in the evening, but had had no opportunity of giving it to her.

The note was a very daring one, considering that their acquaintance was so short.

> "DEAREST DAISY,—*Accept this rose as an offering of my devotion. Sweets to the sweet, you know. I am your champion against all corners. If you're ever in danger only say the word, and you'll find Harry Banks ready. 'Here we are again' is my motto, and while I live you'll never want a friend.*"

Daisy kissed the rose, and placed it with Joe Dimity's fifteen shillings under her pillow.

This was wet with tears of gratitude that night, but there was no tender response in her heart to Harry Banks.

She liked him as a friend; she thanked him as the preserver of her life.

But as regarded tender affection, or an atom of love, it did not exist.

The treasures of that little heart were as yet hidden, ready to be bestowed upon the first person who roused the latent passions of her gentle bosom.

She would have laughed with real scorn had she been told that she had already met her fate.

But in very truth she had.

Not that she knew it.

She had never looked upon his face.

But, nevertheless, she had been in his presence, heard his voice, his hand had touched hers, his breath been warm upon her cheek.

And yet she did not even know his name.

Happy dreams visited her that night.

She forgot for a time the tragedy which had so suddenly clouded her life.

Everything seemed *couleur de rose*.

She saw again in her dreams the glare of footlights, the flickering lamps of the "Theatre Royal."

But they were magnified tenfold.

The glare was that of a London theatre.

The audience was numbered by thousands.

Sweet music and the perfume of flowers filled the air, then came the roar of applause, and a handsome youth knelt at her feet.

Again came a rapid change, the youth disappeared by magic, the huge theatre seemed to contract, the lights grew dimmer, and Harry Banks, the clown, came leaping up through a vampire trap,[38] shouting, "Holler, boys! here we are again!" and bore her through clouds of vapoury mist just as he had borne her through the black turbid waters of old Father Thames.

She awoke to find herself in the little warm bed at the inn, and her companion, Agnes Dymot, lying with her arms firmly and fondly clasped round her.

"I wonder who that youth was?" thought Daisy, as she turned over to go to sleep again; "he was very handsome."

She little knew what was coming.

---

[38] Trapdoor in a stage.

Little knew that the strollers were, by stopping at Barnet, leading her into the greatest danger of her life.

But they were doing so unconsciously.

It was a danger of which they little dreamed!

The swoop of the hawk into the dove's nest.

CHAPTER XIV.
SIR ROLAND ASHTON IN A NEW CHARACTER—BEHIND THE SCENES.

THE news of Ralph Ashton's arrest was received by Sir Roland Ashton with mingled emotions.

He would have been glad if his enemy could have been hung out of his way without further to do.

He was quite indifferent as to what fate befell him.

But he had no wish to be involved in it.

The trial of Ralph for murder would bring up, undoubtedly, the most trying reminiscences, and would produce, perhaps, the most awkward revelations.

He had never bargained for Ralph's arrest.

When he had spread about the idea that Ralph was the murderer of Herbert Leigh, he had trusted to his good sense to keep out of the way and fly to another country.

He had never bargained for the determined sprit which would make him stick to his own home to unravel the terrible mystery which hung over his life.

"This arrest is very awkward, Caleb," said the baronet to his steward, when the latter brought the news; "something must be done to prevent the trial."

"Are you afraid he will be hung?" said the man, cynically.

"No, indeed; that would be a mercy for which I could not be too thankful," replied Sir Roland; "but I fear the revelations which may be made at the trial. You see, there is no direct evidence against him. How are we to draw the net round him without implicating ourselves."

"We must manufacture witnesses," said Caleb.

"But how?"

"We have one."

"Whom do you mean?"

"Job Joskins. He saw some one standing by the body of Herbert Leigh up at the ruins."

"That was Spring-Heeled Jack."

"Yes—yes; but he can swear that he saw Ralph Ashton there first, and that he was going to denounce him, only that he was frightened away by this demon."

"Well; but his evidence doesn't count for much," said Sir Roland. "Ralph might declare that he was passing by accidentally and came suddenly on the body. The murder was committed in London, so that Joskins could not prove much."

"No; but it is a link in the chain," said Caleb.

"No one can connect him with the murder in the Mint," replied the baronet.

"That is easily managed," said Caleb.

"How?"

"We must produce some one who will swear that he saw him enter the house on the night of the murder."

SPRING-HEELED JACK,
THE TERROR OF LONDON.

By the Author of "TURNPIKE DICK, the Star of the Road."

"WHAT WANT YOU WITH THIS LADY?" ASKED THE STRANGE BEING, SEPULCHRALLY.

"Well, I must leave all to you," said Sir Roland, "it will not do for me to mix myself up too much in the affair. Get your witnesses together, prove him guilty, and a thousand pounds are yours."

"And as much more as I want afterwards," said Caleb Masters to himself.

But he said aloud—

"Many thanks, Sir Roland. I will do my best, and in order to do so I must go to London at once."

"That means that you will want money," said his master. "I will write you out a cheque. Don't be afraid to spend it; only see that you link the chain properly. Don't let us make mistakes, for that would bring disaster upon ourselves."

It was on the day after this conversation that Sir Roland, strolling through the town, saw the flaming posters announcing the arrival of the Joe Dimity Troupe, and giving portraits of "Maria" in her most ravishing undress.

Daisy Leigh had not yet attained to the honour of being on the bills.

Those on the walls were old ones.

But Joe had it in his mind to have new ones printed soon, on which Daisy was to figure in all the glories of her tights and trunk-hose and plumed hat.

However, "Maria" was quite sufficient attraction to Sir Roland.

Anything in the female line caught his sensual fancy.

And so he resolved, in spite of his position, to figure at the performance that evening.

That was the second night of performance.

He was not there, consequently, to see Daisy's triumphant first appearance.

Occupying a corner where he was as far as possible screened from observation, he sat, with one or two of the young bloods of the neighbourhood, who had come on a similar errand to himself, rather to quiz[39] the play than enjoy it.

Of course it was a queer affair to those accustomed to the real theatre.

But there were good points in it.

Maria's dancing was really first rate.

And when she came leaping on in her short muslin skirts as premiere danseuse, making a liberal display of her superb lower limbs, there was a genuine burst of applause.

The baronet's mind was at once inflamed.

He was one of those cynical ignoramuses who scoff at the virtue of the stage.

He thought that because a woman does not mind coming on the boards in partial undress she must be ready to listen to his fulsome adulation and submit to his loathsome caresses.

In Maria's case he was most woefully mistaken—never so much so, in fact, in his whole life.

She was a clever woman.

She could show all kinds of trinkets, good and bad, which had been given her.

Maria was poor.

She accepted them because she might want them in some case of future necessity.

But the return she made for them was very scanty indeed.

A smile or a pressure of the hand.

There was a tradition in the Dimity Troupe of an unrehearsed dramatic performance

---

[39] Make fun of.

which had occurred on one occasion, when a "swell," who had obtained access to the wings, and had presumed to embrace her, was sent flying on to the stage by a well-directed blow delivered straight from Maria's plump shoulder.

He flew against Harry Banks, the clown, cannoned against old Toppledown, the pantaloni,[40] and fell over into the orchestra, where he subsided into the big drum head first.

For the moment the audience thought this a great joke, and applauded.

But when Joe Dimity explained matters—told them that the "swell" had insulted his "leading lady," and made him dub up the price of a new drum—the mingled hisses and cheers were tremendous.

And, of course, when Maria reappeared she received quite an ovation.

"Eyes on and hands off" was her motto.

But on the stage she was the most daring, rollicking soul that ever trod the boards.

Sir Roland and his set were in raptures.

They had never expected such a treat.

But presently there was a buzz of expectation.

Daisy's name was not on the bills.

But her fame had travelled.

Those who had seen her on the night before had talked.

So the audience waited eagerly.

The dancing was over.

The play began.

Joe Dimity and the tragedy queen, knowing there were "real nobs"[41] among the audience, exerted themselves to the utmost.

But presently Daisy entered as the page, bearing a note for the "Baron de Montfort, of Montfort Grange."

Her nervousness had greatly subsided.

But she looked as ravishing as ever.

Her eyes were now turned more boldly towards the audience, disclosing their exquisite depth and clearness; her hair fell in soft ringlets on the dazzling bare shoulders, so dainty and delicate as to resemble a living statue; her form and limbs were perfect in unison and proportion.

For an instant the audience were spellbound with surprise.

Then came a sudden and spontaneous burst of applause on all sides.

"By Jove!" exclaimed Leicester Lambton, one of the baronet's companions, "she's simply lovely. Deuced shame to have such a superb girl in a strollers' booth!"

"You're right," said another; "she looks a perfect lady, and her figure's beautiful. Why, what the deuce is the matter, Ashton? You look as if you had seen a ghost."

No wonder he expressed surprise.

Sir Roland had turned deadly pale; his eyes had retreated into his head, leaving black rings round them, and he had grasped the rail of the orchestra for support.

"I think I have," he said; "her face reminds me of one I knew long—long ago. She has made me feel quite ill. I will go out into the open air for a moment."

He hastened away as he spoke.

---

[40] A stock character in *Commedia dell'arte*, representing money and finance.
[41] Gentry or aristocracy.

"Queer fellow that Ashton," cried Lambton, as he went, "making a fool of himself over a little stage beauty."

"She's enough to turn any man's head, if that is what she's done," said the other. "She's a dream of beauty! but she doesn't look as if she would stand any nonsense."

Meanwhile Sir Roland strode out upon the common, where the "pitch" had been made. His heart was in a flutter and his brain in a whirl.

"Who can this girl be?" he muttered, as he paced to and fro. "The same face—the same expression! She is the very ghost of Augusta Leigh!"

He glanced round him to see whether anyone was watching him.

But, seeing no one near, he walked rapidly towards a spot where a light seemed to indicate something in the shape of a stage door.

"Yes, the very ghost of Augusta Leigh," he said, as he went; "only more perfect, perhaps, in symmetry. I must and will see her. What joy—what triumph to enjoy the caresses of the daughter of the woman who despised me, and then to fling her away— crush her beneath my feet in triumph! For she must die! If she is the daughter of Herbert and Augusta Leigh, she must die—and soon!"

The hideous fiend who thus lived in the guise of a human being walked quickly and eagerly forward.

At the door a man was sitting on a chair, just, inside the opening.

He rose on seeing a stranger.

"Are you the stage-door-keeper?" asked Sir Roland.

"Yes, sir."

As the man spoke the baronet seemed to recognise a loafer[42] whom he had often seen prowling about the neighbourhood.

"Are you a member of the company, or are you only employed for the week?"

"Only for the week, sir. I live in Barnet, sir."

"Do you know me?"

"You're Sir Roland Ashton, what lives up at the Hall," said the man, readily. "My name's Tugwell—Bob Tugwell. You may often 'a seen me about."

"I have," said Sir Roland, significantly recalling to his mind a day when he saw this fellow leap through a hedge with a brace of rabbits in his hand; "but tell me, my good fellow, do you want to earn some money?" The man grinned.

"Do I not?" he said, "you try me!"

"Very good, then;" said Sir Roland, as he took out his purse and presented the man with a coin; "here's something to buy yourself a drink when the play's over. Now listen. I don't want to stop here talking, because it will look suspicious. Do you know the boathouse down by the river?"

"Yes, sir."

"Be there to-morrow evening then, an hour before you have to come here, and I'll tell you what I want you to do. It's nothing very bad, only what's done every day."

"I'll be there."

"At what time?"

"Five o'clock."

"Very well. But tell me first what's the name of that young girl that came on dressed

---

[42] An idler.

as a page?"

"Lottie Day; she's a stunner, ain't she?"

"Lottie Day!" mused the baronet, sauntering away without answering the man's remark. "Ah! well, that makes no difference. It is an assumed name, of course."

And with his breast full of evil triumph he rejoined his companions.

And unsuspecting any calamity, knowing nothing of the cloud hanging over her, poor Daisy received the plaudits of the audience with radiant smiles.

She was happy for the time, and grateful for her success.

But the tempest was louring.[43] The destroyer was at hand!

Her dishonour and her death were both planned by the same demon who had compassed the death of her father.

CHAPTER XV.

RALPH ASHTON IN PRISON—A DESPERATE RESOLVE—TIMMS' MISSION.

THE feelings of Ralph Ashton, when he found himself a prisoner under lock and key, were terrible indeed.

He was not satisfied of the power of Sir Roland to prove his complicity in the murder of Herbert Leigh.

But there was the forgery.

He would inevitably bring that forward.

Of course, he was innocent of this, also.

But he was powerless to prove even that.

The net which Sir Roland had woven round him was such that it seemed impossible to escape from it.

Hopeless, indeed, was everything in the future.

But he did not despair.

Such a feeling was foreign to his nature.

Yet who could aid him?

This was the thought which filled his mind with unrest.

The only being to whom he could look in his trouble was Constance.

But how to send a letter to her?

The warder who guarded the corridor in the prison where he was stationed was a young man of pleasant but somewhat weak and crafty face.

Surely he could be bribed to take a letter to Constance?

Of course, Ralph knew nothing of the change that had been affected in the young girl's rooms.

But this was not to be thought of as an impediment to his scheme.

The man must find for himself some means of communicating with her.

He lost no time in putting his plan into execution.

When the warder brought in his dinner he at once commenced the attack.

"You must have a dull time of it here," he said.

"Yes; not very amusing."

"Do you have any holidays?"

---

[43] Lowering i.e. descending.

"Yes; I'm off on one to-morrow."

Ralph's eyes glistened.

"Ah! that's the very thing," he exclaimed. "How long will you be gone for?"

"Two days."

"Which part of the world are you going to?"

The man laughed.

"You're very inquisitive to-day, sir?"

"Aye, I am," said Ralph; "but you'll be well rewarded for it. I can put ten pounds in your pocket easily."

The man shook his head.

"Ah!" he said, "all prisoners say that; and then they want such outlandish things done that it's waste o' time to listen."

"Oh! this is not at all outlandish," said Ralph. "All I wish is to get a letter to my sweetheart."

"If that's all I daresay I can do it," said the young man, eagerly.

"Well, then, if you come in towards night I'll have the letter ready."

"Where does the young lady live?"

"At Barnet."

"That'll do for my country trip, then," said Timms, the warder. "Get the letter ready and I will be here to time."

Ralph's letter to Constance took considerable time and trouble.

He had to explain to her particulars which anyone of weak mind would not have been able to grasp.

But he felt confidence in her in everything.

What he asked her to do he knew well she had power and will to perform.

The end of the letter was of the tenderest kind, and hopeful in every way.

It is not given to us to read the future, and it was fortunate for Ralph and Constance that they could not.

Timms was true to his word.

Though it was not his turn to visit Ralph in the evening he contrived to do so; and without loss of time the prisoner proceeded to explain exactly what was required of him.

"When you reach Barnet," he said, "you must inquire for Ashton Grange—that is where Sir Roland, my uncle, lives, who denies my being his nephew. I am in reality the baronet, Sir Ralph Ashton, son of Sir Guy Ashton; but he has suppressed the papers which prove this, and consequently I am powerless."

"If that is the case, it would be better to let the trial come on," said the warder.

"No. He has me too securely in his clutches," said Ralph. "I have not a human being or one single document to prove my innocence. If I were acquitted of the murder of Herbert Leigh I should be convicted of the forgery. There is not the slightest chance of my showing my guiltlessness of that. No; my only resource is escape, and," he added, seeing the scared look on the face of the warder, "that, of course, is impossible."

"Well, to say the least, it isn't very likely," said Timms, sententiously.

"No. Well, as I was saying, Miss Constance Mayfield, to whom this letter is directed, is kept under lock and key by Sir Roland, for fear she should take it into her head to elope with me. He wants her, I believe, for himself."

"Yes, sir."

"The difficulty you will have to surmount is the placing the letter in her hands. If it falls into those of Sir Roland or any of his hirelings all is lost."

"I quite understand. But if she's locked up in a room, I don't see the use of my trying."

"Yes. There is a man called Job Joskins about the place—a foolish, loutish fellow, and about as big a coward as you could find in a day's march. You must ask to see him; use bribes, threats, what you will, but discover in what room Constance Marfield is confined. Then you must hang about till night-time, and climb up in some way to her window. I have done so over and over again by the ivy."

"In that case you can tell me in what part of the house her room is?"

"No, indeed, I cannot, because she may have been shifted to another apartment; but I can say this: when last I saw her she was in the third bedroom on the first floor on the left side of the portico which faces the ground adjoining the high road. See here, I will sketch the place."

He did so roughly and rapidly.

The man was naturally crafty and ingenious, and his wits were sharpened by the prospect of money.

"I think I see it all correctly," he said. "I will to-morrow afternoon, and try and see this Job Joskins. What is he?"

"Well, he's a groom, a coachman, a spy, anything. A paid satellite of Sir Roland is the best name for him," said Ralph. "He'd do anything for his master—tell a lie, pick a pocket—cut a throat, if he had the pluck. Well, here are five pounds. When you bring me the answer of Constance Marfield I will give you five more. If through your aid I escape from the consequences of Sir Roland's persecution, you shall have fifty more."

"Good," said Timms; "I'll do my best."

He took the letter, concealed it in a waistcoat underneath his uniform, placed the five pounds in his trousers' pocket, and prepared to go.

"Beware of Sir Roland Ashton," said Ralph. "He is the fiend incarnate. If you come across him don't trust him with a word."

"Never fear," said Timms. "I'll be as sly as a fox. It's my interest to bring this thing through properly, for, if I do, I shall be able to marry my girl that I've been waiting to get spliced to for more'n a year."

"Then I hope, for my sake, you'll marry her soon," said Ralph, with a smile.

If Timms, the warder, had had any idea that he was aiding in an escape from prison he would never have attempted such a thing as he was now about to experiment upon.

He simply looked upon it as a desperate attempt upon the prisoner's part to obtain through Constance Marfield's agency the papers which he could not obtain elsewhere.

But the truth was far different.

Ralph meant simply to escape from gaol.

He saw plainly that once in a court he had no chance.

Out from those stone walls he must go no matter what happened.

Timms lost no time.

The next day at noon found him at Barnet.

Half-past found him at Ashton Hall.

He had been "in the force" two years before he became a warder.

Consequently he had a little of the detective instinct about him.

He knew that the yokel mind was not, as a rule, of a very high order.

He had in his time experienced the ease with which a man of this kind can be persuaded into remembering a thing that never happened, especially when he is made to see a personal advantage in it.

So he passed through the lodge-gate boldly, keeping his eye on the front of the house, and soon making out the whereabouts of the bedroom mentioned by Ralph.

Presently he saw a servant approaching.

He at once accosted him.

"Which is the way to the stable-yard?" he asked.

"Round there to the right," replied the man. "Whom may you be wanting?"

"Job Joskins."

"Oh! yes; he's round there. Shall I go with you, and fetch him?"

"If you please," said Timms, who, never having seen Job, naturally felt anxious about identifying him.

And so they hurried on.

At the Corner Pin Timms had discovered that Job was in the habit of frequenting that noble house of entertainment, and having a social glass in the parlour, accordingly he knew how to open the conversation.

They were soon in the stable-yard, and John Timms, alias for the moment Bob Wright, was presented to Job Joskins.

The latter touched his forelock, and looked sheepish.

"Day, sir," he said. "What do you please to want, sir?"

Timms slapped his leg and laughed loudly.

"Why, don't you know me?" he cried.

"No; I don't," reiterated Job.

"Well you are—but there, I won't insult ye," said Timms. "You've got no memory. Job. Often's the time we've been at the Corner Pie and drank till all's blue."

Job began to think that, whoever he was, this stranger wasn't a bad sort.

So it wasn't worth while to offend him.

"Well, I'm not a good one at remembering at any time," he said. "I daresay you're right and I'm wrong. What is it you want with me?"

"Nothing very particular," said the disguised warder. "I've come here on a holiday; got a good berth in London now, and have two days' off. I thought I'd like to see some one I knew, so I came here to hunt you up and ask ye to have a drink."

Job Joskins glanced doubtfully round at his companions.

"Oh! all right, go on, Job," said one of the others, with a laugh.

And thus adjured, the groom grinned and went.

The warder did not intend quitting the grounds so quickly, however.

"It's a fine place this of Sir Roland's," he said. "How do you find things? Much about the same as usual, I suppose?"

"Yes; no improvement at any rate," said Job. "The guv'nor is just as glumpy[44] as ever, and now he's taken on with Caleb Masters things are worse."

"Ah! yes; I should think so," said Timms, meditatively.

He didn't know Caleb from Adam.

---

[44] Morose or ill-humoured.

So he didn't venture much.

"But," he added, "how is the young lady you used to speak to me about so much—Miss Constance Marfield? That used to be her room. Many a time I've seen her looking out of that window, so melancholy like, on the meadows!"

Ah! Timms, you ought to have been a detective officer!

Job was quite taken in.

"Ah! that there isn't her room now," he said; "she's t'other side. But ye see the window's barred now, so she hasn't much chance o' seeing out."

"A barred window! that's a rum thing to have in a private house," said Timms; "show it us?"

Job Joskins meditated.

He hadn't had his drink and he was always thirsty.

But, then, what on earth could his old boon companion[45] want to know about Constance and her barred window?

He looked doubtfully at his companion.

"Well, you see," he said, "I should get into a fine bother if Sir Roland knew that I showed you anything about the house. If he thought I even spoke about it it would be bad enough."

"It won't do any harm," said Timms.

"No, I don't suppose it will," returned Job Joskins, "especially as he's away from home. So we'll take a turn round."

Timms laughed outright.

"Well," he said, "I don't see it's necessary to take me all over the place to see Miss Constance's bedroom window. But I wanted to look round the place and see what it's like, as I often have heard of it."

Job Joskins did not say anything, but quietly passed along the broad walk.

Timms glanced round him everywhere—admiring the place, and taking note of every point.

Presently they came upon an angle of the building where the windows looked out upon the wide, glassy lake with its stately swans.

He noted at once the casement which was barred. The ivy was growing densely round it.

"That'll be easy enough to climb up," thought Timms, with intense satisfaction.

"Ah! well, this is a nice old place enough," he said aloud (after observing. that the park led through a wide avenue of beeches towards the lodge gates); "but I don't think I'd go without my dinner for it. Let's go and have a snack at the Corner Pin."

Job Joskins was nothing loth.

He had seen all the beauties of Ashton Hall until he was sick of them, and so off he went down the high road as soon as they reached it, and led the way at a swinging pace.

Timms let him go on in advance.

He was well wrapped up in his own thoughts,

"If I can get a letter to Constance Marfield through those bars, what's to hinder me giving her the things to escape with?"

Such were his cogitations.

---

[45] Close friend.

And when he reached the Corner Pin he became so full of his own ideas that Job Joskins voted him a bore.

However, the grog flowed freely, and Job, under its influence, became very communicative.

In an hour's time Timms learned more in regard to the arrangements of Ashton Hall than he had dreamed of.

Job Joskins knew not what he was saying.

But he did not disclose any of the real secrets of the prison house.

He was too much linked in with the interests of the house—too deeply in the circle of its crimes to divulge anything.

But Timms saw that there was a skeleton in the house.

"It 'ud be worth a man's while to skirmish about here a bit," he said to himself, when presently he saw Job relapse into a drunken sleep. "If Ralph Ashton escapes, I'm hanged if I don't offer to go partner with him in routing out the secrets of this old place. I shan't have much trouble, I'm thinking, in getting that letter into the hands of Lady Constance, and while I am doing that I'm a fool if I can't give her a little help otherwise."

"My friend Job seems in for a long sleep," said Timms, addressing the landlord. "While he's snoring off his whisky I'll take a stroll round."

And so off he went.

He knew very little about the locality, but he had observed that there were some shops near, and he at once made his way towards an ironmonger's.

Here he purchased a couple of excellent files, and a few other necessary articles, and, having done so, he turned to go back to the Corner Pin.

As he passed round the corner of the lane a man sauntered up to him.

"You're Job Joskins's pal, ain't you?"

Timms felt the detective instinct being awakened in him again.

"I am," he said, smiling.

"You're square?"[46]

"Well, I ain't a rounder."

The man laughed.

"If you ain't, Job is," he said. "He's talking about that little affair he was in up at Johnson's Farm years ago, when the plate was nabbed,[47] and if you don't take care you'll get into trouble."

"Hurrah!" was Timms's inward cheer.

"I'll go back at once," he said; "and I'll stand a drain or so. Here's half-a-crown for you, and mind you keep 'mum!'"[48]

"Thank ye!" said the man, grinning; "it's no interest of mine to tell anything."

"Ye see," said Timms, reflectively, "he's been in a good many jobs before he got in favour with the squire—Sir Roland I mean. Do you mean the plate robbery up at Johnson's Farm?"

"Yes; I said so."

"Well, ye see," said Timms; "I wasn't in that job. I was in London. Tell us all about it."

---

[46] Honest.
[47] Stolen.
[48] Keep quiet.

"You must know," replied the man (who said it wasn't his interest to tell anything), "five years ago there was a ball going on at Johnson's Farm, top 'o the hill like, leastwise as ye get nearly top, and after supper, when the servants went down to clear away, every bit o' plate was gone."

"Yes; I remember. Well?"

"Job Joskins was seen a-running like mad across the grounds with another fellow—Bob Taylor."

"Yes."

"Well, they nabs Job, but they lets Bob off, for he went like a greyhound. Job got off 'cos there wasn't any evidence against him; but it was a case of touch-and-go with him, and if Bob Taylor had only been found, and split, Job 'ud a got five years."

"Yes—so he told me," said Timms, complacently. "But I hope you don't open yer mouth to everyone like this."

"Not I. Only you being a friend like—"

"Just so. Here's another half-a-crown," said Timms. "Run into the Corner Pin again, Order two glasses of grog, and tell Job Joskins to 'stow his jawin' tackle,' as the sailors say, for I shall be back in a minute."

He turned and hastened back to the iron-monger's shop.

There he made a singular purchase—something like a horse's bit.

With this in his pocket he made his return to the Corner Pin, and found Job awake, very much the worse for his inebriety and his subsequent snooze.

He looked washed out and half-foolish. "Drink up and come along o' me," said Timms, in a half-whisper. "You've been opening yer cussed mouth about that affair at Johnson's Farm."

"What affair?" asked Job, with feeble bluster.

"Nabbing the plate."

"Why, who the devil are you, then?" groaned Job Joskins, helplessly.

Timms laughed loudly.

"Ha, ha!" he cried. "I thought you didn't remember me properly!"

Then, bending forward, he said, in a low voice, in Job's ear—

"I'm Bob Taylor!"

<h3 style="text-align:center">CHAPTER XVI.</h3>

TIMMS HAS A NEW ADVENTURE—CONSTANCE MARFIELD'S DARING ESCAPADE—RALPH ASHTON DISAPPEARS MYSTERIOUSLY— SPRING-HEELED JACK AGAIN COMES TO THE RESCUE.

THE effect of Timms' words upon Job Joskins was positively electrical.

They sobered him, at any rate.

He drew himself back in his seat, and stared at his companion with glossy eyes and crimsoning cheeks.

"If you're not a-jokin'," he cried, "you're a ghost!"

"A very substantial one, then," said Timms, who was becoming jovial in anticipation of the success he was bent on achieving. "But I want to be off now. Come along— you've drank enough for to-day. Let's be going before you get queer again."

Job was like a lamb.

Whatever Timms proposed he would at this moment have consented to.

In a few moments they were in the road, once more on their way to Ashton Hall.

"Now then, Job," said Timms, when they were out of hearing of everybody, "let's come to business."

"Business!" growled Job. "I'm afraid I've done a bad stroke of business to-day."

"Strikes me you have, if you don't look out sharp," said Timms. "But, come, listen to me. I've a note in my pocket that I want delivered to Miss Constance Marfield."

"Well, I'll give it to her."

"I'm very much obliged to you," said Timms, "but I'd rather not. I'm going to deliver it to her myself at her bedroom window to-night. You've got to put a ladder ready for me this afternoon; hide it away among the shrubs and ivy, you know. To-night you must be under the window about midnight, and keep watch while I speak to her."

Job Joskins made a feeble attempt at a smile.

"Only I know you're joking, he said, "I'd think you were mad."

"Mad! Why?"

"Cos it 'ud be as much as my place was worth to dream o' helpin' you."

"You've got to do it though," said Timms, in a tone of authority; "so understand me at once, and don't waste time. If you refuse to help me I'll go straight to Sir Roland and tell him all."

"You'd get into trouble same as me," blustered Job Joskins; "everyone knows that Bob Taylor was in it."

"Oh! that's your game is it?" said Timms. "Then what do ye think o' this?"

And he suddenly bent forward. Then there was a slightly clicking sound, and Job Joskins found himself handcuffed.

His face grew deadly pale.

"Wha—t's th—is me—an?" he stammered.

"It means, my boy," said Timms, forcibly taking him by the arm as in his old policeman days, "it means that you are my prisoner, and anything you say will be used against you, so you'd better shut up and come along quietly."

"Oh! lor'—oh! lor'," groaned Job. "Bob Taylor turned bobby? What'll the world come to next?"

"Ye see that was a little playful deception of mine," said Timms. "I'm no more Bob Taylor than the man in the moon. I know all about that burglary up at Johnson's Farm; but if you'd only consented to do as I asked you, I'd have winked at it, and let you off. Now, of course, you must take the consequences."

"Where are you going to take me to?"

"Straight to Sir Roland Ashton," returned Timms; "he's a magistrate, and he'll give me the order for your committal to prison."

Job groaned. That was the very thing of all others that he dreaded.

If he could only go to the lockup he might get off without being exposed to Sir Roland at all.

"Oh! dear—oh! dear," he cried, "this is awful! Who'd a thought I should be such a fool as to be taken like this?"

"You should have looked after your own interest, and not refused to do what I asked," said Timms.

"Is it too late?"

Timms shook his head.

"Ah!" he said, "I don't know whether to trust you."

"You could tell Sir Roland if I deceived you."

"True; but then you might run off and leave me in the lurch."

"No; I've got too good a berth."

"Well, I'm inclined to give you a chance."

"I swear I'll do as you ask.

"Very good," said Timms; "I'll try you. But, remember, if I find you trying any of your games I'll round on ye in a minute."

"Never fear," said Job. "You won't have to round. I'll do anything you like."

For a moment Timms thought that he would ask him to let Constance out of her captivity through the house.

But then Job might blunder. Constance would be placed perhaps in another room, and then all their plans would be ruined.

This would not suit Timms.

He felt certain that if he successfully carried out this campaign he would be handsomely rewarded.

So he was willing to risk a good deal.

"All I want you to do is to bring round the ladder and hide it, and be there at twelve o'clock to-night ready for me."

"I'll be there like a shot," said Job, "only pray, Mr. Constable, do take off these irons. There's the farmer's boy at Johnson's coming up and—"

In an instant he was released.

Timms placed the irons in his pocket with a kind of warning jingle.

"Ye see there's a man's life depending on this," he said, "so if ye do play me false look out."

They parted at the lodge gates.

Job turned in, much pleased to have escaped. Timms betook himself saunteringly to a little beershop not far off to rest and eat.

At length night came.

Constance, knowing that from some reason or another she had nothing to fear from Sir Roland for the next night or two, retired to bed early.

The secret which Mrs. Levine had confided to her had roused her spirits, and given her a kind of sense of security.

She slept on quietly until the midnight hour arrived.

When she was awakened by a slight sound at her window.

She started up.

Then she plainly heard it once more.

Tap, tap, tap!

She began to glide from the bed in the dim lamplight as Timms peered through the glass.

Timms gazed at the beautiful creature and was so entranced for a moment that he forgot his mission.

Never had he seen such creamy skin, such softness of outline, such abandon, and luxurious contours.

But after a moment he pulled himself together and tapped again.

"Hist!" he said.

Constance, of course, imagined that her visitor was Ralph.

There was no necessity, therefore, to make any elaborate alterations of toilet, and, consequently, she rushed eagerly to the casement bare-necked as she was.

"Who's there?" she cried.

"A messenger from Ralph Ashton."

"How do I know that to be true?"

"I have a letter here from him."

Constance opened the window slightly.

The letter was pushed through.

Leaving the window still open, Constance hurried to the lamp, turned it up, and tore open the missive.

As she read, her eyes glowed with amazement, her cheeks flushed, and her breasts heaved tumultuously.

It ran as follows—

> "DEAREST CONSTANCE,—*I do not suppose that you have heard of my danger. If you have, do not despair, for the innocent are not allowed to suffer for the guilty. I am in prison on a charge of murder—the murder of Herbert Leigh, of which you, more than anyone else, know me to be innocent. But there is no proof of my guiltlessness, and therefore I must abide by the consequences. The only one in this world whom I can trust is you, Constance. If you fail me, then I must die."*

Constance paused, and pressed her hand over her heaving bosom.

"As if I should fail him?" she murmured.

And then she read on—

> *"By the aid of my messenger you can escape. When you do so, do not take him with you, but ask him to wait for you at some inn. For him to know my secret or guess at it would be a disaster which I fear to contemplate. When you quit the Hall and leave Timms, I wish you to make your way towards the pile of old buildings known as East's Mill. This, as you know, is a ruin. Beneath it is a vault; and, going down the dilapidated staircase, on the right you will find a small cupboard with a brass knob. Press this, and within you will discover a small box. Bring that to me; trust no one else with it. This is the task which I demand of you, which it seems to me is so great, because I do not see how you can properly do it. The only way I can suggest is for you to adopt some disguise. How and where you are to adopt this, I cannot tell. Do not think me selfish; I feel bewildered. I can only hope that out of all this chaos, and confusion, and trouble, I may find a means of escape for you and me for ever."*

The white bosom of the reader rose passionately at this.

"No," she said to herself, "no! You shall not lose name and honour through me. If you persevere I feel that you will succeed, and if you do not, it will not be from any fault of mine, my darling."

Then, for the first time, she remembered that there was someone present at this dainty rehearsal.

She simply threw something over the creamy shoulders, which had made the unfortunate Timms imagine himself in Mohammed's Paradise, and approached the casement.

"Are you Timms?" she asked.

"Yes."

"Where is Ralph now?"

"In prison, as he told you."

"But where?"

"In London."

"How am I to get out?"

"Here," said Timms—the warder, the guardian of the public safety, the ex-constable—"are two very fine files; if you will file that side of the bar—just there—I will file away on the other side—just here—and will have you out in a jiffy."

"I can't get through that little space."

"Oh! no. But I'll enlarge the hole. Never you fear, miss," said Timms; "once that first bar's away I'll wrench away the rest. Then down the ladder you go, and away to London."

"Not so!" thought Constance.

But she did not say this to Timms.

"Very well," she answered; "if you file the iron that side, I will this side. I only hope it won't be heard."

She lost no time in commencing.

But how about disguise?

This was the part of the play which worried her mind.

All the time that her little steel instrument was surely but slowly eating through the iron she was wondering how she should obtain a dress suitable for concealing her person.

At length an idea struck her.

The young groom's clothes would fit her exactly.

"Stay," she said to Timms; "one word!"

"Yes, miss," returned the enraptured constable.

"You must have a confederate in all this?"

"I have."

"Who is he?"

"Job Joskins."

"Where is he now?"

"Within earshot."

"Then tell him to go into the house to the room of Harry Lang, the groom, and by some means or another get his best suit of clothes. They will fit me, and I know if Harry only knew it was for me he would be glad."

"We mustn't wait to see if he's glad," said Timms.

And down the ladder he went.

He was absent some time, during which Constance was not idle.

Before he loomed up again through the darkness she had filed through the bar.

In his hand Timms held a bundle.

"There you are, miss," he said; "and while you're putting on the togs[49] I'll just wrench

---

[49] Clothes.

out the rest of these bars."

Poor Constance!

How her breast was heaving with hope and fear.

Success meant so much.

A union with Ralph, for which she had never hoped, an escape, equally unexpected, from the clutches of Sir Roland Ashton.

And then a marriage with her lover, and happiness ever after—at any rate, through the long vista of human life.

In a very short time she was entirely metamorphosed.

From a lovely plump girl she was changed into a handsome young gentleman; for the groom in whose clothes she had dressed herself was "quite the gentleman," and was regarded as a "great swell" by the girls of the neighbourhood.

The warder Timms had scarcely completed his work when she was waiting at the window.

"Now then, Miss Constance," said he, "I'm ready to help you."

She cast one look round the room to see if there was anything which she desired to take away with her.

Then she stood upon a chair, threw the window half-way up, and stepped out.

Timms, the quiet warder (now Timms the enthusiastic) held out his arms to receive her.

But there was no need.

Constance laughed lightly.

"I want no help," she said; "pass down and I will follow you."

Timms—no matter what his idea might be—knew that to earn the money he desired and hoped for he must do exactly as Ralph Ashton wished, and act also in such a manner as not to offend Constance Marfield.

So he went swiftly down the ladder.

He was followed quite as quickly by the brave young girl, and in a few moments they were making their way in company across the grounds.

Without taking any notice of Job Joskins be it said.

Timms said "Good-night" to him in a chuckling undertone, which Constance did not hear.

"I wonder," she said, "that Joskins was so pleasant."

Timms laughed.

"Ah! I'll explain to ye another time why he was so pleasant, Miss Constance. Come along; don't run the risk of anyone seeing us."

After this nothing more was said.

The two went on together.

Out across the grounds into the lane.

Then Constance took Timms by the arm.

"Ralph told me I could trust you," she said.

"You can."

"You will do just as I tell you?"

Timms thought of the lovely vision he had seen through the window—those gleaming shoulders, that delicious bust, those expansive limbs—and he thought that he could do anything under the sun to win her favour.

"Yes; need you ask?" he said.

"Well, that is settled," she continued. "You must go on to the Corner Pin."

"Yes."

"I am going to East's Mill."

"That is a lonely part."

"I know it; but I must go by myself," replied Constance. "You must get two horses ready at the inn, and when I reach it there must be no delay. We must dash off at once."

"I know you are right," said Timms. "I will make no delay. I know there is no time to lose."

Constance was far better acquainted with the neighbourhood than Timms, and when she left him she paused only for a moment, and then made her way across the fields in the direction of East's Farm.

The particular building to which she had to direct her steps was the old mill where Ralph Ashton had met with his adventure with the victim of the Black Brotherhood.

Advancing towards this, the brave girl showed no hesitation, and, only glancing round her to see if she was watched, she made straight for the building.

Appended to the letter, of which we have given a part, was a full description of the spot—so accurately given that she was able at once to discover the rope, and make her way into the place by the same way that Ralph was in the habit of entering.

It was a most uncanny place for a female to enter at such a time of night; and there was, of course, a tumultuous feeling of excitement in the bosom of Constance Marfield.

But she restrained it well, and repressing an inclination to cry out or else fly from the place, she at length made her way down to the exact spot where Ralph had told her the box was that he wanted.

Not a sound disturbed the stillness of the place.

And yet she was watched.

Could she have seen how she would have been, terrified, perhaps, to death.

But, fortunately, so intent was she on the purpose of her visit to this dark and mysterious spot, that she did not allow her glances to roam far.

Had she done so, she would have seen lying in the corner of the cellar where Ralph's mysterious box was a strange and ghastly object.

A man with his head tied up in blood-stained bandages; his face white and apparently death-stricken; his eyes glassy.

A man who looked, in fact, as if he had risen from the dead; as if he had been the victim of the Brotherhood whom Ralph had flung into the stream, who had come suddenly to life.

He seemed too weak to be capable of speech, but he watched her every movement, not knowing, of course, that she was a woman.

In the darkness he could not observe the graceful voluptuousness of the form which would show itself even in manly garb.

He only regarded her as an intruder, and watched her accordingly.

She was not long there.

Ralph had explained to her exactly where she was to find the precious box whose contents were to work his way out of prison, and accordingly with far less trouble than she had imagined probably, she quitted the place, and began to make her way towards the spot where she was to meet Timms.

Her natural woman's curiosity made her anxious to know what was in the box.

But as evidently the matter was one of life and death to Ralph, she determined to forbear.

She was not long in reaching the rendezvous.

Her steps were hurried by the aspect of the surrounding country.

In the deep darkness which preceded the dawn she fancied that she saw all kinds of shadowy figures leaping round her and beckoning to her.

She had been so long a prisoner that the sense of freedom was in itself oppressive, and she possessed a wrought-up feeling which caused her imagination to run riot.

Again and again she experienced an inclination to hide away somewhere, and leave all idea of advance until morning.

But when she remembered Ralph's deadly peril, when she thought of him eating his heart out in prison, she braced up her courage once more, and pressed onward.

Timms was waiting impatiently.

If Constance Marfield failed in her adventure, whatever was its object, so would he fail.

So when he saw the dainty figure come tripping up in its manly attire he pressed forward with enthusiasm to meet it.

"Have you succeeded?" he asked.

"Yes."

"Would you like a rest before we start?"

"No; let us press on. Are the horses ready?"

"Yes; they can be here in a few minutes."

"Get them quickly, then," said the young girl. "I am all impatience to be off."

Within ten minutes they had mounted their steeds and started.

Constance felt very awkward at first.

She was a good rider on a side-saddle, but with her legs crossing the horse like a man she felt a strangely uneasy sensation.

However this wore off as she proceeded, and she, moreover, determined to preserve her male incognito.

At first she had intended to put on her female attire again as soon as she neared London.

But now she had matured a plan in her head in which her male garb would stand her in good stead.

Meanwhile, as his intended rescuers were hastening towards him, Ralph, as may be imagined, was in a high state of excitement.

He had had a long consultation with his lawyer.

But the result had been anything but satisfactory.

Mr. Fortescue, the solicitor, was a man of high standing in his profession, and his mind was capacious enough to admit even the smallest piece of evidence.

But he seemed to see no loophole of escape.

The evidence all tended to eliminate Ralph.

"You see, false swearing will go a long way," he said. "As you have been leading what is termed a vagabond life, having no fixed habitation, but living here, there, and everywhere, while hiding from justice, you cannot very well plead an alibi."

"Indeed, I cannot," said Ralph. "Even on that night—the night of the murder—I was very close to the murdered man's dwelling, and if the prosecution only get hold of the right persons they could prove it."

"Let us hope they will not."

"And yet, you see, Mr. Fortescue, if I do not admit my presence near at hand I cannot bring the guilty man to justice. Ned Wilmot was the man who killed Herbert Leigh, but how can I prove it."

"Daisy Leigh, the daughter, could aid you in doing so."

"Yes; but how to find her?"

"We must advertise, I suppose," said the lawyer. "I will see that several papers have it in to-morrow. It is strange that she should not have turned up before to punish her father's assassin."

"She has most likely been spirited away," said Ralph; "that is the only solution of the mystery."

What a frail chance of life!

The finding of poor little Daisy, who, in the new life among the genial Bohemians of Dimity's show, never saw or thought of a newspaper.

However, even this was an off-chance, and poor Ralph clung to it.

"I do not see why you should lose hope," said the lawyer. "I can't see how they can hang you on such very circumstantial evidence. But they may. You see, juries are very fickle, and judges are apt to be biased. But the forgery business is clear, and, taking one thing with another, you are sure to get it hot, if you are convicted."

"Never mind, where there is life there is hope," said Ralph; "save me from the scaffold, and I shall not fear."

Strangely enough the man of law left the presence of the prisoner only a few moments before Timms entered the cell.

He was not alone, however.

One of the other warders was with him.

But he was able, by a variety of signs, to intimate to the eager man that he had succeeded.

"I see you have Mr. Fortescue for your legal adviser," he said; "you couldn't have a better one."

"I think he is a very clever man," said Ralph; "but I don't imagine he will have much chance to get me off with all the false swearing that will be done."

"Don't despair," said Timms; "help will come to you when you least expect it."

This was said in such a manner as to intimate to Ralph that he had succeeded in his venture; and the heart of the captive beat so high with hope that the light of a renewed life came into his eyes.

But there was no chance of a private conversation.

The second warder, having seen to the cell and uncovered Ralph's dinner, and placed it before him, sat down while he partook of it.

Timms would not run the risk of saying more.

Only when the meal was over, and he and his comrade were about to leave the prisoner once more alone, he said—

"Mr. Fortescue's clerk is coming this evening with the notes of his speech, &c., and if you want to write down anything ready for him you can have pen, ink, and paper."

"I should be very grateful," said Ralph.

This was suggested by Timms in the hope that he would be able to bring the materials, and explain the result of his visit to Barnet.

But in this hope the friendly warder was destined to be disappointed, for another man was sent with the materials.

Ralph was again, therefore, doomed to endure suspense.

But he did not despair.

He saw by Timms's manner that he had achieved some kind of success, and even that was a solace to his mind.

At length the weary day passed.

Evening seemed never coming; but just as dusk set in there was the welcome sound of footsteps in the corridor.

Then the door opened, and Timms entered, escorting a young gentleman with a large blue bag.

There was only one long, searching look given by Ralph.

Then his arms were opened, and the lawyer's clerk was sobbing on his breast.

"A good job that Lumsden wasn't on duty instead of me, Mr. Ashton," said Timms, when Ralph had finished his kissing of the ripe, red lips. "However, I mustn't stop now. Compose yourself, Miss Marfield. I shan't be able to return to-night, and so a stranger will come to let you out. Be as quick as you can in whatever you want to do."

"I only want a few minutes' conversation with Miss Marfield," said Ralph Ashton, "and then all will be prepared for my escape, I hope. How am I to give notice when my lawyer's clerk has concluded his business?"

"Knock loudly at your cell door three times," said Timms; "when Miss Marfield has gone I may have a chance of coming to your cell for half an hour, and then I'll tell you how I got on with Job Joskins."

"What happiness this is!" cried Ralph, when Timms had gone, and the young girl had sat down upon his knee and yielded herself up to his passionate caresses; "not only is there a chance of my escape now, but you are free from the loathsome attentions of Sir Roland."

"Yes; for ever, I hope," she said.

"We will get married as soon as I am outside these walls," said Ralph, "and then I shall ask you to accompany me to America. It is of no use attempting to carry on this uneven contest any longer."

"That is right," said Constance, "I will willingly go. I see no other chance of escape from this vile persecution. We must trust in time to prove your innocence."

"You have brought the box?"

"Yes; it is in my bag."

"Let me have it quickly, then."

Ralph had soon possession of it, and tenderly lifting her off his knee he turned his back to her, opened it, and took out several small articles.

These he concealed in his bed, and returned the box to her.

"I shall soon be free, I feel sure of it," he said, with a radiant smile. "When you quit this place where will you go?"

"I know of no one in London to whose house I can go," she replied.

Ralph reflected a moment.

"I know of no one now," said Ralph; "there was a person at Weybridge who would have been just the sort of individual to go to. But now circumstances have altered, and we had better trust to strangers. Go to the Lion Hotel at Islington, it is at the corner of Broughton-street, and await me there. Have you any money?"

"No," said Constance, blushing, "I have not."

"I have not much more than I need," said Ralph, "though I know where to get more. But take this sovereign. It will last you until I join you."

"What about my dress; do you think I had better change it?"

"Well, in the glare of hotel lights, I am afraid you won't pass muster as a lad, you are far too pretty," said Ralph, fondly. "If you can find a chance I would put on good female attire again; but be sure to wear a veil. And, now, dear, for the first time in my life I am in a hurry to get rid of you."

"Why?"

"Because every moment lessens my chance of escape," said Ralph; "it will take me some little time to prepare my plans, and so good-bye, my own darling. Be careful, do not let the happiness of your freedom disarm your suspicions. I do not yet know what kind of disguise I shall adopt, but whoever asks for you by the name of Waters will be myself."

One more embrace (so fond and fervent that it seemed to be born of a presentiment of the terrible future), and then Ralph Ashton gave three wavering knocks at the door.

Within five minutes it was opened by one of the warders.

Constance had by this time recovered her composure.

She at once prepared to go.

"Do you want this pen and ink any more?" asked the man.

"If you please."

The warder looked Ralph straight in the face as he spoke, and was able afterwards to swear that he had noted his features well.

"All right! But in an hour it will be 'lights out.' Don't forget."

The man spoke very kindly.

He liked Ralph, as, in fact, did all the warders; and consequently he was always willing to oblige him.

"I won't forget," said Ralph, smiling. "I've a lot of business to get through, but I think there will be time."

Then with a careless nod to Constance, in her capacity of lawyer's clerk, he turned and resumed his seat at the table.

The door was closed.

Ralph listened to the footsteps, dying away in, the distance.

Then he rose and raised his eyes and clasped his hands as if murmuring a prayer.

In another moment he was at work.

What this work was will be seen on a future occasion.

Suffice it that it was a plan of escape.

About half an hour after the departure of Constance Marfield, a strange suffocating odour began to pervade the prison.

The warder's room was at the end of the corridor leading from Ralph's cell.

Here the odour crept in subtly, making them sneeze.

"What's up?" said one, who was making some toast.

"Smells like brimstone," replied a comrade. "I hope the prison isn't on fire!"

At these ominous words they all leaped up. "We'd better go and see, at any rate," cried the head warder.

And so they hastened off in different directions.

Presently two of them reached the door of Ralph's cell.

Here the smell was overpowering.

"He's set fire to his bed clothes and suffocated himself," said one. "Open the door."

In an instant the order was obeyed, and a dense suffocating vapour rushed out.

The men fell back a moment, and then hurried in again.

"Where are you?" cried one.

There was no reply. The cell was in complete darkness, except for the dull red glow of flames leaping up from the bed and clothes of the prisoner. "Quick—bring a light!" cried Timms, who was one of the party.

In a moment it was brought.

The whole party peered in.

The room was full of dense and choking smoke.

But there was no sign of any human being.

"Where are you, Mr. Ashton," cried Timms, in alarm.

"Ha! Ha! Ha!"

Such was the reply ringing out through the cell and the corridor.

"He's gone mad!" said one. "I should think he's the devil if he has a voice like that."

Again there was a loud and deafening peal of merriment.

And then amid a mass of sulphurous flames they saw a hideous form.

The form of Spring-Heeled Jack attired in the most terrific of costumes; his mouth breathing forth flames, his eye-balls glaring, his bat-like wings extended.

"You talk of the devil and he is here," said a voice which had nothing of human intonation in it. "What want you with me?"

With cries of horror the warders fell back. The awful being pressed forward and they retreated more quickly.

And in the corridor, which was arched and lofty, he leaped with one bound over their heads. But he made no effort to escape. He seemed only too anxious to indulge in his demon antics.

He leaped backwards and forwards over them while they cowered down, until reaching the end of the stone passage he vaulted over the iron railing down into the principal entrance hall.

His appearance here was greeted with yells of horror.

The porter fled, leaving the keys on the hook.

In an instant Spring-Heeled Jack seized them, opened the door and bounded out into the courtyard.

The gate of this was a very lofty one.

But it presented no obstacle to Spring-Heeled Jack.

With one upward tremendous leap he was on the summit of the gate.

Then with a downward swoop he was in the street.

SPRING-HEELED JACK,

THE TERROR OF LONDON.

By the Author of "TURNPIKE DICK, the Star of the Road."

OVER THE HEADS OF THE OFFICERS AND ON TO THE BRIDGE FLEW THE MONSTROSITY.

6.

Now there was no difficulty in his way. With bound after bound he was off and away.

Over groups of people, over cabs, and coaches, and carriages, and omnibuses he went, screams of terror following him as he went.

Here he selected a dark and gloomy court, near the Angel, known as Mercer's-alley, and diving down this he disappeared in a cloud of smoke and flame before the very eyes of a constable, who afterwards declared that he had seen Satan of a certainty.

When the excitement at the prison had somewhat subsided, it was found that under cover of the horror produced by the appearance of Spring-Heeled Jack, Ralph Ashton had, in some way, contrived to escape.

In his room was left only the charred wooden bedstead, a table, and two chairs.

The bedclothes, and the bed, and everything of the kind were burnt up to a cinder.

What it all meant it was rather difficult to determine. The fact remained, however. The prisoner charged with the murder of Herbert Leigh was gone.

About ten o'clock that night Ralph Ashton, disguised as an elderly gentleman, put in an appearance at the tavern which he had mentioned to Constance Marfield, and asked for her under the assumed name upon which they had agreed. No such person as he named had been there.

Neither by name or description could he discover anything in regard to her.

He did not get alarmed at once.

He was of too sanguine a nature to give way to fear.

A hundred causes might delay her.

For one, she might not have been able to obtain clothes of which she was in search.

But as the hours went by he began to get nervous.

At length the place closed.

He had engaged a bed, but he did not remain.

Some untoward accident must have happened.

Nothing else would cause her to be untrue to her appointment, and he resolved to hang about the spot till daybreak.

He accosted a constable presently.

"I'm in a queer fix," he said, "perhaps you can help me."

He happened to be a jovial member of the force, and he laughed.

"Well, we often help those who are in a queer fix," he said; "tell me what is the matter, sir?"

"It is a curious case, and a very painful one for me," said Ralph, aping well the manner and talk of an elderly man. "You see I expected a young lady here to-night, at this hotel, and I know that she would not of her own accord have disappointed me. She has never arrived, and I'm getting fidgety."

"Just so," grinned the constable; "someone you're sweet on, I expect."

"That's right. She's my daughter you see, hend she is going to be married this week; but she's got enemies about, and she might have got into trouble."

"Well," returned the constable, sobered in his manner by the word "daughter," spoken impressively by Ralph. "It may be that after all you've hit on the very right person to help ye."

"I hope so."

"It's this way. My mate, John Loftus, was brought into the station with a broken head, and to account for it he told a very queer story. He said that while on duty a couple of hours ago, he saw a young lady came round the corner of Leman-street very quickly, and just as she did so, a four-wheel coach came dashing up. Two men leaped out and seized her!"

"Great Heavens!" cried Ralph.

"Stay," cried the constable, "have patience. She seemed confused at first, struck all of a heap. But after a minute she gave a shriek, and hollered out 'Ralph! Help—help!' The constable made a dash forward to help her, but a blow on the head struck him down."

"Ah! then he saw no more?"

"Just as his senses left him he fancied he saw one of the men pass a handkerchief or something over her face. And then he knew no more until he came to at the station."

"It is she—it is she!" cried our hero, dejectedly; "the one whom she loves is named Ralph. I have lost her after all."

"Don't say that, sir," said the constable; "if you take my advice you will go round to the station at once and see the inspector."

"Yes, I will," said Ralph, mechanically.

Then he gave the man a piece of silver and went.

But not to the station.

He had no desire to show himself in that disguise in the bright light of a police station

Accordingly he betook himself once more in the direction of Mercer's-lane.

This dismal alley was in the same state of gloom as it was when Spring-Heeled Jack had gone leaping into it.

It was a place which, as a rule, was shunned by the police.

It was full of strange-looking shops, where very little show of goods was made, where customers seemed few and far between, but which seemed to be able to keep open.

One of these was a kind of "dolly shop," as it is called, where second-hand goods of all kinds were to be found for sale.

This was kept by a Jew—one Moses Robarts—who, if he liked, could have told a fine tale in regard to the disguise assumed by gentlemen "known to the police."

To this shady den Ralph Ashton made his way when he left the constable.

His mind was full of anxious and wretched thoughts.

To have held Constance to his breast—to have felt her heart beat against his—to have feasted on her kisses, and then to lose her thus!

It was simply maddening.

But it had the effect of making him desperate.

"No America for me now," he cried. "I will devote my life to secure her happiness. Poor Conny! What may be her fate now?"

Ah! what indeed.

Half an hour after Ralph's entrance into the shop of the old Jew there issued from it an old and white-haired man.

He was attired in an ancient kind of cloak, and walked with a bent and feeble gait.

Was this Ralph?

Whoever it was he passed swiftly away, and made haste towards Barnet.

CHAPTER XVII.
SIR ROLAND ASHTON PURSUES HIS VILLAINOUS SCHEME—DAISY'S DANGER— SPRING-HEELED JACK'S WARNING—THE ABDUCTION DECIDED ON.

SIR ROLAND ASHTON was punctual to his appointment with Robert Tugwell.

Five o'clock found him down by the old boat house.

A queer old place.

A place, too, which is destined to figure in our story as the scene of a terrible tragedy.

It is as well, therefore, to describe it somewhat minutely.

It lay at the very extremity of the grounds, where they adjoined a wide and somewhat deep stream known as the Brent.

To reach it from the gardens you had to pass through a piece of heavily-timbered ground, which was left to tangle "at its own sweet will," and was scarcely ever entered by any one.

The ordinary way to the boat house was by a wide path along the river's side, which in its turn was reached through an avenue at the edge of the park.

On either side of the boat house grew some tall poplars, and on three sides the undergrowth had grown high as well as bushy.

There was very little boating done at the Hall.

It was too dull an amusement for Sir Roland Ashton.

His active and crime-haunted mind longed for other and more exciting things to wile away his time.

The boats lay neglected, therefore; the house itself was green and uncleaned.

In this dull autumn weather it looked like a veritable murder hole; and so thought Bob Tugwell as he shiveringly waited.

Not for long.

In such matters as those which had relation to the gratification of his own selfish desires it was rarely Sir Roland was late.

"Good evening, Sir Roland," said the man, with a grin, as his patron approached. "I'm here to time, ye see."

"Good; but let us have a little less grinning," said Sir Roland; "the matter is a serious one for me, I can tell you."

The man saw at once that he was to deal with one who would not on any account allow himself to be treated as an equal.

"I beg pardon, sir; I'm all attention," he said, touching his hat.

"Very well," continued Sir Roland, lowering his voice; "I spoke to you in regard to that young lady—Lottie Day—at the show."

"Yes, sir."

"I want to speak to her to-night. Can it be managed?"

"Well, it's a risky thing to try."

He put on a doubtful expression of face as he said this, and shook his head.

Like all people of his class he knew how to "put the pot on."[50]

"Yes, yes—I know all that," said Sir Roland, testily; "if it were not a risky job I should

---

[50] To make his intentions clear.

not meet you in secret, or, in fact, think of employing you at all. Here are a couple of sovereigns. Now you must let me pass through just as she is going on the stage or coming off. It doesn't matter which, so that I catch her in the stage dress."

"Very well," said Robert Tugwell; "but if you take my advice you'll come the day after to-morrow. To-night there'll be a regular squeeze in the little passage; but the night after to-morrow she's in a piece where all the people are on the stage for a long time, and she has to go off and on secret like. You'll catch her alone then."

"Agreed," said Sir Roland, though he by no means relished the idea of delay. "At what time shall I come?"

"About nine."

"Good; I will be there," said the baronet, "and in the event of her not listening to my words, as I wish her to listen, there is another job in prospect for you by which you may earn fifty pounds."

The man fairly gasped.

"Fifty pounds!" he cried.

"Aye! that's the sum."

"And what am I to do to earn it?"

"If I fail—which I hope I shall not—in persuading her to quit the show, I want you to find me a lonely cottage, some few miles distant, where no cries or disturbances can be heard."

"Yes, sir; I can do that."

Do it!

What would not the ruffian have done for fifty sovereigns?

"You must get some woman to become tenant of it; and all the time you must keep the show in your eye. I don't want to risk anything down here. When the Dimity Troupe have disappeared from this neighbourhood I want this girl carried off to the cottage. When that is done, and she is in my power, you shall have the fifty."

How lavish was the villain with other's money!

The man could but stammer out his thanks.

"It'll be a fortune," he said.

"Yes, to you. Well, now all is arranged you had better be off. On the night after to-morrow I shall be at the stage door punctually at nine. Even if I fail I will meet you here at noon on the following day."

Why was there no listener?

Why did not the dull breezes of that heavy autumn day waft the burden of this hideous conspiracy to other ears?

Alas!

There was no one to learn the peril of poor doomed Daisy.

The hawk was about to swoop into the dove's nest.

There was no fowler near to strike it down. After a few more words the two villains parted. Sir Roland, having nothing better to do, strolled down to the booth at opening time, to feast his eyes on the lavish charms of Maria and the gentle graces of his intended victim.

When he returned home he was slightly the worse for wine, and retired to rest at once.

The morning brought him news of the flight of Constance.

That was a black letter day[51] in the household at Ashton Hall.

Never had the servants or Mrs. Levine known Sir Roland in such a terrible passion as he was on this day.

He had a double reason for being disgusted and put out by the disappearance of Constance.

There was a family cause which induced him to desire a union with her by marriage.

And also he had become so inflamed by her beauty that he wished to unite pleasure with business.

Every effort was, of course, made to discover her whereabouts.

Searching parties were sent out in all directions. Heavy bribes were offered to everyone on the estate if they found her whereabouts.

But up to the time when he went once more to the stroller's booth no tidings had been received.

At length the night came when he was, by the aid of Bob Tugwell—the villainous door-keeper—to have his private interview with Daisy Leigh, or Lottie Day, as she was now called. Still Constance was not forthcoming. Job Joskins had held his peace. For his own sake he dared not disclose one word.

He lived in constant dread of the mysterious man with so many aliases, who had pounced upon him, and caused him to divulge his secrets.

There were no flashings of telegraph wires from one police office to another in those days, and consequently no intelligence had yet reached Barnet of the escape of Ralph.

News of this would, of course, have redoubled his fury.

But his passion evaporated as he approached the spot where he was to meet Daisy.

His plan in regard to her was just such as would suit his hard and cruel heart.

He was utterly bewildered by her beauty and grace.

And he resolved to make her his own. He felt a vengeful and terrible joy at the notion of enjoying her caresses for a time, and then devoting her to death.

There would be a month or so of love and delight in the lonely cottage.

And then a beauteous form would be found rigid and voiceless, and the awful mystery would never be divulged.

We shall see presently how his plans succeeded. At present they promised well. On reaching the booth he found Bob Tugwell at his post.

No one else was near.

"It's all right," he said, in a whisper whose hoarseness proclaimed that some of the golden bribe had gone in ardent spirits. "You've come in the nick of time. They're all on the stage now, and Lottie Day'll be out in a minute."

"Which way shall I go in?" asked the eager baronet.

"This way," cried Bob Tugwell. "You see that curtain?"

"Yes."

"Well, stand against that and she'll come out right against you."

Sir Roland lost no time.

He pushed by the door-keeper, and in a few moments he was posted near the old faded curtain, which served as the means of exit from the stage.

He had not long to wait.

---

[51] Day of great misfortune.

Presently there was a round of applause, and Daisy came out flushed and excited with pleasure.

She started in amazement and fear as she saw the form of a stranger.

A thrill of dread seemed to invade her frame.

Why she knew not.

She had never seen Sir Roland Ashton, or heard his voice.

And yet there was that in his appearance which seemed to tell her that he was an enemy.

"Be not alarmed," he said; "I am only here to ask you a few questions, and tell you something which, perhaps, may rejoice your heart."

He smiled at her in a way which he intended to be reassuring.

But she could not help, innocent as she was, observing the bold looks of admiration which he cast upon her bare white shoulders, her bosom tremulous with the excitement of the stage, her lower limbs exhibited in all their superb contours by the tights of her bayadeer[52] costume.

"Who are you, sir?" she asked.

"It is of no use," he said, "to tell you who I am until I know whom I am addressing. I have my suspicions, but I cannot say if I am correct. Have you a few minutes to spare for me?"

"Ten minutes only."

"That will be abundance," said Sir Roland, as he took her hand and raised it to his lips. "I saw you from among the audience, and I at once recognised in you a likeness to an old and dear friend of mine."

"Indeed!" cried Daisy, opening wide her sparkling blue eyes, and scanning his features more curiously than before.

"Yes; your name is Lottie Day."

"Such is my stage name."

"Shall I tell you your real name?"

"If you can.

"It is Leigh."

Daisy recoiled in some dread now.

Who could this be who had penetrated her disguise only by scanning her features?

"Ah! I am right," he cried, triumphantly.

"I have told you," she said, impatiently, "that my name is Lottie Day."

"Yes; you have told me so," cried Sir Roland; "but that is no reason why I am to believe you. I am sure that your name is Leigh, as mine is."

"Yours?"

"Yes," he said, as he repossessed himself of her soft little hand, and pressed it warmly. "If, as I believe you are, Miss Leigh—Daisy Leigh, daughter of the Herbert Leigh who was so cruelly murdered not long since, then I am your cousin, George Leigh."

A look of hope for a moment overspread her face, and took the place of an expression of incredulity.

"Can it be possible?" she murmured.

"Yes," he said, coming nearer and passing his arm round her waist. "I am your cousin George, and we have the same interests and the same enemies. We must love one another, and work together, and all will go well."

---

[52] A female dancer.

And then, before she could prevent him, or, indeed, know what was his intention, he had bent and rifled a kiss from her cherry lips.

She blushed brightly, all over her cheeks, neck, and bosom, and drew back.

"How dare you?" she cried, with flashing eyes and heaving breast.

"Do not be angry!" he cried. "I knew I had a cousin, but I had no conception that I had such a pretty one; for that you are my cousin I feel quite convinced."

Daisy could scarcely tell how to act in this emergency.

She had not the remotest conception whether this man was telling her the truth or not.

That he was Sir Roland, of course, she could not guess.

In fact, except the fact that he lived at Barnet, she had no reason to fancy that she was within the range of his power.

At any rate, she was resolved not to allow embraces and caresses from this suddenly discovered cousin until she was satisfied as to his identity.

"It is almost time that I returned to the stage now," she said, with as much hauteur as she could assume. "After the performance you can come and see me again, and tell me and Mr. Dimity all about it."

He could have uttered a curse at this.

It was by no means what he had bargained for.

As he gazed at her he could almost have wished for the moment that she was not Daisy Leigh.

Her beauty inflamed him—with her dainty bust and softly sculptured shoulders and rounded limbs.

If she were not Daisy Leigh then his title and his money might cast a glamour over her.

But he felt sure in his own mind that she was the girl he had stated her to be.

If so, as George Leigh, her cousin, he could pretend to aid her against her enemies; could work upon her innocent heart, and by gradually winning her confidence succeed in ruining her.

Surely never did arch-demon hatch so foul a plot.

He restrained his malediction.

To win her he must be calm and self-contained.

"Very well," he said, "it shall be as you wish. But as I am watched by one who is our mutual enemy, I will quit the place now. If I am not able to return to-night I will leave a note at the stage-door with the door-keeper. Good-bye."

Again he bent suddenly and kissed her, and clasped her lithe form to his breast.

As he did so there was a loud burst of applause in the little theatre, and mingling with it an ominous Satanic peal of laughter.

He started and turned pale.

That laugh was one well known to him.

Often and often he had heard it of late.

The weird terrible laugh of Spring-Heeled Jack. "Ha! ha! ha!"

Still convulsively clutching the hand of the young girl, whom he hoped would soon fall into his toils, he drew aside the curtain which separated them from the stage, and peered into the auditorium.

As he did so, a fearful form leapt with one bound up the few steps from the stage-door, and came noiselessly to Daisy's side.

It was Spring-Heeled Jack!

The young girl trembled, and glanced at him in terror and amazement.

But she had seen the strange apparition before–it had befriended her; it had saved her life and her honour; and so, though her heart beat with increased swiftness in her bosom, she did not scream or cry out.

The weird being raised one hand warningly and with the other he clutched her white and rounded arm.

"Beware!" he whispered, in such low tone that none but herself could hear. "That is your worst foe—Sir Roland Ashton."

All this occupied but a moment.

With a muttered curse Sir Roland dropped his hold upon the curtain, and again turned toward Daisy.

"The devil's in it—" he began.

And then, as he saw the hideous apparition before him, he gave a smothered shriek and fell.

It seemed as if his words had acted like an incantation.

Daisy was in a dilemma.

It was her turn in another moment to make her reappearance on the stage.

How could she leave this man here alone?

When he had fallen, Spring-Heeled Jack had disappeared as he had come, in a cloud of vapour.

She rushed to the head of the stairs and called out—

"Mr. Tugwell—quick!"

She was a brave and sensible little girl.

Although her bosom was panting with fear as she saw Sir Roland lying in a dead faint on the floor, she knew that to scream out near the curtain would disconcert every one on the stage and cause a panic throughout the establishment.

But there came no reply.

"Mr. Tugwell!" she called out more loudly, and in spite of the cold wind, which made a shiver run through her bare shoulders and scantily draped limbs, she crept down the steps.

No wonder there had been no reply.

Bob Tugwell was in much the same condition as Sir Roland.

He had—as we have said—been imbibing very freely with the baronet's hush money, and when he saw Spring-Heeled Jack his excited imagination had caused him to exaggerate its terrible aspect.

The horrible apparition was bad enough as it was in all conscience.

But magnified by the fumes of whisky and brandy, Spring-Heeled Jack was a creature of terrific size as well as terrible shape.

What was to be done?

Her tender little heart was all in a flutter.

But she had the sense to see that Tugwell would be very much the worse for any more liquor, while a small drop would, perhaps, revive Sir Roland.

Seeing a bottle of spirits standing, with a glass beside it, on Bob Tugwell's rickety table, she poured some out, and, running upstairs, knelt down by the side of her arch-enemy and poured a little between his lips.

Foolish Daisy!

Why did she not leave him to his fate?

Why did she not permit the evil life to pass out of existence—the life which would strive so persistently to ruin hers?

As he opened his eyes the look he gave her when her dazzling beauty revealed itself again to him as she bent her creamy shoulders over him ought to have warned her.

But she saw it not.

The "cue" was given on the stage.

"Ah! our page returns. Now the mystery will be solved."

And in an instant, pale and flurried, yet still exquisitely beautiful, she was on the stage. Almost at the same moment Sir Roland, recovered his senses and staggered to his feet.

"My plan has failed," he muttered; "I must quit this place at once. But she must be mine. Her beauty dazzles me, and, though she is an enemy, I feel as if I could be tender to her in spite of all. But to remain here would be madness. I know not how much that arch-fiend has told her."

He crept down cautiously.

He expected, of course, to find Bob Tugwell at his post.

He found him, on the contrary, still senseless on the floor.

A shiver ran through his frame.

"Then it was not a vision!" he cried. "This wretched creature has seen it also. Curses light on the fiend, whoever he is!"

And he strode out into the darkness.

He liked not very much the idea of his solitary walk across the moor, and along the lane leading to Ashton Hall.

But he had no inclination now to return to the booth, even to enjoy afresh the beauties of Daisy and Maria.

He wished to be at home to think.

On the way towards the Hall, however, he was haunted by the strange presence.

Every now and then a whirring sound was heard near him, and he saw a huge creature, like an exaggerated bat, leap over his head and disappear behind a hedge or a clump of trees.

He could hear the "Ha! ha! ha!" echoing wildly afar off, and a chuckling close to him.

He could smell the vaporous air, he could see the glaring eyeballs, and the phosphorescent light EVERYWHERE.

At length, overcome by accumulating horrors, he took to his heels and ran—still pursued by the demon-laughter and the demon-presence—nor stopped until he reached the porch of his own domicile.

As it was opened in answer to his violent summons, Job Joskins met him.

"Miss Constance has returned," he said.

But his words fell on unhearing ears.

At any other time he would have smiled with fiendish glee. Now he made no reply.

"Give me that light. I feel ill, and must go to my room. Bring me up some wine as soon as possible."

The wine having been brought he bade Job retire at once, refusing to listen to the story of Constance Marfield's return.

"It is enough that she is here," he said; "I am too ill to listen to more."

Left to himself he poured out a large bumper of wine,[53] drank it, and set his fiendish mind to work to hatch fresh plots of mischief.

CHAPTER XVIII.
SHADOWS OF THE NIGHT—A STRANGE BURGLARY.

THAT night strange things had happened and were happening at Ashton Hall.

All the evening Caleb Masters had been "on the fidget," as Mrs. Levine expressed it.

In the morning he had received a letter from London, which had flustered him considerably.

He had turned colour and given vent to an oath as he read it, and had straightway betaken himself to the out premises to avoid everyone.

Evidently something had gone very wrong with him.

Again and again it seemed as if he were about to confide his sorrows to Sir Roland.

Once he went so far as to approach Sir Roland, when he met him near the stables, but then he wheeled round and walked off before a word was spoken.

When Constance Marfield was brought home in a state of half-insensibility to the Hall the hubbub and wonder created by her reappearance turned the tide of curiosity, and Caleb was left to his own devices.

He sat in his own room writing till very late, and, indeed, till some time after Sir Roland returned.

Then, when all was quiet, he rose, went to his door, and listened:

All was quiet.

"Just the night for my enterprise," he said, with a grim smile, and, reclosing the door, he proceeded to light a small lantern which he took from the cupboard.

This done, he went out into the passage once more, and cautiously crept up the stairs.

He made his way in the direction of that part of the building which had once been visited by Ralph Ashton in search of papers.

This was, as we know, in a part of the building which was seldom used or frequented.

The great diamond-paned windows looked out upon a part of the grounds which seemed in grim accord with that portion of the house, with long dreary terraces, green with age and neglect, and with tall poplars nodding their heads along their edges.

To-night the house was wrapped in utter silence.

Caleb's footsteps—in his stockinged feet—fell but lightly on the polished floor of the corridor.

At length he reached the part of the building furthest from the inhabited portion.

Here he produced a bunch of keys and let himself into a large room, at the end of which, opposite the window, was a high, old-fashioned bureau.

He smiled grimly as he entered and closed the door.

"How long I have waited and expected this hour!" he muttered; "but I did not know that it would come so suddenly. Two thousand pounds, or dishonour and gaol! Of what use would it be to ask Sir Roland? He would laugh at me. No—what I want I must take. It is of no use to dream of anything else. He will never suspect me."

---

[53] He filled the glass to the top.

Sitting down before the ancient bureau, he began manipulating the lock.

He did not know what key it was that opened it, and he had to try key after key.

But at length the bureau yielded to his pressure, and as the lid of the lower drawer flew open he beheld rolls of notes and gold.

The sight made his eyes glisten and his fingers clutch nervously.

He had come there to rob his master of a certain sum.

But the greed of gold was upon him.

"What will it matter?" he thought. "There's an old proverb and a trite one—'You may as well be hung for a sheep as a lamb.' If I take the lot there can be no more row than if I took only what I came for."

His greedy eyes were devouring the glittering treasure, his eager hands were already clutching the gold, when a terrific crash behind him caused him to start back on his chair and utter a smothered cry of terror.

As he turned round he saw an awful apparition, which seemed to freeze his blood and his speech.

For there behind him stood the form of Spring-Heeled Jack, just as he had crashed through the window.

One glance the wretched man fixed upon the spectre.

Then, with a gasping cry, he fell headlong to the floor.

Spring-Heeled Jack emitted a low, chuckling cry—

"Ha! ha! ha!"

But the man did not hear it.

His senses had left him.

Spring-Heeled Jack went to the door and cautiously opened it.

Then he listened intently.

All was still.

The household was evidently slumbering profoundly, and the sounds in this far-off wing did not reach them.

He reclosed the door, and locked it on the inside.

Then he approached the bureau, and took from it the gold and notes which had so overcome the senses of Caleb Masters.

These he placed in a strange-looking kind of wallet, and then he calmly commenced opening the other drawers.

One after another the contents were examined.

But they were quickly cast aside.

Evidently what he required was not there.

Presently, with a grunt of disappointment, the strange being rose, and once more approached the shattered window.

Through this in another moment he leaped.

Alighting on the broad terrace without, he at one more leap reached the ground below, and disappeared among the trees.

It was some time before Caleb Masters awoke.

The fresh air on his face, however, at length revived him, and he sat up, glaring round him in terror.

The awful apparition had photographed itself on his brain.

But all was still.

He had expected to hear the fiendish laugh, and to see the glaring eyeballs and the sulphurous flames of the strange being as it bent over him.

But it was gone. The room was empty.

The lantern burned with a dim light on the table.

The bureau was open; the window was shattered to atoms.

But the author of the mischief was gone.

And so was the money.

Caleb, even in his slate of terror, crawled to the bureau to look for this.

His heart seemed to stand still with terrible disappointment as he saw the loss.

But he had no time for much reflection.

He must quit the room at once.

To be found there would be to be accused of the robbery, and of having an accomplice who carried off the booty.

So with what little strength he had left he crawled to the door, to make his return as quickly as possible to his room.

But it was, as we know, locked.

With a sickening presentiment of coming evil he turned to search for the keys.

But they were gone.

Spring-Heeled Jack had taken them with him.

A cold sweat broke out on the body of the would-be thief.

Here he was—locked in, with the evidences of robbery.

What was to be done?

He strove with all his might to force the door open.

In vain.

It was of strong massive oak, and the lock was in accordance with it.

"What can I do?" he muttered. "Accursed wretch that I am!"

Then the thought occurred to him that if he kicked and shouted loudly he should rouse someone in the household, and he could pretend that he had been assaulted by the thieves, and locked in.

With renewed vigour, therefore, he began battering at the door.

The sound went echoing along the corridor, and out into the night.

But with no result.

The inmates of the hall, even if they had not been fast asleep, would not have been aroused by a sound so far away.

With a feeling of despair he turned to the broken window and looked out.

If Spring-Heeled Jack had quitted the building in that way, surely he could!

Not so.

Below lay the terrace, dark and gloomy—far, far below.

Caleb Masters shuddered.

"It is of no use to attempt it," he muttered. "I should be dashed to atoms. Life, even in my desperate state, is too sweet for me to take the risk. I must remain here till morning, and trust to chance."

Morning!

Who would hear him in the morning more than then?

The part of the grounds overlooked by the shattered window was very rarely frequented, and the domestics whose sleeping apartments were nearest to the disused wing would be dispersed in the lower rooms, further off still.

It gradually dawned upon him that he might remain there and be starved to death.

He knew that Sir Roland had plenty of loose money about him, and therefore there would be no occasion for him to visit the room.

These thoughts came crushingly into the mind of the villain.

Hope began to desert him.

The more he considered over the matter the more the terrible thought resolved itself into certainty.

He would be starved to death!

Again he battered at the door.

He threw himself against it and shouted.

All in vain.

The echoes went mockingly along the corridor.

But no answer came, and Caleb, overcome with his terror, swooned again.

Next morning, Sir Roland Ashton, when he sat down to breakfast in the pleasant sitting-room opening out upon the front gardens, observed by the side of his cup a little packet neatly done up and addressed.

On opening it he found the bunch of keys and a note, which said—

> *"You will find Caleb Masters in your private room in the west wing, which he visited last night for the purpose of robbing you. As I wanted the money myself I took it.*
>
> "SPRING-HEELED JACK."

Sir Roland sprang from his chair with a terrific oath and rang the bell.

Mrs. Levine appeared, bland and genial, as usual.

"Send Job Joskins here!" roared Sir Roland.

Mrs. Levine was astonished.

She had never yet seen him in such a furious passion.

She had been a witness to some of his rages; but now his face was livid, his eyes sunken, and burning like coals of fire, while foam flecked his lips as he spoke.

"Is anything the matter?" she asked.

"Matter enough!" he cried, "when I have been robbed by the very people whom I have trusted. Read this."

And he handed to her the letter he had received from Spring-Heeled Jack.

"It is some mistake, no doubt," she said, when she had perused it; "or it is some ruffian who has robbed you and is striving to put the blame on the shoulders of Caleb Masters. Let us go at once and see into it. To let Job Joskins have anything to do with the matter would be to spread the news all over the neighbourhood."

This was common sense, and Sir Roland yielded.

"Follow me, then," he cried, and, seizing the keys, he strode from the room.

It is needless to say what they found.

Caleb had recovered from his swoon, but he was pale and shivering, and half-stunned.

He staggered to his feet as the baronet entered, however.

"Ah! master," he cried, in his hypocritical whine, "I am, indeed, glad to see you. I have been nearly murdered, and have had to see you robbed before my very eyes."

"You expect me to believe this?"

"It is the solemn truth, sir."

"And who is the thief?"

"That fellow whom you have seen prowling about; the impostor whom the people call Spring-Heeled Jack," said Caleb. "I was just crossing the end of the corridor, when I heard a strange noise, and wondering who could be in this part of the building, I came along the passage, and seeing a dim light and the door open, I entered this room."

"The door open," said Sir Roland. "Where were the keys?"

"In my pocket."

"And yet the door was open?"

"Yes, sir. I could see no one in the room at first, but the bureau was open, and all your notes and gold exposed to view. Just as I sat down to fasten it up again, there was a frightful crash, and Spring-Heeled Jack sprang into the room. His appearance alarmed me so that I fell into a swoon. When I awoke I found that I was locked in and the money gone."

"A very likely story," sneered Sir Roland; "very likely, indeed. I suppose this Spring-Heeled Jack tale is to deceive me. You have had some confederate here, stolen my money, and invented this to deceive me. You'll find yourself mistaken, my man. I shall have you instantly arrested."

For this Caleb cared not a rap.

Although guilty in intent, although he had gone to the spot for the purpose of committing a robbery, he had not absolutely taken one farthing.

There was not, therefore, anything to fix the guilt on him.

Accordingly he spoke boldly, and, without the slightest hesitation, declared his innocence.

Sir Roland began to doubt.

"The affair must and shall be sifted to the bottom," he said. "I shall send for the head constable and put the matter entirely into his hands. I will be guided by him."

"Very well, Sir Roland," said Caleb; "and as you evidently suspect me, I think the best thing I can do is to let someone else hold my position until my innocence is proved."

"Quite so. Take the keys, Mrs. Levine," said Sir Roland. "You had better remain on the premises, however, Masters. If you attempt to escape I shall have you seized at once and kept until the police come."

"No fear of my escaping," said Caleb; "I want it all proved and cleared up as much as you do."

And so he waited sullenly while the baronet delivered up the keys to Mrs. Levine and stalked out of the room.

When Sir Roland reached the breakfast-room again he found a constable awaiting him on the terrace with the news of Ralph Ashton's escape from prison.

"Troubles do not come alone," he muttered, gnashing his teeth; "but there is one thing to rejoice at—Constance is once more in my power. She shall be my wife before a fortnight is over her head. First to dispose of pretty Daisy, and then, by fair means or foul, Constance shall be Lady Ashton."

The constable had arrived very opportunely.

He was taken at once to the scene of the robbery.

But no evidence of any kind was found to connect Caleb Masters with the robbery except the uncorroborated word of Spring-Heeled Jack.

Mrs. Levine was invited to partake of breakfast with Sir Roland when the constable had gone.

"This seems a most mysterious affair," she said. "This Spring-Heeled Jack has so alarmed people that even the police are frightened of him."

"No wonder, if he can break through prison bars and release prisoners, as he has done," said Sir Roland. "It was he who gave freedom to Ralph Ashton."

"He seems to direct all his energies against this house and its inmates," said Mrs. Levine.

"Yes," said Sir Roland; "whether he is mortal or not, he is my enemy."

Mrs. Levine laughed incredulously.

"I am not so superstitious as you, Sir Roland;" she said. "I don t believe in ghosts, and supernatural beings, and so on."

"I fired right through him and did not hurt him," said the baronet. "Human or not, he bears a charmed life, and I fear that I shall yet be the victim of his vengeance."

"You are becoming morbid and ill, Sir Roland," said the housekeeper, thinking it a good opportunity to broach the one idea that was nearest to her heart. "You want someone to be more of a companion than I, as housekeeper can be—to be with you in your lonely hours and comfort you with her love."

She was sitting very close to him, and her plump white hand stole into his consolingly.

"You are quite right, Mrs. Levine," he said, pressing the hand, "quite right. I was about to speak to you on the very subject."

"Indeed!" said the widow, brightening up, though a deep sigh escaped from her ample bosom. "I am pleased, indeed, to hear that."

"Yes; I was about to say that I wished you to speak to-day to Constance," he replied, "to tell her that my wishes must he carried out at once. I will no longer put up with delays and subterfuges. Her flight proves that she does not possess much affection for the one whom she professed to desire to save; and, consequently, if she refuses to do as I wish, the person whom she desired to save shall be handed over to the authorities."

He felt Mrs. Levine's hand tremble with emotion as he spoke.

He was not blind.

He had long seen her preference for him though he refused to countenance it.

But in order to afford her no chance of making a scene, he rose to his feet, after squeezing her little hand confidentially.

"Yes," he said, finding she did not speak; "yes, tell her within a fortnight she must be my wife."

Mrs. Levine had risen too, now.

"Do you think that you are acting rightly," she said, in a broken voice, "in marrying a young girl who has no affection for you—who, in fact, does not even like you, who speaks of you in terms of loathing—when there is one who dotes on you, who would study your every whim, whose love would make you happy and contented?"

"Really," cried Sir Roland, somewhat embarrassed, "you bewilder me."

"You pretend not to understand?"

"Indeed, madam, I protest—"

His words were in vain; the next moment she was weeping on his breast, her arms around him, her voluptuous bust panting beneath the lace covering, which veiled but did not conceal her emotion.

"Really, Mrs. Levine, this is madness," he stammered; "it is something of which I never thought. You must forget this scene. I must have Constance for my wife. It is a happiness of which I have dreamed for years. Pray accept my kindest wishes for your welfare, and the hope that our friendship will last long and unbroken. But be assured that my scheme in regard to Constance cannot be altered."

Mrs. Levine had cards to play of which he knew nothing whatever.

In fact he could not have believed it possible for her to indulge in so wild and extravagant a plot.

He was surprised somewhat, therefore, when she suddenly drew back, saying—

"You are right, Sir Roland. We must both forget this little scene. I will do my best to ensure your happiness in the way you wish, though I had hoped it would have been otherwise."

And so she quitted the room.

Though discomfited for a time she was not conquered.

In her inmost heart she nourished a feeling of anger against Sir Roland.

Yet still she resolved she would achieve her end.

"Constance shall never be your wife if I can help it," she murmured, as she went. "She will aid me."

Aye! so it might be.

But she little dreamed of the terrible cloud of disaster which was hovering over her, and which she was doing her best to hasten.

A cloud of treachery and murder foreign even to the fated house of the Ashtons.

Sir Roland smiled to himself when she quitted him.

"Bless me!" he murmured. "I had no idea that Mrs. L. was so lovesick. By Jove! she's a fine woman too! Hang me if a good many men would not prefer her to Constance! She has a splendid figure, and—but I must forget both her and Constance for a time. Daisy—pretty little Daisy Leigh—must be my care first. What a pity it seems that she must die; but she must!"

CHAPTER XIX.

THE SCENE ON THE HIGH ROAD—THE BLACK BROTHERHOOD AGAIN—
SPRING-HEELED JACK IN A NEW CHARACTER.

THE consternation in Joe Dimity's Troupe when they heard of the swoop of the hawk upon the dove's nest was great indeed.

Maria hugged and kissed Daisy till further orders, so Harry Banks expressed it.

"To think you were so near us, and in such danger too," said Maria, "and were too brave to cry out and spoil the performance! It was all through the fault of that fellow Tugwell."

Tugwell, of course, had to bear the brunt of it to a certain extent.

But, fortunately for him, and, unfortunately for poor Daisy, there was nothing to connect him with Sir Roland.

He pleaded that he had been indulging in some extra drink, and that Sir Roland must have drugged him.

As for the appearance of Spring-Heeled Jack, he denied it altogether.

To acknowledge that he had seen the apparition would have been to confess that he had admitted the baronet to the booth, as Jack's appearance was long after the entrance of the former.

"We had better get out of this neighbourhood as soon as we can," said Joe Dimity.

"Oh! pray," cried Daisy, "do not quit the place for me. Do not let me be the means of your losing money."

"I should lose more money by losing you, my dear," he said; and indeed the showman would not for the world have dreamed of parting with her trim little figure from the show. "We've made a pretty tidy thing out of Barnet, and I think we can afford to look for another pitch after to-morrow."

Daisy was, of course, well pleased.

She feared Sir Roland.

She had heard enough of him from her father.

And now she had seen him, had observed the looks he had cast upon her form, had proved his falsehood even at a first interview, she felt eager to be out of his reach.

What object he had in view in telling her that he was her cousin, George Leigh, she could not conceive.

But whatever it was it could be nothing but evil.

She had, of course, only the word of Spring-Heeled Jack to prove he was Sir Roland. But to her that was enough.

She could not forget how this mysterious being had before rescued her from Ned Wilmot, and she never questioned his truth.

During the day she received a letter, brought to the booth by a boy.

It was from Sir Roland, but signed "George Leigh."

He had not heard, of course, the warning words which Jack had whispered to Daisy, and consequently the treatment he had received from Daisy at the end of the interview had had little effect upon him.

The note ran thus—

> *"Dear Daisy,—I write to you thus because I know you are Daisy Leigh, in spite of your being called Lottie Day on the bills. I am not able to come to the booth to-night because I am being watched by the mutual enemy of whom I spoke. But before I go from this neighbourhood I wish to see you, in order to mature a plan for the restitution of our rights. Send me a letter addressed 'G. L.,' to the Corner Pin tavern, saying when and where you will meet me, as I want to go to London to-morrow or the next day. If I can venture near the booth I will, but that mountebank fellow of yours, dressed in the garb of Satan, has been haunting me ever since."*

Of course, it is needless to say that this letter was written, not for the purpose of obtaining an interview, but of putting Daisy off the scent.

"Don't send any answer, said Joe Dimity, when Daisy told him. "Let him think what he likes."

"I'll take the reply myself," said Harry Banks. "I'll go to Ashton Hall and confront the villain!"

"My occupation's gone!" cried Audley Harcourt. "Banks has gone in for tragedy."

"Perhaps I might go in for manslaughter," said the clown, "if he comes hanging round here any more. But the difficulty is how to identify the rascal."

Then, as it occurred to him that he might "kill two birds with one stone"—that is, find out the author of her trouble and have her to himself also for an hour or so—he said—

"Come for a walk with me to-day, Miss Lottie, and I will see if we can't find this rascal out."

Daisy at once assented.

With stalwart Harry Banks by her side she was in no fear of anything.

And so out they went for a stroll.

There was a delicious sense of Bohemian freedom in that walk.

For Daisy, at least.

When with her unfortunate father she had resided in London, she had always been hiding away in back slums.

It was a new sensation, therefore, to find herself out in the lanes and green fields on this frosty, bright day, in the exhilarating air, which made a brisk walk a new joy.

Harry was in ecstasies.

He had completely lost his heart.

Every time he had to help her over a rough piece of road, or a stile, or a rustic bridge, the contact of her little hand sent a thrill through his very being.

Her eyes seemed to him the sweetest and softest in the world.

Her trim little figure, as it trotted jauntily along, appeared moulded with the grace of the angels.

Poor Harry.

Poor brave heart beneath the motley cloak!

He did not know what misery he was heaping up for himself by indulging in these love dreams.

On reaching Ashton Hall, Harry boldly turned in through the open gates.

He had made up his mind what to do.

If he met Sir Roland Ashton, and he proved not to be the man who had called himself "George Leigh," he would apologise for the intrusion, and say that they were mere strangers, and that they thought the park was open to the public.

If, on the other hand, he proved to be the man, he would beard the lion in his den, and boldly accuse him of his villainy.

He was saved from much trouble.

As they passed through the gates, unseen by the lodge-keeper, a gentleman on horseback swept by them.

He gazed in some astonishment at Daisy and her companion, but did not pause.

The lodge-keeper, roused by the sound of the galloping horse, came out and touched his hat.

"That is the one who said he was George Leigh," cried Daisy, whose heart began to beat high now with a dread conviction.

Harry Banks, without replying, stepped politely up to the lodge-keeper.

"Who is that gentleman?" he asked.

"That is my master—Sir Roland Ashton."

"The villain!" muttered the clown audibly.

Then, turning to Daisy, he added—

"Let us be going, Miss Day. These grounds are private, after all."

Daisy said nothing, but turned slightly pale.

She did not, in fact, speak or show any sign of emotion until they had got some distance from the Hall, and had reached a stile, leading the nearest way to the common where the booth was pitched.

Here she fairly broke down, and, leaning her arms on the top of the stile, burst into tears.

This was too much for Harry Banks' susceptible heart.

He gathered up the lithe form in his arms, holding her closely to him till he could feel the pulsation of her bosom against his breast, and kissed her again and again.

For a moment she did not repulse him.

It was pleasant to feel his strong, protecting arms around her.

And so, as their lips met, she yielded to the intoxication of the instant, and said nothing.

Harry Banks, poor fellow, took this for consent, and he redoubled his caresses.

"My darling—my own Daisy!" he murmured, between his kisses.

This recalled her to herself.

She drew gently away.

"Don't, Mr. Banks," she said; "please let us return to the booth."

"Not for a moment, Daisy," he cried; "let me tell you now what I may not have another chance of telling you. I love you, Daisy, with all my heart and soul. I loved you from the moment I held you in my arms that night when I saved you from the river. I know I am not well off, but I feel I have bright chances before me, and I know that you have brilliant talents. Between us we can make a stir in the world. Be my wife, Daisy; give me the right to protect you, and not all the villains in the world shall have a chance of molesting you."

Daisy drew herself away still further.

"I am sorry to give you pain, Mr. Banks," she said, in a gentle voice; "but I had no idea of this, believe me. I thought you only looked upon me as a friend. It must be so. I cannot give you my love. I do not seem to have any to give. I know not, indeed, what the feeling can be like. Forgive me if I seem unkind, but—"

"Say no more," said the clown, gently, though his heart was torn with emotion.

He saw that she was in earnest, and he resolved not to distress her.

He pressed her little hand, and raised it to his lips.

"Is there no hope for the future?" he asked. "Must I think that I am doomed all my life to be without your love?"

"Pray—pray, do not speak to me of this any more," cried Daisy. "There will never be any hope. I am sure I shall never be able to love you as a wife should love her husband. I will always love you as a sister, but no more. Pray, let us return now."

Harry Banks said no more.

He helped her over the stile, and took her in the direction of the Corner Pin.

Arrived there, he entered, and brought her out a glass of port wine, which he insisted upon her drinking, and then, asking her to wait a moment, he re-entered, called for a pen and ink, and indited an epistle to "G. L."

It ran as follows—

> *"Sir Roland Ashton, alias George Leigh,—Your little game is found out. If you want a good horsewhipping, call al the stage-door of Joe Dimity's booth on the common, and ask for—Yours truly,*

> "Harry Banks."

He wrote this with the utmost equanimity, and handed it politely to the landlord.

"I expect someone will call for this," he said.

"Oh! yes; 'G. L.,' that's quite right," smiled Boniface.

And so Harry Banks, well pleased, went out once more, and meeting Daisy with a pleasant smile, as if his very heart-strings were not being wrung, proceeded to escort her home.

"I've left a letter for 'G. L.,'" he said, "that will do him ever so much good. He won't come to the booth any more."

And Daisy, glancing up shyly at his handsome face and stalwart form, almost wished that she could find it in her heart to love him.

But she knew it would be impossible.

Her love-dream was yet to come.

That night the roads round Barnet were dark and gloomy, and queer characters began to show themselves about as the dark hours came on.

As I have before said, the days of mounted highwaymen, with swords and so forth, had passed away at the period of our story.

But highwaymen of a sort were still to be found in the bye-lanes, and so on, armed with pistols and bludgeons.

The coaches which still ran on the road were armed in the old-fashioned manner, and often had to be defended in the old-fashioned way.

On the night when Harry Banks had walked home with his unwilling sweetheart, whose form as he saw it on the stage was his waking and sleeping dream, there were many persons going to and fro from a large ball in the neighbourhood given by Lord Eustace Elmore.

One carriage in particular contained a young lady and her mother returning after an evening spent in delightful enjoyment.

The old lady, wrapped in shawls, snoozed in one corner and dreamed of conquests in the olden time.

The young lady in the other corner was awake, thinking of the pleasures of that night.

She was, with the exception of a cloak, attired as she had been in the drawing-room.

Her dress was very low, with merely bands for sleeves, so that not only her large and rounded arms, but her breasts and shoulders were left bare.

Her face was very lovely; her hair dark, and worn in wavy curls, which fell upon her neck and caressed the fair white bosom as it rose and fell.

Her complexion was dazzling, her eyes deep blue, her lips rosy red, and her form altogether delicately moulded.

She had enjoyed herself to the "top of her bent," and was now conning[54] her conquests over again, when there was a sudden stoppage, and the horses were thrown nearly on their haunches.

The old lady leaped up with a "Bless me, what's that?" and the young girl was about to look out, in spite of her bare shoulders, to see what was the matter, when the door was opened, and they saw before them four men attired in black from head to foot, and wearing black masks.

The girl seemed quite stupefied.

She had often read about highwaymen, and now she had met them face to face with

---

[54] Thinking over.

a vengeance.

"Excuse me, ladies," said one of them, advancing closer, and talking in a tone of excessive politeness, "but I must trouble you to step out a moment."

"Oh! dear me," cried the old lady, "how dreadful! We shall catch our death of cold."

"Very sorry," said the man; "very sorry. We will not detain you long, however. Pray step out."

The young girl, upon whose bare shoulders the chill air of the wintry night struck keenly, recognised in the man's voice and manner an authoritativeness which would not be gainsayed.

She, therefore, tripped lightly out of the carriage.

"What is your pleasure, sir?"

"Your money and your jewels," said the man.

She placed her hand in her pocket and drew forth a tiny purse.

Then she handed him two rings.

"Thank you, fair lady," said the man, as he placed the cash and jewels in a safe receptacle, "and now I will trouble you for that necklace."

She started away from him.

"No—no!" she cried, "not that. It is a present from one I love, and I cannot part with that. Anything but that."

"I cannot think of lovers," said the man, rudely; "give it to me, or I shall take it."

As he spoke he made a grasp, as if to snatch it from her neck.

She cowered down, holding both hands up as if to protect her diamonds, and at the same time she uttered a long, piercing scream.

As she did so there was a loud peal of laughter.

Laughter well known to many now.

The "Ha! ha! ha!" of Spring-Heeled Jack.

The leader of the Black Highwaymen drew back in dismay, and even the young girl, to whose aid the apparition had come, cowered still more with a cry of horror.

"What want you with this lady?" asked the strange being, in his deep, sepulchral voice.

But there was no reply.

The man, with a wild cry, had fled through the hedge.

"Fear not, fair lady," said Spring-Heeled Jack, "I am here for no harm. Tell me only who you are, and I will see that your jewels are restored to you."

But he was speaking to empty air.

The young girl had fainted.

Spring-Heeled Jack lost no time, but, dashing forward, he caught her up in his arms, and bore her swiftly towards the carriage.

The two man-servants were kneeling down in abject fear: the old lady, stripped of her jewels and her money, was insensible within the vehicle.

Spring-Heeled Jack searched in her pocket and in that of the young girl to try and discover a smelling-salts bottle. But in vain.

He, therefore, placed her gently on the widest seat, and with his claw-like fingers made a slight scratch on the fair bosom, now chilled with the night air, and scarcely moving with her scanty breathing.

Quitting the carriage, then he turned to the two man-servants.

"Your enemies have gone," he said; "mount your box quickly, and hasten to the nearest house or doctor's. Both your mistresses have fainted."

The other three highwaymen had not seen the apparition until it had caught up the young girl in its arms and approached the carriage.

They had then, with yells of horror, sprang towards their horses, mounted, and ridden off.

As soon as he had spoken to the two domestics, Spring-Heeled Jack turned towards the trembling steed which had been left behind by the leader of the highwaymen in his alarm, and, approaching it, leaped upon its back, and dashed off at furious speed in pursuit of the other robbers.

A strange and weird and terrible object he looked as he fled along thus on horseback.

It was the first time that he had ever been seen on a horse, and the few persons who caught sight of him uttered involuntary screams of terror and fled.

He looked, in fact, far more weird and terrible than he did when on foot, with the strange, phosphorescent light gleaming from his eyeballs, the vaporous smoke issuing from his mouth, his bat-like covering fluttering in the wind.

The horse, as if he knew that he had some strange being on his back, seemed to go at increased speed.

It appeared to fly along, scarcely touching the earth as it went, and this, added to its black colour, caused it to be partially invisible to those whom it did not approach nearly.

But the Black Brothers had obtained a long start, and when Spring-Heeled Jack at length drew rein, some miles along the high road, he had not obtained a glimpse of them.

CHAPTER XX.

NED WILMOT—THE ATTEMPTED MURDER—
RALPH ASHTON JOINS THE BLACK HIGHWAYMEN.

TWO days after the attack on the carriage, which caused such dismay on the country side, and yet gained for Spring-Heeled Jack a far better reputation than he had yet attained, a traveller, mounted on a black steed, made his way out of the wood known as Barlow's Coppice, and rode slowly along in the direction of Weybridge.

This was none other than Ralph Ashton.

He was not, however, so daring as to appear in public without disguise.

A large beard partially concealed his face, while a kind of soft felt hat was pulled low down over a bushy head of ruddy-coloured hair, which was most unlike his own chestnut locks.

Notwithstanding his last reception at Mrs. Barton's, he was about to venture there again (to the house to which she had hastily removed) in order to obtain from her some papers, which were of the utmost importance to him.

He had in his mind, too, a plan, by which he hoped to punish Laura in some measure for the cruel and brutal revenge which she had taken upon him.

Passing along the somewhat desolate road—not, perhaps, so desolate looking to him as it appeared to those who were unaccustomed to night adventures—he became conscious that he was being watched, or, at any rate, that someone was moving along in concert with him.

The moonlight was bright at times, though at others the silver goddess was obscured behind banks of clouds.

But when any light showed itself he could see a form flitting along on horseback among the trees or rushing along behind hedgerows.

Who it was he could not guess.

His adventure at the Mill, the avenging dagger and the scroll, signed by the chief of the Black Brotherhood, told him that the days of mysterious associations were not past, and that there was still danger lurking on the roads for those who had secret enemies.

He was well armed.

In spite of all changes in social manners, he never went out without his pistols, and his hand naturally clutched the butt-end of one of these as he transferred his heavy riding whip to his left hand.

Presently, as he reached the old-fashioned rugged bridge which spanned the river, the trees became few and far between, and the hedges gave place to palings.

There was nothing to conceal a horseman here, and, consequently, if the rider wished to cross the bridge, he would have to do so openly.

"I think the fellow is a highwayman," said Ralph, to himself, as he put spurs to his horse. "I expect when we pass these few cottages he will show his teeth."

Between this point and Weybridge there were two good miles without a sign of any human habitation.

It was for this lonely tract of country that Ralph knew he must prepare, if any danger lurked in the mysterious actions of the unknown traveller.

So he rode very swiftly, and kept his pistol ready.

Scarcely, however, had he crossed the bridge when there was a loud clattering of hoofs, and a man, mounted on a tall, grey horse, came dashing after him.

He put his horse on its mettle, but the stranger seemed to possess the better steed, for he surely gained on him.

At length Ralph suddenly pulled up.

The stranger thus shot past him; but, after a moment, he also reined in his horse.

"Am I going right for Weybridge?" he cried, in a loud voice.

Ralph Ashton knew the tones full well.

They were those of Ned Wilmot.

"What a strange meeting!" thought Ralph. "Is it a coincidence, or has he followed me for some fell[55] purpose?"

"Yes," he said; "go straight on."

He had hardly spoken when he saw the right arm of the stranger raised, and a flash of light was followed by a report.

A stinging pain in Ralph's left shoulder told him that he was wounded.

"Ha! ha!" laughed Ned Wilmot. "I have guessed all along the road that it was you, Ralph Ashton, in spite of your disguise; when I heard your voice I was sure."

He fired again as he spoke.

But by this time Ralph had recovered his presence of mind.

He had felt dazed for a moment by the shock of the wound, and had failed to retaliate.

---

[55] Sinister.

SPRING-HEELED JACK,

THE TERROR OF LONDON.

By the Author of "TURNPIKE DICK, the Star of the Road."

"I AM YOUR FATE—YOUR AVENGING DEMON!" REPLIED THE APPARITION.

No. 7.

But now his pistol was raised, and he fired point-blank at his foe.

The darkness, however, was such that he was prevented from taking good aim, and, with a loud laugh, Ned Wilmot fired again.

Ralph made a side rush, however, at the moment, and was upon his adversary before he could attempt another shot.

"Cowardly murderer, you shall repent this!" said Ralph, as he raised his heavy riding-whip and aimed a tremendous blow at Wilmot's head.

Wilmot saw the blow coming, and caused his horse to swerve.

But, nevertheless, the butt-end of the whip caught him on the side of the head, and he staggered in the saddle.

Now came Ralph's opportunity.

Raising his weapon once more, before Wilmot could recover himself, he slashed him again and again across the face, leaning forward, seizing his bridle by the left hand, while he dealt rapid blows with the right.

Ned Wilmot was surprised, dismayed, bewildered.

But he was not daunted.

In his evil and bloodthirsty heart there was an abundance of real courage, and he strove hard to recover his position.

But Ralph did not give him a chance.

His arm went like a piece of machinery, while Ned could only make a feeble resistance.

Suddenly, however, he remembered himself, and drew from his belt a long knife like a bowie-knife.

He raised this aloft swiftly.

Ralph Ashton's head was close to him.

In another instant it would have crashed through skull and brain.

But our hero's time had not yet come.

There was a sudden rush, a leap of some dark form, and a pistol shot struck the murderous blade front the hand of the would-be assassin.

In the excitement caused by this strange and unexpected interruption Ralph let go the reins of Ned Wilmot's horse, and the murderer of Herbert Leigh, sticking spurs into his horse, fled.

Ralph did not attempt to follow him.

He could not dare under present circumstances to give Wilmot into custody.

And so he must wait until he could meet him under conditions which would be favourable to an act of retribution.

As Ned Wilmot disappeared along the dark road Ralph Ashton saw who it was who had befriended him.

It was one of the Black Highwaymen.

One of the Brotherhood whose mysterious doings had been revealed to him that night at the old mill.

"That was a close shave, my friend," said the masked man. "Was he a highwayman fighting in that strange fashion, or do we claim you as one of our fraternity?"

Ralph laughed.

"No," he said; "I am not one of the gentlemen of the road, nor is the man who assailed me. He is an assassin. I know him as the murderer of Herbert Leigh, whose fate you may have learned through the printed placards of the police."

"I have," said the man; "but if so, why do you not denounce him to the police?"

"I dare not, because I am accused of the crime myself," returned our hero.

"Are you Ralph Ashton, then—the one who escaped the other night from a London gaol, when they said that the devil helped you?"

"The same."

"Then follow me. We will give you protection."

"Many thanks," said Ralph; "but I desired to visit Weybridge to-night on important business."

"I warn you not to go, then," said the masked man, "for the place is swarming with constables. There has been a great robbery there, and the police are everywhere."

Ralph hesitated.

Yet one night would not make such a very great difference.

"Are you in the neighbourhood?" he asked.

"Yes; close by."

"Then lead on."

The man turned, and at the same spot that he had appeared took a flying leap over the hedge crying—

"Follow me!"

Ralph Ashton did not hesitate.

He knew not to what scene he was about to be introduced.

But he was exhilarated by the freshness of the scene, excited by the rencontre with Ned Wilmot, and, altogether, curious to learn the nature of the company to whom he was about to be introduced.

The horse he bestrode was not one to which he had been accustomed, and he was naturally doubtful whether or not he could trust it for a high jump.

But he did, and the powerful brute carried him over beautifully.

The man in the mask still silently led the way through a wood, until presently they reached an old building which looked like a deserted farmhouse.

It was white, or, rather, had been white, for wind and weather had now discoloured it; and there were great patches here and there which made it seem as if it was never used for human habitation.

There were the usual out-buildings.

But these, with the exception of the stables, were untenanted.

In the latter were a number of horses.

"We will put up our animals here," said the masked man, as he led the way towards the stables; "and then we will go into the house. I don't know whether anyone will be there except you and me, or we all went different ways tonight."

The door being opened, the horse which Ralph bestrode walked in as naturally as if she had been there all her life.

"Peggy knows her way, doesn't she?" said the highwayman, laughing.

Ralph glanced at him inquiringly.

"Do you know this horse, then?"

"I do well. It is mine."

"Yours?" cried Ralph, incredulously.

"Aye. I lost it one night when we attacked a lady's carriage, and the devil himself or one of his imps appeared on the scene, and spoiled all our fun."

"Ah!" said Ralph. "Well, I found her standing by the hedge; and as I am not in a position to go about horse-dealing at present, I took it."

The man laughed.

"I thought the devil had flown away with it," he said.

And then they passed out and entered the farm-house.

The place within was almost as dilapidated-looking as it was on the outside.

Warmth was obtained by immense fires lit through the building, but the paper was hanging from the walls and the ceilings, which had given way here and there, and had never been repaired.

When they entered the front room, however, there were two things which struck Ralph strangely.

The one was the extraordinary incongruity of everything in it.

The floor was sanded.

The chairs and tables were of common wood.

But on the walls were many oil-paintings of singular merit, and here and there were sketches which seemed to Ralph very familiar.

"These diggings of yours are odd enough," he said. "Have you been here long?"

"Yes. We have."

"It seems deserted except for you."

"You are right. After the awful things which have happened here, we don't run much risk of being disturbed," replied the highwayman. "It just suits us, for we pay no rent."

"How about the landlord, then?"

"Oh! he wouldn't come near here," said the other; "he was too frightened the last time he came."

"You speak mysteriously," said Ralph. "You may as well inform me what the story is."

"I will," said the highwayman, "it is a story which you ought to know. But before we begin let us call Elsie, and have something to eat and drink."

To this Ralph made no objection.

In the first place he didn't know who Elsie was, in the second place he was hungry and thirsty, and in the third place he was eager to hear the story of the house whose pictures seemed so oddly familiar to him.

In answer to the bell which the highwayman rang an old woman entered the room, a strange old woman, whose hair was not white but a kind of dappled grey.

She was bent with age and infirmity, and her eyes were so hidden beneath the heavy lids, so watery and bleared that she could not see well, and, indeed, she seemed scarcely to know whether there was one person or more in the room.

The name of Elsie had raised in Ralph's mind a vision of some beautiful girl, queen of the highwaymen, and he was utterly astonished and amused when he saw the old hag.

However he said nothing.

He had no desire to annoy his companion.

In some way or another he felt that this house had some mysterious connection with him, as if it would play an important part in his future life.

"Bring us some supper and some grog, Elsie," said the highwayman, "and be as quick as you can, for I want to talk business with Mr. Ashton before the others return."

The old woman stood as if petrified.

For an instant she appeared as if she had lost the use of her tongue. Then she mumbled out—

"Ashton! Ashton; that name's accursed. I hope there's no Ashton here!"

The highwayman winked at Ralph.

"No—no!" cried he, "it's only my fun. This is Mr. Jones, from London."

The old woman, only half satisfied, hobbled her way out.

But in a very short time she returned and brought with her some fine cold roast beef, bread, and the et ceteras, with a bottle of brandy, which she soon supplemented with the necessary sugar and hot water.

"That'll do now, Elsie," said the highwayman, "take this toothful, old girl, and then leave us to ourselves. If you hear our friends coming, give us notice."

Both Ralph and his companion were very hungry, and they attacked the solids first with good zest.

But after they had satisfied their hunger they drew their chairs up to the fire, and filled their grog glasses.

"Now, Sir Unknown," said Ralph, "will you be kind enough to tell me the story you promised? I am all impatience."

"Very well, you shall be impatient no longer," said the highwayman; "and as for being unknown, my name is Paul Pender. They call me Paul Jones sometimes, and say I'm a land pirate. But that is my name, and until I joined the Black Brotherhood I don't believe anyone could have said a word against it.

"But I'm not going to say a word more about myself.

"You want to know the story about this house, and you're not far wrong in doing so.

"To tell it you rightly, I must take you down to the Cornish coast one stormy night.

"That was a night, if I am to believe those who told me.

"A night when sea and sky were as black as ink, when a wild wind was raging round the coast, when fisherfolk trembled for their kindred at sea, and wreckers rejoiced at the prospect of plunderous murder.

"At this time a family of the name of Vernon lived at this farmhouse.

"They had a good many friends in America, and among them was a family of the name of Leigh.

"Nay, now, Mr. Ralph, don't jump up and get inquisitive too soon.

"These Leighs wrote over from America to say that they were coming home—coming home to seek a fortune to which they were entitled, or, at any rate, part of it; and as they were strangers to this part of England they asked the Vernons to meet them at Penwreath.

"At the proper time the father and his eldest son went there, leaving at home Mrs. Vernon and a daughter, Ada, and the servant, Elsie.

"While they were absent the women folk were visited by a gentleman and a kind of groom, who asked innumerable questions, said he was a relation of the Leighs, and promised to come down and see them all again when the American importations arrived.

"The gentleman dined and teaed[56] in this farmhouse, and went away amazingly good friends with every one.

---

[56] Had tea.

"But in the morning Mrs. Vernon and her daughter Ada were found dead in their beds, and a medical examination proved that they had died of poison.

"Elsie was like a mad woman.

"She loved her mistress and her child, and knew not how to express her grief at the loss she had sustained.

"When Mr. Vernon and Tom Vernon returned they were stupefied with horror, as were also their friends from America.

"It was all the more horrible because no clue could be discovered in any way to the murderers and their motives.

"However, this tragedy was nothing.

"Elsie was accused, but instantly acquitted.

"But in the course of one week the blood-stained chronicle of this house began anew.

"One wild and stormy night four men, armed to the teeth, arrived at the door of this house, and demanded admittance.

"They were all masked.

"Their noisy summons roused all the inmates—George Leigh, his wife, and son, as well as Mr. Vernon and Tom, but when they came down to learn what was the cause of the unseemly intrusion they were shot down without an answer.

"Not one of them survived.

"Old Elsie saw it all, and was found in a corner of the hall next day by the constables half insensible and idiotic.

"Nothing definite could be extracted from her.

"Only the few words—

'Ashton knows. I heard them say "Come on, Ashton!"'

"Not one of the victims was even breathing when the constables arrived.

"The men had been shot dead as they came down the stairs, while George Leigh's wife was found with her throat cut in the bedroom.

"As if it was to be, Elsie was spared on both occasions.

"Some day she may yet tell tales, but her intellect is terribly clouded now; and, though she often mumbles the name of Ashton and talks of hidden papers, and so forth, none of us can make much out of her."

Paul Pender paused.

"Is that all?" asked Ralph.

"Well, it is to a great extent all," replied the highwayman. "It is all the story connected with the house, except that the landlord was so horrified by the succession of awful events that he has never once entered the house since they occurred. Elsie was given sole charge, and the place left to go to decay, until we found it in one of our forays, and decided on making it our headquarters."

"Did not Elsie object?"

"Not at all. She was persuaded that we were sent by the landlord, and that was enough. Do you not see how you are interested in all this?"

"I should be a fool if I did not," said Ralph.

"When you know more of my story, you will see that this is one of the links which will form the chain that will gibbet[57] Sir Roland Ashton."

---

[57] Hang.

At this moment a strange shrill whistle was heard without.

Paul started up.

"Here they are!" he cried. "Now I can introduce you.

"You know little of me."

"More than you think."

"To my knowledge we have never met before."

"There you are wrong. We met at the Old Mill," said Paul, "where you found a dead body in the cellar, with a dagger in its breast, and flung it into the river, but of that anon."

And he ran to the door and opened it just as some horsemen, dressed all in black, as Paul was, dismounted from their coal-black steeds.

Old Elsie had tottered to the door also.

To her they delivered over their horses, telling her to take them to the stables, and then strode into the front room, their spurs jingling, their pistol-butts gleaming, their hangers[58] concealed beneath their cloaks, clanking against every obstacle.

It was a scene fitted for the olden times—the times of Tom King, and Blueskin, and Jack Sheppard.

"Whom have we here?" cried the leader in a gruff voice.

"Ralph Ashton," said Paul Pender.

"He who is accused of murder?"

"The same."

"He is welcome, then. But does he know our rules?"

"I have told him nothing yet."

"That is well. I see that you are wounded, Mr. Ashton."

He pointed as he spoke to Ralph's left shoulder, which had been bound up by Paul.

"Yes; I was nearly murdered on my way hither," said Ralph, "else I should not have been here at all."

Paul quickly narrated the incident.

"You have done well by taking our friend Paul's advice," said the leader, "in not going to Weybridge. The place is alive with constables. There has been a burglary up at Newstead Hall, and there's the devil to pay all over the place."

"I am grateful I did not go there, then," said Ralph; "more especially as it has been the means of bringing me into such generous company."

"Good!" cried the leader, significantly. "Since you cannot quit our place without an oath of secresy, we will unmask. We are all both hungry and thirsty after our adventures, and, consequently, they would interfere with our comforts."

They all at once unmasked.

There was the usual dissimilarity of feature.

But there was one likeness among them.

Everyone had black hair and a black moustache.

The one who was evidently recognised as leader had a sword-cut right across his forehead.

A cut which nothing but a bandage could have hidden.

By this Ralph could always have sworn to him.

---

[58] A short sword.

An hour passed in merry-making, and then the chief, addressing Ralph, said—

"When my comrades have retired, Mr. Ashton, I should like to have a private chat with you."

"With pleasure; I was about to suggest it to you," replied Ralph.

When, therefore, the Black Highwaymen had eaten, and drank, and sung to their heart's content, they retired to their rooms, and the "private chat" took place between Ralph and the leader, whose name was Josh Lorimer.

Whatever it was, it proved eminently satisfactory to both sides.

It resulted in a great access of wealth to the highwaymen—in an oath to be taken by all to use no violence on the road, and to molest no women.

Next day, when Ralph rode out towards Weybridge, he had on his left arm a black cross.

He was enrolled for the future as one of the Black Highwaymen!

CHAPTER XXI.
JOE DIMITY'S TROUPE TAKES ITS DEPARTURE FROM BARNET—
THE HAWK ON THE WATCH.

IF Joe Dimity had intended to remain for any length of time in Barnet what had occurred in relation to Daisy would have determined him to change his mind.

He had taken a wondrous fancy to the new member of his troupe.

He was making money freely.

But when Harry Banks' experience at the Hall had proved the truth of Spring-Heeled Jack's words, he resolved to go.

Maria and Mrs. Dimity concurred.

"If once the poor dear gets into the clutches of that villain," said Mrs. Dimity, "I know what will happen."

"I know," said the clown.

"What?" asked Joe.

"There'll be a special and unrehearsed performance in the public streets by one of the Dimity Troupe when I horsewhip Sir Roland if he annoys her, and send a pistol-shot through his head if he injures her!"

"And if your arm gets tired I'll go on with the performance," said Aubrey Harcourt.

It was all very well for the kind-hearted people of Dimity's Troupe to speak thus and to look forward, almost with pleasure, to the chance of chastising the man who was persecuting Daisy.

But they did not know the depth of his villainy, never guessed how diabolical a plot was being hatched against her.

Sir Roland Ashton had due notice of the intended removal of the people of the booth, and was informed by Robert Tugwell of the fact that the route was Weybridge.

It was strange, indeed, that by some unaccountable coincidence Daisy was once more to follow in the footsteps of Ralph Ashton.

Were they destined to be all in all to each other after all?

These two, who had never yet met face to face or exchanged words of love!

At any rate, fate was weaving a strange web round Daisy Leigh.

Robert Tugwell, acting under instructions from Sir Roland, asked permission to join the troupe as door-keeper and general help.

"Wages are no object," he said, when Joe Dimity mentioned the slender state of the exchequer; "all I want is to get away from this 'ere place. It's too hot to hold me. I've got a lot of enemies about here, and if I can only pick up a bit of bread and cheese, and such like, I shall be quite satisfied."

Except that drinking bout, which had been the result of Sir Roland's bribe, Joe Dimity had had nothing to complain of in anything that Tugwell had done.

He had not the slightest conception that he was a traitor.

So Robert Tugwell was tacked on to the Dimity establishment, and when at length they began to move towards Weybridge, Sir Roland was duly informed of it.

"Nothing could have been better for my plans," muttered the baronet when he heard this. "I have a secret mission to perform there, and I can kill two birds with one stone."

CHAPTER XXII.

LAURA BARTON STILL PURSUES THE PATH OF TREACHERY—
SIR ROLAND'S VISIT TO THE COTTAGE—
SPRING-HEELED JACK SECURES THE PAPERS.

LAURA BARTON, when she found that Ralph Ashton had escaped, was enraged beyond measure. Her nature was one of those fiendish and desperate ones which soften at nothing.

To her love had never been a soft and tender passion.

It was a fierce, all-devouring flame, scorching up her better feelings, and rendering her oblivious of reason and conscience.

She had allowed herself to be overcome by her desire for union to Ralph to such an extent that when she found that he was indifferent to her, her senses seemed to become deranged.

From loving she hated.

Not with a quiet, slumberous hatred, but with a hatred which would devote life to the accomplishment of revenge.

Well known is the truth of the old poet's words—

"Hell holds no fury like a woman scorned."

Such, truly, was the case with Laura, and her anger at his escape was furious.

Her mother could not comprehend her feelings.

She had always liked Ralph Ashton, and was, moreover, convinced of his innocence; and the vindictive feeling which induced her daughter to endeavour to hatch up some fresh treachery against him was beyond her comprehension.

Laura, however, was about to have helpers in her diabolical schemes whom she little guessed at.

Sir Roland Ashton had learned from the constables, and from the reports, too, of the capture, that it had been effected at the house of Mrs. Barton.

He at once, therefore, placed himself in communication with Laura, who was publicly spoken of as the one who denounced the prisoner; and, in reply to his letter, he received one which brightened his hopes greatly.

She informed him of the fact that Ralph Ashton had left in her mother's care a quantity of papers concealed in an old chest, and that on a certain night he was coming to the cottage to claim them.

"You know best what to do," she said; "he has wronged and insulted me, and I wish to see him recaptured. I will aid you in any way I can."

On receipt of this Caleb Masters was at once despatched to have an interview with the beautiful demon who was to be Ralph's betrayer.

Caleb was by no means delighted at his errand.

His affection for his master was of the very smallest, although he could not help feeling somewhat grateful to him for the fact that he had not given him into custody over the robbery discovered and rendered abortive by Spring-Heeled Jack.

But still, in the face of everything, he could not refuse.

When he saw Laura, he could scarcely conceive it possible that she could be guilty of the terrible cruelty she contemplated.

But when he beheld her smile he was satisfied.

It was the smile of a demon!

"When can Sir Roland come?" she asked, when Caleb had made known his identity.

"To-morrow night."

"That will do well. My mother, I know, expects him then," returned the girl.

"We will be down here early, then," said Caleb, "for two things—the box, and the capture of the escaped prisoner!"

"Just so!"

But could we not arrange to secure the box at once?" said Caleb, insinuatingly; "my master would be willing to pay a good sum for it."

The young girl laughed.

"No; I could not make any such arrangement," she said. "I want my revenge as well as Sir Roland. I wish you to come for the papers at the same time as Ralph Ashton. You can then take them from the box, while the constables arrest him."

"Very well," said Caleb, "at what time are we to be here?"

"At nine o'clock," said Laura. "That is the hour when Ralph is expected."

"And who will admit us?"

"I will. My mother will be asleep. I will see to that."

And she laughed maliciously.

She accompanied Caleb Masters to the door, and there they arranged a few further preliminaries.

They were evidently very particular, for they talked so earnestly that they did not observe a dark form glide up from beside the shrubbery, and plant himself close to where they stood near the gate.

He was enveloped in a cloak, so that no one could recognise him, and, indeed, so covered up was he that as he stood near the thickly-growing trees he could not be distinguished from the heavy shadows.

He listened patiently to all that was being said, never moving from his position, never seeming to be instinct with life.[59]

Every word spoken by Caleb and Laura was heard by him.

He waited until the former had gone; then he moved forward, as if to accost Laura.

---

[59] Animated by life.

But as he did so two other forms appeared, creeping, crawling towards him.

Two constables, armed to the teeth!

Ralph, for it was he, was perfectly unconscious of their presence.

He had come down, as he had intended, on the evening before, when he was attacked by Ned Wilmot.

The next night was that on which he had told Mrs. Barton he would reach her cottage.

But circumstances had arisen which had made it better for him to come this evening.

Laura, as she leaned over the wicket-gate and glanced at the retreating form of Caleb Masters, saw not the figure approaching her, or the stealthy forms of those who were crawling up behind him.

Suddenly, however, a voice recalled her to herself.

"Laura!"

The well-known voice startled her.

"Ralph!" she cried, starting back, and almost gasping for breath as her heart leaped in her bosom.

"Aye! Ralph, whom you betrayed to his enemies, though you knew him to be innocent!" cried our hero. "But never mind. Your conscience will punish you best. I desire to utter no reproaches. Is your mother at home?"

"No."

"Can I enter?"

"No—that is to say, with my permission!" cried Laura, holding the gate desperately.

"There is no hurry. I can come again," said Ralph.

"To-morrow night, at nine."

"Ah! yes," thought Ralph, "to meet Caleb and Sir Roland. Fear not," he said, aloud— "I shall be here!"

The men's forms were coming nearer and nearer.

The ominous rattle of the handcuffs was heard faintly.

One came gliding up on one side, one on the other.

Laura, retreating towards the house, suddenly saw the two men, and, though astounded, was sufficiently self-possessed to relieve herself by a gasping sigh, and still keep retreating to the house.

The men were within arm's length when Ralph suddenly turned.

He saw the situation directly.

"Ha, ha!" he laughed, as he struck one of the constables a sudden blow in the face; "I am betrayed before the time."

The blow was delivered so swiftly and surely that the man staggered back.

But Ralph was not to escape so easily.

Both the men were, as I said, well armed, and the second at once drew a hanger and made a blow at Ralph's head.

Dead or alive the arrest was to be made; the reward was to be the same.

They were not yokels, but London constables—resolute and clear-headed men—who, besides fighting for a good reward, considered themselves to be doing their duty.

But they were unprepared to find such a determined resistance.

They knew Ralph to be a brave man, and, in fact, they had only come down to reconnoitre.

But when they found that he was there alone they had resolved to risk all and endeavour to make a capture.

The evil heart of Laura Barton beat with a joyous triumph as she saw the struggle.

Had she had physical courage equal to her mental she would have dashed in and joined in the affray; but, as it was, she stood leaning against a tree, gazing at the men engaged in their deadly struggle.

Did no compunction enter her heart?

Did no tender feeling invade her bosom?

No.

She was proof against all.

There was no womanly doubt or softness in Laura Barton; she had been wronged, as she thought, and her revenge made her stubborn and unyielding.

The blow which the man aimed at Ralph missed its aim, or our hero would have ceased to figure in this story.

He contrived to avoid it, and then taking from beneath his coat a short, stout bludgeon, he proceeded to wield it with such goodwill that the man had to act on the defensive.

The one who had received the blow on the face had quickly recovered, and returned to the attack.

But a well-directed crack on the head sent him sprawling after a moment, and left Ralph to deal with his companion alone.

The latter was a stout, broad-shouldered man, and quite up to his work.

But Ralph seemed possessed of unnatural agility, and though the man made constant cuts and blows, our hero remained scot free.

Laura, with despair in her black heart, saw the officer suddenly struck down at the side of his companion.

And then Ralph came up to the wicket-gate.

"Traitress!" he exclaimed, "you are foiled again. Heaven protects the innocent, and will not permit a wretch like you to triumph."

With these words, and waiting for no reply, he bounded into the dark lane and disappeared.

"I hope he heard nothing to put him on his guard," she said, as she reluctantly took her way into the house. "To-morrow he shall be caught in a different way."

Eagerly she looked forward to the hour when Sir Roland and Caleb would arrive, and she determined to put in practice a cowardly and cruel ruse.

She knew that her mother not only believed in Ralph's innocence, but would do all she could to help him.

Accordingly, on the morning following the scene with the officers, she took her way after breakfast towards London.

She had always been a mysterious girl, and had had acquaintances of which her mother knew nothing.

Proceeding, therefore, to the north of the metropolis, she took her way to a street of dingy and doubtful aspect, which was composed of small houses, flush with the street, and shops full of odds and ends, that appeared as if useless to any one, but where, nevertheless, a good trade was done.

Entering one of these as if she was quite familiar with it, she found herself in the presence of an old woman whose appearance was as dingy and doubtful as the street itself.

She had a thin face, but a large red nose, which, with her bleared eyes, gave the idea that she was a friend to the bottle.

Her eyes had a shifty, cunning expression, and as she raised them to look at her visitor, she seemed as if looking her through and through.

One look was enough, although Laura was veiled.

"Ha! Miss Barton," she said; "glad to see you. Anything I can do for you to-day?"

"Yes, Mrs. Corcoran," replied the girl, unblushingly. "I want two sleeping draughts—strong ones, that have no taste, and are safe, too."

"A sleeping draught!" exclaimed the woman, in surprise; and laughingly, "won't your conscience let you sleep."

"Don't waste time in talking nonsense, Mrs. Corcoran," said the girl. "One of the draughts is for my mother, and the other for a man—a friend of hers, whom I want to give into the hands of the police. He's a double-dyed villain, and has quite imposed upon her, though the constables are after him for awful crimes. I want to stop the visits to our place if I can."

"Very well, miss," said the woman; "you needn't explain what you want it for."

Mrs. Corcoran was not many minutes absent, and returned with two small bottles of colourless liquid.

"Am I to give the whole of one of these to one person?" asked Laura, eagerly.

"Yes, the whole," said the woman; "but be careful not to give more, as it might send the person off into a sleep from which he would never wake again."

For an instant the breast of Laura beat high with excitement.

Would it not be a great revenge to give Ralph Ashton the two bottles, and have the pleasure of telling him to his face that she had destroyed all his hopes in life—that she knew him to be innocent—that she had given him a poison to which there was no antidote?

For such a potion as Mrs. Corcoran had given her would, if taken in too great quantities, work so subtly into the system as to render all antidotes of no avail.

The mad impulse to do murder, however, quickly passed away, and she saw it in all its folly.

She must be patient.

If she only bided her time she would be sure of her revenge.

"I will be careful, Mrs. Corcoran," she said, "never fear. If I gave an overdose, I should be a fool, for I should spoil my own game."

She paid the exorbitant price demanded by the woman, and then with an eager heart she took her departure.

Ralph little knew his danger.

The woman of all others in the world who was his deadly enemy had got him in her power, to the best of her belief.

She had in her possession the means of sending him into a deep sleep, or of destroying him.

At any moment her evil heart might change, and she might prefer a swift revenge.

She knew well that at her mother's house she would be able to administer the sleeping draught to Ralph if he came, for he and Mrs. Barton invariably had a cup of tea together, and at times something stronger.

How eagerly the wretched girl waited that evening!

But Ralph did not put in an appearance.

The time passed on.

Mrs. Barton in a disappointed way bade Laura bring in the tea.

The drug must now, at any rate, be administered to her, in order that Sir Roland Ashton and Caleb Masters should be able to enter the house.

The unsuspecting woman, therefore, partook of the tea, and by nine o'clock was sleeping profoundly in her arm-chair, in a slumber which would bind her for hours.

Precisely at the time named a timid knock was heard at the door.

The new arrival was Caleb Masters.

Much as he desired to aid his employer in receiving the box of papers, and, perhaps, also the person of Ralph Ashton, he had no wish to meet the latter suddenly.

It was quite on the *tapis*[60] that the door of the cottage might be opened by the latter himself, and that would be a consummation most devoutly not to be wished.

He kept slightly aloof from the door, therefore, and waited until it was opened, in readiness for flight.

But when he saw the treacherous face of Laura, brilliant in its demoniacal beauty, he advanced reassured.

"Is all well?" he said. "Is it safe for my master and I to enter?"

"Yes, most certainly," returned Laura. "No one is here save myself and my mother, and she is sleeping. I have drugged her so that she will not wake until midnight at least."

"And Ralph Ashton?"

"He is not here."

Caleb wasted no more time in questions, but turning in the direction of the garden gate, beckoned eagerly.

Evidently Sir Roland had been hiding behind some of the thick clumps of trees, for he appeared at once, and, advancing, entered the house.

"This way," said Laura. "Follow me."

She led the way up the stairs into the room where Ralph's box was.

It was a little apartment on the second storey; a bedroom neatly furnished and clean as a new pin.

Laura drew the box from beneath the bed and gave Sir Roland the key, which she had previously stolen from her mother s pocket.

"I will keep watch," she said.

Sir Roland was too eagerly occupied in what was going on to take much notice of Laura, or his evil heart might have felt something congenial in the beauty of this soulless girl, whose vengeful feelings had so completely taken possession of her.

She looked specially beautiful on this night in her demoniacal way. Her face pale and stony, but her eyes blazing with a light which was almost supernatural.

The dress she wore fitted her like a glove, and being cut square, revealed just a tempting glance of her delicate bosom.

But Sir Roland cared for nothing of all this.

His mind was fixed only on the possession of Ralph's papers, and, perhaps, the capture of Ralph himself.

He placed his lamp on a shelf where it would cast a bright light over that part of the

---

[60] Under consideration

room where Caleb Masters was about to commence his dishonest work, and then the man, kneeling down, opened the box.

It was filled with clothes and papers; but there was also a bag of money.

The latter Caleb at once spotted.

"I'll have that while I'm handing him the papers," he thought; and when he gave his master the first bundle he quietly transferred the treasure to his pocket.

Sir Roland opened the documents as Caleb gave them to him, and as he did so he indulged in a running commentary—

"Ah! a copy of the very document which I thought I only possessed. What's this? George Leigh alive! Ha, ha! George Leigh, the miser! What wondrous fortune is this? If Constance only knew! We must unearth him. Let me see his address—Lone Farm, Berkhampstead! What a good name! Now, Caleb, some more; I have exhausted these things!"

Caleb at once handed up to his master another set of papers; and he was grabbing them with the same eagerness, when there was a sudden crash, a wild and unearthly peal of laughter, and, before Sir Roland could well realise what had happened, the papers were snatched from his hand.

"Ha! ha! ha!"

The weird and unnatural laughter rang through the place, and echoed out through the open window.

Caleb, glancing up from the spot where he knelt, by the side of the box, saw his master standing speechless, and Spring-Heeled Jack near him, holding in his hand the papers.

The man was as paralysed as his master, and knelt, still glancing up at the terrible apparition, with open mouth and glassy eyes.

For quite a minute both of them stood thus, while Spring-Heeled Jack seized upon all the other papers which the box contained.

Sir Roland at length reeled back from the position where he had stood so fixed and stone-like.

He rested his right arm against the head of the bedstead.

"Strange being!" he cried, in a hoarse voice, "who are you who are thus ever on my track? What want you with me? Who are you that you follow me wherever I go?"

"Your fate—your avenging demon!" returned the apparition, in so strange and hollow a voice that it chilled them to listen to it. "Until the hour when you die a shameful death I shall follow you. I am a spirit who is not to be appeased until vengeance is secured for all the wrongs you have committed. I cannot appear against you before a human tribunal, for they would not listen to me; but I will so work that the evidence I procure will be forthcoming before such a tribunal, and then your day is over."

Without waiting for a reply, the apparition leaped across the room towards the open door.

Laura was waiting in the hall below, listening, and looking out upon the night.

She had heard a crash, but she had no conception what it could be, until she heard a terrible laugh, and saw a figure descending the stairs, such as curdled her very blood.

She also stood for awhile transfixed with horror.

"Ha, ha, ha!" cried Spring-Heeled Jack. "Demon! traitress! you fear me now! How will you fear me when your great day of reckoning comes? Betrayer, cruel-hearted fiend, beware! Thus do I mark you as my own for ever!"

He sprang towards her.

The girl was powerless to resist him.

She leaned, panting and breathless, against the wall.

His sulphurous breath nearly choked her; his glaring eyes were so close that it seemed as if she could almost see into their fiery depths. As her hand was put out it touched his body—smooth, hot, panting.

"Ha! ha! you shrink. Murderess, for such you are in heart," cried Spring-Heeled Jack, as he clutched her round the waist with one arm, thus then I mark you with the brand of Cain."

And raising his right claw-like hand he made the mark of the cross on her forehead, tearing the white flesh as he did so.

Then he flung her from him, and she fell fainting on the floor.

In an instant he had opened the door ready for escape.

But he could not resist returning to the room where he had left Caleb and Sir Roland.

He leaped up the stairs again, therefore, and found Sir Roland kneeling near Caleb, who was lying in a dead faint.

With one clutch he was at the back of the baronet's neck, and had seized him and flung him across the room.

He gave a gasping cry and sunk into insensibility.

Then Spring-Heeled Jack bent for a moment over Caleb Masters; and, turning, sprang again down the stairs.

He leaped with one long powerful spring across the garden.

Then he was about to pause, when a shot came whizzing by his head.

"Ha! ha! ha!"

The laugh re-echoed weirdly over the landscape, and the terrible apparition sprang over the gate.

Then he darted along the lane.

But the place was alive with foes.

Again and again the shots of enemies rang out over the landscape.

Spring-Heeled Jack paused.

This was an unusual experience.

Who could be these suddenly-roused foes?

He turned and leaped towards the cottage. But there again he was intercepted.

As he neared the cottage a shot came so near to his face that it scorched him.

The mysterious being, however, though he evidently did not like the annoyance of this attack upon him, was not distressed about it.

He leaped and sprang from side to side, over hedges, across the lane, in and out the trees, as if to draw out his enemies.

After a while he took to the open fields, and' there began a series of gambols and outrageous antics which must have been intensely annoying to those who were attacking him so seriously.

In a few moments his *ruse* had its effect.

From different parts of the hedges around the open meadow came Bow-street Runners.[61] They had been sent down to prowl about for the purpose of arresting Ralph

---

[61] Professional police officers, rather than the informal, privately funded officers. They were called runners" owing to their pursuit of criminals.

Ashton; but finding that they could not affect this, they resolved to endeavour to make another capture, which would redound[62] quite as much to their credit.

The capture of Spring-Heeled Jack.

Already his name had become a bugbear.

Already it had become the terror of London.

Nursemaids used it as the nursemaids of thirty years before used the name of Napoleon, "the Corsican ogre," to frighten the children.

In various parts of the metropolis he had been really seen.

But where he had not been seen the brisk imagination of servant girls had manufactured him.

In fact, "Jack" was an excuse for a great many things which would have surprised him.

At any rate, quite a little cloud of London constables came out from the hedgerows, and disposed themselves about the field as if they were suddenly resolved to play a game of cricket by moonlight.

Spring-Heeled Jack was certainly in an awkward predicament, if, indeed, he was of such a nature that earthly troubles affected him.

But he was in no way discomfited.

He leaped about in the most extraordinary manner, perfectly puzzling to his would-be captors.

But it was a tiring game even to a being who was able to leap continually over the heads of his tormentors.

Had he had a mind he could, no doubt, have sprang away like some supernatural kangaroo, and distanced them all.

But evidently he was waiting for someone or something.

Suddenly, when another volley of bullets came whistling uncomfortably round his head, he gave a loud sepulchral laugh, followed by a. strange, shrill cry, and in a moment afterwards the whole scene was changed.

From two sides of the meadow came a rush of horsemen, who leaped the hedges and charged down upon the Bow-street runners.

They were masked, and were dressed in black from top to toe.

They were none other, in fact, than a band of the Black Brothers.

The constables recognised in a moment that they had a difficult foe to deal with, and, consequently, they directed their attention more to the new comers than to Spring-Heeled Jack.

And well they might.

The Black Highwaymen swept all before them.

The constables, as we have seen, were by no means devoid of courage.

But the charge was like that of heavy cavalry and it came, moreover, on two flanks.

They made an attempt to withstand their new enemies.

But in vain.

They were cut down, or ridden down, and in the midst of it all, Spring-Heeled Jack, with a loud "Ha! ha! ha!" made his escape.

The Black Highwaymen did not stop to follow up their victory.

They were contented at seeing their opponents dispersed in all directions, flying as if

---

[62] Have an advantageous effect.

for their lives.

With loud laughter they affected to pursue them.

But as soon as they had seen that the constables were fairly beaten, and had entirely given up all hope of capturing their victim, they rode off in various directions, apparently with the notion of making a night of it on the road.

Three of the constables—resolved to make the best of their way back to London, and attempt, moreover, to make arrests of any kind that night—hastened towards the banks of the Brent, with the idea of crossing over to the other side, to the Eagle and Hound, a tavern where they could not only obtain some refreshment but a seat in the coach for London.

They had crossed over in a boat, and had left it by the bank.

Towards this they now made their way.

"That's a rum go about this Spring-Heeled Jack, George," said one of them, addressing his companion. "Can you make anything of him?"

"He's the devil, I should think," said the man addressed.

"I kept firing at him again and again," put in the other man; "but you might as well fire at the moon for all the effect it takes on him."

"I fired, too," said the one addressed as George; "but it's no use."

"It can't be a mortal man," said the other. "Oh! Lord preserve us!"

No wonder was it that he gave vent to this exclamation.

For as he spoke a cloud seemed to come between them and the moonlight, and Spring-Heeled Jack alighted in front of them.

"'Ha! ha! ha!'"

The terrible laugh echoed dismally and weirdly over the landscape.

It was a blood-curdling laugh, and the men, with trembling limbs and chattering teeth, were preparing to fly back in the direction they had come, with what little strength they had left in their legs.

But the apparition went flying on far in front of them, and in a few moments disappeared.

Not one of those men was there who did not wish himself safe in the neighbourhood of Bow-street.

"Ugh! I shall dream of this for months," said George, "and I shall feel a funny feeling, I don't know what, creeping up behind me!"

"Don't doubt ye! I know I shall," said the other.

The third was hurrying on ahead to secure the boat.

It was not long before they reached the river.

The boat was there and they eagerly re-entered it, congratulating themselves that they had seen the last of Spring-Heeled Jack, at any rate, for the night.

Alas! for the futility of human hopes.

They had scarcely left the shore when again there came a small cloud between them and the moon.

And with a crash, which threatened to destroy the boat, or, at any rate, to upset and immerse them all in the water, Spring-Heeled Jack bounded into it.

They were about to leap up.

But a loud and deep sepulchral voice restrained them.

"Hold! Be not mad! Sit still and row on towards the bridge! Ha! ha! ha! You ought to row quickly now, for you have the devil's luck with ye!"

The men mechanically seated themselves at the oars.

They seemed possessed of superhuman strength.

The boat appeared to rush through the water as if by magic.

The sensation was a pleasant one.

But it made their hearts beat terribly.

It was altogether uncanny.

The swiftness with which they sped along was, perhaps, imaginary.

Their feelings at their strange position were, doubtless, to be blamed for any unusual exultation.

A strange position in very truth.

Rowing in a boat along that silent river, with the very being whom they had tried to arrest—a being whose eyes glowed above them like lamps, whose mouth vomited flames, and about whose form a sulphurous vapour hung.

A being who had defied their bullets and fled from them, and then came voluntarily back to keep them company.

They said nothing—only plied their oars mechanically in the direction of a rudely-constructed bridge, which spanned the river some distance above the water.

The courage of the Bow-street runners had begun to creep back.

With safety came a desperate resolve.

They saw people moving about on the bank.

What if Spring-Heeled Jack was only an impostor, hiding away from some one; and what if they asked these people to aid them in catching him?

As they neared the bridge it seemed as if the monstrosity who had so long defied their efforts had divined their thoughts.

He gave vent suddenly to a loud—

"Ha! ha! ha!" and, with one spring, which shook the boat, he went flying through the air, chuckling as he went, and alighting on the rustic balustrading of the bridge.

The constables (one of whom, in the excitement consequent upon the hope of capture, had already grasped his staff of office like a club), looked up aghast as the extraordinary being sailed above their heads.

Then, as he alighted on the bridge, and went leaping away with his usual terrible laugh, they figuratively took to their heels.

They would have done so had they been on dry land.

But, as they were in the boat, they pressed on as swiftly as possible towards their destination, after arriving at which they lost no time in making their way to London.

Their courage, as regarded Spring-Heeled Jack, had evaporated.

"Never no more, George!" was the expressive observation made by one of them as they found themselves once more in safety.

And that sentence, incomplete as it was, expressed the ideas of all.

Spring-Heeled Jack had certainly impressed his enemies that night with a forcible idea of his power.

He had scored three victories.

He had routed ignominiously the myrmidons[63] of the law.

---

[63] Faithful followers, named after a people ruled by Achilles.

He had proved to the enemies of Ralph Ashton (for whom he had so mysteriously taken up the cudgels) how he could defend him.

And he had left an impression upon the minds of Caleb Masters, Sir Roland Ashton, and Laura Barton that would never be effaced.

When Sir Roland and his worthy servitor had recovered from the deadly stupor into which the sight of Spring-Heeled Jack and his words had thrown them, they crept downstairs in the hope of obtaining some refreshment in the way of spirits to give them, at least, "pot-courage."

Their lamp had, fortunately for them, not been extinguished, but its light revealed to them at first a sight which was far from refreshing or likely to revive their spirits.

In the hall, where Spring-Heeled Jack had left her, was Laura Barton, still in a dead swoon.

The blood was pouring still from the wound in her forehead, where the claw-like hands of the strange apparition had marked the cross.

It had stained her face hideously, and trickled down upon the white breast, whose faint pulsations alone spoke of the presence of life.

"This must indeed be the devil!" muttered Caleb Masters; "it can be no man that thus defies every law, and laughs to scorn the endeavours of everyone to catch him."

"No, he is not the devil," said Sir Roland; "he is some mysterious being who has some dealings with those who understand the black art. There must be necromancers in these days, in spite of all they tell us."

And the baronet, laden as he was with crime, shuddered at the thought.

Caleb said no more, but moved towards the parlor, where a light was gleaming faintly.

Here they found Mrs. Barton in a profound slumber, as her daughter had said.

A bunch of keys lay on the table, and seizing these, the steward, who had been followed quickly by his master, searched in the cupboards and found a bottle of brandy.

It was like "manna in the wilderness" to those two men, who had lost all courage, and almost all physical strength through the apparition of Spring-Heeled Jack.

They poured two cups full and drank them off at a gulp.

Then Sir Roland bethought himself of Laura.

"Come, Caleb," he said, "show a light. We must see to the girl. We don't want to run the risk of being mixed up in such an affair as this."

Passing into the hall, the baronet raised the senseless form of Laura from the floor and bore her into the parlor.

Here he tore open her dress, and placed his hand upon her breast to see if the fluttering of life still existed.

Only faintly.

But as the air came to her, and a little brandy was poured down her throat, her eyes slightly opened.

She glanced somewhat vacantly around her, and her magnificent bust rose and fell for a moment tumultuously.

The baronet raised her to a sitting posture.

"What means this wound on your forehead?" he asked, as he handed her a small drop of brandy.

"It is the mark of that accursed thing which haunts this neighbourhood," said Laura, drinking her brandy, but unable, nevertheless, to repress a shudder. "I only hope that some means or another may be found to stop his strange antics, or he will cause the death of more than one of us."

"Aye!" said Sir Roland, with a shudder, having time now to view well this beautiful traitress, and see how handsome she was; "aye! I know that twice running he has nearly killed me."

"What believe you he is?" said Laura, eyeing the door timidly.

"The devil, I should think," cried Caleb.

"Certainly he seems to bear a charmed life," said Sir Roland. "I have fired point blank at him only a few yards off, and the ball has taken no effect. But we must be going, Caleb. Miss Barton, what reward can I offer you for your attempt to-night to do me a signal service?"

"I need no reward, Sir Roland," said Laura, "more especially as we have so miserably failed."

"Nay, we have not failed altogether," said the baronet. "I have obtained a clue to something which will be of wonderful service to me. If I find that this clue leads to anything, you shall be rewarded handsomely. In the meantime accept this ring as some small recompense for all the trouble you have gone through this night for me."

He drew a handsome ring off his finger as he spoke, and, taking Laura's hand, placed it on its engaged finger.

Of course this was purely accidental, and Laura knew it to be so.

But it assumed the proportions of a strange coincidence in her mind.

"It would be by no means a bad thing to be Lady Ashton," she thought.

She knew him to be bad, cruel, selfish, unscrupulous.

But what mattered that?

Was she not the same?

So when he placed the ring on her finger she smiled sweetly at him.

Caleb had gone to get the horses ready, and so Sir Roland was at liberty to exercise at will his fascinations over this beautiful demon.

And beautiful, indeed, she looked, in spite of her wounded brow, with her dark hair falling in masses over her shoulders, her large eyes flashing, her pouting lips red with renewed life, her splendid bust revealed still by the *deshabille* which had been necessary to recover her from her faint.

The sparkle in her eyes emboldened him.

He raised her left hand with his right, intending to salute it; but a sudden impulse made him forget himself, and, slipping his arm round her waist, he drew her to him, and kissed her ripe lips.

One long, clinging kiss it was, and then she started away.

"Forgive me, Miss Barton!" said Sir Roland, who was almost as nervous at his act as herself, for, knowing her character, he could scarcely tell how she would construe it.

She smiled sweetly up in his face.

"Of course I forgive," she said, forgetting her *deshabille*, and wondering at his looks of admiration. "I put everything down to the strange and exciting events of the evening. But pray go now. My mother, as you see, shows signs of waking. She must know nothing of your visit. All the upset in the house can be put down to the visit of Spring-Heeled Jack."

Sir Roland, in spite of the false position he was putting himself into, looked very much as if he would like to rifle another kiss from that cherry mouth.

But Laura drew prudently away.

She was not the one to make herself too cheap, and Caleb's heavy tread, too, was heard approaching.

So with a smile he took her hand, pressed it warmly, and saying—

"Good-night, Miss Barton. Keep that ring, and if you are in any trouble, come to me and you will not find me forgetful."

Within five minutes after the baronet and his servant were riding away in the direction of Barnet.

As they neared the adjacent village, they resolved to pause and partake of some refreshments, fluid and solid; and ascertain if anything had been bruited about in the neighbourhood in regard to the doings that night of Spring-Heeled Jack.

The tavern was that to which the constables had gone when they had fled from the river's side after their row with Spring-Heeled Jack, the Eagle and Hound.

But it was certainly no constable's voice which was now roaring forth the refrain of a boisterous song.

As they neared the place the words of the ditty were heard plainly, and they paused in utter astonishment.

"You hear, Caleb?" said the baronet; "it is about Spring-Heeled Jack, as they call him—that hideous monstrosity which haunts our path everywhere. Listen! It is encored. Let us hear it out."

In response to loud shouts of applause and laughter, and banging of pewter pots on tables, the man with the stentorian voice once more sang out the words to a quaint, rude melody:—

"The constables boast of their valorous hearts,
And their merry deeds under the moon;
But there's a sly dog among them just now—
That scatters them off pretty soon!

'We'll take him in charge for a rascally knave—
Come on lads—come, no holding back!
Ha—ha! in a crack,
Comes Jack—Spring-Heeled Jack,
And away goes the curs in a pack!

'There's many a lass and many a lad
Gets robbed on the dark highway;
But there's never a one, living under the sun,
Can call Jack a thief, anyway."

The thieves, like the constables, boast of their pluck,
How they'll lay him right soon on his back!
Ha—ha! in a crack,
Comes Jack—Spring-Heeled Jack,
And away go the curs in a pack!"

SPRING-HEELED JACK,
THE TERROR OF LONDON.

By the Author of "TURNPIKE DICK, the Star of the Road."

"CONSTANCE MARFIELD! CONSENT NOT TO THIS UNHOLY SERVICE!" SAID SPRING-HEELED JACK.

No. 8.

"Curse that fellow!" said Sir Roland, as he dismounted and prepared to enter the inn with Caleb. "He's getting too much for us. I'd give a thousand pounds if I could find a man to destroy him or fathom that mystery."

Ah! there were many who thought the same, Sir Roland Ashton.

But who succeeded?

"I'm afraid all the thousands in the world will never find out the mystery," said Caleb, with a growl; "and if people are going to sing about him, and make him popular, his pranks and antics will become worse than ever.

They had intended to go into the room for refreshment.

But one glance around determined them not to do so.

Within were such a rough crowd that the place was nearly crammed full; while near the fire were two men, dressed all in black, one of whom had been roaring out the rude ditty we have given above.

These, though they were not masked, were evidently members of the Black Brotherhood.

"I don't like the look of that crew," said Sir Roland, as they paused an instant at the door. "We'll have something warm at the bar, and then we'll ride home as fast as we can. Over supper I have something of importance to tell you."

And so, in a few moments, master and man were riding off again, full of their villainous schemes.

CHAPTER XXIII.

DAISY AND HER ENEMIES—THE LONE FARM AT BERKHAMPSTEAD— THE MURDER.

BEFORE a roaring fire and an ample supper at Ashton Hall the ruffian baronet and his associate forgot for a time the terrible adventures of the night.

That is to say, they forgot the awful part of it—the tendency which it had to utterly unsettle their future.

"Caleb," said Sir Roland, "I'm almost obliged to believe that you know something about the disappearance of that money from my room in the west wing."

Caleb was silent.

"Well," he thought to himself, "perhaps it would be as well to tell him; and yet if I do he may send me flying."

He glanced up at his master's face resolutely.

"I wonder what he means?" he thought, as he saw the enquiring look that met his.

"Come on, Caleb," said Sir Roland, with a strange laugh; "speak out. Don't be afraid."

"I am not afraid of anything," said Caleb; "but may I tell my story in my own way?"

"Yes."

"Very well, then, sir," returned the steward; "you see since I've been in your service you've spoiled me, and made me more used to good things, and so on, than I ever expected to be. Well, I got extravagant, and—"

His master interrupted him.

"Ah!" he said; "just so. Don't make a long song about it. You've got into trouble, and you owe a lot of money. Don't be afraid to say how much."

"I'm almost ashamed to say how much," said Caleb, beginning to look very sheepish.

"I will tell you, then," said the baronet, calmly refilling the two glasses; "two thousand pounds! Nay, hear me out! What you found in the west wing was three thousand—a thousand more than you required to pay back the amount of that forgery. However, you failed over that; a more artful thief than yourself stole the cash, and you are now as penniless and as much in want as you were before you crept up to the west wing in the darkness when you thought I was asleep."

"I may as well confess that this is all true," said Caleb.

"Well, what would you do if I were to cancel all this—forget that you ever tried to rob me—and give you a cheque for two thousand pounds as well?"

Caleb raised his glass and drained its contents.

"I should think you the most generous of masters," he said; "but I can't say any more, for you might ask me to cut my own throat, and then I shouldn't be able to enjoy my life or your money either."

"No, I shan't do that," said Sir Roland. "I merely wish you to sign a paper saying that you did rob me, and then I will sign a cheque now for the two thousand you want, and tell you how you can earn a thousand more to set you going."

"Pray tell me, then, master," said Caleb.

"Replenish your glass and listen," said Sir Roland. "I am going to tell you a secret which I would not tell to everyone, and which I certainly would not divulge to you if I did not know that I had you pretty well in my power.

"George Leigh, of Lone Farm, Berkhampstead, is a perilous relation of mine.

"He is more perilous to me than Ralph Ashton, for the simple reason that were everything to turn up wrong between me and Ralph, he could only claim the title, for the fortune is nearly exhausted.

"Were I a coward I should say that I had only enough to enjoy myself for a time, and then blow my brains out.

"George Leigh is the one of all the family who has plenty of money, and from him are all our hopes of fortune.

"And, you see, Caleb, his money can be got at without lawyer's fees."

He paused, knocked the ashes off his cigar unconsciously, and continued, seeing that his companion and associate in villainy did not quite comprehend him—

"I have been trying for years to find out where he lived, so our chance visit to Mrs. Barton's hasn't turned out badly. I've found out now. There's no use in beating about the bush any more. Three nights hence I want to go down to the Lone Farm, and I want George Leigh's money. Do you get at my meaning now?"

"I think I do. You want me to assist you in ransacking the miser's place?" said Caleb, feeling ten thousand times more at his ease.

"I do, for the papers he holds, combined with what I have now discovered at Mrs. Barton's, proves that once George Leigh was dead—"

Caleb recoiled a little.

He had no desire for deliberate murder,

"Dead!" he said.

Sir Roland was "full of wine" now.

He did not care who heard him.

"Ha, ha!" he cried, "are you becoming squeamish? That is truly funny. Do you think we can enter the Lone Farm and obtain George Leigh's wealth without sending him to his eternal rest? Confound me, sir, are you a fool?" roared the baronet, who was warming to his work. "Do you think there is any other way to get at George Leigh's coffers except by a knife through his heart? Do you understand me now?"

"I do."

"Then drink and understand me again!" said Sir Roland. "At the time I have named we make our way towards Berkhampstead. I will endeavour to work my way into the old miser's house gently and coaxingly. If I fail then the bullet or the bludgeon must settle it. I am in desperate straits, I can tell you, Caleb, or I should not trust in you."

Caleb had done his inward reckoning now.

"Very well, Sir Roland, I will do my best to help you," he said; "but I know one thing you will have to see to first."

"What is that?"

"Your marriage with Miss Constance."

"What know you about it?"

"I know this, Sir Roland, and I hope you will not be offended," said Caleb. "That Tom Harland, the supposed father of Constance Marfield, is about the place again. That he boasts of the fact that he has you in his power, but that he will not betray you, which I think about tells his own story—he can't."

"Just so."

Sir Roland said these two words inquiringly and doubtingly.

He was beginning to feel uncomfortable.

"Well, you see," continued Caleb, "in one way or another I've picked up a few facts about things, and those facts tell me that if Miss Constance Marfield ain't another of the big family—ain't Miss Constance Leigh, for instance—I'm a Dutchman."

"You're about right, Caleb," said Sir Roland; "and so my plan is this. First we go down to the Lone Farm."

"Yes. That's the miser's."

"Then we settle his business and collar his coin," (the baronet was now getting drunk, and did not choose his English well) "and after that the great object of my life is to be achieved."

Caleb did not say that that would never be achieved.

He dared not.

He thought the more though, as he replied—

"I do not understand, sir, what that is."

"My marriage with Constance. That is the crowning point. Once Ralph Ashton is out of my way, and Constance my wife, every farthing of the Leigh and Ashton money is mine. For we will see that George Leigh makes no will, will we not, after to-morrow, at any rate, eh, Caleb?"

"Quite right, Sir Roland," said the man, with an ugly grin.

"With the money we take at the Lone Farm," continued his master, "I shall be able to put myself right, and give you enough to get yourself out of your difficulties."

"Thank you, sir," said Caleb, "and I can assure you that you will not find me squeamish."

"Very good," said Sir Roland. "Then to-morrow afternoon we will start for Berkhampstead. That business over we must hurry over my marriage with Constance.

She shall marry me now whether she likes it or not."

"Let me suggest that there is one thing which will simplify matters most wonderfully," said Caleb.

"And what is that?"

"Let me obtain a drug—a narcotic, which will deaden her faculties without rendering her unable to speak or move. She will go about then like an automaton."

"A good notion," said the baronet, smiling.

The idea just suited him.

There was something delightful in the notion of having her entirely in his power—in marrying her while she was unable to offer any resistance—at the notion that she would wake up in the morning to the fact that she was his wife irrevocably.

"Then I will go to London on the day before that fixed for the ceremony, and procure the necessary drug," said his accomplice. "I know exactly where to obtain it."

"Here's to our success, then," said the baronet, as he refilled their glasses.

The two villains accordingly pledged each other in bumpers,[64] and then separated for the night.

On the next day, at the appointed hour, they took the coach, and were soon en route for Berkhampstead.

They did not go straight to their destination, however.

That would have been wilfully placing themselves in peril.

They quitted the coach at Houghton, and, after showing themselves at the Sun there, doubled back on the London road, and then began to cross the fields.

It was, of course, by far the longest way, and they knew that it would be early morning before they reached the old place.

But for this they did not care.

They were well aware that such an adventure as that on which they were about to start could not be carried out all at once in a rush.

They must have time to reconnoitre, and so forth.

On reaching the town and entering, which they did considerably after midnight, they made some alterations in their attire and general appearance.

Both Caleb and Sir Roland put on false beards and round caps, and hid their overcoats in a clump of trees by the roadside, showing underneath clothes of a far rougher material.

In the pockets of these coats were pistols and a couple of bowie knives.

"I think we've put the people off the scent," said Sir Roland, as they took their way along the lane which led to the Lone Farm. "If anyone was watching us anywhere, we have entirely altered our looks."

"The devil himself would not know us now," said Caleb.

Sir Roland shuddered, and looked round.

"Pray do not invoke his satanic majesty," he said, "or we shall have his imp, or substitute, Spring-Heeled Jack, appearing to us.

"Ugh! I hope not," grunted Caleb. "But here we are; keep your stick handy for fear of dogs and prowlers."

In another moment they had broken through the hedge and were making their way to the house.

---

[64] Toasted each other.

The Lone Farm well deserved its name.

It stood on the top of a wind-swept hill, with tall trees surrounding it—great poplars, that bent, and moaned, and swayed in the breeze.

It was a tall, gaunt, stuccoed building, that had once been white.

But now the wet and moss of years had made it green and stained everywhere.

Its flat face resembled nothing so much as a lunatic asylum.

Near it were red-tiled farm buildings, where the tiles were broken here and there, leaving great gaps for the water to come through.

A long narrow lane ran between these and the house, and a broad side ditch went stagnantly by, which had once been a trout stream.

Here and there in the house itself the windows were broken and the roof dilapidated.

Within, all was indicative of decay.

The house had at one time been full of splendid furniture; it had been upholstered, in fact, by a London firm once, regardless of expense.

That was when George Leigh had determined to take to himself a wife and to retire altogether from the grip of the rapacious relations who would have wrung every farthing from him and made his life a misery if they had known he was about to marry.

George had made heaps of money abroad, which, added to his paternal acres, made him a very wealthy man. But no one dreamed that George was a marrying man.

He was tall and gaunt, and ungainly, with an odd-looking face, though he had large earnest dark eyes.

Everyone, however, who thought him incapable of love was wrong.

George Leigh had his love-dream, like all others.

Only it came to him in a peculiar way.

He had gone down to a little country place, a mite of a seaside village, and he had taken lodgings at a house of a worthy couple, who had a daughter scarcely sixteen years of age.

She was a bonnie wee lass, a miniature little woman.

At first he took her for very much less in age than she was.

He treated her as a child.

He used to kiss her, and nurse her on his lap, and wonder at the depth of her great childish eyes.

But the idea of love never once occurred to him.

So things went on.

Everyone trusted him with Lily.

He used to take her out for walks on the cliffs, and out for rows in his boat.

At last came a summons for George Leigh to go to London.

It was only when this came that he knew how dear Lily Mayford had become to him.

They were sitting on a bench at the extremity of the garden when the letter was brought to him.

His arm was round her waist, and her head on his shoulder, and he was showing her some pictures.

She felt him thrill and his grasp tighten round her as he read.

This surprised and alarmed her, and she said, quickly—

"What is the matter, Mr. Leigh? Any bad news?"

He turned his head from the paper he was reading, and glanced down into her face.

In that face he read the fact that she was not a child.

And in his own heart he knew that he loved her.

"Well, it is bad news, little one," he said. "I am going away."

"Going away?"

The words to her young heart were expressive of great sorrow, and, without thinking how her action might be construed, she clung to him.

"Oh! don't say that," she said; "pray, don't say that."

"Would it be so bad for you, then, my little one?" he whispered.

"Yes—yes!"

"Do you love me, then?"

And he gathered her up in his arms.

"Yes; I do love you," she cried. "Do not leave me."

And then their lips met in long passionate kisses, and their hearts beat madly in unison.

When they were calmer George Leigh told her what had happened.

A dear friend of his to whom he had made a vow that he would come to him any distance if he were dying had written to claim his promise.

He must start for Paris without delay.

"But I shall not be long absent from my little darling," he said. "Only be true to me— be true to me!"

And out there, amid the sweet-scented flowers, they had exchanged vows of everlasting love and truth.

The departure of George Leigh was too hurried to admit of any explanation to the father or mother.

They saw when the two said good-bye that they were more than common friends; but they made no remark.

In their own minds they had long ago settled it that George Leigh and Lily were to be man and wife, and, though quite content that it should be so, they made no effort to find out how the land lay.

For some reason best known to herself Lily Mayford said nothing.

She preferred, perhaps, to keep her little love story to herself.

At any rate she said nothing, and George Leigh went off to Paris.

He was detained there far longer than he had intended. His friend was a long time dying, and during the whole time he received no news of Lily.

He had not asked her to write.

He had only asked her to be true to him, to wait for his return; and he was quite content to dream of her, to think of her delicate beauty, and to realise in imagination the delights which would be his when she was really his own.

At length he was free to return.

The friend who had claimed his presence died at last, and George eagerly returned to the village which held his treasure.

What did he meet with there?

Not the reception which he expected.

The Mayfords were there.

But where was Lily?

He knew there was something wrong directly he saw their faces.

But what was it?

"Was Lily dead?" he asked.

Alas! it would have been good for him if she had been.

It was not she but her heart that was dead to him; for three months after he had left her she had fled with a winning young cousin of hers, who had only brought his handsome face and fascinating manners into her company for the first time a few weeks after the lovers' parting.

To describe George Leigh's grief would be almost impossible.

He had such a strange way of showing it.

He grew deadly pale, his features became stony and rigid.

Scarcely a word crossed his lips, but what did pass was terribly expressive.

"With her then be accursed all womankind," he cried.

Then he at once set his plans in motion.

He knew that his relations were eager for his death, in order that they might clutch the wealth which he could not alienate from them.

Accordingly, looking upon them with as much hate as he did Lily, he resolved to beat them.

He accordingly sold off and let all he could, and through his lawyers he contrived to amass together a large sum of gold.

He had bought the Lone Farm when he had first felt his love for Lily Mayford, and had had it furnished in the very tip top of fashion; and had pictured to himself the joy of taking home his bride to the old place.

That was years—long, long years—before the time when Sir Roland Ashton and Caleb Masters made their way across the fields with murder in their hearts.

Ever since then George Leigh had lived in the old house alone, save for an old serving man.

He refused to see any neighbour, and, save for two rooms, he used the old place in no way.

No horses stood in the stables, no pigs filled the styes, no cows were in the sheds, no poultry made the farmyard lively.

It was the very picture of utter desolation, and ruin.

The rooms were now mouldy and musty-smelling, the furniture was falling to pieces, and the whole house was as if it had been given up to ghosts.

For years and years George Leigh had never looked upon the face of a human being, save John Dobbs, his servant.

This faithful old domestic was a tall, stalwart man, gaunt like his master, and of such fierce and furious aspect that when he was put out by any of the neighbours who presumed to be too inquisitive they went off alarmed.

He was just the one to guard such an abode of mystery as Lone Farm.

And seeing his fidelity and determination, and finding him in every way true and obedient, George Leigh began to be absolutely fond of him.

Of course it was useless to deny the fact that George was a miser.

He seemed to take a delight in keeping himself without creature comforts.

He never spent a penny which he was not compelled to spend, and, of course, he expected John Dobbs to be of the same mind.

And so Dobbs was.

Only when his master was reading his quaint, old books, and dreaming away his life, he made a little money for himself, so that when the master of Lone Farm was dining off dry bread and a herring, his man could afford a steak not paid for by his master's money.

Three nights before the arrival of the two murderous ruffians in the neighbourhood of Lone Farm George Leigh called John Dobbs into his private room.

It was a dingy room, with scarce a handful of coke fire in the grate, and two flickering candles giving their unpleasant light.

The furniture was massive and good, as was all furniture in the house, but it was discoloured and dirty.

The apartment looked, as indeed was the truth, as if it had never been cleaned for twenty years or more.

"Dobbs," he said, motioning him to a chair, "those letters you brought me last night were very important."

"Indeed, sir," returned Dobbs.

"Aye! the one told me of the death abroad of Lily Mayford. She died abroad—not very happy—and sent me a line to ask my forgiveness. Ah! well, she ruined my life, but I cannot keep back my pardon on the brink of the grave."

"No, sir," said John Dobbs.

He was used to his master's strange fits of melancholy.

"The other letter," continued the owner of Lone Farm, "was from Mr. Fortescue, the solicitor, who had in hand the case of Ralph Ashton. There seems to me, from what he tells me, there is not the remotest doubt of his innocence. And there appears no doubt, moreover, that he is the son of Sir Guy Ashton, and consequently the heir to the baronetcy and the estates."

"From what you have told me, I have always thought so," said Dobbs.

"So you see, Dobbs," continued George Leigh, "I want to make my will."

Dobbs looked scared.

His master smiled.

"Don't be alarmed, Dobbs," he said, "in my will you will be well remembered. Get out a piece of foolscap and a quill, and write to my dictation. To-morrow you can go to Berkhampstead and bring me Lawyer Smith, and the whole thing can be done at once.

The old man reluctantly obeyed.

He knew, in fact, that it was useless to rebel.

But with many others he held the superstition that the making of a will was a preparation for death.

In concise terms George Leigh made his will.

There was no bungling or doubtfulness about it.

With the exception of five hundred pounds to John Dobbs, it left the whole of the property to Ralph Ashton.

Dobbs was more than satisfied.

He was an honest and trustworthy servant, and he could, had he been so disposed, have helped himself often to some gold.

But he had never felt the temptation, and the wish of his master to place him above want for the rest of his life brought tears into his eyes.

"Don't be foolish, my good man," said the master of Lone Farm, with a smile. "You have deserved that and more, but I know you do not covet more. It will do to keep you from want for the rest of your life."

The next day John Dobbs went in search of the lawyer.

He was away.

"He will not return for several days," said Dobbs, when his master asked him anxiously.

"It matters not," said George Leigh; "now that it is off my mind I am quite contented."

On the fourth night the wind blowed "great guns."

The trees in the plantations began to sway to and fro, and howls swept over the whole country-side, like the wailings of lost spirits.

It seemed as if there were some wild and supernatural beings at work.

Though every window and every crevice in the Lone Farm was closed up, a searching wind penetrated into the house.

Icy particles were driven by the wild wind against the windows, where they rattled like the tapping of skeleton figures.

"A wild night this, Dobbs," said George Leigh, as, in a fit of sudden extravagance, he placed a small lump of coal on the fire to rouse it up. "I think we will both have a small glass of spirits to keep out the cold—a very small glass, Dobbs, because too much spirits, you know, are bad."

And so he doled out a small drop of brandy to John Dobbs, who accepted it with becoming gratitude and solemnity, though he was looking forward to a good stiff "nightcap" in his own room.

Left alone, George Leigh poked the fire, and leaning his head on his right hand, gazed into the embers.

As the wind roared round the house, and swept down the wide chimney, something seemed to remind him of days gone by.

He called to mind a wild and stormy night by the seaside, when he and Lily Mayford had crept down to the shore, and watched the tossing ships at sea and listened to the shrieking and moaning of the wind among the jagged rocks.

He could hear her voice again, he could see her face, he could feel the touch of her warm little hand.

Little did he imagine that at that moment there were creeping towards him across the grounds two ruffians who sought his life.

Such an idea would have been the very last in his mind.

He had lived so long free from anything of this kind that the idea of robbery never entered his head.

"Poor Lily! she's dead!" he murmured, almost fancying he could see her face in the glowing embers. "I wonder how long I shall be before I follow her? Forgive her! How could she doubt it? I have wrestled with my hate and anger long since."

As he spoke the wind lulled slightly.

And, as he naturally paused to listen, he fancied that he detected a strange, clicking sound.

What could it be?

At present certainly it was not in the house.

He rose and approached the window.

The sound apparently came from beneath this, so opening it, in spite of the chill wind, he leaned out and listened.

All was still.

Save for the voices of nature.

So he drew back, and was about to close the casement again, when once more his ears were assailed by the strange sound.

His ears were very sharp.

All who have been travellers, used to sleeping in strange places, have acute hearing, and are ever on the alert.

"Thieves, by Jove!" was his inward comment.

He made no outcry.

He knew, in fact, that it would be useless, for the Lone Farm stood such a distance from the high road, that it was not possible for any one to hear any alarm, unless he rang the long disused bell in the turrets.

And besides, the place was looked upon as so uncanny, that no one cared to have much to do with it.

He closed the window, therefore, as noiselessly as he could, and proceeding calmly to the bureau he took out a pair of pistols.

Then, quitting his own room, he walked towards the chamber occupied by John Dobbs.

The wind seemed to make the place haunted that night to George Leigh.

He expected his servant to be awake and ready to receive to him.

He was a selfish man, and, having always lived within himself, he could not understand well the feelings of other people.

John Dobbs had, on the other hand, been his servant so long that he was used to his ways, and if, perhaps, he had heard a cry in the night, he would not have made an effort to see what it meant.

There had always been strange cries since George Leigh had returned from his love adventure.

He had heard him calling out for his "lost darling," and had rushed to his room, only to be told to go back and mind his own business.

So he had got into the habit of mugging himself up with a little "extra drop" of a night, and retiring, quite confident that he would hear no more of the master.

He was wrong in this.

His good old heart had no idea of the heart-burnings through which his master had to pass.

He never saw his sleepless nights, his tremulous views of daylight in the morning, when he viewed again the terrible loneliness of the next few hours.

It had become, then, an habitual thing that when poor George Leigh—poor, lonely George Leigh—retired to his own apartment, John Dobbs said "Good-bye!" to him, and never much troubled himself as to what the morning was to bring forth.

The servant looked upon the master as a slipshod, weary man.

When George Leigh tapped at the door, and finding no answer, entered, John Dobbs was astounded.

He saw before him a man, calm, resolute, and determined.

"Master!" he cried. "What is the matter?"

"Thieves," said George Leigh. "At last the scent of my riches has gone abroad, and I have to fight them on my own ground. Here are my pistols. Come, John Dobbs, let us show them that we are not afraid."

Dobbs rose at once.

He also had had disturbed dreams.

He had heard strange noises in and about the old house.

In a few moments he was ready to follow and accompany his master anywhere.

As soon as John Dobbs had indued himself into as many things as he thought absolutely necessary he descended the stairs with his master.

They went down in the dark.

Neither Dobbs or George Leigh had a spark of cowardice in them, and they were walking about in a house which was well-known to them, with no boots or slippers on.

It was better for both of them if they could only drop upon their enemies unawares.

By the time they had glided down to the big hall—the grand old central hall—which seemed as if it contained a special ghost in each shadow, the interlopers had become more venturesome. They could hear plainly the work of the thieves (for Sir Roland and Caleb were no better), as they endeavoured to work their way thither.

Dobbs glanced at his master.

He knew, like an old soldier, that his commanding officer was right under any circumstances, and no matter what were his inward thoughts, he had sufficient confidence to know that if he followed his master he was not going far wrong.

"What are we to do, Mr. Leigh? he said, as they placed themselves in the darkness opposite the place where a chink of light told them the robbers were at work.

"Take this pistol, Dobbs," whispered Leigh, "and when I fire, you fire also." George Leigh then advanced to the door.

"Who is there?" he cried.

No answer.

"I ask you once more—Who is there?"

Still no reply.

"By Heaven! if you do not answer, I will fire through the door. We are early people here, and do not like strangers in the middle of the night. If they cannot account for the business which brings them here, we generally conclude they have no business at all, and we treat them accordingly."

A rude and boisterous laugh greeted these words.

But no answer was vouchsafed.

In an instant George Leigh was as good as his word.

He made no further remark, but aiming straight at the point of attack, fired point blank.

There was no cry of pain.

Only a hoarse laugh.

Then a furious bashing at the door, the timber gave way, and George Leigh was face to face with his enemies.

Sir Roland Ashton and Caleb Masters.

For even as a boy Caleb had proved himself a scorpion.

Of course, as we are aware, the baronet and his accomplice were in disguise.

But something seemed to tell George Leigh that they were familiar with him and his surroundings.

As the two villains sprang into the hall the master of the Lone Farm challenged them.

"Who are you?" he cried, "and what do you want that you burst into a man's house thus in the night? If it is money you seek you are wrong."

Sir Roland Ashton laughed hoarsely. "Money! Aye! we do come for money, and before we go we will have it, too!" cried he. "Send off that scarecrow servant of yours, and then we can talk together."

"Who are you?" asked George Leigh.

A coarse laugh was the first answer. "I think, as you and your man are the only persons in the house, that I can safely tell you my name. I am Sir Roland Ashton."

George Leigh drew himself back with a convulsive start, and John Dobbs was also similarly affected.

But the two men took the news in a very different way.

Dobbs saw the intrusion only in the light of an intrusion.

His master knew well that it was an attack, not only upon his property, but his life.

"If you are Sir Roland Ashton," he said, "you are the greatest enemy I have in the wide world, and I cannot see why you are here, except it be to rob me or take my life."

"I will do both, old man, unless you comply with my wishes."

"And those are—what?"

"Dismiss your man and I will dismiss mine," said Sir Roland Ashton.

"Very well. John Dobbs, keep this man company awhile," said George Leigh, "and see that he does not move from his place here. After what I have suffered I have no faith in any body."

With an evil smile, which Caleb Masters quite understood and was prepared to act upon, Sir Roland Ashton made his way to the library with George Leigh.

"Do you suppose," he said, when the door was shut, "that I am going to stand any more of your hypocrisy?"

"I am at a loss to understand you," Leigh said. "I can't understand what it is you are aggrieved at. My money and my property are my own to do with as I choose. You are evidently excited, and it would, consequently, be better for you to leave my house and return at another date. You see I don't like intrusion. I have kept myself aloof for a long time, and I am resolved never to unbend to a coward, a villain, and an alien, as I believe, like yourself. Leave my house, Sir Roland!"

The words were bravely spoken.

The baronet knew that they were, and felt the full force of them.

He rose from his seat and listened.

The hour had come.

He must choose now, once and for ever.

"Is this your final answer?"

"Yes."

There was no further reply in words.

Sir Roland took one leap and gripped the unsuspecting man by the throat.

"Villain! murderer!" gasped Leigh.

He struggled violently.

But his strength was as nothing compared with the desperate iron-muscled adversary with whom he had to deal.

Poor John Dobbs—even had he been within hail—would have been useless.

As it was he had been left in charge of a wretch quite as ruthless as the master of Ashton Hall.

Caleb Masters, knowing the great stake at issue, and inspired by the desperate, murderous spirit of his master, attacked John Dobbs, hoping to silence him at the same moment that Sir Roland silenced the long-suffering George Leigh.

Leigh had his pistols ready, as we have before seen.

But the spring of his enemy was so sudden that it was impossible to use them.

As he endeavoured to fire at his foe, the weapon went off, burying itself in the old wainscoting.

Sir Roland made no remark.

A deep sigh of relief escaped his breast.

Relief that he had been fortunate enough to be saved from such a sure shot.

And without a cessation of his exertions, he still continued bearing his enemy to the floor.

At length by a sudden jerk he did so.

"Coward and villain!" cried George Leigh, whose white face showed how the terrible struggle was playing upon his disabled body; "what want you?"

"Your life!" cried Sir Roland.

The grip of the baronet tightened round his throat. Then his hand sought his belt, and his long knife was produced.

It gleamed a moment, then descended, and was buried deep, deep in the miser's heart.

It was scarcely a sigh of satisfaction with which Sir Roland Ashton withdrew the reeking blade.

The struggle had been a desperate one, and he had succeeded in his hideous purpose.

But, nevertheless, he had committed another awful and deliberate murder, and he could not but feel how the crimes were accumulating surely and heavily on his soul.

But there was relief in his heart at the thought that there had been no interruption; that they had not been discovered in their awful villainy.

At the very moment that this idea crossed his brain a cry of agony awoke the stillness of the old house. Turning to see what it was, he saw Caleb Masters stagger and fall.

He had reckoned without his host.

John Dobbs had proved his master, and at the very moment that Caleb bad imagined that he had won the day, and that the wretched man was at his mercy, he drew a small poignard[65] from his pocket and thrust it into Caleb's throat.

The wound was instantly fatal.

Masters fell with a sudden thud, but Sir Roland, with his bowie knife still smothered with the blood of his foe was upon the serving man.

Against this red-hot assassin John Dobbs had no resource.

After a fearful struggle he succumbed.

Sir Roland was alone with three dead men.

But his villainous heart was too full of joy to allow him to act the coward.

Glad almost of being rid of a man like Caleb, who knew so much of his affairs, he began at once to ransack the place.

---

65 A long, slender dagger.

Money and papers in quantities soon filled his pockets.

But he was unable to take all he wanted, and so the sickening task devolved on him of disposing of the bodies. A tedious and horrid duty.

One by one the slain men were dragged down the stairs of the house, every crack of the boards causing the assassin to start and tremble.

At length the ghastly work was over, the signs of murder obliterated, and George Leigh's will destroyed.

But the wealth for which all this blood had been shed had not yet been discovered.

He must close up the old house, as it often was closed up for weeks together, and return after awhile to reap the blood-stained harvest.

He locked the place up carefully, and glided out through a window at the back.

"When I come next," he said, "there'll be a flare in the sky, and the mystery of the murder will be hidden for ever!"

CHAPTER XXIV.
THE FORCED MARRIAGE—SPRING-HEELED JACK AND THE CLERGYMAN—
THE WEDDING NIGHT—THE MORNING AFTER—
A SURPRISE WITH A VENGEANCE.

NO ONE who saw Sir Roland Ashton at the Hall, after the cruel crime which had been committed by him and Caleb Masters at the Lone Farm, would ever have suspected that he had such a terrible thing upon his conscience.

He was just as gay and light-hearted as ever and he went about with such a smile upon his face that the servants declared it to be quite a treat.

The change was especially grateful to Mrs. Levine.

She had quite matured now the plan which she had so long been thinking out, and the confession of which to Constance had caused the blushes to mantle in the young girl's cheek.

The baronet was especially gracious to her.

There was no wonder in this, because Mrs, Levine was absolutely indispensable to his plans.

Now that his monetary affairs were somewhat more settled there seemed no necessity any longer to delay the marriage with Constance.

Apart from the fact that her money was necessary to him he had an eager desire for this union.

Her personal charms—full, large, and voluptuous—were just such as suited him, and he resolved to put the matter off no longer.

The plan suggested by Caleb Masters was the one decided on; a special licence and an opiate would set all things to rights.

There was no longer any need for the Tom Harland farce.

No necessity to ask her to wed him to save a father from the scaffold.

It would all be carried out while she was in a state of semi-unconsciousness, from which she would not awake until the morning told her that her fate was irrevocably sealed.

On the third evening after the shocking occurrence at the Lone Farm, Mrs. Levine entered Constance's room.

"My dear," she said, "the crisis has arrived. The wedding is to take place to-morrow night."

Constance's face became rosy red, and her bosom rose and fell in one tumultuous heave, and then fluttered tremulously.

"Are you sure that all will be well?" she said; "that you will be able to succeed?"

"Oh! yes, my dear," cried the housekeeper, with a smile. "I shall succeed right enough. There is no fear of that. You may depend upon that. I shall do my best, for it is my heart's dearest wish to do as I have told you."

"I only hope that all will be well," said the young girl. "What a terrible scene there will be when he knows he has been deceived!"

Mrs. Levine laughed.

"Oh! I will chance all that," said she. "I will risk everything for such a consummation. I have thought it all over, and know what danger I run in doing what I am going to do. But I care not. I am determined to save you and please myself at the same time."

"And what part do you wish me to take in this farce," said Constance.

"You must dress yourself as a bride, and prepare apparently to carry out the programme as Sir Roland wishes it. Appear to consent thoroughly. Let nothing in your manner let him suspect that all is not as he wishes it."

"But he will wonder at my being so willing, after all."

"You must not appear too willing," said the wily Mrs. Levine. "You must appear to give way reluctantly at the last moment."

"And are you sure that all the arrangements can be carried out as you wish? It all seems so impossible and mysterious."

"The mystery will all be over the day after to-morrow," said Mrs. Levine, with a laugh. "I know the risk is a great one, but I do not mind that."

On the following day Sir Roland let Mrs. Levine into the secret of the sleeping-draught, and gave her strict injunctions how it should be used.

"Will she be able to walk about when she has taken it?" she asked.

"Yes, just as before, except that she may be somewhat mechanical in her movements," replied Sir Roland.

"But how will she give the responses?"

"Easily. That will be all right."

"And when will the effect of the opiate go off?"

"Not until to-morrow morning."

"She will be completely in your power then."

"Completely."

"And how soon before the ceremony do you desire the draught to be given?"

"About half an hour."

"Very well," said Mrs. Levine; "all shall be arranged satisfactorily. The marriage, you say, is to take place at eight. The drug shall be administered at half-past seven in a cup of tea."

"Do as you like," said Sir Roland; "arrange all things properly, and you may depend upon it you shall be rewarded."

"I hope so," said Mrs. Levine, with a smile—a smile so significant that it was as well he did not see it.

About half-past seven, just before the clergyman arrived, she brought into her master's room a couple of glasses and a bottle of port.

"Shall I pour you out a glass, sir," she said, "or will you wait until the clergyman comes?"

"Oh! pour one out now," said the unsuspecting baronet, "and one for yourself. Let us drink to the bride's health!"

With her back turned slightly towards her master, Mrs. Levine did as she was directed.

"Here's the health of Constance, soon to be Lady Ashton!" cried the baronet, as he drank his wine off at a draught.

"Here's the bride's health with all my heart!" cried Mrs. Levine, with another queer smile.

And she drank her wine off also.

At eight o'clock precisely Sir Roland, feeling very strange and confused, and yet excited, passed with the parson and his clerk into the room where the marriage was to be solemnised.

It was a square room on the first floor, the window of which opened out upon a terrace.

Already the bride was there with the witnesses—the housemaid, and Job Joskins, and Mrs. Levine.

Constance looked pale and unhappy, but still wonderfully lovely.

She wore a plain dress, and also a bridal veil.

Mrs. Levine, on the contrary, was attired in a dark-green velvet, cut low, and affording a lavish display of her large and well-formed bust.

The ceremony began.

Sir Roland seemed dazed and bewildered.

"Been drinking, I expect," thought the parson.

But the fees were good, and he didn't marry a baronet every day, and so he held his tongue.

Anyone entering the room would have imagined that it was Mrs. Levine who was being united to Sir Roland.

Constance appeared utterly afraid, and the housekeeper accordingly had to support her.

In doing so her hand took that of Sir Roland, and it looked as if he were about to place the fatal circlet upon her finger when a strange and terrible incident occurred.

There was a loud outcry of demoniacal laughter without.

The wild discordant laughter of Spring-Heeled Jack.

Then there came a terrific crash, the window was smashed in, and the awful apparition, which had so often alarmed Sir Roland and his associates, stood by the clergyman.

Both the latter and his clerk stood speechless and appalled at the unexpected phenomenon.

No one in the room, in fact, seemed able to utter a sound.

He advanced grimly, with outstretched talons, towards the baronet.

As he did so the flapping wings knocked against the table, on which the wax candles stood, and overset them.

The room was now in complete darkness, save for the feeble radiance of a wax-taper on the mantelpiece and the sulphurous flame emitted by the lips of Spring-Heeled Jack.

"Beware! Sir Roland Ashton," he said; "if you carry out this nefarious plot, your race will be run quicker than if you paused awhile to consider. Constance Marfield, beware how you consent to go through with this unholy service; and as for you, Mrs. Levine, vengeance will find you out when you least expect it."

"You," he added, turning to the parson and his clerk, "had better go away at once. Close your sacred books and leave this den of infamy."

No one answered.

Job Joskins and the housemaid were locked in each other's arms, and hiding their faces as if for mutual protection.

Mrs. Levine alone seemed as if unawed and unalarmed by the aspect of the awful being.

Constance clung to her, gaspingly.

"Beware, all of you!" cried Spring-Heeled Jack, once more in his solemn and terrible voice. "If you persist in going on, retribution will surely overtake you. My vengeance will fall swift and sure."

Then with a leap and a spring he passed through the broken window and disappeared.

"Go on—go on!" cried Sir Roland, in a hoarse, unnatural voice, "we have a taper's light. The Devil himself shall not step between me and my bride!"

"Really, Sir Roland," stammered the clergyman, "matters have taken such a strange turn that—"

The baronet rapped out an awful oath.

"Proceed," he said, "or I'll horsewhip you, and if that will not bring you to your senses, I'll blow your brains out."

The baronet seemed truly beside himself.

His face was deathly pale.

His features worked convulsively.

"Pray continue," said Mrs. Levine, in a low voice. "Pray continue!"

The priest accordingly went on, and in a few moments all was over.

Sir Roland advanced staggeringly to salute Constance.

But Mrs. Levine restrained him.

"Not now," she said, in a whisper. "You are upset—the wine and the excitement have overcome you. Let us sign the register and then retire to the drawing-room."

The register was soon signed, the certificate given to Mrs. Levine, and then the party, with the exception of Job Joskins and the housemaid, retired.

The parson received his fees, drank a glass of wine and departed.

The baronet was by this time dazed and idiotic, but he chucklingly expressed his satisfaction at all that happened.

Mrs. Levine sat down beside him, and he at once placed his arm round her waist and kissed her.

He was too far gone now with the strange drug to know who she was.

At a sign from Mrs. Levine they took away all the lights save one little lamp at the extremity of the room.

The master of the Hall and his housekeeper sat in front of the blazing fire.

The drug, whatever it was, had quite dulled his perception.

Otherwise he would certainly have been astonished at the warmth with which his kisses were returned, and the quietude with which his somewhat daring caresses were received.

He felt intoxicated with delight.

"My darling Constance," he cried, as he again pressed his lips to the responsive mouth, "now that you are my bride, I feel contented. Life will be joyous for me where it was blank and lonely before."

"I will do the best to make you happy," said Mrs. Levine, in a low, tender tone, as she drew his head down upon her ample bosom.

She knew that he would soon be asleep if she could only coax him into it.

The warmth of his new resting-place had apparently a soothing effect upon him.

In a few minutes he was in a sound and heavy slumber.

As soon as by speaking to him and shaking him she had ascertained that he was safe and sure, she gently placed his head upon a pillow, and glided from the room.

She hastened at once to that of Constance Marfield.

The young girl was already dressed for a journey.

"Come quickly," said Mrs. Levine. "I have left him fast asleep. He is not likely to wake now until the middle of the night; but still I shall feel more satisfied when all is over and you are gone."

Tears of joy stood in the face of Constance Marfield.

"You cannot be as eager for my going as I am to go," she said. "I am quite ready."

"Have you sufficient money?"

"Yes, thank you."

"And you are decided as to where you are going?"

"Yes."

"Then let us lose no time," said Mrs. Levine. "I shall see you as far as the Corner Pin and into the coach. As this is Sir Roland's wedding night," she added, with a laugh, "no one will think of disturbing him. So we will pass through the drawing-room where he slumbers, and go through the French windows on to the terrace. By these means no one will see us go out, and no one will even suspect our absence.

"Lead on. I am entirely in your hands," said Constance. "I am only anxious to be away."

Mrs. Levine said no more, but eagerly, though cautiously, passed out of the room.

They descended the stairs noiselessly, and, passing through the room where Sir Roland slept still soundly, went out on the terrace.

No one was about.

The moon was shining brightly, and they could see around them an immense distance.

But to all appearance not a living being was anywhere to be found.

The two women eagerly descended the steps, crossed the broad gravel path, and hurried across the grounds in the direction of the Lodge, where Harry Banks and Daisy Leigh had seen Sir Roland Ashton ride by.

They did not pass the little house, however.

Even at this hour they dreaded discovery if they attempted to open the gates with Mrs. Levine's duplicate key.

So they swerved slightly to the left, and making their way through some shrubbery they found a gap in the hedge and passed into the high road.

Still all was quiet and lonely.

The distance to the Corner Pin Tavern was not great, and at length they reached it in time to see the coach come swinging up for its ten minutes stoppage, ere it dashed off again on its last stage.

The task of booking a seat was an easy one, and Mrs. Levine bade Constance adieu.

"I dread your going back," said the young girl, kindly, to the woman who had been so cruel to her, save at the last moment, and then only changed from motives of self interest.

"Why?"

"Because I am sure harm will come of it."

Mrs. Levine laughed.

"There is some danger, I admit," she said; "but then it is worth some risk to be Lady Ashton."

And after kissing the girl, who was going away alone into the wide—wide world, she hastened away.

Scarcely had she passed a few hundred yards along the lane when the now well-known laugh, was heard—

"Ha! ha! ha!"

The woman heard it, glanced back, and saw Spring-Heeled Jack come leaping over the hedge.

She uttered a shrill cry of fear and cowered down, in the road.

But it was not to her that Spring-Heeled Jack devoted his attentions.

He went leaping and springing towards the stage-coach, on arriving near which he was greeted by a loud scream of terror.

Those on the top doubled themselves up in as small a compass as possible and hid their faces; those within, consisting only of two ladies besides Constance Marfield, fainted clean away as the awful apparition came to the door.

Constance herself felt a terrible sinking of the heart and an inclination to contract herself into the smallest possible space.

But, nevertheless, she did not lose her senses.

"Constance Marfield," said Spring-Heeled Jack, as he stood there, with his glaring eyeballs and sulphurous-breathing mouth, "fear not! I mean you no harm. You have taken my advice and fled from that house of iniquity before it is too late. If you desire to see Ralph Ashton, be at the Queen's Arms, near Sadler's Wells, to-morrow night at eight. Ask for John Gray and you will have good tidings. Meanwhile, be brave and patient, and be sure that Spring-Heeled Jack is watching over you."

The young girl made no reply.

All this had taken but a moment.

But it was some time before the spectators of the scene were sufficiently recovered to pursue their ordinary avocations.

At length, however, by the administration of stimulants, the two ladies within the vehicle were aroused to consciousness.

The driver and the guard were restored to something like common sense, and the travellers on the roof felt brave enough once more to glance around them.

A general rush was then made to the bar of the inn by the male part of the company, where sundry cups of strong waters were partaken of amid disjointed exclamations and wondering comments upon the astounding apparition they had witnessed.

At length, however, the driver and guard mustered up courage again to make another start, and presently, the travellers having been mustered together, the mail coach was swinging away towards London.

Meanwhile Mrs. Levine hastened back with all speed in the direction of the Hall.

Her heart was in a strange flutter of mingled triumph and fear.

She had played a bold and desperate game.

SPRING-HEELED JACK,
THE TERROR OF LONDON.

UP WENT SPRING-HEELED JACK INTO THE AIR AND THEN PERCHED BEHIND JACOB.

And—for the moment—she had succeeded.

Although she felt sure that this mysterious being was friendly, that he meant to do her good, she could not avoid feeling an awe in his presence—an awe which prevented her from speaking.

She was pleased, in spite of the glad tidings that he brought, when he took a step backwards, leaped over the steaming, snorting horses, and disappeared.

But would the result be what she anticipated?

Everything appeared to favour her.

Not a human being had, to all appearance, seen her departure and return, and Sir Roland Ashton was still sleeping heavily, just as she had left him.

A smile of triumph wreathed itself over her lips.

"All goes well," she said, to herself; "my plot has succeeded so far. But when he wakes and finds who is really his bride, how will he take it? What storm of passion shall I not have to endure?"

She passed gently from the room and dismissed the servants to bed, telling them that she would take Sir Roland's supper into his room.

When the baronet awoke in his bedroom in the grey of the morning, after a sleep full of strange visions, he saw that he was not alone.

Lying beside him, fast asleep, was the form of his bride.

But what did it mean?

Had he suddenly gone mad?

Where were the fair tresses of Constance?

Those dark, waving locks belonged surely to another.

The sleeper's back was turned towards him, and, raising himself on his elbow, he leaned over and took a glance at the sleeper's face.

He drew back in dismay.

It was that of Mrs. Levine.

"What mad thing is this?" he muttered, lying back on his pillow.

Then, as he lay still, trying to recall the events of the previous evening, he saw a paper pinned to the curtain of the bed near the watch pocket.

He seized this eagerly, turned up the lamp and read it.

It was a marriage certificate between Sir Roland Ashton and Constance Ruth Levine, widow.

A demoniacal smile overspread the features of the baronet.

"She has tricked me somehow," he said; "but I will trick her in return. She shall think that I accept my fate; but the day will come when she will regret this hour. She has courted death by this fatal victory of hers. However, I will dissemble. I will meet her craft with cunning as deep. She shall have her own way. She shall reign as mistress of the Hall for a brief space of time, and then, swiftly and surely, the blow will fall. Constance Marfield shall be mine yet."

At first the idea of marriage with his ward had only occurred to him as the means of securing to himself the property.

Since then the idea had developed itself in a different way.

He had noted her charms of person, and his wish to make her his wife was now founded on a double feeling of interest and passion.

Never, perhaps, in her life, had Constance Marfield been in greater danger, as regarded Sir Roland's plans and desires, than at this moment, when he awoke to find Mrs. Levine lying by his side, installed by her clever and mysterious ruse as Lady Ashton.

CHAPTER XXV.
DAISY LEIGH ONCE MORE—THE HAUNTED COTTAGE.

JOE DIMITY'S next "pitch," after leaving Barnet, was at Weybridge.

This was not taking Daisy very far out of danger, it is true.

"But," as he was fond of quoting, because, he said, it so exactly suited his case always, "needs must when the devil drives."

"And he's always driving me," he would say, with a queer little comical smile.

The old posters were now all used up, and the fresh ones flaunted on the caravan and the wails of the village, announcing the new "star," Lottie Day.

This was perilous work, since the baronet knew that this was her assumed name for stage purposes.

But the whole company was on guard.

Little Daisy had become the pet of the troupe, and every one in the caravan was one of her bodyguard.

She seemed to grow prettier every day.

The sorrow at the loss of her father was wearing off now, as such sorrows will.

Her eyes were lighter and more unclouded, while the exercise of dancing, which Maria was teaching her, was giving grace and firmness to her lower limbs.

Her appearance on the stage always created a good first impression, and she always went off amid a perfect roar of applause.

"That girl's worth her weight in gold," Joe Dimity would say.

And Harry Banks would sigh like a furnace, and think what a foolish girl she was not to accept him as a husband, so that they could go to London and try their fate on the legitimate boards.

Poor Harry!

He knew she was not for him.

But he couldn't help loving her, and would have protected her with his life.

She had good need of protection.

Robert Tugwell, though outwardly a friend to all in the show, and a most diligent servant, was a never-failing spy.

Every little incident was faithfully reported to Sir Roland.

His letters were in some cases exaggerated, just, as he expressed it, "to keep up the game."

But he told every word which seemed to suggest a change of ground; and Sir Roland was able to shape his plans accordingly.

Sir Roland had no wish to be in a hurry.

He preferred maturing his plans.

He had fallen in with his fate, apparently, with cool nonchalance.

In fact, except in one sense, matters were little altered at the hall.

Mrs. Levine was now no longer housekeeper.

She was Lady Ashton, and his wife.

So, for a time, he accepted her as a companion, until he could mature his other plans, in spite of the confession she had made that she had drugged his wine, and forged a letter to the parson, getting the name altered in the special license he brought in his pocket.

She took to her position well.

By caresses and endearments she endeavoured to coax him out of his secrets.

But it was useless.

He treated her in every way as a wife, but his black heart was a sealed book.

His plans, as regarded Constance Marfield and Daisy Leigh, were kept hidden in his own heart.

He was well aware that his wife would not be the one to aid him in anything which would tend to lessen her own power.

To ask Mrs. Levine (or as we must now continue to call her Lady Ashton) to assist him in any scheme having regard to Constance or Daisy Leigh would be ridiculous.

Accordingly he made no sign.

Certainly he had no fault to find with the new Lady Ashton in many ways.

She was good-looking, possessed a splendid figure, which, in her new style of dress, showed to its best advantage, and altogether behaved herself in the household as one upon whom her new dignity sat well.

So, yielding to the influence outwardly, and pretending to accord her all the respect which was due to her, he was secretly plotting against her; arranging so that she should serve his purpose for a time, and then be flung aside swiftly as soon as it suited him.

His fury at the escape of Constance Marfield was intense.

But even this he kept under.

He secretly sent messengers in every direction to discover her whereabouts.

In vain.

Wherever she was she was so well concealed that it was out of all question that he would be able to find her.

In regard to Daisy he was kept well informed, as we have said, by Robert Tugwell.

She could wait.

He always knew exactly in what place she was, and, consequently, there was no need to precipitate matters.

Yet it turned out in the contrary way.

Robert Tugwell had spent all his ready money, and was longing for more.

So one morning by the first post there arrived a letter for Sir Roland.

It was very brief, but lo the purpose—

> "RESPECTED SIR,—*The Dimity lot are talking about going abroad. We shan't stay long at Weybridge. I haven't had time to take the place you asked me to look out for, but I have seen a place just like what you wanted. It's an old cottage just in the middle of a wood. It's called Lilac Lodge, and it's supposed to be haunted. If you want the job done it had better be done at once, for I don't know, where we may be in a week.*
>   *"Your obedient servant,*
>   *"ROBERT TUGWELL.*
> *"P.S.—A little money would be acceptable, as I have run quite short."*

The baronet smiled at the last words.

"Run short, eh?" he thought; "why, I don't suppose the fellow ever had so much money for spending purposes in all his life before. But it's no use grumbling. If you deal with such people you must expect to pay through the nose."

The reply went down at once—

"I will be down to-morrow night. I enclose a fiver.[66] *Try and arrange about the cottage."*

On the following day Sir Roland went out for a ride alone.

He said he only intended to ride over to South gate on business, and return for lunch.

But, of course, this was pretence.

As soon as he had got well out of range of Ashton Hall he turned his horse's head, and, putting spurs to his steed, he dashed off furiously.

The way to his destination was not very long.

But he was eager and impatient.

He was eager to see Daisy, even if he was unable to compass her destruction yet.

His passion for Constance Marfield was mingled with a mercenary feeling—a feeling that he would by securing her, secure also a certainty of the property, without any possible rivals springing up to oust him from his post.

The housekeeper who had forced herself into the position of Lady Ashton had no hold upon him whatever—not even her life was safe in his hands.

But towards Daisy he experienced a different feeling altogether.

Her gentle grace, her childish beauty, her budding charms, had roused in him a mad passion, which was not dulled or in any way affected by the knowledge that she was to be devoted to certain death.

Ralph Ashton he regarded as an obstacle which would soon be got rid of by the ordinary course of law. Constance could be secured by marriage.

But poor little Daisy, heiress to wealth which she knew not of, was a far more dangerous opponent.

All these things coursed through his brain as he rode swiftly along towards Weybridge.

There was another thought that occurred to his mind, and that was a most disquieting one.

Where was Spring-Heeled Jack, and would he, as before, interfere just at the moment when he was in the presence of the one for whom he had such a mad passion?

As he rode along swiftly through lanes and highways he kept glancing round him to see if any signs of the mysterious being was to be observed.

But no.

Spring-Heeled Jack seemed for the moment to have given up his wild gambols in the vicinity.

The country-side, in fact, was strangely still, and when presently he crossed a wide expanse without tree or building he felt convinced that, any rate, his *bête noir* was not on his track.

Reaching the Weybridge Arms, a tavern not far from the spot where the Joe Dimity Troupe had made their pitch, he put up his horse, and, having partaken of some refreshment, he at once made his way towards the booth.

Tugwell was at the door. That fact Sir Roland observed in a moment, although the

---

[66] Five pounds.

spy did not recognise his master.

On his way across the common the baronet had placed on a wig and a false beard, and, with a slight assumed stoop, he was not recognisable as the bold, resolute villain, Sir Roland Ashton.

Pleased with this proof of the value of his disguise, Sir Roland did not at once reveal his identity to his accomplice, but, paying his entrance fee, strolled into the auditorium.

The play was at its height, and presently Daisy entered.

She was received with thunders of applause. Evidently the audience had already begun to appreciate her value.

She was looking ravishingly beautiful. She had on her page dress, as when Sir Roland had first seen her; her attire was more elegant, but still as daring—displaying the firm, small, budding bust and the rounded lower limbs to their full extent.

"She is distractingly lovely!" thought the insatiate villain, as he gazed upon her. "What would I not give if I could have her for my wife? But the law says 'No,' and, as she cannot be Lady Ashton, and is a perilous obstacle in my path, she must die. Poor girl— how beautiful! I will keep her alive as long as it is safe, and that will be very long if she can only be retained in security. In this lone and haunted cottage of which Tugwell speaks there would be very little chance of her communicating with the outer world."

Having feasted his eyes on Daisy's beauty as long as she was on the stage, he took his way from the auditorium and passed round to the door where Robert Tugwell was seated.

"Good evening, Tugwell," he said, in his own voice.

The man started and looked up. But, though the tones were familiar, he did not recognise him. "Good evening, sir," he said, constrainedly.

There was an abundance of rabbits on his conscience, and he had a wholesome fear of the constabulary.

The baronet laughed.

"Well," he said, "since you do not know me my disguise must be good. I am Sir Roland Ashton."

Tugwell jumped up with a ready apology.

Sir Roland was by no means pleased at this. "You are a very bad accomplice," he said, in a low voice, which, however, was full of anger. "If you cannot keep our mutual secret, of what use is it to attempt to work together?"

Tugwell, who had responded so eagerly because he already scented some more gold, made abundant apologies and sat down.

"How soon will the performance be over?" Sir Roland asked.

"In an hour."

"Come then to The Weybridge—not the Weybridge Arms; my horse is put up at the latter place and I might be recognised. Be as quick as you possibly can after all is over."

"If I can," said Tugwell, hesitatingly, anxious to enhance his services.

But he was wrong in his estimate of the baronet.

"Can!" cried Sir Roland, with an oath. "If you can't do what I require there are plenty who can. So make no favour of it, but say at once. Are you going to help me or not?"

Tugwell saw that his line wouldn't do.

"I beg your pardon, sir," he said. "I didn't mean no offence, only I might be kep', and then if you was waiting long you might think I wasn't coming."

"No—no! I'll wait for you," replied his villainous employer. "I'm not going to return to Barnet until this affair is over now."

"Do you mean her?" said the man, jerking his right thumb over his right shoulder.

"Yes; Lottie Day, as you call her. I wish no further delay in the matter. I'm certainly not going to let her slip through my fingers by going away. Don't fail."

And, hearing a sound of someone coming, Sir Roland hastened off.

The Weybridge, which he had noticed on his way to the booth, was a large inn, a square modern building, with stone steps running up to the door of the private bar, all kinds of indiscriminate buildings at the back, and a long row of livery stables running at right angles with it, though not connected with the general structure.

He entered in his disguise, and in a few moments had got into conversation with a respectable specimen of the "oldest inhabitant" class, who could give him minute descriptions of nearly every place in the neighbourhood.

"I have never been in this place before," said Sir Roland, "and I don't know, therefore, if there is anything worth seeing."

"Oh! well, the place isn't without attractions," said the other. "It has its lunatic asylum, its haunted house, and many other things worthy of notice."

Lunatic asylum!

Why did those two words strike him so forcibly?

Was it that they spoke of an easy way to rid himself of little Daisy, or was it Mrs. Levine, now Lady Ashton, that presented herself to his mind in this way?

Whatever it was he pursued his enquires.

"Can anyone look at this asylum, and this haunted house?" he asked.

The man laughed.

"Well," he said, "you can look at the asylum from the outside; but I don't think that unless you had a very special introduction you would obtain an entrance. Dr. Catchem is a very particular man, and I don't fancy he likes people prying about."

"Then I won't go there," said Sir Roland, "on any account; I don't like prying of any kind. But tell me about this haunted house; where is it? That I suppose has only a few ghosts to defend it, and so I should have a better chance to pry."

"Oh! the house is easily got at," said the oldest inhabitant; "it is in the woods. Only a little place, but with a big story to it. They say that an awful murder was committed there some time since, and that the spirit of the murdered woman walks round it by night, dressed in white, with a gaping wound in her breast, from which the blood stains trickled on her muslin garments."

Sir Roland laughed.

"A real old woman's story," he said. "Who lives in the place?"

"No one."

"It is to let then?"

"Yes."

"Then, by George, I'll rent it if I can!" said Sir Roland; "I'm fond of all kinds of mysteries, and if I could only bowl out these ghosts and prove them impostors, I should be in the seventh heaven of delight."

The oldest inhabitant was highly amused at this.

"You won't have any difficulty about that," he said, "I can assure you. The agent, Mr.

Parker, of Gracechurch-street, will only be too glad to let it to you. The only question which will be raised will be the length of the term for which you will take it. Plenty of tenants have taken it, but a week of it has generally settled them."

"Thank you for all this information," said Sir Roland; "of course, you mustn't take all I say as *au serieux*. Perhaps I may never think of this foolhardy idea again. But at any rate I thank you for your kind information."

Then they drank together and otherwise fraternised until at length Robert Tugwell appeared.

He entered the bar somewhat confused, for he had met certain persons on the road whom he suspected of being on the watch, and he had had to go out of his road somewhat to avoid them

Two men, dressed entirely in black, whose faces were hidden by black masks, and who looked more like a couple of old-fashioned highwaymen than modern denizens of the world.

They had followed him nearly all the way from the booth, and he had only escaped them by dodging through a hedge and lying *perdu*[67] in a ditch until they had ridden by.

"Good evening, sir—hope I see you well?" said he, as he met Sir Roland.

He gave expression to no name because Sir Roland had not suggested one.

"Oh! Barnes, I am glad to see you," said the baronet, airily. "Didn't think you'd know me after all this time!"

"Oh! yes, I should have know you anywhere, Mr. Crawford," replied Tugwell, hazarding the first name that came uppermost in his mine.

"Well, then, have something to drink," said Sir Roland, "and then, if you have time, I want you to show me the way to High-Street, Weybridge."

"All right, sir," said Tugwell.

He knew he was expected to do what he was told, or, at any rate, what was hinted at, and consequently he guessed it was proper to say, "Yes."

The "old inhabitant" laughed.

"You don't mean that you're so struck with the appearance of the place that you mean taking it offhand?" he cried.

Sir Roland joined in the merriment.

"No; not quite as bad as that," he said; "but I am so fond of anything in the ghost line, that I feel as if I mustn't let the opportunity slip. So I shall see this Mr. Parker at once, and learn all particulars. I should not think of taking a place without knowing what it was like."

They took leave of the man soon after, and in a few minutes the two accomplices in guilt were hastening towards the High-street.

It is needless to say that Sir Roland Ashton did not go to Mr. Parker's that night.

He had only made that an excuse in order to get away with Robert Tugwell.

The information given him by the old man had been useful to him.

But before he dreamed of making use of it, he was resolved to wait until morning and have a good view of the place, to see if it was suited to his deadly purpose.

"I have heard some particulars of your haunted cottage, Tugwell," said Sir Roland, as soon as he and his accomplice were beyond ear-shot of anyone.

---

[67] Concealed.

"Indeed, sir, if you think anything of it I can take you straight to it—if you ain't afraid of the woods."

"What should I fear in the woods?" demanded Sir Roland.

"Nothing, Sir Roland; only they do say Spring-Heeled Jack—"

Tugwell paused and glanced nervously round.

He seemed to dread even the mention of that name.

"Tut! I do not fear him, even if he be the fiend he pretends to be; but it is my belief he is the greatest thief unhung. It shall go hard if I do not unmask him and bring him to justice."

This speech, instead of encouraging Robert Tugwell, seemed, in spite of its boldness, to have just the opposite effect.

He kept much closer to Sir Roland's side, and started at the slightest sound.

Sir Roland noticed this, but deemed it wise not to mention it.

They had now entered a lonely road which passed through a wood.

It was pitch dark, and the wind moaned through the trees in a most melancholy manner, so that Tugwell fancied that he heard weird voices and demoniac laughter.

Even Sir Roland paused sometimes to listen, and seemed half-inclined to turn back; but, uttering a scornful exclamation, and making an impatient gesture, as if ashamed at faltering, even for a moment, he then pushed on at greater speed.

At last they came to the cottage, a miserable place, which had at one time, without doubt, been used as a hunting lodge.

But the days of its glory had vanished, and it looked ghastly.

Well could anyone believe that ghosts and goblins haunted the dreary place.

The windows were mostly boarded up. Those which were not so were broken, and all of them were as dark as midnight, or the proverbial wolf-throats.

It was an awful place, fit for murders and all kinds of crimes, and, if report spoke truly, such had been its history of terror.

"It is a fearful place," said Tugwell, in a trembling voice.

"But one, Master Tugwell, just suited to my purpose," replied Sir Roland, with a fiendish laugh. "Come, Master Tugwell, be more of a man, and cast aside these fears. Those who would serve me must be bold and resolute. I pay well, but my service is of some danger."

"Of a truth, Sir Roland, you do pay well, and with drink a man may defy the devil. I will serve you."

The baronet gave one glance of scorn at his companion, and said—

"You have pleased me much in this matter. But. how are we to enter the house?"

"By a window at the back of the premises. I made that all right."

"Good! Have you the means of procuring a light?"

"I never travel without that, because of my pipe. Come, Sir Roland, and let me introduce you to this ghostly residence."

Cautiously they crept round the house, and were soon standing beneath a low window.

"Jump on my back, Sir Roland; from thence you can climb on to the window-sill. The window opens inward. Push it, and the catch will give way.

"And how do you intend to follow me?" demanded Sir Roland, suspiciously.

"I can scramble up by this old piece of pipe, and you can give me a help into the window. My clothes are so bad that a tear or two more will not hurt them."

"Serve me faithfully, and you shall not want for clothes or for money to spend on your favourite drink. Now help me up."

Tugwell bent down, and, placing his head against the wall, made what is generally known as a "back".

On this extemporised platform the baronet leaped, and was soon in the window.

"Now then, there," he whispered, "come on up. I will help you in. Come!"

Tugwell did not pause an instant, but scrambled up the old piping, and was soon standing by Sir Roland's side.

"Now for a light; but stay. We must first close this window."

"And better cover it over in some way. It is not very likely that anyone will be passing, but it's best to be on the safe side. Who knows? Some poachers might be about, and carry some story down to the village that lights had been seen in the haunted house, and then all kinds of inquiries would be raised."

"True. I had forgotten that, and in these cases one cannot be too careful. See, here is an old screen here. We can place that before the window, and then think what is to be done."

The screen was soon placed so as to conceal the light—that is, when it was struck, and then Tugwell produced flint and steel, tinder, and a dark lantern.

"There! that is all right," said he, when he had lit the lamp. "It is not so brilliant a light as old Dimity's in his 'Halls of Dazzling Delight,' but it suits us, and is better for our purpose."

"After all, I do not suppose that it would matter much if people saw the light," replied Sir Roland. "The ignorant bumpkins would put it all down to ghosts."

"They would, Sir Roland, and would not come near the place for a hundred pounds. But, then, suppose these men should not be ignorant country bumpkins, but quite the reverse; that would be rather awkward. I mean people who are only a little, if anything, less knowing than Spring-Heeled Jack himself. What then?"

"I do not understand you. You must speak out plainly to me."

"Why, sir, they do say that there is a band of men about here, half-highwaymen, half-political offenders, who have a strange power of knowing everything that passes. Have you heard about them?"

"Yes. They are called the Black Band, I believe."

"Just so; and I have seen some of them in this wood."

"Say you so? If that be the case, we had better search this old house. Who knows if we may not have fallen into a nest of theirs?"

"No, Sir Roland; I do not think that. I think even they would not venture too much in this old house."

"Light the way—we must search at once," said Sir Roland, impatiently.

Tugwell did as he was commanded, but his heart was full of terror.

Sir Roland drew his sword, and, holding his pistol ready, advanced boldly.

If the outside had been dreary, the inside was forty times more so.

The furniture had not been removed; but it had been left to decay away, or become the spoil of the rats.

The curtains, which were of the richest damask, were covered with dust, and festooned with cobwebs.

There hung bloated spiders where once were festoons of flowers.

The hideous beetle slowly crept into corners, and there remained at ease.

They had lost all fear of their natural enemy—man.

Now and then a startled rat would dash away at full speed; but once having gained his hole in the wainscot he would turn and take an indignant survey of the intruders, much like an old landed proprietor might view a poacher.

"S'death! I think we are safe enough here, Tugwell," said Sir Roland.

"Do you think so, Sir Roland? Well, I am glad to hear it; only—"

"Only what? By Heaven! you croak like a raven. No fit companion for such a place as this. Speak out, and tell me what you mean."

"I mean that it is scarcely a fit place to take a young and beautiful girl to. I fancy she will scarcely like her lodgings."

"True! In thinking of my companion I had forgotten her feelings. Tut! I know not why I should consider them. What room is that yonder?"

"I know not, Sir Roland. Shall we enter and see?"

"Do so."

They found the room door bolted, but Sir Roland and his followers soon forced the bolts back, rusty as they were.

The door creaked upon its hinges and opened with some difficulty.

All the rooms had been dark, damp, and musty, but this one was fearful.

The windows had been barricaded up, the very chimney stopped.

The furniture had been overturned; the chairs and mirrors broken.

The lamp, and table upon which it had no doubt stood, were overthrown, and there were patches in the carpet where the flaming oil must have burned large places before it could be stamped out.

Everything gave proof of a most desperate struggle—one of life and death.

Could any further proofs be wanted they were not hard to discover.

Here on the wall were large and horrible plashes,[68] the deep colour of which told their nature.

The place smelt like a charnel-house, and, as if to tell the terrible history of the room still further, here lay a small white satin shoe, over there a piece of blue ribbon, and further off a small, delicate glove.

"Let us leave this room," said Sir Roland, with a shudder; "some awful crime must have been perpetrated here. Phew! how close the air is: I cannot breathe."

He hurried from the room, plucking at his throat as if he really were choking.

"Bolt the door after you, and follow me," he cried.

"It strikes me that will soon come to be the only haunted apartment in this house!" muttered Robert Tugwell, as he hurried after Sir Roland.

Sir Roland entered the apartment by the window of which he had gained admittance to the house, and, throwing himself on a chair, wiped the perspiration from his forehead.

"You don't seem well, Sir Roland," said Tugwell. "Will you do me the honour of drinking a little of this?"

And here the fellow produced a large flask bottle of whisky from his pocket.

The bottle being half empty sufficiently showed Sir Roland where the man's courage had come from. However, he made no reply, but drank deeply of the spirit.

"That puts fresh fire in a man," he cried. "I feel now able to face the devil. We must

---

[68] Light splashes.

to work at once. To-morrow, in the name of Crawford, I will take this house. I know a woman who will come down from London and set things in some kind of order, and keep Daisy company."

"Will that be safe?"

"Fear not, Mrs. Corcoran is in my power. She dare not disobey."

"Good! I understand. Only women are not always to be trusted."

"She is," said Sir Roland, who suddenly began to notice that Tugwell was becoming very familiar, and wished to keep him in his place.

Fool! were they not bound by the common tie of crime, a bond which knows no distinction? The titled profligate is no better than the lowest scoundrel of Seven Dials.

"All right, your honour. I meant no offence. Only in these things—and in this, you see, I am somewhat interested—I like to be on the safe side."

"Fear not, I will make all right. I will hire the coach to carry the girl off, and will have trustworthy servants down from London to carry out my plans. Let us leave this place. When I come here again I will have it made more cheerful. Curse it! What was that?"

The two men had started to their feet, and gazed at each other with horror.

From the room—the dreadful room which they had just left—a terrible scream arose, followed by cries for mercy.

Then the furniture seemed hurled about, and the two awe-struck men knew in their trembling hearts that the terrible tragedy, whatever it might be, was being rehearsed.

Ah! how often had it been rehearsed?

How often had those vain cries for mercy echoed from that blood-stained room and rung through the house? Was it doomed that the terrific tragedy should be enacted nightly until the Day of Judgment?

Even Sir Roland, bold villain as he was, turned pale at the thought.

As for Tugwell, he had gathered so much false courage from the bottle of whisky that he had become positively defiant.

"I will solve this mystery," cried Sir Roland, "Let the danger be what it may. Follow me, and hold the lamp steady."

The last two orders were not the easiest to carry out by Tugwell.

Follow he did, but the lamp was certainly not steady, neither was the bearer.

The door was reached, the bolts drawn back, and the two men stood upon the threshold peering into the room, unwilling to enter it.

Had they seen the phantom of the victim and the murderer they would not have been so horrified with surprise as they were.

The room was empty—just as they had left it—not a particle of furniture had been touched. No one was there, and all was quiet.

"Tut!" said Sir Roland, as he banged the door too. "Some deception of the senses, and—but what is this?"

As he spoke he held out his hand in horror.

It appeared really and truly to be stained with blood!

At first both men stood aghast and then Sir Roland, seizing the lamp, examined the door.

"Tush! look here Tugwell, and see how easily men can be fooled if they have not courage to look into things. Do you see that patch of what appears to be white?"

"I see it, your honour, and see that blood appears to be running from it."

"That is a kind of cochineal, the little insects in which gives forth this crimson fluid which so much resembles blood. Had we time, I doubt not that we should be able to explain the strange noises we have heard as easily as we have done this."

"I think it would take a precious long time!" said Tugwell, to himself.

"But I have no time to spare, just now," said Sir Roland, as he wiped the stain from his hand with his handkerchief, taking care to cast the latter from him and not to replace it in his pocket. "I have now formed all my plans, and we need remain here no longer."

Tugwell was not sorry to hear this, and prepared with alacrity to depart.

The lights were all extinguished, the screen moved from the window, and both men, although they would not say so, breathed much freer in the open air then they did in the stifling atmosphere of the haunted house.

CHAPTER XXVI.
THE WARNING IN THE WOOD.

"PAH! that place leaves a nasty taste in the mouth," said Sir Roland, as he spat on the ground. "But old Mother Corcoran is used to such things, and in a few hours will make the place look as cheerful as need be."

"I think, your honour, that it would have been almost better not to have taken that house. I don't think Miss Lottie Day will like it."

"That matters but little," laughed Sir Roland. "She will not stay there long. I doubt not that I shall tire of her caprices before a month is out."

"And then?"

"How should I know what she will do? I know as little as I care."

This cruel speech made even Tugwell look surprised.

"Oh! it's nothing to do with me, sir. Only as I am so well-known at the theatre, don't you think that it would be better if I did not appear to have any hand in the abduction?"

Sir Roland looked rather suspiciously at his henchman.

But, being satisfied that the fellow was faithful, he said—

"Perhaps it would be as well that you should keep in the dark."

"I think so, too; until I leave the theatre to enter your service."

"My friend, do not make a mistake. For some time you will not leave the theatre, although you will be in my service. You must remain at the theatre and be one of the chief ones to mourn the young lady's disappearance."

"Ah! I am to play a double character?"

"Just so. You must play the spy and keep me well informed as to what may be going on, so that I may be able to prevent any rescue, and throw all suspicion from myself. Do you understand?"

"I understand, your honour, and will carry out your orders to the letter."

"I shall send at once for my secretary, and it will have to be through him that you communicate. Again, do you understand?"

"I do, and it shall be done."

"To-morrow you shall hear my plans for carrying the lady off. At present we will keep all secret. I will not venture to breathe these plans, even in this lone place. This time I'll prove myself equal to Spring-Heeled Jack."

"Ha! ha! ha!" rang that sepulchral laugh through the woods. "Ha! ha! ha! Who dares defy Spring-Heeled Jack?"

The baronet and his henchman started back in greatest amazement. They gazed all around but could not see anyone.

"Mysterious being," cried Sir Roland, "whoever thou art, tell me why thus you thwart my schemes; who, with some diabolic purpose, crosses my path to frustrate my purpose. Who art thou?"

"Who I am matters not. At the present it pleases me, Roland Ashton, to keep the matter secret. What I am, and who I am, you shall one day know."

"Tut! think not to frighten me with these juggling tricks. I am no ignorant peasant or timid boy to be frightened by such pranks. Tell me who you are, and what you want, and then leave and trouble me no more?"

"Ha! ha! ha!" rang the fiendish laugh through the wood. "Think you that I am to be commanded by such as you, Roland Ashton? You do not believe in me, yet you dread me. Beware, Roland Ashton, your career of crime and folly draws near an end. Repent whilst there is still time."

Again the woods rang with laughter, but this time it was Sir Roland who laughed.

"Be warned by you? Why, if you are what you appear to be, you are the fiend himself, and advice from you would be dangerous to take. Nay! you are but a cowardly impostor after all, and dare not show yourself, but by fits and starts, to take people by surprise. Begone, lest I should discover your whereabouts and treat you as a mountebank deserves."

"Look!" replied a deep, stern voice.

A small blue light, no bigger than that given by a glowworm, appeared upon one of the highest branches of a tree.

This grew stronger and brighter, until it was some seven feet high and four feet broad.

Then, as if appearing from a luminous cloud, the horrible figure of Spring-Heeled Jack was seen, his arms raised above his head, and his bat-like wings spread out to their full extent.

Instantly Sir Roland, who had been watching for this opportunity, drew forth a pistol and fired point-blank at the supposed fiend.

For a moment Spring-Heeled Jack remained still glaring down upon them.

Then, with a deafening yell, he plunged forward and seemed as if he would have descended upon their very heads.

But he passed over them and disappeared in the darkness.

"By Heaven! I have wounded him," cried Sir Roland, triumphantly.

"Ha! ha! ha! Roland Ashton, you did not even touch me!" came the terrible voice of Jack out of the darkness, seeming almost at the baronet's elbow. "Ha! ha! ha! You have done that to-night for which you will be sorry. Do what you will. Remember! you are watched. Every sin which you commit will be registered against you—a fearful list of blackness of heart, but for every one of which you shall pay the utmost farthing. You are lost—lost, and for ever!"

For a moment the baronet seemed stricken with fear, unable to speak.

Then he plucked up courage, and in a bold voice made answer—

"Be it as you will. If I am condemned for ever, no worse fate can befall. Therefore I will not repent, but will have a short life and a merry one. He who has forfeited hope must find relief in despair. So, farewell, good Master Devil—if devil you be. Henceforth we are foes, and I promise you that I will try the bullet-proof of your skin each time we meet."

"Farewell, Roland Ashton. We shall meet again, and that speedily. Injure not the daughter of Herbert Leigh, the man whom you caused to be murdered. Keep that sin from off your head, or vengeance will follow quicker than is now intended. Farewell!"

Another eldritch shriek and the deep laugh, then the whole wood seemed alive with fearful sounds.

These only lasted a few moments, and then died away until the same dread stillness prevailed.

"Sir Roland," whispered Tugwell, "do you still hold to your fell purpose?"

"Firmer than ever," cried the baronet, as he stamped his foot in rage.

"You are a determined man, Sir Roland. But be not rash—be careful."

"Away with all thought and care," cried Sir Roland. "If, as this fiend says, all hope hath gone, then let me meet my fate with the bold defiance which becomes a man. No more words. To-morrow Jacob Butler" (a worthy successor to the defunct Caleb Masters, who had expiated his sins at the Lone Farm in the moment of triumph) "will be here, and you shall receive an earnest[69] of your future reward, if you are true to me. If you are false, your life shall answer it."

CHAPTER XXVII.
THE THREE JOLLY ANGLERS—"NEEDS MUST WHEN—"

"WELL, I can't make it out, Giles. That a gentleman should go for to shut himself up in a place like that when he's got lots of money fogs me."

"I 'gree with you, Luke; but then, these gentle-folks have all kinds of whims and fancies, they takes a liking to all sorts of queer things."

"They never took a liking to me," said Giles, scratching his head.

Nor me, either," replied Luke; "but I heard that this Mr. Crawford was what the world calls a hypocrite—a fellow as loves solitude and melancholy."

"You mean a hypochondriac," said a tall, dark man, who was seated at a little distance front the speakers.

"Maybe I do, sir. I never was no wise particular as to the language I use, so long as I makes myself understood."

A murmur of assent ran round the company, who evidently agreed with Luke's noble sentiments.

The conversation just related took place in the snug little taproom of the Three Jolly Anglers, and the people conversing were men of the agricultural class—good honest fellows, but somewhat rough in their way, and much given to beer and tobacco.

The time was evening, when the grey twilight was quickly deepening into night.

The lamps had not been lighted yet—or we ought to have said candles, for lamps were luxuries for the rich, not for the poor, from whom in those days the very light of day was shut out by Mr. Pitt's window tax,[70] whereby every window had to pay a certain duty. The bowls of the men's pipes with their charges of burning tobacco gleamed like red fiery eyes

---

[69] Token.

[70] The window tax was first introduced in 1696, and was tripled by Prime Minister William Pitt in 1797; in older buildings in the UK, it is common to see windows that were bricked up to reduce the tax. Many felt that the tax was unfair as it restricted natural light, hence the expression 'Daylight Robbery'.

in the darkness.

"I spoke in no ill-will, friend," said the dark man, quietly. "But could you tell me who this Mr. Crawford is, and where he is about to reside?"

The men saw that the tall dark man was evidently a gentleman.

Now, "gentleman" is a very vague term, especially as some people use it. Money has nothing to do with it—manners and absence of false pride everything. In a word, it means the man who is gentle to his fellow-creatures; and so these rough working-men at once perceived the stranger to be, and therefore at once took a fancy to him.

"Well, you see, sir, we don't rightly know who Mr. Crawford is. He came down here all of a hurry. A nice kind of free-and-easy gentleman, as it seems, only somewhat glossy. Well, he takes the Lone—or Lilac—Lodge in the woods."

"For what purpose?"

"How should I know?" said the man, almost indignantly. "Gentlemen with a heap of money, like Mr. Crawford, do not give reasons for their actions."

"True! I hear this Mr. Crawford is very rich?"

"I should think so!" replied the man, with that strange admiration which many poor people have for rich ones. "He has untold wealth—millions!"

In his admiration of such boundless wealth, the man threw out his arms, and in doing so managed to knock over his jug of ale.

Not only was the ale spilt but the mug was broken.

"Dang my buttons!" said the poor fellow, scratching his head. "I'm in for it now. Well, it can't be helped. I must pay for it."

"Stay—stay, my good fellow!" said the stranger. "You met with this accident in doing me a service. Let me settle for this and supply you with some more. Ho! there, landlord; bring hither a couple of mugs of ale for these honest fellows, and take also for this mug which has been broken."

The astonishment of the men was only equalled by their gratitude.

They seemed to think that a gentleman so lavish with his money must be as rich as Mr. Crawford.

They now became as communicative as at first they had appeared to wish to preserve silence.

Indeed, so communicative were they, that a great deal of fiction became mingled with their story.

"Was the lodge really haunted?" demanded the stranger.

"Haunted? I should think it was," cried one. "Why there are nothing but ghosts in the whole place, as well it may be so, seeing the numbers of murders which have been committed there."

Here followed a number of blood-curdling stories that made one shudder, and if a tenth part of them were true the lodge must have been the scene of bloodshed from the time it was built to the time at which our story takes place.

"You indeed horrify me," said the stranger, while his lips curled with a sneer. "And so Mr. Crawford has taken this terrible house?"

"Who speaks of Mr. Crawford?" demanded a man, as he turned into the room. "If you fellows will be warned by me you will keep your tongues between your teeth. My master, sir—I mean Mr. Crawford—is not to be trifled with, I can tell you, and you had as well offend the devil as offend him."

No sooner had this man, who was no other than Caleb Masters' successor, Jacob Butler, entered the room, than the stranger pulled his hat firmly over his brow, and drew back into the darkest part of the room.

"We ask your honour's pardon," said the poor men, humbly. "We only ventured to answer this gentleman a few questions, and I hope there is no offence done."

"Egad! I am not so sure of that. Men in the position of Mr. Crawford do not like to have their business discussed in a common alehouse by labourers over their vulgar pots of beer."

The men began making a humble apology again, when the stranger spoke.

"Surely there is no harm in men talking of their neighbours? If there were, conversation would soon be very small indeed."

"Neighbours! Do you class these men with Sir—I mean Mr. Crawford—that you call them his neighbours?"

"Why not? Are they not his neighbours! They live in his neighbourhood and therefore must be his neighbours."

"And who are you that you dare to speak thus of—of a gentleman?"

"A man, and not a slave. Why should not these honest fellows speak of a new comer to the neighbourhood—especially one who comes in such a mysterious manner."

"Mysterious manner? I do not understand you. Mr. Crawford does not believe in ghosts. He is rich, hears of this house, and, to please his fancy, determines to take it. Is there anything wonderful in that?"

"No; but something more than strange. Does he mean to call up the spirits from the vast deep?"

"Perhaps he does, and perhaps he does not. That is his business, and not yours or mine. All I know is, that finding the house was so cheap, for none of the people hereabouts would have anything to do with it, he bought it."

"Bought it!" exclaimed the stranger in astonishment.

"Aye! have you anything to wonder at or complain about that?"

"Not I; but he must have a very queer taste The house, as I have heard, is in ruins, and although furnished, the furniture is in such a fearful state that no one could use it."

"Phew! What of that? What cannot money do?" and here he slapped a heavy wallet which hung by his side, and winked—"and there is plenty of it here."

"Mr. Crawford is fortunate in possessing so much wealth, and so careful a man of business, who will not let his master's affairs be talked about," sneered the stranger. "I wish you good evening."

Bowing low he strode from the room.

Mr. Jacob Butler saw that he had made a fool of himself,

But what could he do to mend matters?

Nothing.

The thing was done and could not be undone again.

Drinking off his liquor, he hastened out of the house, called for his horse, and having inquired his way to Lilac Lodge, galloped off in that direction.

We have described the way to the lodge as very lonely, but the path which the ostler had directed Jacob to take was far more lonely.

It led down between two large embankments, in fact, was a cutting to save a steep hill to the river, then Jacob was directed to turn to the right, cross over a meadow by a bridle-path, and so find his way to the wood, in the middle of which stood the lodge.

Although Jacob was no coward, he would scarcely have ventured on that road if he had heard the other's muttered speech as he left the inn yard.

"A curse on you as a mean, swaggering hunks! No: a sixpence, although I touched my hat to him as if he were a gentleman. Well, I have had my revenge. I've told you the worst and the longest road, and I hope you will meet Spring-Heeled Jack on your way."

But Jacob heard not the fellow's grumbling, and galloped serenely on his way, communing with his own thoughts.

"I wonder what devil's work Sir Roland is up to now," he mused. "No good, I'll be bound. he has been a hard master to me, although I have served him well. Never mind, I think I have my plans laid to catch Sir Roland, and when I do I'll have revenge for all the insults he has laid upon me. Ill swoop down upon him like—"

"Ha! ha! ha!" The sepulchral laughter rang in the air. A blaze of light shot upwards, and discovered to the awestruck Jacob the horrid form of Spring-Heeled Jack.

Jacob cowered down upon his horse's neck, and tried to urge the animal on.

But the horse reared and shied so as nearly to unhorse its rider.

The next moment, with his awful laugh, Jack made a high bound into the air, and then, descending on the horse just behind Jacob, seized the reins from the now terrified man. The horse was now entirely in Jack's hands, and he urged the animal on at a fearful pace, at the same time shrieking into Jacob's ear—

"Ride, Jacob Butler, ride! You needs must when the devil is the driver. Ho! ho! ho! Your master expects you. Sir Roland is all impatience for the arrival of his faithful secretary. Ha! ha! ha!"

"Mercy! Mercy!" groaned Jacob, who really believed he was in the clutches of the devil. "Mercy! mercy! In serving Sir Roland I must have served you at the same time."

"True; but I expect more from my servants than anyone else."

"Ask me what you like and I will do it," groaned Jacob.

"Obey me, then, and I will spare your life a little longer."

"What would you have me do? Tell me, and I'll do it. Only let me go."

"Give me that leather wallet."

"But you can't want gold and notes, Mr. Devil, and my master will almost murder me if I do not take him the money in safety."

"What care I for that? Let him—it will be the first good action he has ever done. Ha! ha! ha!" roared Jack, at this joke, the fun of which, we need scarcely say, Jacob failed to see.

"I must not part with the wallet," he said, sulkily; "I cannot."

"Then part with your life. Look before you. That is the river to which we are dashing with such headlong speed. Refuse to do as I order and I will wring your neck and throw you into the stream."

This was said with such determination that Jacob had no room to doubt that the horrible phantom, or monster, would carry it out.

"Take the wallet," he said. "I would sooner be murdered by Sir Roland than you. Now go, and leave me."

"No, no, Jacob Butler; we part not like that. You must be punished."

Jacob remonstrated, but in vain.

The river drew fearfully near, and, as he saw the dark rolling waters, his heart fell within him.

On—on—on they sped, until they reached a high embankment, overlooking the river.

Then Spring-Heeled Jack gave one of his fearful screams, and leaped from the horse's back to the ground.

But the horse, with Jacob on his back, plunged forward over the steep embankment, and both horse and rider were soon swimming in the river.

"Ha! ha! ha!" laughed Jack, as he waved the wallet aloft. "Go, seek your master, Sir Roland, or Mr. Crawford, as he now chooses to be called. Tell him that Spring-Heeled Jack is on his track, and will never rest until he has hunted him down and brought him to justice. Hold to your horse, he will save you. Go with the stream, you will find a bank lower down, where you can land. Ho! ho! ho!"

And with a wild yell the horrible creature dashed away.

"Curse me, if I don't think he is the devil after all!" muttered Jacob. "Devil or not I will be equal with him yet, and have my revenge."

CHAPTER XXVIII.
HOW JACOB REACHED THE LODGE AND HIS ADVENTURES ON THE WAY—
SIR ROLAND'S RESOLVE.

JACOB BUTLER scrambled out of the water by the side of his horse, for he had found that it would be safer to get off the animal's back and partially swim whilst he clung to its neck, than to weigh it down with his weight.

But Jacob's troubles of the night were not yet at an end.

No sooner had he reached the shore than he began wringing the water out of his clothes.

Taking advantage of being thus liberated, the still frightened horse dashed quickly away, leaving Jacob alone and disconsolate, standing on the banks of the river wherein he had been so perfectly drenched, and had lost his hat and whip.

"Now confound the beast! I do believe that he must be in league with the fiend also. To think of serving me such a scurvy trick as this!"

He looked ruefully at the dark, rolling waters, and began to think what he should do.

"Well, I have made a pretty night's work of it, and no mistake. Over a thousand golden guineas gone, my clothes spoiled, my hat lost, and gold-mounted whip gone. Then there's the horse—that has bolted. I shall have to pay for that out of my own pocket—Sir Roland will not."

Presently a broad smile came over his face as he said, with a wink—

"Won't he? It shall go hard if I do not make him. I have the key of his money chest, and also of his conscience, and if I do not make him dub up the expenses of this night it will be my own fault."

He turned round and glanced about him.

All dark and desolate—not a light to be seen in all the country.

"Confound it!" he muttered. "I think I must have been misled by that fiend into the wilderness. Surely this place must have some habitations near, and I would give something to dry my clothes and have something hot."

Well might he wish to do both, for the wind began to blow icily off the Thames, and

Jacob shivered again.

"Well, it's no use standing here; I shall be chilled to death."

He climbed up the embankment, and once more gazed around him.

In the distance he saw a streak of light, which he guessed to be some town, but far too distant for him to reach on foot.

Then, to the left, he made out a thick wood.

"That must be the place," he growled; "and I had better make my way there. I hope Sir Roland will not show his temper to-night, for I am in no humour to stand it."

So, growling, he began plodding over the fields, which he had the pleasure of finding covered with mud.

Shivering with cold and gasping with rage, he at length reached the wood—scarcely a place a man would like to pass through at any time, but after such an experience as Jacob had, not at all inviting.

But Jacob had no choice. So he made a virtue of necessity, and entered the wood, humming a song as loudly as he could to show he had no fear.

He had passed on some way when he saw a glimmering light among the trees, and stopped to examine it.

"Surely that comes from some house. It may be the lodge or a farm. I don't care what it may he. Whatever it is, I shall make my way to it, and demand hospitality. I could not go much further; my limbs are completely numbed."

So he turned out of the narrow path he had been pursuing, and struck across the wood.

No easy matter this to do, for not only was the night dark, but, once off the path, Jacob Butler found himself floundering into ditches, fighting with brambles, which tore his clothes, and tripping over briers, which made him stumble forward and fall on his face.

"May all the curses of Egypt alight on Sir Roland's head for this!" he said, as he picked himself up from a heavy fall. "I think he has supernatural powers, and knows that I have lost his money, and so has bewitched me. But what is this? Surely the light is now further to the left."

He paused and looked anxiously around him and then at the light.

"Pish! this night's work has unhinged a brain and set my nerves dancing. The light is much nearer. If I hallo now I have no doubt they will hear me."

Suiting the action to the word, he put his hands to his mouth and sent up a loud cry for help.

Again and again he repeated it, and at last a faint "Hullo! there" came from the direction of the light.

"Is there any path that will lead me to your house?" cried Jacob.

"What do you ask for?" returned the voice. "We care not for strangers in these parts."

"I have lost my way. I seek one, Mr Crawford, who has taken up his abode at Lilac Lodge. If you cannot direct me to the lodge I pray you give me shelter."

There was a pause for a moment or two, as if the man was consulting some one, and then the voice cried again—

"I cannot direct you to the lodge. So come here. You will find a break in the hedge a little to your right. Pass through it and advance boldly."

Jacob Butler at once followed the fellow's advice, but had not advanced far when he found himself sinking into a swamp.

"Help! Help!" he cried, "I am sinking in a swamp. Help! I have lost my way. Help me to find it and you shall be well rewarded!"

"Ha! ha! ha!" burst forth the terrible laugh and high overhead Jacob Butler beheld Spring-Heeled Jack leaping from tree to tree, his eye gleaming with a lurid light as he glared down upon the secretary.

"Ho! ho! ho! Jacob Butler," he cried, "why do you not hasten on your journey? Your master awaits your coming with impatience. Fly to him and tell him how well you have carried out his orders. Ha! ha! ha! he wants the money. Ho! ho! ho!"

Although this strange being seemed so delighted at the miseries of the secretary, he seemed to halt near him, as if unwilling that he should encounter any actual danger. In that case in all probability Jack would have assisted him.

But Jacob was able to crawl out, and then the monster, with another fearful shriek, disappeared as suddenly as he had appeared.

Swearing and vowing vengeance, Jacob, much trouble, managed to find the road again and staggering on he succeeded at last in discovering the lodge.

No sooner did he announce himself than he found Mrs. Corcoran, who was already installed as housekeeper, awaiting his arrival anxiously.

The two had met on several occasions before and knew each other's business thoroughly that no compliments passed between them.

"Well; so you have come at last. A pretty state Sir Roland's in, and you are in a pretty state also. Why, how in the name of evil did you get into that plight?"

"I have no time to gossip now. Get me some brandy, you hag."

"You would not have time to drink it if the hag did get it for you," sneered the old woman. "There goes Sir Roland's bell again. He has not ceased ringing it for the last two hours every five minutes. I would not be in your shoes for something."

"I must wash some of this mud off before I go into the presence of Sir Roland," cried Jacob.

"I know nothing of that," chuckled the woman. "I shall go and tell him you are here. Then you can settle the matter between you, and I shall not be to blame."

With that she hobbled away and entered the room which Sir Roland was pacing.

No sooner did Sir Roland hear of his secretary's arrival than he thundered forth an oath, and commanded that Jacob should instantly appear before him.

"Now, for impudence and courage to defend me!" thought Jacob, as he walked boldly into the room.

"Well?" cried Sir Roland, angrily. Then, pausing in surprise, he said—"What is the meaning of this appearance?"

"Wait!" said Jacob, quietly, and, walking to the table, he filled himself from a decanter which stood thereon a bumper of brandy, and tossed it off at a draught.

"What is the meaning of this insolence? Are you drunk?"

"No!"

And he filled himself another glass, and drank as before.

"Mad?"

"Almost. You would be quite so, if you had seen and heard what I have to-night."

"Where is the money?" demanded Sir Roland, who began to think that his secretary must be overcome with drink.

"I don't know."

"Don't know? Have you not procured it, as I directed?"

"Oh! yes. I procured it all right; but it is now in the hands of Spring-Heeled Jack. Be patient, Sir Roland, and I'll tell you all. Besides, I have a message—a terrible message to you."

"Be brief, then, for I have but little patience to hear you out."

Then Jacob Butler commenced a history which did more credit to his imagination than to his truthfulness.

Never had Spring-Heeled Jack appeared half so hideous, terrible as he was, than as he appeared to Jacob, and never had he done such astounding tricks.

He had by a wave of his hand made the secretary powerless. Then he had taken away the money. After which by another wave of the hand he had rendered the horse mad, so that Jacob was thrown into the Thames.

Not content with this, Spring-Heeled Jack had sat himself upon the waters, and floated down the river by his side, laughing and jeering at him.

"Can this be possible?" exclaimed Sir Roland, in surprise.

"Perfectly, I assure you, Sir Roland. I do not ask you to believe it, for I think I should almost doubt it myself, even if my own father had told me, and he was a man who always stuck to the truth."

"And this message that this impostor sent me?" stammered Sir Roland.

For a moment Jacob looked down, and seemed unable to reply.

"Why do you hesitate?" demanded Sir Roland, suspiciously; "you have not completed your story?"

"I fear your anger, Sir Roland, if I repeat the fiend's very words."

"Fear not; I have met the fellow, and we have come to a bargain."

"And if I had, sirrah, what would that matter to you? I can look after my own affairs."

"Well, Sir Roland, I mean no offence; but, if that be the case, after what I have seen to-night and heard to-night, I wish you would look after your own affairs. I reckon I am a match even for lawyers, but I am not in it when it comes to the devil."

The earnestness with which the artful villain said this made an impression even upon Sir Roland Ashton.

"Nonsense—nonsense! Jacob, you must know that I would not do that."

"Well, I must own, Sir Roland, he did not speak in a friendly way about you—in fact, he was so uncomplimentary that I scarcely like to repeat what he did say."

"Fear not; I shall not blame you for what he said. Take some brandy and proceed."

Jacob did take some brandy, and, as he drunk it, began to consider what he should say.

Then the time came, and he plunged into the matter at once.

"'Tell Sir Roland,' cried this fiend, 'that I know that he has no right to the title and the estates he holds; that he caused the murder of Herbert Leigh—aye! and many others too. Tell him that Harland hath summoned me to his aid, and we have sworn never to let him have rest until he is stretched cold and dead, as many of his victims have been. Warn him that his only chance is repentance and reparation, if not his doom is fixed, and no hand can stay it.' Then the terrible fiend disappeared, and the numbness of my limbs ceasing, I swam ashore, and made my way on foot here. I trust I may never pass so fearful a night again."

SPRING-HEELED JACK,
THE TERROR OF LONDON.

SPRING-HEELED JACK EFFECTUALLY PREVENTS THE CONSPIRACY.

Sir Roland, although he attempted to conceal the fact, was greatly moved by the story he had heard from Jacob Butler.

He paced up and down the room several times, muttering curses to himself.

At last he paused at the table, and having drank off a glass of brandy, laughed—

"This Spring-Heeled Jack, in one way, is a fool. Does he think to terrify me by his threats and absurd pranks. If so he is mistaken. My mind is made up and my plans formed, and nothing, no, not even the devil himself, shall turn me aside."

"Out of the great respect and affection I have for you," whined Jacob, "I would implore you to consider before you make any rash step, sir."

"Silence, hound! Do you think that I have the same cur-like spirit as you have? No; I defy those who threaten me, and by fair means or foul I will carry my own way—aye! and have my revenge."

"Another insult," thought Jacob. "You shall not be the only one, Sir Roland, who will have his own way AND REVENGE."

"I have already defied this fellow, but cannot bring him to book. Now he has robbed me twice, and I will set the runners on to him. To-morrow see that five hundred pounds reward is offered for him dead or alive. Fear not, I will arrange matters with the Government."

"A bargain! You don't mean to say that you have sold yourself to the devil right out?"

"You had better let me communicate with the Home Office first, Sir Roland. A reward for the capture of a man who has robbed you. To capture him alive is nothing—a reward for his death means murder."

"Well, well, Jacob, do as you please; but I doubt not that my vote in the House of Parliament would outweigh the death of a fellow who has proved himself a dread and nuisance to all London. But do it your own way, only let it be done quickly."

"It shall be done, Sir Roland, as you order. Of a truth, being so threatened, you need the greatest protection. Shall I date my letter from here, Sir Roland?"

"Are you mad? No. From Ashton Hall. My presence here must be kept a profound secret. Nobody must know it."

"One does."

"What do you mean? Here I am thought to be Mr. Crawford. No one knows—"

"Yes; one—Spring-Heeled Jack."

"Confusion! is this fellow ever to dog my path? I tell you, Jacob, that come what will I will carry out my purpose. My plans you shall hear afterwards. I must—I will succeed."

"I trust your worship may. You must have spent a fortune here."

"Aye!" cried Sir Roland, as he waved his hand towards the handsome fittings of the rooms. "I came here, and I found this place a hovel. See what I have made it—a palace—a perfect palace! Truly your modern magician's wand is made of gold."

"In truth it is wonderful," said Jacob, as he glanced round in envy and admiration. "It must have cost a fortune."

"Tut! what of that? It may bring me one. Take that lamp and lead the way, and I will show you what I have made of this house."

Jacob did so, and his master led him through a suite of elegant rooms.

"There, Jacob, and when I came here spiders hung and built in the curtains, beetles crept on the floors, the damask of the furniture was eaten by the moth, whilst the rats ran rampant round the rooms."

"It is amazing, Sir Roland, truly amazing, and all this done in a few weeks?"

"You might almost say in a few hours. But more. When I came here I found the windows broken, and all are now repaired with coloured glass. Then the place hath the rich services fit for a countess."

"Wonderful! and what are the wonders in that other room, which is so closely barred and bolted?" demanded Jacob, as he pointed to the door of the haunted chamber.

A cloud passed over Sir Roland's brow.

"There is a mystery about that chamber, and therefore I propose to keep it closed."

"Haunted?"

"The idle gossips of the place say so—but then they say all the house is. Suffice it that I do not care to have that door opened. See that my orders are obeyed."

"Your will is law, Sir Roland, to your humble dependent, Jacob Butler."

"'Tis well. You see I have had strong oaken shutters put here to keep out thieves and ghosts. I think now that I can defy, in this stronghold, even Spring-Heeled Jack."

"Ha! ha! ha!" came the dreadful laugh from the haunted chamber, making both men start back in alarm.

"Keep out Spring-Heeled Jack!" came the dreadful voice. "Only the walls of the tomb shall do that, even if they succeed. Ha! ha! ha!"

Sir Roland drew his sword, and quickly unbolting the door, rushed in, to find the room empty and just as he had left it.

Staggering from the place, he closed the door and fastened it.

"Not a word of this to anyone," he whispered. "Do not breathe it to yourself."

"And do you mean still to follow up this—this—I know not what to call him."

"Most assuredly. The letter shall be written to-night to the Home Secretary and the police, doubt not that in less than twenty-four hours Spring-Heeled Jack will be in Newgate."

Whether the baronet's belief came true our story will show.

CHAPTER XXIX.

THE ABDUCTION—SPRING-HEELED JACK'S WARNING.

THE night had come when Daisy, or Lottie Day as she was now called, was to be carried off.

Sir Roland Ashton had taken every precaution to prevent failure.

Everything was suited to his plan, and the men whom he had engaged were hardened, unfeeling wretches, ready for any crime.

These men had been ordered to attend the theatre and having stationed themselves at different parts of the house, to be ready at a given signal to leap on to the stage and seize Lottie Day, and bear her off to a carriage, which was to be kept in waiting ready at the corner of the Street.

Sir Roland Ashton had taken his seat in the stalls, and watched the performance with the greatest interest, so that he might discover the most opportune moment for the dastardly action.

Daisy appeared on the stage with a light bound.

The audience gave a roar of applause as Daisy entered, and as the Fairy-queen sang a topical song, full of meaning and hits at the aristocracy, and in praise of the working classes.

A song by no means truthful, but it told with the gallery and pit, who applauded to their uttermost.

It was near the time when the baronet had determined to give the signal, and he glanced round to see that all his people were in readiness.

When Daisy had finished her song, she stamped upon the stage and cried—

"Spirit of the lonely brake,
Where there hides the venomed snake,
Bounded though the atmosphere,
Obey my call. Appear—appear!"

Scarcely had she said the words when the other trap flew open, and a yell of horror arose from the audience, for the demon that appeared was not the fantastic and picturesque one which usually shot up before the audience, but Spring-Heeled Jack!

The ladies of the ballet fled in fear, leaving Daisy alone with the demon on the stage.

Almost swooning she crouched at his feet gazing up at his terrible face.

"Daisy Leigh!" he cried in stern tones. "I have already warned you of the danger which surrounds you. Beware! for to-night the danger has come to a climax. There sits the villain who would ruin you for life. He calls himself plain Mr. Crawford, but he is Sir Roland Ashton."

"'Tis false!" cried Sir Roland, as he sprang to his feet. "Seize that mad impostor. There is a reward of five hundred pounds out for his capture, and I will double that amount to anyone who will take him dead or alive!"

"Ha! ha! ha!" roared Jack. "Let them who value their lives keep from my path. And you, Sir Roland, know from me that the day of your doom rapidly approaches. When it comes expect no mercy at my hands, for your sins have been so many and fearful, that to lighten the punishment for them one iota would be a crime. Your fate is sealed."

Uttering a sepulchral laugh, Spring-Heeled Jack bounded into the air, flew over the heads of the startled and terrified audience, reached the gallery, and turned round and faced the people as if he would have addressed them.

But he either altered his mind or perceived that they were too much afraid to listen to him.

With another fearful laugh he bounded through an open window and disappeared.

Before the actors or audience could recover from their terror Sir Roland sprang upon the stage, and, seizing the fainting Daisy, lifted her in his strong arms. Calling upon his retainers to follow him, and prevent any attempt at a rescue which might he made, he dashed off the stage with his lovely burden.

The cry aroused the actors and the audience to a sense of the crime which they had seen committed before their eyes. They rose to attempt to rescue the poor girl. But Sir Roland's men had been well selected, and were proficients in the noble art of self-defence.

The low comedian, Harry Banks, made a desperate rush after the baronet, but was received with a fearful blow from one of the pugilists that sent him flying into the orchestra. And now the fight became general. Blows were dealt right and left, many of them landing on the faces of those for whom they were least intended.

Women shrieked and fainted, men cursed and swore.

Never was there a scene of greater confusion inside a theatre, and, to make things worse, Robert Tugwell had, by the direction of Sir Roland, turned out the gas when the confusion was at the highest.

Luckily Joe Dimity preserved his coolness in the midst of all this confusion.

He had the gas turned on again and speedily re-lit. Then, placing himself in the centre of the stage, he cried—

"Ladies and gentlemen, I pray you to resume your seats. I can see that this is a plot to ruin me. Or, perhaps, the person who has done it considers that it is only a joke. If so, when I have brought this cruel night's work home to him, I can assure you that he shall find it no joke, or I'll have him punished if he be peer or peasant. A—"

He paused, for at that moment Harry Banks hurried on the stage, pale and trembling with excitement and rage.

"She's gone, guv'nor!" he cried. "The villains have carried her off. Old Tugwell declares that he was collared and held while some of the rascals bore her away."

"Who has gone?" demanded Dimity, who, in the confusion, had thought Daisy had escaped with the rest of the ladies.

"Lottie Day!" almost screamed the infuriated actor. "The best and prettiest woman on the stage. She has been carried off by that scoundrel the baronet; but I'll find him out and then let him look to himself."

"Do you hear that, ladies and gentlemen? There has been an outrage in my theatre. You have all been witnesses to it."

"And a pretty set of witnesses they are?" said a voice in the gallery.

This remark, in spite of the terrible scene which had just happened, caused some laughter, as well it might, for black eyes were very popular; torn dresses and tresses seemed suddenly to have come into fashion; indeed, respectable as the audience really were, they had not that appearance.

"Don't laugh!" cried Mr. Dimity, angrily. "A young and beautiful girl has been ruthlessly dragged from my charge by villains. What may be her fate I know not. She may be the heiress of a large fortune, for a mystery overhangs her birth. Be that as it may, I here swear that I will not leave a stone unturned until I have found her, and punished the cowardly rascal who has caused this outrage to be committed."

Applause of the loudest kind met this announcement.

"I am not a rich man, by no means, but by hard and honest work I have managed to make some money. Now some of you may come across traces of this girl. Let them come to me at once, and let me know them. If these traces should lead to her discovery, I will present the person—man, woman, or child—with twenty pounds, and old Joe Dimity cannot say fairer than that."

"Three cheers for honest old Joe Dimity," cried Harry Banks.

After he had embraced the kind-hearted manager, and the audience having responded most lustily to the call, then slowly they arose and departed.

Gloom reigned over the company of Joe Dimity's theatre, for Daisy was loved by everyone.

The male part of the company hurried about, making inquiries at the inns and hotels, but to no purpose.

All they could learn was that a carriage had been heard driven away at a furious pace in the direction of London.

Then all clue ended, and, meanwhile, Daisy Leigh was in the power of her cruel oppressor.

She was thrust into the carriage, the baronet jumped in by her to support her with his arms; the door closed with a loud bang, and the coachman lashed the horses into full speed.

Away they dashed, and soon reached the wood.

No sooner had they entered its gloomy depths than Spring-Heeled Jack's demoniacal laughter could be heard—now from the right, now from the left, now in front, and now behind.

At length, with a terrific bound, he plumped down on the top of the carriage.

The coachman, in his fear, would have checked the horses.

But Sir Roland shouted from the inside of the carriage—

"Drive on—drive on! or, by Heaven! I will put a brace of bullets through you."

"Aye! drive on as if the devil was behind you. Ha! ha! ha! who knows but what he is—who knows? How are you, Sir Roland?"

And now Spring-Heeled Jack leaned over the top of the carriage and glared spitefully at the baronet through the right-hand window.

Sir Roland drew forth a pistol to fire, but Spring-Heeled Jack had disappeared before he had time to carry out his purpose.

"Ha! ha! ha!" yelled Spring-Heeled Jack, looking in at the left-hand window. "Ha! ha! ha! I see you have procured your lovely prize. But it shall never be yours."

"Who dare say so? I have her in my power and will keep her."

"I say so. Spring-Heeled Jack tells you that she shall never be yours."

"Fiend, I defy you!" cried Sir Roland; and thus I prove it!"

As he spoke he discharged the pistol right in Spring-Heeled Jack's face.

The smoke cleared off and the malignant face still grinned on.

"Ha! ha! ha! Sir Roland. If that is the way you mean to defy me I think you had better try another plan. I will tell you good news. The constables have arrived and are on the search for me. Let them look out. Perchance they may meet me when they least expect it. For to-night, farewell."

With one of those wild supernatural yells which had in a great measure made his appearance and disappearance so terrible, he made a sudden leap, seized a branch of a tree which hung some distance above his head, swung himself up in it, and was gone.

"What am I to do, Sir Roland?" asked the terrified coachman.

"Drive on, you coward, or this girl may die. I will soon have this fellow in the bilboes;[71] that will soon put an end to the lightness of his heels."

The carriage dashed on at full speed and soon arrived at Lilac Lodge.

Here they were received by Mrs. Corcoran.

"Ha—ha! Sir Roland," laughed the woman, right merrily, "so you have returned at last, and successful, I see."

"Yes," replied Sir Roland, somewhat sharply. "Don't stand there chuckling and crowing like an old hen, but lead the way to the room intended for this lady as she has swooned."

---

[71] In shackles.

"Or pretended to do so; I understand all about it. This way, Sir Roland—this way. A bold heart commands success, and it deserves to do so."

"Ah, me! I have seen the time when—"

"Silence, woman," said Sir Roland, sharply, as he placed the still fainting Daisy on a sofa. "Silence, and get some wine to restore this lady."

Sir Roland, had he seen the scowl upon Mrs. Corcoran's face, would have doubted if he had done a wise thing to insult her.

She poured out a glass of wine, and throwing back the cloak which still enveloped Daisy, grumbled to herself.

"A nice lady, certainly—a common ballet girl! But she is beautiful, I must confess. Well, well, well! handsome is what handsome does—we shall see what this does."

The old woman, having relieved herself of these jeers at Daisy, set to work to bring her round.

The wine warmed her heart and made it beat with more activity.

The colour came back to her cheeks and lips, and, after having one or two deep sighs, she opened her beautiful eyes and gazed wonderingly around.

"She has come to herself Sir Roland," whispered Mrs. Corcoran. "Shall I go and leave you alone with your charmer?"

"No, I will not speak to her to-night," said Sir Roland, hurriedly, in a whisper. "See that she has the finest raiment and the richest fare. Do not tell her who I am, but state that I love her dearly and will marry her."

The old woman looked up and gave a peculiar smile.

She had heard all about the strange marriage of Mrs. Levine.

"Ah! I know what you want," she said; "it shall be done. I agree with you that it is better that you should not be seen here alone on this night. The violence that has been used to capture her will make her less inclined to believe your protestations or to listen to your suit; it will be so fresh upon her mind."

"Do you think that she will ever forget it?" demanded Sir Roland, as he admired her secretly from a distance.

"Pish! of course she will. Is she not a woman? Give her fine clothes, dainty food, warm wines, and plenty of amusement, and she will forget everything."

"I trust in you," said Sir Roland, as he stole from the room. "See, she is awake."

No sooner was the door closed than Mrs. Corcoran hurried up to the couch where Daisy reclined.

"So, so, my pretty darling," she began, "you have recovered yourself at last? Upon my honour I thought I should have to send for the surgeon at one time. But you are better now. Your cheeks and lips, which had lost their tone, are now firm as in the fullness of health. Take this to drink."

Daisy, who was naturally thirsty from the excitement she had passed through, drank the contents of the glass which was offered her.

It was wine, and naturally increased her vitality.

"Come now, that is better. You will soon be as right as ninepence, and we shall be so jolly together. Have another glass. It will do you good."

Daisy waved the glass away and turned her weary head on the pillow.

"Well—well, perhaps. you had better not at first take too much; but you will soon grow to like it. But good wine should never go a-begging, so I'll drink this."

And in one gulp the good wine had disappeared.

"Where am I?" demanded Daisy. "Who brought me here?"

"Ah! that's tellings," chuckled the old woman. "Don't you be alarmed, dearie. You are with them who will take good care of you."

"But why should I not know who I am with?" demanded Daisy.

"Because his lordship forbids it, miss—that is all I know."

"His lordship?" exclaimed the girl, in surprise.

"Lah! to think that I should have been so foolish as to let that slip out. But there—there, I know that you, who are a dear, good girl, Daisy, will not get a poor old woman into trouble for the slip of the tongue."

"I have no wish to get anyone in trouble, replied Daisy. "But why have I been brought here?"

"Because his lordship loves you, and would make you his lady."

With eyes flashing fire Daisy leaped from her touch and faced Mrs. Corcoran.

"Do you think that I would be forced into marriage with a man I do not love—nay, a man I do not know Never!"

"Think, dearie, think! He is a fine gentleman—immensely rich—a nobleman! Look at that! Why, you ought to be thankful that he has carried you away from those disreputable strolling actors you were with."

"Thankful! Whoever he may be, I hate him for it. What right had he to take me away against my will? They were honest and good people, who, out of kindheartedness, did their best to help me, a poor, ill-used stranger. Let me go back to them. I remember all now. Let me go back to them."

"If so be that you are really foolish enough to prefer a mummer to a lord all I can say is I truly pity you," replied Corcoran.

"You pity me? Then you will be my friend—you will help me to leave this hateful place?" pleaded Daisy, misunderstanding the other's words.

"Nay, child; I dare not do that. You do not know the power his lordship has. Why, my head would not be safe on my shoulders two minutes if I did that. Great men like he fear no crime. They are tried by their peers, and their peers forgive them."

"Then what am I to do?" cried Daisy, imploringly. "I will not stop here."

"Hush! hush!" said Mrs. Corcoran, seeing the advantage she had gained over Daisy by saying that she was sorry for her. "Do as I tell you and all will be well. I have great influence with his lordship."

"You?"

"Yes; I am his foster-mother. Do you see? I will tell him that you do not love him—that you wish to rejoin your friends. Oh! he is a good-hearted gentleman, and will do much for me. Then your pretty pleading ways and sweet tearful face must move him to compassion. But you must not cross him."

"Must not cross him? I know not what you mean."

"Tut, child! Are you a schoolgirl? To-morrow his lordship will come to pay you his respects. Receive him kindly with smiles—"

"Never! The man who so ruthlessly tore me from my friends can only receive scorn from me."

"You little fool!" cried Mrs. Corcoran, stamping with rage she could scarcely help showing. "You little fool! will you not be guided by me? If not, look to yourself. I wash my hands of the whole matter."

Daisy feared that she might in her indignation nave lost a good friend, and therefore hastened to ask what she should do to win the favour of the old lady.

"Why, dearie, there is not much to do," said the old woman, coaxingly, to the trembling girl. "His lordship, I tell you, wishes to make you his lady. Well, he don't like those theatrical things, and wishes you to put on these fine clothes and jewels, which he has had prepared for you. No great hardship in that, I should think."

"Perhaps you would not, but I should prefer my humble garments," replied Daisy.

The old woman looked snarlingly at the girl, as she answered—

"But his lordship would not. Do you think the tinsel gewgaws can give pleasure to a nobleman? No; I tell you it must be done to win his favour."

"Why should I try to win his favour?" demanded Daisy.

"In that you may please yourself, but I warn you not to gain his anger. He is a man who never forgives—a man whose love is a fierce passion, and whose hatred is a rage. Beware! Will you wear the clothes? They cannot hurt you. The jewels are handsome."

"I care not for them."

"Would they were mine."

"I would they were. You are welcome to them for my part."

"Ha! that is all very well, but what would his lordship say?"

Mrs. Corcoran continued to speak of his lordship; for, although she knew Sir Roland had no right to that title, yet she fondly imagined that it would make some impression on Daisy.

"Well, well—what next?" demanded the girl.

"That you will partake of these splendid viands and wines," said Mrs. Corcoran, as she indicated with her hand a small table on which meats, fruits, and wines were spread. "That is all. Surely you cannot object to that. Now, shall I help you to change your clothes?"

"No," said Daisy, quickly; "leave me a little while alone so that I may think the matter over and determine how to act. My head aches."

This request was so reasonable that Mrs. Corcoran would have injured her own cause by complaining at it.

She therefore put on the best grace she could, and bidding Daisy to rest awhile and think, for she would not return for an hour or more to hear her decision, she left the room, closing the door after her.

Daisy waited some few moments listening attentively.

Being satisfied that she was not being watched, she crept to the window and looked out.

Nothing to be seen but the dark branches of the trees as they tapped with twig-like skeleton fingers against the panes.

She then tried the sill, but found that shut and securely fastened—she could not tell how, for there was no sign of bolt or bar.

Still it was so fastened that she could by no means shake it, let alone open it.

She next turned her attention to the door.

That appeared bolted on the other side and unopenable.

She knew that she was a prisoner, and throwing herself upon her couch gave way to grief.

After a time her grief subsided, and, girl-like, she began to admire the jewels and dresses. They were, indeed, of the richest and finest kind, and moved the young heart to longing.

In the midst of this occupation she was startled by a strange voice.

She started up and gazed around.

In the corner of the room was a handsome, old-fashioned screen, and from behind this she felt the strange voice must come.

"Who are you and what do you want with Daisy Leigh?" she demanded. "Speak, and do not fill my heart-with dread!"

"Fear not, Daisy Leigh, I am a friend of yours, as I was to your father, and will serve you as I would have done him had I been nearer. May I approach you?"

"First tell me your name!" cried Daisy, who, after having gone through so many dangers, was naturally afraid of new enemies.

"Hush! speak not so loudly," replied the voice. "My name at present I dare not tell, but men know me by the title of Spring-Heeled Jack."

Daisy's first idea was to rush to the door and scream for help. Then she remembered that whatever the character of the strange creature was, to her he had always proved a true friend.

For all that it was not without some little trepidation that she bade him approach.

Then from behind the scene the gaunt figure of Spring-Heeled Jack appeared, but his face wore not that hideous aspect which it generally did, it was calm, and no phosphorescent light played round the mouth or eyes,

"Fear not, maiden," he said, in a calm voice, "believe me, I am your friend."

"I do believe it. Why should I do otherwise? Have you not proved yourself so?"

"I have tried to, but not always succeeded," he said, with clouded brow.

"Ah! you failed at the theatre, to-night," said Daisy, sadly.

"Not altogether, Daisy Leigh," he replied. "I had wished to save you and spare one for a little further time, but, perhaps, now that it has happened, it is all for the best. Fear not but that I will protect you here. I have a power over this man which he cannot shake off, and dare not defy. Know you who this man is?"

"No; but I have heard that he is a lord, a noble."

"He is no true noble. He is a scoundrel who has raised himself by every class of villainy a man could practice. Be warned, Daisy Leigh, wear not those dresses, touch not the wine and fruit!"

"If I refuse, the good woman here who has promised to protect me may cease to be my friend."

"Good woman! there is no good woman here except yourself."

"How?" cried Daisy, in the greatest alarm. "I understand you not."

"This woman, whom you call good, is by profession a poisoner."

"Great Heavens! then I am indeed lost," exclaimed Daisy.

"Not so. Avoid what they give you to eat or drink; refuse boldly to wear their clothes, and all will be well."

"The food indeed may be poisoned, but the clothes and jewels?"

"Are stained with blood!"

"Blood?"

"Aye! your father's blood! This man, who calls himself Sir Roland Ashton, was the cause of your father's murder. Although he himself did not strike the blow he directed the hand that did so. But fear not; your father's death shall be fully avenged. Be firm. Refuse all that they offer you, and all will be well. Each morning and night a store of provisions shall be placed behind that screen, to which you can help yourself, and fitting clothes shall also be placed there for your use. Will you obey me?"

"I will."

"Till then, sweet girl, adieu! When the hour of trial comes I shall be near to save you."

With remarkable grace he waved her a kiss and disappeared behind the screen.

She waited some moments and then peeped behind the screen.

Spring-Heeled Jack had gone. Gone, but how she could not tell.

But he had already kept his word, for there was a basket of provisions, wine, and some simple but good female attire placed ready for her use.

Of the latter she quickly availed herself; and feeling sure that she had true friends near her, threw herself upon the couch, when she wondered over the mystery until, worn out with fatigue, she fell asleep.

CHAPTER XXX.
THE CAPTORS CAPTURED—OR, THE CONSTABLES IN A TRAP.

"DICK CATCHPOLE, I tell you that we are going the wrong way."

"And I tell you, Elias Grabham, that we are making our way to the inn, as straight as we can go. Look there, Grabham; there is the light. Now what do you say?"

"Well I certainly admit that there is a light, which nobody can deny, but I don't think that it is the light we want."

"You are so stubborn."

"And you are so obstinate."

"Come, come, Grabham, it won't do for you and I to quarrel. When we came down here we agreed that we would go shares over this matter of Spring-Heeled Jack, and I am willing enough to stick to my word; and I'm sure, as an old pal and brother officer, you are to stick by yours. If we have lost a day looking for the fellow it can't be helped, and if we share the reward, five hundred pounds, that is two fifty for each of us, I do not think we should grumble."

"Right you are, Dick Catchpole, and there's my hand upon it. But you will pardon me for saying that I don't think this is the right way to the inn."

"Then you're a fool," replied Grabham, forgetting his peaceful intentions.

Dick Catchpole was about to make a somewhat sharp answer to this speech, which was certainly more true than polite, when a tall figure, dressed in a very long black cloak and slouched hat, stepped from a side-path and addressed them politely—

"I beg your pardon, gentlemen, but I heard—at least I fancy I did—some dispute about yonder light. As I am a native about this part of the country, perhaps I can tell you what it is and settle the dispute."

"I say it is the inn," said one.

"And I say it is not," said the other. "When we left it we came the other way."

"You are both right, gentlemen—both right—only when you left the inn you must have left it by the front door."

"Of course we did."

"Well, that light comes from the back entrance, so you are both right, one declaring it was the light from the inn, and the other that it was not the light from the entrance where you left. So, at least, I understood you. Therefore you are both quite right."

"Dash my buttons if I ever thought of that!" said Catchpole.

"By the Lord Harry, but you are a sharp one," said Grabham; "you would make a first-class constable."

"Oh! no; do not flatter me. I could never hope to be so clever as those gentlemen are. Am I mistaken in thinking that you gentlemen belong Ito that noble body of men?"

"You've hit it again," said Mr. Catchpole. "We hail from Bow-street."

"Ah! I thought so. May I ask the nature of the business which has brought you down here?"

"Not if I know it," said Mr. Grabham, placing his forefinger to his nose.

"Oh! I only asked, not out of curiosity, I can assure you, but because I fancied that I might know something of the matter, and so put you on the right track of the person for whom you are seeking."

"Well, I don t know, but perhaps you might. But who do you think we want?"

"A fellow who has wondrous agility, and is called Spring-Heeled Jack."

"By Jove! governor, what a fellow you are! I You know everything."

"Not quite, but I do know something of this fellow. He will be very difficult for you to catch."

"Bah! Once let us get our claws on him, and he shall not escape, I warrant you. You country folk know very little of what we town-bred men can do. Let me once get hold of Spring-Heeled Jack—a firm grip, you know—and I warrant that he will not leap out of my clutches."

"Neither will he out of mine," laughed Catchpole. "Sir Roland Ashton has put too much on his capture for that. I only wish I had him now."

"Your hands, my good fellows. I see you are men of courage."

"We have to be, seeing the work we have to do," replied the men as they shook hands with the stranger.

"And would you really seize upon this desperate character, man or fiend, Spring-Heeled Jack, and capture him?"

"Only give us the chance. Don't I tell you that he shall not escape if once we get hold of him? You seem a good-hearted fellow. Come and show us the way to the inn, and over a glass of grog tell us what you know about this remarkable fellow."

"I cannot spare the time to-night. Besides, I have nothing much to tell that the whole of England does not know; only I know that he is in this wood to-night."

"Are you sure of that?"

"As certain as I am here. I saw him not long ago, bounding over these hedges and ditches more like a kangaroo than a man."

"And were you not frightened?" demanded Catchpole.

"Not I. As far as I have heard Spring-Heeled Jack never did any harm to anyone who did not propose to do harm to him. Therefore, I do not fear him. But you—"

"Well, what of us?" demanded Grabham, quickly. "What of us?"

"Why, if you have come down to seize him at the instigation of Sir Roland Ashton I do not think that he is likely to treat you with much respect, for he has—or at least it is supposed that he has—a bitter grudge against that person. Whether it be right or wrong I will not pretend to say."

"Right or wrong we don't care. We have nothing to do with the justice of the case. We have our orders to lock him up, and we will, too."

"Aye! that we will. We care nothing about the prisoners' guilt or innocence. All we have to do is to get them into prison, and then the judges can hang or pardon them as they think fit. We get our reward, and that is all we care about. Ain't it, Dick?"

"I should think so, Elias," laughed Dick; "and. now we know that our man is so near us we will make our way down to the inn, and if our friend here will accompany us to drink to our success why he is welcome. That is all I have to say about it."

"I thank you kindly for your offer, but must at the present refuse. Perhaps I may join you later on. Tell them I wish you all the success your high merits deserve. This road takes you straight to the inn—you cannot miss it. I shall most likely meet you again. Until then I must bid you adieu."

The stranger bowed slightly, pulled his cloak further round him, and strode away.

"A strange fellow that!" muttered Dick Catchpole, uneasily.

"What's strange about him? I don't see anything strange in him. You are always so precious suspicious."

"And you are always so stupidly trustful. I don't like that man."

"I do," retorted Elias Grabham. He was a thorough gentleman, for did he not refuse to drink at our expense, and yet warned us about this Spring-Heeled Jack?"

"That's just what I don't like. No honest man ever refuses a drink, especially at somebody else's expense."

Now, these two men, Dick Catchpole and. Elias Grabham, were sworn friends, and really and truly loved each other like brothers.

They hunted up thieves together; they shared the rewards they gained, and when in London lodged in the same house.

Yet for all this they never missed wrangling and jangling with each other.

Nay, they very frequently sulked with each other for days.

They even went so far as to come to blows, but they very soon afterwards shook hands, and were as thick as it is said those gentlemen are whom it was their duty to capture— namely, thieves.

Marching along the road to the inn Mr. Catchpole managed to make himself particularly disagreeable, and consequently Mr. Grabham had retaliated with more than his ordinary insults.

On this occasion the sulks set in, and that to a very unusual degree even for these fellows.

Hands thrust in their pockets, heads bent sullenly down, they walked on in silence, when suddenly Mr. Grabham's foot kicked against something.

He muttered an oath and kicked what he considered a stone into a ditch.

Now Mr. Catchpole's sharp ears had caught the chink of gold; so he walked quietly to the ditch and picked up that which his comrade had so carelessly and angrily kicked away.

He thrust it in his pocket, for it was a bag of gold, and humming a tune walked on his way.

Grabham's curiosity was aroused, but the sulks. would not let him speak.

As they reached the inn, however, curiosity overcame temper, and he asked—still in a surly tone though—

"What was that you picked up just now, Dick Catchpole?"

"What is that to you, Elias Grabham?"

"Well, I know it is something of value, or you would not have stooped to pick it up."

"May be it is—may be it is not, growled Dick. "At all events, it is mine."

"I cry shares," said Grabham, now convinced it was of value.

"Too late," replied Catchpole; "you should have called 'halves' when I picked it up."

With that he walked chuckling into the parlour of the inn.

Now, as the reader will perceive, neither Dick Catchpole or his comrade were pleasant men, or affable ones; but for all that we must own they were honest, at least, to each other.

Catchpole had not the slightest intention of disputing his old friend's claim to shares; but Elias had put him out, and he enjoyed putting Elias out.

The tap room was empty, so seating himself at a table, Catchpole called for a bottle of rum and two glasses. That being brought, he filled the glasses, and with a triumphant smile playing round his lips he pushed one glass over to his friend and invited him to drink.

"I don't want your rum," growled the other. "I want my share of what you found."

"Oh! if you won't drink you must leave it alone," replied the other. "I like my liquor too well to quarrel with it."

And he tossed off another bumper of neat spirits, and then another.

The temptation was too much for Grabham to withstand.

In the most absent manner possible he drew the glass towards him.

Then he let it remain for a little while untouched.

Then he raised it to his lips, and drank off the contents, and filled again.

"That's better. Now we will finish the bottle, and say no more about my find."

"Your find! Come, I like that. Wasn't it as much my find as yours?"

"Most certainly not. Did I not pick it up?"

"Yes; but then I was walking with you. We agreed to share over this job as we have done over lots others."

"We agreed to share over the capture of Spring-Heeled Jack, I admit, but this has nothing to do with him."

"How do you know that? I want my share;" this in a bullying tone.

Both men had been drinking freely, and became heated.

"Then you won't get it. Besides, you kicked it away."

"Then it is as I suspected. I did find it first. At least show it to me."

Catchpole could not refuse this, and drew forth what proved to be a good-sized bag of gold.

How Elias Grabham's eyes glittered when he beheld this!

He was now more determined than ever to have a share of it.

"Come, Catchpole," he said, "this is too good a find for you to keep all to yourself. I must have my share."

"Not a guinea. Ha, ha! don't be in such a hurry to kick things out of your path another time. Lor'! this will be a standing joke against you as long as you live."

"Look here, Catchpole!" cried Elias, now fairly mad with passion at his loss, "you know, as well as I do that you have no more right to that gold than I have. It ought to be returned to. its lawful owner. Now, finding it don't make it yours."

"Don't it? Possession is nine points of the law, and I mean to keep it."

"Now, if you don't share half-and-half with me, I will give notice to the authorities of the find, and also to the lord of the manor, and we shall soon see where you are then."

"You will, will you? Do your worst; I defy you. Go and round on me, old pal."

"You are a nice one to call yourself a pal," sneered Elias Grabham; "you, who will not go fair shares with him."

"Not a guinea! I ain't one to give way before threats, I can tell you."

As he spoke he reached forward to take the bag, in order that he might replace it in his pocket.

This was more than Elias could stand, and he seized the bag also.

A struggle instantly ensued. Both men were broad built, strong fellows, and with hasty tempers.

The bag of gold was dropped upon the table, and they grappled together.

Backwards and forwards they pulled each other, now one seeming to have the mastery and now the other.

At last, from wrestling they came to blows, and fought manfully.

Who was the better man it was hard to tell, for they fought until they were quite exhausted, and, separating, paused to take breath.

At that moment the window flew open, and Spring-Heeled Jack bounded into the room.

Seizing the collar of Catchpole's coat in one hand and that of Grabham in the other, he swung them round with wonderful strength—such was his tremendous power—and dashed their heads together as if they had been boys instead of grown-up men.

"Ha! ha! ha!" he roared. "What think you now of Spring-Heeled Jack? Is he to be so easily caught? Do you think that you will have the reward? Ha! ha! ha!"

And at each question he dashed their heads together.

"Mercy! help!" gasped Catchpole, who now was bleeding fast.

Elias Grabham said nothing, for he could not speak on account of his teeth being knocked down his throat.

"Mercy! Oh! you ask for mercy, do you? You, who never granted it to any one whom you seized—you, who are thieves yourselves."

"No, no, Mr. Spring-Heeled Jack; we are not thieves, but good, honest men, whose duty it is to protect all worthy citizens from criminals."

"Nice protectors, truly. Call you Sir Roland Ashton an honest man? And you would do his bidding, let it be what it might!"

"No, no, sir. Oh! do let us go, and we promise never to take you."

"Promise never to take me. Ha! ha! ha! Why you could not do it."

"Oh! if we once get away from you we will never cross your path again—we swear it."

"If I thought you would do otherwise I would take one under each arm and fly away with you."

"No, no; think of our wives and children, good Mr. Devil," implored Catchpole.

"That money on the table is mine; I placed it there for you to find. I knew you could not withstand the bait of gold. Gold, which is a blessing or curse to man, as he uses it."

"You may have the gold, sir. We do not want it!"

"Ha! ha! ha! You are generous with that which does not belong to you. Listen to me, and obey my orders, or worse will come of it."

"We will—we will! We'll do anything for you. Only leave us."

"Seek out Sir Roland Ashton; you will find him at the house in the wood. Tell him what has happened; refuse the pursuit of me."

"Oh! that we will," cried Catchpole, eagerly.

"You had better, for this is little to what shall happen to you if you dare disobey me; and now, farewell."

Hurling the men on one side, he seized the bag of gold and leaped out of the window.

"He's the devil himself," groaned the affrighted Catchpole.

CHAPTER XXXI.
ROGUES IN COUNCIL.

SIR ROLAND was surprised when the two constables called upon him at Lilac Lodge, but hearing their business from Jacob Butler, who had at first declared only Mr. Crawford lived there, he at once admitted them to his presence.

Two more unfortunate-looking creatures than these luckless men could not well be imagined.

They had bruised themselves pretty considerably in their fight; but that had been nothing to the contusions which Spring-Heeled Jack had showered upon them, or, rather, had caused them to give each other.

Blackened eyes, swollen noses, cheeks bearing what the gentlemen of "the science" are pleased to call "mice," were among the number.

To add to this their clothes were stained with blood, and their linen collars and shirt fronts had the appearance of having been mangled in a very improper way.

The baronet looked at them with considerable surprise.

"Well, gentlemen," he said, at last, "you have found me out."

"Yes, Sir Roland—if you are Sir Roland," said Catchpole.

"I am Sir Roland. Now, my men, to your business quickly."

"All right, your honour; only we have a message for Sir Roland's ear alone, and when we came here we were told that only a Mr. Crawford lived here."

"Mr. Crawford and Sir Roland Ashton are one. "It is a name I take when I wish to be in perfect privacy. Doubt not that I have reasons for it. But who has pierced my secret and told you that I am here?"

The two men looked at each other as well as their blackened eyes would let them, and then glanced nervously round the room.

"What ails the fellows?" cried Sir Roland, who had watched their movements with surprise and anger. "What do you fear? Speak out!"

"The creature that sent us," said Catchpole, "was no other than Spring-Heeled Jack."

"Ha! But you can tell him from me that I have no dealings with him."

"I would not do it for a thousand pounds," replied Catchpole.

"Bah! you need not fear him. I have two constables from London who will soon have him in prison."

The two men shook their heads and sighed sadly.

"Those two constables will never place hands on Spring-Heeled Jack,"

"What do you mean, fellow? Do you doubt my word or the force of the law?"

"Neither, Sir Roland. Constables may be found who can arrest this Spring-Heeled Jack, but not the two who came down here. *We are the two constables!*"

"You!"

"Yes."

"Then what is the meaning of this disgraceful appearance? I ordered—and was told my orders had been obeyed—two of the smartest men in the force."

"And as such we are reckoned. Truth to tell, I don't think any two men in all the body of constables in Great Britain smart more than we do at this precious minute. Do you, Elias?"

Elias groaned and shook his head sadly, then groaned again.

"What has happened to you? Why does not that fellow speak?"

"Because he can't. He hasn't a tooth in his head."

"What has he done with them?"

"Swallowed them. Couldn't help it, poor fellow. They went against his stomach, but he was compelled to do it."

"Compelled! and who by?"

"Spring-Heeled Jack!"

Every time this name was mentioned the men glanced nervously round, as if they expected to see the dread phantom behind them.

"Confusion!" cried the baronet. "Is this fellow always to cross my path?"

"He says he will," says Catchpole, and then he delivered Spring-Heeled Jack's message.

"We shall see to that," said Sir Roland, with a hollow laugh. "Perchance I may be more than a match for him. Return to your duty, my brave fellows; catch this man, dead or alive, and I will double or even treble the reward. And, hark you, my men, if you can manage to kill him by accident you know I would give you another hundred pounds each. Do you hear?"

"Very much obliged for myself and partner, Sir Roland, but it cannot be done."

"Not be done! Why, what do you mean?"

"I mean that I don't think there is a chance of killing this fellow. He is not a man, but a demon from the deepest depths of the bottomless pit."

"What can this man be who changes you from brave men—and such I heard you to be from your officers—into cowards?"

"A devil!"

"A devil! Well, devil or not, I will face him and conquer him yet. Would that he were here now."

Scarcely had he said the words than something darkened the window of the apartment.

The constables crouched down, and in silent horror pointed to the window, where there appeared the terrible form of Spring-Heeled Jack.

"Ha! ha! ha!" yelled the creature, as he spread out his long, bony arms. "Ha! ha! ha! Sir Roland, am I not kind in granting your wish? You desired to see Spring-Heeled Jack, and he is here to oblige you."

For a moment the baronet seemed overtaken with fear.

Quickly recovering himself, however, he rushed to the table and caught up a pistol.

He presented it with a rapid and good aim, and then fired.

The glass was smashed by the bullet, but as the smoke caused by the discharge cleared away Spring-Heeled Jack was still at the window.

He gave one of his horrible laughs and cried—

"Farewell for a time, Sir Roland—we soon shall meet again!" and with a bound disappeared from the window.

Sir Roland and the men hurried to the window and gazed out. They could not believe Spring-Heeled Jack was unhurt.

But they were mistaken. There he was, gamboling through the woods as merrily as ever; now and then glancing up at the window with a diabolical grin, as if he could see his foe and enjoyed his discomfort.

"The fiend is in him," muttered Sir Roland, loud enough to be heard.

"It's my belief that he is the fiend, Sir Roland," said Catchpole.

"And mine," mumbled Elias Grabham.

Sir Roland walked to a buffet, and taking therefrom a decanter of brandy and some glasses, filled one for himself and pointed to the men to do the same.

The two men eagerly accepted the offer, but when Grabham had taken his into his mouth he hastily spit it out, curled up, and writhed about, making the most hideous faces one could imagine.

"Why, what is the matter with the man?" demanded Sir Roland, angrily.

"Don't be angry with him, Sir Roland," said Catchpole. "It's the brandy has burned his gums. That's what it is. Take another glass of the spirit and toss it over your gums, down your throat. It will warm your heart and do it good."

"Aye! warm your heart; you need have something to warm your hearts if you are cowards enough to put up with the insults and injuries which you have received from that monster."

"Ah, the fiend!" said Catchpole, who since the money had gone had quite returned to the love of his old friend. "That fellow is the fiend, and no mistake. It's no good trying anything against him."

"Cowards! By your own confession you have been trapped, and that in a way which I do confess does more credit to his brain than yours. Be more cautious another time— assume disguises, and you may not only have your revenge, but become rich for life."

"Ah! it's all very fine to say get rid of your foe like that, but how are you to do it? I candidly confess that I don't see my way clear to manage it. I wish I could."

"Take some more brandy," said Sir Roland, who quickly perceived that he had made some impression upon the men. "Take some more brandy, and then draw near the table, and I will place before you a scheme which I have formed, and one which I think will be successful."

The men drank deep bumpers of brandy, and then drew up to the table.

"This is my scheme. This Spring-Heeled Jack has ordered you to London?"

"Yes, and in no very polite language either," said Catchpole.

"And you mean to go?"

"The moment I leave here, Sir Roland, I take the road to London."

"And you will do quite right," replied Sir Roland, quietly.

Messrs. Grabham and Catchpole were evidently much relieved by the baronet's approval of that movement, and, to show they were so, took advantage of his pushing the bottle towards them to drink a deep draught again.

"Yes; you must go. This fellow is evidently a very artful one."

"A good deal too artful for us," groaned Mr. Catchpole, sadly.

"Ah! you were duped. The stranger whom you met in the wood—he who directed you to the inn—he was Spring-Heeled Jack, and planned all this."

"Impossible! He did not look a bit like him," cried Catchpole.

Elias tried to make some remark, but, after a few gutteral sounds, he clapped his hands to his mouth, and became mute with agony.

"Lord love you, Sir Roland, I know what my pal would say."

"Indeed! You must be very quick of understanding then."

"Ah! but I have known him for years. We always agree to disagree."

"A very agreeable arrangement I should say," sneered Sir Roland.

"Well, I don't know that; but it works well. You see by that means we get to look at both sides of the question. He goes on one side, and I go on the other, and so between the two we knock out a happy medium, and very often nab the right man."

"And very often the wrong one," thought Sir Roland, but he did not say it.

"Ah! perhaps that is not such a bad idea after all, although I should be liable to find it a little bit confusing. But, then, I know nothing compared to you."

"I should think not," chuckled Mr. Catchpole, delighted at the compliment.

"Just so. Now, what I was going to suggest is this. You should return to London at once, report your failure and ill-usage to your superiors and then retire on the sick-list; you need it."

"We do, we do. Nobody needs it more than we do. Curse the fellow!"

"Ah! he has done me much less injury than he has done you. But I swear I will have the deadliest revenge that wealth and power can command. Now, listen to me attentively."

"We are listening, Sir Roland."

"Good. When on the sick list I will allow you five pounds a week each."

"Five pounds a week each!" exclaimed Catchpole, and Elias clasped his hands in delight.

"Yes—on conditions. This Jack of the light heels goes about in all kinds of disguises. You must do the same. I am convinced that he is connected, with some band of thieves or spies, who carry the information to him which he appears to gain by supernatural means, and help him in his cruel pranks. For all I know there may be two Spring-Heeled Jacks, and that is how he appears to travel so fast."

"By the Lord Harry, I never thought of that," cried Catchpole, smacking his leg. "You've hit it, and you have given me fresh life again."

"Then you agree to do as I order? Examine all the thieves' dens in London—in disguise, mind—and trace out this fellow. Do you agree?"

"We'll have him yet," cried Catchpole, who had grown valiant over the brandy. "We will pay him out for his treatment of us."

"Remember, the reward holds good either dead or alive."

"I sha'n't forget the extra two hundred if he be shot in a scrimmage."

"Ah! it would be sad; but I should not regret it, I must confess."

Mr. Catchpole winked violently, and chuckled.

"Here is a week's salary for each, in advance," he continued, smiling.

"Thank your honour's honour kindly," cried Catchpole, as he and his companion took up the notes the baronet had placed upon the table. "Don't you fear, we'll put Master Jack in a box soon—a long black one—out of which he won't jump for a long time. Ho! ho! ho!"

Was that an echo, or was the laughter dimly repeated down below their feet?

"For myself and partner I do," said Catchpole.

"Good. Now go. Your remaining here longer would look suspicious, and we must keep this fellow in the dark."

Sir Roland saw the men waver.

He gave them more brandy, and then made them go.

"I will have revenge on this fellow," he said, when he was alone. "But I must smooth my features, as I must now visit my pretty little Daisy."

CHAPTER XXXII.

SIR ROLAND TRIES TO TEMPT DAISY—HE MEETS SPRING-HEELED JACK FACE TO FACE, AND HAS REASON TO REPENT IT.

DAISY had been left undisturbed in her handsome apartments, but kept a close prisoner.

She soon found that Spring-Heeled Jack had been true to his promise.

He had not deserted her, but had kept her well supplied with provisions and wine as he had promised, all of which had been placed behind the screen in the mysterious manner in which the first had been placed, but she had never seen him again.

Mrs. Corcoran had expressed much astonishment as to where Daisy had obtained her new clothes, which she knew she had never supplied to her.

But as the girl simply said she had found them in the room, and, as far as Mrs. Corcoran could see, she had no other means of procuring them, she had to be content.

But there was the food and the wine; why was that not touched?

That was a greater mystery to Mrs. Corcoran than the clothes.

Not even one of the beautiful peaches had been tasted, and she felt certain that not a stopper had been removed out of one of the decanters. She was sure of this, for she examined them herself so often; and yet Daisy looked as fresh and well as ever.

The knowledge of a true friend being near had given her courage, besides which, in one of the baskets of provisions which Spring-Heeled Jack had left for her, she had found a small Spanish dagger, on which was tied a label hearing the words, "Strike and fear not."

This she had carefully concealed in the fold of her dress, taking the greatest care that the handle should be kept near to her hand, so that she might be able to draw it forth at the slightest show of danger.

Now and then she could hear the weird laughter of Spring-Heeled Jack as he played his pranks and gambols through the woods.

She liked to hear it. She had long since ceased to fear it, and knew that sometimes it was given to show that a friend was near.

So matters had gone on for two or three days and nothing had happened.

Mrs. Corcoran came in now and then to visit Daisy, and although she could not conceal her ill-humour at the girl's refusal to don the apparel placed for her, or to eat of the different viands, yet she always spoke kindly and encouragingly to her captive.

SPRING-HEELED JACK,
THE TERROR OF LONDON.

On the evening of the day on which the constables had called upon Sir Roland, the old woman—who had persuaded Sir Roland not to visit the girl until she was better prepared—entered the room, and with a winning smile, said—

"Why, Daisy dear, how pale you look! Come, come, you must not fret. I tell you you will be at liberty soon. Ha! Ha! that has brought the roses to your cheeks. Now you look your own beautiful self again."

"Mrs. Corcoran, how often have I told you that I cannot bear these compliments?"

"Compliments, forsooth! It is no compliment to tell a pretty girl she is pretty."

"It were better left alone," replied Daisy, with a wan smile. "Trust me, when a girl is pretty she will soon find it out for herself without anyone having to tell her."

"T'faith, you are right there, and such praise sounds fitter for a fine gentleman's lips than from those of an old woman like me. Am I not right?"

"If you mean it would sound well from the lips of the man who so foully tore me from my friends, I at once declare that it would not. I would sooner a hundred times hear him curse me. I hate him!"

With such vehemence and dramatic effect did Daisy say this that the old hag was startled.

"Nonsense, Daisy," she cried; "you must not speak like that. Remember, this fault, if it was a fault, was done out of love to you."

"Love to me!" exclaimed Daisy, in the greatest scorn. "Do not desecrate the word love by applying it to a man who could stoop to such an action. Do you think if I loved a bird that I should keep it in a cage if I saw it beating its wings and crying for liberty? No, it should go free, and if it loved me so little that it would not come back to my call, I should let it go and pray that it might be happy."

"You are a fool!" cried the old woman, startled at this outburst, and annoyed at finding that her pretended kindness had not had the effect she had hoped it would have, "Would you go back to those wretched strollers, and live a life of hardship when you might have one of luxury? Think! To be called 'my lady,' how delightful that would be—to be courted wherever you go—to have enough to spend on silks and satins, to—"

"Hold!" cried Daisy, in horror. "Are you also false? Can I trust no one in this horrible place? Am I alone? No; I defy his lordship's power, for I know there is one who will save me."

This speech gave the old woman no little amount of alarm.

In the first place, Daisy had placed a very strong emphasis on his "lordship."

Could she have found out that Sir Roland was not a lord?

If so, how had she done it?

She had been a captive, and yet knew who her captor was.

She had believed that he was a lord when she—Mrs. Corcoran—had first said so. How, then, had she so suddenly changed? Then, who was this one on whom she relied so much for protection?

Who could protect her in that solitary house, let alone save her? No one.

The old woman felt sure of this, and banishing her fears, replied, curtly—

"I did but speak for your good; but as they say wilful men will have their way, what are you to expect from a woman? They are always more wilful than the men."

And here she burst into a loud laugh, and hurrying to the side table she poured out some wine into a tumbler.

Then with a quick action she drew from her bosom a small vial and poured into the wine a few drops of reddish fluid, after which she filled another glass of wine.

All this was done most carefully, so that Daisy should not see what she did.

"Come, dearie," she said, in the kindest tones she could assume, "come, we must not quarrel, you know, we must be friends. You know, dearie, that I would do anything to help you. Come, drink a glass of wine with me."

And she handed the doctored glass to Daisy, who took it almost in thoughtlessness.

"There's a good girl," chuckled Mrs. Corcoran. "Now we will drink together."

Daisy looked at her in a firm manner, but the old woman was so convinced that she had conquered that she did not notice this.

"Now let us drink good fortune to each other!" cried Mrs. Corcoran. r

"Stay!" cried Daisy, as the old woman raised the glass to drink. "You have taken white wine and given me red."

"It's better for you, dearie," replied the old woman, with a smile on her lips and a scowl on her brow. "It is more strengthening, and will do you good."

"If that be true, good mother," said Daisy, who now suspected the old woman's truthfulness, "you should take the red wine and I the white."

"Nonsense, child, nonsense," said the old woman, quickly, "You are fretting, and need keeping up. Although I am old—and I would I were not—I need but little stimulant. A glass of the lightest wine would be quite enough for me

"And me," replied Daisy, quietly; "I need no stimulant at all. My wrongs support me. So, my good Mrs. Corcoran, we will exchange glasses if you please, and then I will drink with you; but not until then."

"Now a plague seize upon her heart," thought old Mrs. Corcoran.

But she did not say so aloud, trying to laugh the girl into drinking.

It was no good.

Daisy was firm and refused all temptation. "Have it your own way, miss," cried the old woman at last. "Do not drink with me if that be the return of all my kindness. I am sure I do not know why I should have plagued his lordship so about you. I had better have let him do just what he liked and closed my eyes to all your prayers and entreaties— all of which I believe to have been quite false. Now you may take care of yourself."

With that the old hag snatched the glass from Daisy's hand and placed it on the table.

Then she emptied her own glass, put that on one side, and hurried from the room, slamming the door after her—the door which closed with a secret spring and kept Daisy a prisoner.

Daisy rose from her couch and smelt the glass of wine.

There seemed to be nothing the matter with it. Could she be mistaken?

So lonely was she that she almost hoped that she had wronged the old woman and that she would forgive her.

"Perhaps if I drink the wine," she thought, "when she returns in a little time, which she is sure to do to wish me good-night, it may please her. Yes, I will drink it and tell her I did but joke to try her, that was all."

She raised the glass to her mouth to drink, but scarcely had the rim touched her lips when a stern voice—which came from where she knew not—uttered a warning.

"Daisy Leigh! Daisy Leigh!—beware. Did I not warn thee never to touch the food or drink supplied thee by thy most deadly foe? Disobey me and you shall perish. Obey me and you will be saved."

Daisy placed the glass down and turned quickly round to discover where the speaker was.

The room appeared to be empty, and yet the voice seemed to come from close behind her. "Generous man, spirit or whatever thou art," she said, "I thank thee for thy warning. Tell me, is this woman treacherous also? Am I to trust no one?"

No answer came to this eager question.

A dead calm seemed to hang over the room almost as a funeral pall.

"Could I have imagined this?" she thought, as she tottered back to the couch.

Again the silence was disturbed by a softly-breathed sentence.

"No, Daisy Leigh, you have not imagined this. The hour is come, the enemy approaches, but the rescuer is near; be courageous, fear nothing, and all will be well."

"Am I mad?" exclaimed Daisy, as she sprang from her couch. "Am I dreaming that I hear this strange voice? At least I will show that I have courage."

With that she seized the lamp, and drawing forth her dagger carefully searched the room. No signs of anyone there, not even behind the screen.

Indeed, her usual basket of provisions was not there, a thing which gave her some uneasiness, for she knew that if the hour of danger were not nigh, Spring-Heeled Jack would never have for gotten that.

Scarcely had she returned to her couch when the door opened and Sir Roland Ashton entered the room.

Daisy pretended to be asleep, but she grasped the hilt of her dagger.

"It is well," said Sir Roland to himself, "she sleeps. Then she must have drank the wine. How beautiful she is."

He stooped down and kissed her cheek softly.

Daisy's heart beat violently, but she never spoke, appearing to sleep still.

Presently, supposing her to be under the influence of the drug, he placed his arm around her waist.

In a moment the indignant girl had thrown him off and stood up boldly facing him.

"What means this intrusion?" she demanded, her eyes flashing fire.

"Intrusion! May I not visit my charming guest?" said Sir Roland, softly.

"Your guest! You mean your prisoner. Do not try to deceive me, Sir Roland Ashton. I know all."

"Sir Roland Ashton!" said Sir Roland, surprised and somewhat alarmed that his true character should be known. "You mistake, fair one, I am not Sir Roland; I bear a higher title."

"Conferred upon you by your housekeeper," said Daisy, scornfully.

"Confusion! can she have betrayed me," cried Sir Roland, furiously.

"Oh! no. She has been true to her trust. In good truth, so plausible was the old wretch that I think I should have been deceived by her had it not been for the timely warning of a friend."

"The timely warning of a friend," cried Sir Roland; "impossible!"

"Impossible it may seem, yet it is true, Sir Roland," replied Daisy.

"Who is this friend?" demanded Sir Roland, passionately. "I insist on knowing."

"And I refuse to answer," replied Daisy, as passionately and as haughtily.

"This must be seen into," cried Sir Roland, and he hurried to the window. "No, the fastenings are all safe. Nothing touched. She must have guessed it."

Consoling himself with this idea, Sir Roland returned to Daisy.

"I know not, sweet one, what has put this wild thought into your head, but believe me it is false. Why should I deceive you?"

"I know not; but that it is for some bad purpose I am sure."

"Nay; you are too hard upon me. What harm have I done you? I took you from low companions not fit to breathe the same air as you—a life of privation and one which must have ended in misery. To what have I brought you? Look round and view this beautiful furniture. Are not these meats and wines of the best and rarest? Do not these diamonds almost dazzle one with their brightness? What more then can I do?"

"Let me leave this place at once. Restore me to my friends. Think you that the wild bird loves its cage because it is golden? No. I ask no reparation for the wrong you have done me, but let me go."

"Nay, sweet one, that must not be. As well might you ask a miser to give up his treasures as me to give up you, who are my treasure. Ask me to bring forth my heart, and I will do it as readily as give up you, for you are my heart. A man cannot live without his heart. You are my life, my love, my soul! Oh! sweetest Daisy, the flower of love, why are you so cold to me?"

As he spoke he moved towards the girl, who stood erect and defiant.

"Keep off," cried Daisy, as she snatched forth her dagger, "or I will kill you."

Sir Roland started back, for he had little expected such a fury. "Daisy," he cried, sternly, "be reasonable. These stage airs must be forgotten when you become my lady. Know that I have made up my mind that you shall be mine, and that on which I have set my mind must and shall be carried out. Tempt me not too far. I would love you and be gentle, if not—"

"You would show your true character, and prove the brute you are. I know you, Sir Roland, and fear you not. You see I am armed. Place one finger on me and I will strike."

"Nonsense, girl. Give me that dagger, it is no toy for women."

"Approach, and you shall find it no toy," replied Daisy, sternly.

"I do not fear it. I have parried many a blow in my time given by more practised hands than yours, fair one. Death at your hands would be sweet. Strike, and you will be so cruel."

With this he boldly advanced towards her, but she assumed so determined an air that he paused a few paces from where she stood.

"Daisy," he cried, "at least tell me why you shrink even from my touch."

"Because your hands are stained with blood," replied the girl.

"With blood! I understand you not. To what crime do you refer?"

"Are there so many that you are doubtful to which I allude?"

This remark was said so scornfully that Sir Roland was stung to the quick.

"Have a care!" he cried. "I am but little given to bear such taunts from one whom I have honoured with my love."

"Honoured with your love! Love from such as you means dishonour. Stand back, I say, or I will strike you to the heart."

"But should you fail, my pretty Daisy, what then? Would it not be better to have my love than my hate? No man has yet been able to brook my hatred—how, then, will a young girl do it? Can you tell me that, sweet Daisy?

"I would dare your hatred sooner than be touched by my father's murderer."

"Your father's murderer! What mean you by that?" exclaimed Sir Roland; turning pale and starting back. "Who could have told you that?"

"So you admit it?"

"I? No. I knew Herbert Leigh, and have heard of his death; but mine was not the hand which struck the blow."

"But yours was the mind which directed it," exclaimed Daisy, passionately.

"Not so. Hear me. By Heaven I swear—"

"Silence!" exclaimed Daisy, drawing herself up to her full height. "Have you no reverence for aught that is pure and holy, that you swear by the Heaven you have outraged? Think you that the angels are deaf to the cries of your victims, that they close their ears to their curses or prayers for punishment on he who has so brutally used them? No! Water sinks into the earth, but blood flies upwards and bedews the Heavens. Repent while there is time. Go and sin no more."

This was said with such deep feeling and intention that even the hardened villain, Sir Roland Ashton, appeared touched.

"Daisy!" he cried, "no woman has ever touched my heart as you have done. You and you alone can save me from despair. Be mine, and—"

"Think you that I will permit you to wed me—you, my father's murderer—sooner a thousand deaths than that. I stand here alone with you, disgraced even by your presence, this dagger my only protection. Still, I fear you not. Such is my hatred for you that death would be preferred to one touch of your hand."

"Be it so," said Sir Roland, purple with passion. "I have tried all means to win you by love—they have failed, and now I care not what I do."

With a quick spring he dashed at Daisy, who made a blow at him with her dagger.

But Sir Roland was on his guard.

He parried the blow, seized her wrist, and in a few seconds had wrenched the weapon from her grasp.

Then with all his strength he forced her back on the couch.

She struggled hard, but what was her girlish strength against his?

The room seemed to spin round her, a dark shadow came over her eyes.

The brain whirled, all thought had gone, and she sank back insensible.

"Mine! mine, at last," cried Sir Roland, as he bent over the senseless girl.

"Never!" cried a stern voice, and Spring-Heeled Jack, who had been watching this scene from behind the screen, bounded over it and stood with outstretched arms over the fainting girl.

Sir Roland started back in horror.

How had the fiend come here?

The place had been securely closed—the windows fastened and the doors bolted and barred.

Still, there was this fearful creature, again baulking Sir Roland.

"Stand back, Sir Roland Ashton—to approach may mean death!" cried Spring-Heeled Jack. "Remember, I have no mercy for you. You, who would ruin the innocent; you, whose hands are stained with blood."

Sir Roland, as we have said, was no coward.

He sprang forward and cried aloud—

"Man or devil—I care not which—you shall not make the heart of Sir Roland Ashton tremble. Thus do I seize thee!"

But Spring-Heeled Jack had noticed his design, and frustrated it in the following manner.

With one bound he flew up to the ceiling, and descended with all his weight and force upon Sir Roland's breast, bearing him to the ground.

The baronet fell with a crash, and Spring-Heeled Jack grasped him by the throat with his claw-like hands, the nails embedding themselves in his throat.

"Now I have thee, Sir Roland!" laughed Spring-Heeled Jack, as he dashed the baronet's head upon the floor. "Now I have thee. If it were my pleasure I would wring the black heart out of your bosom. But, no, I will spare you at present—live on, sin more, and make your punishment here and hereafter more severe. Ha! ha! ha!"

At each of his fiendish laughs, Spring-Heeled Jack dashed the head of Sir Roland upon the ground, and fairly stunned him.

Then with a final blow, a bumper at parting, he sprang off the baronet.

Sir Roland was some minutes before he recovered himself.

When he did he staggered to his feet and gazed vacantly round.

"The fiend has gone!" he muttered. "Can this creature really be a devil sent to plague me? Impossible! I will not believe it. He is some maniac whose madness adds to his strength. I will match him yet, and, once in my power, I will crush him."

"Ha! ha! ha!" came in hollow, sepulchral tones from the cellar.

"Can this man—madman, or whatever he may be—pass through these substantial walls as easily as he seems to pass through the air? Let him do what he likes, I still will defy him. I have defied the devil often enough, and of a truth I shall not draw back from defying Spring-Heeled Jack. And now for my pretty little Daisy," he continued, turning to the couch.

He started back in angry surprise, for the couch was vacant.

"Gone!" he exclaimed; "impossible. Even if this demon should be able to pass through walls, ceiling, or floor, she could not; and yet she has gone."

He dashed behind the screen.

No one was there.

He hurried to the window.

It was fastened, and not a pane of glass broken.

The door bolted and fastened as securely as he had left it.

Then he staggered back to the table, and, seizing a glass of wine he found there, drank it off.

No sooner had he done so than a strange dizziness seized on him.

He tried to cry for help, but his tongue clove to the roof of his mouth.

He staggered hither and thither, trying to resist the drug, for he had drunk the wine which Mrs, Corcoran had drugged for Daisy.

A chill like that of death seized on his heart, and then he fell senseless on the floor.

CHAPTER XXXIII.
THE HAUNTED CHAMBER.

SIR ROLAND ASHTON, when he came to himself, was furious with rage.

Not only was he dazed by the drug, but his body was bruised all over.

What could he do? He summoned Mrs. Corcoran and Jacob Butler.

The old woman and the man were thunderstruck.

They had heard no noise—indeed, by Sir Roland's orders they had kept out of the way. No one had passed the door; that they were ready to swear.

Where then could Spring-Heeled Jack and the girl have gone?

That was the question they all asked, and that was the question which no one could answer.

"Follow me. I will have the place searched!" cried Sir Roland.

Having armed themselves the three started on their search.

Room after room was ransacked. but without any result.

The rooms only echoed back their footsteps and whispers, for even Sir Roland spoke with bated breath, as one who walks in a churchyard at night.

Softly they stole along, almost seeming like the ghosts which were said to haunt the rooms.

At length they came to the room which led to the haunted one.

Sir Roland examined the door of the ghostly chamber carefully.

It was securely fastened, and appeared to be untouched.

"The search is useless, quite useless," he muttered. This fiend has managed to baulk me even in this; but I will be equal to him yet."

He was about to turn from the door of the haunted apartment when a strain of sweet melody filled the room. From whom could it come? As far as Sir Roland knew, there was not a musical instrument in the place; and yet now the air which floated around seemed filled with soft, dreamy music, like that of a harp when gently touched.

"What new wonder is this?" exclaimed Sir Roland, sharply.

"In good truth I cannot tell, and I like it not," said Mrs. Corcoran.

"Neither do I," grumbled Jacob. "I am not frightened of any man; but devils!—who can fight against them? Only saints, and we are not of that order."

Certainly Jacob Butler had never said a truer word in his life.

"Tut!" cried Sir Roland. "I do not believe in devils."

"Humph!" said Mrs. Corcoran, "I am not so sure about that."

"Are you afraid?" demanded Sir Roland, sharply.

"Not I. I have long since made up my mind to my fate, and fear it not."

"What a pleasant old lady!" thought Jacob; but he deemed it as well to be quiet, lest she should cast some spell upon him.

Mrs. Corcoran had an idea of her own about casting spells.

Certainly not a very poetic one, but one which was very effectual.

"Bah!" said Sir Roland, with a bitter laugh, "there is evil enough in this world without having it in the next. I will not believe in it."

Suddenly a low wail sounded, and then became louder and louder.

Then a sweet voice was heard as from a distance, which faintly sang—

"Why should mortals fear grim death?
Tell me why—tell me why?
'Tis but a gasp of fleeting breath;
All must die—all must die.
The flesh to earth we must return;
A painful tribute all must give—
From worldly hopes and pride we turn,
The soul shall live—the soul shall live."

Sir Roland stood entranced as he listened to this song.

Never had he heard anything so wildly plaintive and beautiful.

But far more than the beauty of the voice was, to his ears, the fact that it was Daisy's.

Yes; he could not mistake her sweet tones, and his heart bounded with triumph as he heard them, or he believed he should now recapture her.

"Unbar that door, Jacob!" he cried, in exultation. "if Spring-Heeled Jack thought to keep his *protégée* safe because he has hidden her in what is called the haunted chamber he is mistaken. Throw open the door and we will unearth this songstress."

It was not without some little trepidation that Jacob obeyed his master.

However, it was at length done, and the door thrown open.

Seated at the dressing-table, clad in bridal dress, sat Daisy.

Her face was turned away, and the bridal veil was down.

She sat as if in the deepest melancholy, with bent down head.

"So—so, mistress," cried Sir Roland, with a merry laugh, "you have not escaped us yet? By my faith, it shall go hard if I permit you to do so a second time, now I have you."

As he spoke he advanced boldly, and threw his arm round her lovely form.

Judge his horror when it collapsed, and a mouldy dust filled the air.

The veil fell off and exposed a grinning skull, which, snapping at the nape of the neck, rolled upon the floor.

A skeleton!

Nothing but a hideous skeleton, the very touch of which was horrid.

Sir Roland uttered a cry of horror, and started back from the fearful thing.

Even Mrs. Corcoran seemed somewhat upset, whilst Mr. Butler did not take any trouble to disguise his feelings, but bolted from the room.

"What can be the meaning of this?" cried Sir Roland, with a shudder.

"How should I know?" replied Mrs. Corcoran. "There is mischief brewing."

"Mischief brewing? What do you mean, you hag of midnight?"

"I mean," replied the old woman, turning fiercely on the baronet, and glaring at him, I mean that vengeance is near at hand. The sword of justice is near, and only a strong arm and powerful will can thrust it on one side."

"How know you that?"

"Can you look at that," here she pointed at the skeleton, "and ask me?"

"I do not understand you. What have these musty bones to do with me?"

"Aye! there you ask too much. How should I know family secrets?"

"Family secrets! Dream you that this woman was one of my family?"

This was said so haughtily that the old crone burst into a laugh.

"In good truth, Sir Roland, I know not much about your family. I only know that death comes to all, and pays no respect to persons."

"Death?"

"Aye! death. Look at those bones. Can you forget that warning?"

"What mean you? I am strong and full of health—passion. I—"

"Stand on the brink of the grave. Be warned, Sir Roland, and pursue this girl no further. She is protected by those who have more power than you, and they must conquer."

"Be my fate what it may I will not retreat!"

"Do as you will; I have spoken," said Mrs. Corcoran. "I say no more."

The words had scarcely been said when a loud laugh sounded through the room, and Spring-Heeled Jack appeared by the fire-place.

"What!" he cried, "does Sir Roland tremble at death? Does he think that he can escape the immortal fate? Fool, your fate will be most terrible! Death and dishonour. Woe, woe! to you, Sir Roland! Look at that fearful reminder of death, and know that before long you shall be even as that is!"

"Fiend! Devil! Whate'er thou art—thus I defy ye!"

Sir Roland sprang forward to seize Spring-Heeled Jack.

But a well-directed blow felled him to the earth, and then, with his usual wild laugh, Jack disappeared.

Jacob Butler and Mrs. Corcoran hastened to Sir Roland's aid.

He was insensible, and bleeding from the mouth.

"This is a nice affair," grumbled Jacob Butler. "After all, I think honesty is the best policy."

"Did you ever try it?" chuckled Mrs. Corcoran, with a leer.

"Well, I can't say I have. Honesty hasn't been much in my way. But I've had serious thoughts of looking into the matter."

"And what keeps you from doing so?" demanded the crone.

"I ain't certain whether it would pay, and one might as well be dead as be poor."

"Better—far better," said Mrs. Corcoran; "but I have made a good long purse, and know how to keep it. Aye! and will, too. That is, until I am married, and then how I shall pet my husband. The late Corcoran—poor dear—had a happy life of it."

"Did he?" said Jacob, simply. "Well, I should not have thought it."

Scarcely politic; but although Mrs. Corcoran looked as if she could have killed Jacob, she answered in as sweet tones as she could assume—"Ah! indeed he did; and a happy life he led. Nothing but pipes and beer all day.

Jacob opened his eyes and licked his lips.

He suddenly appeared to find charms in the withered old woman he had not seen before.

"Oh! he was a happy man. Never did a day's work in his life."

"Hum! You—you are a good woman, Mrs. Corcoran," said Jacob.

"I have tried to be, Jacob Butler, but the world is so censorious." "Let it be; as long as we do our duty and look after ourselves, what does it matter?"

"What you think—I think. Oh! Jacob, don't look at me like that."

"I wasn't a-looking at you, that I know," replied Jacob. "I was thinking of a debt I owe."

"A debt! Gracious goodness! you are not in debt, Jacob Butler?"

"Well, it's only a little affair, and I can square it with him."

Here he pointed to Sir Roland and gave the old woman a queer glance. The deed was done.

Jacob had fallen into the trap, and nothing could save him.

Mrs. Corcoran was the octopus which threw her deadly arms around him.

Unlucky man—miserable Jacob!

His fate was sealed, and the old harpy Corcoran knew it.

"Jacob—" she whispered to him, "Jacob, would you like to be rich?"

Jacob scratched his head and declared that he rather should.

"Then," whispered the old woman, "you can become so in a little time."

"Can I? Tell me how?"

"Marry me."

"The devil!"

"No me."

"Well, it's much about the same thing," growled Jacob Butler.

"You are very complimentary, certainly. I forgive you."

"You are very kind—very; but I have said nothing of marriage."

"But I have. Now listen, Jacob Butler. I know a great deal about you."

"No harm, I hope, Mistress Corcoran," said Jacob, quickly.

"No, not much; only enough to hang you," replied Mrs. Corcoran.

"To—to hang me! You don't mean to say that?" cried Jacob.

"I do; and not only do I say so but I will do it," grinned Mrs. Corcoran.

"Who—who could have told you?" gasped Jacob Butler.

"He did—he who lies there. Jacob Butler, I tell you that his day is nearly over. Join me and we will rule all. Who knows but that we may be the master and mistress of Ashton Hall. Do you consent?"

Jacob looked at the hag. and felt inclined to murder her.

But there was that about the old woman's face he did not like—a firmness and sharp determination he could not understand.

"In a few days," she continued, "I shall have that man under my thumb. I know what he means. Now, will you marry me or not?"

Mr. Jacob Butler felt that he was pretty well under the lady's thumb, at any rate.

His spirit groaned within him; but the old witch had fixed him with her eyes, and he dared not refuse.

"Come," she said, "I have taken a fancy to you, Jacob, and I mean to marry you. Sooner or later you must give in, and it will be much better for you to accept at once. Marry me, and you shall be better than the master of Ashton Hall."

"I suppose I must," groaned Jacob.

"Then that's agreed. Now, to prove how much I love you, Jacob, I will let you into a few of my secrets. Lean over to me, Jacob dear, and I will tell you my plans."

Jacob leant over and listened intently to what the old woman said.

It was a terrible tale—a fearful plot of the darkest crime.

Jacob Butler was not a particular man—very far from it.

But even his hair stood on end "'like quills on the fretful porcupine."

"Gadzooks! you are a wonder. It isn't a five-barred gate that would stop your wild career. Why, Mazeppa[72] would not be in the race with you!"

---

[72] A Cossack leader.

"I should think not. Mark me! to get on in this world you must get rid of all scruples of conscience. Now, Jacob dear, do you agree with me?"

"I'll agree with you in anything, so long as you find me in plenty of money."

"That's right, Jacob—perfectly right. But, see, Sir Roland is recovering."

"Not a word to him of this," said Jacob, eagerly. "It might spoil all."

"Never fear! I can keep my counsel, and—ha! ha! ha! he shall find you money."

"Ha! ha! Ha!" roared the terrible laugh of Spring-Heeled Jack. "Do your devil's work and fear not that you shall be rewarded. Ha! ha! ha!"

The two conspirators glanced around but no one was to be seen.

Sir Roland raised himself upon his elbows, and passed his hand over his forehead.

He gazed around. as if thoroughly dazed, and murmured out—

"Where am I? Who has done this deed? Jacob, where are you? Come here!"

"I am here, your honour, and wish I wasn't! I don't like it."

"What has been the matter, Jacob?" demanded Sir Roland.

"Why, you have been knocked down with a blow from Spring-Heeled Jack."

"Ever to be crossed by that man! Jacob, to the stable, have out the carriage and the horses. We will start to-night for Ashton Hall. If Daisy has rejoined the company Tugwell will keep me well informed as to her movements. Jacob, come here."

"Jacob, go to your master," said Mrs. Corcoran, "and attend to him."

"Are you there?" growled Sir Roland. "Bah! the blow is shaking my brain."

"Do you not think that you had better go to bed, Sir Roland?" said Jacob.

"No! I will leave this house in an hour. You two shall accompany me."

"Hoity-toity! You speak finely," cried Mrs. Corcoran, flaring up. "Do you think nobody has a right in the world but yourself. I would have you to know differently. Those people who stoop to crime cannot be choosers of their friends. Crime, I have heard the parson say, is the same as death. Death makes all men equal; so does crime, and you, Sir Roland, have steeped yourself well in that. We are equal by crime, if not by birth—equal, Sir Roland! What think you of that?"

Sir Roland looked at the man and woman with amazement.

"What means this change?" he cried, as he started to his feet.

"It means, Sir Roland, that we are masters of the situation," said Mrs. Corcoran.

"You?"

"Yes—Jacob and I. We have come to terms. Jacob is going to make me Mrs. Butler, and we are going down to live at the Hall."

"Live at the Hall? Impossible! What would Lady Ashton say?"

"What care I what Lady Ashton says? Besides, if I carry out your orders, Sir Roland, Lady Ashton will not have much to say in the matter. We settle these things by a way which is much quicker than arguments."

And here the crone gave a shrill laugh, which was positively fiendish.

Sir Roland Ashton poured himself out a glass of wine and drank it off.

"And you, Jacob Butler," he said, "you mean to marry this woman?"

"I beg your honour's pardon, but it strikes me that the boot is on the other leg, and she means to marry me."

"Fools! You will live to repent this," muttered Sir Roland.

"Most people who marry do live to repent it," laughed Mrs. Corcoran.

"You speak from experience, I suppose?" snarled Sir Roland.

"Yes; my own and other people's. Poor Corcoran passed away in peace. His last few hours were the most peaceful ones he had after he married me."

"That I can believe," said Sir Roland, dryly, while he cast a quick look at Jacob Butler. "I only hope, for Jacob's sake, that he may have as peaceful an end. Do what you like; so long as you please me, I do not mind. But mark this, both of you. Serve me; and serve me faithfully, then I will be a kind master to you; let me see one sign of treachery, and I will dash you to pieces like I do this glass."

Taking the glass from the table he hurled it on the floor, shivering it into a thousand pieces.

Jacob turned pale as death, and even Mrs. Corcoran shivered at the baronet's fearful energy.

"Enough now!" he cried; "to-morrow we will leave here and start for the Hall. Be faithful, and you will not repent having served me. Swear that you will be faithful to me!"

"Swear! Ha! ha! ha! ha!" came the sepulchral voice of Spring-Heeled Jack.

"Heed not that impostor!" cried Sir Roland. "Swear!"

Mrs. Corcoran and Jacob swore upon their honour.

Could they have sworn on anything less substantial?

"Enough, Jacob; see that all is prepared for our journey. To-morrow we start for the Hall."

"And I go, too," came the voice of Spring-Heeled Jack. "Ha! Ha! ha!"

CHAPTER XXXIV.

HUSBAND AND WIFE.

LADY ASHTON, formerly Mrs. Levine, reclined upon her sofa in the-drawing-room of Ashton Hall.

She had quite changed from the soft-spoken Mrs. Levine.

She had now become haughty and tyrannical, so that all the servants hated her.

Nothing was good enough for her ladyship. Indeed, had she been born the heiress to millions she would not have been so exacting.

Dinners had to be cooked in the most *recherché* style.

As for diamonds and dress no lady in the county could equal her.

Her maids dressed as ladies, and waited upon her hand and foot.

She had been a servant herself once, had felt the sharp taunt and scorn of a master's tongue; but instead of teaching her a lesson of humility, it had made her more imperious than ever. If she ruled the servants with a rod of iron when she was housekeeper, one may fancy what she did now she was mistress.

As we said before, Lady Ashton reclined upon her drawing-room sofa. She was reading a novel, and placed it languidly on one side as Sir Roland entered the room.

"So, Sir Roland," she said, quietly, "you have returned home at last?"

"Yes. I do not suppose you have felt my absence very much."

"No," yawned the lady; "I have amused myself with my monkey, Coco."

"Whom you love better than your husband. Ours was a pretty love match!"

"Love match! who could have put that into your head?"

"You loved me when you married me, I suppose?" said Sir Roland.

Ha! Ha! ha! ha! Who could have put that foolish thought into your head?"

"You did; you declared you did the morning after we were married."

"Ah! those were the early days. You would not have a woman speak her mind during the honeymoon! No—no, Sir Roland, that comes afterwards."

Sir Roland uttered something which was certainly not a compliment to his wife.

But it was his interest not to quarrel with her, and so he answered kindly—

"Come, come, my dear. If business called me away from you so soon after our marriage, it was not my fault."

"Business! Sir Roland," said Lady Ashton, raising her eyebrows. "Are you sure it was not pleasure?"

"Pleasure, my dear. What pleasure can I have away from you?"

Lady Ashton made no reply, but throwing her arms above her head burst out into a loud fit of laughter.

"How now, Lady Ashton?" cried Sir Roland. "What means this most unseemly mirth?"

"It means this, Sir Roland. That you cannot and shall not hoodwink me. I am not blind; you hate me, and your death would not cause me a moment's sorrow. But since we are husband and wife, our interests are the same, and that being the case, I will work with you. But let us understand each other. If our interests were not the same I should work against you."

"Candid, at all events," muttered Sir Roland.

"I meant it to be. Now, Roland, look here; I know what your object in life is. If you do as I wish, I will help you; if not—now mark my words—I will spoil every plan you have. If I benefit, well and good; if I do not, look to yourself!"

Sir Roland ground his teeth but could make no reply.

He knew too well that this woman had a fearful will of her own, and that, fight against it as he would, he was subservient to it.

"Be it as you will. Now we understand each other we can talk openly."

"Oh! certainly," replied the lady. "And to begin with, read that letter!"

Here Lady Ashton threw over a note to Sir Roland.

Sir Roland picked it up, opened and read it.

It was an exact account of what had happened between Sir Roland and Daisy.

This note was signed by Spring-Heeled Jack.

"Has that cursed villain been here?" demanded Sir Roland.

"I have not seen him," replied the lady, carelessly; "but I have written to him, and, as you see, he has written to me."

"You have written to him? And may I ask where you have written to?"

"A man named Lorimer brought the letter and carried back the answer."

"And what was the answer?"

"I do not know that I shall tell you, if you are going to poison me."

"It seems to me that you have some strange ideas," said Sir Roland, but turning pale.

"The strange ideas have come through a very good authority."

"What authority?"

"Spring-Heeled Jack!"

"What! has the scoundrel dared accuse me of such a purpose?"

"Aye! and proved it also. Mrs. Corcoran is a skilful woman, but she will have a great deal of trouble to match me."

"So you think that I would be guilty of murder?"

"I know you have been," was the calm reply; "and it shall be my purpose to prevent your being so again. I have no wish to be a heroine at the expense of my life."

"You know that?"

"Yes, Sir Roland; I do know that, and a great deal more. I advise you to be careful. You will find me a better friend than foe. Dear me! do you think I am ignorant of all your plans? No! I know them all."

Sir Roland bit his lip and glared with rage.

Here were all his plans upset by his arch enemy, Spring-Heeled Jack.

How could he have done it? With what swiftness he must have travelled!

"You wrong me," said Sir Roland. "I had no more intention of wronging you than—"

"Marrying me," laughed the lady; "but having done the one I will take care that you do not do the other. I have told you that if you are subservient to me I will aid you in your plans. Try to upset me and I will hang you."

Sir Roland looked at this woman, and in spite of himself admired her.

She was handsome, strong, clever, and determined.

Might she not be the one who could overthrow the power of Spring-Heeled Jack?

At all events he determined to try it, and made answer—

"I will not disguise from you the truth. Our marriage, as you know, was not intended by me."

"Far from it," said the lady, quietly. "I intended it, and had my own way, and mean to have it. You understand me?"

"Perfectly," said Sir Roland; but his cheek grew purple with passion.

"And you will obey me. That Mrs. Corcoran must leave the house!"

"Let it be so. Do you think that I want the old woman here? No, let her go."

Scarcely had he said the words than he saw one of the curtains which were drawn over the windows move, and the hideous face of Mrs. Corcoran appear.

Mrs. Corcoran was always hideous, but now she appeared more so than ever.

Placing one skinny finger on her blue lips, to warn Sir Roland to silence, she pointed with the other to Lady Ashton, and then grasped her hands with a terrible motion, as if she clutched someone's throat.

There was no mistaking the sign.

It asked as plainly as words could have done.

"Shall I strangle her?"

Taking advantage of his wife having glanced on one side, Sir Roland nodded his head, and the old hag Corcoran glided softly from behind the curtain.

"The next thing that I must insist upon," said Lady Ashton, "is the dismissal of Jacob Butler. He knows too much of the family matters, and must be silenced."

"Be it as your ladyship wills," said Sir Roland; "I care not for the fellow."

"I am glad to find you so obliging, Sir Roland," smiled her ladyship.

"Yet, my lady, I would have you think for a moment," said Sir Roland. "Jacob has been a good and faithful servant to me, and has never divulged my secrets."

"True, but your secrets would be safer when he was dead."

"Ah! madam, talk not so lightly of death. It is often nearest to us when we think it furthest away. It would be better to be more charitable."

Lady Ashton opened her eyes in wonder; then burst into laughter.

"Why, Sir Roland, something dreadful is surely about to happen! I have heard that the devil can quote Scripture to suit his own purpose; but that Sir Roland Ashton should moralise is more than I could have believed. Wonders will never cease."

Meanwhile the old hag had crept nearer and nearer to Lady Ashton.

In one hand she held a napkin and in the other a bottle, from which she poured a colourless fluid on to the napkin.

Whether Lady Ashton noticed something peculiar in her husband's eyes, or whether she heard the creeping step behind her, no one can tell, but certain it is that she turned suddenly round and faced the murderess.

She sprang to her feet and cried aloud for help and mercy.

Help! mercy! When had these virtues ever entered the heart of Sir Roland?

Mrs. Corcoran sprang upon her, and thrust the napkin in her face.

There was a horrible stifling sensation—a faint, sweet smell, a dizziness, and Lady Ashton fell back insensible.

Then the old hag pressed the napkin over her ladyship's mouth and nostrils so firmly that to breathe was impossible.

A few faint struggles for life and then her limbs were stretched out in death.

"There," said Mrs. Corcoran, as she removed the napkin and gazed down at the horrible work she had done. "There; she won't trouble you again, Sir Roland. Ha, ha! my lady, you would have me turned from the house! Poor old Mother Corcoran was to go forth homeless! Ah! you were a kind, merciful lady—you were! But I was more so; I have found you a home from which you will never rise until the end of the world—the grave. Ha! ha! ha!"

"Have you no feeling—no remorse for the cruel deed which you have just now committed?" cried Sir Roland, as he gazed down at the livid face—now fast becoming rigid.

"Remorse! Ho! Ho! ho! I like that! Have you no remorse? Who ordered me to kill her? You. You talk to me of remorse, and I reply that while such men as you are to be found, such women as I am will always be ready at hand to carry out your plans. Who is the worst? The head that plans the deed, or the hand which carries it out?"

"Silence, woman!"

"I will not be silent, Sir Roland," cried the old woman. "Henceforth I would have you to know that I am your equal. I have heard it said that in some eastern country, many—many years ago, that if a man murdered his wife the body was chained to the murderer, who had to drag it about with him, until the loathsome thing caused him to die with terror, or gave him some pestilence from which he died. You will bury this body, but you will drag about with you the ghost—the true corpse—remorse!"

Sir Roland paced up and down the room in the wildest agitation.

"Woman! fiend! Devil!" he cried at last, "have you no remorse?"

"No. I was born poor, and learned in the school of privation that conscience was a luxury the poor could not afford, if they wanted to get on in the world. I have obeyed my orders. Yours be the blame—not mine."

The woman spoke so calmly and coolly that Sir Roland could not answer.

He felt that he was in her power, and bowed before her will.

"Be it as you like," he muttered; "he who once ventures on the path of sin must continue to the end. Step by step he sinks lower and lower into the quicksand of crime, until, powerless to move, the tide of time overwhelms him, and he sinks never to rise again."

"Ah! you have found that out, have you?" laughed the old woman.

"Alas! yes, and you have no feeling?"

"None! I have seen too much of life for remorse. But what is to be done with this pretty piece of death. Shall we not rouse the house and declare that her ladyship died suddenly? It would be as well to send post haste for a doctor. I have certain drugs which I can use to remove all odour of the drug I used. Trust to me, Sir Roland, I have had too many cases like this on hand to make any mistake about it. None will find us out."

"Ha! ha! ha!" rang a sepulchral laugh through the room.

The two guilty wretches turned round and gazed with horror at the window from whence the sound came, and there they beheld the horrible features of Spring-Heeled Jack.

"Ha! Ha! ha! Sir Roland," roared Spring Heeled Jack. "Do you think that this crime will go unpunished? No! Murder will out, and although you escape for a time at last your meed[73] of punishment will come; then you shall know who Spring-Heeled Jack is. Ha! ha! Ha!"

And with a yell of laughter the horrible creature bounded away.

"Will this fiend ever haunt me?" cried Sir Roland.

"I suppose so," remarked Mrs. Corcoran; "but what harm does he do you? Be a man, Sir Roland, and defy the devil himself. Shake off this trembling cowardice, and knowing that you have little to hope for in the world to come, make the best of this. Now call up the servants."

Sir Roland knew the old crone was right and acted on her advice.

He seized the bell-rope and rang with all his might as he shouted—

"Help—help—help! Her ladyship is in a fit! Help—help—help!"

The sounds of hurrying feet—the confused murmer of voices.

Then Mrs. Corcoran flung herself down at the side of the couch, and began rubbing the hands of the dead woman, while Sir Roland bent over her as if in the most abject grief.

In rushed the servants, Jacob Butler at their head.

"What is all this?" cried Jacob, as he gazed in horror at the dead.

"I know not, Jacob. Your mistress was talking to me when she was taken with a sudden faintness and—and became insensible, and—"

"She is dead!" said Jacob, as he placed his band over his mistress's heart.

"Dead—impossible!" cried Mrs. Corcoran, putting on a look of the greatest surprise.

"Dead—my darling dead!" exclaimed Sir Roland. "I cannot believe it!"

Jacob looked uneasily at the servants as he made answer.

"I don't know about its being impossible, all I know is that it is true."

Sir Roland cast himself upon the body and kissed it passionately.

Far more passionately than he had ever done in her lifetime.

"Fly, Jacob, fly!" he cried, apparently overpowered with grief. "Seek a doctor at once. My darling—my darling! She cannot be dead."

"She's a precious good imitation of it," said Jacob, as he left the room.

---

[73] Reward.

"Don't overdo it," whispered Mrs. Corcoran, to the baronet, "or they will suspect something."

Then, in plaintive tones, she continued, aloud—

"Moderate your grief, Sir Roland. The poor dear angel has gone. All the tears in the world will not bring her back to life again. Ah! this is a wicked world, and in the midst of life we are in death."

"Who can know my grief? Who can fill her vacant place?"

Mrs. Corcoran felt inclined to say that she could, but prudence forbade her, and yet the old crone had some idea that she might throw over the servant and take the master.

But that, she thought, had better be left for the future.

The doctor came—a pompous country practitioner, who would have done anything to oblige Sir Roland Ashton.

So everything was arranged to the liking of Sir Roland Ashton and Mrs. Corcoran.

"This is a nice thing you have done," whispered Jacob to Mrs. Corcoran, as she and he left the room together.

"Yes; I think it is, Jacob," said the old woman, complacently. "I told you that you should soon be as good as the master of Ashton Hall—marry me and you will be, for I have him under my thumb."

CHAPTER XXXV.
THE BULL IN TOP BOOTS.

DOWN in the Borough there is, or rather was, a noted public-house with the somewhat mysterious sign of The Bull in Top Boots.

Whether it had been originally intended for John Bull[74] in the usual top boots in which he is so constantly represented, history says not; but the sign showed a good big bull, with long horns, curly pate, and fiery eyes, pawing the air with his front hoofs, whilst his hinder ones are encased in huge top boots—a particle of dress which, to say the least of it, must be rather inconvenient to the bovine animal, seeing that he has no feet to keep them on.

However, there was the sign and there the house, and a most disreputable one it was.

Gentlemen in flash clothes, who rode blood mares, and whose business took them out mostly at rights, and who had a horror of Bow-street, lounged about the place all day, drinking, smoking, and diceing.

Then there were a much rougher set of fellows.

Men who did not seem to have washed or shaved for weeks.

These men appeared to have a kind of veneration for the men who kept the blood mares, and called them all "captains," although not one of them could claim to have been in their country's service; indeed, the only service they could do this country would be to hang themselves, and so save the country expense and the sheriffs trouble.

In a word, the house was a resort of highwayman, thieves, and the worst of characters, and it is to this place we must conduct our readers.

It was a dark, stormy night; the wind blew cold and chilly up the Thames. The rain fell in fitful showers, and the distant thunder told that a storm was not far off.

On such a night a crowd of men and women of the character we have described were

---

[74] A figure who symbolically represents England.

seated in a long room of the Bull in Top Boots, rejoicing in their usual pastimes.

Two men were away from the rest, and as they drank their grog and smoked they watched the others keenly.

These two men were no others than Dick Catchpole and Elias Grabham.

They were carrying out Sir Roland's orders, and were ever on the watch.

"By the power, Bill Blarney!" cried a tall Irishman, dressed in a lace coat, doeskin breeches, and top boots almost as high as the prancing bull wore. "By the powers, Bill Blarney; but that was a rare song that you gave us just now."

"Hold your whist, Pat Kelly; I'm not in the mood for singing."

"Now, Bill, I want a song," said a blooming: lady of some thirty summers, with a complexion like a Dutch doll, and rolling eyes, which she used freely. "So tip us a tune, or maybe I shall take another lover."

"Arrah! Judy," replied Bill, "if you make me jealous, you beauty, it's meself that will murder the man who dare come between us!"

"Then sing me a song at once," said Judy.

Like most women, Judy knew how to get the best of her lover.

Bill Blarney submitted to the will of his charmer, and said—

"Shure, Judy, you know that I would never displease you. Only, maybe some of the company may not care about a song," and here he cast a quick glance towards Messrs. Catchpole and-Grabham.

"If anyone objects to your singing, Bill, let them speak to me," said Judy, putting her arms akimbo and glancing fiercely round.

No one did object; in fact, every one seemed anxious to bear the song.

"Which one shall I sing, Judy, 'The White Boy's Lament,' or 'Bad Luck to the Deyil?'"

"Give us 'Bad Luck to the Devil;' that always appears to me a kind of religious song," said Judy.

Thus urged, Bill Blarney struck up the following beautiful ditty—

BAD LUCK TO THE DEVIL.

"Oh! bad luck to the Devil, he's dead!
He gained but a sad notoriety;
But his very worst foes never said
He ever gave way to sobriety.
He liked both to drink and to dice,
Loves lasses whose eyes brightly shone;
'Tis true he has many a vice,
But pity him now he has gone."

"Chorus, gentlemen!" roared Judy; and amidst the rattle of pewter pots, the clinking of glasses, and stamping of feet, the chorus was roared out—

"Oh! bad luck to the Devil, he's dead!
He gained but a sad notoriety;
But his very worst foes never said
He ever gave way to sobriety."

Encouraged by the success of the first verse, Bill continued.

"Oh! bad luck to the Devil, he's dead!
He always went in for variety;
He is missed—at least, so 'tis said—
In the highest and lowest society.
But what they will do with his soul,
I'm sure I really don't know—
Above he'd break all control,
And be quite at home down below."

"Chorus, gentlemen!"

"Oh! bad luck to the devil, he's dead,
He gained but a sad notoriety;
But his very worst foes never said
that he ever gave way to sobriety."

"I'm not sure that the devil be dead," said Catchpole, breaking into the conversation directly the applause had ceased. "I've heard people speak about a kind of devil that goes leaping about frightening people out of their wits."

"You mean Spring-Heeled Jack?" said Grabham. "I've heard of him."

"And it's meself that has seen him," said Bill Blarney.

"You have seen him! Where?" cried the rest of the company.

"Well, I was riding, but it don't matter where or for what purpose," said Mr. Blarney, suddenly remembering that his midnight frolics might be dangerous to repeat. "Anyway, I was having a canter over the country on my mare, quite at my ease like—"

"That's more than any gentlefolk would have been if you had met them," laughed Judy.

"Hold your whist, Judy!" said Blarney. "Sure and you are not the girl to peach[75] upon a lover?"

"I should think not. And let me catch the man who dares to peach upon my sweetheart—I'd precious soon wring his neck! But go on with your story."

"Well, the moon was sailing up aloft, and I was cantering over the heath, just humming a stave to myself, and wondering if Providence would kindly put some piece of good fortune in my way, when I heard the wheels of a carriage.

"In luck, Bill, my boy!" laughed Pat Kelly. "You always were a lucky dog."

"I don't so much know about that," said Bill Blarney; "but I did believe that I was, and that's the truth of the matter. Well, I puts my tit[76] into a gallop, and away we went over the heath. A carriage came in view, and as I presented one of my pistols I invited the coachman to stop, which he did in double quick time."

"Quite polite and gentlemanly," laughed Pat Kelly—"a true Irish boy."

"But, oh! such a screaming and a squalling was set up that you never did hear."

"Women?" said one of the men, laconically.

"Ladies," replied Bill Blarney, in a tone which might lead one to think that he thought women and ladies two very different kinds of animals. "Ladies as highly born as any of us here."

---

[75] Inform.
[76] A worn-out horse.

SPRING-HEELED JACK,
THE TERROR OF LONDON.

"DAISY LEIGH IS THE LASS I LOVE BEST, SIR ROLAND!" CRIED GEDGE.

Some people might not have thought this a great amount of praise.

But it seemed to meet with the approval of the company, and Bill, being applauded, looked round with the greatest satisfaction.

"Yes, gentlemen, they were ladies, and I fancy that ladies are rather partial to me."

Here the Hibernian highwayman coughed and pretended to be modest.

A thing he quite failed in, and set Pat Kelly off into shrieks of laughter.

"Be they women or ladies," said Mistress Judy, "they had better not let me catch them at any of their flirtations with my boy. However, go on."

"Well, I rode up to the carriage window, and, taking off my hat, said, after making the most graceful bow that I could—

"I ask pardon, lady, or ladies, as the case may be, but I have a very painful duty to perform. It is suspected that a load of jewels are being carried over the country to help the Pretender,[77] and I must examine you to see if you have any about you. Loyalty, and only loyalty, compels me to make this demand. Do not think that I would he so rude as to interfere with ladies, if it were not for the king and for the country. Perish the thought! It's meself as would scorn the action. But I have my duty to perform, and must do it. So please hand over your jewels, my pretty dears, and we will see what your purses contain!"

"I warrant me you made a good haul?" laughed Judy.

"There you are wrong, Judy. The women flopped down on their knees, the coachman squealed like a stuck pig, and rolled off the box.

"I had them quite at my mercy, and was about to remove some articles of value which looked somewhat suspicious, when a dark cloud seemed to overshadow the moon.

"I gazed upward, and there, leaping down on the top of the coach, was that infernal imp of his chief, Spring-Heeled Jack."

"Did you seize him?" cried Judy, eagerly.

"No," replied Bill Blarney, somewhat ruefully. "On the contrary, he seized me."

"But you grappled with him?" demanded the warlike Judy.

"Well, I can't exactly say I did, for no sooner had he bounded on to the top of the coach than he bounded off that on to my back. Planting his knees. firmly into my back, whilst he grasped me by the throat, he forced me down on to my face, where he held me firmly."

"And you did not kill the fellow?" said he fiery Judy, her eyes flashing.

"No, I did not. I should have liked to do so, but somehow he had the best of it."

"Had the best of it! What do you mean?" demanded Judy.

"Well, my jewel, he had me face downwards on the ground, and he held on with the power of a giant. I can't say he was too gentle, for I had reason to remember that there were stones upon that heath."

"You mean that he beat your thick head upon the ground?" cried Judy, indignantly.

"Well, Judy, darling, it must have been something like it, or I had a most powerful dream. But the next morning I found my head all bumps, and a cruel sensation of cramp down my back, as if someone had been kneeling on me and kneading me with their knees."

"In other words, you were jolly well whopped," said Judy, indignantly.

"Sure that was my opinion of the matter, my darling, but I did not care about mentioning it at once, and before company. Those things are best kept to one's-self.

---

[77] Prince Charles Edward Stuart, also known as Bonnie Prince Charlie (1720 1788) was one of the Stuart claimants to the throne, descended from James II who was deposed in 1688.

Sure, Judy, darling, you would not blame me because I could not fight the devil?"

"I would fight the devil and all his imps, if he came across me!" said the valiant Judy.

"Be gorrah! Judy. You have the courage of the devil, but you never met Spring-Heeled Jack. I wish he were here now, to let you know the fiend he is."

"Whatever he was, I should not be frightened. Well, what did you do?"

"Well, Jack held me down, and battered my face on the ground."

"And did you do nothing?"

"Oh! yes; I bellowed like a bull; but I soon found that the more I bellowed the more he bumped, and so I thought discretion was the better part of valour, and then I heard the monster cry—

"'On your box, coward, and drive for your life, or Spring-Heeled Jack will serve you as he has done this ruf—gentleman, I mean.'"

"Ruffian, you mean!" said a stern voice from a dark corner of the room.

The men turned round and glanced eagerly at each other.

Not a soul was there, and yet all had heard the voice.

As if to make the idea more ghostly the rain came down in fearful storms.

Then the lightning flashed through the windows, and the deep-voiced thunder rolled.

"Phsaw! who was that who spoke?" demanded Bill Blarney, as he wiped the perspiration from his forehead. "Surely Spring-Heeled. Jack is not amongst us?"

This idea seemed almost to terrify the valiant Judy, but she was too much of a woman to show it.

No; sooner than give way, Judy Bulgrudery resolved to defy anyone.

"To think that you men should fear a fellow of that sort!" she said.

But as she spoke she glanced nervously over her shoulder.

"And do you not fear him, mistress?" asked Dick Catchpole.

"Me afraid of him? I would he was here now that I might tell him my idea of his high pranks. Bah! had I been a man he would have been in prison long ago."

Crash! bang! A livid flash of light and then the deep war of heaven's artillery sent forth its fearful file!

Every one in the room was nearly blinded and even the courageous Judy seemed overcome, for covering her face with her hands she bent her head down and screamed.

The very air seemed impregnated, with sulphur, and the glasses were shaken by the heavy thunder clap.

All were blinded for a time with the flash, but when they had recovered from the shock they looked up, and to their horror beheld a tail dark man, dressed in a riding cloak, which hid his figure from his neck to his feet.

He wore a hat slouched over his face, his hair was long, and his moustache turned up in the Mephistophelian style.

"I hope I do not disturb you, ladies and gentlemen, but, the weather being somewhat stormy, I thought I would take shelter here. Madam, your glass is empty—permit me to fill it?"

And with the greatest coolness possible the stranger drew from his pocket a black cased bottle, with which he replenished Judy's glass.

The people all looked in horror at the man.

And yet, so far as they could see, the man was a handsome one.

Judy at first seemed inclined to refuse the drink: but the smell of it was too tempting, and she drank it off with great gusto.

"It's nectar!" she cried. "It's drink for the gods!"

"I am glad you like it, madam. You shall have some more anon."

"Who the devil are you?" demanded Bill Blarney, in amaze.

"Exactly so. My dear sir, in a society like this I am careful about giving my name."

There was nothing which one could call positively unpleasant in the man's manner, and yet there was a way about it which offended, because it appeared to claim authority.

"Men who will not give their name are to be suspected," growled Bill.

"Suspect as much as you like," replied the stranger, quietly. "It cannot hurt me.

There was no boastfulness in all this. It was done quietly and firmly.

"You speak boldly," said Bill, "Do you know who me and my pals are?"

"Yes—vagabonds—rogues—thieves! You may be worse; I don't know," replied the stranger.

"By the Lord Harry! I will not stand that," cried Bill Blarney, as he jumped up. "I'll teach you to respect the company you are in."

With that he sprung towards the stranger, making a clutch at his throat.

But, stretching forth a pair of muscular arms as he threw the cloak on one side, the stranger grasped him with a power which was fearful to witness.

The man's very bones seemed to crack beneath his grip.

Holding the man in his arms he lifted him up as easily as if he were a child.

"So," he cried, "you would attempt to rule me! Learn that I am above you all Oh! you may call for help," he continued, as the men started up to rescue their companion from hi; grasp, "but I tell you, if anyone dares to place one finger on me, I will strangle this fellow first and his friend afterwards.!

The people drew back in alarm, and Bill Blarney called aloud for mercy.

"Mercy!" cried the stranger. "What mercy do you deserve? But go! Too long have I defiled my hands with you."

With that he dashed the man across the room, throwing him on a table that was filled with bottles and glasses.

Loud was the crash he made in his descent, and louder still the cry Judy made at the overthrow of her lover.

Bully him herself she would to any extent, but would not permit anyone else to do the same.

With hands like claws and outstretched arms she flew at the stranger.

But he caught her easily in an embrace, and waltzed with her round the room.

So lightly, so deftly, and gracefully did he lift the woman that the people appeared surprised.

It was the dance of a demon.

Now they were pirouetting on the floor, now they were making the most extraordinary bounds into the air.

Judy was breathless, and could not speak, although she would have fain asked the stranger to desist.

Up and down, here and there, he danced all over the place.

The "Devil's Fantasia" would have been the fitting music to have played to it, for never was such a horrible impish dance.

It was now here we go up, up, up; here we go down, down, down.

Judy Bulgrudery gasped for breath and sighed for mercy.

But the stranger would not cease. He seemed endowed with special strength.

He whirled her about as if she had been a fairy, whilst his long legs were thrown up so high that the people started back, so as not to have their hats knocked off.

At last Judy did indeed grow faint, which no sooner did the stranger perceive than with the greatest kindness he placed her on a chair, and handed her a glass of punch, which, much exhausted as the lady seemed to be, she drank with the greatest eagerness.

"Now, gentlemen," said the stranger, as he bowed lowly, "and especially you, Catchpole and Grabham, I trust you will have a good remembrance of Spring-Heeled Jack."

"Then you are—" cried Catchpole, jumping forward.

"Spring-Heeled Jack!"

And with a loud laugh the stranger bounded over their heads and disappeared through the door.

CHAPTER XXXVI.
CATCHPOLE AND GRABHAM HAVE REASON TO REPENT THEIR VISIT TO THE BULL IN TOP BOOTS.

THE company at the Bull in Top Boots could scarcely speak. They were not men or women given to much fear or superstition.

But here, before their very eyes, had come a fantastic fiend whose nature they could not make out,

Even the redoubtable Judy Bulgrudery seemed scared.

"It's the fiend himself," she gasped, directly she could recover her breath. "Never did I have such a devil's dance, and may the saints protect me from such another. Although I do confess he behaved like a gentleman to me."

"Faith! he knew I was present, and thought he had better behave himself."

"What are you talking like that for, Bill Blarney?" cried the woman. "Don't you know he would just have treated you as a terrier would treat a rat—give you a good shaking and throw you over his shoulder."

Bill Blarney did not like this speech for two reasons. In the first place he had been the cock of the walk at the Bull in Top Boots, the admired of all and now his comb had been cut. Secondly, Judy's speech seemed to partake more of admiration than horror at the grim goblin, and as he really did like Judy he was naturally somewhat jealous.

"Faith! and you need not be so proud of your dance with the devil, Judy."

"I don't see that. He can shake as pretty a leg in the dance as ever I saw," replied Judy, who saw Bill Blarney's jealousy, and was determined to make the most of it, woman-like, "and I don't see that he is so ugly."

"Hold your whist,[78] Judy," said Pat Kelly, who would always stand up for his leader, be he right or wrong. "What's the good of annoying Blarney? Sure, no man can fight the devil, although some women can get over him. Faith! I've heard it said that most women are more than a match for him."

"So much the better for the women," laughed Judy; "but those two gentlemen over

---

[78] Be quiet.

there seemed to know more about him than anyone."

It was a most skilfully-timed remark of Mistress Judy.

She liked Bill Blarney, and certainly had no desire to quarrel.

So having, as it were, established her supremacy, she turned on the unfortunate constables.

"We? We know nothing of this fellow!" stammered Dick Catchpole.

"Less than nothing," put in Grabham. "We are honest folk."

"Ha! ha! Ha!" came the fearful laugh of Spring-Heeled Jack, sounding as if it came from the very roof tree of the inn. "Honest men! Ha! ha! Ha! Two constables—two spies in the pay of Sir Roland Ashton. Honest men! Ha! Ha! ha!"

The hint had been given and was soon taken by such a company.

"Hillo!" cried Bill Blarney, as he started up and glared fiercely at the constables, who were now as pale as death. "Is this true?"

"Of course it is," cried Judy. "Look at their faces. The white-livered cowards dare not deny it. Now, lads, let us show them our metal!"

"Stand back!" cried Dick Catchpole, as he sprang up and produced his staff of office—a little round piece of wood, much like an office ruler with a brass crown at the top. "Stand back! I am a sworn-in constable, and I claim the protection of the laws."

"Laws!" cried Blarney; "who cares for the laws? Hillo! lads, listen here."

The men who frequented the highly respectable establishment of the Bull in Top Boots crowded round Blarney, so that Messrs. Catchpole and Grabham found themselves prisoners.

"Beware!" cried Grabham, producing his truncheon; "this is felony."

"Oh! is it. Well, I think we have been pretty used to that. Eh, boys?"

"I should think so. Let us give 'em their quietus,"[79] growled one brawny fellow.

"Take care—take care! The first one who places a finger on me I shall arrest."

This useless threat caused the people to burst into loud fits of laughter.

Among the merriment could be heard the wild shriek of Spring-Heeled Jack.

"No, no, lads," cried Judy; "we had better not do that. Let us give them a lesson which will teach them better manners, and cause us some amusement. What do you say to tossing in a blanket?"

The suggestion was met with shouts of applause from everybody in the room save the two most interested—namely, Messrs. Catchpole and Grabham, who somehow did not seem quite to view the matter in the same comic manner as the others.

"Ladies, gentlemen!" urged Catchpole, as a number of horny, but far from honest, hands were laid upon him; "you do me a wrong and yourself an injury. The law should be respected by everyone but lawyers. I do not wish to threaten you, but as one of the lower members of the law—"

"Shut up!" said a sturdy fellow, giving the constable a severe shaking.

"I protest, I—I—Let us go, gentlemen, and we will depart in peace."

"No!" thundered Bill Blarney; "that we will not do; but as one day we may be nabbed and compelled to take our trial we will give you the same fair chance as we shall have. Bring the prisoners forward and bind their arms."

---

[79] Either settle their debts, or death.

Vainly did Messrs. Catchpole and Grabham try to escape and implore for mercy.

They were dragged ruthlessly forward and bound.

Bound, and that not in the gentlest manner, for it must be admitted that these gentlemen of the road and light-fingered people were not given to tenderness at the best of times, and when the men to be tormented were constables they looked upon the matter as a duty combined with pleasure.

"So, gentlemen, you are come here as spies," said Blarney, who had seated himself at the end of the room, and had put Judy by his side, as if she had been his queen. "Do you think that we will have spies at the Bull in Top Boots? No!"

"Mercy! kind sir," said Catchpole, as he dropped down on his knees.

"Mercy!" cried Grabham, doing the same; "we did not come here to spy upon you, but to see what we could find out about that horrible monster Spring-Heeled Jack, whom folks call the Terror of London."

"By my faith! but you have found out something about him," said Judy, laughing. "You see, he can appear like a gentleman, and not like a devil, which I hold that it is more than you can do, you spalpeens."[80]

"You are right, Judy, my darling," said Blarney; "as you always are."

"Besides, may not this Spring-Heeled Jack be one of us?" continued the lady, being thus encouraged. "I have heard that he can make pretty free with other people's gold. In fact, I believe him to be a regular romany" (gipsy), "and a swell high-toly man" (highwayman), "who just puts on this disguise to frighten the constables. At all events, if the constables hate him he must be a pal of ours."

"Bravo—bravo!" cried the men. "Spring-Heeled Jack is a friend of ours!" shouted the men. "Whoever heard of his doing a poor man an injury? Long live Spring-Heeled Jack!"

"That's right, boys!" cried Judy Bulgrudery, as she seized up a glass from a table and filled it with neat spirits—"that's right! and whatever be our faults—and I don't pretend to say that we have not some—forgetfulness or treachery to our friends is not amongst them. So join me, lads, in drinking to Spring-Heeled Jack."

This was not quite what Mr. Blarney had reckoned on.

But what was he to do? The toast was received with such loud cheers that he felt even with the power he had over the men, he would not be able to stop them.

So, like the cunning fellow he was, he pretended to join in the cheers.

In fact, no one drank the health of Spring-Heeled Jack as loudly as he.

In the first place, he greatly doubted if Spring-heeled Jack was a thief.

In the second, he came to the conclusion that if Spring-Heeled Jack really was a thief he would soon get the command over the others, and in that case it would be as well to keep friendly with him, so that he might be his lieutenant.

"Better be captain than lieutenant," he argued; "but better be lieutenant than nothing."

And so he became suddenly the most complimentary of all to Jack.

"Jack is a giant!" he cried; "but, although he did me a little injury just now, I bear him no grudge, and so I'll drink his health again and again."

And so he did, and so did the rest of the company, much as they would have drunk the health of the devil himself, if only for the drinking sake, for the customers of the Bull in Top Boots were thirsty souls, as the landlord well knew to his profit.

---

[80] Scoundrels.

"Ha! ha! ha!" came the stern laughter of Spring-Heeled Jack, as if he held them all in contempt.

They glanced nervously round, but no sign of Jack was to be seen.

"Leave Jack alone and let us turn our kind attention to these gentlemen."

So spoke Judy Bulgrudery, and the two miserable constables cast looks of pleading towards her, for they saw plainly that she ruled and their fate was in her hands.

But there was no pity in the Amazon's face or manner.

She was as cold and stern as a statue. Pity! She enjoyed their pain.

"Oh! do have some mercy, ladies and gentlemen?" groaned Catchpole. "Consider that we are married men, and if you have no pity for us, think of our wives and have pity for them!" exclaimed Grabham.

"Wives! You are nice men to talk about wives. Do you pity the wives of the poor fellows you take up and have sent to Tyburn?"[81]

The constables had a very good answer to this most unfair charge.

They might have said they only did their duty and obeyed orders, and the thieves did not.

But they dared not speak out boldly. Besides, there was a horrible practice at that time which made the constables hated even by honest, respectable men. I mean the fearful custom of giving blood-money!

This was managed in the following way—

A man started as highwayman, cracksman,[82] or some other illegal profession.

The constables knew where to lay their hands upon him at any moment.

But, no.

They considered their own interests and not those of the public.

Of course a reward was offered for the arrest of the culprit.

But it was not enough.

More crimes were committed—more money was offered for his arrest.

At last the amount offered came to a large sum. and then the constables, who had treated the man almost like a friend before, swooped down upon their victim and carried him off.

They had all the evidence cut and dried, and escape was impossible.

So off in a cart, seated on a coffin, with his back to the horses, went Dare-Devil Dick, or Jolly Jack of Blackheath, and many others, who seemed to think it rather a noble thing, instead of a most degrading one.

Ladies wept and threw them nosegays. Noble lords, who were not a bit more virtuous or decorous than they are now-a-days—in fact, it seems to be the privilege of the aristocracy to remain like stagnant water, so still that it stinks; noble lords sent them cambric shirts to be hanged in, and laughed and chaffed the miserable wretches as they went to their doom.

Of course the clergyman was there to pray. But who listened to him?

Not even the doomed man who stood on the threshold of eternity.

How could he pay any attention amidst the cheering, yelling, laughing crowd, formed of the scum of the people and the ordinary run of the senseless, heartless aristocracy— the so-called nobles who have for so many centuries degraded England?

---

[81] Location of the execution scaffold.
[82] A burglar, especially safebreaker

The fatal noose was tied and—well, we draw a veil over the last scene.

There hangs a man who a little time back was full of life and hope.

Wicked, we do not deny; but were the gay ladies and his noble patrons less so?

Worse—far worse. They were rich, and yet they had all the desires to act as amateur hangmen, even as a titled brute did the other day.

Then the constable pocketed his blood-money and went home to rejoice.

What wonder the people looked with hatred upon the constable, who far more encouraged crime than prevented it!

And so it was that not one look of compassion came in the face of man or woman when Catchpole and Grabham pleaded for mercy.

"No! we will have no mercy upon you," cried Judy, her eyes flashing. "Did not you, or some of you fellows, hang my poor husband for the blood money?"

"Hang them—hang them!" shouted the excited crowd. "They deserve it."

"No; we will not hang them, because I am not sure they are the men who led my husband on, and then seized and sold him to the gallows."

Catchpole and Grabham were delighted to hear this, for they now recognised the virago and knew that they had been the very constables who had sold her husband, and a pretty pull they had made out of it.

"No; we will not hang them. Bill Blarney, order in two bowls of punch as hot as the people can make it."

Catchpole and his companion seemed greatly relieved at this order, as they thought that all they would have to do would be to "pay their footing," as it is commonly called—that is, pay for the two bowls of punch, and then be permitted to depart in peace.

Unhappy men! How little did they know what was in store for them! The punch was brought, and then Judy Bulgrudery, who had become suddenly as imperious as the Empress Theodora,[83] ordered two of the strongest men in the company to take the bowls and compel the unfortunate constables to drink them—one each.

Vainly they implored to be spared, declaring that the punch was so hot that it scalded their mouths.

Their prayers were not listened to, or perhaps it would be better to say, were only derided.

They were compelled to drink not only the health of Spring-Heeled Jack, but of the whole company.

Resistance was useless, and with many a gulp they drunk off the punch.

The liquid being potent as well as very hot, soon had the desired effect upon the constables.

They staggered to their feet and began singing all kinds of songs.

"Now bring in the book and swear them in members of the Black Highwaymen."

This proposition seemed to sober the constables a little.

"Stop—stop" they cried; "to do what you wish would make us liable to be hanged."

"That is just what we know," replied Judy, with a laugh; "and just what we want."

The company roared at this piece of pleasantry, and called on them to sign.

But here the men were obstinate.

Their necks might depend on it, and they would not do so.

---

83 Byzantine empress in the 6th century.

"Well, then," said Judy, with a laugh, "since you will not do that you shall join the merry company of Moonrakers."[84]

"Any company sooner than that dreadful Black Band."

"Let it be so. Take them away, lads, and we will soon instruct them."

The miserable wretches were seized and dragged out into the porch of the inn.

Here they were placed back to back, at the mercy of the storm, which now raged fiercely, whilst the others took shelter in the doorways of the hostelry and the stables, all laughing with delight; and even the landlord came forth, pipe in one hand and a foaming tankard of brimming ale in the other, to witness what he was pleased to call the fun.

Presently a large blanket was produced, and six men seized it.

One of these stalwart fellows stood at each corner, and the other two took up their position one on each side.

Each grasped the blanket firmly with both hands, and then two others, lifting Mr. Catchpole up, threw him into the centre of the blanket.

Then the men who held the blanket ran all together, paused a moment, and sprung back suddenly, so that the blanket was stretched to its fullest extent, the consequence being that the miserable Catchpole was jerked some dozen feet in the air, from whence he fell back into the blanket.

Up he was thrown again, and this was repeated at least twenty times, until the unhappy wretch was so dazed with his flight through the air and the effects of the punch that he could do nothing but sigh and yawn.

The sport thus began to lose much of its excitement.

When he had been able to beg for mercy and yell as he sped upwards, the laughter had been uproarious, but now it was over.

Over for Catchpole, but not for his comrade, Elias Grabham.

Catchpole was removed from the blanket and Grabham forced to take his place.

Up he went, and being a somewhat lighter mass than his companion, he flew up higher and came down much lighter, so that he lasted longer. and the inhuman merriment was again resumed whilst Judy and some of the other viragos clapped their hands, and sang in chorus something like this—

> *"There he goes, up! up! up!*
> *There he goes, down! down! down!*
> *Here he goes, head over heels,*
> *And falls on his feet or crown."*

Surely never were two men so fearfully tormented as these two!

Mr. Grabham lasted out so well that the pleasure he gave them seemed inexhaustible.

But pleasure is fleeting, and after cursing, imploring, and shouting, he became as silent as his companion.

But the fun had become so fascinating that it was not to be easily relinquished.

Catchpole had somewhat recovered, and a cry arose that he should be put back and receive another dose.

Then somebody more fiendlike than the rest suggested that the pair of them should

---

[84] Smugglers.

be put in and tossed in the blanket together. With a yell of delight the proposition was accepted by the crowd.

Catchpole, pale and trembling, was lifted up and thrown with but little ceremony upon the body of his panting companion.

The additional weight needed additional strength, but for such work as this hands are never needed.

A dozen volunteers sprang forward, and up shot the luckless wights high in the air.

But now the so-called fun was redoubled, for the two constables knocked against each other as they flew up in the air or fell in the blanket.

There they bit, kicked, and scratched each other as well as they could, considering that their arms were bound.

Then Judy led off the chorus as before, singing—

"There they go up! up! up!
There they go down! down! down! &c"

The chorus had been sung once through, and the repetition had come to the "Down! down! down!" when the words became prophetic, for Catchpole and Grabham came down clinging together.

The weight was too much for the blanket.

It split, and the two constables rolled through with a crash to the ground.

Amidst sneers and laughter they were lifted up and conducted back to the parlour of the Bull in Top Boots.

Here they were once more ordered to take the oath and sign the book of the Black Band.

They no longer hesitated, but signed at once.

"Now, mark what I have to say," said Bill Blarney, who had dictated the oath and witnessed the signature. "If you break that oath, or in any way, by word or deed—by writing or hinting—you try to betray the band, you will be dead men before twenty hours have passed over your heads. You, knowing this, still swear to be true to your comrades, and acknowledge me your captain?"

The constables gulped down the curses which rose to their lips, but made no attempt to utter them, only stammering out a weak, tremulous—

"Yes."

"Boys!" cried Blarney, "you have heard what they have sworn, and can bear witness to it?"

"We can!" shouted the men.

"And if they break their oath in the slightest degree the penalty is—"

"Death!" replied the stern chorus.

"We—we will be true to our word!" cried the trembling men.

"Ha! ha! ha!" came as the fellows said this, and a vivid flash of lightning showed the terrible figure clinging batlike to the window, glaring in with demoniacal pleasure at the scene.

Then came a loud burst of thunder, and when the people had recovered from their horror and astonishment the fiendlike figure had disappeared.

"By the horns of the devil it is a terrible night," said Blarney, with a shudder. "I think, lads and lasses, we had better separate."

Blarney did not care to own the truth of the matter, but the fact was that he did not like the constant appearance of Spring-Heeled Jack.

Judy by this time had drunk so much that she would have faced the devil, as far as courage went; but the drink had deprived her of all powers of movement, and she leaned back in her chair snoring loudly.

So, as the rest of the company prepared to depart, Blarney made her as comfortable as he could on a settle, placing some old clothes, which he borrowed from the landlord, over her to keep her warm, and a sack rolled up by way of a pillow beneath her head.

In this comfortable position Captain Blarney left his charmer to sleep off the drink.

Then, pulling his coat lightly around him, he bade the landlord good-night, and having given some orders as to Judy's care and comfort, ventured out into the night.

The night was indeed a rough one.

The wind howled amongst the chimney pots—the rain came down in heavy showers, the lightning flashed through the dark, heavy sky, and the thunder roared and rattled like a battery of artillery.

Blarney made his way to Blackfriars Bridge, when the storm increased so in violence, that he took shelter under one of the dark arches, little dreaming what adventures this would lead to.

CHAPTER XXXVII.

THE MEETING BENEATH THE ARCH—THE ROW DOWN THE RIVER.

AS Blarney stood beneath the dark arch of the bridge, and glanced down the river, the sight he beheld was grand in the extreme, but terrible and wild.

The sky was as black as ink, only being lit up by the vivid flashes of the forked lightning.

The wind rushed along in fierce gusts, which it was hard to stand up against.

It howled through the arches, screaming like so many fiends, invisible to the eye, but palpable to touch and hearing.

A night on which witches and warlocks would hold their revels.

At his feet rolled the dark, swollen river, moaning and groaning as it hurried on to the sea.

Blarney believed himself alone, but, to his astonishment, a flash of lightning more brilliant than those which had gone before showed him a tall man, masked, and clad in a long cloak.

On his head was a slouched hat, and his legs and feet were clad in heavy riding-boots, the rest of his dress being hidden by his cloak.

There was something supernatural in the fellow's look that Blarney did not like, and he drew a little on one side whilst he eyed the dim outline of the stranger with the greatest suspicion.

"You need not fear me, Captain Blarney," said the stranger, in deep tones.

"By the powers! But he knows my name. Who are you?"

"One who has employed you more than once," replied the other.

"If that is the case, who are you—friend or foe?"

"A friend, and one who will reward you well if you serve me faithfully."

"Sure, the faithfulness of most services depends upon the pay."

"Of the payment you need not doubt. That shall be certain and good."

"Wurrah! but that's the kind of thing which suits Bill Blarney."

"The services I require will not be performed without some danger."

"What! now, and is it a coward you take me for? What would an adventure be unless it had a spice of the devil in it?"

As he said these words a fearful flash of lightning illuminated the scene, and Blarney again saw the stranger perfectly, and it must be confessed that he did not like his looks.

"But stop!" he cried. "Maybe you are the devil himself? I know Father O'Flaherty used to declare that I served him more than anyone else, and, be jabers! I believe his reverence was right."

"I can fully believe that," replied the stranger, with a bitter laugh.

"True for you, sir; but at the same time there's a difference between serving his Satanic Majesty directly and indirectly. The last you may do by accident, but the other—well, maybe it would be awkward."

"Fear not; I have not the honour to be his Satanic Majesty, or even one of his imps as yet. But I have no time to waste. Here are ten pieces of gold. Say that you will obey my commands and they are yours."

The temptation of the gold almost overcame all scruples on the Irishman's score.

But still he hesitated, and men, like women, when once hesitating, are lost.

"Well, your honour," he began, "I am sure I would do all I could to oblige you, but times are hard, and the ten pieces of gold would go only a little way."

"Do as I bid you, and when to-night's work is done the ten shall be doubled."

"Shure! and what a coaxing way you have," said Blarney, in the tones his name implies.

"Enough of that. Is it a bargain, or is it not?" cried the stranger, impatiently.

"Yes, sir, I'm on. Now what am I to do before I touch the shiners?"[85]

"There are the ten I promised you. You see I keep my promise."

"And by the piper who played before Moses I'll keep mine."

"See that you do, or it will be the worse for you. I was at the Bull in Top Boots to-night."

"The deuce you were! I did not see you there," cried Blarney.

"I had no intention that you should. But I saw all the treatment that the two constables received, and their having to take the oath to the Black Band."

"Then you saw as pretty a little bit of sport as you ever did see or will again."

"And I saw Mistress Judy's pretty dance with Spring-Heeled Jack."

Blarney scratched his head, but said nothing to this.

"That does not seem to have pleased you quite as much?"

"Curse the fellow—no!" cried Blarney, quickly. "It's my belief that he is the devil himself. He has cast a spell upon Judy, and that's sure. I never saw her go on so before."

"He is no devil, but a man. I have often met him, and know what I say is true. One day, if it suits his purpose, he will carry your dear lady off, as—as he has done some others. I know the brute's character."

"If he dare lay a hand upon Judy Bulgrudery I'll have his life."

"I applaud your sentiment, Captain Blarney. I, too, have sworn to kill this monster whenever I get the chance. In that, at least, we agree."

"May your shadow never be less for those words," said Blarney.

"And now to business. You know the Thames-wall?"

---

[85] The coins.

"No one knows it better. I have had too many jobs on it not to."

"Good! And you can manage a boat well?"

"Divil a Thames waterman better, above or below bridge."

"Good again. You also know one Gedge Foote, a deformed scoundrel?"

"What man who has been on the road does not know Gedge?"

"Ah! I thought so. He is a 'fence'—in other words, a receiver of stolen goods?"

"You seem to know him almost as well as I do," replied Blarney.

"Yes, I know him and what he is; but the business I have with him is very different from yours. You know his house?"

"What the old one down by the Mint? I should think I do."

"I must go there immediately," said the stranger.

"It's a jolly long walk," replied Blarney; "and such a night, too!"

"But I want to go the quickest way, and that is by water."

"Impossible! The river is far too rough for that—the boat might be swamped."

"I am aware of that, and have provided myself with a boat so broad in the beam that she will be safe even in this fearful night. You must take one oar, and I will pull the other."

"And when we have arrived there what are we to do?"

"You will have to ground the boat whilst I visit Gedge Foote."

"And after that—what then?"

"We must pull to some place of safety, where I will pay you the return money."

"It's dangerous work, but it shall be done. Where is the boat?"

"Here—moored close by the side of this pier," replied the stranger.

"Stay one moment. How did you know that I was here?" asked Blarney.

"Why I followed you from the Bull in Top Boots."

"Yes, yes, I know that; but about the boat—how did that come here? You had not time to get it since we left the tavern."

"Certainly not, most suspicious of men. That was placed there before nightfall. I had made up my mind to visit old Gedge Foote, but wanted someone to guide me."

"Why did you not go in the daytime, and by land?"

"For two very good reasons. In the first place, I do not wish to seen. You can understand that?"

"Yes; I have been placed in the same circumstances myself."

"I can well believe that. The other reason is that Gedge Foote does not care for visitors before this time of the night. He has reasons for that."

"I know he has," laughed Blarney. "Well, the pay is good, and I have often risked my life for less money, and so, sir, I am on with you. We had better start at once, as the tide will turn shortly, then the work we shall have before us will be almost more than we can manage."

The two men entered the boat, the painter was cast off, and the boat swirled out into the tide.

"Keep her head straight, your honour—keep her head straight, as if she gets broadside on to the tide we shall be lost. Curse it! what is that?"

The last exclamation was caused by a sudden thump on the bow of the boat, which made it nearly dip under water.

Neither of the men dared leave off rowing because of the rush of the water, and therefore they could only glance over their shoulders.

Not a thing was to be seen, and the boat now sped through the water.

"Bah! it's nothing," said the stranger; "pull on as quickly as you can."

They pulled with all their might and main, but both men seemed to think that there was something wrong with the boat.

"I should think this a bad boat to pull against tide," growled Blarney.

"It should not be; the man from whom I bought it declared it a splendid one for pulling. But we must be close on the house now, and in a few minutes shall once more be in safety. Give way, my lad!"

They did pull with might and main, and were soon under old Gedge Foote's house.

This house was one of those old buildings which had once been a mansion—almost a palace—but had long fallen into decay, and had become as miserable looking and as low as the neighbourhood had become in which it was situated.

The basement wall was only two feet from the river, and the balcony above overhung the stream.

The windows, save the one which was by the balcony that overhung the stream, were all securely barred and bolted, in such a manner that they seemed as if they would defy the most expert burglar.

One light, and that a dim one, was alone to be seen, and that shone from the window in front of which the balcony ran.

"The miserly wretch is at home," said the stranger. "Ship your oars and make the boat fast."

Bang!

And once more down went the bows of the boat; but this time they could see the cause.

Bounding from the boat on to the stone quay, Spring-Heeled Jack flew into the air, and then turning round, cried—

"Ha! ha! ha! I thank you for my row, Sir Roland. One day I will make you and your servants suffer for this wickedness. Would it were that I was at liberty to denounce you now! but I cannot. No thought of mercy should hold me back. I would strike and spare not. So go on your wicked way; but, remember, the day of reckoning is growing nearer and nearer."

"Fiend!" cried Sir Roland, as he drew a pistol, "thus will I—"

But before he could level the pistol Spring-Heeled Jack had disappeared.

"Aid me to land," said the stranger, who was none other than Sir Roland, "and wait for me here. Fear not! I will not keep you long."

Sir Roland leaped ashore, and hurried down a narrow lane, so as to reach the front of the house.

CHAPTER XXXVIII.

SIR ROLAND'S BUSINESS WITH GEDGE FOOTE IS SOMEWHAT INTERRUPTED.

OLD Gedge Foote sat in deep meditation in his own room, scanning some books of accounts by the aid of a single dip candle.

Three times did he go over one column of figures, and at last cast down his pen in despair.

"Confusion seize the girl!" he exclaimed, as he rose from his chair and paced up and down the room. "Confusion seize the girl! Has she bewitched me? She must have done, or I, Gedge Foote, who has laughed at the tears of beauty when pleading for mercy, either for themselves or for those they loved—not only laughed, but enjoyed it—would not now be so overthrown that I cannot pay attention to my dear books. I must be bewitched."

Throwing himself back into the chair he made another attempt, but without success.

Once more dashing down his pen, he sprung up, and was about to resume his march, when he was startled by a loud knocking at the door.

"Who can this be?" he muttered. "I expected no one, and few call on me who have not made an appointment."

He glanced hastily round the room to see that there were no valuables left about.

Then he carefully put away his books, and taking a brace of pistols from the wall, candle in hand, left the apartment.

No sooner had he done so than the catch of the window was forced back, and Spring-Heeled Jack entered the room.

Wrapping the cloak—which being bound to his arms and legs gave him the bat-like look which he had when he leaped through the air—round his body, he crouched down in a corner and waited to see what would happen.

He had carefully closed the window, but not fastened it, before this.

Meanwhile, Gedge Foote had crept down to the front door, and opening a small trap, not more than an inch and a-half in diameter, which was placed in the centre of the door, thrust forth the barrel of his pistol, at the same time exclaiming—

"Who are you, and what want you here at this time of night?"

"A friend! Open, Gedge Foote, and you will not repent it," said the voice.

"I open to no man who does not give me his name," said Gedge.

"Are you as particular with all your customers?" sneered Sir Roland; for it was he.

"Not all; but then, I know their voices—I do not know yours."

A muttered oath was all that this remark called forth.

"Begone!" said Gedge, sternly. "Begone, or I fire. My pistol never misses."

"Wait, and I will put my name under the door.".

This seemed to satisfy Gedge Foote, who watched for the slip of paper.

But as he did so he took care not to withdraw his pistol.

The paper appeared, and Gedge Foote, having removed his pistol, quickly closed the catch and then picked up the scrip.

"Sir Roland Ashton!" he exclaimed. "What can he want with me?"

Once more the knocking sounded at the door.

"He once was a good customer of mine, and I must not refuse him admittance."

"Confound it, man!" cried Sir Roland; "am I to be kept here all night in the rain?"

"Patience—patience, Sir Roland, and I will unbar the door."

"There is no need to publish my name all over the Mint," Said Sir Roland, as he walked in and shook the rain-drops from his cloak.

"It would not be the first time it has been heard there, or in Alsatia[86] either."

"Bar the door. I would speak to you in private," said Sir Roland, not noticing this last speech.

"As you will, worshipful sir. I am at your commands."

---

[86] An area in Whitefriars known for its lawlessness, and a refuge for criminals.

Saying which, Gedge Foote closed and barred the door carefully.

"This way, Sir Roland—this way. It is a terrible night, and the business ought indeed to be urgent that has brought you out in it. This room I use as my office."

And with that the old miser lighted the way into the room where we first discovered him.

"Be seated, Sir Roland—be seated," said Gedge Foote, as he motioned towards a chair opposite his own by the table. "It is many years since we did business together. What is it now?"

"The cry that is made by most men, and which I had never let out of my mouth when I was young—"

"And that cry, Sir Roland?" demanded Gedge Foote, suspiciously.

"Money—the universal want. I want and must have a large sum of money."

"What! you the rich Sir Roland Ashton in want of money? Impossible!"

"It may seem so to you; but it is not so in fact. I have drawn largely on my estates. For all the money that is paid my agents is stolen."

"Stolen!—how? Do you think, Sir Roland, that I have had anything to do in this matter?"

"Far be it from me to think so," replied Sir Roland, "although I know, at one time, Gedge Foote knew as much about the gentlemen of the Mint as most men."

"Ah! that was when you were one of the captains of the Black Band."

"Hush! the least said of that the better," exclaimed Sir Roland, hastily.

"And the least said about my past affairs the better, Sir Roland," said Gedge.

"Well, let that be agreed; and now about the money?"

"Impossible! I have no money to lend," cried Gedge Foote.

"Tut! do not tell me that; I know you are wealthy, very wealthy."

"You mistake, my dear Sir Roland; I have lost all my money."

"And how did you lose all your money?" demanded Sir Roland.

"The same way as you did," replied Gedge, taken off his guard.

"And may I ask how that was?" returned Sir Roland, sharply.

"Stolen!" grinned Mr. Gedge Foote, with a look of triumph, as much as to say, "I have matched you there, my fine fellow—one lie for another."

"Do not think to do me, Gedge Foote," said Sir Roland. "Remember, I know the history of the sunken pit, or well, or whatever you call it. What I want is gold, and that I mean to have. But mark you this, Gedge, you shall have twenty-five per cent interest, and that safe, upon it."

"With security?" demanded Gedge, rather puzzled.

"Aye! with security. You know the Meadow Farm? Well, I will place all the deeds of ownership in your hands as security. Will that not suit you, you old Shylock?"

"Humph! How much do you want?" growled Gedge Foote.

"Two thousand pounds."

"Two thousand pounds! Are you mad?"

"The farm is worth five thousand pounds at least."

"Then there is the interest on my money."

"Which is more than covered. Come, Gedge, let us go and fetch the money, and then we will have one of your old bottles of Burgundy."

"You mean honourably to me?" replied Gedge, doubtfully.

"Of course I do. Why should I not?"

"True! Well, come with me. I know you know the secret of this house."

"I ought to. Was it not in my family for years? Aye! built for them, I believe."

"Then," hissed Gedge Foote, why did they make that well?"

"I don't know," said Sir Roland, calmly, but his face showed that he was much annoyed; "to cool their wines, I suppose."

"Or drown their wives!"

"Silence, hound!" cried Sir Roland, passionately; "one word more and I quit this house."

"Do, and I'll keep my money. Good-night, Sir Roland—good-night!"

"Don't be a fool, Gedge. You know very well I don't mean that. Come, let me have the money, and then for the wine."

Jolly old wine—jolly old wine!
The ruddy juice which flows from the vine."

Followed by Sir Roland, old Gedge Foote, candle in hand, led the way down to the cellars of the house.

With a massive key he opened one.

A deep, dark, dank cellar, in the middle of which there appeared a pit.

They knew the pit, or well, but they did not know that Spring-Heeled Jack was close behind them—stealthily watching all their movements.

A looped rope over a pulley, which was fixed to the roof, hung over this well, and taking the candlestick in his teeth, old Gedge descended into the well.

It was with difficulty that Spring-Heeled Jack could keep himself from springing on Sir Roland and hurling him down the pit.

However, he did; and, presently, by means of the double rope, the miser hauled himself up again to the top, with two heavy bags of gold slung round his neck and a well-crusted bottle in his pocket.

He was evidently used to the double rope, and landed himself safely without assistance.

No sooner did Jack see them reappear, than he lightly bounded up the stairs and hid himself behind a partition.

"There is the money, Sir Roland; now the title deeds of the Meadow Farm."

"Here!" cried Sir Roland, as he smacked them down. "Now, my dear fellow, let us drink to the lasses we love best—yours, Gedge?"

"Daisy Leigh!" cried Gedge, throwing himself back in his chair and raising his glass.

"Daisy Leigh!" cried Sir Roland, in horror. "You dare not say to my face that you have presumed to raise your eyes to a lady of my family?"

Before Gedge could answer, the sepulchral laughter of Spring-Heeled Jack rang through the room and he leaped upon the table, leaving them all in the dark.

CHAPTER XXXIX.
SIR ROLAND PLANS A DEED OF ROBBERY.

SIR ROLAND and Gedge Foote staggered to their feet in astonishment, and were just in time to see Spring-Heeled Jack throw open the window and rush on to the balcony.

Sir Roland dashed after the monster, and Spring-Heeled Jack leaped upon the balustrade, and turned as if to defy them.

"Ha! ha! ha!" he roared, as he shook the money-bags which he had snatched up in Sir

Roland's very face. "This gold shall go to the poor. It shall not be used for the vile purposes to which you would put it."

Sir Roland's hands had nearly clasped him when, with another. yell of demoniacal laughter, Jack leaped into the air, and with an aim and precision that was perfectly marvellous dashed down into the boat, staving it in.

Blarney yelled for help, while Spring-Heeled Jack leaped ashore, laughing loudly at the mischief he had created.

"The fiend has escaped!" cried Sir Roland, mad with rage.

"Yes," groaned Gedge Foote; "and he has taken all the money with him."

"Help! help! help! The boat is sinking and I shall be drowned!" roared Blarney.

"Never mind the gold, Foote," said Sir Roland, making for the door. "My man is in danger, and for reasons I cannot explain I would not have him killed for twice the gold."

"Would you? For reasons I need not explain, I'd rather save the money than the man," said Gedge Foote, mournfully; but nevertheless he hurried after Sir Roland and unbarred the door for him.

"I'll stand here, Sir Roland, and wait your return," he said. "Remember, three slight taps on the door will be enough to call me to re-open."

Sir Roland nodded assent and hurried away to rescue Blarney Bill.

No sooner had he gone than old Gedge, ever suspicious, began to think if he had done right in letting the baronet depart so easily.

"May this not have been a trick to do me?" he muttered. "May not this so-called fiend be in the pay of this Sir Roland—a servant, a friend?"

Gedge shook with rage when he thought of this, and at last gasped out—

"If I thought so I'd—I'd murder him; I would indeed! He would not be the first one whom I have throttled."

And he held forth his long, bony hand, and cleaved the air as if he had someone's throat in his grip.

A more horribly fiendish-looking fellow could not be imagined.

"He talks about his family. Well, it was a good one. But who disgraced it? Sir Roland Ashton—the man with the iron will and no conscience. Ho! ho! ho! Sir Roland Ashton, I know enough of your past history to make you dread me—deformed old miser that I am. Ha! ha! ha!"

"Ha! ha! ha!"

Gedge Foote turned round in affright.

Surely he had not imagined that he had heard the laugh of the fiend!

And was it only fear which made him think that he saw a dark form like a huge bat bound lightly up the stairs?

But the light given out by the dim candle, which he had taken the precaution to relight before he followed Sir Roland, did not show him anything distinctly enough to convince him.

Then the laugh had been so subdued that it might really have only been an echo of his own.

"I am nervous—the loss of the money has made me so. But Sir Roland shall pay it me back. It was through him that I lost it, and he is answerable for it."

And so Gedge Foote consoled himself. Even fear giving place to the love of money.

Meanwhile, Sir Roland had hurried down to the river-side.

The boat had sunk, but Blarney had managed to catch hold of an iron ring in the stone wall, where he clung with desperation.

"S'death, Blarney, what a night we are in for!" laughed Sir Roland.

"Don't stand there laughing at me!" roared Blarney. "I wish I had never seen your dirty face. Here are my legs floating about up to my knees in the water, and the saints alone know how much deeper I shall sink if I leave go my hold. Pull me out or I must go down. My hands are as cold as ice."

"Give me your hand and I will pull you out," said Sir Roland, laughing.

"It's meself that will do that, and I never grasped the hand of a friend with greater eagerness. Sure, my top boots, which Judy admired so, have become nothing but leather 'Black Jacks,'[87] full of water. Oh! that thief of the world—that Spring-Heeled Jack—to serve me a trick like this. What harm have I done him? But I'll have my revenge on the ruffian—be he man or be he devil."

By this time Sir Roland had pulled the fellow out of the water, and he stood shivering on the bank.

Certainly up to the knees he was soaking, and his top boots were wet through and thoroughly filled with water.

"Come," said Sir Roland Ashton, "I will put you in a way to gain that which will repay you for all that you have suffered."

"Do you think now that what you have promised me will repay the trouble, not to say the disgrace, I have been through? Devil a bit of it, Sir Roland! I like your pay better than your service, and you must either increase the former or decrease the latter. Here, stay a moment. I feel as if I was walking in Biddy Malone's washing tub. Boots! they are buckets."

He paused a few moments, and, in spite of Sir Roland's impatient protests, pulled his boots off, and poured the water out of them, and even the baronet had to confess that they were full of water.

"Oh! be jabers. Now I have got them off I cannot get them on again," groaned Blarney, as, seating himself on a projecting stone, he made desperate attempts to pull them on.

"Then throw them away," cried Sir Roland, impatiently. "We have no time to lose."

"What! throw them away. The boots Judy admired so? Go in my stocking feet?"

"Take your stockings off will be the wisest plan," replied Sir Roland.

"Och! and I think you are right, for it is penance I should do to be with you."

"Silence, fool! I tell you that if you obey me to-night, not only shall you have money enough to buy fifty pairs of boots, but a full-blood mare, a pair of snappers, fine clothing—aye! even finer than most gentlemen wear."

"You can? That can't be done on thirty shiners—you must know that, Sir Roland!"

"I know that perfectly well. But it can be done on a thousand!"

"A—a what?" cried Bill Blarney, who seemed struck all of a heap at the sum.

"Upon ten hundred pounds and my especial favour," said the baronet.

Mr. Blarney made no further reply than flinging his boots—the boots which Judy had so loved—into the Thames.

---

[87] Boots.

SPRING-HEELED JACK,
THE TERROR OF LONDON.

SIR ROLAND SEVERED THE ROPE AND THE UNHAPPY WRETCH DISAPPEARED.

No. 13.

Then pulling off his stockings he rose up and quietly observed—

"Show me the way to do that, governor, and I'm with you. It is not every day that a fellow gets such a chance, and I'm not the boy to give it up."

"I knew you would not. Now be careful and listen to me."

Here Sir Roland whispered something in Blarney's ear, which made even that hardened villain turn round and look queer.

"Do you mean it?" he asked, in a hoarse whisper. "Can't it be done without—"

"Are you mad? Would you have him wake up the Mint?"

"Well, I should not mind that with most men; but Gedge Foote is a power in himself. Even the Master of the Mint is under obligation to him."

"True; and, therefore, we must run no risks. You understand?"

"Yes; but Gedge Foote knows me too well to trust me in his cellar with him."

"Well, it must be done, and I have a way of doing it. Do not doubt, he will not suspect—and—well, I have the means of making him trust to my word. Come."

"There is only one thing I fear," said Bill Blarney, and he shrank a little back, as if wishing to withdraw from the arrangement.

"And what is that?"

"The Devil, otherwise Jack o' the Spring Heels."

"Tut—nonsense! I will do the deed; you must get the gold." Bill Blarney thought for a moment, and then said—

"I'm on, Sir Roland—I'll do it. The price is too much for anyone to refuse. I'll stick to you until all's blue."

"Then keep quiet. Gedge Foote is here, and we must go into his place unless he suspects something. Be sure to play your part well, and we must succeed."

CHAPTER XL.

THE MURDER IN THE MINT.

GEDGE FOOTE was pleased to see Sir Roland return, but he eyed Blarney somewhat suspiciously.

"What! don't you know me, Gedge?" cried Blarney, as he slapped the old man on the shoulder.

"No—stay a moment. It's Bill Blarney, or Blarney Bill!" he cried.

"That's right, old cock-of-the-walk,[88] and it's many a good bargain I've brought to you."

"Aye, aye! but let bygones be bygones. I have given all that up now."

This Gedge Foote said as he fastened the door securely.

"Given that up? Why, you will never do that until you are in the grave, and then, if they bury you near a family vault, I believe you would steal all the coffin plates and handles, if they were silver."

"Then the coffins would not belong to any of your family," growled Gedge. "They were all buried in the prison precincts, I believe. Ho! ho! ho! I had you there."

"If you do not keep a polite tongue between your teeth I'll pull it out."

"Come, come, no quarrelling. I will not have that," said Sir Roland.

---

[88] An over-confident person who thinks they are better than others.

"Then let him look to himself," replied Bill Blarney; "I'm in no mood to jest."

"Neither am I," said Gedge, with a grim smile. "I don't jest, as a rule, and I think I am a match in strength for Bully Blarney."

And here the deformed wretch stretched forth his long arms so as to show their muscles.

There was no mistake about it; they were immensely powerful.

"Tut, tut, Gedge Foote," said Sir Roland; "we all know your courage and strength. What man in the Mint could doubt it? Did you not wrestle and overpower the Giant Blacksmith, as people called him? I remember it as well as if it were only yesterday, although I was only a lad then."

"Ah! but I was a much younger man then. Not that I think I have lost much of my strength or skill," and here he glanced longingly at Bill Blarney, as if he should like to have another turn with him. "I think I could break a man's neck in a fall, as I did the Giant Blacksmith's, even now."

"To be sure you could—to be sure you could!" said Sir Roland; "so one would not like to try jokes on you. But come upstairs and let us be jolly. I wish to settle about this money and speak to you about dainty Daisy."

Overcome by the praise which he received, and also anxious to hear what he could about Daisy, Gedge Foote led the way upstairs into the room we have before described, and placing the candle on the table motioned the others to be seated.

"Why, how is this, Blarney?" he said, with a chuckle, "Where are your boots?"

By the powers! how should I know? They are floating away somewhere down the Thames. Shure! that thief of the world, Spring-HeeledJack, treated me with a ducking up to the knees, and a pretty state I should have been in walking about with my boots full of water. So that I should not spoil your elegant carpet, I just took them off and threw them away."

"You are very considerate, Bully Blarney, I am sure," sneered Gedge Foote.

"Come—come! no more compliments," said Sir Roland, who was secretly enjoying this sparring. "Give him a pair of boots, Gedge Foote, for as we have lost our boat we shall have to spend a night in the Mint."

"Not the first time you have done that, Sir Roland Ashton," laughed Gedge.

"Nor will it be the last, I daresay," replied Sir Roland, carelessly.

"'Sdeath! I should think not. But if I give Bully Blarney boots, who is to pay for them?"

"To the devil with you, you spalpeen! Do you think that I want any one to pay for my boots?" cried Blarney. "There's a guinea for you," and he threw a guinea on the table.

"Not enough by half," said Gedge, coolly, as he thrust back the guinea.

"Oh! the thief of the world," cried Blarney, "to take advantage of a man's necessity. Shure! then, you are worse than a heathen Jew down Petticoat-lane."[89]

"Make hay while the sun shines, you know," laughed Gedge Foote.

"But devil a bit of sun is there shining. Come, Gedge, out with the boots and a pair of warm stockings, and I'll spring another half guinea."

But Gedge Foote, the miser, was not to be done by Blarney.

It was not until another guinea had been advanced that the articles of clothing were produced and Bill Blarney made comfortable.

Then, Sir Roland having promised to pay all expenses, a large stone jar of brandy was

---

[89] A market site which still exists today.

produced, and the trio set to work to make a jovial night of it.

At least Gedge Foote imagined so. Little did he think how the night would end!

"See that that window is securely fastened, Gedge Foote," he said, as he poured out a bumper of brandy. "I have no taste for any further intrusion on the part of Spring-Heeled Jack. Even Bill Blarney has had enough of him."

"I should think I had. If I never see the devil again I shall not be sorry."

"If I see him again I'll have my arms round his throat," said Gedge.

"And do you think he would stand still and let you?" demanded Blarney.

"I should not ask him," replied Gedge Foote, with a chuckle, as he fastened the window securely, taking the greatest care to place a heavy piece of furniture in front of it, in doing which he was assisted by Sir Roland and Bill Blarney. "Once my hands are round a man's throat I don't think he has much chance of escape. What think you, Sir Roland?"

"I think that a fellow might as well try to get out of the pulley as your grasp."

"Ha! ha! ha! You have seen my handiwork, Sir Roland?"

Sir Roland shuddered, for he had seen Gedge Foote's performance, and a ghastly piece of work it was. But he deemed it wise not to say anything, and so passed it off with a laugh,

"We will not talk of these matters now," said Sir Roland, laughing; "but now let us have a jolly night."

Pipes were lit and glasses filled, and then many a tale was told—stories of such a nature that we certainly shall not write them down here, but which were received by the company with words of applause.

"Come, Gedge!" cried Sir Roland; "you used to sing a good song. Now let us have one."

"Nay, Sir Roland," laughed Gedge Foote, who had taken a great deal more drink than was good for him; "my singing days are over. I have no ear for music."

"Tut! man; let me see—this is how that song used to run in the jolly days of the Mint?" And Sir Roland trolled out—

"THE MARQUIS AND PAIR.

"I had just drank a cup and kissed the barmaid
And of lies I had told her a few, I'm afraid;
When William, the ostler, says—'Here, Captain Dick,
I think if you ride to the health, and ride quick,
With a couple of snappers, you may do the trick
On a marquis, who rides in his carriage and pair!'"

"Hurrah!" cried Gedge Foote, who had now drank deeply of the spirits; "chorus—

"On a marquis who rides in his carriage and pair!"

Then Sir Roland, who had thrown himself entirely into the party, sang—

"So I mounted my mare, and I galloped along,
Just humming the tune of an old drinking song;
And beneath the dark tree used by old Turpin, Dick,
I managed to do that neat little trick—
For the gold of the marquis I quickly did nick,
Then left him alone in his carriage and pair."

"Bravo!" cried Gedge Foote. "But how about that brandy? Who's to pay me for that?" Gedge Foote had been drinking freely and felt quarrelsome.

"I will; don't think you shall lose by it. If you doubt me, here is my note of hand for it."

And, tearing a leaf out of his pocket-book, he wrote out an I O U.

Gedge Foote took it up, examined it carefully, and then placed it on a side-table.

"Will that satisfy you, Gedge?"

"Yes; that will do. But mark this—if it is not paid in time I shall be down at Ashton Hall with the bailiffs in no time."

"And we will give you as merry a meeting as you have given us in the Mint," laughed Sir Roland. "Now let us fill up our glasses, and Gedge shall sing us a song."

"It's many years since I sang a song," said Gedge, who was in that peculiar state of drink that he had left off being quarrelsome and had become morose.

"Nonsense, man. Have you forgotten the song that poor devil of an author, who had to seek the precincts of the Mint, wrote about you? Let me see, what was its name?"

"I know," cried Bill Blarney; "it was called 'My Character.'"

"Ah! that was it," cried Sir Roland. "No song was better known in the Mint than that, and no man sang it better than Gedge himself, or enjoyed the humour more."

Gedge Foote was tickled by this—his vanity was pleased and he did not fail to show it. "Ha! ha! ha! I was a wild dog in those days. Ho! Ho! ho! ho! Ugly as I am, the girls did not dislike old Gedge Foote. He used to win them."

"Buy them," whispered Blarney to Sir Roland, who nodded assent.

"Ha! ha! there was many a dainty little chit there; but none so dainty as little Daisy. Come, let us drink the health of dear little Daisy. Daisy, gentlemen, drink!"

Sir Roland's face turned red with passion, but he drank the toast.

"And now for the song," cried Blarney, and Gedge, who had drunk deeply, sang—

"GEDGE FOOTE'S HISTORY AND CHARACTER.

"In childhood's hours, called sunny,
I never could delight
In jokes some folks called funny,
But dearly I loved spite.
My grandma's nice, soft cushions,
I stuffed quite full of pins;
With bruises and contusions,
I filled my brother's shins.

"For, oh! I'm a character—oh! I'm a character,
The like of which no one saw before;
Oh! yes, I'm a character—yes, I'm a character,
That people all do call a bore."

"One day I got a blister,
And in the dead of night;
I wrapped it round my sister,
It drew her out of sight.
I've been a money lender—
I've kept a gambling den;

Paid dividends most slender,
And ruined many men.

"For, oh! I'm a character—oh! I'm a character,
A thing which no one can deny.
Yes, I'm a character—yes, I'm a character,
Who does deny it tells a lie."

"Bravo! bravo!"

Gedge bowed his thanks to the gentlemen who had so kindly praised him, and drank off his glass of spirits and water.

"Look here, Roland Ashton," he said, with sudden tipsy gravity, as he filled up another jorum[90] of grog, "I'm not going to be gulled by you. I must have that money returned."

"So you shall, Gedge," replied Sir Roland, "have I not told you so?"

This was said in the most conciliatory manner, but there was a nasty twinkle in his eye Gedge Foote did not fail to notice.

"Told me so, yes—you have told me so; but I know what faith to put in your word. Bah! man, I never would trust anybody's word, and least of all would I trust that of Sir Roland Ashton."

"I know not why you should doubt me," replied Sir Roland, sharply.

"Pish! you are a bad man, Sir Roland; and bad men never care about their words."

"You ought to be a judge in such a case!" sneered Sir Roland Ashton.

He appeared to be very calm, but his eyes flashed.

Bill Blarney looked at Gedge Foote and opened a large clasp-knife beneath the table.

"I am a judge in such cases," said Gedge Foote, shaking his head.

"I should think very few good people had any dealings with you, Gedge Foote," laughed Blarney.

"So much the better, Bully Blarney, or I should not have you here."

Gedge Foote little thought how fast he was building up his own fate.

Then he cried, in a boastful tone. "I don't want the money—I have heaps of money— money I keep in a safe place, as you know, Sir Roland. Gad's life! I believe I could buy up Ashton Hall and all the estates belonging to the family and not feel the poorer for it."

"And where do you keep all this vast amount of wealth?" asked Blarney.

"That's my secret, Bully Blarney," laughed Gedge Foote.

"We all know you are rich, Gedge," said Sir Roland, "and so you should be, considering the self-denying life you have led. Living all alone like a rat in a hole, how could you spend your money?"

"Ha! ha! ha! I've not been quite such a dull dog as you think."

"Indeed. I never heard that you were given to any gaiety, save now and then indulging in a social glass, as we have done this evening."

"Oh! I have had my fun," cried Gedge Foote, "only I was not such a fool as to let other people know it. Ask old Mrs. Foster, and she will tell you that Gedge Foote loves a girl's lips as much as most men. Ha! ha! ha! It was from her house that my dainty little Daisy gave me the slip. Pretty, dainty, little Daisy!"

Sir Roland bit his lip when he heard this hideous monster speak so of the charming

---

[90] Drinking bowl.

girl allied to him by ties of blood-relationship.

But he made no remark, and bent his eyes down on the table, so that Gedge should not see their angry expression.

"Now look here, Sir Roland," continued Gedge, who kept on drinking freely, and who grew more impertinent as he drank; "you owe me two thousand pounds!"

"You seem to forget that I never had the money," said Sir Roland.

"What of that?" cried Gedge. "I have the acknowledgement of it safe enough, and, better still, I have one or two of your secrets, Sir Roland."

This was a dangerous thing for Gedge to have said, but he had drank too much to notice that.

"Ha! ha! Sir Roland. The lads of the Mint love old Gedge Foote, and would resent any injury done him. Be sure of that, and you, too, Bully Blarney. I'm not only free of the Mint, but I am one of the chief rulers. Ha! ha! ha!"

Sir Roland and Blarney exchanged glances with each other.

"I tell you, Sir Roland, that if I were to give the signal I could call up a number of men who would come to the rescue."

"I do not doubt it. I know that the rules of the Mint are very stringent," replied Sir Roland; but Bill Blarney noticed that he drew forth a sharp dagger made to cut as well as thrust—more like a hunting knife, in fact.

"Well, Sir Roland, I'll tell you what I will do. I'll not only forgive you that money, but I will advance you as much again, on one condition."

"Gedge, you are a prince of good fellows. Let me know the condition. It will be hard indeed if I cannot comply with them for such a sum."

"The thing is easy enough," replied Gedge. "Your cousin, Daisy Leigh, must become my wife!"

"Your wife! Are you mad? Have I not told you the thing is impossible?"

"Tut! Sir Roland. Do you think I care for what you say? I have an argument that will overcome all your scruples."

"And what is that argument?" asked Sir Roland, breathing heavily.

"The argument that moves all the world—money."

"You speak like a book," said Bully Blarney. "Money rules all."

"True," replied Sir Roland; "and as far as I am concerned, I should not care who married Daisy Leigh—whether it be our good friend, Gedge Foote, or anyone else. But I do not know where she is."

"That won't suit me, Sir Roland," said Gedge, as he lolled back in his chair. "You don't think that I was such a fool when I had once taken a fancy to the pretty little Daisy to lose sight of her?"

Sir Roland ground his teeth with rage, but answered, lightly—

"You speak to me in riddles, Gedge Foote; I do not understand you."

"Ho! ho! ho! None so hard of understanding as those who will not understand," roared Gedge Foote with a burst of coarse laughter, and he tossed off another bumper of neat spirits "Ho! ho! ho! That's a good one, that is. Do you think that I did not set my people to work? Of course I did, and they precious soon ferreted something out. They knew all about her being at old Dimity's Theatre, and how she was carried off by you to the lone house in the wood, where, I suppose, she is now."

"So far I must admit that you have gained true information," said Sir Roland, quietly. "But you have not heard all the rest."

"The girl has not come to a violent death?" demanded Gedge, savagely.

"Not that I am aware of. I know not what has become of her."

"Don't humbug me. I'll not believe it. You carried her off."

"I do not deny it. I carried her off with the most virtuous designs in the world. I wished to save her from marrying a rascal so much beneath her—one Harry Banks, a clown."

"You protect her! A pretty protector you are, Sir Roland. Ha! ha! ha! Sir Roland Ashton setting up for a protector of innocence. That is rather too good a thing. No, no, Sir Roland—that will not do for us. We know a thing worth two of that."

"You may be remarkably knowing, Mr. Gedge Foote," said Sir Roland, calmly, "but I can assure you that such was my purpose. Not only did I do this at great expense to myself, but even whilst I was expostulating with the maiden in her folly, that fiend, Spring-Heeled Jack, bounded in at the window and carried her off, even as he did your money-bags."

"It's a lie!" roared Gedge Foote, who now, mad with drink, sprung from his chair. He leaned over the table, his blood-shot eyes glaring with rage, and his tongue hanging out of his mouth like a dog with hydrophobia. "It's a lie! Don't think to put me off with such stories, because I will not believe them."

"They are not stories!" thundered back Sir Roland Ashton.

"Oh! don't bully me. I am not to be bullied, I can tell you," retorted Gedge Foote. "A pretty thing, indeed, to try to make me believe this story. I suppose soon you will try to make me believe that Spring-Heeled Jack will come and bear me away?"

"I wish to Heaven he would!" cried Sir Roland, springing to his feet.

The gesture was not a threatening one, but Gedge Foote seemed to think so.

He likewise sprang to his feet and the two men grappled.

Sir Roland was a powerful man, but Gedge was much more so.

He twined his bony fingers round Sir Roland's neck and pressed him back.

"Blarney! Blarney!" cried Sir Roland; "strike this fiend down, or I am strangled."

Blarney, whom, truth to tell, had little reason to love Gedge, as few men of his class had—for they knew that the deformed dwarf would sell them to justice as soon as they were of no further use to him—sprung up, and swinging his chair round brought it down on the head of Gedge with such force that the blood spurted out.

Gedge Foote reeled back and gazed with horror around.

Yes; he saw it all now—the two villains were prepared for murder.

He had seen too many terrible cases in his time to doubt that.

The looks of the two men were like leaves from the Book of Fate, which he was doomed to read and find unalterable.

One quick gaze at the two and then he turned and fled.

Fled, shrieking and yelling for help, and pursued by Sir Roland Ashton.

Bully Blarney attempted to follow; but he had drank so much of the spirits that his foot catching against the table he fell flat on the floor.

Gedge flew out of the room like mad.

Sir Roland followed him as quickly as he could.

Away flew Gedge Foote through the place, yelling and crying for help. Up the stairs he flew and at last caught a bell rope.

"Dong, dong, dong!" the bell tolled out, and Gedge shouted in glee—

"The alarm bell is rang and the people of the Mint are aroused."

"Curse you!" cried Sir Roland. "You, at least, shall never live to tell the story."

Away—away! The chase of death, the victim first, the murderer following, and behind them retribution.

Sir Roland bounded up the stairs and Gedge Foote flew before him.

The house, as we have said before, was an old and handsome one, and, like most of these old-fashioned mansions, it had two staircases—one for the owner and his friends, and the other for the servants.

Gedge dashed down the back staircase, and was closely followed by Sir Roland, whilst Blarney took the other staircase, so as to cut off the miser s retreat.

But Gedge Foote saw through this movement, and darted off in another direction.

As if by a natural instinct he made for the cellar where he kept his gold.

Sir Roland was close upon his track, but fear lent Gedge Foote wings.

He reached the cellar, and at once seized the rope which hung over the well.

With this he swung himself over the yawning gulf, and began to descend the well.

"Saved! Saved! saved!" he cried, in triumphant glee.

"Confusion! You shall not escape me!" cried Sir Roland.

As he spoke he made a dash with his knife at the rope.

At the same time he caught the other end of the rope, which passed over a pulley, and prevented it descending.

The strands of the rope were half cut through, and the miserable miser hung over the abyss, screaming and crying for mercy.

Sir Roland chuckled with delight as he beheld the fellow's agonies.

"Sir Roland—Sir Roland Ashton, spare me—spare me!"

"Not I, my dear Gedge Foote. I told you that I would pay you back the money, and I will. Ha! ha! ha! Egad! they say that there is truth at the bottom of a well. When you go there it will be the reverse. Lies, lies; nothing but lies!"

"Mercy, Sir Roland! Let the rope a little lower down, and then I can reach the secret passage where I keep my money."

"I thank you for having given me the information, Gedge. Would you not like to leave a lock of hair for your dainty little Daisy?"

"Sir Roland—Sir Roland!" he cried, "have mercy upon me. I will do all you wish; I will give you half my money."

"What care I for half your money? I will have all. Ha! Ha! ha!"

"Take it all, but spare my life. I am not fit to die!"

"I don't know whether you are fit to die, but I do know that you are not fit to live," laughed Sir Roland. "I shall be your heir and spend your money on pretty little Daisy."

At this moment Spring-Heeled Jack glided into the cellar.

He was about to spring forwards to the rescue, when Sir Roland severed the rope and with a despairing shriek the miser plunged into the well.

Then Sir Roland turned and fled, calling on Blarney.

But as he fled the wild laughter of Spring-Heeled Jack sounded through the house.

Scarcely had he gone when Spring-Heeled Jack sprang to the well and lowered himself down by the remainder of the rope.

Down, down, down, he went; but at last he touched the water.

Clinging with one hand to the rope, Spring-Heeled Jack felt about until he grasped the miser.

Then using the double rope, he hauled himself and Gedge up.

He reached the brink of the well and swung himself over it.

It had taken all his herculean strength to drag Gedge up, but he had done it, and stood panting with exhaustion at the top of the well.

No sooner had he recovered himself than he turned his attention to the miser.

"He is dead!" he muttered. "The world has one villain less, but for all that I wish I had been in time to save him. But I hear the murderers approaching, and they must not see me at present."

With that he propped the dead body of Gedge—hideous in life, but far more so in death—up against the wall, and then hid himself behind some lumber.

"This way—this way," said Sir Roland, as he guided Blarney. "Now we can grasp the miser's gold. Half-way down this well there is a landing which leads to a secret passage. There you will find the gold."

"Begging your pardon, Sir Roland, since you know the place so well, do you not think that you had better go down and get the money?"

"No, no," said Sir Roland, quickly. "I do not care to go down there."

"In point of fact, neither do I," said Blarney, coolly. "It's not inviting."

"What have you to fear? Nothing. I will stand by this double rope and lower you down. I murdered Gedge Foote and I dare not go down that place."

"Well, I don't like the looks of it," said Blarney. "Are you sure the gold is there?"

"Positive. Did I not tell you that Gedge Foote brought up two thousand pounds from that place?"

"Two thousand pounds! Perhaps that was all he had," said Blarney.

"I tell you that Gedge Foote was a miser—a money-lender; rich—very rich."

"Well, he ought to be. He's been one of the meanest old fences in London"

"And one of the most successful. I tell you that there is a fortune below?"

"You are sure of that? Now look here, Sir Roland Ashton!"

"Well, what is it?" asked Sir Roland, impatiently. "We lose time."

"Do you mean fair by me? I mean fair by you. Indeed, as long as I live I mean to stick to you. You are the sort of man I like, and I am the sort of man who will suit you. Now, are we agreed?"

"Yes," said Sir Roland, giving the vagabond his hand in apparent friendship.

"Good!" cried Blarney, as he wrung the baronet's hand in the warmest manner.

Sir Roland shrank from the familiarity, but had to return the grasp.

"Now, Sir Roland. Just you look well to that rope. Remember, one slip may send me to keep company with old Gedge. Bad enough it was to keep company with him when he was alive, but now he is dead it would be fearful."

"Tut! man, what hast thou to fear? You did not kill the old rascal. If ghosts really appeared I should be frightened, but I am not. Gedge Foote rests at the bottom of that well, and there he will remain until the Day of Judgment."

CHAPTER XLI.

WHAT THE ALARM BELL BROUGHT—
SIR ROLAND AND BILL BLARNEY FIND THE MINT TOO HOT TO HOLD THEM.

IT WILL be remembered that Gedge Foote in his frenzied flight had sounded the alarm bell.

Neither Sir Roland Ashton nor his villainous accomplice had thought of the consequences of the act of the man so cruelly murdered.

In the excitement of the moment, and in their greed for gold, they had given heed to nothing.

And yet those loud sounding notes had told their story of alarm only too well. Strange-looking men of the roughest description poured from the houses of evil repute—hurried shouts rent the air.

Torches were lit, and flashed on bare knives and pistol barrels.

"Gedge Foote has rung the alarm bell!" shouted one gigantic fellow, who took the lead. "This way—this way!"

The mob increased every moment.

Their hoarse cries rent the air.

On they came yelling, cursing, and making the night hideous.

Let us now turn to Sir Roland Ashton and Bill Blarney.

At the very moment that they were about to descend into the well in search of the miser's treasure Bill Blarney started back and held up his hand.

"What is that?" he cried. "Don't you hear?"

"Hear what?" Sir Roland Ashton demanded. "Fool! do you want to make a coward of me as well as yourself?"

"I thought I heard a murmur as of a crowd of angry people."

"Bah!

"Sneer away," said Bill Blarney. "You are too clever. Have you forgotten what Gedge Foote said about being on friendly terms with the people in the Mint? Have you forgotten that he rang the alarm bell?"

Sir Roland Ashton turned pale and trembled in spite of himself.

"Hush!" he said; you may be right. Let us listen."

At this moment a hoarse roar came to their ears.

Then came a banging at the outer door, and a hundred voices demanded admittance.

"What are we to do?" Bill Blarney whined. "If we stay here we shall be killed to a certainty. What are we to do?"

"Hold your tongue!" Sir Roland hissed. "Let me think the matter out. I have been in a worse fix than this and yet have laughed at my enemies in the end."

Bang! Crash—crash!

"They are getting impatient," said Bill Blarney, alluding to the men who were thundering at the door.

"Let them," Sir Roland replied. "The bolts and locks will hold yet for some time. Keep quiet, and if I do not find a way out of this muddle never trust me again."

For some moments he paced up and down.

Bill Blarney watched him, wondering whether his meditations would ever come to an end.

Meanwhile the noise at the door became deafening, but Sir Roland paid no more attention to it than if the street was silent.

"We had better go upstairs again," he said at last. "I must confess that this place is just a little too warm for us at present."

"But what is the use of going upstairs?" Bill Blarney groaned. "That will be worse than staying down here. They will surely search the upper rooms first, and we shall be as helpless as a couple of caged rats."

"You idiot!" Sir Roland replied. "Has not this house a roof? And is there no hope in that direction? Stay where you are, if you like, I am going."

So saying he dashed up the back staircase.

Bill Blarney followed after a moment's hesitation.

As they reached the ground floor they heard a crash.

"Be jabers!" Blarney gasped; "they have knocked in the upper panels."

"Gedge Foote—Gedge Foote!" roared a voice; "where are you?"

"Here!" Sir Roland cried, imitating the miser's voice as well as possible.

"What did you ring the bell for?"

"I was wondering whether it would act well in a case of emergency."

"Open the door, then," shouted the first speaker. "You will have to stand something handsome for bringing us out at this time of night."

"All right," Sir Roland replied. "Wait a minute. Don't be in such an infernal hurry."

"That is not Foote's voice," cried another man. "Down with the door, I say—batter it down! There has been foul play at work."

Sir Roland waited to hear no more, but bounded up the stairs.

Bill Blarney was in the act of following, when his foot slipped.

His head came in violent contact with the edge of one of the stones, and he lay stunned and motionless.

"So much the better," Sir Roland said, as he continued his upward flight. "Foote's friends will put him out of the way, and rid me of a troublesome fellow. Ha! ha! ha! Knock away. I suppose you will be satisfied with one capture?"

At this moment the door gave way with a crash, and a number of men poured into the house.

Bill Blarney was correct in his notion that the upper rooms would be searched first.

"Hold!" cried the leader of the gang, raising the torch he held above his head, "hold! Here is the body of a stranger."

He had come to Bill Blarney's inanimate form, and in a moment a crowd gathered round it.

"Kill him—stab him!" shouted a dozen of the men.

"No, no," said their leader. "He is only stunned, and may be able to give some information. We will bring him round and settle accounts with him afterwards."

Two of the strongest raised Bill Blarney up and began to chafe his hands and rub his ears in no gentle manner.

Suddenly Bill Blarney opened his eyes.

He closed them again immediately, and his heart grew sick with fear.

"Now, then," said the leader of the men, "no shamming. Here, Rolley, just give him a tap over the head with your hammer, just to show him that we are in earnest."

"No—no!" Bill Blarney howled. "Don't do that, good gentlemen. I am sure that you would not like to hurt an inoffensive man."

There was a roar of hoarse laughter at this.

"Where is Gedge Foote?" demanded the leader.

Through all the gloom of apprehension Bill Blarney saw a ray of light.

"He has been drinking?" he replied. "He rang the bell, and when I told him how stupid he was he knocked me over the head."

"Well?"

"And then he ran into the cellar."

"That's a very likely story," the man said "but as there may be some truth in it we will go and see for ourselves. Light fresh torches there, and bring this rascal along."

"I'm afraid I shall have to leave you, kind gentlemen," Blarney said, in his most persuasive manner. "I have a very particular appointment on London-bridge, which I must keep."

"That's not bad," said the leader. "It's just likely that you will have to keep an appointment in the river below London-bridge, if you don't keep a still tongue in your head and do as you are told. Pass a cord round his wrists and hold him tight. Forward, there!"

If ever a man felt inclined to shrink into his boots that man was Bill Blarney.

As his wrists were tightly bound, and as the men dragged him along, he gave up all hope.

A dull red mist gathered before his eyes and his lips became flecked with foam.

Death stared him in the face and mocked him.

The man who did not scruple to shed blood like water was an arrant coward at heart.

Down the stairs they went, a motley crew, and at last reached the cellar.

"See here," shouted the leader in a stentorian tone of voice, "one of the ropes has been cut."

"Mercy—mercy!" Bill Blarney screamed, falling upon his knees. "I will tell all if you will spare my life."

"We make no promises," the leader said, sternly "but if you do not speak, and that instantly, you will never have another chance on earth."

"Sir Roland Ashton—"

These were all the words that came from his lips, for a long gleaming knife flashed before his eyes.

Speech failed him.

His tongue clove to the roof of his mouth, and, falling back upon his captors, he swooned away, and lay like a log of wood in their arms.

Just at this time Sir Roland was making his escape good.

He contrived to reach the roof—but how was he to find his way to the ground?

This was a question which puzzled his brain.

As he looked down the height made him giddy, and he clutched at an old iron rod supporting a stack of curiously-twisted chimneys.

One false step, one slight mistake, and he would be dashed to pieces.

Below he could hear the voices of the avenging crowd.

He knew that Bill Blarney had fallen into their hands, and, moreover, that they were dragging him down to the cellar.

Though he chuckled to himself over this the suspense was awful.

Bill Blarney might turn informer as to his whereabouts, and then men, thirsting for his blood, would rush upon the roof.

Sir Roland fell upon his hands and knees, and, crawling along to the edge of the coping, looked down.

The flickering oil-lamps, shedding feeble jets of ghostly light, seemed to blink mockingly at him.

What was he to do?

In this direction there were no possible means of escape.

Suddenly a thought occurred to him.

Why not hide himself in the chimney?

By pressing his back and knees against the brickwork he could lower and raise himself at will.

No sooner did the idea flash into his brain than he commenced to put it into action.

Trusting his weight to the iron rod, he climbed and was soon seated on top of the stack.

What was his dismay to find that the aperture of each flue was too wide for him to support himself in the manner he had decided upon.

Back he went, and standing upon the roof pressed his hands to his throbbing brow.

Something must be done.

There was not a moment to lose.

He carried his life in his hands.

"I must try the other side," he said. "There may be a pipe or something by which I can lower myself. All still below—I wonder what can have happened?"

He looked down through the open trap-door by which he had gained the roof and listened for a moment.

Then he crept cautiously along the roof until he had reached the other side.

It was dark, fearfully dark.

The lowering sky frowned upon him, and London at his feet looked like a yawning pit ready to receive him.

As he felt along the coping his hand suddenly came in contact with something.

It was the top of a gutter down which the rain poured from the roof.

"Saved!" Sir Roland murmured, triumphantly. "I defy you all. An Ashton was never beaten, and the day is far off when I shall succumb to my foes."

Grasping still lower down with his hands, Sir Roland Ashton clutched the piping.

It was old and crazy.

It creaked and groaned under the very pressure of his hands, and Sir Roland uttered a curse as he thought it might give way beneath his weight.

What would follow?

He shuddered as he pictured himself a mangled corpse on the rough jagged stones below.

But there was no time for reflection.

Escape meant life, freedom, and the fulfilment of his plans.

To remain there would be courting certain death.

Keeping a firm hold on the rusty piping, he swung his legs gently over the coping, and then thrust his knees against the wall.

He went down hand over hand, expecting each moment to be his last.

How that pipe cracked and groaned!

Some of the holdfasts came out, and went jingling and rattling below.

But as the distance between Sir Roland and the ground decreased, he gained courage.

A mocking laugh rose to his lips as his feet touched the earth.

"Hurrah!" he hissed, "I am free. Where is all your cunning now, Spring-Heeled Jack? Where are all your plans of vengeance? Ha! ha! ha!"

He checked his ill-timed mirth, and looked about him.

"Which way shall I go?" he said, under his breath. "Ha! I cannot do better than take to the river. Once on the Surrey-side, I know a house in Southwark which will give me safe shelter, good food, and a warm bed."

So saying, he ran towards the river, where the tide was roaring and rushing, as if battling with a pack of fiends.

Down courts and alleys Sir Roland fled, never stopping to look back, or to take breath.

His way was fraught with danger, for at any moment he might be stopped and asked to give an account of himself.

Grim, and gruesome, and evil-smelling was the old Mint. Its very atmosphere seemed to reek with the blood of the betrayed and murdered!

Soon Sir Roland heard the churning and roaring of the foaming river.

Then he halted.

"It will be a great chance if I find a boatman hereabouts," he mused, "and if I do, he may perchance be an evil customer who would not scruple to rob me and give me a dip in the water afterwards."

As he reached the river bank he paced it to and fro.

All was still.

The night had grown so black that he could not see his fingers by holding them close to his face.

Suddenly he heard the sound of approaching footsteps.

Sir Roland stepped back and hid himself behind a pile of rotten timber.

The footsteps came on.

Sir Roland's heart beat almost audibly.

Was the stranger a man or a woman?

If a man, would he prove a friend or a foe?

CHAPTER XLII.
HOW BILL BLARNEY WAS HANGED—SIR ROLAND AT SOUTHWARK—
THE BLUE ROOM, AND WHAT OCCURRED IN IT.

THE leader of the gang, known by the name of Luke Spry, regarded Bill Blarney with a look of disgust and contempt.

"I did think that he would prove a little more game," he said. "Bah! I have a good mind to order him to be pitched head first down the well; and I'd do it, only I want information from him. Wake him up!"

"That's all very well," laughed one of the men who held Blarney; "but how is it to be done? He's as heavy as lead, and, to all appearances, as dead as a door-nail."

Luke Spry cast his eyes around.

He detected a bucket in a corner.

It was half full of water.

"I think this will do the trick," he said, swinging the bucket in the air. "Put him on his back and stand aside; I'll treat him to a bath."

Swish went the water over Bill Blarney's face.

"Help!" he murmured, feebly.

"Oh! yes, I'll help you," said Luke Spry. "Here, fill this bucket again, somebody!"

"No, no," Blarney pleaded, sitting up. "I don't want any more. Where am I? Who are you?"

"Come, come," said Luke Spry, "this sort of game won't do for us, you know. It's all very well with a woman, but it won't wash with you. Get up!"

Luke Spry accompanied these words with a kick that lifted Bill Blarney an inch or two in the air.

Spry's men laughed, but it was no laughing matter for the unhappy victim, who, bound as he was, ran to the other end of the cellar, and crouched down in a corner.

"Mercy!" he gasped. "Don't ill-treat a man who is in your power."

"Listen to me," Luke Spry said, drawing a pistol from his belt, and cocking it. "You may see at a glance that I am not the sort of man to be trifled with."

Bill Blarney did see it, and said so with a groan that came from the depths of his throat.

"Well, then," said Spry, pointing the pistol at Blarney's head, "listen to me a moment. Just before you fainted away, like a squeamish girl you mentioned some man's name. Repeat it."

Bill Blarney's lower jaw fell.

He seemed to be pondering on the wisdom of such a course, but a glance at the muzzle of the pistol told him that unless he made a clean breast of all he knew that in all probability his brains would be scattered against the wall.

"I came here with Sir Roland Ashton," he whined. "I am only his servant—his miserable, wretched servant."

"I will take that for granted," Luke Spry said. "Go on, and don't keep me waiting, for when I grow impatient I am likely to pull the trigger."

"He owed Gedge Foote some money, and—"

"He murdered him?"

Bill Blarney nodded his head.

"Where is the body?" Luke Spry demanded, "Tell me, you dog, or make up your mind that your last moment has come."

Bill Blarney pointed to the well.

"Oh! down there," said Luke Spry. "Very clever, I dare say. Well, where is your master—this Sir Roland Ashton?"

"I don't know."

"You lie."

"I speak the truth," Bill Blarney avowed. "I would swear it with my last breath."

"Then," said Luke Spry, "he must be in the house."

"Unless you left the door open."

Luke Spry uttered a furious oath.

"What fools we were not to guard it!" he said. "But at any rate we have you to deal with. Bring him here."

The command was made to some of the men, who immediately proceeded to obey.

The strength died out of Bill Blarney's legs, and the men dragged him forward, grovelling abjectly on his knees.

His head had fallen upon his breast; his hands shook as if smitten with the palsy.

In truth, no more pitiful spectacle ever presented itself on earth than the wretch who but one short hour ago had been so bold and boastful.

"What shall be done to this man?" Luke Spry demanded, turning to the men. "What does he deserve?"

"Death! death!" they shouted.

"You hear that?" Spry said, laying a heavy hand upon Bill Blarney's shoulder. "What have you to say against the sentence? Is it not a just one?"

"Not according to law!" Bill Blarney shrieked. "I demand to be tried before a judge and jury of my country."

This seemed to tickle the men of the Mint immensely.

Luke Spry alone remained grave and stern of feature.

"The law likes us not, and we like not the law," he said, with bitter sarcasm.

"But don't kill me without a fair trial," Blarney moaned; "some of you might fall into the same trap, and then how would you like to be served like this? I ask you how would you like it?"

"About the same as you," Spry returned. "But enough; we have wasted too much time already."

Again he turned to the men.

They were a strangely composed body, and the light of the torches lent almost fiendish expressions to their countenances.

"Comrades," Spry said, folding his arms, and drawing himself up to his full height, "you have now justly condemned this miscreant to death. He is in your hands; it is for you to decide how he shall die."

"By the rope!" shouted a dozen voices.

"Over the well where Gedge Foote lies a murdered man," added one of the crowd.

"No—no; anything but that!" Bill Blarney howled. "If I must die, shoot me through the head and put me out of the world that way."

"No—no!" roared the angry crowd. "The rope—the rope! Hang the cowardly, murderous dog!"

"Your doom is sealed," Luke Spry said, addressing the unhappy wretch. "If you have anything more to say we will give you just one more minute, and no longer."

As a drowning man clutches at straws so did Bill Blarney faintly hope that help, in some shape or other, would come before that short space of time came to an end.

He counted and begrudged the moments.

How quickly they went by!

Surely time never flew so swiftly before.

When the last came he begged and prayed for more time.

"Only a moment," he said; "I have something to say. I can reveal things such as you never heard or dreamt of. I know a hundred secrets which will be useful to men like you. I know where treasure can be had for the asking, and—"

"Cease your prating," Luke Spry said. "Your tongue has wagged too long in this world already. It must now be silenced for ever. Come, let it be said of you that you died like a man, and not like a cur."

Bill Blarney raised his eyes to the roof of the cellar.

Could it be that he would never see the sunlight again?

Was he mad or dreaming?

The iron grip on his shoulders convinced him of the dread reality of his position.

He uttered an agonised cry and clasped his bound hands.

"Only a moment! Only one short, fleeting moment!" he cried. "Give me a drink of water. You can't find it in your hearts, hardened as they be against my appeals, to refuse me that!"

Luke Spry made a motion with his hand.

"Put a handkerchief over his eyes, and let there be an end to this scene," he said.

"I'll not die in the dark," Bill Blarney howled.

He struggled, but ineffectually.

In the hands of the men who held him he was as helpless as a child.

He was blindfolded and the rope passed round his neck.

Then hot blood rushed into his brain.

Every innocent scene of his youth and every darker one of his mis-spent life seemed to rise before him.

In the one short moment as he hovered between this life and eternity he lived an age—an age of awful terror and excruciating agony.

"Let him go!"

He heard these words.

They seemed to linger upon his ears for a long period, and then—

"It is all over with him," Luke Spry said. "Halloa! what is this? See, the rope is dangling loose. It must have shifted from his neck."

"I heard no splash," said one of the men.

"Nor I," said another. "Is there anything that he could catch his feet against?"

"No."

"Then the very deuce[91] must have had a hand in this."

Luke Spry took the rope in his hand, and, drawing it from the well, examined it.

"As I live," said he, "it has been cut! Confusion! What on earth can this mean?"

"Why, that Gedge Foote is not dead yet, and—Oh! horror, what is this?"

One and all started back as Spring-Heeled Jack appeared.

He bounded from the well as if he had been shot from the mouth of a cannon.

"Back!" he cried. "Leave this house. You are not wanted here. Leave me to deal with that man."

The men glared at him in terror-stricken silence, but made no answer.

"Gedge Foote is dead," he said. "Let that suffice. The money shall be placed in proper hands. Go! I am master here."

---

[91] Devil.

The men retreated before him as he advanced with long, elastic strides.

"Man or fiend," said Luke Spry, "I will speak to you, though I fall dead at your feet. Tell me who you are."

"Spring-Heeled Jack."

This was enough.

Most of the men of the Mint turned pale at the mention of that awful name and retreated towards the staircase.

Luke Spry still lingered.

Instinctively he laid his hand upon a pistol, but in an instant the weapon went hurtling up to the ceiling.

"Do as I tell you," Spring-Heeled Jack whispered. "Don't tempt me to do you an injury. Leave everything in my hands and all will be well."

As he spoke he rose, as if by magic, and disappeared down the yawning mouth of the well.

"Mercy on us!" Luke Spry cried; "this is no mortal. It is a fiend who has the keeping of Gedge Foote."

With these words he followed the rest of the men.

Darkness and gloom now reigned in the cellar, as it did upon the river bank, where Sir Roland Ashton stood hidden behind the pile of timber.

As the footsteps increased in sound he saw a dull flash of light.

It came from a lantern with horn windows, such, as may be found even at the present time in old-fashioned farmhouses.

Then Sir Roland heard a voice.

The man was singing, and in such a jovial tone that he must have been a light-hearted fellow to give vent to melody on so bad a night.

"This is no night-prowler or robber," Sir Roland said. "I'll hail him. Hullo, there!"

The man halted and broke off in the middle of a verse.

"Who calls?" he demanded, holding the lantern above his head. "Is that you, Bill?"

"Hang Bill and all his family!" Sir Roland thought.

He then walked out of his hiding-place.

"My friend," he said, "I am desirous of crossing the river. Can you assist me?"

He spoke in the direction of the light, for he could not see the man, from the fact that he was now holding the lantern before his face.

"Why?" said the man. "What does a gentleman like you do down in these parts?"

"I am a stranger to London and have lost my way," Sir Roland replied.

"Then you may think yourself lucky that you are not knocked on the head, and floating down towards Gravesend by this time."

"Indeed!" said Sir Roland, with an air of innocence. "Is this, then, a dangerous locality?"

"Not to those who live in it and know it well," was the reply. "But, my lord, or duke— for I see that you are one or the other—that diamond brooch glittering in your cravat would tempt many a half-starved wretch picking up his living by the waterside."

"You shall have it if you will row me across the river."

"What?"

"I mean exactly what I say, and no more or less, my friend!"

"Oh! I see," said the man, lowering the lantern. "You want to get across the river very particularly. How am I to know what game you have been up to? It strikes me very forcibly that you are not such a stranger to these parts as you pretend to be."

"Tush! man," said Sir Roland Ashton, impatiently. "The simple question is this, will you row me over or will you not? If you say 'No,' why there is an end of the matter."

The man was tall, and roughly clad, wearing a fur cap upon his head and a spotted handkerchief about his neck.

He grinned and rubbed his chin thoughtfully, as he stared at Sir Roland, who winced under the steady, suspicious eyes.

"Well," said the man, "if I don't row you across I know that nobody else will."

"Then why do you hesitate?"

"Because I might get into trouble if I tried to get rid of that brooch," the man replied. "I might be asked how such a fellow as me became possessed of diamonds."

"You prefer gold?"

"I do."

Sir Roland took his purse from his pocket, emptying the greater part of its contents into the palm of his hand.

"Here are ten guineas," he said; "I have left myself only five, so you see—"

"Oh! yes, I see," the man interposed; "but there happens to be a little difficulty in the way."

"What difficulty?"

"I have no boat."

Sir Roland Ashton muttered an oath under his breath.

"What is to be done, then?" he asked; "I cannot stay out here in the open all night, and I certainly should not think of trusting myself in one of these houses."

"I have it," said the man; "I will show you the way through the Mint."

"That will not do."

"Why not?"

"Because it will not," Sir Roland said; "and let that suffice. I had horrors enough getting here, without wishing to go back by the same road."

"Then," the man replied, "I suppose I may say that I am ten guineas out of pocket?"

He made a movement as if to walk away, but Sir Roland called him back.

"You seem to be an honest fellow!" he said. "Can you think of no way of getting me out of my difficulty?"

The man shook his head and became thoughtful again.

"No," he said, "I cannot. But stay. Why should I not borrow a boat? There are plenty here swinging idly on the tide. Who would be the wiser, eh?"

"Who, indeed!" said Sir Roland, delighted beyond measure at the idea.

"I wonder I did not think of it before."

"Never mind," said Sir Roland, jingling the gold in the palm of his hand, "fetch the boat, man. There is not a moment to lose—I mean that I shall be only too thankful when I am on the opposite shore."

"Right you are," the man replied. "Stay where you are. I shall not be long. Would you like to have the lantern? I can find my way very well in the dark."

"No," Sir Roland returned, with a shuddering glance at the distant houses. "Take it with you. Do be quick, there's a good fellow. I am as cold as an eel, and miserable to boot."

SPRING-HEELED JACK,
THE TERROR OF LONDON.

SLOWLY THE BLACK SHADOW CREPT ACROSS THE FLOOR.

The man went away swinging the lantern before him.

Sir Roland watched the rays as they flitted to and fro with wistful eyes and deep-drawn breath.

As he had said, there was not a single moment to lose.

The men of the Mint might arrive at any moment.

Sir Roland fully knew what amount of mercy to expect at their hands, and he thought of what the stranger had said, and repeated the words.

"'You may think yourself lucky that you are not knocked on the head, and floating towards Gravesend by this time.'"

"Most truly," Sir Roland said, "I do think myself lucky. My curse on the fellow, how he lags! If he had been through what I have he would make better use of his limbs."

Sir Roland could not see the light of the lantern now, for the man had gone down to the water-edge, and was making his way through lanes of stranded mooring-piles and a chaos of all sorts of river craft.

He waited and waited until it seemed to him that hours had passed.

More than once a shout rose in his throat, for he thought he heard the hum of many men's voices in the distance.

Was it fancy or conscious guilt?

Remembering a simple but effective way to hear the approach of vehicles or footsteps, he stooped down and placed his ear close to the ground.

Nothing was stirring, save the wind, which sighed and moaned as if in grief that the night should hide so much wickedness.

Sir Roland rose to his feet, and as he shaded his eyes with his hand, he was gratified with the sight of the lantern.

"This way!" shouted the man. "Keep straight on, and fear nothing. Hallo! What's up now? The beacon in the old Mint is alight."

"The beacon!" Sir Roland gasped.

"Yes; look there!"

Sir Roland turned his head, and saw some rubbish mingled with tarred logs burning fiercely in a brazier fixed to the top of one of the houses.

"What does that portend?"

"That something is wrong," was the startling reply. "Possibly it means that a stranger who has found his way into the Mint is wanted."

"Ha! ha! ha! That sounds like a joke."

"It may to you, perhaps," the man said; "but it wouldn't be to me if you happened to be the stranger in so great request. I am afraid, sir, that I cannot row you across the river."

"You cannot? Give me your reason."

"Because I dare not," the man replied.

Sir Roland Ashton tore his hair and ground his teeth in an impotent fury.

"See here, he said. "Take all—money—brooch—everything. I will confide in you. I got into trouble to-night, and it is just possible—"

"That the beacon is burning for you?"

"Yes."

"Then there is an end to the bargain. It is as much as my life is worth to have you in my company."

"Stay—stay, for mercy's sake!" Sir Roland said. "Surely you would not see an innocent man murdered before your eyes?"

"No; I will not wait to see."

As he spoke he scampered away as fast as his legs could carry him, and no sooner had the sound of his hurrying footsteps died away than there came another borne on the wings of the wind.

Sir Roland Ashton glanced up at the beacon and then at the flowing river.

"I suppose I must row myself across," he said, groping wildly and blindly about for the boat. "What shall I do—oh! mercy, what shall I do?"

He tried to utter the word "Heaven," but it stuck fast in his base throat.

"The boat at last!" he cried, joyfully.

He dragged at the chain mooring the frail craft, but it held fast.

Meanwhile the beacon burned brightly, and other lights were approaching the water's edge.

He heard his own name shouted by a number of voices.

The men of the Mint yelled to him to surrender.

"Not while I have an ounce of strength left in my muscles," he thought. "Curse the chain! how is it to be undone?"

It gave way unexpectedly, and he fell headlong into the boat.

Bruised and bleeding he sprang to his feet, seized the sculls, and settled himself to work.

The murkiness of the night did him a good turn.

It hid his form from the sight of his pursuers.

A yell of execration burst from their lips as they heard the click—click of the sculls in the rowlocks.

Sir Roland was pulling for his life, and if life was ever dear to him it was now.

On he went with long, sweeping strokes, little caring where he landed so that it was on the opposite shore.

"Boats! boats" he heard his foes shouting.

This way. Murder! The villain must not, shall not escape!"

By this time Sir Roland was fairly in the middle of the stream.

Strong as he was, the ride forced the boat along out of its course, and it suddenly occurred to Sir Roland that if he rested on the sculls a few moments and allowed the boat to float as it chose, he might baffle his pursuers much easier than by attempting to reach the Surrey shore at once.

So feasible did this notion appear that he adopted it, and with such success that he heard Luke Spry and his men cursing with rage.

Suddenly several reports rent the air.

The men of the Mint were firing at random.

Sir Roland Ashton felt inclined to give a shout of defiance, but he checked it upon his lips.

It was well for him that he did so.

Luke Spry and three other men had taken to a boat.

Two of them pulled, one steered, and the fourth, standing in the bows, whirled a torch above his head.

Sir Roland Ashton saw the lurid light falling in flashes upon the dark, troubled waters, but it did not reach him.

He sat perfectly still and the boat floated on, now whirling as an eddy caught it, and now dashing along with the racing tide.

Something blacker than the night loomed before Sir Roland's eyes.

He knew that it was the hull of a ship, and grasped the skulls frantically, and only just in time to save his life.

In spite of himself he uttered a cry of terror, and a man watching on board the vessel leaned over the side and tried to pierce the pall-like gloom.

Burning lights from other vessels were seen to twinkle and gleam, and Sir Roland, having made sure that he had eluded pursuit, began to think of landing.

Pulling vigorously he succeeded in running the boat aground and stepped out ankle-deep in mud.

But to a man in such a predicament a little discomfort was nothing, and he breathed a sigh of relief as he clambered up what appeared to be a ship yard.

Here, again, caution was necessary.

There might be a watchman about the place or a dog, which would be a still more unpleasant customer to tackle in the dark.

But the wharf was deserted and as silent as the grave.

Sir Roland came to the conclusion that he had floated about a mile down the stream.

He was about right in his conjecture, but it took him some time to reach Southwark.

He made his way towards an ancient house over which hung an enormous sign, representing the figure of a wounded hart, and by such name was the inn known.

There was not a single light in any of the windows, and Sir Roland stared about him in perplexity.

"It is just like my luck," he said. "If I had not come Witchardson would have set up half the night drinking and playing cards. However, I must have him out of bed if he snores like the seven sleepers rolled into one."

He struck heavily at the door several times with his fist, and then waited for a response.

Was it the moaning of the wind or a warning whisper that caused him to start as he stood beneath the old-fashioned porch?

It might have been either, but he thought it was the latter, and stared up and down, as if expecting to see his inveterate enemy, Spring-Heeled Jack, appear at his feet.

"Accursed apparition!" he hissed, "I will find means to silence you yet."

Then he listened for the mocking, weird, unearthly laugh, but he listened in vain, and then he renewed his attack upon the door.

Crash! crash!—bang! bang!

He struck at it with wild fury and until blood spurted from beneath his finger-nails.

A terrible sensation came over him. He compared himself to a hunted animal, but in reality he was more like a malefactor escaping from the sword of justice.

Suddenly one of the upper windows opened and a nightcapped head appeared.

"Hullo!" roared an angry voice, "what's the meaning of this row?"

"I want to come in," Sir Roland said, breathlessly.

"I daresay you do," responded the wrathful voice, "but perhaps you'll oblige me by keeping out. Go away you scoundrel, or I'll give you the contents of this blunderbuss."

Sir Roland crept closer to the wall as he saw the bell-shaped muzzle of the ponderous weapon, a terrible one in close quarters, for it was capable of belching forth half a pound of lead.

"Witchardson—Dick Witchardson," he said, in a conciliatory tone, "don't you know me? Surely you have heard my voice often enough to recognise it now?"

"Why, bless my heart, it is Sir Roland Ashton!"

"The same."

"I beg your honour's pardon, I will be down in less than a minute."

Back went the nightcapped head and down went the window.

Sir Roland's fears increased every minute.

He knew that Luke Spry and his men were prowling about not far away, and, moreover, he was perfectly aware that they would not give up the search until all hope of finding him had fled.

A smile of exultation played on his lips as he heard the rattling of locks and bolts.

"Thank you, Witchardson," he said, as he passed through the open door. "You look surprised to see me."

"Well, Sir Roland," the landlord replied, "I'd just as soon have thought of seeing the— well never mind who. Come into the parlour; the fire is not out, and a drop of something warm will do you good. You are as pale as a ghost. I hope you haven't seen one."

"No, no," Sir Roland said, laughingly. "I want you to let me have the blue-room. I don't care about going to bed, as I have something particular to think about."

"Certainly, your honour," Witchardson said, "I'll see to it myself. But won't you—"

"No," Sir Roland interposed, "I don't care to stay down here. You need not ask questions, for I have my own reasons, and you know I prefer a silent man to one with a long tongue."

The landlord, who was a short, stumpy, and rather a jolly-looking little man, eyed Sir Roland Ashton curiously.

"Of course you know best," he said, as he led the way up a fine old staircase. "It is not for me to argue that point with my superiors, but I am afraid that your honour will find the blue-room just a trifle damp."

"The fire will soon put that all right," Sir Roland replied; "and, Witchardson?"

"Yes, your honour."

"Have you a brace of pistols that you can lend me?"

A troubled expression spread over the little innkeeper's face.

"I have, your honour," he replied; "but don't you see—well as you are not likely to require such things, why—"

"Do you think that I want to blow my brains out?" Sir Roland interposed. "Nay, my friend, I am too fond of life to make such an ass of myself. I never care to be alone without some weapon of defence. We live in troublesome times, you know."

"We do," Witchardson said, turning back and stopping half-way up the staircase. "They say that Prince Charles Edward will establish his right to the throne of England yet. Do you think so?"

"How should I know?"

"Oh!" said Dick Witchardson, staring up at the ceiling, "I thought you gave me a sign that's all"

"What sort of a sign?"

"To keep my tongue between my teeth," Dick Witchardson replied.

Sir Roland Ashton laughed again, and the discussion dropped as the blue-room was reached.

It was a handsome, stately apartment, and had sheltered many a distinguished personage.

Here cavaliers, true to the cause of King Charles, had plotted and sang and drank, making fun of Cromwell's followers, who so very soon turned the tables by making fun of them; and, so at least the legend ran, Bluff King Hal[92] had quaffed a measure of sack in the room and complimented the landlord on the quality of the liquor.

The furniture was almost as old as itself, but, though faded and tarnished, it was still strong and capable of doing its duty well.

The fire, composed of logs resting on steel dogs, was soon ablaze, and Dick Witchardson, setting the lamp down upon the table, stood before his guest and rubbed his hands softly.

"Can I bring your honour up anything?" he asked.

"Yes," Sir Roland replied, "a bottle of your best wine. Then you can leave me for the night, as I shall do very well."

The wine and pistols were brought up, Witchardson withdrew, and Sir Roland Ashton, left alone to his reflections, pressed one hand to his brow and stretched out the other towards the fire.

"So," he muttered, "I have given them the slip at last. I am safe, for who would dream of coming here? Ugh! the dying glare from Gedge Foote's eyes haunts me, and it will be many a day before I forget them."

Rising, he advanced to the table, and, pouring out a glass of wine, swallowed it with the gusto of a man parched with thirst.

"Ha!" he said, "I feel better now. Wine warms a man's heart and braces up his nerves. I feel another man now, and could face almost anything."

He drank another glass of wine and then re-turned to the chair at the fireside.

A deadly stillness had fallen upon the night—the Street was silent, and the only sound that Sir Roland heard was the rustle of the dying embers as they fell upon the hearth.

"I must end this," he said. "I must hasten back to Lilac Lodge, and once Daisy is in my power again she must never quit it. We will go abroad, where Spring-Heeled Jack cannot follow us. Ha, ha, ha!"

"Ha, ha, ha!"

The laugh was so much like the echo of his own that he glanced round the room in astonishment.

"How strange," he said.

"Strange," the echo repeated.

Sir Roland sat still and watchful.

The brace of pistols lent to him by Dick Witchardson were in his pocket, but there seemed no necessity whatever to draw them.

The door was closed and locked, the windows were guarded with shutters and curtains—might not somebody be lurking behind them?

Sir Roland made sure that such was not the case, and then sat down to think out his plans for the future.

---

[92] King Henry VIIi (14911547).

"I must not give way to idle fancies or idle fears," he said. "I have been a fool to stay so long in the field of danger. Daisy, pretty Daisy, you shall be mine in spite of yourself."

"You lie!"

Sir Roland could not have been more startled had a thunderbolt fallen at his feet.

In that moment of terror he never gave Spring-Heeled Jack a thought.

"Who speaks?" he asked, in a whisper.

"Your foe!" was the reply. "I, who would have been your friend."

As these words were uttered Sir Roland Ashton saw a shadow creep slowly along the floor.

It was so dark and so sharply-defined a shadow that it seemed as if it might be palpable to the touch.

Onward it came, and Sir Roland Ashton's hair bristled as he recognised in it the shape of Spring-Heeled Jack.

The guilty man had passed through many horrors in his time, but he had never seen anything like this.

If Spring-Heeled Jack, who was for ever treading upon his heels, had appeared in the form of flesh and blood, Sir Roland would have done his best to put a bullet through the strange creature's brain.

But he could not grapple or fight with a hideous black shadow.

There it lay, almost at his feet, and he felt his blood turn as cold as ice, and then course madly through his veins with the heat of molten lead.

"Accursed fiend!" he yelled, "show yourself. I am prepared for you."

"I am here," said the voice of Spring-Heeled Jack. "This is one of the forms I am permitted to take. Do your worst."

Sir Roland almost swooned.

He stretched out his hand to grasp the bell-rope, and then the shadow vanished amid a peal of wild, mocking laughter.

Sir Roland's hands fell to his side. "What horrible witchery is this?" he gasped. "Am I never to be free? Surely Spring-Heeled Jack could not enter this room? Am I going mad?"

His flesh crept upon his bones as he heard a strange, ghostly, rustling sound.

Glancing over his shoulder he saw that one of the white window blinds was fluttering.

The shutter had been thrown back and the window was wide open.

"How is this?" Sir Roland cried, starting to his feet. "Am I to have no rest?"

Drawing a pistol from his pocket he advanced towards the window.

"If I can only get a shot at the fiend," he said, grinding his teeth with fury, "I'll see if cold lead can penetrate his unholy body."

"Unholy! Ha, ha, ha!"

It was the voice of Spring-Heeled Jack, but he was nowhere to be seen.

With his finger on the trigger Sir Roland passed out on to an old wooden balcony that overlooked the street.

There was not a creature in sight.

The clouds had rolled away and the moon shone clear and bright.

"It is impossible that all this should be imagination," Sir Roland said. "When I entered the room all the windows were safe and—"

A gigantic bat-like form hovered over him for a moment and then, descending with the swiftness of a thunderbolt, struck Sir Roland down.

As he fell, uttering a cry of dismay, the pistol exploded harmlessly in the air, and Sir Roland Ashton lay stunned and motionless upon the balcony.

The report startled the echoes of the night, and Dick Witchardson started from his bed.

Pale and trembling with horror he hurried on his clothes.

"Mercy on me!" he gasped. "What a fool I was to give Sir Roland the pistols; he has committed suicide!"

"Help—help!"

The ostler, the boots, and the chamber-maids were running all over the house like scared rabbits.

"Keep quiet, will you!" Witchardson roared, as he opened the door of his bedchamber. "Silence, you fools! Silence, you hussies!"

"Help—watch![93] we shall be murdered in our beds," screamed the fat cook.

"How the devil should that be, when you are all up?" Witchardson bellowed, almost beside himself. "Where's Tom?"

"Here I am, sir," the ostler replied. "Lor! a-mussy, what's the meaning of all this 'ere?"

"Come with me," Witchardson said, grasping the blunderbuss. "Get back to your rooms, you women."

"We won't—we can't—we shan't—oh!" shrieked the bevy of beauty, who were all of a heap on the landing.

"Then stay where you are and I hope you'll catch your deaths of cold," the landlord said, adding anything but a blessing on the heads of the ladies. "This way, Tom. Something has happened in the blue-room. Where's that coward, Bill the waiter?"

"Here I be," Bill squeaked; "but I ain't a coward."

"Then go in front with the lamp and show us the way upstairs."

Bill was a thin, musty gentleman, with weak knees and large sprawling feet, which were constantly getting in each other's way.

He did not seem to appreciate the idea of going in advance, but it so happened that Dick Witchardson, whether by accident or design, presented the blunderbuss at him, and the unhappy waiter skipped up the stairs, shedding oil and sparks as he went.

Suddenly Tom the ostler uttered a howl.

"What's the matter now?" Witchardson demanded.

"Hot fat," Tom gasped. "I've got about a quarter of a pint down my neck."

"I'll kick the lot of you into the Thames if you can't keep quiet," Witchardson growled. "Now then, here's the blue-room."

He knocked at the door as he spoke, but of course there was no response.

"What are we to do?" he said. The lock is strong enough for a prison."

"I think," said Bill the waiter, every tooth in his head chattering with fear "that we ought to call the watch"

"Call the devil, you mean," Witchardson replied. "We shall have the Charlies[94] here quick enough, never fear. We must break down the panels."

Witchardson was a strong man, but the panels were stronger.

They defied his efforts for some time, though he rained blows upon them powerful

---

[93] Watchmen were tasked with providing security at night.
[94] Police.

enough to have felled an ox.

"Sir Roland must be dead or dying," he groaned, as he desisted in his efforts. "Tom, run downstairs and fetch a crowbar. We must get into the room somehow."

The ostler did as he was told, and soon the sturdy panels succumbed with a crash.

All three rushed into the room, and then they stood gazing at each other in blank astonishment and dismay.

Sir Roland Ashton was nowhere to be seen.

The windows were closed and fastened, and nothing in the room had been changed.

On the table lay the pistol which Sir Roland had fired, and under it a scrap of paper.

"What's this?" Witchardson said, as he picked up the latter. "Hang it, I told you to send for the devil, and it strikes me that he must have been here."

"Eh!" the waiter said. "Oh! lor', you don't say so, sir?"

"Listen to this," Witchardson said, as he held the scrap of paper at arm's length.

The document had been written with a red liquid that looked like blood, and ran as follows:—

"Trouble yourself no more about that villain, Sir Roland Ashton. His arch-enemy, Spring-Heeled Jack, will take good care of him. Beware! Shelter him no more, or dire trouble will fall upon your house."

"Well, I never," Bill the waiter said, dodging behind Tom. Don't you smell something like sulphur?"

"I do," Tom the ostler assented. "I'm a sinner—an awful sinner."

"So we all are," Witchardson said; "but we have done no harm. Where on earth has this mysterious being who calls himself Spring-Heeled Jack carried Sir Roland to?"

"To an earthly purgatory," said a voice behind him.

The landlord of the Wounded Hart started and grasped his hair with both hands, as if afraid that it would fly off his head.

"We can do no good here," he said. "Ha! I hear voices. The Charlies have arrived at last. Let them in, Tom, for this is a case for the law to inquire into."

"I wouldn't go down them blessed stairs alone for a thousand pounds," Tom declared.

"I begs to give warning," the waiter said, faintly. "Show me a man and I'll fight him if he be big as a house, but I can't battle with hobgoblins, and—"

At this moment Bill thought he felt the pressure of an icy hand on the back of his neck, and dropped the lamp.

The room was instantly plunged in darkness, and a general stampede took place.

Dick Witchardson discharged the blunderbuss, and made a hole in the celling as big as the crown of a man's hat.

Tom the ostler laid hold of Bill's ears, and rolled comfortably down a flight of stairs with him. The women screamed, a dog in the yard barked and howled furiously, and outside the watch hammered at the door, and demanded entrance in the name of the king!

At last something like order was restored. The front door was opened, and several old men, armed with staves, carrying lanterns, pushed forward to enter the house.

The first person they encountered was Bill the waiter, who was in such a mortal hurry to leave the place that he forgot everything except a strong desire to make himself safe.

But a rap over the head with a club about as thick as a broomstick checked his progress.

He retired into a corner, and having sat down in a violent hurry, gazed up at the ceiling and smiled in a sickly kind of fashion.

"Witchardson," croaked one of the old men of the watch, "somebody has been discharging firearms in your house. What does it mean? Is it a duel, a murder, or a suicide?"

"I know no more than the man in the moon," the landlord replied. "Sir Roland Ashton came here about two hours ago and took the blue-room, but he has been walked away by a spirit, or a—a—"

"Corpse—candle," Bill the waiter suggested, feebly. "I can see lots of 'em flitting about now."

He was looking in a dazed kind of manner at the lantern, and that accounted for the delusion.

"Hold your idle tongue," Witchardson said. "Gentlemen of the watch, I invite the fullest inquiry, for this matter has disturbed my mind more than you can think."

"It is a likely story to begin with," said the Charlie who acted as spokesman. "I suppose Sir Roland Ashton didn't come here with a well-filled purse?"

"What do you mean?"

"Why that he must be found," the watchman replied. "It's all nonsense about his being spirited away."

"Well, then, perhaps you will find him," the innkeeper said; "and when you do I hope you'll keep him, so that he does not trouble me again. Make what use you like of the house. It is entirely at your service."

"Give 'em something to drink," Bill suggested, sitting up, and rubbing his smitten cranium. "I could do a drop o' something warm myself."

This was not a bad idea, and the watchmen seemed to agree with it.

They refreshed themselves to a considerable extent, and then went upstairs to the blue-room, and came back just as wise.

"Well," said Witchardson, "what do you make of it? Nothing, I suppose? But now I have something to show you. Just glance at this slip of paper."

The watchmen gathered round and inspected the document, and having read it thought that it was time to go.

They had all heard of Spring-Heeled Jack, and the fact that he had been in the house and might be there still was more than a sufficient reason to give them a sudden dislike to the Wounded Hart and its vicinity.

"This," said the leader, "is a case for the Bow-street runners. We must go back to our duty. Disperse, men, to your stations; and if you should see this Spring-Heeled Jack, why, of course, you will take him into custody."

Of course they said they would, but every man made up his mind to shut himself up in his box and keep there until the sun rose and awoke the world to activity.

CHAPTER XLIII.

**THE PRISONERS—GOLD MERE DROSS—THE WELL BEGINS TO OVERFLOW—
RATS! RATS!—SPRING-HEELED JACK SOFTENS HIS HEART.**

THE READER will remember that Spring-Heeled Jack brought the body of Gedge Foote from the well and propped it against the cellar wall.

The ghastly object was deposited in a corner of the gruesome place, where pall-like shadows lurked.

Thus it was that Bill Blarney, ignorant of what had been done with the body, pointed to the well when questioned by the men of the Mint.

He thought that the remains of Gedge Foote were still in the well, and his captors were too much excited to search the cellar; but at the time when Bill Blarney was being examined by the lawless tribunal and prepared for execution the sightless eyes of the murdered man were directed at him as they had been in life.

When Blarney was hurled into the well with the rope about bis neck he felt the jerk and all the horrors of strangulation.

He experienced a sensation as if wheels of crushing weight and fitted with red hot tyres had passed over his neck.

Jagged flashes of vivid light danced before his eyes, his tongue enlarged and filled his mouth, and his heart and brain seemed to take fire and burns fiercely.

If he had lived an age as he stood on the brink of the well, he was suffering an eternity of awe now.

His senses reeled, a thousand mocking, devilish voices rang in his ears, and then he became plunged into a boisterous sea of molten metal, which rolled over him in furious waves.

All was over at last.

Oblivion came to the wretched man's rescue. Suddenly he experienced the sensation of returning life.

And life was now a hideous reality to him, for as his blood began to circulate, it set his veins tingling with icy coldness and then with burning heat.

Bill Blarney passed his hands up to his neck.

A piece of rope still encircled it, and the agonised wretch groaned and writhed like a cut worm, with an agony that has no name.

"Is this perdition?" he moaned. "Have I finished my earthly career to suffer torture for ever and for ever? Oh! no, no! Mercy!"

A sound he had heard often before fell upon his ears.

It was the drip, drip of the water of the well.

"I am not dead," Bill Blarney said; "I am in Gedge Foote's secret haunt. How did I escape? What miracle saved me? Hush, hush! I must not speak, or my enemies above will—"

"Your enemy is here," a stern voice interposed.

A light flashed up, and Bill Blarney gathered up his aching limbs in horror as he saw Spring-Heeled Jack bending over him.

The strange being held an old-fashioned oil lamp in his hand, and its light fell upon Gedge Foote's secret hoard.

What was the miser's gold to him now? His lifeless hands could not bathe in it as they had been wont to do.

His eyes could not gloat over the shining metal, and no longer was its ring music to his greedy ears.

"So," said Spring-Heeled Jack, "you have your wish at last, Bill Blarney. Here is a king's ransom. Help yourself."

Bill Blarney only groaned and rolled over on his side.

"What?" said Spring-Heeled Jack. "You will not speak? This is poor gratitude to me for saving your life."

"Give me a cupful of water," Bill Blarney pleaded.

"There is plenty in the well."

The prisoner shuddered. "Coward and murderer!" Spring-Heeled Jack cried, in a voice of thunder. "Your hapless victim has gone to his last account, but his body shall keep you company. Ha! ha!"

"Spare me that!" Blarney cried, clasping his hands. "Bring it not here. I shall go mad if you do—I shall go mad!"

"And would not that be a just punishment for your crimes?" Spring-Heeled Jack demanded. "It is said that when a wicked man goes mad that they live their horrible lives over again, for them there is no present, no future, no hope."

"Being of mystery," Bill Blarney said, in a despairing tone of voice, "if you took the trouble to save my life you will have mercy upon me now?"

He clasped his hands above his head and grovelled abjectly on the ground.

"No, no!" Spring-Heeled Jack replied. "You have brought this upon yourself. What mercy can you expect of me? You are my prisoner now, but soon you will be the prisoner of the dead. Ha, ha!"

Bill Blarney's blood ran cold with horror, and it seemed, in his over-wrought imagination, that Spring-Heeled Jack's form enlarged, and that flashes of lurid light came from his eyes.

Suddenly Spring-Heeled Jack extinguished the lamp and left the secret passage.

In a frenzy of fear Bill Blarney attempted to follow, but ere he was half across the damp, reeking floor a pair of arms, iron-like in their grasp, hurled him back.

Bill Blarney, thus thwarted, and, indeed, more dead than alive, gave up all notion of attempting to escape, and lay still and moaning as he thought of his hideous fate.

To have the body of the murdered man with him would be too awful. It could not be true.

He was mad—the drink had maddened him, and he would awake presently and find that he had been dreaming.

So Bill Blarney endeavoured to persuade himself, and so he tried to hope, but the sudden creaking of a pulley put an end to all such ideas.

Spring-Heeled Jack, bearing the body of Gedge Foote in his arms, entered the secret passage.

"There is your companion," he said, placing the lamp upon the floor. "I will leave you the light, for the best of company cannot be jovial in the dark."

Bill Blarney pressed his hand to his eyes to shut out the awful sight.

Spring-Heeled Jack's mocking laughter rang in his ears, and the wretch crouched like a hound under the lash.

"I have another companion for you, and I will bring him soon," Spring-Heeled Jack said.

"You are going then?" Bill Blarney said, removing his hands and casting a wistful glance at the demoniacal figure.

"Yes, but not before I have taken precautions to prevent you running away."

The prisoner's heart sunk as heavy as lead as Spring-Heeled Jack produced a strong cord.

"You hurt me," Blarney whined, as he was being bound, "the cords cut into my flesh."

Spring-Heeled Jack only grinned, which gave his face so horrible an expression that Bill Blarney almost fainted.

"Now," said the uncouth creature, "you may escape if you can, and I wish you joy."

"Don't go?" Blarney gasped. "Don't leave me here alone with the corpse. Kill me if you like, but don't—don't. Oh! mercy! Stay another moment?"

But Spring-Heeled Jack was already away, and the prisoner, bound and helpless, managed to crawl to the mouth of the secret passage.

Gazing below he could just see the water of the well.

A flickering ray from the lamp fell upon it and lent a ghastly hue to its black surface.

Bill Blarney thought of suicide.

He had only to crawl along a few more feet and then his miseries would be at an end.

He had heard that death by drowning was an easy one; but, sick at heart, he turned away, only to see the eyes of the corpse staring blindly at him.

Oh! it was awful.

Those eyes followed him everywhere, and when he closed his own matters became worse.

The body moved; it advanced, stretching out its stiffened joints.

The under jaw wagged mockingly, and Bill Blarney, unable to bear this pressure of terror, gave vent to a prolonged shriek and fainted.

*

The dawn of day was slowly creeping over London.

Night had hidden its secret sins and crimes, and the broad, glorious sun would soon rise and cleanse away pollution with a flood of golden light.

A heavy mist hung over the river.

Few craft were moving about, but from the decks came the sound of preparation, for sailors are early risers.

A man leaning over the side of a vessel saw a boat emerge from the gloom like a shadow, and disappear silently and swiftly.

The man put his hand to his ear, and listened for the sound of the sails, but he could hear nothing save the plashing of the water against the hull of the ship.

The tide was running up, and in another hour it would reach high-water mark.

The boat was going against the stream—a fact that caused the sailor to rub his nose thoughtfully, and speculate as to what sort of thing it could be that could go at such a rate against wind and tide.

All sailors are more or less superstitions, and this particular son of Neptune did not feel at all comfortable.

"What on earth was that lying at the stern?" he said. "It looks like the body of a man made ready to be shot overboard. Hang me if I don't speak to the captain about this!"

He did and was called a lubber for his pains.

The captain was all the more wrathful because his vessel was outward bound and ready to sail as soon as the sun came up.

"Do you think I am going to muddle my brains about who comes and who goes on the river?" he said. "You're a fool, Tarline!"

"Thank 'ee!" Tarline said, scratching his head.

"Don't you give me any of your insolence!" the captain roared. "Go about your duty and think yourself lucky that I don't report you to the owners."

Tarline went forward, grumbling under his breath.

"Well," he said, "I daresay I am a fool, but I can believe my own eyes, and if it wasn't old Nick[95] in that boat it must have been his first cousin. Mark me, something will happen to this 'ere vessel afore it returns to England, if ever it does."

Consoling himself with this rather mournful reflection, Tarline went about his work, but the memory of the spectral boat haunted him, and if he saw it in his mind's eye once during the day he saw it a hundred times.

The boat which had so alarmed the old salt[96] contained Spring-Heeled Jack and Sir Roland Ashton.

A heavy cloak enclosed the baronet's form, and he was unconscious of his journey upon the river, and of everything until he was roused by hearing a peculiar chanting sound, which ceased as sense and feeling revived.

Sir Roland opened his eyes and stared about him in wonder.

He was in the very room in which he had met Gedge Foote on the previous night.

There was the table, the empty brandy bottles, and the dirty glasses, still reeking with the fumes of the fiery liquid.

Sir Roland rubbed his eyes and shrugged his shoulders.

He was chilly, shivering, and feverish.

"Let me think it out," he said. "Have I been in a trance? Is it possible that Gedge Foote drugged me, and that I have—no, no! It is all real. That fearful row across the river—the blue room—the appearance of that fiend—"

"Who appears before you again?" Spring-Heeled Jack cried, entering by the door. "Sir Roland, I bring you back to old quarters. Have you no word of thanks?"

Sir Roland Ashton was dumbfounded.

He could not speak, but only sit and stare at the weird form towering exultingly over him.

He noticed that Spring-Heeled Jack carried a long cord in his hand, which trailed upon the floor like a serpent.

"What new devil's prank is this?" he contrived to gasp out.

"If I am a devil," Spring-Heeled Jack replied, "it is you who have raised me. But I have no time to waste words. The hours fly, and I must away."

Sir Roland's face paled as a thought flashed into his brain.

"I know where you go," he said.

"Yes; to Lilac Lodge."

"My bitterest curse upon you?"

"Of what avail are curses or blessings from such a man as you," Spring-Heeled Jack said, sternly. "If I followed my own inclination my hands would be at your throat, but— bah! I have no more words for you. Come!"

Whirling the cord above his head in a series of loops, he encircled Sir Roland and drew him upon his knees.

A few hastily-tied knots, and the baronet presented a rather ridiculous appearance.

He looked like a trussed fowl, and his struggles to get free only added to the security of his bonds.

"Wretch—uncouth wretch!" Sir Roland yelled, "my hour is yet to come!"

---

[95] The Devil.
[96] Sailor.

"It has," Spring-Heeled Jack assented. "Look a well to it. Search your heart and ask yourself what you are. Uncouth, forsooth! Ha, ha, ha! You have travelled the long lane of debauchery, deceit, and murder, but retribution is at band. Come with me and I will give you gold. You shall eat of it, you shall drink of it. To the well—to the well!"

Sir Roland Ashton felt his heart grow cold as he heard these words.

His features assumed a livid hue, and he made a supreme effort to burst his bonds.

His struggles were fearful to behold.

His eyes protruded from his head, and the veins upon his forehead stood out like bosses of whip-cord.

Spring-Heeled Jack raised his prisoner as easily as he would have picked up a child from the floor, and leaped from the room at a single, bound.

His feet, if they touched the winding staircase, made no noise.

He seemed to be treading upon air, and Sir Roland became giddy as he was made a party to a fiendish waltz over balustrades, through archways, and in and out of rooms.

But at last the mad journey ended.

Dazed and bewildered he discovered that Spring-Heeled Jack had planted him upon the very brink of the well, so near the brink that one touch would have sent him headlong into the black abyss.

But such were not Spring-Heeled Jack's intentions.

Seizing the rope with one hand, Spring-Heeled Jack clutched Sir Roland with the other, and began to descend.

To Sir Roland the journey was filled with as many vague terrors as if he were crossing the river Styx in company with the ghostly ferryman, Charon.

"Hah!" cried Spring-Heeled Jack, as he sent his prisoner flying into the passage half way down; "here we are."

"Oh! the devil!" cried Bill Blarney. "Is it yourself, Sir Roland? It's much obliged that I ought to be to you for leaving me to take care of myself."

Sir Roland Ashton made no reply.

His hair bristled, his knees knocked together, and the marrow of his bones congealed.

"Gedge Foote—Gedge Foote—Gedge Foote!" he shrieked.

"Yes; to bear you two company," Spring-Heeled Jack said, mockingly. "What, do you not like the look of him now? He can make no more bargains. See, here is the gold that he loved to call his own. It is yours now. I, the trustee, make you a present of it. Now you can take Daisy Leigh abroad. What is there to hinder you?"

The next instant the prisoners were left alone.

"Your company is better than none, Sir Roland," Bill Blarney said; "but I would do my best to get out of it if my hands were at liberty."

"I am in no mood to talk over what has taken place," Sir Roland replied, sulkily. "I wonder what fate is in store for us."

"By thirst while water is near you, and starvation with wealth within your grasp," cried the voice of Spring-Heeled Jack.

"He cannot mean it," Bill Blarney whined. It would be too cruel, Sir Roland."

"Well?"

"Let us try to get rid of that body."

"How is it to be done?"

"By pitching it into the well."

"My hands are bound behind my back."

"Be jabers! I didn't notice that before," Bill Blarney said. "Spring-Heeled Jack has been more merciful to me than you. But we must get rid of the body somehow."

"I would not touch it," Sir Roland said, shuddering. "What is that?"

It was a low, gurgling sound, followed by the plash of water.

"Perdition!" Sir Roland cried. "The well is rising. We must perish."

Bill Blarney threw himself down upon his face, and began to howl dismally.

"Listen!" Sir Roland exclaimed. "It must be as I said. Do you not hear—do you not hear?"

"Yes," Bill Blarney yelled. "Will these horrors never pass away?"

The water was bubbling up furiously, and would soon reach the secret passage.

Presently a number of sewer rats, driven from their haunt, appeared, their red eyes gleaming fiercely.

They came in swarms, scampering about and squeaking, to the terror of the prisoners, who huddled into a corner and expected each moment to be their last.

"It be all over!" Sir Roland groaned. "If we are not drowned we shall be devoured. Oh! for one more hour of freedom."

The water was now running into the secret passage, and soon Sir Roland Ashton and Bill Blarney were ankle deep.

"Oh! for one more hour of freedom," the baronet repeated. "Is there no hope?"

"Yes, if you will promise to lead a better life," said the voice of Spring-Heeled Jack.

"I will," Sir Roland panted. "I will do anything you ask!"

"Swear?"

"I swear by all that is holy."

As Sir Roland breathed the last word, he felt his bonds cut through with a sharp instrument of some sort.

The severed cords fell at his feet, and wading through the fast rising waters, he seized the dangling ends of the rope, and began hauling himself up.

Breathless and drenched to the skin he reached the cellar, and was presently joined by Bill Blarney.

"So," said the baronet, you are free, too, are you?"

"Why, yes," said Blarney. "Do you think that yours is the only life worth saving? But I am not going to stay here to talk, or Spring-Heeled Jack may repent of being so merciful, and make short work of us. Good-bye, Sir Roland, and when you want more dirty work done you must seek a meeker pupil than me."

CHAPTER XLIV.

**THE VALUE OF A BAD MAN'S OATH—SIR ROLAND BEGINS TO PLOT AGAIN—
A PLAN TO CATCH SPRING-HEELED JACK.**

IT was a beautiful morning.

The sun shone gloriously, and the air was fresh and bracing. The aspect of the landscape from Lilac Lodge was lovely in the extreme, but Jacob Butler had no eyes for it.

He was as miserable as a man could be, and the prospect of becoming the husband of such a hag as Mrs. Corcoran did not help to lighten the gloom, but quite the reverse.

"Ugh!" he said shudderingly, "I wish I had nothing to do with this place or Sir Roland. I wonder where he can be? Four days have passed away and he is still absent. Well, for my part, it would be a relief to my mind if I heard that he had broken his neck."

He was standing with his back to the door and did not hear it open, and was unconscious of the fact that Mrs. Corcoran was stealing upon him, and listening to every word he said.

"If I marry that old. wretch 1 am sure I shall poison her or myself," he said.

"Yourself if you like, Jacob dear, after a month or two, but. not me," said the hag.

Jacob Butler started, and his hair moved as if disturbed by a sudden current of air.

"Ha, ha! I was only joking," he said, forcing a feeble laugh. Of course, I knew that you were behind me."

"Of course you didn't, you contemptible liar!" The old hag's eyes flashed green with fury, and Jacob Butler could not help thinking that if she had lived in the time of James the First she would have been denounced as a witch and met death by burning or drowning."

"Hard words won't do any good, lovey," he said.

The last word nearly choked him, and it cost him an effort to get it through his lips.

"So you will poison me?" said Mrs. Corcoran. "Ho, ho! Well, your chance will soon come. To-morrow we shall be man and wife."

Jacob Butler turned livid, and looked at the window as if he contemplated hurling himself out of it, and thus avert his impending fate.

"Listen, you fool!" Mrs. Corcoran said. "I care as little for you as you care for me. We hate each other, but as we both have the same secrets in keeping it is necessary that we should make ourselves safe."

"Just so," Jacob gasped. "For my own part, I wish I had done it before. Lor'! how limp I do feel about the knees."

"We have Sir Roland under our thumbs," Mrs. Corcoran went on, casting a sidelong glance of contempt at her future husband. "He must and shall find money. Listen! that girl is singing again."

"I hear her," said Jacob Butler "but where is she? We never see her in the day time, and yet at night I hear her walking about the house."

"Or the ghost of Lady Ashton?"

"Don't," Jacob groaned; "I can't bear to hear you talk about such horrible things. Do you believe that there are such things as ghosts?"

"I am sure of it."

"Have you ever seen one?"

"I have."

Jacob Butler pressed his hand to his waistcoat, and brought his chin down almost to his knees.

He was fated, not only to marry the ugliest old woman on the face of the earth, but a ghost-seer to boot.

"Whose ghost was it that you saw?" he contrived to ask.

"The spirit of the woman you hear prowling about this house at night," the hag replied. "You think it is Daisy Leigh, but it is not."

"Are you sure of it?" said Jacob, quaking in such a style that he could not keep a single joint still.

"I am sure of it. Listen!"

Jacob's mouth and eyes were open to their utmost limits, and his ears drank in every word the hag uttered.

"Two nights ago," she croaked, "I was sitting up late. I got it into my head that Sir Roland would return, and I did not care to be roused out of my bed, so I thought that I would wait and get him such refreshment as he might require."

"You always were a thoughtful creature," Jacob said, in a piping tone of voice.

"Peace, fool, and let me finish my story."

"Oh! it's only a story, then," said Jacob, much relieved. "When I was young I used to like fairy tales and—"

Mrs. Corcoran hooked one of her claw-like hands upon his ear and gave it such a wrench that Jacob Butler howled with pain.

"That's the way I have when I am playful," she said, grinning. "Now then, just be quiet, or I will turn my attention to the other side of your head."

"I'll be as dumb as a dram with a hole in it," Jacob promised.

"Well," said the hag, "I was telling you that I was waiting for Sir Roland. I was reading a beautiful book, full of such nice pictures. Ha, ha! Would you like to know the name of it? You may speak."

"Yes."

"It was De Foe's 'History of the Devil.'"[97]

"Oh!" Jacob groaned. "I don't think I should care about reading that after dark."

"I did, because it interested me," Mrs. Corcoran said, with a hollow laugh. "As I sat glancing through the pages I thought the lamp began to burn dimly, and then I heard something that sounded like the rustle of a silk dress on the staircase."

Jacob Butler turned a sickly green, and he hung on to his waistcoat as if he felt very bad indeed.

"Hah! thought I," the crone continued, "that girl Daisy is about. Now is the time to catch her. I took the lamp in my hand and opened the door, and right in front of me stood the spectre of Lady Ashton."

As she spoke the rumbling of thunder came from a distant cloud, and Jacob Butler looked as if he was going to have a fit.

"I challenged the ghost to speak," Mrs. Corcoran continued; "but it remained speechless and motionless. Its eyes were fixed upon me—they fascinated me and held me powerless—but I did not lose nerve."

"You never do?" Jacob said; "you are all nerve."

"I could see right through the apparition," the hag resumed, taking a hideous delight in every word she uttered, "or I should have thought it was some trick to frighten me. Suddenly the ghost spoke."

In spite of all warning Jacob Butler could not keep his tongue still.

He felt that he must either speak or shriek like a maniac.

"What did it say?" he asked. "Make haste to tell me. The storm is coming, and you know that thunder and lightning makes me feel dreadfully bad."

"Woman!" said the ghost, "if you repent of the share that you had in my untimely

---

[97] Daniel Defoe. Written in 1726, *The Political History of the Devil* discussed the Devil's involvement in human affairs.

end, you must turn your thoughts to vengeance, and Jacob Butler must help you."

"It was very kind of the ghost," said the wretched Jacob, "but I'd rather—oh! dear— oh! dear! I wish I was dead. I wish I may die if I don't."

At this moment the sky darkened.

Clouds of inky hue were rolling up from the westward and soon the storm burst in all its fury.

Jacob Butler grovelled on the floor and hid his face in his arms.

"The house will be struck!" he cried. "We shall be burnt to cinders. Was there ever such a place as this? It must be next door to the infernal regions."

Mrs. Corcoran looked at him contemptuously as he kicked spasmodically and wriggled about like an eel on a fish-hook.

The hag cared nothing for the storm, but seemed to delight in it, and clapped her hands as the jagged lightning rent the murky clouds asunder.

"She'll fly up the chimney on a broomstick presently," Jacob muttered; "I wish the devil would come and rid me of her!"

As he gave expression to this amiable wish a thunder-bolt fell with such a terrific explosion that Lilac Lodge rocked upon its foundation.

A dreadful smell of sulphur pervaded the apartment, and as Jacob Butler skipped to his feet, with the intention of taking refuge in the coal cellar, there came a furious knocking at the outer door.

"Who is that?" Jacob replied, starting back aghast, and almost swooning.

"Sir Roland Ashton," the hag replied. "You might have seen him riding through the rain and lightning if you had not covered your cowardly eyes. Let him in. We will bid him welcome. Ho! Ho!"

Half dead with terror, Jacob Butler took his tottering limbs down the staircase.

He opened the door, and slipped aside to allow Sir Roland Ashton to pass.

The baronet paid no attention to Jacob, but passed along the hall like a man in a dream.

Sir Roland's face was deadly white, and his eyes fixed, as if he were walking in his sleep.

On he strode, up the staircase, and then shut himself up in a room.

"He's mad," Jacob said. "Everybody is mad here. Oh! murder, what a flash. If this storm goes on the house must fall."

He was making a dash towards that haven of refuge, the cellar, when a bell rang violently.

"That's Sir Roland," said Jacob; "I wonder what he wants? He came stalking in like a ghost, and now he kicks up a row. Let that old beast of a woman answer the bell; I won't."

"Yes, you will," she said; "Sir Roland wants to see you particularly, and me, too."

Jacob Butler felt inclined to sink into his boots, as he saw that Mrs. Corcoran was looking over his Shoulder.

"Very well," he said; "but this will be the death of me, and then you can't marry me. So much the better."

The hag took him by the shoulders and twisted him round.

"If I hear another word of complaint from you," she said, thrusting her face close to his, "I'll weave a spell about you that will fill you with such pain that you will wish yourself dead a hundred times an hour."

"I knew it," Jacob groaned, under his breath; "she is a witch and in league with the devil."

Limp and damp with cold, clammy perspiration he followed his betrothed up the creaking staircase and entered the room into which Sir Roland had previously taken himself.

The baronet sat at a table with his face to the window.

"Sit down," he said; "this storm is in keeping with my feelings. Since I went away I have suffered the tortures of perdition. But enough! we will talk of that anon. Where is the girl?"

"Ask the booming thunder and the quivering lightning, for I know not," Mrs. Corcoran replied. "She may be in the house for all I know, or she may be a thousand miles away."

"Them's my sentiments," Jacob said, mildly.

He would have liked to add—

"And I wish I was a thousand miles away, too."

But he checked himself, for the hag's watchful eyes were upon him.

Before Sir Roland had time to speak again Daisy's voice was heard.

The dulcet notes rose clear and sweet, and seemed to lull the storm, for the clouds parted, and began to roll away.

"She is here!" Sir Roland cried, exultantly, "and she shall yet be mine! Daisy, my darling—Daisy, my love!"

"Beware!" said a voice, proceeding apparently from the massive wall. "Remember your oath!"

"I will remember nothing!" Sir Roland hissed. "An hour hence the house will be surrounded, and nobody will pass in or out of it without my permission. Ha! ha! I triumph at last."

Mrs. Corcoran rubbed her skinny knees, and Jacob Butler gave vent to a feeble chuckle, because he thought it was required of him.

It was a great relief to his mind that other people were coming to Lilac Lodge, as he saw some hope that his marriage with Mrs. Corcoran might be postponed, and thus give him a chance of escape.

"I left two officers in a hut in the wood," Sir Roland continued. "They will be followed by soldiers, and this fox who calls himself Spring-Heeled Jack will be unearthed and killed."

"Ha! ha! ha!"

"Laugh on," Sir Roland cried. "My hour of triumph is at hand and I will repay you with torture for torture."

"This is a most uncomfortable state of affairs," Jacob Butler said, glancing nervously at the wall. "There always was something wrong where women are concerned since the world began."

"Hold your tongue, idiot!" the hag hissed. "If you have nothing more sensible to say, keep your tongue between your teeth."

"Certainly, my dear," said Jacob, looking as if strangling her would have given him an appetite. "I will make no more remarks. hah! Hear the knock. More visitors."

"The officers," Sir Roland said. "Admit them at once. I will see them alone."

"In this room?"

"No; in the library," Sir Roland replied. "When I have been there this haunting fiend has never troubled me."

Jacob Butler ran joyfully downstairs and admitted Catchpole and Elias Grabham.

"You're a rum object to look at," Grabham said. "What do you call yourself?"

"I don't call myself anything," Jacob returned, wrathfully. "I leave that to other people and I expect them to be civil."

"I s'pose you know who we are?" said Grabham, drawing himself up to his full height.

"You are police officers?"

"Right you are! And you had better mind how you behave while we are here."

"Oh! indeed," said Jacob Butler.

"Yes, indeed," Catchpole chimed in. "Me and my mate don't take sauce[98] kindly. Now, then, take us into a room and get us something to drink, for we are as wet and cold as frogs."

"I hate the country!" said Elias Grabham, as he and his brother officer followed Jacob Butler. "The houses leak, and the roads are like sponge. Only think of that blessed place we had to put our heads into! Give me London and its mud and fog, I say, to all the trees as ever was growed!"

"And the fields full of spiders and grass-whoppers!" sneered Catchpole; "likewise the wopses[99] and the bumble-bees—ugh!"

"There you are!" said Jacob Butler, flinging open the library door. "You'll find a decanter and glasses on the table. Leave a drop for Sir Roland. He will be down presently."

"And so will you—on the floor, if you don't behave better to your superiors," Grabham said, loftily. "Come along, Catchpole, my boy, and we will make ourselves comfortable while we may."

They had not much time to carouse, but they made the most of it, and drank a great deal before Sir Roland had time to get down.

The baronet put on a smiling face and a bland demeanour before the officers.'

"We have had our troubles, gentlemen," he said, "but the reward in store for us will make the memory of them sweet."

"I ain't so sure of that," Catchpole said, shaking his head. "I'd willingly forget all about that 'ere Spring-Heeled Jack."

"So would I," assented Elias Grabham, glancing over his shoulder. "You are quite sure that he can't see or hear us?"

"Quite," Sir Roland replied; "I have had the walls examined and the chimney bricked up. This room seems to be the only one which he has no power to enter. You may speak freely."

"But," said Catchpole, with a knowing air, "it will be just as well not to talk too loud; we don't want to holler, you know."

"Quite so," said Sir Roland. "You have come down here to catch Spring-Heeled Jack, and the first question I have to ask you is whether you have hit upon any plan likely to be successful?"

"We have," Grabham replied. "The only thing we can think of is that it must be done with nets."

"With what?" Sir Roland demanded, in astonishment: "Did you say nets?"

"I did say nets and I means nets," Grabham replied.

"In fact," Catchpole remarked, "we both means nets, and I am sure, Sir Roland, that you will give us credit for a clever dodge when you have heard all about it."

"Well—well," said Sir Roland, "I am willing to listen to anything you have to say.

---

[98] Rude remarks.
[99] Wasps.

Unfold your scheme as quickly as possible."

"It is this," said Grabham. "We mean to catch this skip-jack of a fellow in a novel sort of way. He goes flying in and out among the trees like a bat, doesn't he?"

"Yes."

"Well," Grabham continued, "supposing we stretched nets across from tree to tree, don't you think he might bounce into one and get nicely trapped?"

"Perhaps so," Sir Roland said; but for the life of me I don't see where the nets are to come from unless you have brought them with you!"

"There you have hit the right nail on the head, your honour," said Catchpole, grinning, "and that is just what we have done."

"Where are they?"

"At the inn; we will go for them as soon as. the sun goes down."

"Capital—capital!" exclaimed Sir Roland, rubbing his hands. "My influence at Court has enabled me to obtain the services of a detachment of soldiers, who, I hope, will be here before nightfall, and then every inch of the house will be well guarded."

"I think we could have managed the business, without the help of the sogers,"[100] Elias Grabham said, looking down his nose. "Howsomever, I shan't grumble if we are well paid."

"I will see to that," Sir Roland said. "Fill your glasses again and join me in drinking confusion to that fiend on earth—Spring-Heeled Jack!"

"I'd like to have him under lock and key," Catchpole growled, as he drained his glass to the dregs. "I'd make it pretty warm for him, as hot, if not hotter, as—What's the matter with you, Grabham?"

"I thought I saw a shadow creeping along the wall," Grabham replied, as he held on to the arms of his chair.

"Which wall?" the baronet demanded.

"The one behind you, Sir Roland," Grabham answered. "Let it pass, for it might have been nothing more than my fancy."

"It was your fancy and nothing else," Catchpole grunted. "You are always seeing something or other which turns out to be nothing at all."

"I think that our interview is at an end," Sir Roland said. "We will meet here again and make merry when you have captured Spring-Heeled Jack. In the meantime, you will now make your preparations."

"Certainly—certainly," Grabham said. "The nets are rather heavy, and we should like your man to help us to carry them."

"Jacob Butler shall go with you," Sir Roland Ashton said.

The baronet touched a bell, and, in about a minute, Mrs. Corcoran appeared.

"Send Jacob to me at once," Sir Roland said.

The hag disappeared, and presently her voice was heard calling for her beloved.

She called in vain.

Jacob was ether hiding or had given her the slip in spite of all her vigilance.

The old woman raved and tore the air with her hooked fingers like a maniac.

"Oh! my dear Jacob, my own manly Jacob," she cried. "How fondly will I embrace you when we meet again. I'll give you such a hug, my pet!"

---

[100] Soldiers.

SPRING-HEELED JACK,
THE TERROR OF LONDON.

SPRING-HEELED JACK SHOUTED TO THE HORSES AND URGED THEM ON.

No. 15.

Sir Roland did not seem much disturbed when he heard that Jacob Butler could not be found, and dismissed the officers.

Mrs. Corcoran stayed behind to have a few words with Sir Roland.

"I tell you," she said, "that this runaway idiot must be found, and at once. There is no telling what he may say or do to make himself safe. The fool thinks that his neck is in danger, and he will blab."

"Say you so," Sir Roland returned, frowning fiercely. "If such an idea had entered my head I would have found means to silence him. What is to be done? Who can we send in pursuit?"

"I will go myself."

"That, I think, will be the very best course to pursue."

"And remember," said the hag, "when I do catch him, I will not be interfered with in my treatment of him. Oh! I'll physic him—I'll physic him."

CHAPTER XLV.

WHAT BECAME OF JACOB BUTLER—

OUT OF THE FRYING-PAN INTO THE FIRE.

AS soon as Jacob Butler had shown the officers into the library the thought flashed into his brain that if he was ever to escape from the fate he dreaded then or never was the time.

He felt almost certain that as soon as Sir Roland went to interview Catchpole and Grabham that Mrs. Corcoran would not be far away from the keyhole of the library door, and he made up his mind to cut and run if it cost him his life.

Passing the hag on his way upstairs, he pretended to be hilarious, and hummed a tune.

"You are fond of music, deary?" Mrs. Corcoran said; "I am glad of that, for you will be able to sing to me when the winter evenings are long."

Jacob nodded and went his way, and Mrs. Corcoran, suspecting nothing, went hers.

After waiting about five minutes Jacob Butler made preparations for flight.

He sneaked like a thief down the stairs, starting and trembling as they creaked under his weight, and expecting every moment to be grabbed by the neck and hauled back to his dreadful captivity.

But fortune favoured Jacob Butler, and he got free of the house.

As soon as he reached the open air he took to his heels and ran at the top of his speed for a mile or so, and then paused to take breath.

"Thank goodness!" he gasped, "I will never be taken alive now. I have done with Sir Roland; and as for that old witch—ugh! I shouldn't wonder if she were to turn herself into a black cat or something as nasty and follow me."

The thought set Jacob Butler going again.

Leaving the highway, he plunged into a wood, plashing through pools of rain-water, and scratching his hands and legs with the trailing brambles.

But a little pain and discomfort was nothing to Jacob now.

All he thought of was how to put distance between himself and Lilac Lodge.

He had not the least notion in the world of what he was going to do, but poverty, starvation—anything, in fact—was better than being forced into a marriage with that wicked old woman, Mrs. Corcoran.

But at last the fugitive grew so tired that he could scarcely stand upon his feet, yet he was afraid to rest or close his eyes for a moment.

It suddenly occurred to him that if he could climb a tree and hide himself among the foliage that he would be comparatively safe.

Selecting an oak for this purpose, he commenced the ascent by grasping one of the lower limbs and hauling himself up.

Jacob Butler was no athlete, and by the time that he had settled himself in a forked branch he was fairly overcome.

"Now for a good long sleep!" he said. "I'm another King Charles. Ha! ha! I wonder what that bag of skin and bones will say when she finds that I have given her the slip? It would be as good as a play to see her dance about like a cat on hot bricks, and hear her swear like a trooper."

Jacob Butler closed his eyes and began to snore.

He was secure enough in his leafy perch, but his slumbers were disturbed by uncomfortable dreams.

He could not get rid of Mrs. Corcoran.

She travelled with him through that misty land of dreams, and refused to part company with him.

Jacob Butler groaned and wriggled in his slumbers, and when he awoke it was in consequence of a firm belief that Mrs. Corcoran had embraced him round the neck with a pair of red-hot arms.

"Hang it!" he said, as he rubbed his eyes. "How real that dream seemed to be! Hallo! what's that?"

A stone came hurtling through the branches and missed Jacob's head by about a quarter of an inch.

Then came another and another.

Jacob Butler dodged and bobbed about until he over-balanced himself and went down heels over head.

The branches broke his fall or the earth would have broken his neck.

He fell flat upon his back and lay staring idiotically at the sky.

"Don t, lovey—don't!" he murmured, feebly. "I wasn't running away, but only taking a little gentle exercise."

He fully expected to see Mrs. Corcoran and feel her sharp nails about his neck; and when somebody jerked him to his feet he howled with terror and fell upon his knees.

"What's the matter with you, you spalpeen?"[101] grumbled a man's voice. "You're a curious sort of oak-apple to come rolling down. Be jabers! if you had fallen upon me there would have been some bones to mend."

Jacob gazed with fishy eyes at the speaker, and found that he was in the hands of a rather rough-looking customer.

But he was so relieved to discover that Mrs. Corcoran was not present that he burst out laughing.

"I certainly had a narrow escape," he said; "but, I say, what did you throw stones at me for?"

"At you?" said the man. "How the divil was I to know that you were up there. I was

---

[101] Rascal.

pelting birds to while away the time."

"Oh! that's it," said Jacob. "Well, as there is not much harm done, it is not worth while making a fuss about it. You seem to have been in trouble my man?"

"Trouble!" cried Bill Blarney, for he it was. "Trouble! No word in the English language or any other will describe what I have gone through lately. Look at me; I have been half-drowned, bound, beaten, cut with stones, torn with thorns, stormed at with lightning—but here I am, scarcely able to believe that I am alive!"

"Lor'! you don't mean to say so?" said Jacob, opening his capacious mouth. "Well, I have had a little taste of the same kind of thing. It strikes me very forcibly that you are escaping from some body."

"You'll be struck still more forcibly if you talk nonsense!" Bill Blarney growled. "Well, well, goodness knows that I have no cause to be uncivil. Did you ever happen to hear of Spring-Heeled Jack?"

Jacob Butler's eyes stood out of his head like hat-pegs.

"Hear of him!" he said, in a hushed tone of voice. "I should think I have, and seen him too."

"Then you're the very man I want," said Bill Blarney.

"What for?" Jacob Butler demanded, starting back in alarm. "I've done no harm to you, and I'll thank you to leave me alone."

"You need not be afraid of me," Bill Blarney said. "I want to ask you a few questions. This part of the country is a favourite haunt of Spring-Heeled Jack's, is it not?"

"It is."

"When was he seen last?"

"Oh! not for nearly a week."

"Good!" said Bill Blarney, rubbing his hands. "Now, the next question I have to ask is—who are you?"

Jacob Butler hesitated.

If he told a lie his face might show it but if he spoke the truth the man might be a friend to him in the hour of need.

"Sit down," he said, "and I will tell you all about it."

He did so, and Bill Blarney listened with an expression of face plainly telling that the story interested him keenly.

"It's strange that I should meet you here in this fashion," he said; "for it so happens that I am going to Lilac Lodge."

"You are?"

"Yes; and you are going with me."

"No, no!"

"But I say yes, yes!"

"I tell you I won't," Jacob Butler avowed. "I wouldn't go back again to that house for all the gold that lies buried under the sea."

"Just listen to me," Bill Blarney said. "I have cause to hate Sir Roland Ashton. He left me like a coward when I lay stunned and help less after doing his dirty work."

"I hate him too," said Jacob, wagging his head; "and that is all the more reason why I don't want to go back to Lilac Lodge."

"Wait," said Bill Blarney. "What would you give to get rid of the old woman who is the torment of your life?"

"Everything I possess."

Bill Blarney took a brace of pistols from his pocket.

"I went down to the Bull in Top Boots," he said, "and the boys lent me these barkers and a few shiners to get along with."

"Very kind of them, I'm sure," said Jacob. "Well, sir, I think I will bid you good-bye."

"If you move until I tell you I'll blow your brains out!" Bill Blarney growled. "You know every inch of Lilac Lodge, and you'll have to come with me to-night and show me how I can steal upon Sir Roland unawares."

"But Mrs. Corcoran will scent me out and murder me."

"I'll put a stopper on her first," Bill Blarney said, flourishing one of the pistols. "What a treat it will be for you to know that she can never worry you again!"

"Ah! if I could only believe it I would go through fire and water."

"But it shall be an accomplished fact, I tell you," said Bill, flourishing one of the pistols.

Jacob Butler shook his head dismally.

"You've no idea of what sort of woman you have to deal with," he said. "She ain't a woman, in fact—she's a witch—a she-devil, and takes a delight in reading and talking about her master with the hoofs and tail."

"So much the better," Blarney said. "If I can get an interview with her I'll pitch a tale that I know where you are, and when I get her in a good humour—bang! over she goes, just as you fell out of the tree. Ha! ha! ha!"

Jacob Butler laughed too, but it was rather a dismal kind of a laugh.

"I have the cold shivers whenever I think of her," he said, "and I get the jumps when I walk about, for I seem to see her everywhere. Just now I could have sworn that I saw her peeping from behind that tree."

"I should like to catch sight of her," said Bill Blarney. "I have rather taken to you, Jacob Butler."

"Thank'ee, I'm much obliged to you."

"Because," Bill Blarney continued, "I should think that you would be the right sort of a pal in a row."

"Do you really think so?"

"I do, indeed."

Jacob Butler tried to look bold, but it was the old story of the ass in the lion's skin, and his true nature came out when the bushes rustled a little louder than usual.

"Here she comes!" he gasped—"here she comes! Hide me or I'm a dead man!"

Bill Blarney opened his mouth and roared with laughter.

"What!" he cried, "a warrior like you afraid of a woman? But this is only your good nature. You are considerate to the fair sex. Let me give you a word of advice, my friend."

"What is it?"

"Not to try to imitate Spring-Heeled Jack by skipping about like a parched pea."

"I can't help it—indeed I can't!" Jacob whined. "You'd be the same if you had suffered what I have."

Bill Blarney touched one of Jacob's ears with the muzzle of a pistol.

"I don't want to kill more people than I can help," Blarney said; "but if you don't do just as I tell you, and keep quiet into the bargain, you certainly will put me to the painful necessity of letting daylight through your head."

"Was there ever such a miserable man as I?" Jacob Butler moaned. "I must have been born under an unlucky star. Why didn't they smother me at my birth?"

"Well," said Bill Blarney, as he restored the pistol to his belt, "your mother must have been very fond of children to have brought you up."

Jacob Butler made no comment on this rather doubtful compliment, but kept a wary eye upon Bill Blarney and his actions.

"Here's a flask full of brandy," Blarney said, suddenly. "Take a pull at it; the stuff is good and will steady your nerves."

Jacob certainly needed some kind of stimulant, for his teeth were chattering in his head and his face was as green as an unripe gooseberry.

"How do you feel now?" Bill Blarney asked, as he applied the flask to his own lips.

"A little better. Ah-h-h! The brandy went like fire through my veins."

"Which showed that you needed it," Blarney said, throwing himself down at full length upon the grass. "What a long day this has been! It seems to me that the sun has made up its mind never to go down again."

"I've lived a hundred years of mortal agony since this morning," Jacob declared. "You are quite sure that you will not let me go?"

"Quite so."

"Then I suppose I must resign myself to my miserable fate?"

"That is the most sensible speech I have heard you make," Bill Blarney said. "We shall not have long to wait now. The sky is growing red, and it will soon be dusk."

"The night is at hand," Jacob Butler muttered to himself. "Shall I ever see the light of day again?"

CHAPTER XLVI.

HOW THE PLOT TO CATCH SPRING-HEELED JACK SUCCEEDED.

THE sun was sinking below the beautiful landscape when those valiant officers, Catchpole and Elias Grabham, arrived at the inn at which they had left the nets.

These were enclosed in a curiously-shaped bundle, and had so excited the curiosity of the customers who had called to refresh themselves with good old ale, that when the constables arrived to claim their property they found it surrounded by quite a dozen grinning yokels.

Both the minions of the law had had quite enough to drink—in point of fact, they were half-seas over,[102] and consequently high minded and lofty.

Stealing up behind one of the spectators, Elias Crabham dealt the man such a crack over the head with the crown-tipped official staff that he saw cartloads of stars, and shot like a rocket into the fender.

This little episode was more than sufficient to leave the way clear, for the yokels, ever in mortal fear of anything in the shape of a policeman, made tracks to the other side of the room.

But even the humblest of rustics have feelings, and when violently banged about the cranium may resent it in a similar manner.

Such was the case with the man who floated so suddenly into the fender.

---

[102] Fairly drunk.

As he rose to his feet he picked up the poker and threw it at Elias Grabham.

The aim was good. The knob of the poker took the constable in that region known to pugilists as "below the belt" and laid him out as flat as a pancake on the floor.

"I'm a dead 'un!" he groaned, curling up. "Catchpole, see that that man is charged with my murder."

Mr. Grabham certainly did look uncommon queer, but all notions of his leaving this vale of tears vanished when his brother officer laughed.

"Catchpole," said Grabham, sitting up and hugging his knees, "you're a hass—a braying ass, that's what you are, and I'm jiggered if you mayn't carry the bundle yourself."

This only made Catchpole laugh all the more.

There was something very funny in seeing a man doubled up with a poker, according to his ideas, and he roared and rolled about until his sides ached and tears rolled down his face.

The rustics thought that they, too, might laugh now without offending the majesty of the law, and they took up the chorus until the rafters rang again.

"There—there!" said Catchpole. "Get up, Grabham, and don't look so sour. You brought it on yourself, you know, and we haven't time to stop to kick up a row. Let us have just one more glass, and then go about our business."

Grabham got up surlily enough, and seating himself at a table, made a remark to the effect that if he had a little more wind in his body that there would be an inquest held upon somebody.

A huge jug of ale was brought in by the landlord, and it proved so good that the constables ordered another.

They quaffed and made merry until Grabham manifested strong inclination to sing and dance; but Catchpole, becoming suddenly aware that darkness had set in, whispered in Grabham's ear that it was time to go.

"Pull yourself together," he said; "you forget that we must see Sir Roland again."

"Who cares for Sir Roland?" Elias Grabham hiccupped. "I don't. Let him catch—"

"Hush! you fool."

"Who's a fool?"

"You are."

Elias Grabham closed one eye and tried to look angry out of the other.

The attempt proved a failure, and after reeling about all over the place for some time he clutched one end of the bundle and hauled it towards the door.

As soon as he got outside he went down, spreading himself out like a turtle, and Catchpole went flying over him, grazing his nose on the ground.

"Oh! dash it!" he said, as tears of agony rushed from his eyes. "Here's a mess! I shall have the gravel-rash for the rest of my life. Grabham, if you don't get up and act like a man I'll kick you in the ribs."

Grabham made no reply, but a sound came from his throat very much like the winding up of an eight-day clock.

"He's broken something," Catchpole gasped. "Cuss this place and everything in it! Grabham—Grabham, what's the matter?"

"Everything's the matter," Grabham howled. "I'm smothered in my own gore."

"Think of the time we are wasting—think of the money we are losing."

This speech seemed to rouse Elias Grabham to a sense of his position.

"Right you are," he said. "I'll pull myself together directly."

After a few minutes he got up, shrugged his shoulders, stretched out his arms, and announced that he was ready to proceed.

"Good!" said Catchpole. "We shall be in time yet. Sir Roland will be pleased with us, and we'll make him shell out handsomely."

It was pitch dark now.

The moon was hidden by dark clouds, and every now and then a flash of sheet lightning quivered in the air.

Catchpole was anything but steady on his feet, but Grabham was much the worst of the two.

He tripped over every obstacle, bumped his head against trees, and suddenly disappeared altogether.

"Where are you?" roared Catchpole, groping blindly about. "What have you done with yourself?"

"I'm in an infernal ditch!" Grabham spluttered. "Lend a hand, can't you?"

"I will when I can see you."

The wretched and unfortunate Grabham was at last extricated and came out smothered in mud and weeds.

"It seems to me that somebody gave me a shove behind," he said. "Was it you?"

"Was it me?" Catchpole cried. "That's a nice sort of question to ask of a friend."

"Well, then, we are being followed."

"Nonsense! Here, catch hold of this bundle. It will be midnight before we get into the park."

It was all very well to say catch hold of the bundle, but where was it?

The officers felt about, and swore as they stumbled and jolted against each other, but no bundle could they find.

It had vanished as cleanly as if the earth had opened and swallowed it up.

"Here's a go!" said Catchpole. "Here's a nice state of things!"

"Nice—nice!—I call it—oh!"

"What's the matter now?"

"I'm caught—I'm fixed!" Grabham yelled. "I'm in one of them confounded nets,"

Before Catchpole could say a word or give expression to his astonishment at this announcement in any way he felt something sweep over him, and in an instant he was in a similar predicament as his companion.

The constables kicked and roared lustily, but all to no purpose.

The more they struggled the tighter they were fixed, and at last got so mixed up with the meshes that they could move neither hand nor foot.

"Murder!" Grabham gasped, as he felt that he was being drawn along the ground. "Oh! please don't! I'm the father of a large wife and a family—I mean a wife and a large family. Help—help!"

"Ha! ha!" laughed a mocking voice, "I'll! show you how to catch Spring-Heeled Jack!"

"Mercy—it's him!" Catchpole yelled, as he was bumped over the ground at a furious rate. "Farewell to everybody—farewell to everything!"

Onward they went in spite of themselves.

Over brake[103] and bramble, dragged through gaps in hedges, turned heels over head in ditches, until the bewildered men began to think that they must have become mixed up in some intricate machine.

At last a halt was made.

But the officers could no longer ask for the help they were in so much need of.

The breath had been jolted out of their bodies, and they were only just conscious of the unpleasant fact that they were being strung up side by side on the stout branch of a tree.

"You will pass the night here," Spring-Heeled Jack said, now appearing before them; "and you may think yourselves lucky that I have let you off so easily. When you are free return to London and think no more of capturing me, and, above all, shun Sir Roland Ashton as you would an adder in your path."

"This is all a delusion," said Elias Grabham "My head is spinning round and round like a whirligig. Catchpole, we didn't ought to have had that last mug of beer. I'm quite satisfied that this is all a mockery."

"It are," Catchpole said, dismally. "It's such a delusion that we are both caught in our own trap."

"Ha! ha! Ha!" laughed Spring-Heeled Jack, "Adieu, my friends. The night promises to be a wet one, but I daresay that you will be able to make yourselves comfortable. Sing him a song, Grabham—sing him a song of warlike deeds and glory."

At this moment the strange creature vanished as if by magic, and the constables, left to themselves, began to rub their aching joints and smooth their rumpled hair.

"Of all the pickles I was ever in this is the worst one," Grabham moaned. "Won't the people laugh when they find us bagged like a couple of hares!"

"I don't care how they laugh so long as I get my feet on the ground again," Catchpole said. "Hush! there's somebody coming."

The footsteps were light ones, but the night was so still that sound travelled far.

Bill Blarney and Jacob Butler were approaching—Jacob, of course, being in the rear, and as limp as a damp-rag.

"Lift your feet up," Blarney said, threateningly. "Shure you hop about like an old washer-woman on pattens."

"I wish I was a washerwoman," Jacob replied, with a smile. "I wish I was anybody or anything than myself."

"You'll be nothing at all soon, I can plainly see," Bill Blarney replied, clicking the lock of the pistol he held in his hand.

"I wish you would put that horrible thing away," Jacob said. "The very sight of it is enough to frighten me into fits."

"It is more likely to frighten you out of the world," Blarney returned, grimly. "Let me see. Where are we now, you white-livered, green-eyed, snivelling slab of misery?"

"Go it!" Jacob gasped. "Call me names. I don't care. You're like old mother Corcoran, she calls me 'Deary' one moment and pitches into me the next. It's a way women have of showing their affection, I suppose—drat 'em!"

"Hold your tongue," said Bill Blarney. "We must be getting near to Lilac Lodge now,

---

[103] Coarse ferns, especially bracken.

but I see no signs of it. Don't they ever burn a light?"

"Yes," Jacob Butler replied; "but they take jolly good care to close the shutters?"

"Ah! that accounts for the darkness, then. Why could you not say so before, you tottering-limbed, green-faced caterpillar?"

"I s'pose I shall be a cabbage soon," Jacob said, meekly. "We are in the park now. I know these trees. Bless my heart! what's this?"

His head had come in collision with the toes of Elias Grabham's heavy boots.

Jacob Butler put out his hands, and as they came in contact with the net he gave vent to a prolonged howl and started back.

"It's alive!" he panted.

"What is?"

"The thing hanging on the trees."

Bill Blarney cocked the pistol again and stood on guard, ready for any emergency.

"Don't fire!" moaned the netted officer. "If you're a man and a brother you'll help me out. Me and my mate have been hung up here by Spring-Heeled Jack. We were going to set nets to catch him, but he caught us."

"He did," Catchpole assented, with a kick and a wriggle, "and very neatly, too."

"Spring-Heeled Jack!" Bill Blarney cried. "Curse the demon! he is ever on my track."

"Spring-Heeled Jack!" Jacob Butler squeaked. "Oh! lor'! Didn't I tell you it would be a foolish thing to go back to Lilac Lodge? It's as much as our lives are worth to attempt it now."

"But we shall, even though a worse death than Spring-Heeled Jack can deal stares me in the face," Bill Blarney said. "I am resolved to be revenged upon that scoundrel, Sir Roland."

"And shoot that virago?"'"

"Yes, if you act like a sensible man and help me.

"But, I say," said Elias Grabham, "won't you help us—a couple of poor fellows in distress?"

"Who are you?"

"Two constables, who—"

"That's enough," said Bill Blarney, laughing hoarsely. "You will hang there for a month of Sundays if it is left to me to take you down. I only wish that each of you had a rope round your neck. Remember your oath, dear boys, and. don't forget that you belong to the band of Black Highwaymen."

"It's Bill Blarney," Catchpole roared.

"Yes," Blarney said, "I thought I would look you up, as I don't like to desert old pals."

Even Jacob Butler rose a little from the depths of his misery and laughed faintly at this small joke.

Had he known what was in store for him no ghost of a smile would have played on his lips.

"We will leave these two gentlemen," Bill Blarney said; "and if we are lucky we will pay them another visit as we come back."

So saying, he dragged Jacob Butler along, accelerating his movements every now and then by touching him on the bridge of the nose with the ice-cold barrel of the pistol.

"If ever I get out of this," Jacob said, "I'll lead a changed life; I'll be a changed man, and go to—"

"The devil!"

Bill Blarney ejaculated these words as a huge red light flared up before him.

It seemed to rush from the ground with the speed of a meteor, and went hissing upwards into the air, and tinged the clouds with red as it vanished.

"I never saw the like of that before," Bill Blarney said. "What was it—what can it mean?"

"That Spring-Heeled Jack is abroad again!" said a deep-sounding voice.

"Then here's my answer to him!" Bill Blarney roared.

Bang went the pistol, and Jacob Butler, overcome with fright, fell flat on his back, and kicked up his heels like an obstreperous donkey.

"Fool!" cried Spring-Heeled Jack, "your bullet has found a billet in the air. Let me see if I can take a better aim."

Bill Blarney caught Jacob Butler up and held him before him.

"Here! I say," Jacob cried, kicking and twisting furiously, "don't make a target of me; it ain't fair."

"You are safe, poor fellow," Spring-Heeled Jack replied. "I will not harm you. Had you placed yourself in my hands you would not have suffered so much misery."

"I will place myself in the hands of any man who will get rid of Mrs. Corcoran," Jacob said. "Let go. will you?"

This was to Bill Blarney, who did not intend to do anything of the kind.

Neither of them could see Spring-Heeled Jack.

He was invisible to them, but they could hear him as he took terrific leaps.

Jacob's faint heart throbbed and beat like the spring of a watch.

He had borne much, but could bear no more.

Squealing like a guinea-pig, he doubled up and sank fainting at Bill Blarney's feet.

"A thousand curses!" the ruffian hissed. "I am once more in the power of Spring-Heeled Jack."

"Go!" cried the voice of the mysterious creature. "I have better things to do than to waste time or words with such a scoundrel."

Bill Blarney felt grateful to hear this, and set about restoring Jacob Butler to consciousness.

This was not an easy task, but at last he accomplished it, and planted him against a tree.

"I saved a little brandy for myself, but you shall have it," Blarney said. Drink it up, and we will get along again."

"Spare me—spare me!" Jacob pleaded. "I have suffered enough horrors for one night."

"It will soon be over," Blarney said, persuasively; "and then you will be a free man to do as you choose."

While this conversation was going on, Sir Roland sat within Lilac Lodge.

He drummed his fingers impatiently upon the table, and listened for any sound that might denote the coming of the constables.

At last, unable to bear the suspense, he rose and paced the floor like a wild beast that suddenly finds itself behind the strong iron bars of a cage

"Will they never come?" he said, clenching his hands. "Have their designs been thwarted—has that accursed fiend, Spring-Heeled Jack, upset their calculations?"

Just then Mrs. Corcoran glided into the room.

"Sir Roland," she said, "the hour grows late. Where are your hirelings—where are the soldiers that were to come to guard the house?"

"Something must have delayed them upon the road," he said; "but I cannot understand the conduct of those constables."

"I can."

"Explain it, then."

"It is as likely as not that they have deceived you," said the crone.

"Nonsense! I would trust them with my life, because it answers their purpose to be faithful to me."

"You have lived long enough in the world to trust to no man," the hag said, with a hollow laugh. "There is but one I mourn the loss of, or rather two—the husband who is gone and the man who was to have taken his place. Ah! Jacob—Jacob! how I should like to have you here for a few minutes!"

"It would go hard with him, I'm thinking," Sir Roland said, smiling grimly. "Hark! what is that?"

"The wind," Mrs. Corcoran said. "The night is dark and promises to be stormy."

A clock on the mantel-shelf struck.

"Nine o'clock and no news yet," Sir Roland said; "but I suppose I must be patient. Leave me, for I wish to be alone. When do you intend to start in search of Jacob?"

"At midnight."

"A strange, unearthly hour."

"It suits me well," the hag replied; "I shall find him huddled up somewhere, and then I will bring him back and set him on the stool of repentance."

"Poor devil!" Sir Roland muttered.

"In whose hands can he be better than in mine?" Mrs. Corcoran demanded. "Remember, Sir Roland, that he has a long tongue, which for your sake must be kept silent."

"And for yours."

Mrs. Corcoran snapped her fingers.

"When I fall who falls with me?" she asked.

Sir Roland Ashton bit his under lip.

"Enough!" he said. "This is not the time to discuss such questions. Did you not hear? I wish to be alone."

"And what if I choose to stay?"

"What!" Sir Roland cried.

"Do you want me to repeat my words?"

"Yes."

"Then what will you say if I choose to stay in the room?"

"But I order you to leave it."

"And I refuse!"

"Woman, beware how you trifle with me!" Sir Roland said. "I am in no mood to have my commands disobeyed, and if you do so it will be at your own peril."

"Peril! Ha, ha, ha! The man standing on the brink of a volcano talks to another of peril!"

"Go! or you will raise all the bad blood in my heart," Sir Roland said.

"I refuse to go, because if you are master of this place I consider that I am mistress of it."

"You are mad."

"There is a method in that madness," Mrs. Corcoran said, contemptuously. "But now, that I have told you my mind, I will go."

She banged the door behind her so furiously that the windows rattled.

Sir Roland examined the fastenings of the shutters before he went back to the table.

"That obstinate old woman must be got rid of," he mused. "She talks of long tongues. What a disturbance she could make if she were to unbridle hers! Yes; I have made up my mind. She must be got rid of. Why should I not do it myself?"

He asked himself this question a hundred times, and a devilish light gathered in his eyes.

Unlocking and opening a drawer in the table, he took out a dagger, enclosed in a morocco sheath[104] inlaid with a filagree of gold.

The weapon was as sharp as a razor and as bright as a burnished mirror.

"One thrust with this," he said, running his thumb along the edge; "only one thrust with this, and all will be over."

But then he began to think of Jacob Butler.

He might repent of his run-away excursion and return.

If so, the first question he would ask would be about Mrs. Corcoran.

"Not to-night," he said, returning the weapon to the drawer. "I must wait the course of events. The constables must leave before I attempt to settle accounts with Mrs. Corcoran."

He sat thinking over the past until he became weary with the suspense and delay.

"Something must have happened," he said, leaning his head upon his hand. "Fate is against me. Mystery of mysteries! how is it that I can hear Daisy's voice, and yet not see her face?"

As he spoke he thought he heard a low, grating sound coming from the direction of the window.

Turning round, he saw the glinting of a piece of fine steel.

It had pierced the shutter, and was moving swiftly to and fro.

"So," said Sir Roland, "there is foul play at work! Perhaps Mrs. Corcoran is at the bottom of this. She may have anticipated the fate I have promised her. And yet she would not set an assassin to work so openly. It must be somebody who expects to catch me napping."

Sir Roland turned down the lamp to a faint glimmer, and then. took a pistol, ready loaded and primed, from his pocket.

"I will give my visitor a warm reception," he said, dropping on his knees behind the table. "How busy he is! I almost envy him his employment!"

The file, for such the instrument was, kept on.

Its teeth soon cut through the iron bars.

The severed pieces fell with a clang.

Then came a pause.

It was evident that the burglar or burglars outside were startled by the sound.

Sir Roland kept silent and motionless.

He held his breath until his face grew hot and flushed.

Presently the shutters began to move.

They opened slowly, and then the head of Bill Blarney appeared.

"The scoundrel!" Sir Roland muttered under his breath.

---

[104] Made of a fine leather.

"How is this, Jacob?" Blarney said. "There is a lamp on the table."

"Is it alight?" came Jacob's voice from below.

"Yes."

"Then I can't make it out," Jacob replied. "I have never known Sir Roland to use this room save in the day time. Hadn't we better bolt?"

"No, fool. There is not a creature in the room, so it is all right, and if there was I have got my barkers ready."

"So have I," Sir Roland thought.

After taking another and a still more careful survey of the room, Bill Blarney stepped from the window-sill and approached the table.

"Somebody was here not long ago," he said. "Perhaps Sir Roland himself. He may return; I will wait for him."

A blinding flash of light and a stunning report caused him to throw up his arms.

Bill Blarney fell back with blood gushing from his shoulder, and a terrible oath escaped his lips as Sir Roland Ashton rose from his place of concealment.

Blarney, filled with anguish, took aim at Sir Roland and fired.

The aim was nervous and badly taken, and Sir Roland had the satisfaction of hearing the bullet strike the wall with a thud.

"Villain!" the baronet cried, advancing with great strides.

"Villain in your teeth!" Bill Blarney replied, snatching up a chair and brandishing it over his head. "The world is not large enough to hold us both."

"I agree with you," Sir Roland replied, coolly. "You came here to take my life and yours shall pay the forfeit of your folly."

Seeing that Blarney held a dangerous weapon in his hands, Sir Roland stepped back to the table and secured the dagger.

The gleam of steel caught Bill Blarney's eyes, and, poising the chair, he hurled it with all his remaining strength at Sir Roland.

Again Bill Blarney missed his aim.

The chair smashed into pieces, and at the same moment strange sounds came through the open window.

Mrs. Corcoran had secured the hapless Jacob, and was dragging him into the house.

This seemed to attract Sir Roland's attention for a moment, and gave Bill Blarney the opportunity he desired.

Leaping backwards, he hurled himself bodily through the window, and fell with a crash to the ground.

"Confusion!" Sir Roland shouted. "He shall not escape me. I thought those idiots of constables were dragging Spring-Heeled Jack along."

Rushing to the window, he gazed below.

Bill Blarney had escaped, and the night was of such pitchy blackness that to have followed would have been an act of madness.

"I will seek him out, and cold steel shall be his reward," Sir Roland said, as he closed the shutters.

They flew open again instantly, and the head and shoulders of Spring-Heeled Jack appeared.

"Ha! ha! Sir Roland," said he, "you are making merry to-night. May I not be also one of your guests?"

Sir Roland hurled the dagger at the ghastly form of his foe, and then retreated back into the room.

Spring-Heeled Jack uttered a cry of exultation and vanished.

CHAPTER XLVII.
JACOB BUTLER HAS A HARD TIME OF IT.

YES, Mrs. Corcoran had caught Jacob Butler.

He was in the act of taking to his heels when the hag caught him.

Fixing her talon-like nails on the collar of his coat, she dragged him along with a strength wonderful for a woman of her age. But there was no need for so much fuss and violence.

If Jacob Butler had ever possessed strength or pluck he lost both the moment the struggle began. "Don't!" he gasped. "Surely you never thought I would run away from the woman I promised to marry?"

"Of course you wouldn't think of such a thing," Mrs. Corcoran said, giving Jacob a twist in the neck that nearly broke it. "Of course you wouldn't, deary. If my poor first husband could look out of his grave, what a sight this would be for him!"

She bundled Jacob heels over head into the house and closed the door.

Jacob lay exactly where he had been thrown, and seemed to be in no immediate hurry to get up.

"Now then, this way," Mrs. Corcoran said, opening a door that led to the cellar.

"What?" Jacob gasped. "You don't mean to say that you are going to put me into such a hole as that?"

"But I do mean it. I will call you early in the morning so as to give you plenty of time to dress for the wedding."

Jacob Butler pulled a face as long as a fiddle.

"Look here," he said, "I will make a bargain with you."

"Well, speak out."

"If you don't keep me under lock and key, I will promise not to run away again."

"How kind you are, deary!" said the hag; "but I don't forget that promises, like pie-crusts, are made to be broken."

"But I'll take my oath, if you like."

"You may swear to your heart's content when you are in the cellar," Mrs. Corcoran said, maliciously. "I will put my ear to the keyhole and listen to you."

Jacob Butler gave up discussing the subject.

He found that it would be mere waste of breath to continue it, for he got nothing but mockery for his pains.

"Well," he said, if I must go I must. If I refuse, I suppose I shall be murdered."

"And buried under the flag-stones in the cellar, instead of being allowed to walk about there like a gentleman."

"When a man is married his wife is bound to obey him," Jacob said, with a spark of defiance. "I'll alter all this sort of thing then."

"You shall have all your own way, my prince," Mrs. Corcoran said, sneeringly. "I'll cook your food, mend your clothes, and give you money to spend in the public-house, and when you come home drunk and silly I'll take your boots off and put you to bed."

Jacob did not relish these entrancing prospects of matrimonial bliss.

On the contrary, they made him look as if he had accidentally swallowed a tooth.

He crawled rather than walked towards the cellar door, and as it closed upon him he gave vent to his wrath in a torrent of abuse.

"You yellow-skinned harridan—you she-dragon—you monster in dirty stockings—you rattling dice-box of mischief in petticoats!" he howled. "I'd go to your funeral with the greatest of pleasure, and take good care not to be late. If I saw you dead at my feet I'd wear a white favour and set the bells ringing."

"You shall wear a white favour and the bells shall ring, too, to-morrow, deary," Mrs. Corcoran said, through the door. "What a happy pair we shall make to be sure!"

"I dread the hour as I dread the thought of seeing the devil," Jacob shouted back. "I won't marry you. I tell you I won't. Give me a rope and I'll hang myself."

"No, no," said the hag; "I can't afford to part with you yet. Life is too short to be always squabbling, so I will leave you."

"I wish you would, and for good and all," Jacob groaned.

"You are only joking. I know how fond you are of me, as you ought to be."

"You lie, you mildewed cat!"

Jacob kicked viciously at the door, but finding that performance brought him no consolation, but hurt his toes, he gave it up and went shudderingly down the damp staircase.

The cellar was certainly not a nice place to be imprisoned in.

In one corner there was a heap of litter and rubbish, the collection of years.

Large flabby masses of fungi grew upon the wall, and two or three red-eyed rats peeped at Jacob as he ran about as if the floor had turned red-hot under his feet.

"I don't want to die, but I'm hanged if I want to live!" Jacob muttered, as he ground his teeth with rage and misery. "Am I a man or a—a monkey? I'm treated worse than a harmless dog. I'm kicked about like a child's play-ball, and then—dash it—it's monstrous I am to be dragged up before a parson and made to swear to love and cherish a beast I loathe and detest."

Jacob Butler kicked his foot against the heap of rubbish and thought he heard something ring.

It was like the sound of glass, and Jacob, being glad to find something to do, determined to investigate the matter.

After pulling away some of the rubbish, he saw something shining, and, pulling it out, discovered it to be a bottle of rare old wine.

"Ha! ha!" he laughed. "I shan't be so bad off after all. I wonder if there are any more bottles?"

Further investigation proved that there were, and Jacob Butler now had it in his power to make a second Bacchus of himself.

Knocking the neck off one of the bottles, he took a long drink.

The ruby liquid was rich and delicious.

It was fit nectar for the gods, and Jacob felt as if a new lease of life had been given to him as he drank.

I wonder who put that here," he said, aloud. "Whoever it was has my thanks."

"I did!" said a voice, which seemed to proceed from the floor.

Jacob started so violently that the bottle almost fell from his hands.

"Who spoke?" he asked, in quavering accents.

"Your master's much-feared foe."

Jacob Butler knew now that Spring-Heeled Jack was speaking, and he shook in his shoes.

"Sir Roland is no master of mine," he said. "I have done with him for ever."

"If you are in earnest I will find the means to set you free."

Jacob clasped his hands, and a thrill of delight went to his very heart.

"If you do I will bless your name as long as I live!" he said.

A light flashed into the cellar, and Spring-Heeled Jack stood facing the prisoner.

The appearance was so sudden that Jacob Butler had not the slightest notion of where the weird form had come from, but he did not trouble his mind on that score.

"Being of marvel and mystery!" Jacob Butler cried, falling on his knees, "have pity on me! Earn the thanks of a wretched, persecuted man!"

"I require no thanks," Spring-Heeled Jack replied. "I know your history and the fate in store for you. Choose between me and that."

"I—I don't know what you mean," Jacob stammered.

"Will you serve me?"

"Yes—oh! yes."

"Well and faithfully?"

"As I value my life here and hereafter I will," Jacob said.

"That oath has paid the price of your freedom," Spring-Heeled Jack replied. "Now listen to me, and mark every word I say."

"They shall be printed on my heart and brain," Jacob declared.

"As soon as I show you the way into the open air," Spring-Heeled Jack said, "make your way across the park, and so along until you come to four cross-roads. Do you follow me?"

"Yes; I understand every word."

"When you get there," said Spring-Heeled Jack, holding up a silver whistle in his hand, "you will sound a call upon this, and you will be answered by a green light which will flash thrice in the air."

"Yes," said Jacob, who in his excitement to get away did not exactly know whether he was standing on his head or his heels.

"Then wait," Spring-Heeled Jack continued, "and you will hear the sound of wheels. A carriage drawn by a pair of powerful horses will come up. A man wearing a slouch hat will be on his box, and as he comes within hearing you must utter this single word to him—'Lucifer!'"

"Oh! Lucifer?" Jacob said; "that's another name for Old Nick, isn't it?"

"Never mind what it is another name for," Spring-Heeled Jack observed. "All you have to do is to utter the word. Can you drive?"

"As well as a first-class coachman."

"Then you will change hats and coats with the coachman, and bring the carriage back to the park."

"What, must I come back again?" Jacob asked, dismally.

"Yes; because my man is more powerful and determined than you," Spring-Heeled Jack replied. "I want him to watch the road. What do you say—will you do all this?"

"Yes," Jacob replied, in a rather shaky tone of voice.

"If you fail me," Spring-Heeled Jack said, sternly, "I will increase your miseries tenfold; but if you serve me well you shall not go un-rewarded."

"I only want my freedom."

Spring-Heeled Jack smiled.

"So men say when they are laid by the heels," he said; "but they soon alter their opinion. The greed for gold is born in the hearts of mortals. Men will do anything and stop at nothing to possess it. Wars have raged, good men have been murdered, innocent children have perished, and great kingdoms have been raised and overthrown for the love of the glittering metal."

"Yes, yes," Jacob said; "but isn't it time I was on my way across the park?"

"Not until I give you the word to go," Spring-Heeled Jack replied. "See here!"

He touched a portion of the masonry of the wall, and one of the huge slabs of stone slid back as lightly as if it had been a mere wooden panel.

"That is the way out," Spring-Heeled Jack said.

"That!" Jacob Butler echoed. "Where on earth does it lead to?"

"To the base of a hollow tree, in which there is a ladder by which you can mount to the top."

"Bless me!" said Jacob, startled into an expression of astonishment. "Whoever would have dreamed of such things?"

"I did, and made them a reality," Spring-Heeled Jack said. "You may go now. Stay! I have one more word to say."

"Yes; I am all attention."

"You will find a portion of the passage alight, and will pass through a part arranged like a room, and furnished," Spring-Heeled Jack said. "It is just possible that you may see a fair-haired lad there. If you do, take no notice of him."

Jacob Butler nodded his head to signify that he understood what was said, and, leaping into the passage, breathed his thanks as he passed Spring-Heeled Jack.

Indeed, Jacob had to exercise great control over himself to prevent a shout of joy escaping his lips.

On he went, finding his way through the underground tunnel without much difficulty, for the floor was as smooth and level as a lawn.

Suddenly he saw a glimmer of light in the distance.

He stopped, for at the same instant he heard the sweet silvery tones which had so often floated through Lilac Lodge.

"What would Sir Roland give to be down here?" Jacob said, grinning. "He little thinks that I, the despised and persecuted, have become the trusted friend of Spring-Heeled Jack."

He went on again, but with a feeling of shame gnawing at his heart.

If he happened to encounter pretty little Daisy Leigh what would she say to him?

She might be armed with a pistol or dagger, and thinking that Jacob had no right in her hiding-place take such measures as would prevent him escaping after all.

Jacob did not feel quite so happy as when he started on the journey.

"Ahem!" he coughed aloud. "Ahem!"

The singing ceased, and Jacob thought he saw a figure flit from one side of the passage to the other.

"That's her," said Jacob. "What a good thing she didn't stop to ask questions? I am sure I shouldn't have the courage to look her in the face."

It was very generous of Jacob Butler to remember his past iniquities, but it may be supposed that he believed in the adage that "it is never too late to mend."

"Yes," he said. "As I told that murdering thief, Bill Blarney, if I ever got a chance I would turn over a new leaf and become a changed man. And so I will; so help me Heaven!"

Presently the passage widened, and he came to the room Spring-Heeled Jack had spoken of.

It was beautifully and luxuriously furnished.

On one side there was an elegant couch, replete with laced pillows and cushions, and on the other was a magnificent harpsichord.

How such things had come there was a mystery to Jacob Butler, and all he could do was to open his mouth and stare in astonishment at everything that met his astonished gaze.

"It's wonderful—it's marvellous!" he said. Why, it's like the 'Arabian Nights' Entertainment' I have heard about. It beats Sindbad the Sailor and his valley of diamonds. Hullo! here comes somebody else."

A tall, fair-haired boy of slender form walked into the apartment and sat down upon a chair, the framework of which was carved ivory.

He took not the slightest notice of Jacob, who, remembering the injunctions he had received, thought it better not to speak. Jacob felt that he was treading upon air as he left this scene of wealth and luxury and once more entered the passage.

It narrowed again, but was dark no longer.

Richly-coloured lamps hung here and there, and the soft glow fell upon walls, which had been built and decorated by a master hand.

"Well, I'm blessed," Jacob thought as he went on, "I wonder what I shall meet next? Perhaps it will be an army of blacks, carrying vases filled with jewels on their heads? Nothing would astonish me now."

But something did, for suddenly Jacob felt cool air blowing upon his face, and, raising his eyes, he saw that he stood beneath the hollow tree.

"How am I to reach the ladder?" he asked himself.

"Stand still and firm, and you will see," said a voice.

The floor began to rise, and Jacob, thinking that this was some new trick to ensure his destruction, uttered a cry of alarm.

"I sink! I fall!" he called out.

"Keep your footing and fear nothing," said the voice. "If you have no faith in me you shall complete your lodging in the cellar."

Jacob said no more, but, closing his eyes, resolved to take matters as they came.

Suddenly his hand came in contact with the ladder, and he clutched at it as a drowning man clutches at a straw.

He mounted with all possible speed, and was soon in such a position that he could look down upon the ground.

Lowering himself from branch to branch of the withered oak, he sped away at the top of his speed.

He drank in the fresh, cool air, and it gave him additional vigour.

As he reached the four cross roads he halted to take breath, and then blew the whistle.

Instantly the promised green light flashed in the air.

Once!

Twice!

Thrice!

Then Jacob Butler stooped down and listened.

The sound of wheels soon came to his ears, and presently a carriage drawn by two horses appeared so close to him that he had to step out of the way to prevent being run over.

"Lucifer!" Jacob Butler said, faintly.

"What? Speak louder!"

"Lucifer!"

"Right; but who are you, my friend?"

"Spring-Heeled Jack's servant!"

"A new one, at any rate," said the man on the box-seat. "Show me that whistle."

Jacob Butler passed it up without a moment's hesitation, and it was presently returned to him with an expression of approval.

"I am to change clothes and places with you," Jacob said.

"My master said he might send somebody," the man replied, taking off his hat and coat. "You see I am pretty well aware of what is required. Now, then, jump up, and make all haste you can."

"What?"

"Don't ask questions, but do exactly as you are told, and no more."

Jacob Butler took the hint, and climbed on to the box as soon as the man had descended to the ground.

The horses were well trained, and, full of fiery metal, dashed away, and the park was soon reached.

"Halt!"

The horses seemed to know Spring-Heeled Jack's voice, and came to a standstill without any effort on Jacob's part.

"Step in," Spring-Heeled Jack said, holding open the door and bowing low.

The fair-haired lad entered the carriage.

"I wonder who on earth he is?" Jacob meditated. "Perhaps he is some young lord or a prince."

"Get down, and I will take the reins," Spring-Heeled Jack said; "get down, but if you care for a lift on the road you may jump up behind."

"May I be so bold as to ask you where you are going?" said Jacob.

"To London."

"Then I will go with you."

"As you will. Mount quick, for we must be away. Ha! ha! ha! I leave you, Sir Roland, free and welcome to Lilac Lodge and all its contents."

He reached the box-seat in a single bound, and grasped the reins in his powerful hands.

He shouted to the horses and urged them on.

They broke into a gallop so headlong and furious that the occupant of the interior of the carriage thrust out his head, and cried out in a tone of alarm.

"There is nothing to fear," Spring-Heeled Jack cried. "Ha! ha! ha! This is glorious."

The wheels whirled round, striking showers of sparks as they passed over the hard flints.

Jacob hung on with his eyes starting out of his head, and expecting that the carriage would be overturned every moment.

It swerved and skidded to a fearful extent round corners, and yet Spring-Heeled Jack kept up the pace.

It might have been a race for life or death, and the horses never tiring swept along over mile after mile.

And all the time Jacob Butler was asking him-self the question—

"Who was the fair-haired boy, and why was Spring-Heeled Jack in such a hurry to get him to London?"

CHAPTER XLVIII.

MRS. CORCORAN MEETS WITH A SAD DISAPPOINTMENT AND A SADDER END.

"JACOB, deary."

It was the gentle, dove-like voice of Mrs. Corcoran calling to her love.

"Jacob, deary," she said again, "are you asleep or awake? Your breakfast is ready, and so is a nice new suit of clothes for you to put on."

As there was no reply to this endearing summons Mrs. Corcoran opened the cellar door and peeped down the staircase.

"Oh!" said she; "you are obstinate, are you? I'll soon show you the way to find your tongue, young man."

As there happened to be a broomstick handy, she armed herself with it and stalked down the stairs with ghost-like strides.

"Now then," she said, rattling the stick on the flagstones, "wake up, or you'll go before the parson with an aching head."

It was so dark that she could distinguish no object clearly.

"Drat the man!" she said. "He has taken quite a new fit in his head, but I'll knock all that out as soon as the ring is on my finger."

Mrs. Corcoran, failing to see Jacob, or to get a word from him, began to feel about for him with the broomstick.

If Jacob had been there it must have come in contact with some portion of his anatomy, but as he was not Mrs. Corcoran got nothing for her pains, and lost her temper.

Suddenly she came upon the empty wine-bottle and, picking it up, stared at it in unmitigated astonishment.

"Why," she cried, "he must have had company down here! Here—here! Confound him! he is no longer here. But how could he have got away? The cellar door was locked and fast, and these walls are as safe as a prison."

The more the old hag thought over the matter the more she was bewildered.

It puzzled and bothered her brains how Jacob could have got out of the cellar, unless he had become possessed of a supernatural gift.

"There wasn't much of him, but he was no ghost," she said, savagely. "At all events, he's gone, and I shall not be married to-day."

But she found it hard to drag herself out of the place where she had thought that her beloved was in such safe keeping.

At last she went upstairs, and just then Sir Roland had left his sleeping apartment, and was coming down.

"Is my breakfast ready?" he asked, in a surly tone of voice.

"No; and not likely to be for some time,' Mrs. Corcoran said. "I have been dreadfully upset this morning."

"What about?"

"I put Jacob in the cellar last night, but he is no longer there."

"Good riddance to him," Sir Roland said. "I am tired of all this nonsense. The fellow is too much of a coward to open his mouth about us, and if he does we can face the matter out and have him sent to prison for slander."

"But," said Mrs. Corcoran, "you must forget that I was to have been married this morning!"

"I know nothing about that arrangement, and don't want to," Sir Roland said. "If Jacob comes back, I wish you both joy; but if he doesn't, he may keep away and go to perdition for all I care."

"You are out of sorts this morning, Sir Roland."

"I am master of my own temper, and shall use it as I please," came the sharp reply.

"But I want you to look pleased and smiling," Mrs. Corcoran said. "Do you believe that dreams ever come true?"

"If they did," Sir Roland Ashton said, frowning, "I should not be here."

"Where would you be, then?"

"I would rather keep that to myself," Sir Roland replied. "At all events, I don't believe in such rubbish as dreams, so there is an end of that matter. Let me pass, woman, and see to my wants as quickly as possible."

Mrs. Corcoran stuck herself up against the wall like an eight-day clock, and grinned hideously as the baronet strode by.

"Ho, ho," she croaked; "his nose and chin are in the air this morning. So he cares not for me, and Jacob may go to the devil. It strikes me he will have to follow you, Sir Roland, much as I hate him."

This thought seemed to give her much satisfaction.

She rubbed her skinny hands and then shook a bony fist in the direction Sir Roland had taken.

"So," she said, "I am only a puppet in your estimation. Pull the string and the figure will dance. The performance is just going to begin. True, Sir Roland—true, but it is the beginning of the end."

Then she began a horrible, witch-like dance and croaked the snatch of a song.

"Why should I not be merry in the face of all my disappointments?" she said. "Why not? Yes, I will; for Jacob will not forsake me. No, no; I'll take good care of that. A little patience and I shall have him back again, and then I must not leave him for a single moment."

"Curse you!" Sir Roland cried, flinging a door open. "What devilish scheme are you plotting now? Are you talking to your broomstick sisterhood. Come down, you witch, and cease that prating."

Mrs. Corcoran's red and rat-like eyes flashed fire as she heard these words from Sir Roland.

"Miserable wretch that he is!" she muttered. "He is foiled and disappointed at every step, and finds no better solace to his feelings than in bullying and cursing."

Presently she began to hobble downstairs, and having set Sir Roland's breakfast before him withdrew.

SPRING-HEELED JACK,
THE TERROR OF LONDON.

THE HAG WAS MOUTHING AND MOCKING AT SIR ROLAND.

No. 44.

"Bah!" said the baronet, pushing his cup and plate aside. "What a farce this is, my trying to eat; my nerves require something stronger than coffee."

He rang the bell and Mrs. Corcoran appeared.

"What now?" she demanded, brusquely. "Am I never to have a moment's peace?"

"Take these things away," he said, gloomily, "and bring me a bottle of brandy."

"You had best beware how you swallow that liquid fire," the hag said. "Men in drink do things past recalling. If you would accomplish the object you have in view, you need a clear head and a steady hand."

"I care not," Sir Roland replied, imperatively. "Do as I tell you. Bring me the brandy."

Mrs. Corcoran croaked out something from the depths of her throat, and hobbled out of the room.

Presently she reappeared with a bottle half full of brandy.

"I suppose you haven't put anything into this?" Sir Roland said, holding the bottle up to the light.

Mrs. Corcoran laughed.

"What put such a notion into your head?"

"Because no notion is too bad to come out of yours."

Mrs. Corcoran laughed again, and this time her voice sounded as if it came from a vault.

"You are complimentary," she said. "What would you say if I told you that I suspected you of similar designs?"

"Bah!" sneered Sir Roland Ashton. "We have had more than enough of this prating. Bring two glasses, and sit down a few minutes."

"I do not wish to drink."

"But you shall."

"Well, if I must I must, and so there is an end of the matter," the hag replied. "Fool that you are to think that I should wish to destroy your life when you are so useful to me!"

As she spoke she placed the glasses on the table, and Sir Roland filled them.

"Drink first," said the baronet, "and drink down to the very dregs."

The old hag did so.

"You do not follow my example," she said. "What is the reason?"

"Because I wish to see what effect the liquor has on you," he replied. "If you had brought me a full bottle, uncorked and sealed, you would have saved yourself all this trouble."

"This is something new, Sir Roland," Mrs. Corcoran said. "What have I done to deserve it? Have I not proved myself trustworthy?"

"Henceforth I trust neither man nor woman," Sir Roland responded, fiercely. "Well, I think I may drink now, for the brandy seems to have no effect on you."

He raised the glass to his lips, but set it down immediately.

There was a great knocking and uproar at the door.

"What now?" he gasped. "Has that villain, Jacob Butler, betrayed us?"

"It may be so," Mrs. Corcoran said, starting to her feet. "Sir Roland, I call you to witness that I am your servant, your slave; I have acted under your instructions, and—"

"Peace, virago," Sir Roland said, interrupting her.

His face grew purple with fury, and he raised his clenched hands as if to strike the old woman.

But he refrained from doing this, for the knocking, kicking, and general confusion was going on with unabated vigour.

"I will sell my liberty as dearly as I would sell my life," Sir Roland said, as he advanced to the window.

Looking out he beheld a number of yokels, who mingled groans with roars of laughter.

At first Sir Roland Ashton could not comprehend the cause of this extraordinary scene, but presently he saw that the centre of this boisterous crowd was occupied by two of the most dejected-looking men he had ever set eyes on.

The individuals were Catchpole and Grabham.

The unfortunate officers had spent a most miserable night in the wind and rain.

Their shouts and cries for help had passed unheeded, and now that they were released they were nothing more than objects of mirth and ridicule.

Strips of netting clung to their uniforms, and their noses, absolutely blue with cold, gave them so comical an appearance that Sir Roland, angry and perplexed as he was, could not refrain from smiling grimly.

"I suppose I had better see this thick-headed pair of fools," he said. "Mrs. Corcoran, let them in, and tell the rest that if they do not take themselves off they will incur my displeasure."

Much relieved at finding that she was not to be arrested and dragged to durance vile, Mrs. Corcoran departed gladly on her errand.

Indeed, so overjoyed was she, that on her way to the door she armed herself with the identical broomstick which she had threatened Jacob Butler with.

Throwing open the door, she laid about her with such hearty goodwill that the yokels changed their bursts of laughter to yells of dismay.

The conflict was of short duration, but the execution was most satisfactory from Mrs. Corcoran's point of view.

At least half-a-dozen rustics scampered away with heads to mend, and the hag chuckled as she gazed at her handiwork.

"I don't think you will come here again in a hurry," she said.

Then she turned her attention to Catchpole and Grabham, who stood trembling and eyeing the broomstick as if they expected a taste of it themselves.

"Come in, you two, if you want to see Sir Roland," she said, flashing her eyes upon them.

"Want to see him?" Grabham retorted, hoarsely. "I should just think we did. I shall never get rid of this 'ere cold. It will be the death of me."

"So it will of me," Catchpole asserted. "Ugh! Oh! dear."

He coughed, making a sound like a trombone out of tune.

"Well, I know nothing about it, and don't want," said Mrs. Corcoran. "Come, or I will bang the door in your faces."

Thus invited, the two crestfallen officers sidled into the house.

"Where is Sir Roland?" Grabham asked.

"You will find him where you left him last night."

"In the library?"

"Yes."

"How now?" said Sir Roland, as the constables entered the room. "What is the meaning of this?"

"It means that instead of us catching Spring-Heeled Jack he caught us," Grabham replied.

"So I should presume, judging by your appearance," Sir Roland returned. "Sit down and tell me how it happened?"

Catchpole and Grabham cast greedy eyes on the brandy-bottle, and Sir Roland, taking pity on them, passed it.

"Now," said the baronet, when both had drunk deeply, "let me have your story, and make it as short as possible."

Still acting as spokesman, Grabham told the story of the capture, and Sir Roland felt amused at it in spite of himself.

"You are a precious pair of noodles to employ," he said. "But what else could I expect? I have only to blame myself for trusting you with such work."

"Wait a minute, Sir Roland," Catchpole said. "I fancy that we have a bit more news which may interest you."

"Well?"

"As we were hollering and roaring in the blessed nets we see a carriage and pair drive into the park."

"Ha!"

"You may well start, your honour," Catchpole continued. "Just as it came near us the clouds shifted, and we could see by the moon who was driving."

"Who was it?" Sir Roland demanded, anxiously.

"The man who ought to have helped us to bring the nets away from the inn."

"Not Jacob Butler?"

"That is the man's name."

Sir Roland drummed his fingers upon the table and looked thoroughly bewildered.

"How in the name of wonder did he become possessed of a carriage and a pair of horses?" he said, musingly; "and more mysterious still, what was he going to do with them?"

"Be patient," said Catchpole, "give me time to tell all. Slung up as we were we could see a long way when the moon shone. All at once Jacob Butler changed places with Spring-Heeled Jack and away went horses and carriage at a speed fast enough to frighten Old Nick."

"Is this true?" Sir Roland Ashton. asked, in astonishment, as he turned to Grabham.

"Every word, your honour."

"Look here, Sir Roland," said Catchpole, with an air of injured innocence, "I am not in the habit of telling lies, and—"

"Tut, tut! I meant no harm," Sir Roland said, interrupting him. "Did you see anybody else?"

"No, your honour."

Sir Roland Ashton swept his hand across his. brow.

"I fancy I know what has taken place," he said, "and, therefore, I wish you to keep what you saw a secret."

Grabham nudged his companion in the ribs with his elbow, and Catchpole grinned.

"Certainly, your honour," said Grabham. "We know our duty to our superiors, but—"

"You want to be paid for it?"

"Exactly."

"And you shall be," Sir Roland said, opening his pocket-book. "I am rather short of money, but as we are likely to meet again you must he contented with five pounds apiece for the present."

"It ain't much, considering how we have passed the night," Grabham growled. "When the moon went down it came on to rain like fury."

"And the wind seemed to blow holes in me," Catchpole groaned, as he was reminded forcibly of his recent sufferings. "Make it ten pounds apiece, your honour, and we won't grumble."

"I cannot just now," Sir Roland replied. "My expenses are enormously heavy, but all will be well in time. Trust to me, and I will—well, perhaps make both of you rich men."

"How?" both the officers demanded in a breath, with their mouths wide open.

Sir Roland cast a glance round the room.

"They say that walls have ears," he said, "and my experience gives me cause to credit the assertion. Listen! Lean forward over the table that I may whisper to you."

The constables did so, laying their heads closely together.

"What would you risk to share an immense treasure with me?" Sir Roland asked.

"Anything—anything!"

"Your lives? Another meeting with Spring-Heeled Jack?"

"Yes."

"Then you shall have the chance," Sir Roland replied. "Do you know Gedge Foote's house in the old Mint."

"Know it?" said Catchpole. "Rather! and the old fence too."

"The old fence, as you call him, is not likely to trouble anybody again," Sir Roland said. "He met with an accident—that is, he fell into his own well and was drowned!"

The constables glanced at each other and then at Sir Roland, but they deemed it prudent to say nothing.

"I will tell you how it happened," Sir Roland began, when Grabham interrupted him with—

"I s'pose your honour was present at the time?"

"It matters not to you where I was, Sir Roland retorted, angrily. "Oh! I beg pardon."

"That's right," said Catchpole, "and mind you don't put your spoke in again. Sir Roland, don't pay no attention to him."

"Gedge Foote hid his treasure in a secret passage halfway down the well," Sir Roland continued, "and he was in the habit of lowering himself into this snug hiding-place by means of a rope. Like the pitcher of old, he went too often—missed his grip on the rope and fell."

"And a good job too," said Grabham. "So there's money there, is there?"

"Yes," Sir Roland replied, "thousands of pounds—hundreds of thousands of pounds, perhaps. Gedge Foote told me—well never mind what he told me. Will you join me in the enterprise?"

"We will!" said Catchpole and Grabham, tragically.

"So far so good," Sir Roland said. "I will leave here for London to-morrow—perchance to-night, and you may make your own appointment where to meet me."

"What do you say to the West-end, your honour?" Grabham asked.

"Anywhere," the baronet replied. "I have no choice whatever in the matter."

"I mentioned the West-end because it is out of the way, and we are not likely to meet anybody we know," the constable said. "Good!"

"Then say twelve o'clock at noon the day after to-morrow at Hatchard's."[105]

"I will be there," Sir Roland said. "You may depend on me."

Soon after the constables took their leave, and a little later on Sir Roland learned that the detachment of soldiers promised from town had arrived.

He had no use for their services now, and, having seen them well-cared for, dismissed them.

"So," said the baronet, when he was again alone, "the miscreant, Jacob Butler, has betrayed me after all, and gone over to the service of my enemy, Spring-Heeled Jack. I know now what the arrival and departure of the carriage means—Daisy Leigh is no longer here; but I will follow and secure her, though the foul fiend stood in my path."

He spoke thus as he stood at the window watching the shades of night as they gathered on the landscape.

"At least," he said, closing the shutters and drawing the curtains close, "I shall be left in peace for a few hours. Oh! for one night's rest. Oh! for the sweet repose that belongs to me as a reward for labour."

Returning to the table he dropped his head upon it, and as he did so his hand came in contact with a piece of paper protruding from a drawer.

He had not noticed it before, and drew it out with a feeling of curiosity.

It was a note to him, and the writing was blood-red.

His first impulse was to fling the paper aside, but remembering that he would know no rest until he had perused its contents, he burst the seal and read—

> *"Your intended victim is no longer here. Sir Roland, you have been in my power a hundred times, but I have refrained from slaving you. I have given you opportunities to repent, but do not tempt me too far. Daisy Leigh will be safe and in good hands by the time you read this. Once more be warned, and be warned in time, or swift will come the hour of retribution and vengeance sure.*
>
> *"SPRING-HEELED JACK."*

Sir Roland crushed the paper in his hand, and was in the act of hurling it down at his feet when he heard a strange sound behind him.

Turning his head, he saw that most horrible of old women, Mrs. Corcoran.

She was mouthing and mocking at him hideously.

One hand pointed at him and the other clutched a dagger.

Sir Roland uttered a fearful oath, and, springing to his feet, overturned the chair.

"So," he hissed, "you thought to steal upon me unawares! Woman, if such you be, give me that dagger!"

"I came here," Mrs. Corcoran replied, defiantly, "not to steal upon you unawares nor to take your life, as you may think."

"Why, then, are you armed?"

"To defend myself against a desperate man who has been foiled in all his undertakings."

"Wretch—witch! I believe not one word," Sir Roland cried. "Give me that dagger!"

With a quick movement he seized her wrist and pinned it against the wall.

In another instant he had possessed himself of the dagger.

---

[105] The oldest bookshop in the United Kingdom.

Then all his evil blood boiled in his veins, and its reflection shone from his eyes.

"When you said that I am a desperate man and stop at nothing," he hissed, "you spoke the truth. Ah! you may twist, struggle, and turn, Mrs. Corcoran, but I have you now, and had you the strength of a giant I could hold you."

The hag felt this to be the truth, and her cheeks grew ashy grey.

"You will not harm me," she said, "for I meant none. Let me go, and I will trouble you no more. I have a little money of my own, and—"

"Yes, I know," Sir Roland interposed; "and you will use it in the cause of my destruction now that you discover I have found you out. I will not give you the least chance; I—"

"Would you murder me?" Mrs. Corcoran cried.

"It would be no murder to rid the world of such a wretch as you," Sir Roland replied.

As he spoke he tightened his grasp, and the hag groaned with pain.

"No—no—no!" she said, feebly. "You do but jest with me. Think of how I have served you! Think, if I die now, what sins I carry with me to the grave!"

"No grave would hold you," Sir Roland said. "Some ghoul would tear you from the earth and bring you back again. You shall burn! You witch, you shall burn!"

"Burn?"

"Aye, burn," Sir Roland repeated. "When you are dead I will fire this place. There will be a red glare in the sky to-night, and your ashes shall mingle with the sparks and burning fragments."

"Have mercy!" Mrs. Corcoran gasped. "Let me implore you on my knees to have mercy. You are only trying to frighten me. It must be so—say it is so!"

"It is not so. You must die."

Death now stared her in the face.

The white and always grim horseman that knocks alike at the door of the palaces of the rich and hovels of the poor, stopped before her, and bade her mount and ride across the shadowy border that lies between this earth and eternity.

Death was so horrible—horrible to her because she, guilty creature, had so many reasons to cling to life.

With a quick movement she struck at Sir Roland with her left hand and buried her nails in his cheek.

A yell scarcely human burst from his foam-flecked lips.

The dagger rose.

It flashed in the air and then descended.

Mrs. Corcoran uttered a gasping cry and fell.

"Oh! I am stabbed," she shrieked. "I am wounded to death. Wretch—villain—murderer—I will haunt you."

She raised herself on her elbow, but he struck at her and knocked her down.

"Seek the spirits of those you have sent before you," he cried, as her eyes dimmed and her limbs stiffened.

"Oh! murder—cold, cruel, heartless murder," the dying woman muttered, faintly. "The Heaven I have defied and wronged so long will avenge this."

These were the last words that passed her lips, and Sir Roland, throwing down the dagger, gazed at her body for some minutes in silence.

"Fool, to tempt me to dye my hands deeper in blood," he said. "Had you served me well, you might have lived out the remainder of your days, but I can have no obstruction in my path. Pah! what a wretched atmosphere is this I breathe. I gasp—I choke."

He placed his hands to his throat and wrenched his cravat off.

"Now to destroy the evidence of this crime," he said, hoarsely. "The fire will purge all. Ha! I must be quick. I will show myself to the villagers and help them to put out the blaze; but before they arrive the flames will be flying in seething wreaths about Lilac Lodge."

Piling some chairs against the wainscotting, he placed the lamp beneath them, and hastily left the room.

When Sir Roland Ashton passed outside Lilac Lodge, he stopped for a moment and looked back.

He thought he heard his name called by the woman he had so cruelly slain.

Sir Roland's face paled, his parted lips sent forth a steam-like vapour, and his knees knocked together.

"What now!" he gasped. "Is she not dead?"

"Sir Roland!"

He heard the voice now above him, and borne on the wings of the soughing wind.

The baronet clutched his hands and fled across the park.

As he reached the road, and saw lights twinkling from cottage windows, he felt more at ease.

Then he turned again and looked towards Lilac Lodge.

"Where is the red light in the sky?" he said. "Surely the overturned lamp has done its work by this time? If the glare does not appear presently, I must go back at all risk. But first to show myself to the people."

Walking hastily towards the inn at which Grabham and Catchpole had so distinguished themselves, Sir Roland entered and sat down.

There was a general movement among the customers to make room for the distinguished visitor, and the landlord dashed into the back parlour to smooth his hair, and to put on a snow white apron.

"Will your honour be pleased to walk into a private room?" he said, as he returned, and bowing low.

"No," Sir Roland replied. "I shall do very well where I am. Put some wine on the table, and let these honest fellows drink to my health."

"Your honour is too kind and condescending."

Sir Roland Ashton waved his hand in a manner implying that he required no thanks.

"I have had a long walk," he said, "and require a little rest and company. I get little of either at Lilac Lodge," he added, under his breath.

The company was made up of labourers, farmers, and village politicians.

They remained silent in Sir Roland Ashton's presence and held aloof from him.

The wine remained untouched upon the table.

"What have I done that you should keep away from me?" he asked, angrily. "Do you think that my presence will breed a pestilence among you? I wish to be merry to-night. When I came in here somebody was singing. Let the song continue."

The vocalist made an attempt to start again, but it ended in dismal failure.

No applause followed, and the men shuffled their feet uneasily.

It was evident that they resented Sir Roland's presence as an intrusion, and the landlord looked sheepish and ill at ease as he poured out the wine.

"Here's to a better understanding between us!" Sir Roland said, raising his glass to his lips.

The next instant it lay smashed to atoms on the floor.

A man with frightened eyes and distraught appearance had dashed into the room.

"Lilac Lodge is on fire!" he roared.

"What!" Sir Roland cried, starting to his feet, "the lodge on fire? Impossible!"

"Come and see for yourself," the man said.

The room became empty in less time than it takes to record the fact.

"This way!" Sir Roland shouted. "Follow me, men! Human life is in danger. Oh! my poor old housekeeper, she may not be able to escape."

He wrung his hands despairingly, and played his part so well that the men who had mistrusted him gave him their pity and help.

The red glow in the sky was fierce and angry.

Huge tongues of flame leaped and roared, as if with joy at the destruction they were creating.

Myriads of sparks danced and hovered over the burning building, and before the men, headed by Sir Roland, were half-way across the park, the roof fell in.

"It is useless—we can do nothing now," Sir Roland said. "The fire must have its own way."

This was so evident that no attempt was made to save any part of Lilac Lodge or anything it contained; but the crowd, augmented by troops of men, women, and children, remained until day dawned, and the sun shone upon the charred and blackened walls.

A search was then made among the rubbish, but no remains of Mrs. Corcoran could be found.

This seemed mysterious to Sir Roland Ashton, and he bit his under lip.

"Surely she was dead when I left her?" he said. "Yes; the flames have done their work only too well, and left no trace of the old hag behind."

CHAPTER XLIX.

CONSTANCE MARFIELD MEETS DAISY LEIGH—
JACOB BUTLER IS SENT ON A PERILOUS ERRAND—
MYSTIFICATION OF ALL PARTIES.

IT will be remembered that when Constance Marfield made her way to London, she did so with certain instructions from Spring-Heeled Jack.

He told her to go to the Queen's Head, Sadler's Wells, and on arriving there she was received by the landlord as if he expected her.

"It is all right, miss," he said; "you need not offer any explanations why you are here. I know all about it, but I am afraid you will have to wait a few days before your friend arrives."

"Indeed!" said Constance. "What course am I to pursue?"

"Remain here, and make yourself comfortable. You shall have every attention, and the best that the house can give is at your service."

"All this is very strange, and it seems to me more like a dream than reality," Constance replied. "I cannot make out why this weird creature, known as Spring-Heeled Jack, should take such an interest in me."

The landlord smiled.

"That you may find out sooner than you expect," he said. "At all events, I have received commands to see that you are well cared for."

Constance hesitated no longer.

She banished all fears and doubts from her mind, and made herself as much at home as possible.

Some days passed away, but no message came.

Spring-Heeled Jack remained absent, and Constance Marfield began to think that something must have happened to him.

Early one morning she was roused from her slumber by the rumbling of wheels and the voices of men.

Rising hastily, and looking out of the window, she saw a carriage, from which a dainty-looking lad was stepping.

A tall, handsome gentleman was handing him out, and then an individual, yawning and rubbing his eyes, dragged his legs down the steps, and looked vacantly about him.

Constance Marfield's heart beat audibly, and a wild cry of joy escaped her lips.

In the handsome gentleman who was paying such attention to the lad she recognised Ralph Ashton.

"Ralph! Ralph! dear Ralph!" she exclaimed, throwing the window open, "do I indeed see you again?"

Ralph Ashton kissed his hand gallantly.

"Yes," he said. "Come down as soon as you can. My heart is bursting to hold you in my arms."

Constance Marfield dressed herself as quickly as possible, and was soon in her lover's embrace.

"Ralph," she said, "tell me what this means. I was sent hither by Spring-Heeled Jack, and now you are here. Who are these people?"

"You must have patience, darling, and I will tell you all," Ralph replied. "As strange as it may seem to you, Spring-Heeled Jack has everything to do with my being here."

"But this man and boy?" said Constance. "Who are you?"

"If you please," said a sweet voice, "I am not a boy, but a girl. I am Daisy Leigh."

"And I am Jacob Butler, or at least I think so," said another voice, which was not sweet, but cracked and harsh. "I never had such a journey in my life. How I got inside the carriage, or how Spring-Heeled Jack contrived to change places with Mr. Ashton, would puzzle that broomstick-witch, Mrs. Corcoran."

"Well, well," said Ralph Ashton, "to put an end to that matter, let us say we are all fairly puzzled. For my own part I have only a confused notion of what took place. At all events, here we are, and safe and sound. Daisy Leigh has escaped from that scoundrel, Sir Roland, and you, Constance, are once more at the side of the man who loves you dearer than his life."

At this moment the landlord's wife, a plump, buxom, comfortable-looking woman, entered the room with a tray laden with all sorts of good things for breakfast.

Jacob Butler was accommodated with a small table near the window, but he was so overcome with astonishment that he could eat but little.

If Mrs. Corcoran had bounced through the window, or had floated down the chimney, he would have taken her appearance as a matter of course.

Meanwhile, the three at the table were chatting on gaily, as if nothing had occurred to disturb their lives, and this helped to reduce Jacob to a state of semi-idiocy.

He stared blankly, rumpled his hair all over his head until it looked like new-mown hay, and listened like a man in a dream.

"We must wait here until we hear from Spring-Heeled Jack," Ralph Ashton said; "that may be in a few hours hence, or days may pass before he tells us what course to take."

"How do you know this?" Constance asked.

"I have Spring-Heeled Jack's word for it."

As Daisy Leigh required rest she went to an apartment prepared for her soon after breakfast, and Jacob Butler, thinking wisely that he was in the way, went below to chat with the landlord and to bother him with a thousand questions.

These the landlord fenced cleverly, and compounded Jacob Butler potations[106] of such extraordinary strength, that Jacob sank lower down into the depths of bewilderment, and finally, stretching himself at full length on the bench, went to sleep.

When he awoke he discovered that he had been put to bed.

Heavy plush curtains hid the room from view, and Jacob, drawing them aside, saw that night had come.

"Is it possible that I have slept the whole day through?" he said, sitting up. "What a fool I must have been to get drunk. I shall get into trouble to a certainty. What account could I give of myself if Spring-Heeled Jack were to appear and question me?"

The last word had scarcely left his lips when the curtains on the other side of the bed parted, and Spring-Heeled Jack thrust his face so close to Jacob that he uttered a yell and rolled himself on the floor.

"Ha, ha!" laughed Spring-Heeled Jack. "So this is the way you do my bidding. Get into bed again, fool, and listen to what I have to say to you."

"I am sure I am very sorry," Jacob Butler replied; "but really the landlord is more to blame."

"Peace," Spring-Heeled Jack said. "What you have done cannot be helped or recalled now. Listen."

"Yes, sir. I am all attention."

"When you rise in the morning you will find that your own clothes have been removed and replaced with others," Spring-Heeled Jack said. "Breakfast early, and as you value your life drink nothing stronger than coffee. Do you follow me?"

"Oh! yes. Oh! lor'."

"I am very angry with you," Spring-Heeled Jack continued; "but at present you have nothing to fear. Trifle with me again, or disregard my instructions, and I will throttle you as sure as you are a sinner."

Jacob Butler gave a wriggle and a spasmodic bounce in the bed, for Spring-Heeled Jack extended one of his long muscular arms and touched him on the neck.

"Don't—please don't," Jacob pleaded; "I will do anything you wish—indeed, I will."

"Good," said Spring-Heeled Jack. "I hope you will do so for your own sake. Now then, to finish my instructions. When you have put on the suit of clothes and other things placed for you, you will find yourself disguised as a farmer. Go then to Charing-cross

---

[106] Alcoholic drinks.

and wait until you see Sir Roland Ashton in conversation with Catchpole and Grabham."

Jacob Butler groaned.

"How now!" cried Spring-Heeled Jack, "what is the matter?"

"Nothing—nothing," Jacob replied, hastily. "I have spasms sometimes, and they make me feel awfully queer."

"You had better dispense with them for a day or two," Spring-Heeled Jack said, grimly, "or you may have one you will not get over in a hurry."

Jacob made no reply, but he hung on to the side of the bed to keep himself from wriggling like an eel.

"The task before you is not a dangerous one," Spring-Heeled Jack continued, "and if you play your part well there will be no risk. Follow Sir Roland and the officers, and when you have seen them to their destination come back to this room, strike thrice with your fist on the panel over the fireplace, and I will come to you."

"I understand," Jacob Butler replied.

The curtains closed again and he was alone.

"Bless me!" Jacob gasped, "this is more awful and confusing than ever. I wonder what I shall be expected to do next?"

"Silence!" said Spring-Heeled Jack's voice.

Jacob Butler buried his head beneath the bed clothes, and kept it there until streams of perspiration poured down his face.

At last he came to the surface and breathing more freely fell asleep again.

When he awoke he found that Spring-Heeled Jack had been as good as his word.

On the chair nearest the bed was a suit of clothes, such as might be worn by a gentleman from the country, and a false beard.

Jacob put the latter on first, and stared at his altered visage in the looking-glass.

"Ha! ha!" he laughed; "I don't believe that even Mrs. Corcoran, clever as she is, would know me now."

This was such consolation to his mind that he cut a few capers, expressive of delight, about the room.

As he proceeded to dress himself his astonishment increased.

"Why," said he, "somebody must have taken my measure when I was asleep. These things fit me perfectly. Ah! well, it is no use wondering about such matters, or I shall lose my head altogether."

In a repentant state of mind Jacob Butler went downstairs.

The first person he met was Ralph Ashton, who eyed him keenly, but said nothing.

"I have seen Spring-Heeled Jack," Jacob faltered.

"I have seen him, too," Ralph replied. "If I had not, I should have made some remark as to your altered appearance. Do your duty, and say nothing more to anybody."

Jacob scratched his head and then shook it.

"We live in a strange world, sir," he said. "Who would believe that less than two days ago I was at Lilac Lodge, and now I am here with a mission?"

"Listen to me," said Ralph Ashton, interrupting him. "You will do well by keeping whatever Spring-Heeled Jack has said to you to yourself. A still tongue makes a wise head."

Jacob Butler rubbed the top of his cranium as if to satisfy himself whether there was any wisdom left in it.

"Well, sir," he said, "I will only say this. Spring-Heeled Jack saved me from a fate which I feared worse than death, and I will do my best to fulfil the task which he has set me."

"Well said," Ralph Ashton replied. "You will find breakfast ready for you in the room on the left."

So saying he turned upon his heel, and Jacob Butler proceeded to refresh himself.

His appetite had now returned and he made a hearty meal.

Suddenly the door opened and the landlord entered.

"Have a drop of brandy, my boy?" he said.

"No, thank you," Jacob replied.

"Just one."

"Not for worlds," Jacob replied; "and I will trouble you to leave me alone. I suppose I am not the only man who has got drunk in your house?"

"Don't lose your temper," the landlord said, grinning. "I thought I was doing you a kind action by asking you. You look all the better for your long sleep."

"If I look it I feel it," Jacob replied. "I suppose you were not disturbed during the night?"

"Oh! dear no—not at all." The landlord laughed in a peculiar manner, and closed the door.

"He didn't seem to believe what I said," Jacob Butler mused. "I—I wonder if he has ever seen Spring-Heeled Jack? If he hasn't I should like to see his face when he does. I'd bet anything that all the beefy colour would fly out of his face and leave him as pale as a turnip."

Having finished his breakfast Jacob left the inn and made his way through the salubrious localities of Clerkenwell and Smithfield.

He had seen nothing that morning of Constance Marfield or Daisy Leigh, and he was wondering whether he should find them at the inn on his return, when he suddenly ran against a man.

It was Bill Blarney, and Jacob Butler, filled with terror, turned cold from the soles of his feet to the crown of his head. "I beg your pardon," Bill Blarney said. Jacob made no reply, for fear that his voice might betray him.

"Are you dumb?" Bill Blarney asked.

Jacob took a hint from this remark, and nodded his head.

"There is no man so dumb as he who chooses to keep his tongue between his teeth," Bill Blarney said.

Jacob Butler pretended not to hear and walked away.

Bill Blarney followed and placed his hand on Jacob's shoulder.

"You are just a little too clever," he said. "It so happens that I have been watching Sadler's Wells, and saw where you came from."

Jacob Butler felt inclined to shrink into his boots.

What he was to do now he had not the slightest notion in the world. Suddenly an idea flashed into his brain. "Since you have found me out," he said, "I may as well tell you the true facts of the case. That little affair got me into trouble, so I thought it better to bolt."

"It got me into trouble, too," Bill Blarney said, pointing to the shoulder which had been wounded. "But what a liar you are."

"Eh?" said Jacob, feebly. "That's rather strong language, you know."

"I repeat that you are a liar, and a contemptible one," Bill Blarney replied. "Look me straight in the face, and tell me who are the people you have been staying with?"

"If you want to know you had better go and ask them," Jacob said, sullenly. "You pressed me into your service, but I want nothing further of you. Leave me to myself or I will call for assistance and denounce you in your true character."

"You had better not."

"I will unless you take yourself off."

Bill Blarney eyed Jacob as if he could have stabbed him with all the pleasure in the world.

"This is neither the time nor the opportunity for me to settle accounts with you," he said; "but we shall meet again, Jacob, my boy."

"I'll take care to be prepared for you."

"In what manner?"

"With a brace of pistols."

Bill Blarney placed his hands on his hips and laughed uproariously.

"Why, you would only shoot yourself you fool," he said; "but perhaps that would be the better way of settling the difficulty."

As he finished speaking two constables turned a corner of the street.

Bill Blarney dived down a court and was lost to view in an instant.

"He is a coward at heart with all his bounce," Jacob said, as he moved away. "I wish I had not seen him—I don't feel quite so comfortable as I did. Hang him and everybody! The very air is full of mystery."

He took the longest route towards Charing-cross, knowing no other.

Passing along Fleet-street he entered the Strand, and then he began to proceed with more caution.

At any moment he might encounter Sir Roland Ashton, and he cast his eyes from one side of the street to the other, with some vague notion that the baronet might recognise him in spite of his disguise, and pounce upon him unawares.

In the days of which we are writing, the West-end of London presented a vastly different appearance to what it does at the present period.

There were but few houses in the Strand, and these were scattered about and standing mostly near the river, in their own grounds, and had fine gardens sloping down to the water.

Charing-cross was little more than a village, and had its fields, lanes, and green hedgerows, until the Mall was reached, and then, as now, fine buildings and handsomely-dressed people stamped the locality as one of wealth and luxury.

Jacob Butler wandered about for hours, but his eyes were not regaled with the sight of Sir Roland, or of the constables.

Jacob did not know whether to go back or not, but at last he decided upon putting up somewhere for the night.

But where?

This was a question that sorely puzzled Jacob Butler.

The sun went down and what promised to be a gloomy night began to set in.

At last Jacob made up his mind to take his way up St. Martin's-lane and enter the first house likely to provide entertainment, for he was not only hungry, but dreadfully thirsty.

"Nobody can say that I have not stuck to my post," he murmured, as he went along. "Hullo! This is a rather queer sort of neighbourhood, but I suppose it is none the worse for that."

Pushing open a door half covered with a red blind, he found himself at a public bar, presided over by a stalwart, beetle-browed man.

"Can I have a bed here?" Jacob asked.

"Yes, if you have the money to pay for it," was the reply.

"How much?"

"Two shillings, or three if you want any supper."

"That is just what I do require," Jacob replied. "I am half dead with hunger. Give me some cold meat and pickles, or anything you may have handy."

"Mary!" shouted the landlord.

"Yes, sir," said a slovenly-looking girl, appearing at the end of the bar.

"Show this gentleman into the parlour and lay the supper cloth."

As the landlord was speaking the door by which Jacob had entered creaked on its hinges. Catchpole and Grabham entered. They wore disguises, but of so flimsy a nature that Jacob Butler recognised them at once.

They looked at Jacob, and he stared back at them with compound interest.

"Beg pardon, sir," said Grabham, "but I fancy I have seen you before."

Now was the time for Jacob Butler to distinguish himself.

For all he knew Spring-Heeled Jack's eyes might be upon him at that moment.

"If you have," he said, "you must have a better memory than I possess. Where was it?—in London?"

"No; in the country."

Jacob Butler winced a little.

"Is not that a rather vague place to talk about?"

"So it is—so it is," Catchpole assented. "Here, I'll put the question straight—"

"Your supper is ready, sir," said the girl. "This way, if you please."

"And I am ready for it," Jacob replied.

It suddenly occurred to him that he had better take the bull by the horns, as the saying goes, and turning, he addressed the officers.

"You can easily see by my attire that I come from the country," he said. "I am going to sup in the parlour, and if you care to drink a glass or break a crust with me, I shall be glad of your company."

Grabham and Catchpole saw a chance of being well treated for nothing, and winked at each other.

They required nothing to eat, but in point of fluids they seemed incapable of pouring enough down their throats.

Then they began to boast and lie.

It was in their nature to do so and they could not have helped it had their lives been at stake.

Jacob listened and chuckled to himself.

He contrived to question them with such success as to discover not only the fact that they were going to sleep in the house, but also the number of the double-bedded room they had taken.

Jacob Butler thought it wise to pay for no more drink.

If the constables took much more they would be too sleepy to talk, and Jacob had made up his mind to listen to their conversation, when they thought they were snug and alone in the room.

This was not a bad notion on the part of Jacob Butler, and how it succeeded we shall presently see.

Neither Grabham nor Catchpole offered to pay for anything, and when they found that their patron had closed his purse-strings, they took themselves away to the upper regions of the house.

Jacob Butler followed in about five minutes.

In the first place he went to his own room, and divested his feet of the thick, heavy boots he had been wearing all day.

Then he peeped out of the door, and looked up and down the long, dark corridor.

It cost him an effort to screw up his courage, but remembering that he would be visited with condign[107] punishment unless he did his duty well, he crept along as stealthily and noiselessly as a cat.

When the boards creaked Jacob started, and there was something unpleasant about the atmosphere of the place.

At last he reached the door hiding the constables from view, and Jacob Butler proceeded to place his ear close to the keyhole.

But woe to him!

His foot slipped and his head came in contact with one of the panels.

Jacob Butler picked himself up and ran for his life.

Tearing madly into his room he slipped off his clothes, and rolling into bed hauled the clothes about his ears, and then began to imitate a prodigious snore.

Presently he heard the sound of approaching footsteps.

They stopped at his door, and then somebody's knuckles began to tap.

Jacob Butler snored louder than ever, and what between fear and chagrin at his failure, he made the most horrible noises in his nose and throat.

Tap, tap, tap!

"Who—who's there?" he demanded, in a muffled tone of voice.

"I say," demanded Grabham, "have you been paying us a visit?"

"Why the devil should I do such a thing as that?" Jacob retorted, wrathfully.

"Well, the devil, or Spring-Heeled Jack, may have something to do with it," Grabham returned. "We were in bed when something rushed against the door and busted in one of the panels."

"It strikes me," said Jacob, as he gained sufficient courage to speak coherently, "that you have both been dreaming. Go to bed again and leave me to sleep in peace."

"We only came to ask you to get up if you hear any more noise?" Catchpole chimed in.

"I'll do that," Jacob replied. "Good-night. You wouldn't hang about there if you knew how sleepy I am."

"There ain't much sleep left for us, I'm thinking," Grabham growled. "Catchpole, why didn't you seize your pistols, and fire them, when you got out of bed? If you had banged

---

[107] Appropriate.

away at the door, you must have hit something on the other side of it!"

"Grabham, my friend," said Catchpole, solemnly, "I followed your example, and kept still."

Mr. Grabham muttered something Jacob Butler could not hear, and then, after a few lively remarks of mutual recrimination, the officers swore to stand by each other until they perished, and sneaked back to their room, trembling every inch of the way.

They were up betimes in the morning, but not so early as Jacob Butler.

He was down and on the alert before they appeared.

Again Jacob took himself to Charing-cross and wandered about for more than three hours.

At last he saw a well-known figure approaching.

It was Sir Roland Ashton, and Jacob Butler dodged behind a broken down wooden fence, and watched with the keenness of a ferret.

Sir Roland looked carelessly about, and evinced neither surprise nor gratification when he was joined by Catchpole and Grabham.

They went away in company, and after giving them a couple of hundred yards' start, Jacob Butler followed, keeping close to the wall, and almost dodging his way from doorway to doorway.

In these days he would have been locked up on suspicion to a certainty, but constables, even in the most frequented parts, were rare articles then and nobody seemed to take much interest in Jacob's movements.

Sir Roland and the officers reached Essex-street and suddenly turned to the right.

They descended the stairs and, hailing a boatman, floated away in the direction of the Tower.

So far all had gone well with Jacob Butler.

Up to that moment his presence had not been dreamed of by the conspirators.

He also hailed a waterman and looked sharply at him.

"Do you want a job?" Jacob asked.

"If I didn't I shouldn't be here," the man replied.

"Well, then, follow that boat at a distance," Jacob said.

"I understand," said the waterman, grinning. "I suppose this is some secret bit of business?"

"Whatever it is you will be well paid for it," Jacob replied, as he stepped into the boat. "Keep away, so that none of those men can recognise me, but pull ashore the moment they land."

The journey down the river was of short duration, as a swift ebb-tide was flowing.

Sir Roland, Grabham, and Catchpole soon stepped ashore; but before they were out of sight Jacob Butler was on their track.

He saw them enter the old Mint.

He followed them until he beheld them standing before the door of the house once occupied by Gedge Foote, and then he retraced his footsteps towards the river.

Now that his work was done all his old fear and horror of Sir Roland Ashton returned.

His face grew ghastly pale, and his legs tottered under him.

"Back again," he said, hoarsely, as he staggered into the boat. "Phew! I am hotter than a furnace."

"That's curious now, for you are as white as a snowdrift and look as cold as one," the waterman observed. "I hope you haven't brought a fever or any catching complaint into my boat."

Jacob Butler did not feel easy until he had landed at Blackfriars-stairs, and not quite safe until he had reached the inn.

It was still broad daylight when Jacob rushed up into the room in which he had seen Spring-Heeled Jack.

As he struck the panel above the mantel-shelf with his fist he felt something moist fall upon his face.

A mist gathered before his eyes and he reeled into a chair.

"Well," said the voice of Spring-Heeled Jack; "have you succeeded—have you seen Sir Roland?

"Yes," Jacob replied. "But what is this? Your voice seems to come to me as in a dream. My head swims. I am sinking. Where am I going? Oh—help!"

"Fear nothing," said Spring-Heeled Jack, "but answer my questions and then you shall rest."

"Did Sir Roland meet the constables?"

"He did."

"And you followed them?"

"Yes."

"Where to?"

"To a house in the old Mint."

"That is well," Spring-Heeled Jack replied; "and now I will leave you in peace. Do you hear what I say?"

"Yes, I hear you, but I cannot see you."

"And yet I am very near you," Spring-Heeled Jack replied. "For the present, farewell."

Jacob Butler wrestled with the sensation of drowsiness that overpowered his senses.

Once he thought he caught sight of Ralph Ashton standing in the doorway, and then his head fell back and he sank into a long and dreamless slumber.

CHAPTER L
DEAD OR ALIVE.

WHAT IS that creeping painfully along the dark road so late at night? The sky is red with leaping flames, and the wind howls a dirge to Lilac Lodge as it sinks under the destroying element.

Owls, bats, and other evil night-birds of prey leave their haunts and fill the air with shrill cries.

The sight is a strange one to them, and with leathery wings they flap and flip from tree-top to the crumbling buttress of the old church, and huddle together for company sake.

And as they crouch and squeak they seem to ask the same question—

"What is that creeping along the dark road so late at night?"

It is a lonely figure covered with tattered rags.

Now it stops as if fainting, and now it struggles along aimlessly until it reaches a pool of stagnant water, and then it stoops and drinks greedily.

It is impossible to say whether the figure is that' of a man or a woman.

A wild cry of rage and agony bursts from its lips as the figure turns into a wood, and then all is still.

Tremble, Sir Roland Ashton! tremble, Jacob Butler! for Mrs. Corcoran, or her spirit, is abroad.

Sir Roland, Catchpole, and Grabham, having entered the house in the old Mint, and, as they thought, unobserved, began to make preparations to carry out their scheme.

"This is a strange place," Catchpole said, shuddering and glancing nervously over his shoulder.

"Yes," Sir Roland replied, grimly, "and I have some strange recollections connected with it. You did not forget to come well armed I hope?"

"No, your honour," Catchpole replied; "both Grabham and I have a brace of pistols and plenty of ammunition. Why did you ask the question?"

"Because you may have reason to be glad of taking such precaution."

The constables glanced at each other as if they did not relish the job they had taken in hand.

"It ain't that I am afraid of mortal man," Grabham said, "but since that we are here I should like to know all about this place and what we are to expect."

"I had a narrow escape with the men of the Mint," Sir Roland replied. "They gave chase to me on the night that Gedge Foote met with his misfortune."

"It was an accident, I suppose?" Catchpole observed, a little dubiously.

Sir Roland paid no attention to this remark.

"I was thinking that this wild crew might think proper to come here again," he said, "and in that case it would be advisable to be prepared for them."

"They may have removed the treasure," Grabham suggested. "If so we have had all this trouble for nothing."

"Gedge Foote was no fool, and did not wag his tongue like some people I could mention," Sir Roland retorted, glancing at the constables.

"Then," said Catchpole, who began to wish himself outside of the old house, "I should like to know how you became possessed of his secret?"

"I was in difficulties and I came here to borrow money," Sir Roland said. "It was not the first time that Gedge Foote had obliged me, and I determined that he should do so again. We—"

"Who's we?" Catchpole interrupted.

"Well, if you must have it," said Sir Roland, "Bill Blarney was with me."

Both the constables started.

"Why didn't you tell us you were in league with that scoundrel?" Grabham said.

"Who said I was in league with him?" Sir Roland replied, with a scornful laugh. "I will be honest and speak out. I made use of him just in the same way that I am making use of you."

"Oh! that's the game, is it?" said Catchpole, who grew more sick at heart and uncomfortable every moment. "It strikes me rather forcibly that you know more about Gedge Foote's death than you care to tell."

"What if I do?" Sir Roland said, coolly. "I told you that I killed him, and that statement was one of simple fact. What course of action do you think you could pursue? Here are you two officers of the law met here with me to plunder a dead man's house!"

Catchpole rose to his feet.

"I wash my hands of this affair," he said. "No man in all the world is fonder of money than I am, but when I know that it is stained with the blood of a murdered man I—ugh!— turn away. Grabham, I think you will agree with me that we have had enough of this business?"

"Just so," Grabham replied. "I wish to Heaven that I had never moved a step towards this place."

"Gentlemen," said Sir Roland Ashton, with a sneering laugh, "I'll trouble you to remain where you are."

"What if we refuse?" Grabham demanded.

"Why, I shall help myself to the treasure, and when safe abroad with it take the trouble of putting the authorities in the way of letting them know what a brace of beauties are trusted with the care of life and property."

"You villain!" Grabham gasped.

"I am not aware that I have ever posed as a saint before you," Sir Roland returned. "Now, let us understand each other. It is you who threw out the suggestion that I killed Gedge Foote. I confess I did. Now, mark me! as sure as you are living men I will accuse you of being accomplices before and after the fact unless you do my bidding. Help me and you shall have your share, and I care not whether I ever see you or hear of you again."

Grabham and Catchpole staggered against the wall and looked helplessly at each other. They were in a fix and could see no way of getting out of it.

"But why should we quarrel?" Sir Roland went on. "Here, almost within our reach, is money enough to make all of us rich and happy."

"Happy!" Catchpole groaned. "I have done many things in my life which I don't care to think about, but this is too horrible."

"This house is not calculated to inspire a man with pleasant thoughts," Sir Roland said, "and the sooner we are out of it the better. It will take us at least five or six hours to raise the treasure from the well to the cellar, so follow me and we will commence work at once."

"Catchpole," Grabham whispered, "what are we to do?"

"I don't know. Where's the use of asking me?"

"I took you to be a man of common sense," Grabham said, mournfully. "I'm in such a wretched state of mind myself that I don't know whether I am on my head or my heels."

"We must follow him through with it now," Catchpole remarked, in a whisper; "but wherever there is the stain of blood a curse follows you can't wipe it out. It is the only thing the earth will not hide. It has a voice of its own voice that is heard in Heaven, and it cries aloud for vengeance."

"What lovely words!" Grabham said. "I feel better after them, Catchpole. Do you think that if we kept half our share of the money and gave the rest to some charity that—"

"Cease that prating and follow me," Sir Roland Ashton interrupted, turning in the doorway. "Ha!"

"What's the matter?" Catchpole demanded,

"I thought I heard a sound below," Sir Roland replied. "Give me a pistol. Good! Now it will be death to the man who crosses my path."

At this moment Catchpole shrieked, and Sir Roland turned fiercely upon him.

SPRING-HEELED JACK,

THE TERROR OF LONDON.

"DIE ! DOG—DIE !" SPRING-HEELED JACK HISSED.

No. 17.

"What now?" he demanded.

"The shadow—the shadow!" was all Catchpole could utter.

"Shadow—shadow?" Sir Roland repeated. "Speak out, man. Use your tongue like a creature of sense and reason, or I will render it useless for ever."

"It was the shadow of that horrible old woman you had at Lilac Lodge," Catchpole blurted out.

The pistol fell from Sir Roland's hand, and he stared in blank dismay at the terrified constable.

"What fool's lie is this?" he cried, hoarsely.

"No lie at all," Catchpole replied. "If I was on my dying bed I would swear that I saw the shadow."

"It might have been your own."

"Am I like a witch?" Catchpole demanded. "Are my fingers hooked like a hawk's and my nails half-an-inch long? I tell you that the old woman is about somewhere."

"Impossible!" Sir Roland ejaculated. "How can that be, when she is—"

His utterance became choked, and a strange, rattling sound came from his throat.

He had seen the shadow himself.

It appeared for an instant on the opposite wall, and then vanished as if a sudden flash of light had been thrown upon it.

"What devil's work is this?" Sir Roland cried, as he recovered his speech.

"Your own!" said a hollow voice.

Grabham and Catchpole clutched each other by the arm and looked towards the door, which was blocked up by Sir Roland's form.

"I don't think it's any use staying here," Grabham said, feebly. "You'll agree with me Sir Roland, that where there is a shadder there ought to be some cause for it."

Sir Roland did not speak, but passed his hand heavily across his brow.

The constables moved slowly towards the door, but the baronet waved them back.

"Cowards!" he said, "are you to be frightened like children by idle conjurings? This is the work of my enemy and yours. Mrs. Corcoran is dead, and if her spirit has been permitted to revisit the earth it cannot hurt us.".

"It strikes me," Catchpole whined, "everybody is either dead or dying. At all events, treasure or no treasure, I am out of this place as quick as my legs will carry me."

Sir Roland Ashton presented a pistol at head.

"Hold up your hands!" he said.

Catchpole did so, and became so limp that he had to lean against the wall to support himself.

"Follow his example, Grabham," Sir Roland said. "Good! I am glad to find you so sensible and obedient. Now harken. I defy ghost and mortal, and will not leave this place until Gedge Foote's treasure is mine."

"Then come," said Sir Roland.

They descended the dark, dismal staircase, and trod almost silently on the thick carpet of dust which had accumulated there for ages.

Huge networks of cobwebs dangled from the filthy walls, and all kinds of hideous creeping things emerged from niche and cranny.

Sir Roland took a dark lantern from his pocket and flashed the disc of light to and fro over the heads of the constables.

He compelled them to go in advance for fear that they might play him some trick or bolt when his back was turned.

Down they went until they came to the cellar door.

A gust of wind from above caused it to sway gently.

Its creaking hinges sounded like the chains of a gibbet, and the constables, more dead than alive, came to a standstill.

"Go on!" Sir Roland said, sternly. "A few more paces and you will see the well yawning at your feet."

They reached the cellar at last, and stood in silence glancing round the fearful region.

Its walls ran with damp and slime, and every now and then a red-eyed rat dashed from one hole into another, squeaking in terror and rage at the appearance of the strangers.

There was the well, with its pulley and dangling ropes, just as Sir Roland had seen it on that awful night when Gedge Foote breathed his last.

Sir Roland advanced and examined the well by the light of the lantern.

A terrible oath escaped his lips.

"We are foiled," he said. "The water has risen above the secret passage and we cannot enter it. We must wait until it goes down."

"What! wait here?" Grabham demanded.

"Yes. We cannot be in a safer place."

Sir Roland took a cord from his pocket, and, attaching a coin to it, tested the depth of the well.

After a few minutes he repeated the experiment.

"The water is going down," he said. "We shall not be kept long in suspense. In less than two hours we shall be out of this accursed place, and each of us carrying enough gold to ransom a king."

To the terrified constables each minute was an age, but at last Sir Roland clutched the ropes and handed them to Catchpole.

"What am I to do with these here?" the constable demanded, starting back.

"Descend by the aid of them, unless you like to jump."

"No, no!" Catchpole exclaimed. "You go first, Sir Roland, and show us the way."

"Phsaw!" said the baronet. "It is easy enough. Lower yourself until your feet come in contact with a ledge. Move forward, and you will find yourself in the passage."

"If I don't find myself at the bottom of the well it won't be any fault of yours," Catchpole howled. "Why don't you go first?"

"Because you would leave me like a brace of curs," Sir Roland replied; "and I don't mean to give you that chance. Quick! or you will fire my blood with anger, and then you may discover yourself making a sudden descent."

Catchpole, finding that there was no alternative but to obey, passed his trembling fingers round the rope and swung his legs over the well.

"Oh, lor'! oh, dear!" he yelled; "I am sinking! I shall fall and be drowned!"

"You would fall and be hanged if I had my way," Sir Roland replied. "Ass! idiot! Lower yourself hand over hand. How long are you going to keep us up here?"

Catchpole closed his eyes and went down, but so slowly that his arms became racked and filled with pain.

At last his feet came in contact with something, and he breathed a sigh of relief.

"I am all right," he said. "Lor'! how hollow my voice sounds here. Who is to come next?"

"Grabham!" Sir Roland replied. "Of course, our old friend, Grabham, is most impatient to join you."

"Am I?" Grabham replied. "That's all you know about it. But, here goes!"

Sir Roland lighted the constable on his way, and when a word told that he was safe the baronet descended himself.

"I never noticed that there was a door here," he said, as he stood at the entrance of the secret passage. "I suppose I must have overlooked it. See, here are some cords; attach them to the bags, and we will haul them up."

As he spoke the dark lantern was dashed from his hand, and the heavy door closed upon him with such force that it drove him against the shuddering constables.

All three rolled heavily upon the floor.

Sir Roland was first on his feet.

"Ho! ho! you are trapped again!" laughed the voice of Spring-Heeled Jack. "This time I will hold you safe. In six hours the water will rise again and flow over the lifeless bodies of three scoundrels!"

CHAPTER LI.
THE ABDUCTION AT THE QUEEN'S HEAD—THE VAULT BENEATH THE CHURCH—TERROR OF CONSTANCE MARFIELD—APPEARANCE OF SPRING-HEELED JACK—FLIGHT OF BILL BLARNEY—THE STRUGGLE ON THE TOWER.

AT that good old inn, the Queen's Head, near Sadler's Wells, matters remained quiet.

Jacob Butler lay still sleeping out his well-earned rest, and Daisy Leigh and Constance Mar-field sat chatting at a window overlooking a pleasant garden.

Fragrant roses and twining honeysuckle grew in the neighbourhood then, and people came from far and near—came to drink the waters of the celebrated well.

It was one of the most fashionable resorts of all London.

Gaily-dressed gallants took snuff from diamond-studded boxes and flirted with the ladies, who, adorned with patches, powder, hooped dresses, and enormous fans, presented odd spectacles.

The comparatively modem crinoline is but an infant when placed side by side with the dress worn by the feminine gender in the days when a monarch spoke the Dutch language[108] from the English throne, and when starched coat-skirts were still in vogue with the male portion of the aristocracy.

From their place of 'vantage Daisy Leigh and Constance Marfield watched the gaily-dressed throng as it moved to and fro with the lazy yet elegant deportment taught in all schools.

The sight was a novel one to the girls, and amused them greatly.

At last they grew tired of the scene, and commenced chatting about themselves and their future prospects.

Ralph Ashton had gone out, giving no explanation as to where he was going or what

---

[108] Deutsche – German.

time he might return.

"You must tell me all about it, dear," Constance Marfield said to her companion. "You have told me how this strange being, Spring-Heeled Jack, rescued you from Sir Roland and placed you in a secret passage running from Lilac Lodge to a hollow tree in the park; but the rest is still a mystery to me."

"And so it is to me, in honest truth," Daisy replied. "Well, I will tell you all I know.

"This secret passage was most elegantly furnished, and so hollowed out in places that a dozen people might have lived there in ease and comfort.

"I had a suite of apartments, if I may call them by such a name, and Spring-Heeled Jack seldom came near me.

"Everything was placed at my hand in the most mysterious way, but when Spring-Heeled Jack did approach me he treated me as if I were a princess.

"One morning when I rose from my bed I found a note pinned to my pillow.

"It told me to dress in a suit of boy's clothes, which I should find in a chest on the other side of the room, and that I was to make up my mind to leave that very night.

"I was not frightened.

"I knew that Spring-Heeled Jack had always acted as a true friend, and why should I fear him when he had rescued me from a fate worse than death?

"I did exactly as the note instructed me, and passed the day in reading, in playing the harpsichord, and singing.

"I was, in a manner of speaking, a prisoner, yet I was furnished with plenty of amusement, and in no instance did the time hang heavy on my hands.

"In the evening, when I was waiting and wondering what was to happen, and where I was to go to, the man who is here with us passed through the secret passage, and I saw him no more until Spring-Heeled Jack had placed me in the carriage.

"How I got there I cannot tell.

"I seemed to me that I was suddenly blindfolded, but I did not struggle, for Spring-Heeled Jack whispered in my ear—

"'Courage! courage! Trust me. I, who have protected you so long, will not desert or hurt you now.'"

"What a strange yet noble creature he must be!" Constance Marfield said.

"As soon as I was placed in the carriage I recovered myself," Daisy went on, "but the pace was too frightful to endure.

"The horses seemed to fly over the ground, and I expected every moment that the carriage would be dashed into a thousand pieces.

"After all I am but a weak and timid girl, and I cried out to Spring-Heeled Jack.

"He only laughed, saying that I was perfectly safe in his hands, so I withdrew my head and resigned myself to my fate, whatever it might be.

"I must have fallen asleep, for suddenly I became aware that I was not alone in the carriage.

"Jacob Butler, looking as if he had just awakened from a trance, sat opposite me.

"I questioned him as to how he came in the carriage; but he could give me no lucid answer.

"All he knew was that he had been lifted bodily down, and that it appeared to him that Ralph Ashton had taken the place of Spring-Heeled Jack on the box-seat.

"And then we came to London, as you see, Constance.

"My story is rather a vague one, and has perhaps left you in the dark as much as ever."

"I must confess that to be the case," Constance replied; "and, moreover, Ralph's conduct mystifies me. When I question him he only laughs, and says that I must seek a full explanation from Spring-Heeled Jack. It is not very likely that I shall do that. Shall we walk in the garden, Daisy?"

"Yes; the air is so fresh and beautiful that it will do us good."

The girls went downstairs, and Constance Marfield, stooping, picked up a tell-tale flower, and blowing lightly upon it, said—"He loves me—he loves me not."

"Yes," cried Daisy; "he loves you, for see there is no more bloom left upon the stem."

She started as she saw the head and shoulders of a man protruding over the neatly-trimmed hedge.

The man wore a slouched hat, pulled low so as to partly conceal his features.

Daisy Leigh started back, but Constance faced the stranger boldly.

"What do you want?" she asked. "How dare you intrude yourself upon us?"

"A thousand pardons, fair lady," the man said. "I crave your charity. I am but a beggar in sore need of food and lodging. Bestow a silver coin upon me and I will pray Heaven to bless you."

Constance Marfield, thinking that the plea was a genuine one, advanced with a shilling in her dainty hand, and as the man took it he pressed her fingers lightly.

It might have been an accident, but it was not lost upon Constance.

"Daisy," she said, as she returned to her fair companion, "there is something about that man I do not like. I am glad he has gone away."

"He gave me a start," Daisy replied. "When I caught sight of his face I thought I had seen it before, but it must have been fancy. Shall we return to the house?"

"I think that would be the wisest course to pursue," Constance replied, "for we may be doing wrong by walking out without leave from Ralph. I wish he would return. That man, beggar as he called himself, may be the agent of one of our enemies."

"Our fears may be groundless," Daisy said; "and yet we had better be cautious."

No sooner had the door closed behind the girls than the beggar-man peered over the hedge again.

Tossing the shilling contemptuously in the air, he chuckled and rubbed his hands as if he had discovered something to invoke his mirth.

"Now, by the bones of Saint Patrick!" he said, "I will fight Spring-Heeled Jack with his own weapons. The Bull in Top Boots shall see me to-night, and the Queen's Head shall lose a guest. Ha, ha!"

Bill Blarney, for he it was, laughed hoarsely.

"What a thing it will be to claim a ransom of this light-heeled gentleman!" he said. "With all his cleverness he never dreamed that I watched his movements, and saw—Never mind that! I know now that cold steel and dull lead will reach him, though he were the dullest of mortals, and the time is not far distant when we shall try conclusions."

He turned away, keeping up the character he assumed by creeping and crouching, and begging of all the well-dressed people he met.

"Stand aside, you hound!" said a gentleman who was whispering soft nothings in a lady's ear.

"Hound!" Bill Blarney ejaculated.

"Yes, filthy hound! Get out of my path!"

Bill Blarney's hand went inside his coat as if to clutch some hidden weapon, but he withdrew it empty.

"Prince Charles Edward is not king yet," he said under his breath; "and there may be yet heads as noble as yours fall from the scaffold on Tower-hill."

The gentleman started, and his face grew ashy grey.

"What mean you by that?"

"That you are an arch-traitor and a conspirator against the peace and throne of King George."

"You know me, then?"

"Yes; almost as well as you know yourself."

"Come away," the lady whispered. "That man's looks and words frighten me."

"Aye, take him away," Bill Blarney said, scornfully, "He forgets the days when he was glad to clasp my hand."

"I clasp your hand!" the gentleman exclaimed, in astonishment. "You must be mad."

He laid his hand upon his sword as he spoke, but withdrew it as Bill Blarney snapped his fingers contemptuously.

"Yes—you, Herbert Stanfield," Blarney said. "Times have altered, and I daresay you find it convenient to forget the past. I never forget a face or a thing that has happened."

"I must speak to this fellow," Herbert Stanfield said, hurriedly.

"Fool!" he hissed in Blarney's ear, "could you not have made yourself known to me in a different fashion?"

"You gave the first offence," the ruffian replied. "So you have made it up with your friends?"

"Yes."

"And changed midnight rides on the highway for lolling about a drawing-room?"

"Hush! hush!"

"Well, well," said Bill Blarney, in a surly tone, "I don't want to harm you, but be careful how you tread on my corns. You know the old Carters, the Bull in Top Boots, in the Borough?"

"I am never likely to forget the den," Herbert Stanfield returned, with a nervous glance at the lady.

"Well, then, come down there any evening after this and stand treat to the boys," Bill Blarney said, in a whisper. "They will be glad to see you and give you a royal welcome. And now I will put matters right with your lady. You have good taste, Herbert, my boy."

Herbert Stanfield's face grew pale with passion, and his fingers itched to strike the scoundrel standing before him to the earth.

"Leave the explanation to me," he said. "Begone! You will see me ere long. I will bring sufficient money to pay my ransom, and then I hope that neither you or any of the band will ever trouble me again."

"Perhaps not."

"What did you say?"

"Nothing," Bill Blarney replied; "I only made a remark about a wound I have in my shoulder; the pain of it is enough to drive me mad."

Leaving Herbert Stanfield to stammer out some excuses to the lady, Bill Blarney slouched away, chuckling and grinning.

"What a stroke of luck to meet him after all these years!" he said. "His ransom will cost him something. I must keep my eyes wide open, and not let him slip through my grasp. Poor devil! he must feel uncomfortable now that he is bowled out."

It was late in the day when Bill Blarney wended his way towards the Bull in Top-Boots.

A feeble oil-lamp was burning in one of the windows, shedding a sickly glare on the rough, uneven road beyond.

There was not a soul in sight, and Bill Blarney, after glancing furtively up and down the street, entered the house.

"Ha!" said the landlord greeting him with a smile. "So you have found your way back at last!"

"Yes; but winged like a sparrow," Blarney replied. "That was Sir Roland Ashton's work, and I owe him a grudge for it."

"What! Sir Roland?"

"Yes, but I have no time to tell a long story," Bill Blarney growled. "Are any of the boys here?"

"No; but I expect several presently," was the reply. "I suppose you are not in such a devil of a hurry that you can't wait a few minutes?"

"Time is no object to me just now," the scoundrel replied; "but I want a job done to-night. Ha! here comes Dick Sleuth!"

A short, stunted, evil-looking ruffian, with shoulders almost as broad as his body was long, entered the house, and was in the act of passing through to the rear of the premises when Bill Blarney stopped him.

"How fares it with you?" the latter asked.

"Rough."

"Short of money?"

"Yes, and short of temper into the bargain," Dick Sleuth replied, with an oath. "Let me pass, unless you are agreeable to wet a thirsty man's lips."

"Give it a name."

"Brandy."

"Put a bottle on the table," said Bill Blarney, winking at the landlord. "Dick is the best fellow in the world when you know how to treat him properly."

"That's so," the landlord returned, as he reached down a black bottle and dusted it with his handkerchief. "Where is your bosom friend and pal?"

"What, Phil Tricker?"

"That's the boy I mean."

"I left him following an old gentleman with more rings and jewellery than he can possibly want; but I expect him here soon."

Dick Sleuth grinned as he made this explanation, as if he had said something comical.

The landlord of the Bull in Top Boots and Bill Blarney laughed in compliment to the speech, and Dick Sleuth's hardened face softened a little.

"I hope Phil will bring some swag back with him," he said. "If not, I will go on the lay with him outside Vauxhall; but people are getting so precious mean now."

"That is to say they take care of themselves."

"Bah!" Dick Sleuth growled; "they are so awfully suspicious, and have their chairs carried into the gardens instead of calling for them outside."

"I think I can put you in the way of a good thing, Dick," Bill Blarney said. "What do you say to running away with as pretty a young lady as ever you set eyes on?"

"That sort of game isn't in my line; I never tried it," Dick Sleuth replied.

"But will you say 'No' if I tell you that there is money to be had for the mere asking?"

"It's money I want, and money I must have," Dick Sleuth replied.

"Then let us sit down and talk the matter over," Bill Blarney said.

He led the way to the room where the band usually met to share the plunder and discuss future plans.

Dick Sleuth did not wait for a corkscrew.

He knocked the neck off the bottle with a blow of his fist, and poured half the contents into a long glass.

"Your health!" he said, taking a gulp which would have choked an ordinary man.

"And yours, my brave Dick!" responded Bill Blarney, sipping his liquor carefully. "Don't spare the brandy. There is plenty more where that came from."

"Leave that to me," Dick Sleuth said, as he took another pull at the fiery liquid. "Ah! this is good stuff. It warms the cockles of a man's heart, and saves him the trouble of eating."

Bill Blarney was a heavy drinker at times, but he could not refrain from gazing at his companion in horror and astonishment, for the brandy went down Dick Sleuth's throat like water.

It did not make him gasp, but a strange unnatural light came into his eyes.

"I—I don't think you had better have any more just now," Blarney said. "I want you to go with me to the Queen's Head, Sadler's Wells, after midnight, and help me to bring away a gal I have my eye on."

"You? Ha! Ha!"

"If you think that I can love, you are vastly mistaken," Bill Blarney said. "I, like you, want money, but I want more—revenge—sweet revenge on Spring-Heeled Jack!"

This remark had the effect of sobering Dick Sleuth a little.

He shook his head and beat his hard, horny knuckles upon the table as if this was a phase in the promised adventure which he did not expect or entirely agree with.

"I never met anyone I was afraid of yet," he said; "but don't you think that will be a rather dangerous experiment to attempt?"

"Nothing risk, nothing have," Bill Blarney remarked.

"Just so," said Dick Sleuth. "But Spring Heeled Jack is not like an ordinary man—if indeed he be man at all. He is here, there, and everywhere at once. His feet have wings, and he comes and goes from place to place at will."

"Then you give up the girl?"

"I did not say so. What is the figure? That is the most important question."

"Five pounds down, and ten more as soon as we get the girl under the vaults of St. Matthew's Church."

"Why do you intend taking her there?" asked Dick.

"Because it is a place only known to even a few members of the band."

"It's an awful place—a horrible place," Dick Sleuth said, with staring eyes. "I shall never forget the night I passed there alone. I heard such sounds and saw such sights as would turn the blood of the boldest man to ice."

"All the better," Bill Blarney returned.

"But the girl will go mad," Dick Sleuth said, "and if she do she will be no use to herself or to—"

"Enough of this!" cried Bill Blarney, interrupting him. "If you won't help me I must find somebody who will. The question I put to you is simple enough. Yes or No? Answer it one way or the other, and then I shall know what course to decide upon."

Before Dick Sleuth could reply the door opened and Phil Tricker entered the room.

He had the appearance of a man who had seen better days, and his tall, commanding figure contrasted strangely with that of Dick Sleuth, whose height was not more than five feet.

Tricker was evidently an assumed name, and as he walked across the room his gait had the bearing of a gentleman.

"Well," said Dick Sleuth, "what have you brought back?"

"Nothing."

"Nothing?" repeated Dick Sleuth, angrily. "What do you mean by nothing?"

"Just what I say," Phil Tricker replied. "When I came up to the old man and looked him in the face he reminded me of somebody I had known years ago. My heart failed me and I turned away."

"You're a nice sort of chicken to have for a pal," Dick Sleuth growled. "How do you think we are going to get along without money?"

"I don't know, and I scarcely care," Tricker said.

Something like a sigh escaped his lips, and his hands twitched nervously as he placed them on his knees.

"You don't care!" Dick Sleuth growled. "We'll see about that, curse you!"

"Come! come!" Bill Blarney interposed. "Leave your quarrelling to some other time. Tricker is a little odd at times, but when he really means business there is no better man to be found in the Bull in Top Boots. Dick, will you help me to-night?"

"Yes."

"Then tell Phil what is to be done, and ask him to join us."

"No," Dick Sleuth exclaimed, furiously. "You

and I can do the trick very well by ourselves. Let the white-livered—"

"Hold!" cried Bill Blarney. "I won't have this sort of thing. We don't want to start with a fight, which might, perhaps, cause us to end with failure."

"Let him say what he likes," Phil Tricker said, snapping his fingers contemptuously. "All the hard words in the world will break no bone of mine. I want to know nothing of your plans, and, to tell you the truth, I am sick at heart of the horrible business carried on here."

"Listen to the repentant sinner!" cried Dick Sleuth, with a laugh that might have come from the throat of a bear. "Perhaps the next thing he thinks of will be to peach on us."

"Not I," Phil Tricker replied. "You wrong me there, but I wish to Heaven that I could get back to the country and live and die there."

Other men walked into the room, and it soon began to fill.

"Perhaps it is just as well that Tricker is not in the job," Dick Sleuth whispered to Bill Blarney. "When I first knew him he was as bold and desperate as the rest of us, but he has greatly changed. Sometimes I think that he must be going mad."

"It would be awkward if he did so and roared out a few things he had seen here."

"It would," asserted Dick Sleuth, screwing up his features. "Ha! There goes eleven. Hadn't we better make a start?"

"There is time, for we are not going on foot."

"How then?"

"I have arranged for a horse and cart."

"Well," said Dick Sleuth, "of course we shall want something to bring the gal away in, but there is another thing to be considered. How are you going to prevent her from screaming?"

"With some wrappers, which will muffle her cries effectually."

"Right you are," Dick Sleuth replied. "I like to know all particulars before I start."

They partook of another glass and then walked out into the open air.

It was a dark, gloomy night.

The wind had hushed its voice, and the almost motionless clouds hung pall-like and heavy over the City of London.

Grim and gaunt were the shadows that lurked in dark entries, and strange and uncouth the people who stole from them.

As may be imagined, many of these night-prowlers were out for no good purpose, but among them were the poverty-stricken and the homeless.

Wretched, shivering beings, clad in tattered rags, crept through the darkness, houseless, miserable, and starving.

Bill Blarney and Dick Sleuth were used to such scenes and paid no heed to them.

A little distance from the Bull in Top Boots was a yard guarded by two high gates.

Here Bill Blarney stopped and whistled softly.

The signal was returned in a similar manner, and then the gates opened slowly.

"All ready?" Bill Blarney asked.

"Yes," a voice replied.

"Then come out and let us get on the road."

A man, shrouded from head to heel in a long coat brought a horse and cart from the yard, and Bill Blarney signified his approval by placing some silver in the man's hand.

"You had better come with us," Blarney said; "for it may take two of us to get the girl out of the house. You haven't forgotten to bring your own pistols, I suppose?"

"No."

"Then all's well. Jump up and we'll get away."

Leaving the three conspirators to travel on their way towards the Queen's Head, we will return to the inn and ascertain what is passing there.

Nothing more transpired to alarm Daisy Leigh and Constance Marfield, but neither of the girls forgot the repulsive face of the beggar-man who had appeared before them so suddenly.

Ralph Ashton did not return, and, as the evening grew apace, Constance became uneasy, and her pale face told what was passing in her mind.

"Don't be alarmed," Daisy said. "A hundred things may have kept him away."

"True," Constance replied; "but, on the other hand, a hundred things may have happened to him."

"Isn't that looking on the dark side of the picture?" Daisy said. "Come, let us banish these vague fears and try to be cheerful. Hark I hear footsteps."

"They are not Ralph's," Constance said.

Just then came a knock at the door.

"Come in," Daisy said.

Jacob Butler put his head into the door.

"A note for you, miss," he said, looking rather oddly at Constance Marfield.

She sprang to her feet, and, taking the paper from his hand, read—

> *"You may not see Ralph Ashton for a few hours, but he is perfectly safe. Fear nothing and be surprised at nothing.*
>
> "SPRING-HEELED JACK."

"Where did you get this?" Constance demanded.

"I found it, miss."

"Where?"

"Nailed to the door of my room."

"How strange!" Constance said, glancing a second time at the writing. "Thank Heaven that Ralph is safe!"

"Yes," Daisy returned; "I say 'Amen' to that. Now, dear, it is time that we were in bed. Shall I come with you to your room and chat for a few minutes?"

"No, thank you," Constance replied. "You must be quite as tired as I am, so let us say goodnight. Light slumbers and pleasant dreams, Daisy."

The girls parted, and Constance Marfield, having reached her room, sat down on a chair by the bedside.

She locked the door, and then examined the fastenings of the windows, though scarcely knowing why.

And yet a nameless, undefined terror was upon her, and she was so impressed that she was not alone in the apartment that she peeped nervously into the cupboards and shook the curtains to make sure that nobody was lurking behind them.

"How silly of me!" she said, trying to laugh at her own fears. "I am as bad as a servant-girl after reading a ghost story."

Walking up to the mirror, she began to undress and to fold her garments neatly.

The bed was a cumbrous piece of machinery, fitted with four tall, carved posts, heavy velvet curtains, but comfortable withal.

It was a bed to woo the drowsy god, and Constance had no sooner composed her limbs and placed her head on the soft, yielding pillows than she fell asleep.

The room was on the first floor, and close to the window was a small outhouse with a sloping roof.

Constance had not been asleep many minutes when a church clock in the neighbourhood struck the hour of midnight.

The sound of the bell disturbed Constance for a moment.

She opened her eyes, but closed them again, and her gentle breathing told that she slumbered again.

A quarter of an hour passed away, and then the dark form of a man stole across the garden.

He was quickly followed by another, and as they met, they stood whispering for some moments.

"Give me a leg up," said Dick Sleuth, pointing to the outhouse. "I suppose you are sure of the room?"

"As sure as you and I are standing here," Bill Blarney replied. "Steady! Mind how you go. The tiles are old and a few of them may be loose. It would be a pretty business if they gave way and you came down with a run."

"Trust to me," Dick Sleuth said, as he ascended to the roof. "Now throw me that wrapper and stand below. I'll drop the girl into your arms and you can make off with her."

"Yes—yes!" Bill Blarney said, impatiently; "but don't stand there talking."

Dick Sleuth took a fine steel instrument from his pocket, and placing it between his teeth he began to crawl along the roof.

One or twice he stopped to glance at Constance Marfield's window to listen.

It was as still and as quiet as the grave.

Little dreaming of what was about to happen, poor Constance Marfield slept soundly.

With noiseless movements Dick Sleuth crawled along, and then with a cat-like spring he reached the window.

Throwing the wrapper round his neck he went to work at once.

Inserting the steel instrument at the side of the window he pulled it sideways, and the fastening slid back with so faint a click that it did not wake Constance.

But now Dick Sleuth had the most difficult portion of his task to perform.

How was he to open the window without making a noise and arousing the sleeper?

The window was one of small diamond-shaped panes set in lead, and opened outwards.

Its hinges might be rusty and creak at the slightest touch.

But Dick Sleuth, having gone so far, was not the man to stand upon trifles.

Opening the window an inch or two, he hooked his fingers over the top, and pressing it downwards, held it fast. In a few moments he was standing in the room.

His feet, encased in list slippers, made no noise whatever.

Swiftly and silently he moved towards the bed, and drawing the curtains, gazed at Constance.

She had changed her position, and was now sleeping with her head pillowed on her arm.

Dick Sleuth unwound the heavy wrapper from his neck and shoulders and folded it double.

Then with a quick movement he threw it over Constance, and pressed it down over her face.

Constance awoke and tried to cry out, but a heavy hand was upon her mouth, and an arm as strong as an iron band was about her waist.

As the poor girl felt herself lifted up, and apparently thrown over a man's shoulder, she gave herself up for lost.

Suddenly she felt herself fall, and then, as she was caught, a voice hissed in her ear—

"Keep quiet, or I will murder you!"

Constance could not have uttered any sound now if she had been ever so much inclined.

All her breath had left her body, and her heart beat so audibly that she thought it must burst.

"Heaven help me!" she thought; "for I cannot help myself. Into whose hands have I fallen? Oh! Ralph—Ralph! it was an evil hour when you left me to endure such an outrage as this."

Bill Blarney, keeping Constance's head well covered, bore her away, and placing her in the cart threw a number of thick rugs over her.

He held her down, but there was no need for such violence, for Constance was so bewildered and terror-stricken that she lay as still as if death had suddenly overtaken her.

The cart jolted on its way, Dick Sleuth running after it and climbing in behind.

"I think I have done my work well and deserve my money," he said, breathlessly.

"You have, old fellow," Bill Blarney replied, "and you'll find me as good as my word."

"Do you really intend taking the girl to the vaults under St. Matthew's Church?"

"Yes. Why not?"

"Will she not catch her death of cold?"

"I can't help that," Bill Blarney replied, brutally. "She shall have the rugs and wrappers, and must make the best use of them."

The church alluded to has long since been pulled down.

It stood on the Surrey side of the Thames—so close to it that the shadow of its tower was reflected upon the water—and commanded a full view of London-bridge.

It did not take long for the cart to reach the church.

It was in a dreadfully dilapidated state even then, and no services had been held for some time.

"Steady!" Bill Blarney said, as he leaped from the cart. "We must make sure that we are not being watched. If you see anybody peering about use your barkers, Dick."

"Right you are," Dick Sleuth replied. "It's all right—there's nobody about. Out with the girl!

"I'll carry her," said Bill Blarney. "Here, take the key and open the vault. You'll find a lantern if you pass your hand in on the left-hand side."

This was but the work of a few moments.

"Give me air," Constance groaned; "I am dying."

Bill Blarney removed the wrapper from the girl's face, and then a wild and piteous cry burst from her lips.

"Ralph, Ralph!" she shrieked. "Oh! come to my aid! Help, help!".

"Curse you!" said Bill Blarney. "Is this how you repay my kindness? Hold your tongue."

But Constance redoubled her cries for help. and Blarney, brute and hound that he was, struck the girl's up-turned face with his fist.

With a bitter moan of agony she sank back in his arms and lay as still as death.

Blarney bore Constance to the mouth of the vault, and pointed to a flight of stairs.

"Down you go!" he said. "Quick, or I will hurry your movements with the butt-end of this pistol."

Constance knew that to disobey was to meet certain death.

"Have you no mercy?" she said, turning to him. "What wrong have I ever done you? For Heaven's sake let me go!"

"Down—down!" was all Bill Blarney could say.

Constance made no further appeal, but descended the steps.

She almost fainted as the trap-door fell with a crash a few inches from her head; and, as she heard the key turn in the lock, she wrung her hands, and hot, scalding tears filled her eyes.

Bill Blarney had flung down some of the rugs after her, and collecting them, she wrapped them round her shivering form.

How cold, dark, damp, and horrible!

A dreadful smell pervaded the place, and Constance had to put great control upon herself to keep herself from going mad.

She shrank back when she thought that she was alone with the dead.

She dared not stretch out her hand for fear of touching some mouldering coffin; and at last she sank down upon the floor and gave herself up to despair.

Exulting in the capture of Constance Marfield, Bill Blarney and Dick Sleuth took themselves back to the Bull in Top Boots.

The house was open night and day for the convenience of its light-fingered customers, and the rascals, who had accomplished their villainous designs, called for more brandy and proceeded to pass the night in revelry.

But at last they tired of drinking and singing, and Dick Sleuth, finding that Bill Blarney had dropped his head upon the table and was snoring like a grampus,[109] took himself away to his lodgings which were hard by.

Presently Bill Blarney felt a touch on the nape of the neck and opened his eyes.

They were heavy and bloodshot with drink, and for some moments he could not distinguish anything with clearness.

At last he fancied he saw something like a huge bird crouching in a corner of the room.

The figure moved and stood erect.

Bill Blarney remained speechless with terror when he saw Spring-Heeled Jack towering over

"Villain! unmitigated villain!" Spring-Heeled lack said, in a deep, stern voice. "What have you to say for yourself? What excuse can you make for this night's work?"

Bill Blarney tried to speak, but his tongue love to the roof of his mouth and his teeth chattered in his head.

"Speak, I command you!" hissed Spring-Heeled Jack, "or this moment shall be your last."

"How did you get here?" Blarney contrived to articulate. "Who betrayed me? Who let you in?"

"That is my business and not yours," said Spring-Heeled Jack. "Let it suffice for you to know that every movement on your part was watched. Come, scoundrel that you are! I have determined to teach you a lesson such as you will never forget."

As he twined his long muscular arms around Bill Blarney the ruffian gave a gasping cry for help.

Spring-Heeled Jack silenced him with a blow between the eyes, and the room seemed filled with stars and jagged streaks of light.

"This is some of your own treatment," Spring-Heeled Jack said in his ear. "Poor, pitiful fool to think of thwarting Spring-Heeled Jack! I could have stopped that infernal cart a dozen times but I thought I would let you run to the end of your tether."

It struck Bill Blarney as Spring-Heeled Jack tossed him into the air and whirled him about until he was giddy that he had run a little bit over his tether.

Suddenly Spring-Heeled Jack stood him on his feet and glared into his face.

"Where is the girl—where is Constance Marfield?" he demanded. "Tell me what you

---

[109] A large dolphin or whale.

have done with her!"

"I thought you knew all about her?" Bill Blarney stammered.

"Never mind what you think. Answer my question, you cowardly dog!"

"I don't know."

"Villain! you lie."

As he spoke he seized Blarney by the throat and forced him backwards.

"Help! mercy! help!" Blarney shrieked.

A door opened and footsteps approached.

"Ha! ha!" laughed Spring-Heeled Jack. "He who can catch me must be a clever man."

Raising Bill Blarney in his arms, the weird creature kicked against one of the panels in the wall.

It flew back, and Spring-Heeled Jack, carrying his burden as easily as if he had a child in his arms, darted through.

Click went the panel as it ran back into its place.

A passer-by in the street beheld a strange sight.

Something flew over his head and went bounding along with gigantic strides, now on the ground and sometimes in the air.

The man raised a cry of alarm and the inmates of the Bull in Top Boots, armed with all sorts of weapons, rushed into the street.

Too late!

Spring-Heeled Jack was away with his prisoner and had reached St. Matthew's Church while the bewildered miscreants at the inn were asking each other questions.

One of the church windows were open, and Spring-Heeled Jack, never relaxing his hold on Bill Blarney, sprang through.

Then Bill Blarney found himself lying flat upon his back on the cold stone flags.

"If your intention is to kill me," he gasped, "do so quickly, and put me out of pain."

"Kill you—yes!" Spring-Heeled Jack replied; "but why should I put you out of pain— you who scruple not to torture others? I will play with you as a cat plays with a mouse. You shall know what it is to feel agony of mind and body, and then—"

"Mercy!" Bill Blarney groaned. "I will tell you where Constance Marfield is. She—"

"Silence!" Spring-Heeled Jack interposed. "If I did not know I could soon force the truth from your craven throat! Villain, I have a surprise for you. You shall see how London looks by night from the top of the church tower!"

"No—no!" Bill Blarney yelled.

He now saw through Spring-Heeled Jack's designs, and grovelled on the ground like a whipped cur.

"Anything but that!" he pleaded. "Spare me such torture as you hope to be forgiven your sins! Let me live a few more hours! You had mercy on me once!"

"And this," said Spring-Heeled Jack, planting his foot on the panting ruffian's breast, "this is your gratitude?"

"Give me one more chance," the wretch pleaded—"one—one!"

Spring-Heeled Jack laughed aloud, and dragging Bill Blarney after him, ascended the stairs of the tower.

That was an awful journey.

As Bill Blarney swung from side to side he was bruised and beaten almost out of his five senses.

He cursed, raved, prayed, and begged most piteously.

But all in vain.

The blood of his strange captor was up, and he paid no heed to any word uttered.

Bill Blarney closed his eyes when Spring-Heeled Jack stopped at last.

Cool, fresh air was blowing on his face and he felt revived.

He knew that he was on the top of the church tower, and that between him and the earth there was a space of fully a hundred feet.

What would happen next?

He dare not think or conjecture on his impending fate.

He felt his hair bristle and his blood run deadly cold.

At last Bill Blarney opened his eyes and saw that Spring-Heeled Jack was sitting down with his legs crossed and his hands on his hips.

"Poor fool!" Spring-Heeled Jack said. "You have brought this upon yourself. If you have anything to say, say it now."

"Is this to be my last hour?"

Spring-Heeled Jack leaned over the crumbling but still massive masonry and pointed downwards.

"Yes," he replied. "In a few minutes you will be lying crushed and mangled beyond recognition."

"Listen!" Blarney said, under his breath. "You will wrong yourself by destroying me. It will do no good."

"It will rid the world of a villain."

"Granted that I am all that you say," Bill Blarney continued; "there are others as bad, and if not worse. Sir Roland is your enemy. Spare me, and I will betray him to you."

Spring-Heeled Jack laughed again, and so loud that the air caught up the sound and rolled it away like rumbling thunder.

"So you think to bribe me?" he said. "No, no; I hold Sir Roland in my power, and can deal with him as I wish. You must die! If you wish to breathe a prayer or to make a confession I will give you five minutes to do so, but no more."

"Only five minutes?"

Not a moment longer."

A sudden thought dawned into Bill Blarney's mind.

There was hope in it, though a faint one, but he clung to it as a drowning man clings to floating straws.

If he could but get a hold of Spring-Heeled Jack he would sell his life dearly.

"I thank you even for those minutes," he said. trying to look very repentant. "I have much to say and much to think of."

As he spoke he moved a little nearer to Spring-Heeled Jack and made a sudden grasp at him.

But Spring-Heeled Jack was on his guard.

He struck up Bill Blarney's wrist, and leaping to his feet, raised the ruffian aloft in his arms.

"Mercy! Oh! horror! Mercy!"

Spring-Heeled Jack brought him down with a thud upon the masonry.

"Die, dog—die!" he said. "Your last moment has come."

Bill Blarney struggled faintly; a gurgling cry of agony came from his throat, and he fell. Down—down—down!

Spring-Heeled Jack turned his head aside and trembled.

The sight was too awful even for him.

Presently he heard a thud. All was over!

Constance Marfield had not moved. She sat thinking and wondering whether her abductors would bring her food, or whether they had determined that she should die the fearful death of thirst and starvation.

What had she done to the villain that he should kidnap her just when her heart was filled with joy at seeing Ralph Ashton again?

She asked herself this question a thousand times, but could find no satisfactory answer to it.

"Oh! Ralph—Ralph," she moaned, "what will be your feelings when you return to the Queen's Head and find that I am no longer there? Oh! Daisy—pretty Daisy!—would that I had never left you for a single moment."

The darkness and horror of the vault were almost insupportable, and she passed her hand to her eyes and brow, thinking that she must be mad.

"Great Heaven!" she cried, "give me strength to bear this. Keep the balance of my brain clear and even. There must be some mistake; this dreadful man will find it out soon and set me free."

Suddenly she heard a sound proceeding from the top of the vault.

She strained her ears to listen, and her heart gave a great bound.

"Who's there?" she called out.

"Your friend!" was the reply.

And Spring-Heeled Jack came leaping down the staircase.

"Heaven be praised for this!" Constance cried, joyously. "Oh! how can I thank you? How did you know that I was here?"

"It matters not, fair lady," he replied. "I came hither to save you, and here I am. I am aware that the scoundrels dragged you from your warm bed and so I have brought this cloak to protect you from the cold."

As he spoke he handed a long, handsome cloak to Constance.

It was richly lined with fur, and Constance was so grateful for it, that she could have thanked Spring-Heeled Jack on her knees.

She was advancing towards the steps when Spring-Heeled Jack confronted her and waved his hands before her face

Thrice he did so, and then Constance felt that she was sinking through the floor, and lost consciousness.

The song of birds and a flood of sunlight awoke her.

She was in bed, and in the room at the Queen's Head, too.

"Marvel of marvels! she said, sitting up and rubbing her eyes. "What can this mean?"

She glanced keenly round the room, scarcely believing that anything she saw could be real.

"Have I been dreaming, then?" she said. "It is impossible. But how comes it that I am here?"

The curtains near her bed were open, and she glanced at the window.

It was fastened, and everything remained as she had left it overnight.

But suddenly her eyes fell upon a deep blue velvet cloak, lined with sable.

Constance Marfield started and turned pale.

"It was no dream," she said. "Spring-Heeled Jack rescued me from that horrible vault, and brought me here in some mysterious manner only known to himself."

Tap—tap—tap!

Somebody was knocking at the door.

"Who is there?" Constance demanded.

"Daisy Leigh!"

"Wait a moment, dear, and I will get up and let you in."

As Daisy ran into the room Constance clasped her round the neck.

"Oh! I have such strange things to tell you," she said; "sit down, and I will tell you as I dress."

Daisy Leigh opened her beautiful eyes wide as Constance narrated her wonderful adventures, and kept silence until she had finished.

"You take my breath away," she then said. "If I had not heard the story from your own lips I should have laughed at it as an idle one."

"Has Ralph Ashton returned?" Constance asked.

"Not that I am aware of," Daisy replied.

"I wish he had," Constance sighed, "I long to tell him what I have passed through. I wonder what can keep him abroad so long!"

CHAPTER LII.

THE PRISONERS IN THE WELL—THE STORM—
THE THUNDERBOLT—FALL OF THE HOUSE IN THE OLD MINT.

IT WAS some time before Catchpole and Grabham could fully realise their position.

They stood and rubbed their bumped heads in fear and amazement, but at last the bitter truth dawned upon them in all its earnestness.

They were in a trap and there was no way out of it.

In spite of his rage Sir Roland Ashton never lost nerve.

He groped his way to the door and passed his hands over it. There was no handle nor lock, so far as he could ascertain.

As he turned away, with a horrible oath on his lips, something chinked under his feet. It was gold, but the sound was no longer music to his ears.

"Curse the demon!" he said. "Why does he not meet me openly? By all the fiends my sword should give a good account of itself."

"I suppose we shall be let out of this crib soon," Catchpole whined. "No man with a heart in him could leave us to die here. It must be a lark."

"A lark be jiggered!" Grabham gasped. "There are three of us, and we must get the door open somehow, or we shall perish."

The place was so pitch dark that they could not see each other, but there was much comfort in talking.

Catchpole sat down, and hugging his knees rocked himself to and fro.

He began to babble and prate like a child, and talk of the scenes he had passed through.

"Hold that row!" Sir Roland said. "What the devil is the good of snivelling? Peace, or I will shatter your skull!"

"That's it," Catchpole moaned, "kick me while I am down. I am only a poor old sinner. I have always stood in my own light, or I should have held a good position before now. Sir Roland, you got us into this mess and you will have to get us out of it."

Sir Roland bit his lips in his rage, and paced the dismal place to and fro.

"Get you out of it!" he said. "I wish I could—and into the well."

"Hear him?" Catchpole returned. "He isn't satisfied with being the cause of all this misery, but would like to kill us into the bargain."

Just then a startled cry came from Grabham.

"What now?" Sir Roland demanded.

"There is a fourth party here," Grabham said, under his breath. "I touched a face, and it was as cold as death."

"It is just possible that you have come across the dead body of Gedge Foote," Sir Roland said.

"Ugh!" cried Grabham, recoiling. "This is too horrible!"

Catchpole wriggled himself across the floor amid the damp and scattered gold, until he came in contact with Sir Roland.

The baronet struck furiously at the constable, but missed him.

He then drew a pistol, with the intention of putting Catchpole out of the world, when an unseen hand struck his arm up, and the weapon exploded harmlessly in the air.

"Coward!" hissed a voice in his ear, "coward to attempt to murder the miserable wretch you have lured here!"

Sir Roland turned his head sharply, and saw that Spring-Heeled Jack was looking over his shoulder.

"How now?" said the baronet. "Do you come here to taunt me?"

"No; I come to grant your wish," Spring-Heeled Jack said.

"I do not understand you."

"Think of the words you uttered just now," Spring-Heeled Jack replied. "Think of your boast. You wish to meet me openly—to try conclusions man to man. Your desire shall be gratified. The door is open, ascend to the cellar. I will follow you."

Grabham and Catchpole made a movement towards the opening, but Spring-Heeled Jack barred the way with his arms.

"Back!" he cried. "Do not attempt to leave. Your time will come quite soon enough."

"We are done for," Catchpole said, as the door closed with a bang.

"I don't think so," Grabham replied. "At the worst I don't think we shall get more than a kicking. Hark! there is a nice rumpus going on overhead."

As Sir Roland climbed hand-over-hand up the rope Spring-Heeled Jack followed him so closely that escape was impossible.

A lamp was hanging from the roof of the cellar, and shed its light upon the foes as they stood face to face.

Spring-Heeled Jack drew a rapier as lithe as a whip.

He bent it in his hands so that the point touched the hilt, and then let it spring out towards the baronet.

"Sir Roland," he said, "you wear a sword. Draw it, and defend yourself."

"You will fight me fairly?"

"Yes."

As Spring-Heeled Jack spoke there came a crash, and the old house was filled with rumbling echoes.

"Is this some new trick of yours to frighten me?" Sir Roland asked, glancing upwards.

"No," Spring-Heeled Jack replied. "A fearful storm is rolling overhead. Heaven is pouring down its wrath upon this wicked city."

Again the booming thunder shook the ruinous old tenement, and its very foundation trembled.'

"Come, Sir Roland," Spring-Heeled Jack said. "You were all impatience just now. We need pay no heed to the storm down here, for the lightning, be it ever so blinding, cannot reach us."

"We are not on equal terms," Sir Roland said. "I must remove my coat. I suppose you will not take a mean advantage of me as I do so?"

"You measure my corn by your own bushel," said Spring-Heeled Jack. "how often have I had the chance to end your wicked life and as often turned my hand aside, thinking that the hour must come when you would see the error of your ways? But enough! We meet at last. This world is too small to hold us both."

Sir Roland threw aside his coat and rolled up his shirt-sleeves to his shoulders.

He then drew his sword and advanced slowly upon Spring-Heeled Jack.

"You will do well to make your peace before we cross swords," Spring-Heeled Jack said, "for I shall kill you."

"You are too confident," Sir Roland replied. "The chances are on my side, unless you wear armour."

"I wear nothing of the kind," Spring-Heeled Jack said; "and base as you are, I would scorn to lend myself to unfairness. You are suspicious, Sir Roland, because you have acted the part of a villain so often."

"Then here's at you!" cried Sir Roland. "Living I have hated and detested you, and if the arch-fiend to whom you belong does not protect you, you shall die!"

He attacked Spring-Heeled Jack with such ferocity that sparks glinted from the rapier.

"Ha! ha!" laughed Spring-Heeled Jack. "Think not to break down my guard in that way. I see that I must give you a lesson in coolness."

"Devil that you are!" Sir Roland hissed, "I will rid the world of you!"

But to the baronet's astonishment his rapier went whirling up to the ceiling.

"Try again," said Spring-Heeled Jack. "Again you see I have your life in my hands. But I will not take it yet. I have promised myself this meeting for a long time, and I will enjoy it until I grow tired."

Sir Roland Ashton's face fell.

He confessed to himself that he had met more than his match, and as he took his sword again in his hand his face was pallid with fear and chagrin.

Meanwhile the thunder was cracking fearfully and the house rocked under the terrible force of the storm.

"I am in no hurry, unless you are," Spring. Heeled Jack said, sneeringly, as he saw that Sir Roland stood hesitating. "Will you attack or shall I? Do your best or worst all is over with you, and this night you shall be sent to answer for your long list of crimes."

As Spring-Heeled Jack finished speaking there came a fearful crash, like the springing of a mine.

Timber, brickwork, and masonry reeled and tottered.

"The saints preserve us!" Sir Roland shrieked. "The house is falling!"

Stunned by the awful visitation, he recoiled on his heels towards the wall, and as he did so he saw Spring-Heeled Jack vanish down the well.

Sir Roland crouched down and shrieked with terror as the walls fell like a house of cards.

The noise was deafening.

Crash succeeded crash.

Huge beams of wood, mingling with blocks of stone and jagged masses of brickwork, cane thundering down in wild confusion.

Was it possible that a human being could escape being crushed under the debris?

Up to the present Sir Roland Ashton remained unscathed, for the terrible shower of death-dealing missiles had taken a slanting direction.

But the house was doomed.

It broke away piecemeal, as if a thousand men were at work upon it with pickaxes.

It was the dwelling of the wicked, the house of bloodshed and crime, and not one stone would remain upon another.

A thunder bolt had struck the roof, and the chimneys, crashing through, carried everything before them.

Sir Roland crouched closer and still closer to the projecting wall.

Presently he felt it moving and settling down upon him.

Then, with a cry scarcely human, he sprang to his feet and flung up his arms.

There was no hope of escape now.

The last ray fled from his heart as he cast his eyes upward and saw the massive wall parting and bulging out towards him.

The well was so blocked up with rubbish that he could not reach it, and Sir Roland, pressing his open hands upon his head as if to lessen the pang of the death-blow, swooned away and fell prone and senseless upon the floor.

CHAPTER LIII.

WHAT THE BARGEMEN FOUND.

DAY had scarcely dawned when Dick Sleuth made his way to the Bull in Top Boots.

Men who drink heavily overnight are thirsty in the morning, and Dick Sleuth was no exception to the rule.

His tongue was parched and cracked, and his hands shook as if smitten with the palsy.

He was a horrible sight to gaze upon, and men on their way to honest labour shrunk out of his path and regarded him with loathing.

"If you want to save my life, give me something to drink," he said to the landlord as he entered the inn. "I am as dry as a limekiln and as hot as a furnace."

"You look like it," the landlord replied. "I should think you poured a couple of pints of brandy down your throat last night!"

"And I feel equal to the task this morning," Dick Sleuth said, grinning. "Where's Bill Blarney?"

The landlord gazed at him in surprise.

"I forgot that you went away before he vanished."

SPRING-HEELED JACK,
THE TERROR OF LONDON.

LOCKED IN A FIERCE EMBRACE THEY WENT HEADLONG OVER THE CLIFF.

"Vanished!"

"Yes—vanished like a ghost, and goodness only knows where he went to."

Dick Sleuth passed his fingers through his unkempt hair.

"I never was a good hand at guessing riddles," he said, "so perhaps you will tell me what you mean?"

"I mean exactly what I say," the landlord replied. "I looked into the back room about three o'clock and Bill Blarney was fast asleep. About a quarter of an hour after I heard his voice shouting for help, and when I ran back to the room he had gone."

"That's curious, to say the least."

"Curious! It is most mysterious and aggravating."

"Perhaps he dreamt that somebody was after him, and went—"

"Went where?" the landlord interposed. "The window is screwed down, and he couldn't fly up the chimney very well."

"That idea is against all common sense," Dick Sleuth said. "I see by your face that you have something else to tell me?"

"Well,' said the landlord. "A fellow in the street created a disturbance, and swore that he saw the devil flying away with a man."

Dick Sleuth smote his forehead.

"I have it!" he cried, "Spring-Heeled Jack has got Bill Blarney!"

*

For a short time we must turn aside from Sir Roland and give some attention to the man who had shared a portion of his career in crime.

This was Bill Blarney, hurled from the top of the church tower by Spring-Heeled Jack.

Down—down went the villain, yet strange to say he never lost his senses.

This made his punishment all the more horrible, and though the descent was but the work of a moment Bill Blarney seemed to pass through an age of horror.

In that one brief instant a thousand thoughts crowded into his mind as the earth seemed to leap up to meet him, and then came the crash.

A bargeman dragging laboriously at his long sweeping oars heard the thud and looked along the river bank.

At first he saw nothing, and thinking that some person had thrown something heavy from a window into the river he whistled and went on with. his work.

Suddenly he rested on his oars and shaded his eyes with his hand.

He was looking at a queer-looking object sticking in the mud.

At first he could make nothing of it. But whatever the thing was it was endowed with life, and the bargeman, filled with curiosity, pulled nearer to the bank.

"Why, dash it all!" he cried, suddenly, "it's a man sticking in the mud! I say, old fellow, how did you get there?"

This was rather an idle question to ask for several reasons, the principal one being that Bill Blarney having had all the wind knocked out of his body, and being shoulder-high in the thick, slimy mud, was not capable of going into any particulars.

"Well, said the bargeman, running his fingers through his hair, "I've seen a few funny things on land and water, but this beats the lot. I suppose I must have him out, dead or alive, or the tide will soon be over him."

The bargeman moored the lumbering craft he had been tugging at to a post, and, pitching a plank upon the mud, stepped gingerly along it, and took a critical survey of

Bill Blarney's mud-bespattered features.

"The more I look at him the more I'm puzzled," he said. "Well, at any rate he looks like a dead 'un, and I suppose I shall get a trifle for his body."

But just then Bill Blarney put all such notions to flight by opening his eyes and glaring vacantly about him.

The villain's protruding eyes, and the dim baneful light that shone from them, startled the bargeman.

He was running to get on board his vessel when Bill Blarney called to him.

"Don't leave me here," he said, feebly, as he thrust one arm out of the mud. "Lend me a helping hand and I will pay you well."

But the bargeman did not seem to care to have anything to do with the job.

He kept at a respectable distance, as if convinced that there was something uncanny about Bill Blarney, and that he might be doing the world a good turn by knocking him on the head.

"Now, then," said Bill Blarney, "if you want to earn a guinea, you can do so by pulling me out and giving me a ride down the river."

"Wait a minute," the bargeman replied; "the first thing I should like to know is how you got there at all?"

Bill Blarney pointed to the church tower.

"Fell off?" queried the bargeman.

Blarney nodded his head.

"Well, then," said the bargeman, shuddering, "you have had a mighty narrow escape, that's all I can say. What a lucky thing for you that you didn't pitch on your head!"

"I shall think it a luckier thing when I am out of this altogether," Blarney growled, as he began to struggle frantically. "How would you like to be in such a position, you dunder-headed idiot?"

"Come—come," said the bargeman, "hard words will do no good. Here's my hand and you are welcome to it without payment."

As Bill Blarney crawled on to the plank he cast a furtive glance at the church tower and shook his fist.

"What are you up to now?" the bargeman asked.

"Nothing—nothing!" Blarney returned, hastily. "Let us get on board and pull away. What an escape I have had! You may land me at the next flight of stairs if you choose."

The bargeman was not loth to do this, as he did not like Bill Blarney's company and was glad to get rid of him.

Blarney tossed the man a guinea, but it was tossed back again.

"What!" cried the ruffian, "are you too proud to accept money?"

"No," replied the bargeman; "I am as poor as most people, but I would rather go without anything from you."

"Why?"

"Because you don't look as if you came honestly by it."

"Fool!" said Bill Blarney, as he went up the stone steps, "I should have thought that honesty or dishonesty made but very little difference to you."

The bargeman stared after the villain until he lost sight of him, and then he, returning to his work, meditated on the strangeness of the adventure.

Meanwhile Bill Blarney made his way towards the Bull in Top Boots.

He was stiff, sore, and aching in every limb, and his mud-covered clothes impeded his progress, so that he could scarcely drag one leg before the other.

People stared at him as he passed and made room for him.

Bill Blarney was certainly a queer-looking object, but he cared nothing for the eyes directed at him, or the remarks that passed from mouth to mouth.

At last he reached the Bull in Top Boots in a state of almost utter prostration.

Staggering into the house he fell upon his face, and the landlord could do nothing but stare at him in surprise.

"Dick Sleuth—Dick Sleuth!" he shouted.

The man came running up.

"What now?" he asked. "I thought by the sound of your voice that all the runners from Bow-street were round the house. Hullo! Who's this?"

"Lift his head and see for yourself."

"Bill Blarney! as I am a sinner," Dick Sleuth cried. "Pour some brandy down his throat. Something very odd must have happened to bring him back here in this state."

"So I should think," the landlord assented. "Pah! How his clothes smell! He has had enough of Thames mud to last him a lifetime."

Just then Bill Blarney rolled himself over on his side and groaned.

"No—no!" he gasped, "any death but that. Mercy—Mercy! Don't hurl me from the church tower."

"Hear that?" said Dick Sleuth, with an oath. "It strikes me very forcibly that poor Bill has had a very lively time of it."

"Spring-Heeled Jack must have had a hand in this business," the landlord said, shuddering.

The mention of that awful name acted as a restorative on Bill Blarney.

He opened his eyes and glared at those who were stooping over him.

"So," he murmured, "it was only a bad dream after all."

"Dream be hanged!" said Dick Sleuth. "You don't dream yourself wet through, battered like a mummy, and smothered with mud. What on earth have you been doing with yourself?"

Bill Blarney trembled from head to foot.

"Put me to bed," he said, "and I will tell you all about it. Don't leave me. Watch over me. Don't leave me for a moment."

"What do you fear?"

"Spring-Heeled Jack," Bill Blarney replied. "Ugh! shall I ever forget that fall?"

CHAPTER LIV.

JACOB BUTLER TAKES A WALK TO HAMPSTEAD HEATH
AND FALLS IN WITH AN OLD ACQUAINTANCE.

THE series of passing events was more than sufficient to upset a man constituted like Jacob Butler.

His notions were hazy and he went about like a man in a dream.

Constance Marfield and Daisy Leigh seldom saw anything of him, for Jacob, when not asleep, resorted to the public portion of the town, and drank himself into a state bordering upon idiocy.

It was during one of these bouts, when his head was throbbing with a splitting headache, that he wandered out of doors.

He was in that condition that he cared not where he went as long as he was out of the way of everybody, and chance took his wandering, erratic footsteps towards Hampstead Heath.

It was getting towards evening when Jacob Butler started on his journey.

"What a fool I am to carry on in this way!" he moaned, as he pressed his hands to his burning temples. "The landlord said I was to have what I liked, but I'll be hanged if it likes me. Ah! how beautiful and pure the air is! Curse the brandy! I wish every drop in the kingdom was turned into the sea."

When Jacob reached the heath he stood on the hill where the stately and ancient fir trees have reared their heads for twice a hundred years and looked in the direction of London.

The sun was going down like a huge ball of burnished copper, and as it sank behind a bank of purple clouds sailing up from the west the sound of distant thunder boomed through the air.

Our readers will remember that Jacob Butler had an innate horror of thunderstorms.

They filled him with a nameless terror even when under shelter.

"Bless my heart!" he gasped, "what am I to do?"

There was not a house of any description in sight, and the clouds were coming up too quickly to admit of him heading the storm and getting back to Sadler's Wells before it burst.

But there was one thing that Jacob Butler did not intend to do, and that was to remain under the trees and stand a chance of being struck by the electric fluid.

A second clap of thunder started him off like a rabbit that hears the sound of the sportsman's gun.

He tore madly down the slope, and taking the wrong road ran on towards Hendon.

It was a wild and desolate part in those days.

Dark woodlands flanked the rough roads, and farmers travelling that way took good care to keep their powder dry, for desperadoes lurked with evil intent under the overhanging trees.

Jacob Butler had no thought of being stopped and robbed.

He had no money to speak of that he could call his own, but he dreaded the quivering lightning and booming thunder.

Onward he went, groaning, foaming, and perspiring.

Oh! for a house, or even a hut, where he could creep in until the storm had passed over.

Suddenly Jacob saw exactly what he desired.

It was a tumble-down, ramshackle sort of building, standing in the middle of a field, and the belated fugitive made for it with hot haste.

Without stopping to knock at the door, or to ask whether his presence would be welcome or otherwise, he dashed in and found himself in profound darkness.

The hole in the wall serving for a window was blocked up with furze and bramble, but as Jacob's eyes became somewhat accustomed to the gloom he saw a few faggots smoking and smouldering in a corner.

"Is there anybody at home?" he asked, in weak, quavering accents. "I'm very sorry to come in so sudden, but there's a precious storm brewing."

No reply was vouchsafed to his remarks, and he, approaching the fire, crouched down before it.

There was no vestige of furniture in the place, and Jacob Butler had concluded that it was used by a shepherd as a watch-house at night when the door opened and somebody hobbled in.

At that moment a broad flash of lightning filled the hut with a lurid glare, and simultaneously a shriek of discovery came from Jacob Butler's lips.

Standing with her back to the doorway, and leaning on a gnarled stick torn roughly from a tree, was Mrs. Corcoran.

She looked so horrible and witch-like that Jacob Butler never for a moment believed her to be alive, and as she stalked with a gliding motion, horrible in itself, across the floor, the wretched man drew his knees up to his chin.

He thrust out his hands to ward off the old woman, but onward she came, and Jacob was soon made acquainted with the fact that there was nothing ghost-like about her.

Raising the stick with her skinny arms, she gave Jacob Butler the full benefit of it.

"Ho! ho!" she laughed, as he rolled on his back. "So we meet again, Jacob dear!"

Mrs. Corcoran's miserable victim was in no mood to reply.

His head had ached sufficiently beforehand, and now that he was treated to a vision of thousands of dancing stars he was not quite sure whether he was dead or alive.

"You thought that I was dead, did you?" said Mrs. Corcoran, with fiendish glee. "Ho! ho! You thought you had got rid of me for ever!"

"I never thought anything of the kind," Jacob replied, feebly. "I knew you would come back to me like a—a—a—"

"Like a what, deary?" Mrs. Corcoran queried, keeping the stick waving about a few inches over Jacob's cranium.

Mr. Jacob Butler was going to say like a devil, but he instituted the word angel, and tried to look as if he meant it.

"That's right, lovey," she said, making so hideous a grimace at him that he turned cold. "I am an angel—your angel, Jacob."

"Ugh!" Jacob ejaculated, rubbing his head.

"You won't rub that off in a hurry," Mrs. Corcoran said; "and if you are not careful I will give you another to keep it company."

"Don't!" Jacob pleaded—"don't! I'm confused and bumped enough already."

Mrs. Corcoran sat down, and, hugging her knees with her arms, rocked herself to and fro.

"I suppose you know that Lilac Lodge is burnt down?" she said.

"No!" Jacob replied, in astonishment. "Who set fire to it?"

Mrs. Corcoran pointed at him with a bony finger furnished with a hawk-like talon.

"You don't?" said she. "Then I will tell you the story. Listen!"

Jacob Butler crept up against the wall and leaned his aching head against it.

"Sir Roland stabbed me and left me for dead," Mrs. Corcoran continued; "then the coward set fire to the place, thinking that the flames would scatter my ashes to the winds."

"That was very wrong of him," Jacob Butler said.

"Do you really think so?"

"Ye—e—s."

"Then I don't believe you," said Mrs. Corcoran, grinning. "You'd give half your lifetime to know that I was buried twenty feet under the ground."

"Have it your own way," said Jacob, despairingly. "You are like the rest of women, and would have the last word if it choked you."

"What a dear, lovely dovey you are!" said Mrs. Corcoran, grinning more hideously than ever.

"Thank 'ee," Jacob replied, with the air of a man who has accidentally swallowed a tooth. "Never mind me. You were talking about Sir Roland and Lilac Lodge."

"So I was, my rose," Mrs. Corcoran replied. "Sir Roland's act saved my life. When the base coward stabbed me he set fire to the furniture, and it was the heat that brought me round."

"Oh!" said Jacob, thinking that he got a whiff of sulphur at that very moment. "I suppose that sort of thing agrees with you."

Mrs. Corcoran knew what he meant, and filled the hut with mocking laughter.

"At any rate, it saved my life," she said. "There is not much blood in my veins, so little could flow, and I dragged myself to the window. Ho—ho! how the flames chased me!"

"I wish they had caught you," Jacob muttered under his breath.

"But I cheated them," Mrs. Corcoran continued, "and when I stood free I hastened away, taking an oath, which I mean to keep."

"You always were a woman of your word."

"I swore to find you if you were above the earth, and never part with you again."

Jacob Butler's face fell, and he would have taken it as a compliment if the earth had opened and swallowed him up.

"And I swore to hound Sir Roland down and bring him upon his knees before me," Mrs, Corcoran continued.

"I have no doubt you will do it," said Jacob.

He found that he was in a trap, and, acting on the peace-at-any-price principle, tried to make himself agreeable.

"It is part of my plan to let Sir Roland believe that I am dead," Mrs. Corcoran said.

"What for?"

"To make the revenge I mean to take on him all the more sweet."

She looked so unearthly and devilish as she spoke that Jacob screwed his head into the mud-wall and groaned.

"And now, Jacob deary," said Mrs. Corcoran, "you must make up your mind to live a happy life with me. This is my place, and I am sure you will be able to make yourself comfortable in it."

"It might be a little—to put it mildly—a little better furnished," Jacob said. "But—but, I say, we ain't married, you know, and so you see it, wouldn't be right for me to slay here."

Mrs. Corcoran became convulsed with laughter.

"Addle-pated fool!" she said, digging him in the ribs with the stick, "that is a matter which can be managed before another day is gone. Don't run away with the notion that I shall let you go out of my sight for a moment."

"But you must—hang it! you must," Jacob gasped.

"We shall see," said Mrs. Corcoran. "Jacob, come over here and kiss me. "

Jacob Butler looked as if he could have bitten her, but he did as he was told, and looked as if he had feasted on early gooseberries.

"Now put your arm round my waist and tell me that you love me," said the hag.

"I can't," Jacob gasped. "I can't, I tell you—I can't. It's against human nature. Why do you torture me?"

"Because I know that you hate me," said Mrs. Corcoran.

"Before you came in my way," Jacob cried, wildly, "I was neither a coward nor a fool. But now I am both, and I feel that I am going mad. Hang it! I'll stand this no longer, for what are you but a woman after all, and an old and ugly one into the bargain."

Mrs. Corcoran smiled as she gave Jacob a sidelong glance.

"Deary!" she said, "I suppose you don't want to be hung, do you?"

"Of course I don't. Who does?" he blurted out.

"Then you certainly will be unless you take my advice and marry me without any fuss," Mrs. Corcoran said. "I have you under my thumb, and a word from me would put the halter round your neck."

"But what about yourself?" he demanded.

"That's quite another matter, deary," the hag returned. "I want you because you will be useful to me."

"As your slave!" Jacob said, clasping his hands in anguish.

"The word was yours not mine, but it suits," Mrs. Corcoran said.

The storm having given free vent to its fury was now rolling, rumbling, and grumbling away in the far distance, and Jacob Butler cast a yearning glance at the door.

"I will make a dash at it when she is not looking at me," he said to himself.

But Mrs. Corcoran never removed her eyes from him.

She watched him as a cat that plays with a captured mouse, and there was something as helpless and terror-stricken as the inferior animal in Jacob Butler.

The gaunt, hideous hag revelled and gloated over the wretched man's misery, but all the time she plied him with endearing terms, which she knew were loathsome to him.

And all the time she kept the stick which had supported her tottering limbs ready for use, and Jacob knew full well what strength lay in her shrivelled arms, and that she could strike a blow of which a giant would not be ashamed.

"Come," said Mrs. Corcoran, "we must be merry. We will celebrate this joyful meeting with music. I heard you sing and saw you dance once, Jacob, and you shall do so now."

Driven to desperation, cold with terror at one moment and boiling over with rage the next, Jacob Butler hit upon an expedient he had never thought of before.

With a sudden nervous movement he shot out his arms with the intention of flooring Mrs. Corcoran and making his escape before she could recover herself, but she was too quick for him.

His fist rattled upon the ever-ready stick, which had parried the blow, and Jacob, recoiling back to his corner, thrust his injured knuckles into his mouth.

"Why, Jacob," cried Mrs. Corcoran, "I never thought that you could be so playful. I forgive you, deary, but don't try that game on again, or I shall be compelled to chastise you severely, and you wouldn't look well going to church with a couple of black eyes and a scratched face."

As she spoke the old crone hobbled about the floor and brandished the stick above his head in a manner that filled Jacob Butler with loathing and terror.

It was beyond human endurance to him now.

Regardless of all consequence she made a dash for the door.

Down came the stick, and Jacob Butler, flinging up his arms, fell prone and senseless upon the floor.

CHAPTER LV.
ON THE ROAD TO DOVER—THE MEETING ON THE CLIFF—
THE WRESTLE—A SHRIEK FOR MERCY—THE FALL.

WICKED men are hard to kill.

What is called luck often favours them, and fate toys with them—buoys them up with hope until the meshes of retribution close finally and escape is impossible.

Such it would seem was the case with Sir Roland Ashton.

Ninety-nine men out of a hundred would have been killed when Gedge Foote's house came rattling down about the villain's ears, but a descending beam caught the wall as it came crashing down and broke the force of its fall.

Covered with bricks and rubbish, Sir Roland Ashton lay fully an hour before he returned to consciousness, and when he, opened his eyes he could scarcely believe that he was still in the land of the living.

His brow had been severely cut, and a stream of blood was running down his face.

He put up his hand to stem it, and as he did so his hand came in contact with the beam which, falling in a slanting direction, had saved his life.

By degrees he dragged himself out of the heap of rubbish, but he could not stand upright.

Crouching down, he felt his way towards where he knew the staircase to be.

At first it seemed to be completely blocked up, but further investigation proved that such was not the case.

Using all his strength, Sir Roland Ashton pulled aside the *débris* until he could gain a firm footing.

Then he began to mount step by step on the wreck, until his eyes were rewarded with a beam of light.

It came from a lantern swayed to and fro by a man, who, amongst others, were surveying the wreck in amazement.

Sir Roland Ashton kept himself perfectly quiet. It took no great stretch of memory to remind him that his last meeting with the men of the Mint was the reverse from a pleasant one; so, ensconcing himself down behind a pile of joists and rotten floor-boards, he resolved to wait until such time as the coast would be clear.

He never gave Catchpole or Grabham a single thought.

Whether they were alive or dead was nothing to him.

The mission on which he had brought them to the place had ended in failure and ruin, and all Sir Roland troubled himself about was how to get out of it himself unobserved.

The men outside seemed to be searching for something very earnestly.

They prodded about the rubbish with sticks and iron bars, but did not approach Sir Roland, as he had taken the precaution to keep himself above the level of the ground.

It suddenly struck him that they were searching for treasure.

Gedge Foote, the miser, might have hidden money in all parts of the building, and the news of its fall brought hundreds of people to the spot.

At last they dropped away one by one, having found nothing to repay them for their trouble, and at last Sir Roland Ashton crept out of his hiding-place.

He was so covered with dust, soot, and cobwebs that he might have been well taken for one of the searchers, and he passed out of the Mint unobserved.

Making his way past the Tower of London, and giving a casual glance at the green on which so many unfortunate heads had fallen under the headsman's axe, he walked swiftly towards London Bridge. Whither should he go?

Lilac Lodge was burnt down and Mrs. Corcoran was dead (so he thought), and that was some consolation.

At Ashton Hall there was no safety, for Spring-Heeled Jack—Ah! was he dead, too?

"He must be," Sir Roland thought. "Both of us could not have escaped those walls. Ha! ha! ha! He is dead, and I am free of his accursed presence forever."

Turning into an archway, he saw that a coach was being got ready for a journey, and glancing at the back of the vehicle, he saw that it was bound for Dover. Why should he not go there too? Anywhere was better than London, and he needed rest.

Give him time to mature his plans, and he would get Daisy within his power yet, for, if Spring-Heeled Jack was really dead, what other friend had she in the world to raise an arm in her protection?

Calling an ostler he borrowed a brush and removed a portion of the dust from his clothing, and after washing his face and hands in a tin pail, an operation which cost him a crown piece, he paid his fare and walked into the bar.

Here he found his fellow-passengers fortifying themselves for their long ride, and called for a glass of brandy.

As he was drinking it he saw a face look in at the door for an instant and then vanish. To the majority of the people gathered round the bar there was nothing in this incident even to create a remark, but Sir Roland's visage changed.

He went to the door and looked out.

There was nobody in sight, and at last he returned and called for more brandy, drinking it neat.

"What a fool I am!" he muttered. "I start and tremble at everything. The fellow was some hanger-on, or, perhaps, some man looking for a friend."

"Time, ladies and gentlemen!—time!" sang out the guard, appearing with a long brass horn in his hand. "This way for the Dover coach, if you please."

Sir Roland had engaged an inside seat, and it was with great relief that he found himself the only passenger so situated.

The coach rattled away to the cheery notes of the horn, and soon after day dawned.

The sun came up bright and beautiful.

The heavy rain had laid the dust, and so refreshed all nature that the air was redolent with sweet perfume.

As London fell back in the rear so the spirits of Sir Roland Ashton rose.

He felt inclined to be merry, and chatted glibly with the guard and driver each time the coach stopped to change horses.

There was one of the passengers who never got down during the whole of the journey.

This was a man so wrapped up with capes, coats, and wrappers as to almost entirely conceal his face.

He had the appearance of an invalid, and this impression was increased when the coach reached Dover.

Sir Roland watched the silent man as he alighted slowly and painfully, and walked slowly away, disappearing down one of the bye-streets.

The baronet thought he could not do better than put up at the inn nearest to hand, and, having engaged a suite of apartments, he ordered a repast and sat down to enjoy it.

The table was near a window commanding a fine view of the sea rippling away until it became hazy and then relieved by the coast of France.

"Peace at last!" Sir Roland murmured. "Oh! how delightful all this is after what I have passed through.

As he spoke he held a glass of ruby wine to the light.

A hundred objects were reflected upon it in miniature, and Sir Roland startled the sleepy waiter into activity by dropping the glass and giving vent to a fierce oath.

"A thousand pardons!" said the waiter, who was a Frenchman. "Is not milor' well? Ah! you are faint."

"It is nothing," Sir Roland said. "The glass slipped through my fingers."

Yes; and on it Sir Roland had seen the face of Spring-Heeled Jack as plainly as ever he had seen it in his life.

What a strange and unaccountable fancy!

How could he account for it but that his brain was overwrought, and that his reason was giving way?

He pushed his plate away, and, leaning back in his chair, sat looking down at the scene before him.

Suddenly the man who had travelled from London to Dover, heavily wrapped and cloaked as before, passed the window.

Sir Roland gazed at him with eyes of suspicion.

There was something about the stranger that he could not make out.

The very way in which he had left the coach and walked painfully away set the baronet thinking, and here was the man again under his very nose and apparently interested in the house.

"Shall I speak to him?" Sir Roland asked himself. "If I could see his face I should be satisfied. He may be some spy sent down to watch my movements."

It is probable that he might have put this notion into practice, but before he had a chance of doing so the man was gone.

"Curse the fellow!" said Sir Roland. "Why should I trouble my mind about him? Bah! I am like a child frightened by an ugly shadow on the wall. Who could possibly know that I am down here?—and, if such be the case, am I not armed and perfectly well able to take care of myself?"

Sir Roland smiled at his own folly, and more particularly that he had seen Spring-Heeled Jack's face mirrored on the wine glass, but the smile was a faint one, and flitting away left a frown upon his face.

The French waiter watched him, and wondered why he could eat none of the good things displayed so temptingly on the snow-white tablecloth, and he was still further perplexed when Sir Roland rose and announced his intention of going out.

"Milor' is not well pleased?" the waiter said, casting a deprecating glance at the table,

"Yes, very well pleased," Sir Roland replied; "but I have no appetite just at present. A word with you, my friend. I am no lord, but a plain, country gentleman, named Livock; but as I do not wish to be troubled with anybody, I shall never be in a mood to receive visitors. Do you understand me?"

"Ah! yes," the waiter replied. "Milor'—monsieur does not wish to be disturbed—Jules understand. He was valet to English gentleman years ago, and knows much."

"You seem to be a sharp sort of fellow," Sir Roland said.

Jules grinned, shrugged his shoulders, and rubbed his hands more vigorously than ever.

"Monsieur pays me a compliment I do not deserve," he said.

"Nonsense!" Sir Roland returned. "How comes it that you are here after serving under an English gentleman."

"I will tell you," said the Frenchman, grinning. "I see by monsieur's face that I may repose confidence in him. I read faces, and I know—"

"You know what?" Sir Roland Ashton interposed.

"That you are no more Monsieur Livock than I am."

"You know me, then?"

"No," Jules replied, with another shrug of his shoulders; "you are wrong there, and yet you are right. I watched you as you sat at the table. Your eyes were fixed on the shores of my country, and I said to myself—'Monsieur has seen troublesome times— he flies from an enemy.' Hah! I see that I am right."

Sir Roland affected to laugh, but he betrayed the truth in the sound of his voice.

"We may become better acquainted," he said. "What other name are you known by besides Jules?"

"Carleon."

"Yes; and now, Jules Carleon, tell me about your late master, and why you left him."

"It is an odd story," Jules Carleon replied. "My master believed in a short life and a merry one. He could shuffle a pack of cards or throw a set of dice—"

"Loaded ones?"

"Hah!" said Jules, laughing. "I see that monsieur has had some leetle experience in such matters. Well, yes. He was clever and won money, but, alas! he went too far. He made a mistake, was caught, and shot dead by one of the party. Shall I ever forget that evening? no, no, no!"

Jules Carleon shed tears, and Sir Roland eyed him favourably, for he knew that he was standing before a villain and a hypocrite.

"You were present then?" said the baronet.

"Alas! yes."

"And what became of you?"

Jules Carleon's sallow face turned an olive green.

"I went out by the window."

"You were pitched out, I suppose?"

Jules Carleon's neck disappeared into his shoulders, and his mouth expanded into a broad grin.

"Monsieur has seen much of the world," he said.

"Are you tired of being here?"

"Oh! very. It's like a prison—so much to do and so little to get."

"I will talk to you anon," Sir Roland said "but in the meantime keep your own counsel and a watchful eye upon any stranger who may come to the house."

Jules Carleon bowed low.

"Monsieur's commands shall be obeyed," he said.

Sir Roland walked out of the room and into the open air.

He was haunted by the man who had travelled all the way from London in gloomy silence.

Sir Roland seemed to see the mysterious individual at every turning, and lurking behind every porch.

Leaving the grand old town Sir Roland approached the splendid line of cliffs.

He walked slowly and in an attitude of thought

He stopped on hearing footsteps behind him and looked round.

There was nobody within sight, and, as he could see for more than a mile each way, he put the sound down to fancy.

And now he began to reflect what happiness might have been his had he led a good and law-abiding life.

But it was too late now.

He had travelled too far upon the road of sin and wickedness to begin a new life.

So a demon whispered in his ear, and Sir Roland listened to the persuasive voice.

"No—no," he muttered. "It is too late. The course I have run must be finished, though it lead to perdition."

"To perdition!" repeated a voice.

Sir Roland Ashton stood transfixed as if a spell had suddenly fallen upon him.

"To perdition," said the voice again.

Sir Roland recoiled as Spring-Heeled Jack appeared from behind a dump of bushes.

It seemed as if he had sprung from the ground and Sir Roland recoiled on his heels towards the edge of the cliff.

"Have a care, Sir Roland," Spring-Heeled Jack said, pointing below. "The beach lies a hundred feet down."

The guilty baronet passed his hand swiftly across his brow. "You here!" he gasped.

"Yes. Why not?" Spring-Heeled Jack replied. "Like you, I came here for fresh air and peace."

"You followed me down?"

Spring-Heeled Jack smiled.

"Yes," he said, "I did. What then?"

"What then!" Sir Roland repeated in a fury. "I had a hope that you lay buried under the ruins of Gedge Foote's house. Curse you! How long will your hideous form cumber the earth?"

"A little longer than your handsome self, perchance," Spring-Heeled Jack replied, mockingly. "I escaped even easier than yourself, and I set your miserable dupes free."

"You mean Catchpole and Grabham?"

"Yes."

"What care I whether they live or die?" Sir Roland said.

As he spoke he put his hands carelessly in his pockets.

"You have pistols there!" Spring-Heeled Jack said, grasping him by the wrist. "Sir

Roland, attempt no tricks with me, or, by Heaven! you shall rue it."

The baronet withdrew his hands, and with a quick movement threw his arms round Spring-Heeled Jack's waist.

"Now my time has come!" Sir Roland hissed. "Had you the strength of twenty men I would hold you now. My hour of triumph has come at last. Ha! ha!"

His grip was like a band of iron.

The light of fierce determination shone in his eyes.

"Rash fool!" Spring-Heeled Jack cried, "what would you do?"

"Hurl you over the cliff!"

"Well said," Spring-Heeled Jack returned. "We will go together!"

Sir Roland Ashton now felt that the tables were turned upon him.

Strong as his grasp was, it was but feeble in comparison to that which Spring-Heeled Jack now put into force.

"Come—come!" said the weird creature. "To travel down the cliff-side will be merry sport for me."

"I did but joke!" Sir Roland cried, as Spring-Heeled Jack dragged him closer and closer to the cliff. "Let go your hold and I will release mine!"

"Nay," said Spring-Heeled Jack, "it is useless! Come—come!"

Sir Roland shrieked and closed his eyes as he felt the earth leave his feet.

Then came a rush of strong air.

A sound like thunder dinned into his ears.

Earth and sky became mingled together as he and Spring-Heeled Jack went down.

Their whirling forms were followed by showers of dust and stones.

The startled birds wheeled and fluttered in flight.

All this happened in a moment, and then Sir Roland lost his senses.

CHAPTER LVI.
CATCHPOLE AND GRABHAM DISTINGUISH THEMSELVES
AND MAKE AN IMPORTANT CAPTURE.

"MATE," said Catchpole, as he hobbled along at the side of Grabham, "I think I shall retire from this line of business."

Grabham rubbed his nose in a reflective sort of way.

"I should like to do it myself," he said, "but what can we do?"

"Anything is better than this life," Catchpole groaned. "I thought we were done for, shut up like ants in that infernal passage."

"Well," Grabham returned, "I must say that we ought to thank Spring-Heeled Jack for letting us out."

"Perhaps he left the door open by accident?"

Grabham shook his head.

"I don't think that," he said. "Perhaps he isn't a bad sort of fellow, after all."

"You can't expect much good from a devil," Catchpole said. "I can't think of him without trembling all over like a jelly, and I'll take jolly good care not to fall in his way again if I can help it."

"We are both agreed on that score," Grabham said. "What a sell for Sir Roland! I wonder if the house settled him?"

"If it didn't, it's a pity," Catchpole growled. "I'd give my last shilling to have the pleasure of putting a bullet through him."

These two worthies had only just got free from their perilous position in the Mint.

Just at the moment when both had made up their minds that they were doomed to perish by the hideous death of starvation they found the door of the secret passage open.

A quantity of rubbish had fallen into the lower portion of the well, almost blocking it up, and the constables, getting a good foothold, crept out and sneaked away like a brace of whipped hounds.

The hour was late, and they did not exactly know how to account for their absence at home or to their superiors.

To peach on Sir Roland would be to criminate themselves.

"I have it!" said Catchpole, suddenly.

"Have what?"

"A notion which I think will get us out of our trouble."

"Well, what is it?" Grabham demanded.

"We must swear that we have been following up the scent of the Black Highwaymen."

"Good!" Grabham cried, smiting his thigh. "I'll stand a drink for that, Catchpole, my boy. Where shall we go?"

"Into the first house we come to, for I am as dry as an oven."

A few yards further on they turned into an inn, and a tankard of ale was placed before them.

Catchpole drank first, and left so little for Grabham that he looked mournfully into the measure.

"I say, this ain't fair, you know," he said. "I thought we made an agreement to share alike in everything?"

"I couldn't help it," Catchpole replied. "I should have done the same had it been a large pailful."

"Well, then, perhaps you will—"

He said no more, for at that moment a horse came clattering up to the door, and a man, alighting in hot haste, ran into the house and called for a measure of wine.

He was in such a hurry to be served that he did not see the constables, who shrank back into the shadow and watched him narrowly.

"Bill Blarney!" Catchpole whispered, under his breath.

"Yes, sure enough," Grabham replied. "Now's our chance. Shall we collar him?"

"No; let him go, and then follow him."

"But he is on horseback."

"Well, we must get horses too. Hush! Hide your face—he is looking this way."

But Bill Blarney was perfectly unconscious of the constables' presence, and, having finished his wine, he asked the landlord where he could find a blacksmith.

"My horse has lost a shoe," he said, "and as I have a long journey before me, I am anxious to get on the road as soon as possible."

Catchpole glided out by the back door and Grabham followed him.

"We have him now right enough," said Grabham. "Run round to the Two-Necked Swan and get a couple of saddle horses. There's some precious game afloat, and we must see what it is. I'll stay here to keep an eye on Blarney."

Catchpole had scarcely left the yard when the landlord appeared.

"Jem!" he shouted.

"Hullo, there!" cried a voice from a hay loft.

"Just run to Naylor's and ask him to step over to shoe a horse," said the landlord. "Here's a shilling for you, and Naylor will get a crown for the job."

"Right you are, sir."

Jem, a shock-headed, thin-legged, wiry individual, put in an appearance and darted past Grabham.

"Here's a lark!" said the constable. "Here's a turning of the tables. Blarney will wish that he had never set eyes upon us. He's as good as on his way to Tyburn."

Some minutes elapsed, and then Catchpole re-turned, but on foot.

"The horses will be ready for us when we want them," he said; "but how are we to know which way Blarney is going?"

"If he goes north he means to take to the Barnet-road, but if south, Shooter's-hill will be his fancy," Grabham replied.

"You think so?"

"It's almost a certainty."

The smith came over and was soon at work, and in about a quarter of an hour Bill Blarney mounted and rode north.

"What did I tell you?" Grabham said, rubbing his hands with glee. "His game is to stop the coach, but we'll stop him with a vengeance. Let him have a good start, or we may come up with him, and then all the fat will be in the fire."

The constables took another drink to nerve themselves, and then walked round to the Two-Necked Swan, where, of course, they indulged in further potations. When they started heavy clouds obscured the moon, and half a gale of wind was blowing.

The night promised to be a blustering one, and people were hurrying homeward.

Catchpole and Grabham did not hurry their horses.

They knew that if Blarney had gone to the Barnet-road that he would have to wait fully an hour for the mail coach, and their idea was to take him red-handed.

When they had reached as far as Highgate they stopped and dismounted.

Catchpole dropped on his knees and placed his ear close to the ground.

"No sound of the coach as yet, but I can hear the cantering of hoofs."

"One or more horses?" Grabham asked.

"One."

"We are on the right track," Grabham said "Blarney is congratulating himself that he is alone in this spree. How far do you think he is away?"

"A mile at least; perhaps more."

"Then we had better lessen the distance. Ha! there goes eleven. The coach should pass the Bald-faced Stag at half-past."

To follow a man is an exciting incident, but it pales a little when he has to be caught.

Catchpole did not feel quite as enthusiastic as Grabham.

He knew that Bill Blarney was a desperate man, and would sell his freedom dearly if not taken unawares.

Catchpole mentioned this to Grabham.

"What?" said he. "Are you going to turn funky? Think of the glory—think of the reward."

"It's all right to think about them," Catchpole said, dismally; "but supposing that Blarney gets the best of us."

"We are two to one," Grabham said, contemptuously. "You may go back if you like, and leave me to do the job alone. I must have money, and don't you see, you fool, that supposing that if we only scare Blarney away that every passenger on the coach will shell out handsomely to us?"

This was putting a new complexion on the matter, and Catchpole's spirits arose.

"You are always right, Grabby, my boy," he said. "I often think that it is a great pity that you didn't enter the army. What a fire-eater you would have made!"

Mr. Grabham put on a military air and gazed ahead of him.

"I fancy I see something," he said.

"Where?" cried Catchpole, reining in his steed. "Oh! Lor!"

"You idiot!" Grabham growled. "You make enough noise to wake the dead."

The object descried by Mr. Grabham was nothing more ferocious than a scarecrow in the middle of a field.

The time was getting on, and the coach would soon be due.

The constables now drew their horses into a lane so unfrequented that it was completely overgrown with grass.

Soon the sound of a horn awakened the echoes of the night.

The coach, with its four spanking greys, was coming at last.

"Nothing alarming up to the present," Grabham said. "All's well. Can you see the lamps?"

Catchpole stood up in the stirrups and peered over the hedge. "Yes," he said.

Grabham gave a grunt of disappointment. "Bill Blarney must have got wind of us," he said. "It strikes me that he has sheered off, and left us nothing but a wild-goose chase."

Catchpole wished in his heart that such was the case, but kept it to himself.

On came the coach, the lights dancing and flashing, the horses going as if they had only just left the stable, and the passengers chatting merrily, glad enough to be so near London. Suddenly a change came over the scene. The report of a pistol startled the air. The horses fell back upon their haunches, the female passengers screamed and clung to the male ones, and the gentlemen turned white with fear.

Coachman and guard swore mighty oaths at this unexpected interruption, and a hasty search was made for an antiquated blunderbuss which ought to have been in the coach, but had been left behind as usual.

"Ladies and gentlemen," said Bill Blarney, "I am sorry to trouble you for your purses, but I must have them. Please to throw them down and save me the pain of discharging my stock of firearms. Coachman, keep your seat. I have my eyes on you, and if you move I will blow your brains out!" The coachman and guard swore again. To make matters worse, they could not see the highwayman, although they could hear him, and the chances were that he was not alone.

In point of fact, Bill Blarney had dismounted and was lying flat on the ground in such a position as to command a sure aim at any of the passengers he chose to shoot at.

But for once he had reckoned without his host.

As he was chuckling at his success and already counting the gains of his adventure he received a fearful blow on the head from a truncheon, and in another instant Catchpole and Grabham were on top of him.

"Hurrah!" Grabham cried. "We've got the scoundrel. Steady, coachman, with those horses, or they will be over us. We are constables."

"Constables!" cried the passengers, joyfully. Then the ladies recovered from their fright and tittered, and the gentlemen all looked brave and said that if the officers of the law had not arrived that they would have tackled the highwayman and cut him into mincemeat.

Bill Blarney was completely stunned, and the constables bound him in such a manner as to make escape impossible when he returned to consciousness.

"There, he is a regular beauty," said Grabham, taking down one of the coach-lamps and flashing the light upon Blarney's face.

"Trussed like a fowl," Catchpole chimed in, with a chuckle.

As Grabham had predicted, the passengers were only too willing to pay for the rescue, coming as it did at a critical moment, and the constables' hats were half filled with guineas.

"The inside of the coach is empty," the guard said; "so you had better let us take you and your prisoner to London."

"That's all very well," said Grabham; "but what are we to do with our horses?"

"Leave them at the Bald-faced Stag."

"Right you are," Grabham returned. "Blarney's horse is not far away. Wait till we have found it, and then we'll all go home together."

The horse was found tethered to a tree and was soon stabled with the others.

Then the wretched Blarney was pitched into the coach as unceremoniously as if he had been a sack of sawdust, and the vehicle rolled away.

The man who had been the greatest coward of all sang a gallant song of love and war, and the ladies chatted glibly and flirted deliciously, for their hearts were filled with thankfulness that the terrible man who might have taken their lives as now as harmless as a child and beneath their very feet.

CHAPTER LVII.

THE SMUGGLERS' CAVE.

"HOLD! Who goes there?"

"A friend!"

"The countersign!"

"Nimrod!"

"Pass friend, and all's well!"

This conversation passed between two men at the mouth of a cave cleft by nature in a cliff.

One man, he who had put the questions, stood at the entrance with a carbine reclining gently on his arm, the other had toiled upwards with a huge bundle on his back, and, throwing it down as he passed the sentry, took a deep breath.

A little way below lay a boat rigged for rowing and fast sailing, and two men lying in easy attitudes glanced up at the sentry as if awaiting instructions.

When it was high tide the waves rose almost to the mouth of the cave, which for the first few yards was narrow, but widened into a spacious apartment.

Here lamps hung from the chalk ceiling, and the place was fitted with benches and tables.

Piles of barrels, full and empty, occupied the corners, and the walls were festooned with muskets, swords, and other weapons of war, some of which were of delicate foreign make.

This inner cave was occupied by about half-a-dozen men.

They were all of the Seafaring type, for indeed they were smugglers.

They lounged about in the manner of men who had done their work well, and were now taking their rest.

There was a rich aroma of choice tobacco about the place, for all the men were smoking, and by certain coloured bottles and glasses placed handy it was evident that the smugglers appreciated the value of good wine.

At the end of this room, as it may be called, was a door with a grating fitted into it, and a stream of lamplight shone through the bars.

One of the men, a handsome, stalwart fellow, rose to his feet and went to the grating and gazed through.

"Still unconscious," he said, turning to his companion. "This is a wonderful thing, and how he escaped without being smashed to pieces is a mystery to me."

"The upper ledge broke his fall," said another. "Dick swears that when he looked up he saw something like a huge eagle clutching the man."

"Bah!" said he at the grating. "Dick has been taking too much French brandy of late. Eagles in these parts! Ha! ha! Well, at all events here the man is, and if he ever recovers he may tell us what he means by coming head downwards into our quarters. It looks like a case of suicide to me."

"Whatever it is, Fielder will be in a fearful rage when he comes back," growled one of the smugglers, emitting a wreath of smoke from his lips. "I pity the poor devil of a stranger who finds himself here."

"There is only one way out," laughed another, "It's a case of a bullet or a jump into the sea with a nine-pound shot for an ornament on his legs."

"Hush!" said the man at the grating. "Here comes Fielder at last."

The men rose to salute their chief.

He was a man of gigantic stature, black bearded, and muscular.

He flashed his keen eyes on the men, and, folding his arms, struck a commanding attitude.

"What is this I hear about a stranger?" he said, in a deep bass tone. "Tom Wary?"

"Aye, aye! sir."

"You have been here all day," Fielder said. "You may speak."

"All I know is that this man," here he pointed to the grated door, "come rattling down the cliff and fell at the mouth of the cave."

"Killed?" Fielder asked, carelessly.

"At first we thought he was," Tom Wary replied. "A shower of stones and earth followed him and covered him up, but when we dragged him out we found that he was still living."

"Why didn't you pitch him into the sea?" Fielder growled.

"We thought we had better consult you on that point, captain," Wary replied. "Of course it can be done now, if you wish it."

"I will have a look at him first," Fielder said. "Give me the key."

Striding across the cavern floor, he opened the door and gazed upon Sir Roland's upturned face.

"A gentleman, at all events," Fielder said, musingly. "There's precious little life left in him, and he would be none the wiser for a dip in the sea. The tide is running up, and—"

A heavy groan from Sir Roland checked the smuggler chief's utterance, and at the same moment the baronet opened his eyes.

"Bring me a flask of brandy," Fielder said.

As it was put into his hand he pressed it against Sir Roland's lips.

"Do you feel better?" Fielder asked.

Sir Roland groaned and closed his eyes again.

"Poor wretch!" Fielder said, and his heart was smitten with pity. "I haven't the heart to kill him now. Watch over him, and when he is able to speak call me."

In obedience to a motion of his hand a ladder was lowered from the ceiling, and Fielding, passing up it, raised a trap-door and disappeared.

Tom Wary dragged a bench to the door of the cell in which Sir Roland lay and sat down.

Whenever the baronet groaned or moved the smuggler plied him with brandy. It was the only medicine ever used in the cave, and the inmates had every faith in it to cure all the ills that flesh is heir to.

After an hour or so, Sir Roland revived somewhat.

"Where am I?" he asked, feebly.

Tom Wary shook his head.

"You must ask somebody else that question," he replied.

"Am I a prisoner?"

"You made yourself one."

Still confused and bewildered Sir Roland attempted to sit up, but he sank back moaning with pain.

"If you wish to see the captain I will call him," Tom Wary said.

"Captain?"

"Yes—my captain; the man I have followed for years."

"I am still at a loss to know what all this means," Sir Roland returned; "but I will see the captain, as you call him, when convenient."

Tom Wary took a whistle from his pocket and sounded a loud call.

The smuggler chief appeared almost instantly and Wary retired.

"Do you know where you are?" Fielder demanded, sternly.

"That is the very question I was about to ask you," Sir Roland rejoined.

"Then I will tell you," Fielder said. "This place is mine, and the man who sets foot in it without my permission pays for the intrusion his life. It seems to me that you were prying about, and met with a fall."

"Let me think," Sir Roland said. "Everything is vague and uncertain. I seem to have passed through a horrible dream. Ah! it comes back to me. Oh! this agony is almost insupportable!"

"Drink!" Fielder said, passing him the flask. "If I am a revengeful man by nature, I do not torture my prisoners."

Sir Roland gulped down the brandy as if it had been water, and then lay still, again endeavouring to collect his thoughts.

"I have no time to spare," Fielder said. "If you have anything to tell me—if your object was to seek me out and hand me over to what men call justice, as others have done, and paid the penalty for their folly, say so."

In spite of his sufferings Sir Roland Ashton smiled.

"No," he said. "I was hurled down the cliff."

"By whom?"

"A fiend known as Spring-Heeled Jack."

"I have heard rumour of him," Fielder said, "but I have no faith in his existence. You lie! This is but a ruse to throw me off my guard and give you an opportunity to escape."

"It is as true as the sky is above and the sea beneath us," Sir Roland replied. "He is the bane and curse of my life."

"Well, I will take your story for granted. Who are you?"

"Sir Roland Ashton, of Ashton Hall."

"The deuce you are!" said Fielder. "I have heard of you, too, from a man I have done considerable business with in London."

"His name?"

"Gedge Foote."

A cry of surprise and alarm burst from Sir Roland's lips.

"He spoke to you of me?" he said. "Well, he will never do so again."

"No? Why not?"

"Because he is dead, and the house he lived in is a heap of ruins."

"Murdered by Sir Roland Ashton!" said a voice so close to the smuggler that he started to his feet and dragged a pistol from his belt.

"Who spoke?" he demanded, hoarsely.

"Spring-Heeled Jack!"

Fielder dashed across the cavern, and entering the narrow portion, seized the sentry by the throat.

"Dog!" hissed the smuggler chief, "how dare you admit strangers here?"

"Strangers!" the man gasped. "What strangers? It is not true, captain. There must be some conspiracy against me."

"Can I not believe my own ears?" Fielder said, in a voice of thunder. "There is a man hidden in some part of the caves. I heard his voice, and——"

"You see him!"

Fielder turned sharply round and at the same instant Spring-Heeled Jack bounded over his head, and taking an upward flight, seemed to vanish in thin air.

Smugglers, like all men that have anything to do with the sea, are superstitious.

Fielder staggered back, and bold and fearless as he was, he cried out in alarm.

The sentry discharged his musket aimlessly, and in a minute all the men were at the mouth of the cave.

A hundred questions were put and answered.

Some suggested that an immediate search should be made for Spring-Heeled Jack, but the chief shook his head.

"This is a mystery which I will endeavour to unravel," he said. "Let the prisoner receive every attention, for I begin to think that his appearance here was not by chance after all."

So saying, he walked away, leaving the men to talk of Spring-Heeled Jack, and to watch for him in vain.

CHAPTER LVIII.

SHOWS HOW KIND MRS. CORCORAN WAS TO JACOB BUTLER.

"I SAY, you have tied my hands and legs," said Jacob Butler, ruefully. "What new indignity will you subject me to?"

"Yes, deary," Mrs. Corcoran replied; "I did that when you were having that nice little sleep."

"Sleep, be—"

"Now, don't swear," said the hag. "You must not use bad language before a lady."

"You brute—you beast!" Jacob Butler howled. "You knock me silly and senseless and call it sleep. Cut these cords or I'll—"

"Oh! yes," Mrs. Corcoran interposed, as she hobbled round him, "I daresay you will. No doubt you are game to do all sorts of wonderful things."

"Was ever a man in such a fix as this?" Jacob moaned.

"Many in a worse," said Mrs. Corcoran. "Better to have a rope round your ankles than round your neck."

"Oh! you she-devil—you vampire!"

"How nice of you!" said the hag, grinning maliciously. "Dear me, what a happy pair we shall make, to be sure! Come, deary, it is time that you had your breakfast, for morning has come. Let me feed you."

She approached Jacob Butler with a bowl and spoon in her hand.

He turned his head aside in disgust.

"Get away!" he said, with a spasmodic gasp. "I hate the sight of you. I'll not touch anything from your hands."

"Very well," Mrs. Corcoran returned; "if you won't eat it for your breakfast it must do for your dinner. Trust me, my dove, that you will return to your appetite before long."

"I won't," Jacob said; "I swear I won't. I'll starve myself, and think myself lucky to escape you in that way."

Mrs. Corcoran set the bowl down on the floor.

"I am going out," she said; "but I shan't be long."

"Where to?"

"To get the marriage license, my pet."

Butler's hair stood on end and his face went as white as a sheet.

"But look here," said Jacob, in dismay. "You are not going to leave me here, trussed up in this fashion?"

"Yes, I am, lovey; because you look so quiet and pretty. If I let you run loose you might get yourself into mischief, you know."

Jacob Butler opened his mouth to its utmost limits, and said certain things about Mrs. Corcoran and her attentions which it would be scarcely wise to repeat.

The old hag, after making sure that Jacob was perfectly secure, and adding a few more knots as an extra precaution, went out.

"I'm done for," Jacob groaned. "What a fool I was to leave the Queen's Head! What an ass I have made of myself!"

In his misery he rolled over with his face to the ground, and as he lay kicking and fuming he heard the heavy plodding footsteps of a man approaching the hut.

SPRING-HEELED JACK,
THE TERROR OF LONDON.

AS SPRING-HEELED JACK APPEARED A TERRIFIC EXPLOSION SHOOK THE BUILDING.

19.

"Here! Hi! Help!" he roared. The footsteps stopped, and it was evident the man outside was wondering where the voice came from.

Once more Jacob Butler lifted up his voice, with such effect that the stranger tried the door.

"It's locked!" Jacob cried, in a frenzy of excitement. "You can't get in that way. Pull the brushwood out of the window and then you can. Make haste if you want to save my life. That she-devil will be back soon, and she's more than a match for half-a-dozen men."

The man, who was a thorough rustic, and consequently as slow as a tortoise in his movements, did as he was told, and grinned hugely as he looked down upon Jacob.

"Quick! man, quick!" groaned the prisoner. "Out with your knife, and cut these cords." But the man was in no hurry. He had to ask himself whether he would be doing right, and Jacob's suspense became so agonising that he positively howled.

At last the rustic crept through the aperture and cut the cords.

"Free!" Jacob Butler cried. "Hurrah! My blessings on you, man, for this service. Here is all the money I have, but you are perfectly welcome to it. Ha! ha! ha!"

He was in such a hurry that as he emptied his pockets the coins flew all over the floor, and leaving the labourer to pick them up, he took a harlequin-like dive at the window, and raced away across the fields.

Jacob Butler felt just then that he could have handicapped himself against the very best man living.

Away he went like an antelope, until the breath left his body and his legs gave way under him.

As he fell sprawling a carrier's cart rumbled round a corner of the road, and the driver, thinking that Jacob had met with a serious accident, pulled up.

"Where—where are you going?" Jacob Butler gasped, as he staggered to his feet.

"To Islington."

"Then if you are a man with a grain of mercy in your heart, you will give me a lift."

"Willingly," said the carrier; "but you must tell me what you are running away from."

"From a woman."

The carrier laughed.

"Well," he said, "I have seen a bigger and a bolder man than you do that. Jump up!"

The cart had no passengers, and as Jacob climbed in under the tilt he sank down exhausted.

At first he had some notion of regaling the carrier's intellect with the story of his woes, but he abandoned the notion.

In the first place, the carrier might either disbelieve him, or call him a coward and kick him out of the cart; and, secondly, the man might fall in with Mrs. Corcoran and give her certain unpleasant information.

So Jacob concocted a story about a drunken, bad wife, who was hunting about for him with a poker, and the carrier laughed until tears ran down his face.

Mr. Butler got down at a convenient distance from the Queen's Head, and completed the rest of the journey on foot.

He sneaked into the inn as if he had just committed a theft, and the landlord hailed him with a roar of laughter, and followed that up with a dozen questions.

"Don't say anything to me." Jacob gasped. "All I want to do is to go to bed and try to forget what I have gone through."

"You're a nice sort of fellow to run away and leave the ladies," the landlord said.

"Ah! I forgot about them. How are they?"

"Well and hearty."

"That's good news. Has Mr. Ashton returned?"

The landlord shook his head, and bestowed a mysterious wink on Jacob.

"You had better ask Miss Marfield," he said.

"I can't talk to anybody until I have had a sleep," Jacob returned, "and so I am off. I say—"

"Well?"

"If anybody asks you about me take your oath I am not here."

So saying, Jacob Butler made a run for the staircase, and was seen no more that day.

CHAPTER LIX.

THE FALSE BEACON—THE STORM AT SEA—
HOW JULES CARLEON CAME TO SIR ROLAND'S RESCUE.

DAVID FIELDER, the chief of the Dover smugglers, sat alone, with his feet resting on the trap-door that opened into the larger cave.

His own apartment was one which had been especially hollowed out for his use, and was furnished in a luxurious manner.

All kinds of things lay strewn about, and it was evident that Fielder had his hand in other things than smuggling tobacco and liquor.

The smuggler's face wore an expression of mingled gloom and bewilderment.

Sir Roland Ashton was in his power.

He had only to say a word, or to hold up a finger, and the baronet would tell no secrets.

But there was Spring-Heeled Jack to contend with.

Who was he, and how came he gifted with the marvellous power of motion?

David Fielder asked himself these questions so often that his brain grew weary, and at last, folding his arms upon the table, and sinking his head upon them, he fell asleep.

As he slumbered a change was taking place.

Heavy clouds shut out the blue sky and a thick, leaden-hued mist arose on all points of the horizon.

The men who watched at the mouth of the cave knew that a heavy storm was brewing.

Night might come before it would burst, but come it would.

The smugglers now became unusually active.

Some climbed the cliff-side and returned with bundles of brushwood, which was piled into a heap; and others prepared different coloured powders, sifting and handling them carefully.

Evening was coming on when David Fielder joined the men.

The wind was rising higher and higher every moment, and the foam-tipped waves tumbled over each other as if they were in haste to reach the shore and escape the doom threatened by the angry sky.

"Give me my telescope," Fielder said. "Ah!" he added, as he took a survey of the ocean, "we shall have some customers to-night. Is the beacon ready?"

"All ready to be fired," a man replied.

"That is well," Fielder said. "We share alike, boys, so the greater the haul the better. What do you make of yonder schooner?"

"She is a Spanish vessel."

"With a rich cargo, no doubt," Fielder said, smiling grimly. "The wind is dead against her, and it will take her from three to four hours to get into port. It will be dark by that time."

It was dark in much less, for the clouds gathered and mingled with the fog, and gloom soon fell upon land and sea.

Then it was that the real battle of the elements. began.

A mighty gust of wind opened the conflict, and a reign of terror and confusion set in.

The waves, hurled against the cliffs in mad fury, sent up showers of white foam as it were in defiance to the clouds.

The scene was appalling.

Gust after gust of wind.

Crash after crash of thunder, and the lightning trailed and quivered along the leaping waves.

It was a night to strike terror into the boldest heart; but it was one suited to the smuggler's tastes, for, as we have hinted, David Fielder not only dealt in contraband goods, but was a wrecker[110] into the bargain.

Suddenly a sound rose above the voice of the storm.

It was the report of a cannon fired at sea, and a plea for help to luckier people on shore.

"I thought as much," Fielder said. "The schooner could not get near enough to take a pilot on board. Light the beacon. But stay, we will show a light first. "

Almost instantly a white light flared up, burning steadily.

It was as suddenly extinguished, and the smugglers waited the result in silence.

Another gun was fired from the ill-fated vessel. The report was louder than the previous one, and it was evident that the ship was drifting on to the cliffs and destruction.

"Now light the beacon," said Fielder. A man took a torch in his hand and walked towards the pile, but ere he reached it Spring-Heeled Jack stood in his path.

"Villain!" cried the mysterious being. Murderer of innocent men and hapless women, your time has come!"

Clutching the man by the belt, and raising him aloft in his arms, he hurled him into the very midst of his companions.

The appearance of Spring-Heeled Jack and his action was so sudden that the wreckers could not step aside, and several were knocked heels over head down the cliff by the strange and weighty missile hurled at them.

David Fielder narrowly escaped sharing the fate of his followers, and he was so alarmed and enraged at what had taken place that he could do nothing but stand and glare at Spring-Heeled Jack.

But at last he recovered himself, and, setting his teeth, advanced with a cutlass in his band.

But the chance of using it was denied him.

Spring-Heeled Jack kicked the unlighted pile of brushwood over the face of the cliff, and, uttering a loud, mocking laugh, vanished into the darkness.

---

[110] One who plunders wrecked ships.

"It's the very devil himself!" Fielder cried, aghast. "Confusion! we are despoiled of our prey. See, there go rockets from the harbour; and listen!—the schooner answers them."

Boom—boom! went the guns.

During this scene of confusion Sir Roland had not been idle.

He had been left alone in the inner cavern, and the craving to get away came strongly upon him.

Opening a large wooden chest he found that it contained articles of apparel such as the smugglers wore.

Exchanging his own garments for these he stood completely disguised.

"Now to run the gauntlet," he muttered. "It is worth risking, for death stares me in the face here."

The storm was at its height as he approached the mouth of the cave, and the smugglers were too intent on the murderous business they had in hand to notice him.

He crept out unobserved, and trusting himself to chance, grasped the bushes that grew on the cliff-side and lowered himself down.

He knew that there were steps hewn for the convenience of the smugglers, but he dare not approach them for fear of being seen.

Clinging, sliding, and slipping, with the spray dashing in his face, Sir Roland got a firm footing.

He stopped and peered through the awful gloom.

His heart beat almost audibly.

At any moment a flash of lightning might reveal his form, and what earthly power could save him then?

Steadying himself by placing his back against the cliff, he pondered on what he should do.

There might be a path down to the beach, but it was unknown to him.

A fatal step would hurl him into eternity, or leave him to battle for life in the raging sea.

Suddenly he felt a strange hand touch his arm, and he recoiled in horror.

"Courage, monsieur!" said a voice. "It is I—Jules Carleon—and I will lead you to safety."

"How did you find your way here?" Sir Roland demanded.

"It matters not," Jules Carleon replied. "It may be that I know more than David thinks or dreams of. Follow me, and I will put it out of his power to do you harm."

CHAPTER LX.

SHARING THE GUINEAS—A LITTLE MISUNDERSTANDING—
A PUGILISTIC ENCOUNTER PUT A STOP TO IN AN ODD SORT OF WAY.

FOR some days after the capture of Bill Blarney the triumphant officers, Catchpole and Grabham, did not meet.

This was not Catchpole's fault, for Grabham had kindly undertaken the charge of the money given by the passengers, and evinced, by his studied absence, a strong inclination to stick to the lot.

Catchpole dodged about the different inns used by Grabham, but he came not, and at last his disappointed colleague determined to seek him at his own home.

Mr. Grabham occupied a portion of a very old house in Cloth Fair, and the windows looked out upon the churchyard of ancient St. Bartholomew's Church.

The place had been tenanted once upon a time by some wealthy personage.

It had broad staircases, stained glass windows, and the wood-carver's art was prevalent on the oak panels, mantelpieces, and doorways.

Thither Catchpole wended his way, vowing vengeance on the man who had cheated him out of his due.

"What a fool I was to trust him!" he muttered, as he turned out of Smithfield-green and entered a dark, narrow street. "But wait until I have dug the fox out of his hole. I'll give him a bit of my mind, and a jolly good hiding into the bargain, if he isn't careful."

Mr. Catchpole looked very fierce, really as if he meant what he said.

"To be robbed like this!" he gasped. "To be robbed by the man I trusted! I have found you out now, Grabham, and hang me if I don't make you grin on the other side of your mouth!"

This little soliloquy brought Catchpole to an antiquated door, fitted with a knocker moulded in the shape of a dragon.

Catchpole laid hold of the monster and awoke the echoes of the house.

The noise was loud enough to startle a deaf man, but it had no effect on the inmates of the tumbledown mansion, so Catchpole repeated the operation, and with such vigour that he damaged the dragon's beauty and symmetry for ever.

A man living over the way came out with a stick thinking that some mischievous boy was giving full vent to his animal spirits, but on seeing that he had a real live constable to deal with he retired precipitately and hid his benighted head under his own roof.

Catchpole's second application produced the desired result, or rather it produced a one-eyed old woman with a visage as sour as vinegar and a head of hair that looked as if it had been tossed about by a rake.

"Is Mr. Grabham at home?" Catchpole asked, in a tone of voice that denoted that the name he had to utter almost choked him.

"How should I know?"

"Doesn't he live here?"

"Yes. But I have nothing to do with him. He lives on the top floor."

"Then how the devil am I to make him hear?" Catchpole demanded.

"Go round the back way and chuck some stones at his window."

Bang went the door in Catchpole's face, and he staggered back into the street just in time to prevent his cranium coming in contact with the iron dragon.

"That's the way with women—hang 'em!" he gasped. "There's no sense or reason about 'em. Chuck stones at the window! What next, I wonder?"

The gallant officer had no other alternative, however, so he marched himself round by St. Bartholomew's churchyard, and, climbing the wall, felt about for a missile.

It was dark, and the gravestones looked so ghost-like that Catchpole felt anything but comfortable.

At last he secured a stone and hurled it up at a window behind which a light was shining, and cracked it.

Up flew the window-sash and out popped a head.

"Now, then," roared a voice, "what sort of a game do you call this?"

"That isn't Grabham's voice," Catchpole said, aghast. "I've gone and chucked the stone at the wrong window."

The constable dropped on his knees behind a huge tombstone, and kept his head well down, for fear that the irate proprietor of the cracked window might retaliate in a similar manner.

"I'll just step down and speak to Mr. Grabham, the constable, who lives next door," said the voice. "He will wake you up, young Jenkins. I know it's you, my lad, for I can see you."

Catchpole grinned.

This little event reminded him of his youth, when he broke windows and laid the blame on other boys' shoulders.

After a pause, during which the man above vowed that he would do all sorts of horrible things to the invisible Jenkins, he withdrew his head and returned to the delightful and aromatic art of making boots.

"Oh! Grabham lives next door, does he?" Catchpole said; "but which is next door. There's a house on each side, and I don't want to make another mistake, or I shall have the whole neighbourhood down on me."

This seemed so probable that the constable hesitated before he took another stone in his hand, and at last he made up his mind to watch for Grabham at the entrance of Cloth Fair.

This was the most sensible course to pursue, for if Grabham was at home his natural desire for stimulating liquors would bring him out-of-doors.

Catchpole had not long to wait.

He shrank back into a doorway as Grabham left his house, and touched him on the shoulder as he passed.

"What! my old friend?" cried Grabham, with a sickly smile.

"Your old friend, be jiggered!" said Catchpole. "You're a nice sort of party, certainly, to talk about friendship."

"Why shouldn't I?"

"Why shouldn't you?" Catchpole retorted, indignantly. "What do you mean by skulking away from me? Where's my share of the money?"

"What money?"

Catchpole was so overcome by this question that he spun round on his heels.

"Don't you give way to delusions," Grabham said. "There were certainly a few coppers—"

"Coppers!" Catchpole interposed, with a groan. "Guineas you mean!"

"There might have been a guinea among them," Grabham said, evasively. "Well, Catchpole, my boy, I want to do what is fair, so if you will walk round to a house I know we will settle the matter. I have been very queer during the last few days."

"Drunk you mean!" Catchpole said, wrathfully. "Drunk on my money!"

"Don't be hard on a man who has shared your joys and sorrows."

"Jigger my joys and sorrows. I want my money," Catchpole gasped. "There were a dozen passengers on the coach, and if they gave a penny they gave five guineas a piece."

"Then why didn't you count your share?"

"Because you took my hat away from me and shovelled the money into your own pocket."

"It was the action of a man and a brother," Grabham said, virtuously, "and to prove it I'll show you what we really got. When I returned home I tied the money up in a red handkerchief, and it hasn't been touched yet."

"Have you got it about you now?"

"Yes."

"Then come on and let me have my half, or there'll be a jolly row."

Grabham led the way through Smithfield and Clerkenwell, until Catchpole grew tired of walking.

"Where are you going to take me now?" he said.

"To the Queen's Head, Sadler's Wells."

"What for?"

"Because it is a quiet house, where we can talk without the fear of being disturbed," Grabham replied.

Little did he or his comrade think who were staying at the Inn towards which their footsteps were wending.

"Very well," Catchpole grumbled. "The house is kept by Ben Jordan, isn't it?"

"That's the very man, and a jolly good fellow he is."

"Is he?" Catchpole observed, dubiously. "I have heard that rather queer sort of people go to his house sometimes."

"So much the better for us. We may be able to pick up a bit of useful information."

"I've had enough information and work to last me a lifetime," Catchpole replied. "I want rest, and I think I shall go in for a road-side inn, with a bit of garden and a pig-stye at the back."

Mr. Catchpole rubbed his hands as he pictured this scene of bliss on his mind, and he dwelt upon it in silence until the Queen's Head came in view.

Opening a door that creaked warningly upon its hinges, and brought Ben Jordan, the landlord, suddenly out of a room, the constables entered and said "Good-evening" in a pleasant sort of manner.

Ben Jordan returned the salutation, and inquired his customers' pleasure.

"Well, you see," said Grabham, "we have a little business to transact, and so we thought we should like to have a private room for an hour or two."

"Certainly, gentlemen—certainly," said the landlord, smiling. "Anything to oblige you, I am sure. Follow me, sirs, and I will see that you are made comfortable."

"You may as well let us have something to drink."

"Wine, of course?"

"Yes; a bottle of the very best you have in the house."

"You honour me," said Jordan. "If I had such customers as you always in my house I should make a fortune in a few years."

He spoke with his tongue in his cheek, for he knew the officers well, and suspected that they had come there with no good intention to him or those in his house.

The room into which he showed Catchpole and Grabham was situated at the back of the house, and both the visitors expressed their satisfaction at the arrangements made for them.

Ben Jordan brought the wine and set it on the table.

"You will ring if you should require me again, gentlemen," he said. "The door sticks, and you may find some difficulty in getting it open."

"Ah! just so," said Grabham, winking at Catchpole. "Supposing you leave the key on our side, though?"

"Certainly," Jordan replied. "What object should I have in doing otherwise?"

"None—none!" Catchpole said, impatiently. "Thanks; but would you mind leaving? We wish to be alone."

Ben Jordan grinned as he left the room and heard the key turn in the lock.

"One good turn deserves another," he said, as he shot a small bolt, "Now we are equally secure, my friends. I don't want to know your business any more than I want you sneaking about my house."

"Now," said Catchpole, dropping into a chair, "out with that red handkerchief, and let me hear what you have to say for yourself?"

Grabham shook his head, reproachfully. "You wouldn't speak in that tone of voice if you knew how I have looked forward to this meeting," he said.

"Ah! I dare say. Well, never mind the meeting, but give your attention to the parting," Catchpole said. "I don't like the look of this place, somehow."

"What's the matter with it?"

"It looks as if it might be haunted by a ghost," Catchpole returned. "Now, then, are you going to produce that money or are you not?"

"Of course I am; but don't jump down my throat or I may bite you."

As he spoke he produced a piece of dirty, red-coloured rag, knotted and secured as carefully as if it contained the wealth of the Bank of England.

"There you are," he said, "and you'll find it all fair and square."

After struggling with the knots he opened the rag and emptied its contents upon the table.

Catchpole's eyes grew dim as he saw the coins displayed to his view.

Some of them were copper, a few silver, and one piece gold.

"How long have you been saving up these 'ere?" Catchpole said, with a grunt. "If you think to delude me with taking half this muck you're jolly well mistaken."

"If you don't like them don't have them," said Grabham, sweeping the coins back into his coat pocket.

No sooner had he done this than Catchpole threw himself into a fighting attitude.

"Come on," he said. "Stand up like a man. You have always looked upon me as a coward, but now I will prove that I am a braver man than you."

Mr. Grabham did not expect this sudden display of hostilities.

Indeed, it was the very last thing he did expect, and he was so upset, not only by the sight of Catchpole's clenched fists, but by the contortions of his face, that he staggered against the table.

"Do you really mean to say that you will strike me?" he said.

"Don't I!" Catchpole growled. "Of course I do. Come a little nearer, you low, mean thief!"

"Then I am afraid that I shall have to take you at your word," Grabham said, "and if you get a jolly good hiding don't blame me."

Now it so happened that the constables knew as much about pugilism as they did about the interior of the moon, and they did little more than hug each other.

A strange incident put an end to the encounter.

Whilst they were rolling and bumping about all over the room a terrific explosion took place.

It shook the house to its foundation, and above the flame and smoke the constables saw Spring-Heeled Jack hovering in the air.

Grabham, howling with terror, made for the window.

Catchpole dashed at the table, but Spring-Heeled Jack, alighting in the centre of the room, checked their progress.

"Stop!" he cried. "Stay where you are, or I'll leave no whole bone under your skins!"

"Oh! sir—please, sir, don't!" Catchpole whined.

"You came here to share money—where is it?" demanded Spring-Heeled Jack, grinning in such a ferocious manner that the constables almost fainted.

"I have it," Grabham said, feebly, "and I am sure that you are welcome to it, if you want it."

"Want it!" Spring-Heeled Jack said, contemptuously, "I want it! Ha, ha! What is money to me? Nothing! But there are the poor and starving—the desolate widow, the starving child crying for bread. They shall have it."

"Certainly!" Grabham said, as he produced a handful of coins. "I intended to give some of it away myself."

"Craven wretch, you lie!"

"Well, it isn't for the likes of such as me to contradict you," Grabham said; "but I would be much obliged to you if you wouldn't look at me like that."

"This is not all," Spring-Heeled Jack said. "You tried to cheat your companion, but you cannot cheat me."

"It is every blessed farden,"[111] Grabham whined.

"Again you lie," Spring-Heeled Jack said. "Turn out your pockets, or I'll hurl you through the window you tried to crawl out of!"

With many a sigh and groan Grabham complied, and Spring-Heeled Jack left him nothing.

"I have nothing to say to you," he said, turning to Catchpole; "but be advised by me, and quit this house as soon as possible."

Catchpole was about to remark that he intended to do so, when a cloud of smoke arose, and Spring-Heeled Jack vanished in the midst of it.

Then the lights were extinguished by an unseen hand, and the constables, startled out of their senses, clung frantically to each other.

They were afraid to move, lest they should fall into some trap set for them; but to remain there in darkness and suspense was horrible torture.

"Let us make for the door," Catchpole whispered, "I shall have a fit or die if I stay here any longer."

"He went through the floor," Grabham replied, in terrified accents, "and it is just possible that he may have left it open. We must creep round by the wall."

At length they reached the door, to their great joy, and burst it open.

A light was in the passage, and the constables hastened below.

Ben Jordan was at his work and smiled at them, but they gave him frowns in exchange.

"What's the matter, gentlemen?" the landlord asked. "I sincerely hope that you found

---

[111] Farthing, a low-denomination coin.

the wine satisfactory?"

"It is not the wine that we grumble at, but the company you keep," Grabham said.

"Company—company?" Ben Jordan repeated, lifting his eyebrows. "I don't understand what you mean."

"Why, that Spring-Heeled Jack is in this house."

"In this house?" Jordan cried, falling back upon his seat. "Nonsense! You must be mad to make such an assertion."

"We ain't mad at all," Grabham replied. "The jumping scoundrel made me turn out my pockets, and took my money, and Catchpole's too."

"Is this really possible?"

"It is," Catchpole replied, with tears in his eyes. "He came through the floor as if he had been fired out of a cannon."

"I don't believe it—I can't believe it," said Ben Jordan. "I'm a law-abiding man, loyal to my king and true to my country, and I'll trouble you not to run my house down. What do you mean by coming here with a view to ruining me? Spring-Heeled Jack, indeed! Now, if Sir Roland Ashton had told me that—"

"Eh?" Grabham interposed, with a gasp.

"Oh! I happen to know something of your little games," Jordan replied, laughing. "I suppose you don't happen to know such a place as Lilac Lodge?"

The constables stared at each other in dismay.

"I think we had better be going," Grabham whispered, clutching Catchpole by the arm. "It strikes me that we have come to the wrong shop."

"Wait a minute," said Jordan. "It seems that you are afflicted with bad memory. You haven't paid for that bottle of wine yet."

"I haven't a farden to bless myself with."

"But your friend has, and I demand my due."

He walked round the bar, and closing the door that opened on to the street, planted his back against it.

"How much?" Catchpole asked, with a groan that came from the bottom of his heart.

"Five shillings."

The wretched constable produced the money as if he was parting with his life.

"Now you may go," Jordan said, as he opened the door, "and the sooner you are gone the better I shall like it."

"Come on," said Grabham, desperately. Somebody will have to suffer for this. Come on, I say!"

CHAPTER LXI.

THE SHADOW ON THE BLIND.

RETAINING Sir Roland's hand, Jules Carleon hurried the baronet along.

The Frenchman seemed to know the locality well, for his feet never once slipped, nor did he hesitate.

Sir Roland found that they were ascending, and that as they went the path improved, until it was almost as hard and wide as a public road.

"Steady now," Carleon said. "The smugglers have means of overlooking this portion of the way and it's just possible that the lightning may reveal our forms to them. If so, monsieur, they will send quick messengers after us."

"Shoot us, you mean?"

"Yes; and they are excellent marksmen."

Sir Roland Ashton did not doubt this statement for a moment.

His experience in the cave had convinced him that the band of men were of no common mould and he saw signs in the faces of some that spoke of gentle rearing and good education.

How, then, had they drifted into such a style of life?

Men who have squandered fortunes in sin and debauchery must find the means of living, and often sink lower than becoming smugglers.

Sir Roland was fully aware of this, and, as he drew a mental picture of his own career, the colour were not very brilliant, though they might be called startling.

"This path is filled with danger," he said, to Carleon. "You are not deceiving me? You are not leading me into any worse trap than the one I have just escaped from?"

"Why should I do that, monsieur?" Jules Carleon returned. "Am I not your servant now?"

"But how did you know that I was with the smugglers?"

"I did not," Jules replied. "I came upon you by accident. When storms rage one may pick up things worth having at times."

"You mean that you join the wreckers in their hellish work?"

"No," Jules Carleon replied; "I am too wise. I play the part of a jackal, and rest contented with such of the feast as the lions choose to leave."

"I see," said Sir Roland, who was crouching down behind a huge boulder. Is the coast clear now? May we advance?"

"The lightning grows fainter and will soon cease altogether, Carleon replied. "Patience, monsieur. Is it your intention to return to the inn?"

"Where else am I to go to, in the name of common sense?"

"I will show you, if you will trust me," Jules replied. "I have a place of my own. It is what you English call cosy. Will you come?"

"Yes."

"And then?"

"I suppose I must think of returning to London."

"Not yet, monsieur," Jules Carleon whispered in his ear. "You and I—your servant— will go to a little village I know of. There you can take the rest you so much need. Do you consent?"

"Yes."

"And you trust me?"

"I do."

"It is well," Jules Carleon muttered.

Sir Roland thought he heard a sound like the closing of a knife, and kept a wary eye on the Frenchman.

"Now we may proceed," Carleon said, rising to his feet. "The wreckers have not done well to-night, and will sulk at home. They will miss you, monsieur."

Sir Roland now thought it better to tell the Frenchman his real name and circumstances.

He did so, and a cunning smile flitted over Carleon's face. His moustache bristled and his eyes gleamed. "Hah!" he ejaculated, "we live in a strange world, Sir Roland. I often wonder what the next is like. Shall we live, and love, and die, and so on, from sphere to sphere?"

"I am not inclined to argue the question," Sir Roland said. "My only desire just now is to get away from the danger that threatens me. Delay no longer, but take me where you will."

The Frenchman, ever polite and smiling, bowed low.

"This way," he said. "You have not far to go."

They went up the winding path, and crossing a broad open space, turned into a lane leading to some fields.

From this point Sir Roland could see the oil-lamps in the streets of Dover flashing and gleaming.

But it was not into the town that Jules Carleon led the baronet.

Suddenly striking off in an opposite direction, the Frenchman dived down a turning, so narrow and remote that the casual eye would not have noticed it, and Sir Roland found himself standing before a low-roofed, one-storied building, which might have done duty either for a warehouse or a stable.

"What place is this?" Sir Roland asked.

"My home."

Sir Roland glanced from the Frenchman to the house as if he mistrusted both.

"Pardon," said Jules Carleon, "but you hesitate?"

"Yes," said Sir Roland. It may be that a long experience has made me cautious. I thought I saw a light flit across one of the blinds."

"You dream, Sir Roland," Jules said. "I am a bachelor, and nobody enters this house but myself. See, here is the key and here am I. If I have played you false I am unarmed and at your mercy."

Sir Roland, feeling somewhat reassured, opened the door, and Jules Carleon fetching down a lamp from a bracket held it above his head.

"I go before you," he said. "There are but four rooms, and, to satisfy you, we will examine them."

"I will take your word," Sir Roland said. "I daresay I am nervous and fanciful. Faith! it would not surprise me if I went mad and saw legions of ghosts."

Jules Carleon turned back upon him with so white a face that Sir Roland felt a thrill run through him.

"Ghosts—the shades of the departed!" the Frenchman said, under his breath. "Do you believe in such things?"

"I know not what to say."

"But if you saw with your own eyes?"

"Then I should believe."

Jules Carleon said no more; but his footsteps seemed to be unsteady as he led the way into a room.

It was oddly and uncomfortably furnished.

A pile of empty boxes covered with a red baize cloth did duty for a table, and a couple of rickety chairs completed the appointments.

"You do not go in for luxuries, I see," said Sir Roland.

"No," Jules Carleon replied. "Am I not a poor man? Am I not the humble waiter at an inn?"

He cast a side glance full of meaning at Sir Roland.

"Yes," the baronet replied; "but probably for your own purpose."

The Frenchman laughed as he produced a pack of cards.

"Will Sir Roland condescend to play with his. humble servant?" he asked. "To-morrow we will change all this, but to-night, since I have done you so much service, I crave your leniency."

"I will not play to-night," Sir Roland said, wearily. "I wish to sleep."

Jules Carleon pointed to a door.

"There you will find your bed-chamber," he said.

"You expected me, then?"

"How you question me, Sir Roland. Perchance I keep a room for visitors. Why not?"

Sir Roland made no reply, but taking up the lamp stepped into the room.

He found this apartment better furnished than the other.

It contained a clean, white bed, an easy chair, and a few strips of good carpet.

Hastily removing the clothes he had borrowed from the smugglers' cave, Sir Roland threw himself upon the bed.

But he could not sleep.

Strange doubts and fears crept into his mind.

They kept him awake and on the alert.

He tried to convince himself that all was well, but in vain.

There was something sly and subtle about this man, Jules Carleon, who, passing at one moment as a humble waiter at an inn, suddenly changed his character into the man with a secret home, and a thorough knowledge of everything disreputable.

"It's a mystery to me how he knew me in my disguise," Sir Roland said to himself, "and now I begin to think that I must have been a fool to. let out so much to him."

The house was very quiet.

Jules Carleon had said good-night as he passed the door, and had evidently gone to bed.

Why then could not Sir Roland Ashton take the rest he was in such urgent need of?

It was because he was so cowardly and base himself that he could trust no man.

Dim notions floated through his mind that Jules Carleon would suddenly enter the room and demand a ransom, and he twisted and turned these ideas into hundreds of shapes.

His eyes ached and burned with fatigue, and at last he fell into a fitful slumber.

There was no repose—no rest in it.

Sir Roland, like a fox, was, in a manner of speaking, sleeping with one eye open, for the slightest and most common sound in the room would have been more than sufficient to rouse him, and set the blood tingling in his veins.

All was still outside.

The wind dropped, the storm clouds parted and dispersed, leaving the fair moon to reign undisputed in the sky.

The sea was still wild, as though it refused to be soothed after being lashed to fury.

All else in Nature lay sleeping.

Sir Roland Ashton had not closed his eyes more than half an hour before he opened them again, and started up in bed.

He had heard no sound.

Nothing had touched him. He had been but dreaming and he seemed to doubt whether he was still awake, for he rubbed his eyes and looked about him, as if to convince himself of the fact.

"Ah! it was but a dream," he said. "She is dead. Dead women, like dead men, tell no tales. And yet, what a curious dream it was. How vivid and realistic I felt the pressure of her fingers upon my throat, and—"

Something, he scarcely knew what, attracted Sir Roland's eyes towards the window.

The moon was shining full upon the white blinds.

But Sir Roland was almost convinced that he had seen something flit across them.

It might be the shadow of a branch swaying about before the gentle breeze, or a hundred other trivial things might have accounted for it.

But Sir Roland was not satisfied.

He rose from his bed and examined the fastening of the window.

All was well there, and, cursing his folly and weakness, he was stepping across the floor when he became partially darkened by some object which had evidently taken its stand at the window.

Sir Roland looked round.

His arms went up with a convulsive movement.

His limbs became rigid and fixed.

If he had been a statue hewn from a block of solid marble he could not have been more motionless.

What was it that he saw at the window?

Only a shadow; but it was the shadow of Mrs. Corcoran.

He could not speak.

He tried to shriek—to cry out; but his tongue refused to utter a sound.

At last the strength died out of his legs, and he fell with so loud a crash that Jules Carleon started from his sleep.

The Frenchman swore in his own language first, and then in English.

He loved his bed, and to be roused from it in the dead of the night was more than he could brook from even a baronet.

"*Parbleu!*" said Jules. between his teeth. "Sir Roland must keep quiet while he is here. What a noise! Perhaps I had better go and see to him."

It was well for Sir Roland that this idea came into his head and that he acted upon it.

Jules Carleon found his new master lying upon his face, looking so white and ghastly that at first Jules thought he was dead.

To all appearances the foreigner was not a man of great strength, but he contrived to lift Sir Roland easily in his arms and place him on the bed.

"A strange creature this," Jules Carleon said, musingly. "Is it that he walks in his sleep? Hah! he looks at me! He speaks! Sir Roland, I am transported with joy to see you once more yourself."

"Take her away!" Sir Roland said, wildly. "Don't let her approach me! The sight of her is death!"

"Ah! there is a lady in the case," Jules observed, smiling. "A little *affaire du cœur,* I suppose, Sir Roland? But you are dreaming!"

"Dreaming!" said Sir Roland, pressing his hand to his brow; "no—no!"

"But I say yes—yes!" Jules said. "We are alone. Who else should be here?"

"I saw the witch!" Sir Roland hissed between his set teeth. "If flames will not consume her, if the earth refuses to bury her ashes, how am I to rid the world of her?"

Jules Carleon smiled to himself and made mental note of every word.

But he had heard enough, and thought it was time to put a stop to the baronet's ravings.

"Sir Roland," he said, gently, "you are not well. Be calm. Let me fetch you a glass of rare old wine. It will warm you to your very heart and do you good."

"Don't leave me," Sir Roland said, clutching him by the arm. "No—no! I will not be left alone. The spectre would haunt me and drive me mad."

"Well, then," said Jules, as he threw the bed clothes over Sir Roland's icy cold form, "I will not go. I will stay until day-light comes and disperses these idle fears."

"Not idle," the baronet said. "Do you remember your own words? You asked me whether I believed in ghosts."

"I did, Sir Roland."

"I have seen one," the baronet replied. "I have seen the spectre of a woman who died a terrible death."

Jules Carleon twirled his black moustache and flashed a keen glance at Sir Roland.

"Was she young or old?" he said.

"Old—very old."

"How did she die?"

"By fire."

Jules Carleon uttered an ejaculation, but sat calm and still.

"You and the lady did not like each other?" he insinuated, after a pause.

"Ask me no more questions," Sir Roland said "How the night drags. Will it never end?"

Jules sat watching the baronet until the pale grey dawn of morning came creeping over the silent town, and Sir Roland, reassured, thanked the man and bade him depart.

Sir Roland was no sooner alone than, rolling over on his side, he fell into a deep slumber.

CHAPTER LXII.

HOW DICK SLEUTH WENT TO VISIT BLARNEY IN NEWGATE—
THE POWER OF GOLD.

WHILE these events were proceeding, Bill Blarney lay in Newgate.

Mentally and physically he was sore and distressed.

His head had been cracked, as recent bandages plainly showed, and his heart sunk at the thought of dying a violent death at the hands of the hangman.

He knew that if such a fate was in store for him it was a deserved one, but he determined, very naturally, to escape it if he could.

To make matters worse, Grabham, in his zeal to do the thing properly, had emptied Bill Blarney's pockets of every farthing, and thus the captive was compelled to live on such fare as the prison authorities chose to provide.

This was neither tempting in appearance nor nice when tasted.

A small black loaf and a sickly mass of gruel was all Bill Blarney got each day.

He received no visitors, for the simple reason that nobody knew where he was.

He might have sent a note for assistance to Dick Sleuth or to some other comrade who inclined to help him.

But no warder would stir an inch without being heavily bribed, and so Bill Blarney fretted and fumed in his cell and rattled his irons dismally. His trial was coming on shortly. In fact he might be called upon to plead at any moment, and what chance of escape would he have then?

Not the faintest.

Sentence once passed all would be over, save the short journey to Tyburn, with all its hideous ceremonies.

Bill Blarney groaned as these things recurred to his mind.

He was not at all smitten with pity for the misfortunes of other people, but he did not relish being strung up for a gaping crowd to stare at. What a cowardly villain he was! Give him liberty and a pistol, and he would as soon rob a helpless woman as eat his dinner.

But now that he was laid by the heels he whined and howled for mercy.

While he was thus engaged and grudging each moment as it flew by, there was consternation at the Bull in Top Boots.

The landlord was perplexed and alarmed at Bill Blarney's protracted absence, and so was Dick Sleuth.

All they knew was that Blarney had borrowed a horse and ridden out one night.

"This comes of being sly," said Dick Sleuth. "If he had said where he was going there would have been a clue to follow up, but now there is nothing—absolutely nothing."

"Well," said the landlord, "matters are getting serious, and by hook or by crook we must try and find out where Bill is. It strikes me that if you went to the Big Stone Jug[112] you might hear something of him."

Dick Sleuth winced.

"That may be," he said; "but I hardly care to undertake the job."

"Why not?"

"Because when I went there," Dick Sleuth replied, "the warders seemed so precious fond of me that they wanted my company altogether."

"But that was years ago," the landlord urged. "I would go myself, but see the position it would place me in. Fancy the landlord of an inn going to see a highwayman."

"Well, then," said Dick Sleuth, "perhaps you will tell me the character that I am to play?"

"His mourning brother-in-law," the landlord replied. "Buy a good book, and present it before the chaplain's eyes, and after he is gone see what you can do with the warders."

This idea was feasible, but it had its objections.

Dick Sleuth shrank from going to Newgate, but at last he made up his mind to do so.

The landlord gave him a sum of money, and on an afternoon of a gloomy day he set out.

As he neared the prison he stopped and looked carefully up and down.

Little as he dreamed that Bill Blarney had been captured by Grabham and Catchpole, he knew these officers full well, and would have taken to his heels had he caught sight of them.

At last he ventured up the steps and knocked at a wicket.

"Now then," growled a voice. "What now?"

Dick Sleuth pulled a long face, and squeezed a couple of grimy tears from his eyes.

"I am in great distress about a brother-in-law of mine," he said, "and I am afraid that he has got into trouble."

---

112 Newgate Prison.

"What is his name?" the turnkey demanded, gruffly.

"Bill Blarney."

"Then you have come to the right shop, for his trial for highway robbery, among other things, will probably be on to-morrow."

"Oh! how dreadful," Sleuth cried, flinging up his hands. "What can I do? What would you advise me to do?"

"Shake hands with him, and say 'good-bye,' for he's booked."

As the warder spoke he whistled the air of a song he was learning to sing, and he rattled an accompaniment with a bunch of huge keys.

"Can—can I see the prisoner?" Dick Sleuth asked, overwhelmed with grief.

"Oh! yes, I daresay you can; but don't kick up that howling, for a man can only die once," the warder said. "Bill Blarney has had his fling, and I don't see what he has to grumble at, nor his friends either."

He threw open the door, and Dick Sleuth stole in.

There was something deathly in the very atmosphere of the prison, and Dick Sleuth, hardened to scenes of crime and misery as he was, shuddered and wished himself back again into the fresh, pure air.

He was received by another warder, who passed him on to yet another, and so on, until he was made acquainted with the fact that he was standing before the door of a cell which prevented Bill Blarney from following an exciting and often profitable mode of taking care of other people's money.

"Here's your dearly beloved brother-in-law come to see you," said the turnkey, who had brought Dick Sleuth to the spot. "Come, Blarney, don't look so down in the mouth. We all said that you would die game. Don't deceive us."

Bill Blarney stretched out his hand to Sleuth and forced a smile upon his lips.

"I suppose we can be left alone a few minutes?" he said.

"Yes; if your friend will satisfy me that he has nothing about him."

"What should I have about me?" demanded Sleuth, rolling up his eyes.

"Short, handy crowbars, files, screwdrivers, wrenches, and the like."

"Oh! I'll soon satisfy you on that score," said Dick Sleuth, throwing open his coat. "You may search me, if you choose."

The turnkey eyed him up and down, and, seeing that there was nothing bulky about his wearing apparel, walked out of the cell and locked the door behind him.

"Speak low," Bill Blarney said. "Thick as these walls are, there are ears which can hear through them."

"Well," Dick Sleuth returned, "I came here to learn how you got into this precious mess, and how you intend to get out of it."

Bill Blarney told how he had been caught, but as to escaping—that was quite another matter.

"I don t see how it is to be done!" he groaned. "Look at these irons—they drag me down, and a warder looks at them every hour to see that they are all right."

"Why didn't you let us know where you were?"

"Because I couldn't without money," Bill Blarney replied. "It costs a guinea down to get a warder to step over the road, and then the chances are that he would get drunk with your money and never deliver the message."

"Well," said Dick Sleuth, "our old friend at the Bull in Top-Boots has come down handsome. He has given me twenty guineas for your use. Now, the next question is, which is the best way to employ it?"

"I don't know," Bill Blarney groaned. "I don't see the good of it at all. All the counsel in the world couldn't get me off, for, you see, I was taken red-handed."

He whined out his words, and Dick Sleuth looked at him in disgust.

"Come, don't be a child," he said. "Money can do almost anything in the world. Can't you think of any idea?"

"No, I can't."

"Then I must for you."

"Do you think there is any hope?"

"There may be; but just listen to me."

Bill Blarney sat down, and as he did so the irons about his limbs clanked ominously.

"They ain't nice things to wear," Dick Sleuth said, "and I dare say you find them uncomfortable bed fellows."

"That's the worst part of it," Bill Blarney replied. "If they would take the beastly things off at night I shouldn't mind so much. But now for your idea. My brain is too confused to think of anything properly."

"Are you on friendly terms with your turnkey?" Dick Sleuth asked.

"Yes; or at least I think so."

"Well, then," Sleuth continued, "didn't you notice how he looked at me when he spoke about the crowbars and such like?"

"No."

"But I did, and I'll tell you what, Bill; that man would be your friend for a sum of money down and a bit more when you are free."

"Do you think so?"

"I am sure of it."

"But who is to put such a question to him?" said Bill Blarney. "Supposing he scorned the offer and blew the gaff? I should be done for, then, to a certainty."

"No doubt about it."

"Well, then, between two stools I am likely to fall to the ground."

Dick Sleuth made an attempt at a ghastly joke and seemed to enjoy it.

"No," he said; "I don't think you would fall so far, unless the rope broke."

Bill Blarney's countenance changed from white to green, and he shuddered as it he had been suddenly immersed in ice-cold water.

"I wish you wouldn't talk to me in that way," he said.

"I thought it would cheer you up a bit," Dick Sleuth replied, chuckling. "Well, well! we will say no more about it. How do you call the turnkey?"

"By kicking at the door."

"Then we'll have him in."

The turnkey answered the summons, and asked gruffly why he had been sent for.

"I wish to thank you for your great kindness to my unfortunate brother-in-law," Dick Sleuth said.

"Your brother-in law. Ha, ha!"

"Why do you laugh?"

"Because I know that you are nothing of the kind."

"Why don't you call me a liar at once and have done with it?"

"I will, if you like," the turnkey said. "If that is all you have to say to me it isn't much. Your time is up and you must come with me."

"Stop a moment," said Dick Sleuth. "Don't be in such a violent hurry."

"But I must, for I have other business to attend to."

Dick Sleuth paid no more heed to this remark than if it had never reached his ears.

He took a handful of guineas in one hand and began to count them into the other.

The turnkey was visibly affected.

His eyes sparkled and he brushed his hand across his mouth, as if the sight of the gleaming gold made it water.

"I not only wish to thank you," Dick Sleuth said, speaking plainly, and emphasising every word, "but to make you a present. Here are ten guineas for you, and there will be ten more if you do me a little favour."

"What is it?"

"Need you ask?" Dick Sleuth rejoined.

The turnkey tried to look innocent, but he looked hard at Blarney, and Blarney jangled the irons upon his legs.

"I think I understand," the turnkey said.

"Of course you do," said Dick Sleuth and Bill Blarney in a breath. "Will you do it?"

"Yes."

And I suppose I may go away and tell my friends that—"

"Tell them nothing," the turnkey interposed; "but you may tell me something. Where am I to come to fetch the rest of the money?"

"Do you know a house called the Bull in Top Boots, in the Borough?"

"Rather."

"Then that's exactly the place where the balance will be paid to you."

The turnkey said no more and Dick Sleuth went his way rejoicing at having succeeded in his mission and not a little proud of his own display of tact.

The sun was going down, and the shadow of the dismal prison was lengthened when the turnkey visited Bill Blarney again.

The prisoner was sitting crouched up in a corner of his cell, but he rose as the man entered.

"Go back to your place," the turnkey said, "and keep quiet."

Bill Blarney slunk back like a dog, and sat holding his breath, wondering what would happen next.

The turnkey had brought a lantern with him, which he set down on the floor and glanced round the cell.

"Blarney," he said, "if ever a man risked his life for another I am about to do so for you."

"I know it," Blarney began, "and—"

"Don't speak yet," the turnkey said, interrupting him, "and don't move after I am gone. When you hear St. Sepulchre's clock strike twelve, you may get up. Place your irons on the bench, and you will find the door open."

"What then?" Blarney said. "Will the coast be clear?"

SPRING-HEELED JACK,
THE TERROR OF LONDON.

"SILENCE, GIRL, OR YOU DIE!" SIR ROLAND CRIED.

"Yes," the turnkey replied. "It will be as clear as a bell as far as the yard. Go to the western corner, and you will find a rope dangling from the wall. I need not tell you what to do then."

The turnkey opened the cell door again, and, having made sure that there was nobody about, returned to Blarney, and so loosened his irons that, had he not held them, they would have fallen to the ground.

Now Bill Blarney seemed to live an age between hope and fear.

The hours which had passed so quickly now dragged themselves snail-like along.

It was scarcely nine o'clock and there were three more hours to wait.

The hands of the clock seemed to travel backwards instead of forwards, and when ten o'clock struck Blarney felt that he had lived through years of suspense.

He thought that some other warder might enter the cell, or that the governor might take it into his head to make a tour of inspection.

Though the cell was cold Bill Blarney's blood almost boiled, and profuse streams of perspiration poured down his face.

At last the time came for him to make a move. Gathering up the irons carefully, he placed them noiselessly on the bench.

Then, removing his boots, he crept noiselessly across the floor of the cell and placed his hand upon the door.

It yielded to his touch; but the hinges were old and rusty, and as they creaked, Bill Blarney started back in terror.

With bated breath he waited, fully expecting that two or more warders would spring upon him.

But nothing of the sort happened, and, after a long and painful pause, he opened the door and looked up and down the passage.

The coast was clear, and the only sound that came to his ears was a sigh or groan from some miserable prisoner.

With cat-like movements Bill Blarney reached the yard, and wending his way to the western corner, found the rope dangling from the top of the wall.

It was a stout piece of hemp, and knotted at intervals so as to make the ascent more easy.

Bill Blarney clutched the rope frantically, and went up hand over hand.

As he threw his legs astride the wall a deep-drawn sigh came from his lips.

He looked down into the street where the oil-lamps glimmered feebly, and was in the act of pulling the rope over, when he saw a man enter the yard.

Bill Blarney shut his eyes as he clutched the wall with his hands and prepared to drop.

The distance was great, and he might break a limb; but there was no time to waste in suppositions, and, letting go his hold, he descended, falling upon his feet.

At the same moment an alarm was given.

The man in the yard fired a pistol into the air, and a bell rang violently.

Though half-stunned and sickened by the concussion he had received in his fall Bill Blarney gathered himself up and took to his heels.

His only security lay in immediate flight, for death stared him in the face, and he ran as he had never ran before.

Twisting, turning, and doubling like a hare pursued by greyhounds, he turned out of

Snow-hill and found himself in a labyrinth of courts and alleys.

Dashing down a dark entry, he discovered that it had no thoroughfare, and hid himself half-fainting in the deep shadow of an old porch.

Presently he heard a footstep, and glancing at the door he saw that it was open, and that a man, bearing a lantern in his hand, was coming out.

CHAPTER LXIII.

JACOB BUTLER FALLS AGAIN.

WHILE these events were passing there were strange doings at the Queen's Head, near Sadler's-wells.

Constance Marfield and Daisy Leigh were on thorns about Ralph Ashton, and at the very moment that they thought something serious must have happened to him he arrived.

He came clad in a splendid suit of velvet, and mounted on a powerful roan horse.

The moment he appeared Ben Jordan, the landlord, ran out and whispered something in his ear.

Ralph only smiled and nodded, for he was all impatience to clasp Constance in his arms.

She met him with a wild cry of joy, and then almost fainted as she hid her pale face on his breast.

"Courage, my darling!" he whispered. "I regret that I have been so long away, but it was no fault of mine. There is yet danger and mischief abroad, and you must remain here."

"Danger! Mischief!" Constance repeated. "Oh! Ralph, those words mean that you must leave me again."

"I am afraid I must," Ralph Ashton said, sorrowfully; "but I shall triumph at last, and our reward will be peace and sweet happiness. Where is Daisy?"

"In the next room."

"And Jacob Butler?"

Constance Marfield laughed.

"I don't exactly know," she replied. "He is a strange man, but faithful, I believe. He has one failing, and that is taking too much drink."

Ralph Ashton frowned.

"That is a failing he must get over," he said, "unless he wishes to displease me. Daisy Leigh—Daisy Leigh!"

Daisy came running out of the adjoining room, and gave Ralph Ashton a hearty greeting.

"I did not like to disturb you," she said, archly. "Mr. Ashton, we have looked upon you as a wilful truant."

"And I am afraid that you will have to form that opinion again," he said, "for I must go away again to-night."

"To-night?" Constance Marfield repeated.

"Yes," Ralph returned. "Come, come! Constance, you must know that I am doing everything for the best. You trust me—do you not?"

"From my innermost heart," she replied; "but I can scarcely bear to part with you."

They sat down in the old-fashioned room, and Constance told Ralph of her abduction and marvellous escape.

"Yes," he said, "the story is not new to me."

409

"Not new to you!" Constance exclaimed. "Who could have told you?"

"The very man who has done me many a good service," Ralph Ashton replied, smiling quietly. "Spring-Heeled Jack."

At that moment a timid knock came at the door.

"Come in!" said Ralph Ashton.

Jacob Butler put his head and shoulders into the room, and his face wore an expression so woebegone, and yet so comical withal, that Ralph Ashton and the ladies could scarcely refrain from laughing outright.

"Well," said Ralph Ashton, "I hear that you have been in tribulation?"

"Tribulation isn't the word for it, sir," Jacob replied. "I have been through such things that now I wonder whether they really happened or not."

"The man who drinks heavily and makes a complete fool of himself is sure to get into trouble," Ralph Ashton said.

He eyed Jacob Butler keenly as he spoke, and Jacob hung his head and looked sheepish.

"Well, said Ralph Ashton, "as you seem to wish to speak to me, tell me what it is?"

"I want to know my position clearly," Jacob replied. "Am I to serve you or Spring-Heeled Jack?"

"You will serve me while I am here, and Spring-Heeled Jack when he calls on you to do so."

"Oh!" said Jacob, rubbing his head, and casting a vague glance at the ceiling. "That leaves me almost as wise as ever; but I suppose I must be satisfied with the answer."

"At all events, you will get no other," Ralph Ashton said; "and if you wish to preserve your peace of mind, you will pay-attention to what I have said."

Jacob Butler, finding that his presence was not required any longer, withdrew himself from the room, and went below.

Ben Jordan was standing with folded arms and gazing through the open window into the roadway.

"Ha! ha!" he laughed. "Well?"

"Eh! What?" Jacob ejaculated. "What are you laughing at?"

"Oh! nothing," Jordan replied. "I thought you might have something to say, that's all."

"I'm losing the power of language as well as the power of thought," Jacob returned mournfully. "I feel sometimes that I could dash my thick head against the wall."

"Why don't you? It might do you good. Will you have a nip?"

Jacob shook his head, but the gleam in his eyes betrayed the wish which was in his heart.

"Well, only one," he said.

"Just so," said the landlord, passing a glass and bottle; "and then take a walk."

Jacob Butler shuddered and turned pale.

"I don't mean to Hampstead," the landlord said, laughing. "You needn't go quite so far."

"If you ever refer to that again," Jacob Butler gasped, "I'll—I'll throw something heavy at you!"

Ben Jordan placed his hands upon his hips and roared with laughter.

"I can picture you and that old woman," he said; "but what an odd story it was she told you."

"I wish she had never lived to tell it!" Jacob said, viciously. "How would you like such a fiend in petticoats to persecute you?"

"I think I should find some means of keeping out of her way," Ben Jordan said. "Ah! well, we won't talk any more about the matter, as I see it pains you. I suppose they are pretty happy upstairs—eh?"

"Happy!" Jacob cried, clasping his hands. "Oh! that such a fate was mine."

"Here is health, long life, and happiness to all three!" said the landlord. "Drink!"

Jacob Butler did so, and emptied his glass. The liquor went down in such a hurry that he scarcely tested it, and when the landlord asked him to replenish his glass he did not say no.

"I say," Jacob exclaimed, "you have made this dose precious strong!"

"Yes, because it is the last."

It so happened that a masquerade was to be held at Sadler's Wells that evening, and as soon as dusk came a number of men set about lighting the coloured lamps, which might be counted by thousands.

Jacob Butler watched the scene as it grew in magnitude and beauty, and an irresistible longing came over him to go out and mingle with the gaily and strangely-attired people who now began to arrive.

As he was ruminating whether Mrs. Corcoran might not assume some disguise and attend the masquerade Ralph Ashton came downstairs.

"My horse," said he to the ostler. "I must away."

"So soon?" Jacob Butler ventured to remark.

"And why not, pray?" Ralph Ashton said, turning sharply upon him. "Am I to ask you when I am to come and go?"

"Bless me! no, sir," Jacob exclaimed, starting back in alarm. "I only thought—"

"Keep your thoughts to yourself," Ralph interposed, "and be still more secret in your thoughts and actions. Do you understand?"

"Yes, sir."

"Then take my advice."

So saying, Ralph Ashton disappeared out of the house, and in a few minutes was riding towards London.

"I've done something to offend him," Jacob Butler said, miserably, as he tugged at his hair. "I suppose I was born under an unlucky star. I never open my mouth without putting my foot in it."

Jacob had some thoughts of running away altogether; but where was he to go to?

He was only too well aware that Mrs. Corcoran would pursue him with all the energy of her witch-like nature, and that if he ever fell in her power again she would either put an end to his life or carry out her promise and marry him, which would be quite as bad, if not worse.

"I'm a miserable man," he moaned. "Nobody cares for me, and I wish I was dead."

"Don't make a fool of yourself," said Ben Jordan, who overheard the last remark. "Take a run out, and go to bed as soon as you come back."

At that moment a band of music commenced playing, and lured on by the soft, melodious strains, Jacob Butler sallied forth, and soon mingled with the vast crowd of masqueraders.

He had never seen such a sight in all his life, and Jacob soon forgot all his troubles in the novelty of the scene.

As he was watching a party of cavaliers, who seemed extremely attentive to an equal number of masked ladies, he felt himself touched on the shoulder.

Jacob turned and found himself confronted by a tall man, wearing a long coat down to his heels, and a conical hat.

The upper part of his face was masked, but the lower was sallow, and a well-waxed moustache bristled on his lip.

Jacob wondered who the man was and what he wanted with him.

"I think you have made a mistake," he said feebly.

"No, *mon ami*—my friend," was the reply. "And yet, pardon. You wear no mask, and, thinking you might have lost it by accident, I called your attention—"

"I didn't come with a mask," said Jacob, interrupting him. "I happen to be staying in the neighbourhood, so I thought I would stroll in and see what was going on."

"Pardon—ten thousand pardons!" said the man, who, by his accent, proclaimed himself to be of foreign origin. "Will you drink?"

A sudden thought flashed into Jacob's brain, and he hesitated before replying.

He had been warned not to talk to strangers, and he cast a hasty glance over his shoulder to ascertain that he was not being watched by anybody from the Queen's Head.

"Well, you see," he said, "I should like to, but—"

"Oh! let us have no 'buts,'" said the stranger, taking him by the arm. "Life is too short to think twice about sharing a bottle of wine with a man. Let us be merry. Ah! this is a charming scene. It shall never be said in my presence that you English are a sad people."

He led Jacob away, half-resisting and half-consenting, and entered a tent erected at one end of the grounds.

Jacob Butler thought that he saw his companion make a sign to a man dressed like a monk, but he paid little heed to the circumstance, as it was none of his business.

The tent contained refreshments of the most luxurious description, and the foreigner, having called a waiter, ordered a bottle of rare old wine.

Jacob Butler now began to think that he had fallen into a good thing, and, raising his glass, he was about to pledge his hospitable friend when he was again tapped on the shoulder.

With some notion that he would find Spring-Heeled Jack at his side, and filled with terror at the thought, Jacob Butler turned his head slowly.

As he did so the foreigner sprinkled something in the glass of wine.

"I wonder who that was!"

"I saw nobody," said the foreigner.

"I—could swear that somebody touched me," Jacob stammered.

"Very likely. There is a great crowd here. It was an accident. Think no more of it, my friend. Come, let us drink!"

They did so, and as they set down their glasses empty, the foreigner removed his mask, and placed it on the table.

The face that Jacob now saw was that of Jules Carleon.

His bright eyes twinkled, and the end of his moustache went up as he refilled Jacob's glass.

"I like you," he said. "Let us be friends—at least, for the rest of the evening."

"It's very kind of you to say so," Jacob Butler replied. "But I can't think why you should choose to take so much notice of me."

He pressed his hand to his brow with a quick yet uncertain movement, and the Frenchman watched him keenly.

"Listen," he said, leaning across the table, and placing his hand upon Jacob's shoulder in a friendly fashion. "You are a poor man. Pardon—I do not wish to offend you."

"Oh! you don't offend me," Jacob replied. "I am poor—poor as a church mouse, and my master, for some reason best known to himself, keeps me very short of money."

"Who is your master?"

Jacob Butler shook his head.

"I can't tell you that," he said, beginning to stare vaguely about him. "I've been sworn to secrecy as to that, and wild horses couldn't drag it out of me."

"Well, well," Jules Carleon returned, "I will not press you, because it is a matter of no interest to me. But you said you were poor. Well, I am rich, and part of the mission of my life is to make other people happy."

"You must be a jolly good sort of fellow."

"You English have a hearty way of expressing yourselves," Jules Carleon said, as he took the wine-bottle in his hand. "Let me fill your glass again. No? Is not the wine good?"

"It is too good," replied Jacob, whose eyes were sparkling and dancing in his head. "It makes me feel so happy and yet so strange. Your voice comes to me as in a dream."

"Ah! said Jules Carleon. "How delicious! What would the world be without wine, love, and music? Did you say that Constance Marfield was pretty, and that Daisy Leigh was charming?"

Jacob Butler started and pressed his hands to his temples.

"What!" he exclaimed. "Did I mention their names?"

"Yes, my friend—yes."

"When?"

"Just now."

"Then I must be mad, or going mad," Jacob gasped. "Curse the wine! I wish that not a drop of it had passed my lips. Let me go—let me go, I say!"

He struggled to rise, but Jules Carleon's hand was upon his shoulder and detained him.

"Bah!" said the Frenchman. "What have I to do with these ladies, save that I love them one and all?"

Jacob's head fell forward, and he began to breathe heavily.

Then the man disguised as a monk advanced and stood at Jules Carleon's side.

"You have done the trick well," he said, in a low tone of voice.

"Yes," Jules Carleon replied. "He will answer any question I like to put to him now; but I must be quick or he will slumber too deeply. What shall I ask him?"

"Where he came from," said the monk, as he glared savagely at Jacob. "Call him by his name."

"My friend—Jacob Butler," said Jules Carleon, whispering softly in the drugged man's ear, "tell me where you are staying?"

"At the Queen's Head," Jacob replied.

"Good!" said the monk; "that is all I want to know. Come away."

Jules Carleon laughed quietly as he rose from his chair, and, following the monk, they left the gay throng, and entering a carriage, were driven rapidly away.

A few minutes later on a waiter approached the table and gave Jacob Butler such a shaking up that his teeth chattered in his head.

"Now, then, timber lids," the waiter growled, "this table is wanted by other people, who are hungry and thirsty."

Jacob Butler only snored.

"He's as sound as a roach," the waiter said; "but surely half-a-bottle of wine can't account for the state he is in. Here! Hi! Wake up, will you! Open your peepers,[113] and cut your stick, or I'll hand you over to the tender mercies of a constable."

Jacob Butler opened a corner of one very fishy-looking eye, and closing it again, snored louder than ever.

"This is a pretty business," said the waiter, looking round. "Does anybody know who he is!"

Nobody knew and nobody seemed to care; but some young gentlemen bent on having as much fun as possible out of the evening, suggested that it would be an excellent thing to blacken Jacob's face and stand him on his head in a corner of the tent.

This probably would have been done had it not been for the appearance of two constables, and, unluckily for Jacob Butler, they happened to be our old friends, Catchpole and Grabham.

As they glared at the recumbent form of the man they had met at Lilac Lodge, the memory of their wrongs came back to them.

"All right," said Grabham, savagely, "we'll take of him. Stand back, ladies and gentlemen, if you please. This man is mad drunk, and there's no knowing what mischief he may do if he wakes suddenly!"

Lifting Jacob up in their arms in no gentle fashion they bore him away.

As soon as they got clear of the crowd Grabham vented his spleen on the unconscious fool by giving him half-a-dozen sound kicks.

"Now," said the constable, "we'll stow him away in the lock-up, and lead him a pretty life as soon as he comes to himself."

CHAPTER LXIV.

THE OLD WATER-MILL ON THE RIVER LEA.

IT WILL be seen by what took place in the gardens adjoining Sadler's Wells that Sir Roland Ashton and Jules Carleon had returned to London.

This was at Sir Roland's express wish, for after having seen the shadow of Mrs. Corcoran on the blind, he made certain that the hag was either alive, or that her restless spirit had been sent from the grave to haunt him.

In vain did Jules Carleon urge that it was all fallacy on the baronet's part.

Sir Roland refused to listen to all arguments, and his one great desire being to leave the country, Jules Carleon consented to accompany him to town.

When they arrived the notice of the masquerade attracted Sir Roland's attention, and he determined to take Jules Carleon with him.

There it was that they fell in with Jacob Butler.

The moment that Sir Roland saw that most miserable of men he put Jules Carleon on the track, and with what result the reader already knows.

---

[113] Eyes.

"So," said Sir Roland, as they were driven away, "Constance Marfield and Daisy Leigh are staying at the Queen's Head. Good! And now, how to trap them. I am convinced that Ralph Ashton cannot be far away."

"Undoubtedly!" assented Jules Carleon, who by this time had been made acquainted with all particulars up to date. "As you say, Sir Roland, Ralph Ashton is not far away, but he cannot always be at the Queen's Head. I will watch the place, and keep a sharp eye on Ralph Ashton's movements."

"What will be the good of that!" Sir Roland demanded, gloomily.

Jules Carleon laughed, and snapped his fingers contemptuously.

"You English have a saying that there is more than one way to kill a goose," he returned, "and I am going to show you the way to kill this particular goose."

"How?" Sir Roland demanded. "I do not understand you."

"You know this Ralph Ashton well?"

"Only too well—curse him!"

"Have you any letters from him in your possession?"

"Yes," said Sir Roland, bitterly. "What then? Still, I do not understand you."

"How dull you are!" Jules Carleon returned, abruptly. "What would be easier than to imitate Ralph Ashton's signature, and to send a pretty little note to one or both of the ladies? This very carriage could bring them to you. Ha! ha!"

"Your plan is a good one," Sir Roland said, meditatively; "but what if the forged letter fell into Ralph Ashton's hands?"

"I will see that such a thing does not take place," Jules Carleon replied. "Only give me *carte blanche* to do as I please, and success will follow."

"Agreed!" said Sir Roland.

On the following morning, as Ben Jordan, the landlord of the Queen's Head, was putting the bar to-rights, Jules Carleon entered, and called for a measure of wine.

Ben Jordan looked the Frenchman up and down with a critical eye.

There was something about him that Ben did not like, and he served him, took a guinea, and gave the change in silence.

"An old-fashioned place this," Jules Carleon said. "I had some difficulty in finding my way here."

"Had you," Ben Jordan rejoined. "I suppose you are a stranger? My ears tell me that you are a foreigner."

"But I have lived so long in this country that I consider myself an Englishman."

"You may consider yourself what you like," Ben Jordan observed, surlily. "Do what you will you can't turn a foreigner into an Englishman, or an Englishman into a foreigner. It's against nature and common sense."

Jules Carleon smiled as he raised his glass to his lips.

"True, my friend, true," he observed; "but when a man gets used to a country and the ways of its people, he is apt to forget that he belongs to any other sort."

"There you are right," Ben Jordan said. "I know that when a foreigner gets his nose in this country he is in no hurry to take it out again."

Jules Carleon's moustache bristled, and a flush of crimson suffused his face.

It was gone in a moment, however, and he laughed as he finished his wine and called for more.

"Will you drink with me?" he asked.

"No."

"And why not?"

"Because I only drink with my friends," Ben Jordan said.

"My new master told me that I should find you a silent, careful man," Jules Carleon returned. "You would not only drink with me, but shake me by the hand, if you knew from whom I came.

"And pray who may that be?"

Jules Carleon glanced over his shoulder and put on an air of mystery.

"Perhaps it will not be as well to say," he whispered. "But see here. Tell me whether you know this writing?"

As he spoke, he took a sealed packet from his pocket, and held it up before Ben Jordan's eyes.

The packet was addressed to Daisy Leigh, and as the landlord of the Queen's Head glanced at the writing a sudden and startling expression came over his face.

"How!" he exclaimed. "You come from Mr. Ralph Ashton?"

"Yes," Jules Carleon replied. "Last night my master met Jacob Butler, and pressed him into some service of which I do not know the nature, and sent me hither. I am to wait for an answer."

Ben Jordan had no alternative but to believe the villain's story.

There was Ralph's writing he had seen a hundred times, and moreover Jacob Butler had not returned on the previous night.

"Stay here," Jordan said; "I will take the letter up to the lady."

The moment that Ben Jordan turned his back Jules Carleon peered into the back parlour, and finding that it was empty he rubbed his hands, and chuckled under his breath.

Drawing a long gleaming dagger from under his cloak he slipped it into his belt.

"I must be careful, in case that the bait does not take," he muttered. "*Parbleu!* it would go hard with any man who attempted to stop my way to the door."

Ben Jordan went upstairs and knocked at the door of the sitting-room occupied by the ladies.

Daisy Leigh's voice answered him, and in another moment the sealed packet was in her hands.

"How strange!" she said. "Ralph said nothing about writing to me."

"Open it," Constance rejoined, impatiently. "I feel convinced that the communication must be of an important nature."

Daisy did as she was requested, and read aloud—

> "*DEAR DAISY,—In the first place give my undying love to Constance, and tell her that I have at last found a place of safety for her and you. The bearer of this will bring you to me and then return for Constance. I have my own reasons for wishing you to come first, which I am sure you will not inquire into. As you have trusted me, so trust me now. I have heard from good authority that that villain, Sir Roland, is in London. Jacob Butler is with me, and I intend to keep him under my eye, for fear that he might make a fool of himself, as he has often done. Hesitate not, but come at once. The bearer will conduct you to a carriage which I have arranged shall wait for you and him near the Angel Inn.— Yours, with every kind wish,*
>
> "*RALPH ASHTON.*"

Constance Marfield took the letter in her hand, and read it through herself.

"There can be no mistake about this," she said; "but yet it is strange that Ralph does not say where you are to go to."

"Well," said Ben Jordan, who still lingered near the door, "if I might make a remark, it would be to the effect that Mr. Ashton thought his messenger might lose the letter, or be stopped on the road and robbed of it.

"Of course," said Daisy. "That is my own opinion, but would it not be better to see the messenger and put the question to him?"

"Certainly," said Ben Jordan. "I will fetch him up in an instant."

He found Jules Carleon standing in a listless attitude, such as a man waiting for a reply a to letter might assume.

"Follow me," Ben Jordan said. "One of the ladies wishes to speak to you."

Jules Carleon did not hesitate for a moment, and as he stood before Constance and Daisy he removed his hat and bowed humbly.

"Where have you been instructed to take me?" Daisy asked.

The Frenchman shrugged his shoulders.

"That is a question I thought mademoiselle would ask," he rejoined, "but it is one that I cannot answer."

"What reason have you for refusing?"

"Because Mr. Ashton made me take an oath that I would not breathe it to a living soul," Jules Carleon replied.

"But I do not know you," Daisy said. "How am I to know that this letter is not a forgery, and that you have been sent to betray me into the hands of an enemy?"

No change came over the Frenchman's face.

He merely spread out his fingers, shrugged his shoulders, and inclined his head with a deprecating gesture.

"You do not speak?" Daisy said.

"Your words took me by surprise," Jules Carleon replied. "Your enemies! Ha! is it possible that one so young and beautiful can have enemies? I have done my duty, and if you mistrust me, mademoiselle, I must return alone, and leave Mr. Ashton to judge of your refusal."

As he spoke he bowed again, and walked towards the door.

"The man is honest," Constance whispered; "go with him."

"Stay," Daisy said; "I am sorry if I have hurt your feelings. I will get ready and be with you in a few minutes."

Jules Carleon did not seem surprised or pleased.

It appeared to be a matter of perfect indifference to him whether Daisy Leigh went with him or stayed where she was, and he walked calmly back into the bar and finished his wine.

Thus thrown off her guard Daisy Leigh commenced dressing for the journey.

Constance Marfield assisted her, and, in a few minutes, she was ready.

"We shall not be apart for many hours," Daisy said, as she kissed her fair companion, "and yet even that short space of time will be too long. Good-bye. I shall count the moments until I see you again."

When she descended Jules Carleon held the door open, and followed a few paces in the rear.

He did not attempt to speak to her or walk at her side until the Angel, then an old-fashioned coaching inn, was reached.

A carriage with drawn blinds was standing under the archway, and Jules Carleon hailed the driver by holding up his hand.

Daisy Leigh had some slight misgivings as she entered the equipage; but she banished them, and as the horses started she drew up one of the blinds and, leaning back, looked out into the road.

Jules Carleon had shared the box seat with the driver, and for more than an hour the horses trotted on in a leisurely way, as if instructions had been given not to hurry them.

The open country was soon reached, and the day being deliciously fine, Daisy drank in the fresh, pure air, and felt extremely happy.

She loved the country with its fields and woods, and a new and brighter colour came into her cheeks.

Onward, still onward, the horses went, until they were brought to a standstill at a roadside inn.

Jules Carleon got down and held the door open.

"Mademoiselle will dine here and rest," he said.

"But I would rather go on," Daisy replied. "Our destination cannot be far distant?"

"We are half-way," the Frenchman replied; "and, mademoiselle, the horses must be fed and groomed."

Daisy said no more, but, alighting, permitted Jules Carleon to conduct her into a room, with a pretty window overlooking the river.

A sumptuous repast had been prepared, and Jules Carleon waited on Daisy at the table, passing the dishes and removing them with a trained hand.

He glided about like a shadow, and never spoke unless he was spoken to.

Daisy Leigh could not help being favourably impressed with the man's conduct, and she felt sorry that she had ever spoken sharply to him, or regarded him with a suspicious thought.

Two hours passed away, and the sun was going down when the carriage was brought round to the door.

Jules Carleon summoned Daisy with as much ceremony as if she had been a princess, and the journey was continued in the same quiet manner as it was commenced.

Now that Daisy had banished all fears and suspicions she began to look forward to meeting Ralph Ashton.

She was sure that he had some astonishing news to tell her, and was eager to hear it.

Sir Roland was in London, and perhaps he had discovered that she and Constance were sheltered under the roof of the Queen's Head, and if that was the case, Ralph's conduct could be easily accounted for.

The shades of night were falling as the carriage turned into a long, narrow lane, overhung with gloomy-looking trees.

Every now and then Daisy caught a glimpse of water through the foliage, and in spite of herself, the old misgivings forced themselves upon her mind.

She was wondering whether the journey would ever come to an end, when she heard a curious splashing noise, and looking out of the window saw that it was caused by the revolving of a water-wheel, over which towered an old wooden mill, overgrown with moss and creeping plants.

It was a gruesome looking place enough, and Daisy withdrew her head and shuddered.

As she did so the carriage came to a standstill, and in an instant Jules Carleon opened the door.

His lips were parted now with a triumphant »mile, and his eyes gleamed and flashed like living coals.

"Mademoiselle," he said, hoarsely, "your journey is at an end, and that," he added, pointing to the mill, "will be your home until a better one is provided."

"That place!" Daisy cried, shrinking back in horror. "No—no! You must be mistaken."

"Indeed, I am not," Jules Carleon replied. "But come. I see Mr. Ashton approaching to meet us."

Daisy Leigh hesitated no longer.

She saw a man approaching and ran forward to meet him.

He caught her in his arms, and pushing aside the broad-brimmed hat which had hitherto concealed his features, revealed the face of Sir Roland Ashton.

"Oh! help! Mercy! Help!" the girl cried, struggling in the villain's embrace. "Oh! horror. This must be a dream! I am mad—mad!"

"Nay, my pretty birdie!" Sir Roland said. "Forgive me for thus caging you, but your cage shall be a golden one. One more kiss—only one more."

Daisy screamed her loudest and buffetted the baronet's face with her dainty hands, but he took no more notice of the blows than if they had been delivered with feathers.

"Help! Help!" Daisy shrieked. "Is there no man of honour here to protect a helpless girl?"

"Sir Roland!" said Jules Carleon. "Her cries may be heard. To the mill with her."

"Help! Help!"

"Silence!" Sir Roland hissed in Daisy's ear. "Silence, or you will find yourself in the water. It flows to the wheel, and the wheel crushes everything it comes in contact with."

"Would you murder me?" Daisy panted.

"Aye!" Sir Roland replied. "I am not the man to stand upon trifles. Silence, girl, or you cease to live."

Both he and Jules Carleon were holding her now, and Daisy's struggles had brought all three to the water's edge.

Again the terrified girl rent the air with her cries, and struggled with the strength of terror and despair.

"You die!" Sir Roland yelled. "Cease struggling, or you die."

At that moment there was a commotion in the water, and a white ghostly form shot under the surface.

It rose and leaped ashore, and Spring-Heeled Jack, reaching Sir Roland with one bound, felled him to the earth.

"Ha! ha! ha!" laughed the weird creature. "So I have arrived just in time. Fiend!" he shouted, turning on Jules Carleon, and seizing him by the throat. "Go to your well-deserved doom."

An unearthly cry went up as Carleon fell with a heavy splash into the water, and as he battled with the swift current Daisy Leigh fell fainting into the arms of Spring-Heeled Jack.

CHAPTER LXV.
JACOB BUTLER DISCOVERS THAT HE IS IN THE HANDS
OF A PAIR OF TARTARS—THE LOCK-OP, AND WHAT HAPPENED IN IT.

JACOB BUTLER lay perfectly still when he awoke.

Where he was he had not the slightest notion, and the only thing that he was aware of was that he was lying upon his back, with something on his wrists that hampered their movements.

By degrees a confused train of thoughts dawned into his brain.

He remembered leaving the Queen's Head, meeting with somebody who gave him wine, that was all.

"Hang it!" he said. "What is this upon my wrists? Oh! lor', I'm handcuffed."

As this fact became palpable Jacob endeavoured to stand upon his feet, but he found that they had also been secured.

"I must be in some dungeon," he groaned; "and here I shall be until I am murdered."

Then an awful thought occurred to him.

Mrs. Corcoran had perhaps caught him again, and manacled his limbs against all hope of escape!

"I'm done for now," he said. "I shall never recover from this shock, and the sooner I am dead the better."

A fresh pang of terror darted into his heart as he heard a key turn in the lock, and the door swing open.

Whoever the visitor was it was not Mrs. Corcoran, for though the hag's voice was rough and grating it was not one of such double-bass tones as Jacob Butler heard.

A light flashed upon his face, and simultaneously a heavy boot was applied to his ribs.

"How are you by this time?" said Grabham, staring down and grinning at his prisoner. "Ha! ha! ha! How are you now, eh?"

Jacob felt considerably relieved when he saw that it was only a constable.

"I don't know that I am any the better for seeing you," he replied, "and perhaps you'll keep your boots to yourself!"

Mr. Grabham gave Jacob another kick, which made him wriggle like an eel.

"Catchpole!" Grabham shouted, "he's come round and looks lovely. Come and have a look at him!"

Catchpole ran into the cell, and in the exuberance of his joy he took a good handful of Jacob's hair and tugged at it viciously.

"Oh! you brutes—you unmanly brutes!" Jacob gasped. "What have I ever done to you that you should treat me like this? Take these things off my hands and legs, or I'll report you to the authorities."

"You'll do what?"

"Report you to the authorities."

Grabham clenched his fist and pushed it with such violence against Jacob Butler's nose that tears of anguish rushed from his eyes.

"Oh! you hound—you devil!" Jacob gasped. "What am I to suffer next?"

Catchpole manifested a strong inclination to take possession of Jacob's hair again, but he refrained.

"Take them things off you!" Grabham said. "Oh! yes; that's likely, certainly. You're a dangerous character, and must be treated accordingly. I suppose you don't remember threatening our lives with a knife, which you picked off the table?"

"No; and I don't believe that I did," Jacob Butler moaned.

"If you contradict me I'll knock your two eyes into one," Grabham said, with an oath.

"That s right! let him have it," said Catchpole. I'll swear to anything you like."

"Don't—don't!" Jacob pleaded. "You can't find it in your hearts to hurt a defenceless man."

"Can't we?" Grabham replied. "That's just where you make the mistake. We've got a long score to rub off with you, and we mean to do it now that we've got the chance!"

Jacob Butler gave a convulsive sigh, and, stretching out his legs, closed his eyes.

"He's been and gone and fainted," said Catchpole. "P'raps we've done a little too much?"

"Fainted be jiggered!" Grabham said. "Fetch me a pail of water, and I'll soon bring him round!"

At the mention of a pail of water, Jacob thought it better to open his eyes again.

"Not a pailful," he said. "Give me a drop to drink; my throat is parched."

"That comes of getting mad drunk," Grabham replied. "My eye, how you did carry on! I can see the old gentleman who you knocked down with an empty wine-bottle. It's a great chance, if he lives, and—"

"Eh! What?" Jacob cried, aghast.

"You nearly as possible killed him," Grabham continued, unblushingly, "and it took a dozen of us to hold you back."

"Lor' 'a mercy!" Jacob gasped. "I don't remember anything about it."

"Of course you don't," Grabham said, grinning, as he piled up the agony. "If the old gentleman dies you will be hung, as sure as eggs are eggs."

"And if he doesn't?" Jacob Butler queried, faintly.

"Why, then, you'll get transportation for life, and ought to think yourself lucky to get off so easy," Grabham replied.

Catchpole rubbed his hands gleefully as he watched the victim's contortions.

"And so," said Jacob, "that is why I am chained down like a madman?"

"Yes."

"Well," Jacob returned, "at all events, I shall have the consolation of saying something about you when I am tried."

"What do you mean?"

"Oh! nothing. Wait and see."

Grabham glanced at Catchpole, and that worthy's face fell until his chin descended to the top button of his waistcoat.

The constables drew aside, and held a consultation in whispers.

"See here, Butler," said Grabham; "if we consent to take the irons off, will you promise faithfully not to be violent?"

"I violent! Ha! Ha!"

In spite of all his grief and pain Jacob could not help laughing.

Grabham removed the irons, and Jacob Butler sat up and rubbed his stiffened limbs.

"Now," said Catchpole, in a coaxing voice, "you can't say that we have been unfair to you. What would you say if we made things easy for you, and only took you before the magistrate on the charge of being drunk and disorderly?"

Jacob Butler had not much sense, but he had just enough to know that what he had said had taken effect on the constables, and he determined to improve the occasion.

"Oh! I don't know," he said. "You have told a lot of lies, and knocked me about. I haven't forgotten your visit to Lilac Lodge, what you came for, and what took place between you and Sir Roland. What a nice kettle of fish there would be to fry, if all the facts came out."

"Hush! hush!" said Grabham, placing his finger on his lips. "Men ain't saints, and if we did exceed our duty a little, why—"

"Oh! yes," Jacob said, interrupting him; "ft course. If I had nothing against you, I should have been half killed, and then convicted on a false charge. Take me to a magistrate. I want to go before one now."

"Just listen to reason," Grabham said. "You are charged with nothing as yet, and if we like we can set you free."

"I don't want to be set free," Jacob replied, boldly. "I want the whole story to come out. My life is a misery with all these secrets hanging about it. I'll claim the protection of the law against that witch, Mrs. Corcoran, and Sir Roland."

The tables were now turned upon the constables with a vengeance.

They did not know what to say or do.

Catchpole, in a frenzy of mind, ran out and procured a bottle of ale, some cold meat and bread, which he sat before Jacob, and invited him to eat, and drink his fill.

"No," said Jacob. "I'll touch nothing from your hands. How am I to know that it is not poisoned?"

"Don't talk such nonsense," said Grabham, whose face had grown pale. "We were only having a lark with you. Catchpole, open the door. There, now! See how friendly we wish to be."

Jacob Butler smiled and shook his head dubiously.

"Oh! yes," he said; "I know your little games. You'll let me go because you are afraid of me, but you will save up your spite for another time."

"No, no," said Grabham. "On the honour of—"

"Oh! don't talk about honour," Jacob interrupted. "Well, if you wish to make terms with me you must fall in with my views."

"What are they?" Catchpole and Grabham demanded in a breath.

"You must catch Mrs. Corcoran and charge her with the murder of Lady Ashton," Jacob Butler replied. "I can't endure life while she is abroad."

"We'll do our best," Grabham replied; "but, you see, the old hag knew we paid visits to Sir Roland, and she might make matters ugly for us."

"Nobody would believe a word she uttered," Jacob Butler returned, contemptuously. "The sight of her will be enough to convict her."

"We agree," said Grabham. "Good-bye, Mr. Butler."

"There is another little matter which must be settled," Jacob said. "It happens that I have no money, so I'll borrow a couple of guineas of you."

Grabham and Catchpole groaned in chorus, but at last the coins were forthcoming, and Jacob Butler went his way rejoicing.

CHAPTER LXVI.
THE ESCAPE TO THE MILL—THE GOLD RETURNED.

HOLDING Daisy Leigh firmly, yet tenderly, Spring-Heeled Jack gazed upon Sir Roland.

The weird creature's gigantic form trembled with rage, and his eyes blazed like living coals, and he seemed about to leap upon the baronet.

But Daisy Leigh had fainted, and Jules Carleon rent the air with agonised cries as he battled with the stream.

The wheel seemed to revolve quicker, as if anxious to clutch him in its ponderous grasp, and the water toyed with him, now dragging him down, and then hurling him to the surface, and whirling him round and round.

The Frenchman's cries at last attracted the attention of some labourers, who were returning home from the fields.

As they came running down to the water's edge they saw a strange sight.

They beheld a huge white figure, bearing something in its arms, making its way with terrific leaps across the fields.

The spectacle was so strange and terrific that for a moment they forgot Jules Carleon, and would have taken to their heels had not Sir Roland Ashton staggered to his feet and hailed them.

"Stop!" he cried, wildly. "You must not let the man die! See! he is nearing the wheel. Ten guineas to the man who saves him!"

One of the men threw off his coat and plunged into the stream.

This example was followed by another, and they reached Jules Carleon just as he was sinking for the last time, and was within a few feet of the mill wheel.

Dragging Jules Carleon to the bank, they held him, almost between the jaws of death, until Sir Roland arrived.

Stooping down, the baronet lent his assistance, and in a few moments Jules Carleon lay upon the shore, motionless, and to all appearances bereft of life.

"I'm afraid he's gone, master," said one of the men. "We'll carry him to the mill, and try to bring him round, if you like?"

"Do so," said Sir Roland. "He is not dead—see! his eyelids quiver."

The mill itself was a short distance from the wheel, and the men made all haste to carry Jules Carleon to one of the upper chambers.

Sir Roland followed, pressing his hands to his bruised face.

The blow Spring-Heeled Jack had given him was a fearful one, and no sooner had the baronet reached the mill than he reeled, and fell half-swooning upon the floor.

"This is a nice business," said one of the men. "I think we ought to send for the constables—eh, Dick?"

"I was thinking so myself," Dick replied. "There has been foul play here. But what the deuce was that thing we saw dancing over the meadows like a will-o'-the-wisp?"

"Hanged if I know; but let us attend to this fellow or he will die."

Dragging off a portion of Jules Carleon's clothes, they set about rubbing him vigorously, and presently their efforts were rewarded with the desired result.

The Frenchman opened his eyes and sighed heavily.

"Where am I?" he asked. "Ah! me. Is this death?"

"You have been very near it," said one of the men. "How did you get into the water?"

Jules Carleon made no reply.

He thought it better to keep silence on the subject, and merely shook his head.

Just then Sir Roland Ashton recovered sufficiently to come to his side.

"My poor fellow," he said, "I told you how foolish it was to trust to the dangerous, slippery banks; but matters might have been worse. How do you feel?"

"Like a drowned rat."

"Well, well," Sir Roland said, "we have much to thank our good friends here for, and they shall receive the promised reward."

The men grinned at the sight of the shining gold, and were about to leave, when Sir Roland called them back.

"I have paid you well," he said; "and now I want you to do me a favour. Keep your own counsel and say nothing about what you have seen, and it may be that I shall be able to put more money in your way."

The men nodded, and then Sir Roland let them go.

"I wonder if we can trust them?" Sir Roland said, musingly, as he watched their retreating forms.

"Oh! yes, so long as you supply them with money," Jules Carleon replied. "Now that we are here, tell me how you became possessed of the place?"

"I purchased it long ago, thinking that it would make a useful retreat."

Jules Carleon shrugged his shoulders.

"It seems to me that it is a place we had better leave as soon as possible," he said. "*Parbleu!* shall I ever forget my interview with Spring-Heeled Jack? No—no!"

"Curse him!" Sir Roland hissed, as he clenched his hands. "Whence comes the power that gives him the means of thwarting me at every turn? The girl has slipped through my fingers. Love has turned to hatred. She must die!"

"Good!" Jules Carleon said. "Such a revenge would be sweet indeed. Ah! how cold it is. Are there no means of procuring a fire?"

"Yes," Sir Roland said. "In the chamber under this you will find plenty of materials."

"We will go in company," Jules Carleon said, shuddering. "For the life of me I dare not go about this horrible place alone."

As he spoke a gust of wind shrieked and moaned about the mill like a restless spirit.

"Let us go," Jules Carleon said, as he hugged his bare shoulders. "I freeze—I perish of cold."

They went down the creaking staircase, and in a few moments some logs of wood were burning brightly.

"This is better—much better," Jules Carleon said.

He spread out his clothes to dry, and crouched before the blaze as if he could have devoured it.

"Do we stay here?" he asked, presently. "You are very silent, Sir Roland."

"We must remain here—at least, for to-night," the baronet replied. "Silent, did you say? My thoughts so madden me that I am afraid to speak. Jules Carleon, I tell you that Daisy Leigh dies, and then I care not what happens."

Sir Roland crossed the floor, and throwing open a cupboard, clutched a dark-coloured bottle and put it to his lips.

"Drink!" he said, passing the bottle to Carleon.

The Frenchman elevated his eyebrows.

"Why did you not tell me that you had such rare stuff here?"

"Because I had forgotten it."

Jules Carleon drank deeply, and then, covering himself up with a rug, rolled over on his side and went to sleep.

"Will this man grow tired of the undertaking, and betray me like the rest?" Sir Roland said. "If I thought so, I would make short work of him. Why not now? The mission I brought him to assist me in has failed—failed most miserably."

Sir Roland crept nearer to Jules Carleon and listened.

The Frenchman was breathing heavily and muttering in his sleep.

"He serves me but to serve his own ends," Sir Roland said. "I am in his power, and his one aim is to make profit by it."

The baronet took a knife from his pocket and glanced along the blade.

As he raised his arm he heard a heavy step upon the floor and the weapon fell with a clang from his hands.

Starting to his feet, Sir Roland saw that one of the labourers had returned.

"What do you want?" Sir Roland demanded, hoarsely.

"I have come back with your money, and here it is," the man replied.

"What!" the baronet exclaimed. "Are you so rich that you can afford to fling ten guineas away?"

"No," the man replied, nervously. "Heaven knows I am poor enough, but a strange thing happened to me and my mates as we were crossing the fields."

"A strange thing? I don't understand you."

"As we passed into the lanes," the man continued, "we were suddenly stopped by a ghostly figure. 'I am Spring-Heeled Jack,' it said. 'Return the money to the villain who gave it to you. His hands are stained with blood; he is a murderer, and every piece of gold will bring its curse.'"

"Bah!" Sir Roland said, contemptuously. "Are you so foolish as to be frightened by this scarecrow bogey? He is but a creature of flesh and blood, and will meet with his deserts like all criminals."

"I care not what you say," the man replied, "Take back your gold."

He flung it upon the floor as he spoke, and turned towards the door.

Sir Roland strode after him and laid his hand upon the man's shoulder.

"A word in your ear," he said. "Pick up the money. Fool that you are to tempt me! I see that you will go to the village inn and blurt out this story. If you do you will rue the day that you were born!"

"Nay," the man retorted; "Spring-Heeled Jack told us to keep the secret."

"And paid you for doing so?"

"Yes."

"That accounts for you coming back here with a virtuous speech and hurling the money in my teeth," said Sir Roland.

"You may think and say what you like," the man returned. "I wish to goodness that I had never seen you!"

As the man moved away his foot came in contact with something, and, looking down, he saw the knife which Sir Roland had dropped.

The labourer glanced at the sleeping Frenchman and then looked steadily into the baronet's eyes.

"It seems to me," said the man, "that my coming here disturbed you. Wake up, man— wake up! There is the scent of murder in this place!"

Jules Carleon started to his feet.

"Who calls?" he said, rubbing his eyes, "What has happened?"

"Nothing," Sir Roland replied, coolly. "I happened to drop a knife, and this idiot has got a notion into his head that I intended to use it for an unlawful purpose. "

Jules Carleon turned pale and thrust his arms into his coat, which was now thoroughly dry.

"I do not trust you much," he said; "but I do not think you would play me such a trick as that."

Sir Roland laughed and snapped his fingers.

"No," he said. "I should be a fool to go against my own interests. But enough of this. I am sick of listening to such nonsense."

The labourer, growling something under his breath, slouched out of the mill, and Sir Roland, closing the door, placed his back against it.

"Which way shall we go?" he queried. "Whither shall we turn?"

"Anywhere out of this infernal place," Jules Carleon said. "In a short time the whole country will be up against us. Stay here, if you will, Sir Roland, but I go."

"Yes; it will be best," the baronet replied. "There is no safety here. What a fool I was to dismiss the carriage, for we must travel on foot. Pick up that gold, and follow me."

Sir Roland placed his hand upon the door, but it did not yield.

"S'death!" he yelled, "we are locked in."

"Ha! ha! Ha!" laughed the voice of Spring-Heeled Jack. "Never words so true fell from Sir Roland Ashton's lips. You are locked in. Ha! ha! ha!"

CHAPTER LXVII.

BILL BLARNEY HAS AN INTERVIEW WITH MRS. CORCORAN.

WHEN Bill Blarney saw the man at the door he felt his heart throb violently against his side and then stand still.

Blarney measured the man's strength against his own, and came to the conclusion that in a conflict success would be on his side; but a sudden cry or the sound of scuffling would rouse the inhabitants of the court.

"I must take the bull by the horns here," Blarney muttered, "and trust to this man's pity."

As he stepped out and the light flashed upon his face the man started back in alarm.

"Who are you?" he demanded. "And what are you doing here at such a time of night?"

Bill Blarney pointed to his bootless feet, which were cut and streaming with blood.

"I crave your mercy, sir," he said. "I have been attacked by robbers and beaten brutally."

The man who confronted Blarney was grizzled and hideous.

His ferrety eyes flashed suspiciously, and he put his hand to his breast, as if to make sure that some weapon he carried in case of emergency was there.

"Robbed!" he said. "Bah! who would steal your boots It is you who come here to rob. Beware! I am old, but not feeble, and I am armed."

SPRING-HEELED JACK,
THE TERROR OF LONDON.

JULES CARLEON TORE MADLY AT THE DOOR AS THE FLAMES AROSE.

"Well, then, I will tell you the truth," Blarney replied. "I have just escaped from Newgate, and the bloodhounds are after me."

"You don't say so!" chuckled the old man. "What, have you slipped out of the great stone jug? Good. Ha! Ha! Come in—come in; I like you for that."

Nothing loth, Bill Blarney accepted the invitation, and as he stepped into the house his strange host slammed the door and secured it with a ponderous chain.

"Now," he said, speak out, and speak truthfully. Who are you?"

Bill Blarney gave a brief account of his history and the old man chuckled hideously and cracked his fingers joints as he listened.

"Good—good!" he said, "You shall have shelter, and safe shelter, too, for nobody cares to disturb Rick Denton in his lair. Ho! Ho! I have other guests."

He led the way up a long flight of stairs, and Bill Blarney presently found himself in a room furnished with stuffy chairs and a lop-sided table propped up against the wall.

Sitting before a smouldering fire was a woman rocking herself to and fro.

Her back was towards Bill Blarney, but something told him that he had seen her before.

"A friend of mine," Rick Denton said, nudging Blarney in the ribs. "Ah! my boy, this is a small world. Only think that you know SÌ Roland Ashton and that she knows him, too."

"She knows him?" Bill Blarney exclaimed, starting.

"Who better than Mrs. Corcoran—the great, the clever Mrs. Corcoran?"

Blarney's brain reeled as this name was uttered.

"Impossible!" he said. "I heard that she was burnt at the fire at Lilac Lodge."

"Was she?" Denton replied. "Ho! ho! that's just where you make the mistake. She shall speak for herself. Mother, here is an old friend of yours come to see you."

Bill Blarney did not feel very comfortable. Mrs. Corcoran turned her ugly, wrinkled head.

The hag clapped her hands and hobbled up to the escaped ruffian.

"Where is he—where's Sir Roland?" she croaked. "Do you bring me news of him? Tell me where he is, that I may have my revenge?"

"I don't know," Blarney replied. "I wish he was where I have just come from."

Mrs. Corcoran looked disappointed.

"I traced him all the way to Dover," she said, "but he gave me the slip. Oh! to have him here! Oh! to watch him dying in agony at my feet! You, too, have suffered, Bill Blarney?"

"Yes," the ruffian responded; "and it will go hard with him when we meet."

"Give me your hand on that," Mrs. Corcoran said. "We have one object in view—his death! We will travel together and seek him out."

"I'd rather not just for the present," Bill Blarney said. "I must keep quiet until this affair has blown over."

"But you shall—you must—you shall!" the hag screamed, as she commenced to dance about in a frenzy of rage. "I have money and the means to get more. Jacob Butler has been faithless to me, but I will have him yet. Yes, yes! you shall take his place, Bill Blarney, and we will live for revenge."

Bad and wicked at heart as Bill Blarney was, he turned away in loathing from the witch-like old woman.

"We'll talk the affair over presently," he said as he sat down. "I'm weary to death. Denton, give me something to eat and drink. Ha! what is that?"

There was a noise in the court below, and Rick Denton held up his hand to enjoin silence.

"The hounds from Newgate have tracked you," he said.

Bill Blarney's face went livid.

"No—no!" he said. "It must be a mistake."

"I wish I-could say so, for your sake," Denton replied. "Hark! they are knocking at all the doors and demanding admission in the name of the King."

"What is to be done?" Bill Blarney said. "Tell me, is there no hiding place? Am I to be dragged back to that slaughter-house?"

Rick Denton seemed to enjoy Bill Blarney's terror, but presently he touched a spring in the wall and a panel flew back.

"You will find a staircase there," he said, "and it leads to the roof."

"A thousand thanks," Blarney returned, as he disappeared. "If I get clear away I'll not forget this."

As the panel returned to its place Rick Denton seized the lamp from the table and went below.

"Hullo!" he said, as he threw the door open wide. "What's all this fuss about? Ah! officers, I see. Good evening, gentlemen."

"You're mighty civil all at once," said one of the men. "Why didn't you come down before? We made noise enough to wake the dead."

"There's plenty of that in the court," Denton replied. "If I were to bother myself about every brawl I should find nothing else to do. Well, why have you come here?"

"A prisoner has escaped from Newgate, and we have traced him here."

"You don't say so?"

"Yes, we do say so," the officer returned, impatiently; "and if you use your eyes you will see that there are blood marks on your very doorstep."

"Why, so there are," Denton replied. "How strange!"

"So strange that we mean to search your house."

"You are welcome to do that," Denton said, with an injured air; "but you will be wasting your time."

The officers did not think so; but finding no trace of Bill Blarney, they left the house and left the court.

As soon as Denton gave the signal that the coast was clear Bill Blarney returned to the room; but it seemed as if peace was to be denied him that night.

The clock was striking two when they were startled by hearing a loud knocking at the outer door.

Blarney started to his feet. "Confusion!" he cried. "Who is that?"

"Hush!" said Denton in a low voice. "You need not be alarmed; you can hide yourself as you did before. Retire into the next room while I question the applicant."

Blarney returned no answer, but stepped into the room pointed out by Denton, and which being only divided from the other by a thin partition, he could readily hear all the conversation that passed.

The knocking was repeated, and Denton went to the casement, looked out, and demanded who was there.

"I am a traveller benighted on my way, and seeking a shelter from the storm. Can you accommodate me?"

"The hour is late," he said; "but are you alone?"

"I am," answered the man, "and am willing to put up with any sort of accommodation. I come to you quite by accident."

"Well," observed Denton, "I have but one bed unoccupied, but such as it is you are welcome to; so stay a moment, and I will admit you."

"Thanks!" returned the man; "I will not fail to reward you."

Denton made no reply to this, but moved towards the door, Bill Blarney waiting with impatience the entrance of the traveller, convinced that the tones of his voice were familiar to him.

The door was quickly unbolted, and the man entered.

"The fire is extinguished, you perceive," observed Denton, "and, therefore, as you are very wet, perhaps the sooner you retire to bed the better."

"Thank you," said the stranger. "I am very tired, so will do as you suggest, if you will be so good as to conduct me to the chamber. I wish to rise early in the morning."

"Very well, sir. Follow me, if you please," said Denton.

He took up a lamp and proceeded across the room, the man following him.

Blarney had silently opened the door of the room he was in just sufficient to enable him to peep out, and as the man passed by the door the light fell full upon his countenance, and it is needless to attempt to describe his mingled feelings of exultation and deadly malice when he recognised in an instant the features of Jacob Butler.

He could not without the greatest difficulty refrain from rushing out immediately from his place of concealment and seizing him by the throat; but he resisted the feeling as well as he could, and the unconscious Jacob walked on and ascended the stairs to which Denton conducted him.

When he had disappeared Bill Blarney rushed from the room and whispered in Mrs. Corcoran's ear—

"Jacob Butler—your Jacob Butler—is here!" he cried.

"It cannot be true!" the hag exclaimed.

"But it is," Blarney said. "It is true, for I saw his face."

At this moment Rick Denton entered the room.

"What brings this fool to me?" he said. "He tells me that he has lost his friends in a most mysterious manner. Why, mother, what is the matter with you?"

Mrs. Corcoran was capering about, flinging her arms above her head, and behaving in such an extraordinary style that both Denton and Blarney shrank from her.

"Into what room have you put him?" she demanded.

"In one of the rooms upstairs," Denton replied. "But what is the matter with you? Why are you so agitated?"

"Agitated!" the old woman shrieked. "I am delighted. Oh! I have rare reasons for being so."

"What do you mean?"

"I mean that he never leaves this house alive, unless he leaves it with me," Mrs. Corcoran replied.

"He looks to me as if he had very little life worth taking," Denton remarked.

"He has everything to me worth the taking," Mrs. Corcoran said. "How sweet to know that his dastard life is in my power! Oh! little did I think that kind fate would lead him to such a secret place as this. Let me see him—I must see him!"

"Wait till he sleeps," Denton said.

"No—no!" said Mrs. Corcoran. "Give me the light. I am too impatient to delay a moment."

"Well, then, since you will have it so," said Rick Denton, "I will go with you."

"Come now—come now!" the hag almost yelled.

Denton, without saying another word, took up the light and led the way.

When they reached the door of the room they stopped and listened.

Jacob Butler was breathing heavily.

"He sleeps!" said Mrs. Corcoran.

Rick Denton nodded his head.

Overcome with fatigue, Jacob Butler had stretched his weary limbs on the bed without undressing himself.

He slept soundly, little dreaming who was near him.

His countenance was pale and careworn, and it was evident that his mind laboured under some fear or anxiety.

"Ha! ha!" Mrs. Corcoran laughed. "'Tis he! Wake, you lovey-dovey traitor! Ho! ho! Wake, Jacob Butler, and meet the woman you have deceived so cruelly."

Roused by the old hag's voice, Jacob Butler did awake.

Starting up from the bed, he rubbed his eyes, and stared about him in stupefied amazement.

His face became ghastly, and his lips quivered as he caught sight of Mrs. Corcoran.

"Is this a dream?" he murmured. "It must be. It cannot be a reality."

"Oh! yes, it is, deary," said Mrs. Corcoran. Consent to marry me, or this moment shall be your last!"

"Hear me!" Jacob Butler gasped. "I am defenceless—I am half mad! I have made a fool of myself. The people who would have been my friends have gone away. Back—back, you hag! Touch me not!"

"Will you swear never to leave me again?" Mrs. Corcoran hissed.

"No—no! I would rather die."

"Then die!" Mrs. Corcoran yelled.

As she snatched a knife from the folds of her dress Denton caught her by the wrist.

"No—no; not here," he said. "I will have no bloodshed in my place."

The hag struggled fiercely with him, but he held her as in a vice and forced her backwards towards the door.

"What madness is this?" Denton cried. "If you kill this man how can you dispose of his body? Listen to reason."

"I will listen to nothing!" Mrs. Corcoran yelled. "I will kill him, I tell you. Let me go!"

As they struggled, reeling to and fro about the room, Jacob Butler thought he saw an opportunity to escape.

More dead than alive, he made a dash for the door and rushed headlong down the stairs.

But his progress was suddenly checked by Bill Blarney.

"Not so fast, my fine fellow!" the ruffian said. "You must settle a little account with me before you go."

Jacob Butler gathered himself up for a supreme effort, and, hurling himself upon Bill Blarney, bore him down.

The action was so sudden that Bill Blarney was taken wholly unawares.

"Help!" he roared—"help! This wretch is choking me!"

Jacob Butler, driven to desperation, tightened his grip.

Blarney's eyes protruded from his head, his face turned purple, and foam gathered upon his lips.

His senses reeled, and had not Jacob heard footsteps descending the stairs it is probable that Bill Blarney would have ceased to live.

Relaxing his hold, Jacob Butler flew down to the basement of the house.

But another obstacle stood in his way.

The front door was locked, and Rick Denton had the key in his pocket!

CHAPTER LXVIII.

RALPH ASHTON REMOVES CONSTANCE MARFIELD FROM THE QUEEN'S HEAD— HOW JACOB BUTLER WAS DESERTED.

DAISY LEIGH remained unconscious for more than an hour.

When she returned to consciousness she found that she was lying within a tent, the folds of which were swaying to and fro in response to the cool night breeze.

Daisy was alone, and she looked about her with that bewilderment which comes upon a mortal awakening to sense and reason after a long illness.

Her head was pillowed by soft cushions, and a fur rug had been thrown across her.

"Where am I?" she murmured. "What has happened? Ah! I remember. Oh! Heaven be thanked that I am no longer in the power of that wicked man, Sir Roland."

As she sat up pressing her hands to her pale cheeks a woman entered.

She was strangely and quaintly dressed, wearing a short dress that scarcely descended to her knees.

Her dark hair was confined by a golden net of delicate texture, and about her waist was a golden zone, inlaid with sparkling gems.

Daisy Leigh did not speak.

She could only stare at the apparition in surprise.

The woman advanced, and kneeling down at Daisy's side, took her hand.

"I am called Lanoni," she said, in a soft, musical voice. "Do not be afraid of me. I will treat you kindly though you are a stranger and a house-dweller, as I see."

"A stranger—yes," Daisy replied. "But did not Spring-Heeled Jack bring me here?"

"Spring-Heeled Jack!" the gipsy replied. "Who is he?"

"The man who rescued me from Sir Roland.

Lanoni shook her head.

"I know nothing of what you are telling me," Lanoni replied. "One of my people found you where you are now. Close at your side was the paper containing gold. I will read the paper to you. 'Keep and protect this lady until I return. A goodly reward shall be yours.'"

"But how is it possible I could have been brought here unseen?" Daisy said.

"I am as much at a loss to know that as you," the gipsy replied. "However, you must make your mind easy. I am queen here, and my word is law. Not one hair of your head shall be harmed."

Daisy deemed it wise to say no more about Spring-Heeled Jack, and after partaking of some soup brought to her, she reclined again, and fell into a deep, refreshing sleep.

Curious eyes peered at her from time to time as she slumbered, and a stalwart man, armed with a musket, was placed near the tent by Lanoni.

"If a stranger approaches shoot him," she said. "This poor lady has gone through some terrible trial, and must be molested no more."

Leaving Daisy to the care of Nature's sweet nurse, we will ask the readers to return to the Queen's Head.

Day dawning found Constance Marfield still awake.

She had watched at the window for the messenger who was to convey her to Daisy until her brow throbbed and her heart grew sick with apprehension.

Her anxiety was shared by honest Ben Jordan, who, as the night advanced, began to think with Constance that some deep-laid plot had been hatched with success to entrap Daisy.

"It strikes me that that fellow Butler has played us false," he said. "By Heaven! if that be so, he had better keep out of the reach of my right arm."

Constance was too terrified to weep. She could only moan and wring her hands. When the dark pall of night lifted and rolled away before the bright sunbeams she sat staring with aching eyes into the street.

"Heaven help me!" she sighed. "What will become of me if matters turn out as I fear? What shall I say to Ralph? Oh! why is he not here to comfort and advise me?"

Scarcely had she breathed the last word when a horse galloped up to the inn door, and Ralph Ashton hurled himself from the saddle with such force that his spurs rang again. His brow was dark and angry. That he had ridden far was evident from the state of his riding-boots, which were splashed with mud and water.

Not a word did he say to Ben Jordan, who opened the door and stared at him with mingled terror and astonishment.

Constance ran to meet Ralph Ashton, but she stopped half-way, for he halted in the doorway of the room, and, folding his arms, gazed sternly at her.

"Where is Daisy Leigh?" he demanded. "Tell me quickly—where is Daisy Leigh?"

Constance Marfield sank down upon her knees. "Oh! Ralph," she said, "was not the letter in your writing?"

"What letter—writing? I know not what you mean."

A bitter cry sprang from Constance Marfield's lips.

"You do not know?" she wailed. "Then all is lost. A man, whose voice had a foreign accent, came here, presumably from you, and produced a letter in your handwriting."

"In my handwriting?" Ralph Ashton said. "I have written nothing. Where is that letter?"

"Here!" said Constance. "Daisy gave it to me that I might read and read it again in the nappy anticipation of meeting you and her."

"Pshaw!" Ralph Ashton said, as he ran his eyes over the paper, "this is a forgery, and who should the forger be but the basest of villains—Sir Roland Ashton!"

Constance Marfield fell forward in almost a fainting condition.

Ralph caught her in his arms.

"I am not angry with you, my child," he whispered, "for you alone have not been deceived. Courage! Daisy is safe."

"I fear the news is too good to be true," Constance cried. "Who told you so?"

"Spring-Heeled Jack."

Constance Marfield clasped her hands in a transport of joy.

"Ralph—dear Ralph," she said, "how much we have to thank that mysterious being for! He outwits our enemies even when they are in the zenith of their triumph."

"Yes," Ralph replied dryly. "You shall see Daisy before many hours. Where is Jacob Butler?"

"He has disappeared. He went away the night before last and did not return."

Ralph Ashton's face grew dark again.

"If I thought he had any hand in this plot," he said, "I would send him to his reckoning without delay. Curse the meddling fool! He must have been tampered with by one of Sir Roland's agents, if not by Sir Roland himself."

Leading Constance to a couch Ralph Ashton paced the apartment with hasty strides.

"I have been much to blame," he said. "It was my duty to leave you better protected. Constance, prepare to come with me, for the roof of the Queen's Head is not strong enough to shelter you."

"I will go with you anywhere," she said. "I am all anxiety to get away. You are sure that Daisy is in safe hands?"

"Quite sure," Ralph replied. "He would be a stout-hearted man who would dare to approach her now."

"How are we to travel?" Constance asked, anxiously.

"On horseback," Ralph replied; "Jordan can accommodate us. We start in an hour."

Ralph went below shortly after, and though Ben Jordan was thankful to hear of Daisy's safety, he was in a terrible rage.

"To think that I should be taken in like this, and by a foreigner, too," he said, bringing his fist down upon the bar counter. "The forgery was well executed."

"It was," Ralph replied; "and only one man in the world could have done it. How cunning the villain is!"

"The Frenchman?"

"Yes; but he cannot hold a candle to his master, who is a devil in the form of a man."

"That I can readily believe," Jordan assented. "Will you not partake of some refreshment? You look worn out and weary."

"Yes," said Ralph. "Constance and I will breakfast together. Let us know the moment the horses are brought round to the door."

"Everything shall be as you wish," Jordan replied.

Late in the evening of the same day, as Ben Jordan was sitting alone in the back parlour and pondering on the strange events which had taken place under his roof, he heard the door open.

Thinking that it was some ordinary customer he rose slowly, placing his pipe carefully on the table.

"What can I have the pleasure of—"

He got no further.

Speech left him as he saw Jacob Butler standing at the other side of the counter.

"I've been in a precious nice fix," Jacob whined. "I was an idiot to take your advice and go to the masquerade."

Ben Jordan recovered his speech and strength of limbs.

Springing nimbly over the counter, he seized Jacob by the collar and shook him till his teeth rattled in his head.

"You blackguard—you graceless villain!" he said. "It strikes me very forcibly that you have been the cause of all this trouble."

"Troub—b—b—bubble!" gasped Jacob, whose head was flying from side to side. "Here, I say, don't shake the life out of me."

"I should like to," said Ben Jordan, "but I'll leave that job to hands more willing even than mine. What have you been doing with yourself, you contemptible scoundrel?"

Before Jacob Butler had time to reply Ben Jordan pitched him into a corner, where he lay huddled up and gasping for breath.

"Oh! lor'," he moaned, "haven't I been treated bad enough already?"

"Not half bad enough for my liking," Jordan said, towering over him in a threatening attitude. "Give an account of yourself, you white-livered hound!"

Jacob Butler did so as well as he was able, and Ben Jordan listened, smiling incredulously.

"And do you expect me to believe this cock-and-bull story?" he asked.

"I can't help it if you don't," Jacob replied. "Please don't ill-treat me any more. I am half worried to death now."

"The best thing you can do is to take yourself out of my house, and never come near it again," Jordan said. "Mr. Ashton has taken Miss Constance away with him, and I don't want you here."

"Very well," Jacob said. "I have no wish to stay where I am not wanted. I own that I have acted the part of a fool, but that I am guilty of anything else I flatly deny."

Ben Jordan pointed sternly to the door.

"I will listen to no more," he said. "Go!"

And Jacob Butler went, houseless and homeless.

He dare not trust himself to the streets, and that it was, after slinking about for hours, he, so fatigued that he could scarcely stand, found his way by chance to Rick Denton's house and into the presence of that most unpleasant female, Mrs. Corcoran.

CHAPTER LXIX.

THE MILL ON FIRE—MOMENTS OF TERROR—
FALLING OF THE OLD STRUCTURE.

JULES CARLEON, white and trembling, started back as he heard Spring-Heeled Jack's voice.

"Mercy!" he cried. "That fiend will betray us!"

Again came the mocking laughter of Spring-Heeled Jack.

"Uncouth, misshapen wretch!" Sir Roland yelled, in a paroxysm. "Though it is given to you to thwart my desires, you can do me no harm!"

"How often have I spared your life?" Spring-Heeled Jack said, now appearing at a barred window. "Fain would I do so now if I thought you would commence a new life and sin no more. Miserable wretch, your life is in my hands, for this mill is on fire!"

"What!" Sir Roland cried, "the mill on fire! Then it was your dastard hand that did the deed!"

"You lie!" Spring-Heeled Jack cried. "But why should I parley with you? Listen!"

The sound of crackling wood came to the ears of the prisoners, and presently wreaths of smoke and tongues of flame began to rise through the floor.

"Help—help! For mercy's sake, help!" Jules Carleon cried, as he rushed to the door and shook it. "If you are a man take pity on us."

"Pity!" Spring-Heeled Jack echoed. "What pity have you ever shown your victims? What mercy would you have shown to an innocent helpless girl? Die, dogs—die, both of you!"

The smoke now became dense and suffocating,

Sir Roland gasped for breath.

He stretched out his hands pleadingly, and his lips moved in supplication, but no sound came from them.

His throat swelled, and the water of anguish rushed from his eyes.

He reeled and fell face downwards upon the floor, leaving Jules Carleon to battle vainly with the heavy door.

Spring-Heeled Jack had removed his face from the window, but, moved to pity even for the heartless villains who so justly deserved death, he hurled the key through the bars.

Jules Carleon heard it fall, but could not see it.

With the hot, lurid flames writhing snakelike on all sides of him, he grasped about for the key.

If he could only find it all would be well, for outside the mill ran a balcony with a bridge of planks attached to it, leading to the shore.

But all his efforts were still in vain.

The heat now became terrific.

He could scarcely breathe and had given up all hopes when his almost paralysed fingers grasped the key.

But now his strength was failing him, and it was with the greatest difficulty that he dragged his limbs to the door.

"The saints preserve me!" he cried. "One more chance—only one! Oh! what horrible agony is this? Must I die thus? No—no!"

He thrust the key into the lock, and, turning it, flung the door open.

"Sir Roland!" he cried; "Sir Roland!"

The baronet did not move, and Jules Carleon, rushing back, dragged him bodily along, and, regardless of consequences, hurled him into the quiet water beyond the door and plunged in after him.

This was scarcely accomplished when, with a mighty, roaring sound, the flames burst through the roof of the mill.

The old structure reeled and collapsed, to charred timbers and red-hot machinery hissing as they fell, a mere mass of *debris*, into the stream.

As this took place Spring-Heeled Jack appeared on the bank and peered right and left.

"I can see nothing of them," he muttered. "Well, the villains brought their blood upon their own heads. The world will not miss them."

And yet he turned sadly away, and went bounding across the meadows to avoid crowds of people who were now on their way to the mill, but too late to do any good.

Some days passed away, during which Constance and Daisy had been removed to a' cottage near the historic house in which the Rye House plot[114] was concocted.

---

[114] A plot to assassinate King Charles II in 1683.

It was a pretty little place with a garden, and Ralph Ashton remained long enough to satisfy himself that the retreat was likely to prove a snug and safe one.

Nothing had been heard of Sir Roland or Jules Carleon, but it seemed so certain that they must have been burned or drowned that the people, after hunting awhile for their bodies, came to the conclusion that they had floated away with the tide.

And now it seemed that happiness was almost within the reach of Ralph Ashton and Constance Marfield, and, indeed, the preparations for the wedding were commenced, and were almost complete, when Lanoni and her people took an affectionate leave of the ladies.

But the cottage was not left altogether unprotected.

A man, armed with sword and pistols, kept within hail during the day, and another patrolled it by night.

Business connected with family affairs had called Ralph Ashton to London, and the girls were sitting amusing themselves with needlework and chatting.

They could hear the footsteps of their guardian pacing the garden walk, and they felt security in the fact that he had only to discharge one of his pistols to bring the people of the neighbourhood down like a nest of hornets about the ears of any intruder.

Suddenly the footsteps stopped, and Constance, thinking that she heard a dull sound, went to the window and looked out.

The night was so dark that she could see nothing; but though she said nothing to Daisy, she felt alarmed until she heard the welcome footsteps return.

"Constance," Daisy said, "Ralph is later than he promised. I am getting alarmed again. The old feeling that something is about to happen has come again. You may call me weak and foolish if you like, but—Hark! What sound is that?"

"I heard no noise," replied Constance, whose white face betrayed her feelings.

"I could almost swear that I heard a footstep on the stairs."

"It could only have been the wind or the effect of your imagination. Come, come, take courage."

"There again," cried Daisy, her face becoming very pale and her lips trembling. "This time I am certain I was not mistaken. There is someone moving in the house."

"Probably the servant," returned Constance, who had herself heard the sounds. "I will go and ascertain the cause."

"No, no, no!" Daisy cried, detaining her by the arm; "do not stir, but—"

Before she could finish the sentence the door hastily but silently was thrown open, and Sir Roland and two or three other ruffians, masked, entered the room and advanced towards the terrified girls, who screamed aloud as they approached.

"Silence!" said Sir Roland, as he seized Daisy in his arms, and two or three of the other villains tried to secure Constance, who, however, was too active for them, and, flying past them, made towards the door, calling aloud for help.

"Curse her!" cried Sir Roland, "her screams will alarm the neighbourhood, and we may yet find some difficulty in completing the business. Secure her—do not suffer her to escape. This girl, at any rate, is mine, and I will away with my prize."

Daisy had fainted, and Sir Roland, raising her insensible form in his arms, rushed from the room and prepared to descend the stairs, while his companions went in pursuit of Constance; but her loud screams drove them off, for the neighbourhood was now alarmed, and men were approaching in all directions.

Sir Roland, fearful of the consequences of delay, made his way down the stairs with all speed, and supporting his unconscious burden on his shoulder, darted across the garden, opened the gates, and hastened to the spot where the vehicle was in waiting to receive him.

Finding that their efforts were not likely to be crowned with success, his base associates followed him, and Sir Roland, having lifted his unfortunate victim into the carnage, followed quickly himself, and the other ruffians, mounting their horses, the whole were soon dashing away at a rapid rate far from the cottage and in the direction of London.

"At any rate, so far I triumph," cried Sir Roland. "I have been revenged, and Daisy is in my power, although Constance has escaped me for the present. But she shall not do so long. No; the time will come when she also shall be in my possession. Oh! this has been a brave night's work! Daisy, you are mine—you are mine, and cannot again escape me! How beautiful she looks, even in her paleness and terror! To obtain such a prize as this, was it not worth every risk? It was, and I glory in my success. She may heap upon me her scornful reproaches; I am fully prepared for them, and will heed them not. I said I would kill her. No, no; she is too young and beautiful to die."

As the villain thus spoke he once more fixed a look of admiration upon the girl, and then dared to pollute her lips with his kisses.

Poor Daisy! she was unconscious of the contamination, or her soul would have shrunk with horror and disgust.

CHAPTER LXX.
A DEN OF CRIME—SIR ROLAND'S TRIUMPH.

NEARLY an hour had elapsed ere Daisy was restored to sensibility, and by that time the vehicle had proceeded quickly and was travelling through a lonely and unfrequented place without any danger of pursuit.

For some seconds she was not quite sensible of her situation or what had happened to her; but the motion of the carriage aroused her and recalled her to recollection, and fixing her eyes upon Sir Roland and Jules Carleon, who had also taken his place in the vehicle, she uttered a cry of horror and sank back motionless in her seat, covering her face with her hands and the blood turning chill in her veins.

Sir Roland attempted to take her hand, but she shrank from him appalled.

"Horror—horror!" she exclaimed. "Has villainy then succeeded, and am I indeed torn from those dear friends who have so long protected me and ran so many risks for my sake? Wretched, wretched girl that I am! When will my troubles cease? For what horrible fate am I still reserved? Oh! is there no human being at hand to help me and rescue me from the power of these miscreants?"

"Be calm," said Sir Roland, who still wore a mask; "for all your cries for assistance would be useless. Fortune has placed you in my power, and they must be keen and bold who can release you from it."

Daisy Leigh started at the sound of his voice.

"Ah! who are you that have dared to commit this cruel outrage?" she demanded.

"Behold!" answered Sir Roland, raising the mask which had hitherto concealed his features.

Daisy uttered a piercing shriek of the utmost alarm and despair when she recognised the well-known countenance of her persecutor.

"Sir Roland—villain—murderer!" she gasped. "Am I indeed in your power? Are, then, my forebodings thus terribly fulfilled? Then am I indeed lost! Heaven help me! for this is more than I can bear."

"Nay, lovely Daisy, but you must learn to bear it with calmness, fortitude, and resignation," returned the villain. "Yes, it is indeed Sir Roland, the dreaded Sir Roland, who has at length triumphed in the accomplishment of the wishes he has for so long a period entertained. Ere a week has passed away Daisy Leigh shall change her name!"

"Wretch!" cried Daisy, her bosom swelling with disgust and indignation. "Still will I set your power at defiance! Heaven will not suffer you thus to triumph in your atrocious designs. Tremble, for even now vengeance is impending over you, and will assuredly descend upon your guilty head in the midst of your iniquity!"

"Sweet Daisy," replied Sir Roland, "you may save yourself these threats, for I heed them not. My purpose, so far, is accomplished, and I will not fail to take advantage of it."

"Mercy—mercy!! exclaimed the terrified girl. "But I plead in vain; for well do I know that you are insensible to that feeling. Oh! help—help!"

"Forbear your cries, for there is no one here to listen to them," said Sir Roland. "We are now several miles from Hoddesdon, and travelling through a part of the country where we are not likely to be molested. My plot has succeeded, and you are mine beyond all chance of escape. And so you and the rest thought me dead? Ha! ha! ha!"

"Gracious Heaven!" Daisy cried, "interpose, I beseech you, to save me. Oh! Ralph, Constance, my dear friends, what has become of you?"

"You will probably never behold them again," returned the villain, "so you may as well make up your mind to the worst, and not indulge in useless regrets or lamentations."

"Alas—alas!" sighed Daisy, "and it is for a fate like this that I have been reserved! Would that death had long since ended my misery, for now, indeed, has life become a hateful burthen to me."

"Say not so, fair Daisy," said the miscreant, "for you may yet find that Sir Roland Ashton, the villain, as you would term me, knows how to appreciate charms such as you possess, and that be—"

"Hold, monster!" cried Daisy; "your words fill my soul with horror. Think not to triumph, for death will yet snatch me from the awful, the revolting fate to which you would consign me. But this must be all some terrible vision—it cannot be true. Oh! what have I done that I should be thus so severely punished?"

Her feelings completely overpowered her, and she sank back in her seat, unable to articulate another syllable.

She placed her hands across her eyes, for she dared not look in the countenances of the wretches with her, and she gave herself up entirely to the dreadful agony with which her heart and brain were filled.

Nothing could be imagined more horrible than Daisy's situation, and it was wonderful that her senses did not entirely leave her.

To find herself in the power of such a monster as Sir Roland, and entirely at his mercy, was dreadful enough, and the lateness of the hour and the wild and dreary place they were travelling through, added greatly to her anguish.

From such a man she had everything to dread, and her very blood froze within her veins when she anticipated the sufferings that were in store for her.

But whither were the wretches conveying her?

Daring, indeed, must Sir Roland be to attempt the outrage he had committed when he was so vigilantly sought after by Spring-Heeled Jack. It showed, at any rate, that his power was not, as it had been imagined, destroyed, and that he would not fail to put his threat into execution, callous as he was to all sense of pity or humanity.

The climax of her fate, Daisy believed, was approaching, and she contemplated it with the most unbounded terror.

That Constance had not also fallen into the power of the wretches afforded the poor girl much consolation, and she wondered that Sir Roland had not taken care to secure her.

While she continued to indulge in these reflections the carriage proceeded at the same rapid rate, but she was suddenly aroused from them by hearing some observations that were made by Jules Carleon, and which immediately struck her and riveted every faculty in alarm.

"Your sword did you good service, Sir Roland," he said; "and I think the young gentleman will never trouble you again."

"Ah!" exclaimed Daisy, starting, and gazing intently in the ferocious countenance of the villain who spoke. "What do those words imply? Ralph Ashton? Speak! is it to him you allude? You surely have not—"

"He was fool enough to arrive at the same time I did and to attempt to obstruct me in my designs, and he has been justly rewarded for his trouble."

"Recall those dreadful words!" Daisy cried. "Oh! tell me that you have not murdered him."

"I merely ran him through the body," said Sir Roland, coolly; "but whether he is dead or not I cannot say."

Daisy could listen to no more.

She gave one piercing shriek, which resounded far around, and sank, senseless and inanimate, to the bottom of the carriage.

What afterwards occurred to her she had no knowledge of, but when she again recovered she found herself still in the vehicle, but Sir Roland and his companion had quitted it, and their places were occupied by two other ruffians.

Daisy Leigh passed her band across her temple and had at first only a confused recollection what she had heard or where she was.

"Whither am I being conveyed?" she cried, "who are you that detain me here, and—ah! I remember now; they told me they had murdered him; they exulted in the monstrous deed.

"Fiends! was it not enough to tear me from his protection, but you must take his life?

"I see his blood still crimsons your hands—that blood cries aloud for vengeance, and it will overtake you. Yes, a most fearful retribution will descend upon your heads for this hideous deed.

"Ralph, noblest of men! and is it I who have been the innocent cause of bringing you to this dreadful, this untimely end?"

The men appeared not the least moved by Daisy's piteous observations, and quite overcome by the tumult of agonising feelings that rushed upon her brain, she sank back in her seat and burst into a paroxysm of convulsive sobs that might have moved a heart of stone to pity.

"'Tis done—'tis done!" she at length ejaculated, in almost inarticulate accents; "misery can go no further; the final blow is struck; he has been foully butchered, and the utmost that villainy can invent cannot inflict upon me any greater torture. Death will soon release me from all my sufferings, and gladly will I welcome it in any form."

Once more the power of her emotions choked her utterance, and she sank into a lethargy of horror, in which every faculty, almost the sense of thinking, seemed for a time to be absorbed.

At length, as a wild feeling of frantic despair rushed across her brain, she once more started from her seat, and fixing upon the ruffians a look which even made them start, she exclaimed—

"Monsters! his blood be upon your heads! May his curses ring for ever in your ears, and writhe your coward, guilty souls with agony beyond all human endurance! Oh! he was good, he was amiable; but you—but where is he, the fiend in human shape—the heartless shedder of human blood? Let me behold him that I may ring my curses in his ears!"

"You may as well save yourself all this trouble and waste of breath, young lady"!" cried one of the fellows, "for upon us it has no effect whatever. The man should not have been mad enough to attempt to oppose Sir Roland and then he might have escaped; but if people will be foolhardy and obstinate they must take the consequences."

"Oh! villains—villains!" groaned Daisy. Ralph Ashton was murdered—murdered in defending her—and torture could go no further.

How long they had been travelling Daisy had no other means of judging than by seeing the dark shadows of night gradually dispersing before the appearance of morning, and she therefore felt convinced, from the rate at which the vehicle had proceeded, that they must have got a considerable distance from the neighbourhood in which she had been sheltered.

She peeped through the window of the carriage, and found that they were journeying through a wood.

Not a human being met her gaze, and therefore she could not entertain the least hope of obtaining any assistance.

The men were riding by the sides of the vehicle, but she could not perceive anything of Sir Roland, and she therefore concluded that he, not feeling inclined to listen to her reproaches, had hastened forward to the place of their destination.

At length the bitter, the almost insupportable, anguish of her bosom found some relief in a copious flood of tears, and she then sank, as it were, into a state of apathy, and was scarcely conscious of the situation she was placed in or what had happened.

But from this she was shortly aroused by the carriage stopping at what appeared to be the back of some building, before which several tall trees reared their heads, and almost concealed it from observation.

One of the ruffians who was riding by the side of the vehicle dismounted from his horse, and, breaking through the foliage, gave a signal at the concealed door, which was immediately opened.

A large cloak was thrown over Daisy's head, and she was lifted from the carriage and led towards the entrance.

"All right," said the man who admitted them; "thanks to my ingenuity, this business has been managed as successfully as could have been wished."

Daisy immediately recognised the voice of Sir Roland, and, unable any longer to support the terror of her mind, she uttered a faint scream and sank senseless in the arms of one of the ruffians.

Sir Roland took her from him, and advancing with her towards a staircase, one of his hirelings preceding him with a light.

"Send old Martha to me immediately, Sampson," Sir Roland said. "She will be able to do everything towards her recovery."

Sampson obeyed, and Sir Roland ascended the staircase with his insensible burthen, and entered an apartment at the top of the house, but situated in such a detached part of the building that not the least sound that proceeded from it could be heard by the persons who frequented the inn, for such the place was.

The door opened with a secret spring, and was formed so as to resemble the rest of the panelling.

The room was gloomy enough, and but indifferently furnished, and it opened into another of smaller dimensions.

Sir Roland placed the insensible form of Daisy in a chair and supported her until an old woman arrived.

She was a shrivelled old beldame, whose disposition well fitted her for the situation she filled and the many deeds of guilt she had seen committed since she had been an inmate of that house, a den of crime and infamy.

On entering the room and beholding Daisy she stood a few moments and gazed upon her, and her looks plainly showed that she viewed her with anything but feelings of pleasure and welcome.

"So, Sir Roland," she said, "you have thought proper to burthen yourself with this girl, who may cause us more trouble than enough."

"Hold your croaking, old she-cat," said Sir Roland, "and mind your own business. The girl will not cause you much trouble, I daresay; and as to my choosing to bring her hither that is my business."

"She-cat!" muttered the old woman, with a frightful look. "Old Martha has lived for something to be thus called. But——"

"Bah!" impatiently interrupted Sir Roland, "let's have no more of this, but attend to the girl, and see that she recovers. I shall expect you to relax a little of your sourness, if possible, for the girl will be under your charge, and must not be treated harshly. Mind this, or I will be the means of stopping your whisky for six months to come."

This threat seemed to have its due effect upon the old woman, for she looked very much alarmed, and somewhat softened the asperity of her tone.

"Well, well," she said, "if it must be so it must, but it is so many years since I did the amiable that I am terribly out of practice, and I am afraid that it will take me some time before I can become proficient in it again. However, I will do my best."

"That's enough," said Sir Roland, "and, mark me, you will lose nothing by doing so. I know how to reward those who render me any service."

"She is a fair thing enough," remarked old Martha, proceeding to use the proper remedies for Daisy's restoration.

"Ay!" Sir Roland returned, as he hung over the insensible girl; "she is beautiful—a fit wife for Sir Roland Ashton. But I will leave her to your care, and when she recovers beware how you answer any questions she may put to you."

"I will be careful," answered the woman; "old Martha knows how to manage her business well enough without receiving any instructions."

Sir Roland returned no answer, but once more gazing earnestly on the pale but lovely countenance of Daisy, he left the room, and hastened to rejoin his companions in a room where an ample store of refreshments was produced to recruit them after their journey, and to make merry after the success of their expedition.

"So you have returned safe, Sir Roland," said the landlord, who went by the name of Sneath.

"Yes," Sir Roland replied; "nothing could have been executed better than this plot, and I give you and the men you introduced me to all due credit for their services."

"They were sure not to fail in their efforts," observed Sneath.

"No; I was pretty certain of that," returned Sir Roland, "or I would not have trusted them."

"And you gained an easy access to the house?"

"Oh! yes. It was late before we attempted to do so, and we took them by surprise."

"But were they not alarmed?"

"They were," replied Sir Roland.

"And offered resistance?"

"Certainly; but of what use was it, opposed to these brave fellows?"

"No; I do not expect it was much," remarked Sneath.

"It would have been much better for Ralph Ashton had they not, for I am inclined to think that he has paid for it with his life."

"Ah!" ejaculated Sneath.

"Yes; I ran him through," returned the villain, "and left him bleeding and senseless on the ground. I hope the wound will prove effectual, for then I shall have gratified my revenge and got rid of my most bitter and hated enemy."

"But you have only succeeded in getting one of the girls in your power."

"No; I was rather unfortunate in that, but another opportunity may present itself, and I will not fail to avail myself of it."

"And which of the girls is it you have brought here?" asked Sneath.

"Daisy Leigh, you have so often heard me speak of," Sir Roland replied.

"Ah! her with whom you acknowledge yourself to be so much captivated?"

"The same."

"And will you persist in making her your wife?"

"Certainly," said Sir Roland, "or why should I take all the trouble and run all the risk I have done to gain possession of her? She is most beautiful."

"No doubt she will offer a firm resistance" said Sneath.

"And of what use will that be? Here she is perfectly secure, and there is no one who will assist her," Sir Roland replied. "We will call in a priest and he can make us one."

"True. But this affair will cause a great sensation in the country."

"That it is sure to do," Sir Roland returned; "but that matters little to us. They cannot possibly have any means of discovering your retreat, and we may therefore set them at defiance."

"We may. But now this affair is settled we must begin to turn our attention to more profitable business."

"Aye!" Sir Roland replied; "you will find me true to my word. You want money?"

"I do," Sneath said. "You have no cause to complain?"

"No," Sir Roland replied; "and should Ralph Ashton have received his death-blow it will be all but complete."

"You say that you have left the girl upstairs in an insensible state?" said Sneath.

"Yes."

"When she comes to know her situation her terrors will probably overcome her, and after all you may be disappointed in your prize, Sir Roland."

"Well, I must take my chance of that," said the baronet; "but I do not despair. I doubt not but that in time I shall be able to conquer her emotions with my usual skill. If Ralph Ashton recovers he will be mad with rage."

"Very true," remarked Sneath. "But he will leave no means untried to discover where the girl is concealed."

"I daresay not," replied Sir Roland; "but he might as well save himself the trouble, for his efforts will all prove unavailing. Daisy is as safe here as if she was concealed in the deepest cavern of the earth."

"She is."

"There is no chance of her escape?"

"None whatever."

"Then what have I to apprehend?"

"Nothing but the death of the girl through terror."

"Oh! I do not fear that," said Sir Roland. "She is not like one who has never experienced any troubles or dangers."

"Yes; no doubt the life she has experienced has not been the most agreeable," Sneath said. "But are you sure that you made your retreat from the house after the abduction of the girl without anyone following you?"

"To be sure I am," Sir Roland replied; "do you think that any person would have been mad enough to venture such a thing?"

"It certainly is not very likely. But the man from whom you procured the vehicle— are you certain that he may be depended upon?"

"Oh! there is no doubt of him; but Sampson will tell you more about that. He is not a man likely to be deceived."

"No, he is not," Sneath replied; so I think we may rest pretty secure."

"Oh! yes; there is no fear of that. But let one of your comrades go and ascertain whether Daisy has recovered yet. Perhaps it may not be so well that she should see me at present."

"True," returned Sneath.

Addressing himself to one of the ruffians, he desired him to do as Sir Roland requested.

He quickly returned, saying that Daisy had recovered for a short interval, but immediately, on becoming conscious of her situation, she fell into a state bordering upon distraction, and was then raving in the most piteous manner, and it was as much as old Martha could do to attend to her.

She had succeeded, however, in getting her to bed, and was doing all she could towards her restoration.

"It is no more than I expected," said Sneath. "I begin to think, Sir Roland, that you will have much more trouble with her than you anticipated, and I do not see that you will be likely to derive much pleasure from having a mad wife. The prize, at any rate, will not be worth the trouble."

"Pshaw!" Sir Roland said, "you are meeting troubles half way. Of course it could not be expected that the girl would rest calm and contented all at once. She will be better by the morning, I have no doubt."

"And if she is not what can be done with her?" demanded Sneath. "She may require medical attendance, and we do not happen to have any doctors among our comrades."

"Old Martha is as good as a doctor," Sir Roland said, "and I have no doubt she will be able to attend to all her wants."

"And a most tender nurse and attendant, I daresay, she will prove."

"She will not dare to act otherwise after the caution I have given her," said Sir Roland. "But enough of this—let us wait till the morning, and mark my word that the result will be more favourable than you imagine."

"Well, I hope it may," said Sneath; "but I would advise you not to attempt to see her to-day."

"Certainly I shall not. I am too well aware of what the consequences would be likely to be. Come, push about the grog, and let us endeavour to be merry after the success of our plot."

The glasses were replenished, the ruffians drank freely, and soon all were engaged in riotous revelry, in which Sir Roland most heartily joined.

His spirits rose to a most exuberant pitch by the success his villainy had met with, and at the manner in which he had eluded the vigilance of those who kept watch over the cottage, and particularly Spring-Heeled Jack.

The old woman remained in constant attendance upon Daisy, who continued in the same state, raving incessantly in the most piteous manner, until at length, completely exhausted, she sank back in her bed in a state of apathy, and seemed to lose all recollection of what had happened to her or where she was.

The ruffians did not separate until a late hour, and when Sir Roland retired to the room prepared for him he sat down, and laughed secretly at the success of his unholy plot.

Presently a knock came at the door.

"Who is there?" Sir Roland demanded.

"Jules Carleon!"

"Come in, then."

The Frenchman glided into the room.

"So Sir Roland," he said, with a cunning leer upon his face, "you are well satisfied, and safe at last."

"Yes; even from Spring-Heeled Jack," the baronet replied.

CHAPTER LXXI.

JACOB BUTLER FINDS THAT LOCKS AND BARS
DO SOMETIMES A PRISON MAKE.

JACOB BUTLER'S agony was great in the extreme when he found the way to liberty barred.

His breast heaved convulsively, and streams of cold perspiration ran down his face.

He shook the door as a newly-caged wild animal shakes the iron bars of its cage, but finding that the result ended in nothing but vexation he looked about for some weapon to defend himself.

As chance would have it there was a heavy cudgel leaning in a corner, and Jacob, grasping it, stood on his guard.

He could hear Bill Blarney cursing, swearing, and choking, as he endeavoured to recover his breath, but, worse still, Mrs. Corcoran and Rick Denton were descending the stairs.

Denton had secured the knife, which only increased the old hag's fury, and well did Jacob Butler know what would happen if she once got her fingers fixed upon his throat.

"Back! Stand back!" he yelled, whirling the stick round his head. "I'll be the death of anybody who attempts to touch me."

Rick Denton stopped and so did Mrs. Corcoran, and the old man whispered something hastily in the hag's ear.

Mrs. Corcoran nodded, and sat down on the staircase as if thoroughly overcome with fatigue.

"Look here," said Denton, addressing Jacob Butler, "it's not a bit of use kicking up all this fuss. I don't want such noisy customers as you here, and if you'll stand quiet a moment I'll open the door."

This was exactly what Jacob Butler required, and a gleam of hope flashed into his eyes.

"I'll be peaceable if you let me go," he said. "I only want to get out of that old witch's reach. Why can't she leave me alone when she knows that I hate the very sight of her?"

Mrs. Corcoran screwed up her features and squinted horribly at Jacob, but she said nothing to him.

"Well," said Denton, "if you'll put down that stick I'll set you free, and think myself lucky to be rid of you so cheaply."

"How am I to know that you will not play me false?" Jacob demanded.

"Haven't I said that I want to see you clear of my premises?" Denton retorted.

"Yes; but that may be only a ruse to get me into another trap?"

"Bah! you fool," said Rick Denton, contemptuously, "I have had more than sufficient visitors here already, and I'll take good care that I don't open my door to another stranger."

"I'll do as you wish," Jacob Butler returned as he put down the stick. "Now keep your promise to me."

Rick Denton descended the remainder of the stairs leisurely.

"Stand aside, so that I can get at the keyhole," he said.

Jacob did so, but still keeping his face towards Mrs. Corcoran, for fear that she might suddenly pounce upon him.

Rick Denton made a great noise with the lock and bolts, and then, catching the luckless Jacob unawares, he tripped him up and laid him flat upon his back.

"Help! murder!" Jacob roared.

"Another cry, and it will be your last," Denton said, planting his hand over the prisoner's mouth.

Mrs. Corcoran came leaping down the staircase, and she was followed by Bill Blarney.

"I'll soon silence him," said the ruffian. "Raise yourself up a little, Denton, and I will stuff a gag into his mouth."

Jacob Butler closed his eyes and groaned dismally as this was done.

Denton then produced a strong cord, and tied him with such dexterity that showed he was an adept at such operations.

"There he is, Mrs. Corcoran," said the hoary-headed old rascal; "and we'll put him into a safe place until he comes to your way of thinking."

"What a blessing it is to see him like this!" said the old hag, with a burst of wild, shrill laughter. "It does my heart good. You may say good-bye to your wanderings, Jacob deary, for you and I shall never part again."

Jacob heard every word, and what he would have said may be well imagined.

"I'm strong enough to carry him now," Bill Blarney growled. "Where shall I take him?"

"Into the little back room on the second floor," Denton replied. "It's a snug little place without a window, and if he gets out of it, I wish him luck."

Blarney tossed Jacob Butler over his shoulders with as much ease as if the wretched creature had been a bundle of feathers, and, running upstairs, laid him down with so little ceremony that Jacob felt every bone start in its socket.

Then the door was closed and locked, and he was left to his reflections.

The place was pitch dark and evil-smelling.

Jacob could hear the dripping of water in one corner of the room, and judged by the sound that there was a leaky tank or cistern in the room.

Sore in body and distressed in mind, the miserable man lay wishing that death might kindly put an end to his troubles.

He had no hunger, though he had eaten nothing for more than twenty-four hours, but a terrible thirst assailed him, drying up his throat and parching his tongue.

The gag in his mouth increased his agonies, and he twisted and turned, gurgling out incoherent prayers for a draught of water.

He felt that his senses were leaving him.

Strange visions floated before his eyes, and dismal sounds rang in his ears.

He tried to shriek, and hideous noises came from his throat.

His brain seemed to be bursting, and he strained at his bonds until they cut into his flesh.

And then he seemed to take the proportions of a giant, and his body enlarge until it filled the whole apartment.

Walls, floor, and ceiling pressed upon him with crushing force.

A fiery wheel bore down upon him, and then Jacob Butler fainted, and knew no more until he felt that water was being dashed over his face.

Looking up with eyes that were heavy as lead and felt like balls of fire, he saw Rick Denton bending over him.

The old villain removed the gag from Jacob's mouth, but some minutes elapsed before he could utter a sound.

"I don't know why you should persecute me," he said; "but since you seem to be in league with these wretches, I shall take it as a mercy if you will put me out of my misery. Anything will be better than the prospect of falling into that virago's power again."

Rick Denton grinned and shook his head.

"I have nothing to do with that," he said. "and as to making short work of you, why that would be a comfortable way of putting a rope round my neck."

"Then have mercy and set me free."

"No—no; I can't do that," Denton returned. "I am paid for what I am doing. You must take your chance."

"Where—where is Mrs. Corcoran?" Jacob gasped, faintly.

"Gone out."

"For what purpose?"

"I don't know exactly," Denton replied; "but I think that Bill Blarney has given her some information she intends to act upon."

"I wish it may lead her into a worse scrape than I am in now," Jacob said, earnestly. "I think I could give myself up to the hangman with pleasure if I only knew that she was dead. Give me some more water. Ah! what is this? You are trying to poison me!"

"Oh! dear no," said Denton; "I don't do things in that style—at least, not without orders. I have only given you a sleeping-draught to send you off nice and comfortable."

The draught soon had its effect upon Jacob.

He ceased to talk.

His lids closed over his eyes and his head fell back.

"Poor devil!" said Denton. "I could almost pity him. Marry Mrs. Corcoran! Ho! ho! ho! What a life of bliss is in store for him!"

At that moment Bill Blarney put his head and shoulders into the room.

"Well?" said Denton.

"It is not daylight yet," Blarney said, "and I was wondering whether it would be safe to make an attempt to reach the Borough."

"You are the best judge of that."

"I want to get there," Blarney said, "for Dick Sleuth and the boys will wonder what on earth has become of me."

"Well, wait a minute," said Denton. "I will go to the top of the road and see if the coast is clear."

CHAPTER LXXII.

**DAISY LEIGH IN THE HANDS OF A VILLAIN—A CHECK—
THE SHOT THROUGH THE WINDOW.**

WHEN Daisy, by the constant perseverance of the old woman, was restored to consciousness, she looked around her, and beholding the frightful countenance of old Martha and the gloom in the apartment she started and trembled with surprise and alarm, and had no immediate recollection as to what had happened.

"Where am I?" she exclaimed. "What fearful place is this?"

"Be calm, young woman," answered Martha, "and do not give way to this nonsense. You are where it is useless for you to complain, and as to your friends, you are far enough away from them now, and where they will not find it very easy to discover you."

Daisy gazed at the repulsive-looking woman with increased amazement, and then passed her hand across her temples to collect her thoughts.

"Ah! I see it all now," she moaned. "I remember all the dreadful particulars. I was snatched from my friends by that fearful man, Sir Roland, who slew my protector and friend. Oh! Heaven, I shall go mad. Even now I see him weltering in his blood—I hear his dying groans. Release me—let me hasten to him!"

"This frantic violence is useless," said the crone; "you cannot leave this place."

SPRING-HEELED JACK,
THE TERROR OF LONDON.

"RELEASE THE BOY, OR YOU DIE!" SPRING-HEELED JACK CRIED.

"Ah!" said Daisy Leigh, "dare you attempt to detain me? Are you a woman, and can you thus act to one of your own sex? Where is the murderer of Ralph Ashton? Where is the miscreant who tore me from my home? He dare not meet my reproaches; he dare not encounter the bitter maledictions I shall heap upon his head."

She burst into a violent paroxysm of convulsive sobs as she uttered these words, which having subsided, she again relapsed into the same state of distraction as before, while the old woman stood by and listened to her in silence, not knowing what to say or how to act.

"And but for me," resumed Daisy, "he might still have been living and happy. Yes; I have been the cause of all. I have ever brought misery upon those who have befriended me. There is a spell—a curse—attached to my destiny.

"But he may still be living! Yes; he calls upon my name! Woman, if such you are, stand aside, and dare not attempt to obstruct my way!"

As the poor girl said this she attempted to advance to the door, but was again prevented by old Martha; and overcome by her emotions, she once more sank in her chair and continued to rave.

The old woman, seeing that it was useless to expostulate with Daisy, did not offer to interrupt her agonised exclamations, until at length the poor girl was quite worn out, and sinking into a state of torpor, Martha was enabled to get her into bed, where she remained for some time in a state of utter unconsciousness.

The old woman could not but admire her extreme beauty, and something like a feeling of pity stole upon her insensible heart; but it was only for a moment, and she became as stern and callous as ever.

Throughout the day Daisy continued in the same state, raving frantically at intervals and then sinking again into apathy.

Towards night she was quite worn out, and fell into a deep slumber, which was a great relief to the old woman, who had not experienced so hard a day's work for many a year.

She had to watch her during the night, and she had, therefore, provided herself with a sufficient dose of her favourite beverage, to which she not unfrequently applied for consolation. Daisy's sleep, however, was disturbed by frightful dreams, and in imagination she saw reacted all the horrors that had taken place. Again she beheld Ralph Ashton sink bleeding to the earth; she beheld his ghastly looks; she heard him call upon her name in piteous accents, and at the moment when she was about to rush to his arms she was withheld by an herculean grasp, and looking up beheld herself in the power of the miscreant, Sir Roland, whose eyes gleamed with exultation as he pointed to the work of his cowardly hands.

The next moment she felt herself hurried along as by a whirlwind, and imagination became buried.

The next morning she awoke just as the sun appeared in the east, and rubbing her eyes, she had but an indistinct recollection of what had happened until she beheld the old woman, who was seated by the fireside, half-dozing in her arm-chair, and then the whole dreadful truth recurred to her memory.

She started up in her bed and looked around. The gloom of the apartment, which was only lighted by one small, grated window, and the general wretchedness of its aspect filled her mind with terror, and she trembled violently.

"Ah!" she exclaimed, "it is true—it was not a dream. Oh! Heaven, I am indeed a prisoner in an unknown place; torn from my friends, and in the power of such a hang-dog villain as Sir Roland."

The sound of her voice aroused old Martha, who started to her feet and hastily approached the bed.

"Where am I? Tell me, woman, I command you!" Daisy said, in a firmer tone of voice than she had before been able to assume. "For what purpose am I brought here? And who are you that is placed over me?"

"As to where you are," croaked forth the old woman, "it perhaps would not afford you much gratification to know. You are in the power of Sir Roland Ashton—of that you are aware. For what purpose you are brought here it is not for me to say. And as to who I am, they call me Martha, and that must suffice you."

"And what is the character of this house?" demanded Daisy.

"I cannot satisfy you, young woman," replied Martha, in her usual surly tones. "I am not here to answer questions, but no doubt you will find out what you wish to know in time."

"Oh! Heaven," Daisy exclaimed, "what will become of me? Is Sir Roland Ashton in this house now?"

"He is," answered Martha.

"You are a woman!"

"Indeed!"

"Have you no pity?"

"I am not allowed to deal in the commodity, and I must confess that I never felt much inclination to do so."

"Can you not feel for one of your own sex?"

"Aye! I might do so upon a pinch," replied the beldame. "But what would be the use of that?"

"Oh!" Daisy exclaimed, eagerly, "if you have one spark of pity within your breast, if you can indeed feel for a poor, deeply-injured, persecuted, broken-hearted girl, you will commiserate with my suffering—you will assist me to escape from the terrible fate with which I am threatened!"

"Assist you to escape?" repeated old Martha, with an ironical grin; "a very modest and reasonable request, truly. But, if you calculate upon that, you will find yourself very much mistaken, for indeed I shall do nothing of the kind."

"There is, then, no hope?" Daisy cried.

"None whatever, if you think to escape from this place," replied Martha.

"Surely," exclaimed Daisy, "surely you will not permit the villain, Sir Roland, the assassin, thus to triumph?"

"No doubt he fully expects to triumph, and for my own part I don't see that he has any reason to think otherwise."

Daisy turned from the old woman with a shudder of disgust and horror.

"The whole of it is," resumed Martha, "you may as well try to make yourself comfortable, young woman, and to submit without murmuring to your fate; for here there is no one to assist you, and Sir Roland is not the man to abandon any designs upon which he has fixed his mind. He has been at some trouble and risk to get possession of you, and, of course, he expects to reap his reward."

"And that should be the gallows," retorted Daisy.

Her fine eyes flashed indignation upon the old woman, who, however, was insensible to every feeling of shame, and took but little notice of what the poor girl said.

"The wretch may flatter himself in the success which has hitherto attended his diabolical stratagems," Daisy continued, "but there is a power that watches over all our actions, and will not fail to visit him with terrible retribution, even when he thinks that his triumph is most complete."

"I know nothing about that," returned Martha. "I never trouble my head with such matters, but I would advise you, young woman, to be a little more cautious in the language you use to Sir Roland, or—"

"What language do you expect me to use to one who has committed so daring and cruel an outrage against me?—to a wretch whom I know to have been guilty of every atrocious crime?" Daisy demanded.

"Well," said the beldame, "you can use your own discretion; but you may rest assured that whatever you may say will not prevent Sir Roland from putting his designs into execution."

"Heaven help me, then!"

"Well, I want not to listen to such stuff; so you may as well spare yourself the trouble of giving utterance to it."

"And can a woman possibly possess no more feeling towards one of her own sex?"

"I have before told you that I have nothing to do with feeling; I have heard of the word, but I can't say that I very clearly understand it."

Daisy looked at her for a moment, and could scarcely believe that such a hateful character could twist under the garb of one of her own sex; but the beldame was well schooled in vice and took no notice of her.

"I see," said Daisy, after a pause, "that it is useless to appeal to you, and I will say no more upon the subject. I will not yet despair; deplorable and alarming as my situation is, something will yet occur to rescue me from the power of the heartless miscreant who seeks to make my life miserable."

"Probably you may find that your sanguine hopes will be rather disappointed," observed Martha.

"Leave me," said Daisy. "I cannot look upon you with any other feelings than those of disgust."

"Indeed! I am obliged to you for the compliment," returned the old beldame, with a bitter sneer.

"Retire, I request of you," said Daisy. "I would be alone—left to the indulgence of my own thoughts."

"Very well," said the old woman, "I have no wish to keep you company. I suppose, however, by this time you will want some refreshment, as you have not broken your fast since you entered this place?"

"I need nothing," sighed Daisy; "there is not anything but liberty and peace of mind that I want."

"I do not undertake to supply you with them," replied Martha, as she quitted the room; "but I will bring you some provisions, and you can please yourself about eating them."

Daisy returned no answer to this brutal and unfeeling speech, and the old woman disappeared.

When she had gone the power of Daisy's feelings found some relief in a copious flood of tears, after which she arose and dressed herself.

Her brain was giddy, and she sank in a chair, for she could not support her trembling limbs.

All the horrors of what had happened and the situation in which she was placed rushed at once upon her imagination, and she was driven almost to the same state of distraction she had been in the day before.

The observations of old Martha convinced her, if she had even before entertained any doubt, that she had nothing whatever to hope, that there was no chance of her escape.

But could it be true that Ralph Ashton had indeed perished by the murderous hand of Sir Roland? The thought was almost too horrible to bear, but yet, after what she had heard, it was by far too probable for her to reject it.

Oh! the pangs that this maddened idea caused her. If Ralph had indeed met so dreadful and untimely a fate all hopes of protection would be at an end, and death would be a mercy to her.

And she had been the innocent means of sacrificing his life; but for her, had they never met, he might still have been living and happy.

Her agony was most indescribable, and her bosom heaved with convulsive sobs.

The poor girl wrung her hands in despair, and her heavy sobs for some time choked her utterance.

She at length arose from her seat and walked to the door of the apartment and examined it; but she found that it possessed neither lock nor bolt, but was perfectly secure.

She could not discover the secret spring by which it was opened, and indeed it was so nicely contrived that it might set detection at defiance. She shuddered at the thought. Here, then, she was entirely at the mercy of her cruel enemy, and could not protect herself against his intrusion at any hour he thought proper.

The dreariness of the rooms struck a deadly chill upon her heart, for they both only received light from a small iron-barred window, and which gave them indeed the aspect of the most dreary dungeons.

"Alas!" she sighed, "what dreadful crimes may not have been perpetrated within these walls! how many poor suffering creatures like myself have lingered out a life of misery and persecution in these very rooms, until the assassin's knife put a period to their wretched existence!"

She walked to one of the windows and looked from it, but the prospect that met her eyes was of the most gloomy description.

Clusters of tall trees, impervious almost to the light of day, alone met her gaze.

It was a place well adapted for the perpetration of any atrocious deed, and which plainly showed her the infamous character of the house in which she was confined from the loneliness of its situation.

There she could never hope to meet assistance, and, therefore, the horrors by she was surrounded were made the more apparent.

The villain, Sir Roland, could not have fixed upon a more fitting place for the execution of his diabolical plot, no place where he was more secure from interruption, and as Daisy contemplated it she gave herself up completely to despair.

How she trembled with terror when she thought of the cruel persecution to which she was sure to be subjected! With what horror did she look forward to the moment when she should again behold Sir Roland!

How could she look upon that guilty man, whose hands were stained with the blood of so many unfortunate victims, and, probably, Ralph Ashton amongst the number?

Surely the sight of him would drive her to madness.

She was interrupted in these reflections by the return of old Martha, who brought with her some provisions, and placed them on the table before her.

"There, young lady," she said, "is a repast fit for a princess, and, therefore, I should advise you to eat, for you must be hungry enough after fasting for so many hours. I never found sorrow weaken my appetite in the least, though certainly I have not experienced much of it in my time."

Daisy sighed deeply, but returned no answer to this ignorant and vulgar speech.

The old woman looked at her with a malicious expression of countenance for a moment or two.

"I suppose you do not require my attendance?" she observed; "for, no doubt, my company is not very agreeable to you; so I wish you Good-morning, and will leave you to yourself."

"Tell me, I beg of you," said Daisy, "whether I am to continue to be confined in this gloomy apartment?"

"For anything I know to the contrary, you are."

"And once more I ask you what is the character of the inmates of this lonely house?"

"Character?" repeated the old woman, "why, as for that matter, I believe they can none of them boast of possessing any other than a very bad one. They are jolly fellows, who live a life of freedom till they are caught, and make the public contribute liberally to their support."

"Thieves!" said Daisy, with a shudder.

"No," answered the old woman; "thief is the name only worthy of a paltry pickpocket; they are gentlemen of the road, and all of them accomplished cracksmen."

Daisy trembled violently, and looked at Martha with an expression of the utmost disgust.

"And can it be possible that a woman," she said, "an aged woman, can associate with such wretches?"

"Why," answered the beldame, "it is all a mere matter of taste, you know; I have done so for many years, and do not feel inclined to alter my situation, for I do not think that I could better myself."

"Wretched woman!" Daisy cried. "May Heaven pardon you for your sins, and bring you to repentance ere it is too late."

"Repentance!—bah! What have I to repent of? But I came not here to listen to a sermon; I have no taste for such matters, and therefore you had better keep your morality to yourself."

"I pity you," said Daisy.

"Pity!" ha—ha—ha! I am much obliged to you. but I do not stand in need of it."

"Answer me one question."

"Well, what is it?"

"Will Sir Roland visit me to-day?"

"I believe he will not," answered Martha; "but you had better be prepared to meet him when he does, for it is not likely that he will delay his visit long."

"The villain!" exclaimed Daisy, warmly; "he cannot but expect that I shall receive him with my bitterest curses and reproaches."

"Which he will pass unheeded as he would the idle wind," remarked Martha.

"Never, by Heaven! will I be his wife," exclaimed Daisy; "sooner would I suffer death than that the monster should triumph. Weak, defenceless girl as I am, he shall yet find that I have the fortitude to resist him, and that I will suffer anything sooner than I will yield."

"Well," returned the old woman, "that is to be seen; but you will find that Sir Roland is a more determined and desperate man to oppose than you seem at present to imagine."

"Well do I know the villain's character," said Daisy; "but Heaven will give me strength, and even at the very time when he thinks his success secure he may be defeated and brought to that punishment his numerous and horrible crimes deserve."

"With that hope, then, I will leave you," observed Martha; "but I rather think you will be disappointed."

With these words the old woman quitted the room, and Daisy was once more left to herself.

The thoughts that rushed in rapid succession through her mind were of the most distracting description, and whichever way she directed them she could perceive no means of consolation.

The desperate character of the men by whom she was surrounded filled her bosom with the utmost alarm.

But how she shuddered at the idea of beholding Sir Roland!

She well knew his reckless and determined character, and that pity was a stranger to his breast, and therefore she had every reason to apprehend the worst.

The horrible character of the old woman also filled her with terror and rendered her situation doubly insupportable, since she had no person to whom she could confide her thoughts, and who would commiserate with her sufferings.

Miserably did that day pass away, but Daisy experienced no interruption, only at the times when Martha came to bring her her meals, and then she avoided entering into conversation with her, so revolting was her character to the girl, and so utterly destitute of pity or common humanity as she was convinced she was.

She judged that she was in a remote part of the building, for not the least sound met her ears, save the moaning of the wind among the branches of the trees that reared their tall heads far above the building.

The fate of Ralph Ashton constantly occupied her thoughts, and indescribable was the anguish that accompanied it.

Sometimes she dared to hope that he still lived, and that something might occur to make him acquainted with the place of her confinement; but that idea was too extravagant for her long to encourage it, and she quickly again relapsed into the most utter despair.

As night advanced her agony became almost insupportable; the dismal silence of all around chilled her heart, and yet she started with the greatest alarm whenever the least sound met her ears, fancying that someone was coming.

She feared to retire, for she had no means of securing herself against the intrusion of anyone in the night, and every description of horrible apprehension beset her mind.

Again she endeavoured to find the secret spring, but in vain.

After some time spent in this manner she again returned to the bedroom.

Her fears were aroused to the highest pitch, and when she reflected upon the cruel deeds that had probably been perpetrated in these very apartments she could almost imagine that she beheld the grim shades of the departed flitting past her in the chamber.

Frequently she started as she was almost convinced she heard dismal sepulchral cries in the pauses of the wind.

But she was soon satisfied that it was only the effect of her disordered imagination, and by degrees she became somewhat more calm.

"I have never injured those that are gone," she said, "and therefore what have I to fear? Ah! no, it is only the living I should dread."

A clock in the house now struck eleven, and suddenly Daisy felt so overpowered by sleep that she could not resist its influence although she endeavoured to do so, and having secured the door of the inner chamber as well as she could, she threw herself on the bed without undressing, and in a few moments a sound sleep stole over her senses.

It was not quite daylight when she awoke, but the grey mists were fast dispersing, and Daisy, not feeling inclined to go to sleep again, arose considerably refreshed.

She walked to the window and watched the sun as its first beams gradually penetrated between the thick foliage.

While she was thus occupied she perceived three men on horseback suddenly emerge from between a cluster of trees, and approach towards the house.

As they came nearer she was enabled to have a clearer view of their countenances.

She became convinced that they were some of the ruffians connected with the building, and she could not but tremble with dread when she reflected that she was in the power and at the mercy of such desperate villains.

They advanced immediately to the house, and she then lost sight of them, but she had no doubt that they had entered by a secret way.

Daisy quitted the window, and, resuming her seat, gave herself up to the dismal thoughts which all the painful circumstances in which she was placed and the anticipations in the future engendered.

Alas! what had she to anticipate, placed as she was among such heartless and lawless wretches, but the greatest cruelties?

And there was no hope, no chance of escaping from them!

Surely no sufferings could be greater than those to which she was exposed, and in vain she endeavoured to find the least consolation.

Martha visited her at the usual hour with the morning's repast, and was about to leave the room again without speaking, when our heroine prevented her by observing—

"I have a question to ask you, Martha."

"I have already told you that it is not my business to answer questions," returned the old woman, in her usual surly tones; "but what is it?"

"Simply to ask you whether Sir Roland is still in the house?" demanded Daisy.

"Certainly he is," said Martha. "You don't suppose that he would venture from it just yet when there is such a hue and cry after him?"

"And will he dare obtrude himself on my presence?" interrogated Daisy.

"That you may depend he will, young woman. He did not bring you here for the mere purpose of caging you up like a bird. No, no; he must have the pleasure of your society, and I have no doubt that you will see him before the day is out."

"Oh! Heaven," ejaculated Daisy, "I can never endure the presence of such a miscreant—such a monster!"

"No doubt that Sir Roland will convince you of your folly, and make you his wife in spite of your obstinate opposition."

Daisy Leigh fixed a look of mingled pity, horror, and reproach on the woman.

"And these remarks are made by one of my own sex!" she said. "But why do I speak to one lost to every sense of humanity? Your connection with the villains who use this dreadful den shows that you are inured to every vice."

"Thank you for the compliment," said old Martha, sneeringly. "However, I have no wish to speak to you, my pretty bird. I will leave Sir Roland to do that, so I wish you Good-morning and much joy. If I were younger, and in your place, I would jump at such a chance. There are not many girls who would scorn such an offer."

As the old woman left the room Daisy Leigh pressed her hands to her face and burst into tears.

"Great Heaven!" she exclaimed, "can nature have formed any human being so base and callous to shame or pity as this woman?"

Daisy rose to her feet and paced to and fro in a state of great agitation.

"Must I be tormented with this villain—Sir Roland?" she resumed. "Must I listen to his advances? His wife? No—no! Heaven spare me from such a fate!"

In her terror she struck her breast, and groaned in the agony of her despair. If Ralph Ashton had perished she had indirectly caused his death, and where had Daisy now to look for a friend, unless that mysterious being, Spring-Heeled Jack, came to her aid again?

Every sound that met her ears caused her to start violently, for she feared that it was Sir Roland approaching.

But several hours passed away, and Daisy was still alone, and the morning passed away without interruption.

But this state of things was not to last long.

Suddenly Daisy heard a door close, and immediately afterwards the sound of footsteps ascending the stairs.

Daisy Leigh felt a deadly faintness steal into her heart.

She trembled violently and sank into a chair for now she was sure that Sir Roland was on his way to the room.

The next instant the door flew open and the object of her fears stood before her.

Daisy Leigh could not help giving utterance a cry of horror as she beheld the villain.

She averted her head and moved to the other end of the room.

Sir Roland Ashton closed the door, and stood gazing in admiration and triumph at the beautiful girl.

He knew what was passing in her mind, he knew how she loathed him, but he cared nothing for that.

"Look up, Daisy," he said, advancing. "I have come to woo you. Tell me what I can do to prove my love?"

"Hold, monster!—villain!" Daisy cried. "Would that I had some weapon that I might rid the world of such a coward!"

"Nay!" said Sir Roland, "this is unkind. Villain, monster, as you call me, you will find that I can be kind and indulgent. I would bury the past, and whilst leading a new life forget it. Daisy, I love you—yes, love you dearly, insensible as you may imagine that such a heart as mine can be to the tender passion."

"What mockery!" Daisy replied. "You love! The word is polluted by such lips as yours. I will not hear you. Away—away!"

Sir Roland Ashton folded his arms and smiled scornfully.

"You must listen to me," he said, "and with patience and indulgence. I am not the man to be foiled in any determination I may have formed. Ralph Ashton is dead, and—"

"But," said Daisy Leigh, interrupting him, "there is yet another who will avenge my wrongs."

"And who may that be?"

"Spring-Heeled Jack."

"Let me whisper a word in your ear?" Sir Roland said.

As he spoke a few words in a low tone of voice Daisy Leigh started and trembled violently.

"Oh! base and cowardly miscreant!" she cried. "You boast of a triumph you have waded through blood to obtain. The curses of offended Heaven are hovering over your head for the crimes you have committed."

"Speak on! Rail on!" said Sir Roland; "your words fall idly on my ear, and yet it is happiness to listen to the music of your voice. You have called me a murderer, but I can justify my crimes, and—"

"Forbear—forbear!" Daisy exclaimed, shrinking still further away from the villain. "Your words shock my ears."

"And yet," Sir Roland said, "you must hear me out."

"Hold! Speak not," Daisy cried. "Do you not fear that your tongue may blister or shrivel? Such a thing has happened to bad men, I have heard."

"Bah!" said Sir Roland, contemptuously. "I heed not such idle cant."

"Heaven help me!" Daisy said, in faltering accents. "Must I listen to this man?"

"You must," said Sir Roland, "and it will be best for you to do so patiently."

Daisy Leigh sat down near the barred window, and lowered her head to her bosom.

"I repeat," said Sir Roland, "that I can justify the crimes of which you accuse me of."

"Oh! villain—villain!" Daisy ejaculated.

"Had it not been for Ralph Ashton," Sir Roland continued, paying no attention to the girl, "I should never have been guilty. He has always stood in my way, thwarted my designs, and made my life a bane and a curse. Now that he is dead he can foil me no longer. I know that his one great idea was to bring me to the gallows in the end, and I exult in the fact that I have forestalled him, and paid him in his own coin!"

Daisy Leigh raised her face and gazed at the villain. Her lips moved convulsively, but for some moments no sound came from them.

"Monster!" she cried at length, "fiend in human form, I despise you. Begone, and harrow my feelings no longer by your detestable presence."

"Humph!" Sir Roland returned. "You speak boldly, but you seem to forget that I am all-powerful here. I command you to consent to be my wife. You must obey. A priest is within hail to make us man and wife, and so we must become sooner or later."

"Never!" Daisy replied. "Never! by all my hopes of future happiness."

"Your obstinacy is but madness," Sir Roland said. "You are in my power, and to my will you must submit. You are mine, Daisy! You shall be my wife."

"Villain!" Daisy cried, "I would sooner face the burning stake, and suffer a frightful death."

"What madness is this?" Sir Roland said; "for you have not the means of braving the death you speak of."

"But Heaven will help me."

"Daisy," Sir Roland said, "I have risked too much to give you the chance of escaping again. You must and shall become my wife. I have the means to support us in comfort and in luxury, and if you will but forget with me the dreary past my future actions shall make ample atonement for the deeds I have committed."

Daisy Leigh stared at him aghast.

Was it possible that a wretch who had been guilty of such atrocious crimes could talk lightly of forgetting the past?

Did he dare to speak of love to her whom he had so cruelly wronged?

Sir Roland's villainy seemed to pass all the bounds of human baseness, and the longer Daisy gazed at her persecutor the more her horror and loathing intensified.

Sir Roland was not at all abashed by Daisy's demeanour, but fixed his eyes upon her countenance in a manner calculated to cause her the greatest alarm.

"Daisy," he said, sinking down at her feet, "here, on this knee, which has never before bent to mortal, I supplicate your forbearance. I plead for that love, which, if you do not entertain for me now, will come after marriage. I sue to you for forgiveness, and to be the means of reclaiming me."

"Help! help!" Daisy gasped. "Devil! your words are echoed by the curses breathed by the shades of your dead victims. They call for retribution on your guilty head, for your hands are scarcely dry of blood. Oh! Heaven—horror!"

"What idle mockery is this?" Sir Roland cried, starting to his feet. "Do you think that you speak to a child? Do you think I am to be scared from my purpose by such prattle? I have marked you for my own. I have struggled, fought—aye! even bled—to gain my purpose, and a few hours hence my triumph will be complete."

Daisy, overcome with terror, started back to the other end of the room.

All the horrors, the utter helplessness of her situation, rushed upon her mind, and despair took possession of her heart.

During all the trials she had suffered she had never experienced such a moment.

Sir Roland remained silent for a minute or two, and seemed to watch the hapless girl's emotions with the greatest interest.

He approached her again and endeavoured to take her hand, but Daisy shrank from him as from the touch of a poisonous reptile.

"Oh! man—if man you are," Daisy said, pleadingly, "cruel as you are, you will abandon this design against my happiness. Let me go."

"Abandon this design!" Sir Roland replied. "Bah! I tell you, Daisy, that all my hopes are fixed on it. Your happiness or misery is in your own hands, for I am determined to hold you here until you consent to be mine for life."

"Never—never!" moaned Daisy, wringing her hands.

"But I will leave you now," Sir Roland continued. "I will give you a week to think over what I have said. Come, one kiss from those ruby lips, and I will be gone. That kiss shall seal my vows, which I have made in all sincerity."

Daisy screamed with terror and escaped from Sir Roland's outstretched arms.

"Heartless, guilty ruffian!" she exclaimed. "Oh! Heaven, why am I subjected to this disgrace and cruelty?"

"Fool!" Sir Roland hissed, "I ask but a kiss, and will not leave until your lips have touched mine. One kiss I say—only one. Ah!"

A ringing report rang through the room.

The window vanished beneath a cloud of smoke, and Sir Roland Ashton, flinging up his arms, fell with a crash at Daisy Leigh's feet.

CHAPTER LXXIII.

HOW A SECRET PASSAGE WAS DISCOVERED IN A MYSTERIOUS WAY.

WE must turn aside from the events just recorded to see how Jacob Butler is getting on.

It was some relief to his wretched mind to know that Mrs. Corcoran was no longer in the house, and Jacob had some hopes that something might occur to prevent her returning.

Mrs. Corcoran seemed to have as many lives as a cat, which is said to have nine, and Jacob Butler, when left alone, began to count how many narrow escapes Mrs. Corcoran had passed through.

"Something must happen to rid me of her," he groaned. "No mortal was ever sent on this earth to be punished and tortured as I am. I wonder what the hag is up to now. There must be mischief in the wind or she would not leave me for a moment."

Rick Denton had relieved Jacob of his bonds, and the miserable man paced the darkened room like a caged Polar bear.

At present he could see no hope of escape, and as he thought of his position and the fate promised him he flew into a kind of frenzy, and after hammering at the door with his knuckles until they were sore, suddenly used his head as a kind of battering ram, and dashed it, regardless of all consequences, against the wall.

The operation proved somewhat painful, but it produced one good result.

To Jacob Butler's astonishment the concussion was not nearly so great as he had expected, and he went flying through an aperture down two or three steps thickly covered with dust.

Jacob had discovered a secret passage in the most peculiar manner possible. In point of fact, the top of his cranium had released the spring of a sliding panel, which, perhaps, might lead to the road of light and freedom.

Mr. Butler picked himself up and rubbed the injured portion of his anatomy ruefully. He found that he had succeeded in producing a lump about the size of a hen's egg, and, moreover, he was regaled with the vision of a large quantity of stars dancing about in violent commotion.

But these things were mere trifles in comparison to the unexpected discovery, and Jacob, as he picked himself up, could scarcely refrain from chuckling audibly.

The noise of his fall might have reached Rick Denton's ears, and Jacob Butler lay perfectly still, gasping like a fresh codfish. All was still.

A deep, solemn silence reigned in the house, and Jacob Butler, satisfying himself that the noise caused by his tumble had not attracted attention, scrambled to his feet and walked back into the room.

His first act was to examine the panel and its spring.

After making himself acquainted with its mechanism he closed it, and removing the dust from his clothes, sat down and tried to look as if nothing had happened.

But this was not an easy task. His head ached and throbbed as if it would fly off his shoulders, but he bore the pain for fear that if Rick Denton entered the room suddenly his keen eyes would suspect that something was wrong.

It so happened that Jacob had decided to act wisely, for suddenly the door opened, and Rick Denton, bearing a basket in his hand, entered.

"Ha, ha!" he said. "I see that you occupy the same old corner. I hope you find it pretty comfortable."

"Not so much of that," Jacob returned; "but, like a beggar, I have no choice, and I suppose I must make the best of my position."

"Wisely spoken," said Rick Denton. "Well, you see we don't intend to starve you. I have brought you something to eat and drink, and you need not fear treachery. Mrs. Corcoran—ha, ha!—said that her lovey-dovey was to be kindly treated, and played no tricks with!"

"Hang her!" Jacob gasped.

"Of course. Just so. I have no objection," the old man said; "but she may have a few."

Jacob Butler was both hungry and thirsty, and he looked longingly at the basket.

"I suppose it is all right," he said. "I say, has she come back?"

"No; and I don't expect her for some time."

"Not to-day?"

"I can't tell," old Rick replied. "Eat, and don't bother me with a lot of questions."

"Oh!" cried Jacob Butler, with his mouth full, "I only wanted to say a few words to her."

"What about?"

"Well, you see," Jacob returned, "I have been thinking over this and that, and I am convinced at last that I have made a fool of myself. In short, I am willing to marry Mrs. Corcoran."

"She will be glad to hear that," Rick Denton chuckled. "You have soon made up your mind on the subject."

"Better that I should do so than lead the life of a dog."

"Just so; and I think you have taken the wisest course."

The old man grinned as he spoke, and glanced suspiciously at Jacob, who sat munching his food very much like a contented monkey.

"Ha!" said old Rick, "I suppose you think that because you tell me that your mind is made up that I shall let you out to ramble about the house?""

"The idea is yours—not mine.

"Of course you wouldn't try to get away or shout out of the first window you came to?" said Denton. "Oh! no. But I don't intend to give you the chance."

"And I didn't expect it," Jacob returned. "Haven't I told you that I intend to marry the old—Mrs. Corcoran, I mean. I wise she were in the house so that she might bear it from my own lips."

"She'll do that fast enough," Denton replied. "Don't eat so quick or you'll choke."

Jacob Butler had been stuffing his mouth as full as possible to keep down the feelings of exultation that filled his breast.

And yet it might be a question, after all, whether he had anything to crow about, for the secret passage might not lead to the open air, but to some cellar or den used for bad purposes by Rick Denton.

"I'll let Mrs. Corcoran know that you are so anxious to see her," Denton said, "and I have no doubt but that she will be overwhelmed with joy at your decision."

"Will she?" Jacob thought. "If she knew what was in my mind she would return quicker than she anticipated."

Rick Denton did not know exactly what to make of the sudden change in the prisoner's behaviour, but Jacob Butler appeared so earnest, and to enjoy the repast brought him so thoroughly, that the old man became convinced that Mrs. Corcoran had prevailed at last.

"So," he said, as he turned towards the door, "you accept your fate?"

"Yes," Jacob Butler replied. "I may as well do so cheerfully, as there seems to be no other alternative. I am tired of being trapped and caged. Hang it! man, you would do anything if you were in my place."

"Well, I don't know—perhaps I might," Denton said. "Mrs. Corcoran isn't a beauty, but beauty only lies skin deep, and I think she and you will make a well-matched pair. I wish you joy."

Jacob Butler dropped his face, for a heavy frown spread over his features, and he set his teeth to prevent himself saying something far from complimentary about Mrs. Corcoran and her chosen companions.

The fact that Jacob Butler relished his food seemed to annoy Rick Denton a little, and he turned, grumbling and scowling, towards the door.

When all was silent again Jacob Butler pocketed the remnants of the food, and then went to the door and listened.

The keyhole was a large one, and a glimmer of light shone through it.

Applying his eye at this draughty aperture, Jacob, having made sure that there was nobody upon the landing, stepped softly across the floor and applied his hand to the spring.

It yielded to his touch, and Jacob, descending the stairs on his feet this time instead of upon his head as before, began to look about him.

He thought it better to leave the panel partly open for fear that he might have to bolt back to the room at a moment's notice.

The secret staircase was very dark, but at last Jacob's eyes became accustomed to the gloom.

There were chinks in the wall here and there, and these enabled him to see where he was going.

Jacob descended the stairs until he came to a small room fitted up with antique furniture.

It was evident by the accumulation of dust and cobwebs that this apartment had not been used for some time.

As Jacob took a hasty survey of this place he noticed an old-fashioned rapier standing in a corner and secured it.

"Now," he muttered, valiantly, and striking a. tragic attitude, "it will be death to the man who attempts to stop my way."

Crossing this chamber Jacob came to a door, which was luckily open, and, descending another flight of stairs, he reached the cellar.

The only way of egress was by a double trap-door, and Jacob Butler was convinced that it led to the court.

The next and most important question was how to get the trap-door open.

Mr. Butler, quaking from his head downwards to his shoes, gazed at the ponderous woodwork with his head on one side, and then noticing an old rusty bolt he stood on tip-toe and tried to wrench it back.

The bolt was old and rusty, and refused to move at first, but after a great deal of wriggling and perseverance on Jacob's part it began to creak and give way.

More than once Jacob thought he heard somebody moving about over his head, and streams of perspiration poured down his face as he wrestled with the obstinate bolt.

Suddenly it gave way.

The two flaps of the trap-door came thundering down, and Jacob, receiving one of them on his head, fell, floored like a nine-pin.

In another instant he was on his feet, and, springing through the aperture, darted up the court and into the street beyond.

Jacob Butler felt inclined to kick up his heels for very joy.

He scampered down one side of Snow-hill and" up the other, but stopped for want of breath as he came in sight of Newgate prison.

As he did so he saw two constables approaching.

"Hi! you there!" he shouted. "Stop, Catchpole—Grabham! I have great news for you. I know where Bill Blarney and Mrs. Corcoran are."

CHAPTER LXXIV.
SPRING-HEELED JACK RESCUES A BOY, AND THIS INTRODUCES
A NEW CHARACTER TO OUR STORY.

DAISY LEIGH shrank back in silent terror as Sir Roland Ashton fell prone at her feet.

She saw blood flowing from his breast, and the shock was so sudden that she could not scream or articulate a word.

Before the smoke had cleared away she heard the bars being torn away from the window, and then she became aware that Spring-Heeled Jack was standing at her side.

Almost at the same instant the door flew open, and the old woman who had attended upon Daisy entered the room.

"Back, back, you hag!" Spring-Heeled Jack yelled. "If you would live to repent of your vile sins keep clear of me."

Old Martha started back at the sight of the strange weird figure towering above her.

Her face grew ashy grey, and, swooning, she fell across Sir Roland's body.

"Speak not!" Spring-Heeled Jack said to Daisy. "All danger is not at an end. Trust yourself to me, and all will be well. Ready!"

This word was addressed to someone outside the window, and immediately the masked face of a man appeared.

Daisy Leigh noticed that Spring-Heeled Jack raised her with his left arm, and that his right hung limp and apparently useless at his side.

The man outside received Daisy, and, throwing her lightly over his shoulder, descended a rope ladder.

In another instant Daisy found herself inside of a carriage, to which two spirited horses were attached.

They dashed away at a furious speed, whirling up clouds of dust, and rocking the carriage from side to side in a style that threatened to overturn it every moment.

All this added to Daisy Leigh's bewilderment, and she was beginning to think that her miraculous escape was but a dream after all, for she could see nothing whatever of Spring-Heeled Jack, when the carriage stopped suddenly.

Daisy Leigh shrunk back, thinking that Sir Roland's hirelings had overtaken the equipage, and then a cry of joy burst from her lips.

The door opened, and Ralph Ashton entered the carriage.

"Welcome, Miss Leigh!" he said. "I congratulate you. Excuse my left hand; I received a slight wound on the night that Sir Roland bore you away."

"Yes—yes, I know," Daisy replied, as soon as her delight would permit her to speak coherently. "How glad I am to see you! Sir Roland told me that you were dead."

"He did his best to make that an established fact," Ralph replied, smiling. "The coward stabbed me in the back, and I lost a quantity of blood."

His face was very pale, and it seemed as if he had gone through some great exertion recently.

"I am at a loss to account for these things," Daisy said. "How came you here? Was it not that wonderful being Spring-Heeled Jack who rescued me?"

"Yes," Ralph replied; "and it was he who sent me hither."

Daisy passed her hand over her fair brow.

"He sent you hither?" she said. "Ah! I know now. You were with him. It was you who appeared at the window, and carried me away from that dreadful house."

"You make a mistake," Ralph replied; "but you must not ask me to tell secrets which I am sworn not to divulge. Sir Roland will not trouble us for some time, and we are going back to the self-same place you came from."

"Oh! how delightful to see dear Constance again," Daisy said, clasping her hands. "Ah! what horrors I have passed through!"

"But not unwatched or uncared for," Ralph Ashton replied. "Spring-Heeled Jack knew of Sir Roland's movements, and only waited to foil his designs when he thought his triumph complete."

"All this is so wonderful that it entirely passes my comprehension," Daisy said. "Who is this Spring-Heeled Jack? Is he mortal or—"

Ralph Ashton placed his forefinger on his lips,

"Hush!" he said. "Say no more respecting him, for he may be listening to us at this very moment."

"He seems to have been wounded like you?"

"Yes," Ralph replied. "But enough. I must insist upon silence. Forgive me, Miss Leigh, if I appear stern, but I have a method in what I say."

It was late in the evening when the carriage reached its destination, and Daisy Leigh and Constance Marfield were once more clasped in each other's arms.

They shed tears of joy over each other, and Ralph Ashton, after dining with them, left the girls to chat at will.

Ascending to his private room, Ralph Ashton threw off his coat.

"Lorrimer!" he said, softly.

"Yes, sir," replied a voice.

"Enter."

A smart-looking fellow entered the room.

"Attend to my shoulder, and help me to dress," Ralph said. "It is time that I was away."

"And should the ladies enquire for you?" Lorrimer asked.

"Say that I am writing letters and must not be disturbed for an hour or so. Now see to my shoulder; it is growing painful again."

*

The full moon was sailing in stately grandeur across the sky.

All nature lay basking in the light of the silvery beams, and the grand old woods were silent, for no breath of wind disturbed the stillness of the scene.

Here and there a party of frolicsome rabbits frisked about or a hare darted from her "form," and went scuttling away from cover to the open fields.

Here and there a bat wheeled and flitted about in its erratic flight, or a solemn, great-eyed owl floated down upon a trembling field-mouse, and committed a midnight tragedy.

Presently the air became disturbed by the sound of footsteps.

A man and a boy were wending their way through the path in the wood, easily discernible in the moonlight.

The man was of a half-caste gipsy type, brutal of feature, and surly of voice.

His companion was a pale-faced, fragile lad, and fatigue had so told upon him that he could scarcely drag one foot before the other.

"Let me rest," the boy said. "I can go no further."

"But you must and shall," the man replied. "We have only two more miles to go, and they must be done to-night, as sure as my name is Jem Basker and your name is Robin."

"Robin what?" the boy asked. "Why do you keep me in this suspense? Why don't you tell me where we are going to, and for what purpose?"

"Hold your chattering tongue," Jem Basker growled. "If you mind your own business and do as I tell you, we shall be friends; if you don't, why——"

"You will beat and illtreat me as you have done before," Robin said, interrupting him. "What a weary life is mine; I have only one consolation."

"And what is that?" Jem Basker asked, laughing hoarsely. "That you will die some day or other, I suppose?"

"We must all die," Robin replied, "but you are wrong. My consolation is that you are not my father. You lied to me; you brought me up in that belief until I happened to meet Lanoni, the gipsy queen, and she told me——"

"Silence!" Jem Basker cried, in a voice of thunder, as he lifted his heavy hand, "Silence, you pale-faced whelp, or I'll not leave a whole bone in your skin."

"Ah! what a coward you are," Robin replied, fearlessly. "I know why Lanoni made you an outcast from her tribe; I know why she placed a ban on you, so that none of her people will converse with you."

"Silence—silence! I say," Jem Basker hissed.

The light of fury came into his eyes, as he spoke.

"You tried to teach me to thieve," Robin continued. "You made out that men who were dishonest lived merry lives; but I know how miserable you are in spite of all your bluster and pretended indifference. Where are you dragging me to now? I will go no further. By the moon that is shining in the heavens I will not."

Jem Basker's face grew pale, and his lips worked convulsively, as the boy threw himself beneath a tree.

"Listen, boy," he said, at length. "You are going to a place where you will never know want again. I can make you rich for life, and so provide myself with money as to leave this accursed country for ever. Get up and follow me, or you will rue the hour that you angered me."

"It will not be the first time that you have left me bruised and senseless on the roadside," the lad said. "Before I move I will know more of your purpose. If you think to palm me off on somebody as a son, stolen in his infancy, I will be no party to the fraud."

Jem Basker recoiled a step or two and whirled a heavy cudgel he carried in his right hand in the air.

"Beware how you tempt me to-night," he said, hoarsely. "The man who sees gold before his eyes does not turn away from it because it is near the fire. The secret you crave to know will be divulged soon. Once more I bid you rise and follow me."

"You shall tell me the story with your own lips first," Robin said, "and I will then say whether I believe you or not."

Driven almost mad with passion, James Basker seized the boy by the collar and swung the cudgel above his head. "Help!" the boy cried, despairingly.

"Help is near!"

The voice was so close to Jem Basker's ear that he turned with a terrified motion and recoiled before an awful apparition.

Hanging by his feet from the branch of a tree, with his arms and wings extended, was Spring-Heeled Jack.

The visitation was so sudden and terrific in appearance that Jem Basker could do nothing but stand and glare in speechless awe at the weird figure.

"Release your murderous hold!" said Spring-Heeled Jack. "I claim that boy."

"With a quick and marvellous motion, Spring-Heeled Jack shook his feet from the tree and alighted upon them on the ground.

"Dog—cowardly dog!" he cried, clutching Jem Basker around the waist. "Thus do I repay such dastardly conduct as yours."

The ruffian went flying away as if fired from a cannon and lay stunned and bleeding from his face.

"My poor lad," said Spring-Heeled Jack, stooping down and taking Robin's hand, "have no fear of me. My appearance may be strange, and yet methinks I have as warm a heart as most men."

"I do not fear you," the boy replied; "but—but there is something unearthly in your appearance. Oh! sir, leave me to my fate! My punishment will be only the greater for your interference."

Spring-Heeled Jack gazed strangely at the boy.

"So," he said, "I have protected you and saved you from savage blows for nothing?"

"Yes—yes, because—"

"Because you fear me?"

"I cannot help it," Robin replied.

"Well," said Spring-Heeled Jack, musingly, "that is not to be much wondered at. If this man will ill-treat you when he comes to his senses, why not trust yourself to my care. You will find that although uncouth in appearance I am not uncouth within. You have a secret?"

"Nay," Robin replied; "one is hidden from me."

"And I will unravel it, trust me," Spring-Heeled Jack said. "Come, follow me. If you do not like the place I take you to or the company you find there, breathe but a word and you shall be as free as the birds now slumbering in the trees above our heads."

"I fear you no longer," said Robin; "I will go with you."

"Spoken wisely," Spring-Heeled Jack said. "Leap upon my back. I am well able to carry your weight, and I must introduce you to one who is more like ordinary mortals than I am."

With the sense of the strangeness of his position, upon him Robin did as he was requested.

A cry of alarm came from his lips as Spring-Heeled Jack swept over the ground in a series of gigantic strides, and the boy nearly fainted from sudden fear.

"Hush—hush!" said Spring-Heeled Jack. "Be brave, and trust me as you would trust a friend."

While these events were passing, Constance Marfield and Daisy Leigh were enjoying each other's company.

"And so," Constance was saying, "Sir Roland is not dead?"

"No," Daisy replied. "His eye-lids were quivering as a sign of returning consciousness, as I was borne from the room. Oh! Constance—Constance, will there ever be an end to this mystery and misery? I feel that I should take my life if I thought I should ever fall into that villain's hands again."

"Hush! Daisy—hush!" Constance said. "We have noble protectors in my dear Ralph and Spring-Heeled Jack. We must be patient, for what can we, two weak, helpless girls, do by ourselves?"

Thus more than an hour passed away, and when a servant entered the room to prepare the table for supper he was followed by Ralph Ashton.

"I was afraid to acquaint you with the fact that I was going out, for fear that you might be nervous," he said, smiling, "but out I have been, and the strangest thing in the world is that I have brought somebody with me."

Constance Marfield and Daisy Leigh looked askance at him.

"Who is it, Ralph?" Constance asked. "Somebody I know?"

"No," Ralph replied, shaking his head; "and the odd part of it is that I don't know him myself."

"It is a man, then?"

"No, a boy. Come in, Robin."

As the pale-faced, care-worn lad entered the room, Constance and Daisy rose to greet him.

"I came upon this lad in a rather uncanny fashion," Ralph continued. "He was lying under a tree, where he said he had been placed by Spring-Heeled Jack."

"That is true, sir," Robin replied. "He told me to remain there until he sent somebody to me."

"And he sent you?" Constance said, looking earnestly at Ralph.

"Yes."

A silence fell upon the little assembly for some moments.

"It would appear," said Ralph, at last, "that there is some mystery about this youngster. He has been in bad hands, and we must take care of him. Indeed, we are commanded to do so, unless we wish to displease Spring-Heeled Jack, who has been so useful to us."

"We will be faithful to our trust," Constance said, as she stooped and kissed the boy on the cheek. "You must try to make yourself happy with us, my pretty little fellow."

"I could not be otherwise with you," Robin replied, with eyes sparkling with joy.

"Spoken like a young gentleman," Ralph Ashton said, heartily. "To-morrow I will see that Robin is better clothed, and then we will have a long talk, to see what is best to be done."

CHAPTER LXXV.
THE PEDLAR'S BOX.

THE moment that Catchpole and Grabham saw Jacob Butler, and heard his uplifted voice, they came to a standstill.

Then they manifested a strong inclination to bolt, but Jacob overtook them.

"Don't go!" he said, breathlessly; "I have had such a dreadful adventure."

"What's the matter now?" Grabham growled. "We're on special duty, and can't stop to chatter, so if you have anything to say, out with it at once."

"I suppose you know that Bill Blarney has escaped from Newgate?" Jacob said.

"Of course we do," Catchpole said. "Who should know it better than we?"

"Well," Jacob Butler continued, "I happen to know where he is."

"Oh! come now, that's too good a tale to be true," Grabham said. "You are trying to make fools of us, but it won't do, my fine fellow."

"It's a fact," Jacob gasped. "If you follow me I'll show you the house where he has taken refuge in, and Mrs. Corcoran, too."

"He's got Mrs. Corcoran on the brain," Grabham said aside to Catchpole.

"Yes," that worthy assented.

"They're gone out together, but will return soon," Jacob Butler went on. "Follow me. The house is down a court—I don't know the name of it, because I found my way there by accident."

Grabham shook his head gravely, and tapped his forehead.

"I'm afeard that you have melted them two guineas in spirituous liquors, Jacob," he said. "but if so be that you are quite certain about what you say, why, of course, it will be our dooty to go with you."

"I am as certain of it as I am alive," Jacob Butler said; "as certain as that I have been near death."

Jacob Butler in his flight had so twisted and turned, that when he endeavoured to retrace his footsteps he discovered that he was completely muddled and mixed.

If he took the constables down one court he took them down twenty.

They knocked at doors without numbers and the curses of unoffending people were heaped upon their heads.

"Well," said Jacob Butler, after at least an hour of fruitless search, "if anybody had told me that I couldn't find the house I should have called that party a fool."

Grabham tilted his hat on one side and gazed pensively at the much-injured man.

"I'll have a few words privately with my mate," the constable observed; "so if you wouldn't mind standing aside, I should feel much obliged."

"Certainly," Jacob Butler said, and withdrew accordingly.

"What do you make of all this?" Grabham asked, in a whisper.

"Why, that he's gone wrong in the upper story," Catchpole replied. "Did you mark the glare in his eyes when he came running up to us?"

"I did," Grabham returned. "He looked like a wild beast just escaped from a cage. What are we to do?"

Mr. Catchpole took off his hat and ran his fingers through his hair.

"I've got an idea," he said, presently. "Grabham, my boy, he will be a source of trouble to us and must be got rid of."

"But how? You don't mean to say that—"

"I would put him out of the way by foul means," Catchpole interposed. "Bah—no! I had no such thing in my mind. But the law doesn't allow mad people to go prowling about."

"Ha!" Grabham ejaculated, "I understand you now. The idea is this: You and I collar Jacob Butler, we take him before a doctor and swear that he is a dangerous character, and bang he goes into a madhouse."

"That's the notion," Catchpole said. "Once we get him in he will be lucky if he gets out."

"Shall we take him now?"

"Yes," Catchpole replied; "but we must be careful how we collar him. He may kick or bite."

Smilingly the constables turned and walked slowly towards Jacob Butler.

"Jacob, my boy," said Grabham, "of course you are right about Blarney and Mrs. Corcoran, only you can't find the house where they are just now. You must have time to think over it, » take a little walk with us and get your head clear."

"My head is clear enough," said Jacob, backing up slowly step by step.

There was something in the eyes of the constable and the way he approached that Jacob did not like.

"You are up to some game with me," he said. "Keep back—you mean treachery."

Grabham rolled up his eyes, and assumed the air of an injured man.

"This is hard after the way we treated you," he said. "We let you go free from the lock-up. We hail you as a brother, and follow you about on a wild-goose chase, and now you want to make out that we are deceiving you."

"I know it," said Jacob, still retreating backwards. "I am quite sure of it."

Grabham looked up and down the street.

There was no living creature in sight, save a boy intent on making mud pies in the gutter.

"Catchpole," Grabham said, hoarsely, "now or never is our time. We must have him. Attack him in the rear, and if he gives us any trouble I'll give him a oner that will make him see a cart-load of stars."

Jacob Butler's countenance turned from white to red, and then green.

"Help! help!" he cried, feebly. "Murder! I won't be taken alive!"

But Catchpole was already upon him, and Grabham, true to his word, gave the luckless Jacob such a tap on the bridge of the nose that tears of anguish flowed down his cheeks.

"He's a dangerous customer, and we must put the darbies[115] on him," said Grabham.

Click, click, went the handcuffs over Jacob's wrists and the unhappy man uttered a groan of despair.

"Now, Catchpole," Grabham said, "just run to the top of the street and fetch a coach. We must take him before Doctor Cuthem at once."

"Before who?" Jacob gasped.

"Before Doctor Cuthem," Grabham repeated.

"Why," Jacob demanded, "what on earth do I want to see a doctor for?"

"Be calm," Grabham returned, soothingly. "Only be quiet and no harm will come to you. You've had a bad shock to your nerves, and a little rest in a nice quiet place, where you will be taken care of, will do you a power of good."

Jacob Butler turned deadly pale.

He guessed the constable's meaning, and his lower jaw fell.

"Listen to me!" he said. "Only hear me. I—"

"I'll listen to nothing," Grabham interposed. "Catchpole, fetch the coach. We are wasting time by standing prating here."

Catchpole, rubbing his hands gleefully, bolted off and presently returned with the coach.

"I call you to witness that this is a vile, horrible plot against my liberty," Jacob Butler said to the driver.

"Don't heed him," Grabham said. "He's very bad. If we were to let him go goodness only knows what would happen. We found him standing on his head and talking all sorts of nonsense about the world being upside down."

"It's a lie—a base lie!" Jacob howled. "I'm as sane as the King of England!"

"Poor devil!" said the coachman, compassionately. "What did he say?"

"That he was the King of England," Catchpole replied.

"I won't go!" he roared. "I'm not mad! Help—help!"

"Lift him in," said Grabham. "Take care of his feet."

The warning came too late.

Jacob, overcome with feelings of rage and terror, let out with might and main.

One of his feet took effect in the centre of Catchpole's waistcoat, and the constable, after a wild backward flight, fell upon his back and lay gazing placidly at the sky.

"I'm afeard he's knocked all the wind out or my mate," Grabham said. "Get down, coachey, and lend me a hand. You'll have to go before the doctor and tell him of this."

"I don't care about these sort of jobs," the coachman replied; "but I see how the wind blows. It's a mercy that the poor fellow has not killed somebody."

Meanwhile Catchpole had somewhat recovered, and had risen to his feet.

Standing against a wall, with one foot raised and his hand pressed upon his waistcoat, he looked very much like a fat overgrown boy suffering from the consequences of a first dose of tobacco.

---

[115] Handcuffs.

SPRING-HEELED JACK,

THE TERROR OF LONDON.

"IT IS POISON," MRS. CORCORAN SAID. "I WANT TO KILL TWO BIRDS WITH ONE STONE."

Jacob Butler gave a gasp of horror and flung himself down on the ground.

The constable was ill—very ill—and before he could take any part in the proceedings Jacob Butler had been dragged into the coach. Grabham was holding the wretched man by the throat, and the driver had taken his seat on the box.

"I'm mortal bad," Catchpole panted. "I'm afeard that I am wounded in a vital part. I haven't the strength of a child."

"If you can't hold him you can sit on him," Grabham returned. "I'm getting tired. Hang the fellow! I never dreamed that he was so strong."

Jacob Butler fought with his manacled hands, and exerted every muscle of his body in the struggle of despair.

But when Catchpole added his bulky weight, which he did by sitting upon the captive's knees and hugging him violently round the neck, Jacob Butler collapsed all of a sudden, and sank back moaning in a half-fainting condition.

"That's better," said Grabham. "He's all right now. Don't quite choke him, Catchpole. Let him have a little air, as we may have some way to go."

Leaving the coach to jolt and rumble on its journey we will take a peep into the interior of a similar vehicle which has just drawn up at the door of the Bull in Top Boots.

Mrs. Corcoran and Bill Blarney were the occupants of this coach, and the nice old lady was crooning and wagging her head from side to side in the most amiable fashion.

"I have heard of this place," she croaked; "but little did I ever think that I should come to it, and in such gallant company. I declare, Mr. Blarney, that if I did not love my Jacob so dearly that I could take quite a fancy to you."

"Could you?" Bill Blarney growled, under his breath, as he let down the window. "The wrinkled witch! you'd talk in another fashion if you knew what I have brought you here for."

Throwing open the door he walked towards the inn.

"Stop—stop!" Mrs. Corcoran cried.

"What's the matter now?" demanded Bill Blarney, swinging himself round on his heels.

"It is the duty of a gentleman to hand a lady from a coach," Mrs. Corcoran said, smirking.

"Ah! so it is," Bill Blarney returned. "Genteel society has been rather out of my line just lately, so you must put my conduct down to absent-mindedness. Come out!"

He jerked Mrs. Corcoran out of the coach in a rather unceremonious manner; but she only laughed.

"You will pay for the coach, deary," she said.

"Deary, be hanged!" said Bill Blarney, in a savage whisper. "Pay yourself. You don't suppose that the warders of Newgate left me much money. Haven't I come here to fetch some. Pay up, or that scarecrow on the box will think there is something wrong."

Blinking and gasping, Mrs. Corcoran dived her hand into the depths of a pocket, which seemed to end somewhere near her heels.

After producing an antique pair of scissors, a skein of thread, a pin-cushion, a reel of cotton, and a lump of dirty beeswax, she brought a greasy purse to light, and fished out half-a-crown, which looked as if it had passed most of its days underground.

"My fare is three-and-six," said the coachman, gazing in disgust at the hag. "It'll be four shillings if you keep me waiting here any longer."

Mrs. Corcoran screwed a malignant squint at the man.

"What thieves you fellows are," she said. "Three-and-six for riding in a mouldy coffin on wheels. Take another sixpence and think yourself well paid."

"I'll think myself lucky to get out of your sight at any price, you broomstick hag!" the coachman said. "I shouldn't wonder if money from your hands was red hot and smelt of brimstone."

"Wouldn't you, now?" replied Mrs. Corcoran, grinning. "Well, that's smart saying on your part, and I take it as a compliment."

The driver snatched the money, and, hissing out an oath, lashed his horses into a gallop and was soon out of sight.

"That man will remember you as long as he lives," Bill Blarney said. "Come into the house. Phew! I was afraid that he would drive away and fetch a constable."

The landlord of the Bull in Top Boots hailed Bill Blarney with delight, but looked rather queer and dubious as his eyes rested on Mrs. Corcoran.

"Who is she?" he demanded. "Where the deuce did you pick up that mummy?"

"Hush!" said Bill Blarney. "She's sharper than any needle and more cunning than any fox. I'll tell you why I have brought her here presently. Let me introduce you to her."

He did so, and Mrs. Corcoran, having partaken of a glass of brandy, addressed the landlord in such endearing terms that he looked inclined to strike her on the head with something heavy.

"Any news?" Bill Blarney asked.

"No," the landlord replied; "Dick Sleuth has been keeping himself quiet for fear that his movements might be watched after you got clear, but I expect him here presently."

"That's well," Bill Blarney replied. "I shall want his assistance, for Mrs. Corcoran can put us on a job that may help to fill our pockets."

"Good!" the landlord replied. "The boys are all hard up, and to tell you the truth my funds are running down like the tide."

Bill Blarney leaned forward and whispered in the landlord's ear.

"Put that old woman in one of the private rooms," he said, "the very sight of her makes me feel ill."

"I am with you there," the landlord replied, in disgust. "A hospital doctor wouldn't give five shillings for her carcase."

Perhaps Mrs. Corcoran overheard this pleasant remark, for she suddenly burst out laughing.

"Come with me," the landlord said, "and I will show you where you can rest."

Mouthing and grinning Mrs. Corcoran insisted upon taking his arm, and when the landlord returned to Blarney his face was pale and damn with cold perspiration.

"I wish you hadn't brought such a South Sea image to my place," he said, as he threw himself into a chair. "Bah! Pass the brandy bottle. I'd rather face all the traps in London than spend an hour in her company."

"But she'll be useful to us," Bill Blarney said, "If I didn't know it, do you think that I should be such an idiot to tolerate her for an instant?"

"Well, well," said the landlord, "let us hope that she may bring us profit, and then—"

"I hope she will live to share it," Bill Blarney said, laughing.

Their eyes met, and then the landlord laughed too, as if his ruffianly companion had made an excellent joke.

"Now tell us all about yourself?" he said.

Bill Blarney did so, helping himself freely from the brandy bottle meanwhile.

"And now," said the landlord, when the story came to an end, "what wonderful story has this old woman to tell?"

"Not one story, but several," Bill Blarney replied. "In the first place she is satisfied that Sir Roland is in London, and, secondly, she is in possession of other information of a valuable character; but how the deuce she got it is more than I can tell."

"Nor can I, until you tell me what it is," said the landlord.

"You have heard of Mildendale Hall?"

"Yes."

"And something of the story connected with the place?"

"Well, yes," said the landlord; "but my memory is none of the best. Refresh it for me, if you can."

"I will," Bill Blarney replied, "and in as few words as possible."

Having gulped down another glass of brandy, he placed his hands upon his knees.

"Lord Robert Mildendale, the owner of the estate and Hall which bear his family name, married a gipsy girl as soon as he came of age.

"The match did not prove a happy one.

"The country people shunned Lord Robert and his beautiful dark-eyed wife, and for one whole year they remained shut up with scarcely a soul calling upon them.

"At Christmas-time a child was born.

"It proved to be a boy, and Lord Mildendale was delighted, for had he died without an heir the estate would pass to his cousin Charles—a man he hated bitterly.

"Lord Mildendale opened the hall, and gave a grand fête, but only the common people attended it, and his lordship in a fury swore an oath that he would train up his infant son to hate his race, and all men and women of his class.

"But Lord Mildendale never had the chance of carrying out his threat."

"The child died, I suppose," the landlord said.

"There you are wrong," Bill Blarney replied. "The boy was stolen."

"Stolen?"

"Yes," Blarney said; "but don't interrupt me, as I shall forget the story myself."

"Matters did not mend at Mildendale," he continued, after a pause. "Lord and lady led a miserable cat and dog life.

"One night—so it is said—his lordship, after drinking heavily at dinner, struck his wife with a riding-whip.

"The blow descended about her bare shoulders and left a livid mark.

"She did not cry out or utter a word.

"Moving towards the door, she turned, and then her lips moved, as if silently invoking some curse upon his head.

"From that day to this she was never heard of.

"She fled from Mildendale Hall, and it was given out that she went back to her people.

"Strangely enough she left the child, and the boy grew apace for three years.

"One day he wandered from his nurse's side, and mysteriously disappeared."

"I suppose he fell into a pond, or something of that sort?" the landlord of the Bull in Top Boots said, indifferently.

"He did nothing of the kind," Bill Blarney replied. "The boy was stolen by a party of wandering gipsies, who had been waiting their opportunity for more than a year."

"How do you know that?"

"Have patience to listen to the end of the story," Bill Blarney said. "Lord Mildendale received an unsigned letter from Spain, saying that he might bid Good-bye for ever to his son."

"Humph! Well, I suppose his lordship took some little trouble to find the boy?"

"Yes; he spent some thousands of pounds."

"And never got a clue?"

"Not the slightest."

"Nor heard of his wife?"

"Yes; she died. A letter in the same handwriting as the first made him acquainted with that news."

The innkeeper passed his hand thoughtfully across his chin.

"Well," he said, "there is nothing very wonderful in the story, after all. It has been told and with truth in the world many and many a time. I see nothing very extraordinary in it."

"Listen," Bill Blarney said. "This bag of skin and bones, this withered skinflint of a woman, Mrs. Corcoran, declares that the boy was never sent to Spain, but sold to a man in England."

"It is all very well to say so, but can she prove it?"

"She says she can," Bill Blarney replied; "and she says more than that."

"That she knows where the boy is?"

"Yes."

"In that case," said the landlord, "I should imagine that there is a pretty good haul to be netted. What sort of a programme do you intend to follow out?"

"Why, to buy the boy back again, if possible, and then to make sound profit out of him," Bill Blarney replied.

"But supposing this man happens to be in possession of the secret?"

"Yes, but Mrs. Corcoran says he is not," the man returned. "The fellow, it seems, is in trouble, and very likely would be only too glad to grab at a handful of guineas."

"I begin to see the drift of all this." the landlord said, after a short spell of silence. "You want me to advance the money."

Before Bill Blarney could make any kind of a sound the front door opened with a creaking sound, and the landlord started to his feet.

"Hush!" he whispered: "it may be a visit from the Bow-street runners!"

Bill Blarney's face changed colour, and he grasped his throat with his hands in an uncomfortable sort of way.

As the landlord made his way to the bar he whistled unconcernedly, and still more so when he saw that the stranger was only a travelling pedlar.

"I have lost my way in this wilderness of streets," the pedlar said; "and, feeling tired, I thought I would come here. Can you board me to-day and let me have a bed to-night?"

"Good accommodation for man and beast," the landlord muttered.

"That is well," said the pedlar, removing a box from his back.

"You carry a heavy load?"

"Yes," the man replied; "I buy and sell jewellery—the real stuff and no sham rubbish—so I shall feel obliged if you will let me keep the key of my room."

"Oh! certainly," the landlord responded, in his blandest tones. "But, sir, there are none here but honest people."

"Don't be offended," the pedlar replied. "He who carries two or three hundred pounds with him need be careful in these days."

"There you are right. You shall have the key, sir. Would you like to see your room now?"

"Yes; because I should like to rest an hour or two."

The landlord of the Bull in Top Boots turned his head aside for a moment.

He was wondering whether Bill Blarney had listened to what had taken place.

The pedlar went to a room, and when alone, and making sure that there was no other door or peephole through which his actions could be watched, he opened the box and gazed with greedy eyes at its glistening contents.

"A good lot and a fine bargain," he said. "What matters it to me where they came from! They are mine—mine, and will bring me a profit of more than a hundred per cent."

Closing the box, he locked it carefully, and placing it on the bed, passed his arm through the strap, and lay down beside it.

Meanwhile the landlord had gone back to Bill Blarney.

The ruffian received him with a grin.

"I suppose I stand in this?" Blarney said, pointing to the ceiling, and indicating that he alluded to the man upstairs.

"I don't know," the landlord replied. "So you heard what was said? Ah! I thought that you would take the trouble to listen."

"A man with a pair of ears in good order can't help listening, unless he stops them up."

"Which you would never take the trouble to do," the landlord said, laughing.

"Well, I can repay that compliment with interest," Bill Blarney replied. "See, here, I will make a bargain with you."

"Wait a minute," said the landlord. "This is a matter not to be in a hurry over. How are we to know that this is not a pitfall dug for us to fall into?"

"We must chance that," Bill Blarney returned.

Leaning forward he whispered something in his companion's ear.

"How do the terms suit you?"

"Well enough," the landlord replied. "I agree, providing that I have no hand in the matter."

"Then you may consider it done," said Blarney.

CHAPTER LXXVI.

THE HAUNTED TERRACE—LORD MILDENDALE SEES A GHOST, BUT NOT THE FAMILY ONE.

STANDING on a verdant eminence, shaded by fine old oaks and elms, the lofty turrets of Mildendale Hall rose in proud and bold relief against the deepening blue sky.

It was evening, and the sun, lingering amid a glory of crimson, purple, and gold, seemed loth to leave so grand a scene of its own creation.

But at last the orb sank below the horizon, and shadows of deep purple hue crept out from their hiding-places in the hill-sides, and chasing across the sky heralded the coming night.

Just as a few stars peeped out bashfully, and twinkled feebly, as if conscious that their light was not yet required, an old man, bent almost double, emerged from an avenue of trees and hobbled painfully towards the ancestral home of the Mildendales.

He leaned heavily upon a stick, and stopped every now and then to wheeze and catch his breath.

Shabbily attired—for he was in rags which fluttered in the wind—this decrepit old man posed in strange contrast to the noble house, ancient but stately, and filled with every luxury that money can buy and skill devise.

His way did not lay by the front entrance, but by a narrow path used by servants and trades-people, and which, as a matter of course, led to the rear of the building.

The mendicant, or at least he had all the appearances of one, seemed perfectly acquainted with the route, though it was so hard for him to travel, and hobbling on, he reached a small door, and knocked timorously at it.

He shrank back a little as he heard a burst of merry laughter.

"Ah!" he muttered. "Man and maid make merry to-day. It is his lordship's birthday. I wonder if there be any joy in his heart?"

Receiving no answer to his first summons, the old man knocked louder, and then the door flew open, and a gorgeously-clad footman appeared.

"What do you want?" he demanded.

"Charity, good sir, charity."

"You'll get nothing of that sort here," the flunkey replied, "and you may think yourself lucky that his lordship is away just now. He will be back presently, and mark my words, he will order me to set yonder mastiff free, should he happen to catch sight of you."

"Indeed!" the old man replied. "So he is no exception to his—I mean, the world. Because he knows not what poverty is, he deems it a crime."

"You had better go, indeed you had," the footman said. "If I had any change I would give you a penny. Bless me, man, why don't you go? Do you want to feel that dog's teeth meet in your shrivelled legs?"

For a moment the beggar raised his eyes, and a peculiar light shone from them.

"If you have no money," he said, "give me food and drink. I am only a poor old gipsy, and—"

The footman threw up his hands and started back in horror.

"Fly!" he cried—"fly while there is time! If Lord Mildendale knew that a man with Romany blood in his veins had been here he will leave no stone in the neighbourhood unturned until he has found him."

"And then," said the old man, coolly, "if his lordship found that man what would he do to him?"

The footman shuddered.

"Why don't you take my advice and go?" he blurted out. "Listen! I hear the sound of carriage-wheels. Go, I beseech you, or there will be more bloodshed in Mildendale!"

"Yes, I will go," the old gipsy replied, "but I and others will return. Tell Lord Mildendale that I, Namon Wallack, wish him and his son—ha! ha! ha!—many happy returns of this day!"

He turned and vanished from view so quickly that the footman stood motionless and dumb foundered.

"An old man forsooth!" he said at length, "It strikes me that he must be young, hale, and hearty to be able to make his departure in such a fashion. Shall I mention this circumstance to my lord? No, He would only fly into a rage, and ask why I did not shoot the fellow down. I will let the matter rest where it is."

As Lord Mildendale entered the hall the sounds of merriment ceased, and the servants moved about with silent footsteps and grave faces.

His lordship was a middle-aged man, but the deep lines on his countenance, which showed that he laboured under no common sorrow, made him look much older.

He scarcely ever spoke, save to state his wants or to give an order to his valet, a staid, clean-shaven man, who seldom left his master's elbow from morn till night.

"Harmer," his lordship said, "give me a glass of wine and fetch me a book—any one will do."

He threw himself wearily into a chair as he spoke, and Harmer, gliding about like a ghost, obeyed his master's commands.

"I have a fancy to be alone," Lord Mildendale said, suddenly; and then he added to himself—"Forty years old to-day. Forty years of unrest and disappointment. Ah! well, I can employ my mind in looking back into the past."

Raising his eyes, he discovered that Harmer had already left the room.

The book fell from Lord Mildendale's hand, for a sound broke upon his ears.

It was the sound of footsteps upon the terrace walk, and he had often heard them when alone.

"Unreal mockery!" he said. "And yet, how they remind me of bye-gone days! They are but the echoes of the past. How often have I heard those footsteps as she paced to and fro with her baby boy in her arms! Oh! my wife—my child—my child!"

Lord Mildendale dropped his face into his open hands, and a great sob of agony rose from his heart.

"I must go out!" he cried, suddenly. "I cannot not breathe the atmosphere of this place; it chokes me. Would to Heaven that I had died long ago and escaped this misery!"

Pushing open the French windows reaching from floor to ceiling, Lord Mildendale stepped out upon the terrace.

The full moon was shining brightly, and every object was as plain and distinct as at noon tide.

Lord Mildendale seemed to be watching something.

He kept his eyes fixed on the further end of the terrace, as if he expected to see somebody there, and as he watched the ghostly footsteps went on.

"She will come again to-night," he muttered. "This is the night in the year when she appears to remind me of the bitter past. Ah! At last!"

A faint, quivering light flashed up ahead of him, but the apparition he saw was not the one he had expected and had been waiting for with a fast-beating heart.

As in the reflection of a mirror he saw a strange, tall form of a man, weird and ghastly, who held a lad by one hand and pointed to him with the other.

"Heaven help me!" Lord Mildendale cried. "What may this mean? Fiend or mortal speak to me!"

But the mysterious form neither spoke nor moved.

Lord Mildendale tottered forward a few steps, and then the ghastly figure raised its hand.

"Beware!" it said. "To approach me is death!"

At that moment the boy turned his face and looked full into Lord Mildendale's eyes.

"My child—my son!" the nobleman cried. "Ah! he lives. Come to these arms and this heart which has yearned for you through many a weary year!"

As the vision had appeared so it vanished in an instant, and Lord Mildendale, gasping out a cry of terror, staggered back to the room and fell senseless upon the floor.

The noise of his fall brought Harmer to his side.

"He will die in one of these paroxysms," the valet said, as he raised his lordship and placed him in a chair. "Poor men envy the rich, but give me poverty to such a life as this man leads!"

CHAPTER LXXVII.

THE PEDLAR'S ROOM—MRS. CORCORAN HAS A TWINGE OF CONSCIENCE.

NIGHT had fallen gloomily upon London, and the great city lay hushed in slumber.

The sky was murky, promising both rain and thunder, and the river ran sullenly, as if lingering to join the coming storm.

All good people were in bed, but here and there bursts of uproarious drunken mirth came from the windows of houses of low repute, and made the night hideous.

For a wonder the Bull in Top Boots was comparatively quiet, and the front of the house showed no light.

This would have been quite sufficient to convince anybody acquainted with the habits and customs of the vile wretches who used the house that mischief was brewing.

Though the windows facing the street were plunged in darkness the back rooms were bright enough, and some score or more ruffians were drinking deeply and singing ribald songs.

"Come, come, boys," the landlord said, as he made his way into the room, where the merrymakers had assembled. "I must ask you to leave presently, for I am almost done to death. This makes the fourth night that I have been up, and if I try the experiment again the Bull in Top Boots will go into mourning for its landlord."

"Well," said Dick Sleuth, who sat at the head of the table, "bring in another bowl of punch and we will be satisfied."

The landlord grumbled out something under his breath as he turned towards the door.

Bill Blarney followed the innkeeper into the passage and tapped him on the shoulder.

"A word with you," he said.

"Well?"

"Make the punch weak, or some of those fellows will get so drunk that there will be no getting them out of the house at all."

"You may leave that to me," the landlord replied, grinning. "In half an hour we shall be alone."

"And then we must wait an hour or so," Bill Blarney replied. "It is very improbable that the pedlar can go to sleep with all this noise of singing under him.

"We must wait!" the landlord repeated, elevating his eyebrows. "What have I to do with it?'

"Well, it is all one and the same thing," said Bill Blarney, impatiently.

"There I can't agree with you," the landlord rejoined. "You make a proposition, and I agree to let you have your way to a certain extent; but that is all."

"You took good care to make terms with me," Bill Blarney said, sullenly.

The landlord swung himself sharply round on his heels and looked the ruffian steadily in the face.

"You owe your life and liberty to me," he said. "I have fed you, supplied you with money, and if I made terms with you it was only to get back what was due to me."

He snapped his fingers, and turning angrily away, walked into the bar.

The punch was soon brewed and consumed.

Then the company began to disperse, some reeling, others shouting and yelling and a few quarrelling and declaring that they would settle their grievances at a more convenient opportunity.

Bill Blarney had kept out of the way, but no sooner was the door locked and bolted than he appeared again.

"Don t be angry," he said to the landlord, "I meant no harm. You have acted the part of a friend to me often I confess."

"Well, well, we will say no more about the matter."

"I thought it best to take Mrs. Corcoran into my confidence," Bill Blarney said.

"More fool you!"

"I don't think so," the ruffian returned. "She knows my character too well already, and my object is now to get her under my thumb, so as to make sure of her silence."

"In point of fact, I suppose you have asked her to help you?" the inn-keeper said.

"You have hit the right nail on the head," Bill Blarney replied. "The old hag possesses some potions, a few drops of which, sprinkled on the face of a sleeping man, prevents him waking, though a thunder-bolt fell at his feet."

"What a nice, pleasant old lady you have brought under my roof!" the landlord said, grinning. "I hope she will not try any of her experiments on me! Ah! here she comes."

Blinking like an old owl in the sunlight, Mrs. Corcoran came hobbling down the stairs.

"I have listened for his breathing," she said, "and he sleeps soundly."

Bill Blarney drew a deep breath and a death-like pallor stole across his face.

"This will not do," he said, striking his chest. "I have either drunk too much or not enough. Give me another glass of brandy and then I shall be ready for anything."

"Yes, yes," said Mrs. Corcoran. "Come at once. We must waste no time. He may wake suddenly. Strange dreams come to men in danger sometimes and put them on their guard."

The landlord's hand trembled as he supplied Bill Blarney with the fiery liquor, and as the ruffian and Mrs. Corcoran turned towards the staircase he went into the parlour behind the bar and closed the door.

The Bull in Top Boots had witnessed many a scene such as was about to be enacted under its evil roof.

Slowly and noiselessly Bill Blarney and the hag crept up the stairs, and they went on without stopping until they reached a spacious landing.

"That is his room," Mrs. Corcoran whispered, pointing to a door. "Are you sure that you have forgotten nothing?"

"Quite. And you?"

Mrs. Corcoran made a hideous grimace as she held up a phial filled with colourless liquid.

"Hush!" Bill Blarney said. "Now to open the door. The hinges are old; they may creak and wake him."

"In that case," Mrs. Corcoran croaked, "you must be quick and sure. He must utter no word or cry. Now!"

Bill Blarney took from his pocket a duplicate key, which the landlord had provided him with, and inserted it in the lock.

The ruffian listened intently as he turned it, but the pedlar still breathed heavily, and lay unconscious that his time on earth was drawing so swiftly to a close.

Slowly, inch by inch, Bill Blarney opened the door, and he and Mrs. Corcoran stole with cat-like movements towards the bed.

The pedlar, who was lying in an uneasy attitude upon his face, moved slightly as Bill Blarney stooped over him, but in an instant Mrs. Corcoran drew the stopper from the phial and sprinkled its contents over the slumbering man's mouth and nostrils.

He uttered one gasping, guttural cry and opened his eyes.

There was a horrible glare in them, as if he knew what was to happen and yet was aware of his helplessness.

The eyes closed again, but Bill Blarney stood hesitating and trembling in every limb.

"Fool!" said Mrs. Corcoran. "He has no more power than a log of wood. Give me the knife."

"No!" Bill Blarney said, hoarsely, as he raised the glistening blade. "Ah!"

The next instant he and Mrs. Corcoran were out of the room, and stood clutching each other, guilty wretches that they were; but the hag was not yet satisfied.

"I must go back," she said; "I must make sure that you struck home."

"No, no!" Blarney gasped; "let us go downstairs."

Mrs. Corcoran released herself from the ruffian's grasp and hastened into the room.

The next instant a shriek burst from her lips.

Bill Blarney's hair stood on end with terror, and he reeled heavily against the wall.

"What now?" he yelled, as he recovered his self-control and dashed into the room.

"Those eyes!" Mrs. Corcoran shrieked, as she sank upon her knees, "they opened again and fixed themselves upon me. Mercy! mercy!"

"Come away," Blarney said, seizing her by the shoulders, "come away, you witch! He is dead, I tell you."

"Yes, dead in body, but not in spirit," the hag moaned. "See there! See how he stalks towards me! He comes! He stands at my side! Oh! horror—horror!"

Maddened with rage and terror by the old woman's cries, Bill Blarney dragged her across the floor and forced her out of the room.

"Silence!" he shouted, "or there will be two deaths in this house to-night instead of one."

Just then the landlord appeared with a light in his hand at the foot of the stairs.

"Curse you!" he cried. "You make noise enough to wake the dead. Stop her tongue, Bill Blarney, or we shall have the night-watchmen surrounding the house."

As he spoke a loud knocking came at the door.

The landlord blew out the light, and simultaneously Bill Blarney seized Mrs. Corcoran by the throat and nearly throttled her.

"Do you know what you have done?" he hissed, "Listen to that knocking and ask yourself who is at the door. Witch! you shall not wait for the gallows."

But for once Bill Blarney had reckoned without his host.

With a quick movement Mrs. Corcoran struck up his hands, and, leaping to her feet, recoiled several paces from him.

"Not yet," she said. "I have had stronger and more desperate men than you to deal with. My feelings overcame me, but I am myself again."

Bill Blarney did not know what to do or which way to turn, and as he stood thus, undecided and cold with terror, the knocking at the door went on.

"Take that woman into the room on the left," the landlord called out. "I must quiet the barking of these bloodhounds!"

Fumbling with locks and bolts, the landlord of the Bull in Top Boots at last opened the door and peeped out.

To his astonishment he only saw Dick Sleuth standing before him.

"What the devil do you mean by this?" the innkeeper demanded. "Have you taken a sudden spite against me? Do you want to call the attention of every constable to my house?"

"Bah!" said Dick Sleuth. "I made sure that there were no traps about before I kicked up such a bobbery. I want to see Bill Blarney."

"He is not here," the landlord replied. "Dick, you are drunk. Go away, and come again when you are sober."

"I am sober enough to know that Bill Blarney is here, and that I must and will see him," Dick Sleuth replied.

"Humph!" said the landlord, as he admitted Sleuth. "You speak boldly. Such words as 'must' and 'will' don't suit me."

"Bah!" Dick Sleuth replied, "don't fly into a temper. Tell Bill Blarney that I have discovered Sir Roland Ashton's hiding-place."

CHAPTER LXXVIII.
SIR ROLAND RECEIVES A VISIT FROM OLD FRIENDS.

SIR ROLAND lay writhing with pain and rage.

He had left the den of infamy into which he had entrapped Daisy Leigh, and was now in apartments taken for him by the ever-watchful Jules Carleon, who followed the baronet about like his shadow.

"Courage, Sir Roland!" Jules said. "All will be well now that the bullet is extracted. In a few days you will be able to go abroad."

"May the hand that fired the shot wither!" Sir Roland said, grinding his teeth furiously. "Just as I raised the cup of pleasure it was dashed from my lips by this foul fiend!"

"True," Jules Carleon said. "But have you not much to be thankful for? You still live, and, therefore, despair not."

"What else can I do?" Sir Roland demanded. "How am I to know that Spring-Heeled Jack is not in the house at this very moment? He seems to possess the power of entering and leaving any place at will."

Jules Carleon shrugged his shoulders.

"It is certainly mysterious," he said; "and yet I have a notion that I shall be able to pay him in his own coin before long. It is time that I went out to purchase the things you require, Sir Roland. You are not afraid of being left alone?"

"It matters little," Sir Roland replied, wearily. "Give me a glass of wine and then go. The pain has abated somewhat, and I will try to get a little sleep."

Jules Carleon left the room, closing the door softly behind him, and Sir Roland, posing his limbs as comfortably as possible, closed his eyes.

He was thoroughly worn out, and in a short time he began to breathe heavily.

He had not been asleep more than a quarter of an hour when a strange clicking sound came from the direction of the window.

Then the curtains parted, and Bill Blarney and Mrs. Corcoran stole across the thickly-carpeted floor.

"See!" Mrs. Corcoran said, "he sleeps."

"Never to wake again," Bill Blarney said, drawing a pistol from under his coat and holding it over the sleeping man. "Ha! what are you doing?"

Mrs. Corcoran was pouring something from a phial into a glass that stood on the table.

"I am killing two birds with one stone," the hag chuckled. "The man who finds Sir Roland's body will turn faint with fear. He will drink, and drink deeply."

Bill Blarney gazed ferociously down at the baronet.

Blarney's finger was on the trigger, but before the hammer could fall Sir Roland started from his sleep and sat up.

Mrs, Corcoran gave vent to a horrible yell, and Bill Blarney, hastily concealing the weapon, started back.

"Mrs. Corcoran! Bill Blarney!" Sir Roland cried. "Do I dream?"

"No," said the hag. "We have found you and thought that we would pay you a visit. "You do not seem very glad to see us."

Sir Roland passed his hand over his brow.

"How did you get into this house?" he asked, "and what is your purpose in coming here?"

Passing his hand under the cushion he produced a brace of pistols.

"Bah!" said Bill Blarney. "If we had intended mischief we could have done it long ago. With regard to how we got here, we came through the window."

"You mean mischief," Sir Roland said, addressing Mrs. Corcoran. "I can see it in your eyes. Keep your distance, or I will blow your brains out."

"Sir Roland," the hag replied, "I have come here to tell you that I have forgiven and forgotten everything. It is absolutely necessary for your safety and mine that our friendship should be resumed."

"Just so," said Bill Blarney, "and they are exactly my sentiments. Are you alone in the house?"

"No," Sir Roland replied, startled at the question; "a sudden cry or a loud sound, such as firing a pistol, my friend, would bring assistance."

Sir Roland moved towards the table as he spoke, and poured wine into the poisoned glass.

"Drink," he said to Bill Blarney.

"No," the ruffian replied. "I have given that; sort of thing up."

"And you?" Sir Roland said, turning to Mrs. Corcoran.

"After you," she said. "I should prefer a little brandy."

"It is there," he said, pointing to the bottle.

Sir Roland tossed the wine down his throat, and immediately a strange and awful expression came over his face.

He clutched his throat.

He uttered gasping cries and tried to speak, but speech failed him, and he reeled back upon the couch.

"Where is his boast about assistance now?" said Mrs. Corcoran. "Nothing can save him. In less than a quarter of an hour he will be a corpse."

Sir Roland still struggled feebly, but at last he became rigid, and a film gathered in his eyes.

"Poor devil!" said Bill Blarney; "he did not like dying at all. I suppose you are now satisfied?"

"Yes, for the present," said Mrs. Corcoran, coolly. "I have settled accounts with one of my enemies, at any rate, and I hope the time is not far distant when I shall have the opportunity of serving them all the same. This affair is over, and I suppose I must remain contented with it as one night's work."

The witch gazed at the ghastly body with fiendish delight.

"Aye!" said Bill Blarney; "and yet it was almost a pity to rob the gallows of its due."

"He was a coward and a villain," Mrs. Corcoran said, "and deserved his fate, even if it had been for that alone. The fool! What mercy could he have expected from me? He should have known me better."

"True; mercy is no ingredient of your nature."

"I never boast of it," said Mrs. Corcoran; "besides, had I spared his life he would doubtless have taken the first opportunity to have sacrificed mine, as he attempted to do before."

"To be sure, that is correct enough," said Bill Blarney, "and perhaps you have acted the wisest part."

"It was an extraordinary circumstance which brought him to this place," Mrs. Corcoran said.

"It was a fortunate one at any rate," said Blarney.

"There he lies," said Mrs. Corcoran; "and the longer I gaze at his odious corpse the more satisfaction do I feel at the vengeance I have obtained. He is gone to his last account, and a very pretty one, no doubt, he will be able to, render. "

"Come, come! we delay," said Bill Blarney, impatiently; "you have exulted enough over the deed, and the sooner we get away the better."

"Stop," said Mrs. Corcoran, approaching nearer to the body. "He may have something in his possession worth taking. It is not likely he would travel without money; I will search him."

She did so, and ransacking every pocket, turned out various sums of money.

"Come," she observed, "this, at any rate, will repay us for our trouble. A goodly sum this. Oh! Sir Roland, I know you were always a famous one to look after the exchequer. But what have we here? Some papers."

"We can peruse them by-and-bye," said Bill Blarney. "Come, come! let us go."

Bill Blarney and Mrs. Corcoran had scarcely made their escape when Jules Carleon returned.

As the Frenchman gazed at Sir Roland his face turned ashy-grey.

"Murdered in my absence!" he cried; "and yet I see no signs of violence."

Seizing the body of the inanimate man in his arms, Jules Carleon bore it to the window.

"Ha!" Carleon said, "the window is open. It is here that the assassins entered. *Parbleu!* it is all over with Sir Roland, I am afraid."

A faint smell came from the baronet's lips, and Jules Carleon guessed the cause at once.

"Poison!" he said. "He may not be dead yet."

Dashing out of the house, he ran to the nearest doctor, and returned with him in haste.

"The man is not dead," the doctor said. "His heart beats. Place him in bed and I will give him a drug which will destroy the effects of the poison."

The doctor's words were prophetic.

Sir Roland Ashton rallied, and when morning came had so far recovered as to eat a slight repast.

But not a word would he say regarding how the poison had found its way down his throat.

He kept his own counsel, and said nothing about Bill Blarney and Mrs. Corcoran.

"There is time yet," he muttered. "They are too clever! I will wait until I can take my revenge at leisure."

CHAPTER LXXIX.

THE FUNDS GROW LOW.

SIR ROLAND ASHTON, having been relieved of the greater portion of his ready cash, found that the funds were getting too low to be pleasant.

He had a few notes left, but they would soon be gone, and he consulted Jules Carleon on the subject.

The Frenchman reflected with his head on one side and his eyes half closed.

"You must tempt fortune," he said. "Why not try the luck of the gaming-tables, Sir Roland?"

"A good idea that, the baronet replied. "It is a long time since I handled a card or shook a dice-box. We will pay our account, Carleon, and remove into a neighbourhood where we can win money, or—"

"Lose it," Jules Carleon interposed. "Fortune does not always treat her clients well at first. Sir Roland, how much money have you left?"

"About two hundred pounds."

"That is a small amount," Jules Carleon said, "but it may prove enough with care. Should that go, how then?"

"Oh! I must trust to chance," Sir Roland replied.

"The estates you spoke of to me are, then valueless?" the Frenchman said.

"I can realise nothing from them at present" Sir Roland replied, bitterly. "If Ralph Ashton were dead—"

"Bah!" said Jules Carleon. "What is the use of waiting for dead men's shoes. Men must keep themselves. Try gaming, and if that fails—"

"Well?"

"You must do as others do—stop at nothing to get your own back with interest."

"You mean that I should turn a common thief?"

"Oh! no," Jules Carleon replied, laughing. "The swindler on a great scale is courted, but the pickpocket goes to prison. When a handsome highwayman is tried all the ladies run to see him and cry and sigh; but who cares for the hungry beggar who steals a loaf?"

"You reason well," Sir Roland said.

The next day saw a great change in the baronet's mode of living.

His time was now passed in one continued round of riot and debauchery, and he was very seldom sober.

But amidst it all, when the circling glass went merrily round, and the ribald jests of his companions made the room resound again with boisterous mirth, could he stifle the voice of conscience?

Could he bury in oblivion the dismal past?

Could he banish from his breast those dreadful apprehensions that rendered his life wretched?

The guilty know no peace.

Winning or losing he drank; he would stagger to his couch and try to sleep.

Sleep! there was none for him.

Frightful forms were continually flitting before his disordered imagination and ringing curses in his ears.

He would start from his bed and rush again to the scenes of wild dissipation, and there increase the torturing anguish of his mind.

Frequently was he upon the very verge of self-destruction.

He carried a loaded pistol with him, and sometimes put it to his head when more than usually despairing, but he shuddered at meeting such an end.

He clung to life in all its misery, for he did not dare to die.

"I am not doomed to perish thus," he would say. "There is another fate in store for me which I shudder to think upon, but which I feel is certain to overtake me. What would I not give were I now as innocent as in the days of my youth! Happy days! doomed never to return."

And then he would beat his breast and remain for some time in a state bordering upon distraction.

Most of the characters with whom Sir Roland had become acquainted were a set of sharpers and blacklegs,[116] who frequented the various gambling-houses then so fashionable in London.

It was not long before Sir Roland was initiated into their arts, and they used him as a dupe and decoy to others.

He became infatuated with their proceedings; for some time they allowed him to be a share in the booty they obtained; and as his own pecuniary means were reduced to a mere phantom of what they formerly were, it offered to him a temptation which it cannot be supposed that a man in his desperate situation could resist.

But this the villains had determined should not last long.

They only watched an opportunity to beggar him altogether.

They formed a plan among themselves by which they should not only obtain the whole of his money, but the share in the plunder he had at different times received from them.

---

[116] Swindler.

The fatal night arrived, and Sir Roland went as usual to the gambling-house, accompanied by two or three of his associates.

There was an unusual congregation of people there, and the play commenced with great spirit. Sir Roland played and won. Elated with success, he staked higher, and won again.

Higher still he staked, and then had to return all that he had won in the two previous games.

Still, nothing daunted, he played again, and once more fortune was against him.

He became somewhat nervous at this unusual bad luck, and looked towards his associates, from whose countenances and observations he could discover that they were bent on winning.

Once more he played for a high stake and was again a loser.

He could not help uttering a curse between his teeth; but desperation urged him on, and again and again he played and lost, until he found himself reduced to a very trifling sum.

The terrors of his situation were now fully presented to his imagination.

He paused for a moment, and scarcely knew how to act; but at length he excused himself to those with whom he had been playing, and going over to his associates, he drew one of them aside, and mentioning the terrible ill luck he had met with, requested the loan of a sufficient sum of money to try his luck again.

A positive refusal, accompanied by some sarcastic remarks, was all he received.

Sir Roland was astonished—confounded, and remonstrated; but an ironical laugh was his only reply, and the fatal truth now became evident to him.

"Villains!" he cried, and clasping his burning temples, he rushed from them.

He went to the table where he had been playing, but those who had plundered him were gone, and he saw the full extent of his misery.

"Duped—ruined! Oh! horror—horror!" he cried, as he darted like a madman from the fatal place and fled he scarcely knew whither.

Oh! the agony of that dreadful moment. He beat his breast and tore the hair from his head in the frenzy of his despair.

He reached the house in which he was living. Jules Carleon met him and saw what had happened.

"You have lost?" he said.

"All!" Sir Roland gasped. "I am a beggar!" I

"Then farewell!" Jules Carleon said. "I must my see to my own interests. Bah! what a fool not to rob instead of being robbed."

The Frenchman passed out of the door, banging it behind him.

Sir Roland's brain whirled, his limbs refused to be support him, and with one intense groan of anguish he sank upon the bed in a state of utter insensibility.

Had that utter insensibility have lasted for ever have been a mercy to him.

But he at length recovered to a full consciousness of his misery.

He looked around him.

His room was buried in profound darkness, but to his distempered imagination frightful objects seemed to flit before his eyes, and the mockery of demons rang in his ears.

He staggered to his feet; the perspiration rolled from his temples in torrents, and a raging fire seemed to burn his brain.

All the events of the evening rushed upon his recollection, and it is a wonder that his reason did not entirely leave him.

"Ruined—irretrievably ruined!" he groaned. "Oh! fool, worse than madman, that I have been to suffer myself to be thus duped by the wretches. And now what is to become of me? Whither can I flee? Where seek for assistance? Assistance! Despair—despair! Oh! I am now indeed fearfully punished for my crimes! And shall I still continue to drag on this life of horror? No; let me die, and at once end this career of crime and anguish!"

He snatched a pistol from the table as he spoke and raised it towards his head.

But again other thoughts rushed upon his brain, and he dropped the deadly weapon from his, hand.

"No, no!" he cried. "I cannot, dare not, die. I dare not meet that terrible eternity where I must render up an account of all the manifold crimes of which I have been guilty. My soul shrinks appalled from the punishment that awaits me. Oh! horror—horror!"

Again the wretched man clasped his burning temples and traversed the room with hasty and disordered steps.

All the torments of perdition were raging in his breast, and he could perceive no ray of consolation, or hope by which to cling.

All was darkness, horror, and despair.

He had but a small sum left, which would only support him for a few days, and then he must become a wretched, wandering outcast upon the face of the earth, with no other resource but to plunge still deeper into crime or to perish of starvation.

The bare thought was enough to drive him to madness, and throwing himself once more upon his bed, the whole of that night he continued to rave in the most delirious manner.

For two days he was in a state of high fever and was unable to leave his room; but at length he recovered sufficiently to walk forth into the fresh air.

He would not visit his former associates, for he now entertained a horror and dread of them, and knew that he should meet with nothing but their scorn and derision.

He wandered from the city into the most secluded part, and where he could commune with his own harrowing thoughts without interruption.

Sir Roland shunned the haunts of man, and prayed that he could have shut himself out entirely from the light of day.

He felt the same bitter hatred for all mankind as he did for himself, and longed that he could flee to some place where he might perish unknown, and his name might be blotted for ever from the memory of all with whom he had been connected.

Here for hours he remained, and did not return to his lodging until the earth was veiled in the solemn darkness of night.

That shelter he must soon abandon, and become a shelterless wretch, unpitied and uncared for.

The time came.

The climax of his misery arrived—his last coin was expended, and he found himself entirely destitute.

No language can properly describe his agony at that time, and again the thought of self-destruction rushed upon his brain, and it was only the fear of dying that once more arrested his purpose.

He was compelled to leave his lodging, but he knew not where to direct his footsteps, and, indeed, all places were now alike to him.

There was nothing but starvation before his eyes, and at one time he thought of giving himself up to the officers of justice and of standing his chance as to the fate which might befall him; but then the idea of an ignominious death upon a public scaffold, amid the execrations and exultations of surrounding thousands, withheld him, and he determined to cling to liberty as long as he could.

The shades of evening had fallen before he prepared to quit his dwelling, and then, snatching up his pistols, and wrapping his cloak closely around him, he cast one glance round the room and quitted it, as he thought, for ever.

Sir Roland hurried through the city, fearful of being seen by anyone, and soon reached the outskirts, where he took the loneliest way he could find, and travelled on he knew not and cared not whither.

"How am I to live," he cried, "without money, without food? Why should I wander on when I know not where to go? And must I remain in this desperate condition until I breathe my last?"

His hand involuntarily grasped one of his pistols, and a fearful idea in a moment shot through his brain.

"Jules Carleon spoke words of wisdom," he said. "I have been robbed of all that I possessed, and why should I not retaliate? Am I to die a lingering death when there are those who have plenty? Have I not already sinned as far as I can go? Am I not a murderer? and why then should I hesitate to become a robber? Away with conscience! I must not, will not, starve."

In that moment the determination of the wretched man was taken.

He looked around him with the hope of beholding some traveller upon whom he might make his guilty attempt.

But not a human being met his view as far as his eyes could penetrate, and he walked on, still fixed and resolved in his purpose.

And now it became still darker than before, and a heavy peal of thunder announced a storm, which soon burst in all its fury.

This increased the misery of Sir Roland's situation, and added to the terrible determination which had taken possession of his mind.

He looked around him to endeavour to find a place of shelter, but nothing of the kind presented itself to his sight, and again he walked on, muttering curses to himself, and fully prepared, in the state of mind he was in, to commit any deed, however atrocious.

Sir Roland continued to travel in this manner for more than half an hour, completely drenched to the skin, and in a most miserable condition, when at last he came to an old shed which stood by the roadside, and gladly availed himself of the temporary shelter it afforded.

He seated himself on a block of wood, and muttered curses on the fate that had driven him to hide his head in such a place.

At length he was aroused by hearing footsteps and looking out, he beheld a man enveloped in a cloak approaching the hut.

Presently he passed by the shed on the opposite side of the road, and Sir Roland saw that, although the man was travelling on foot, he was well dressed and probably possessed a well-filled purse,

Again he grasped the pistol, and watched the traveller with greedy eyes.

His arm was nerved.

He thought of his destitute condition.

There was probably the chance presented to him of replenishing his purse and saving himself from a lingering death.

Sir Roland could not resist the fatal temptation, but stealing out with stealthy and silent footsteps, he pursued the unconscious traveller. He came within a few paces of him, and then he paused.

A deathly sickness came over him, but it was only for a moment; he raised the hand which grasped firmly the fatal instrument of death and shot the stranger down.

His unfortunate victim gave but one frightful groan and then fell lifeless at the feet of his cowardly assassin.

For a moment the villain stood and gazed appalled at the work of his hands. All the horror of his guilt rushed upon his mind, and even then he would have fled from the spot without seeking the object that had tempted him to the deed; but terror transfixed him to it, and he trembled in every limb.

The thunder rolled more heavily than before, as if in anger at the horrible crime, and the lightning flashed, imparting fresh horrors to the scene.

But the fear of someone approaching, and that he would be detected, at length aroused the murderer from the lethargy of horror into which he had fallen.

Stooping down, he turned the corpse of his unfortunate victim on its back.

The lightning flashed on his livid and bloodstained countenance, and again Sir Roland trembled violently and started aghast as he gazed upon it.

Distorted though the features were by the agonies of the violent death he had met with, Sir Roland could see that he was a handsome young man, apparently not more than four-and-twenty years of age, and the elegance of his apparel plainly showed that he was of no mean rank.

With trembling haste Sir Roland searched his pockets and secured a well-filled purse.

He waited for no more, but fled precipitately from the spot, he knew not whither, nor did he stop to ascertain until he had got to some distance from the scene of his dreadful crime, when he found he was returning towards the city.

Sir Roland paused and deliberated within himself how he should act, but at last he determined that he would return to his late lodging, the other inmates of the house not being aware that he n intended to leave it for ever, and, therefore, suspicion of his guilt, he thought, was less likely to be excited.

It would be impossible to describe the feelings of the assassin at that moment.

The fearful groan uttered by his victim still rang in his ears, and every sound that he heard he imagined was that of pursuit.

But the deed was done beyond recall, and there was nothing now left for him to do but to look to his own security.

The murder had been committed in the darkness of night in a lonely spot.

No one had witnessed its perpetration, and, therefore, what had he to fear, unless his own terrors and the tortures of his guilty conscience betrayed him?

No one could suspect that he had done the crime; or even supposing that they should, they had no proof by which to convict him, and, consequently, he was safe—safe from all but the vengeance of offended Heaven, which assuredly, sooner or later, would overtake him.

SPRING-HEELED JACK,
THE TERROR OF LONDON.

THE ROPE FELL CLEAN OVER JULES CARLEON'S NECK.

Fearing, however, that the body of his murdered victim might be discovered by some travellers and a pursuit commenced, he resumed his way with hurried steps, and reached the city without meeting with any individual on the road.

The storm had now entirely subsided, and Sir Roland slowly retraced his steps towards his lodging, which he entered without being observed, and, throwing himself on a seat for a few moments, was completely overwhelmed with remorse and terror.

"So, then," he muttered to himself, "I have again become a murderer; I have now stamped myself a monster of the blackest dye. Lost—lost! no penitence can now avail me, for what penitence can wash out the stain of the awful crimes of which I have been guilty? My days may be prolonged, but what will they be? Those of horror and unceasing torment. And must I not yet plunge still deeper into crime? Oh! yes, unless the avenging arm of Heaven stops me in my career and brings upon my head that retribution which I have so long feared."

He could proceed no further, but rocked his body to and fro in a state of the most inconceivable agony.

The silence of all around even added to his fears.

There was nothing whatever to interrupt the gloomy horror of his thoughts, but still he imagined at intervals that the dying groan of the murdered stranger rang in his ears, and at such moments he would start from his seat and gaze around him, trembling in every limb, and expecting to behold me dead man's ghastly shade standing before him.

At length he became a little more calm.

He opened the purse of which he had plundered the corpse of the unfortunate gentleman and examined the contents.

There was a considerable sum, and Sir Roland wondered that the man had travelled unattended and on foot at that hour, and in so lonely a place, so much property about him.

But he turned pale with horror at the sight of the glittering booty.

Sir Roland had long been hardened to crime, but now a reaction set in.

He had slain an unsuspecting and innocent man for the sake of his money, and each piece of gold seemed stained with the blood of the unfortunate victim.

It would be impossible to describe the tortures which Sir Roland endured on that dreadful night.

Sometimes he threw himself upon the bed and tried to go to sleep, but that was utterly impossible.

His over-wrought imagination pictured all kinds of awful horrors.

The murdered man was always near him.

The dimmed, glassy eyes followed him about, and the voice of vengeance rang in his ears.

At last day began to dawn.

The fitful light crept across the sky; but at last the bright, glorious sun rent the curtain of night asunder, and called upon the living world to be up and doing.

Pale and haggard to ghastliness, Sir Roland filled his hands with water, and dashed it upon his burning face.

Feeling somewhat refreshed, he walked to the window. Opening it, he looked out, and saw some men on their way to work.

How different were they to him?

They were poor, but cheerful.

He had squandered away a fortune in vice and debauchery, and had at last committed a fearful deed to recruit his funds.

But what was he to do when the ill-gotten gold was exhausted?

He could only return to his career of crime, and add to his list of atrocities.

"Miserable, guilty wretch that I am," he groaned; "the dying gasp of the murdered man will ever ring in my ears."

All day long he kept within the house, but as night closed in again his mind was so filled with horrors that he felt compelled to go out into the open air.

Suddenly a thought occurred to him.

Why not go back to the gaming-tables and try his luck once more?

He would now prove a match for the villains who had robbed him before, and he knew them too well to fear that they would ask how he became possessed of fresh funds.

As he made his appearance in the room he was greeted with frowns and jeers, but as he took a handful of gold from his pocket the demeanour of the gamblers changed.

"Why, Sir Roland," said a man, who went by the name of Pilkington, "have you been robbing the Mint, or have you been trying your luck on the road as a highwayman?"

Sir Roland Ashton winced, and went white to the lips.

"No matter," he said, hoarsely. "It is sufficient for you to know that the money is not yours. I am here to play, and not to talk."

"As for that matter," Pilkington replied, "I am perfectly willing to give you your revenge."

The same story was repeated over again.

Sir Roland lost, and saw with glaring eyes the gold swept into the pockets of the scoundrels who were too lazy to do an honest day's work, and lived by preying upon the foolish and weak-minded.

What chance had Sir Roland against such an army of knaves?

When all the money was gone, save a few guineas, he rose from the table and walked out of the room without saying a word.

A peal of mocking laughter followed Sir Roland, but he paid no attention to it beyond shrugging his shoulders and grinding his teeth.

He felt tempted to snatch the pistols from his pocket and put an end to at least one of the gamblers, but he abandoned the notion and strode into the street.

"I have been successful once in my new career," he said. "I must try again."

He paused and started.

A sepulchral voice murmured in his ears.

"Forbear!"

"Bah!" he said, looking round. "It was but my disordered imagination."

"The wages of sin is death," said the voice.

"Base, unreal mockery!" Sir Roland cried, snatching a pistol from his pocket. "Think not to deter me from my purpose. If the voice comes from that foul fiend, Spring-Heeled Jack, let him appear and try conclusions with a desperate man!"

The voice spoke no more, and as Sir Roland could not see a living creature, he walked on through the dark dismal streets until the houses became less.

He was walking in a southerly direction, and presently he came to a stream spanned by a rustic bridge.

Sir Roland stopped, and leaning his arms upon the rail looked down into the water.

"I will make my venture here," he said. "The night will not pass without somebody passing this way."

Even as he spoke he heard the sound of footsteps, and so near him that Sir Roland started violently.

Suddenly the form of a man loomed out of the darkness, and gazed at Sir Roland with astonishment, but with no expression of alarm.

"Ah! my friend," said the stranger, whose features were concealed by a broad-brimmed hat, "what are you doing here? Not contemplating suicide, I hope?"

Sir Roland grasped a pistol tightly and confronted the man.

"What!" the stranger cried. "Would you obstruct my way?"

The voice was familiar to him—or, at least, he thought so.

"I am a desperate man!" Sir Roland said, as he recovered himself. "I am armed with pistol and sword. I must have money. Give it to me, and pass on your way without injury."

"Daring ruffian!" the stranger returned. "If you think you will extort money from me by threats, you will find yourself vastly mistaken. Begone before I punish you!"

"I claim your money or your life," Sir Roland said. "Give me your purse, or take the consequences of your refusal?"

"Stand from my path, you villain," said the stranger, "or, by Heaven! this will be the worst night's work you undertook."

"Since you will not comply with my demands, I must use other means!" Sir Roland yelled.

He presented the pistol at the stranger; but in another instant the weapon exploded harmlessly in the air, and Sir Roland s wrist was held in a vice-like grip.

"Ah! curses on this mischance," Sir Roland cried. "You have gained the better of me. Your name?"

The stranger threw aside his hat and revealed the features of Ralph Ashton.

"Sir Roland," he said, "your career is at an end. I followed you, knowing your purpose."

"The torments of perdition seize you!" Sir Roland gasped. "Have I lived for you to triumph—to be defeated at last? Well, do your work, and do it quickly. My life is in your hands."

"I will not take it in the cowardly fashion you would have taken mine," Ralph replied, scornfully. "Dog as you are, I will fight you fairly. There is light enough for us; for, see, the moon has burst through the clouds. Draw your sword and defend yourself."

As Ralph Ashton uttered these words he flung Sir Roland from him with such force, that the baronet spun round and struck his shoulder heavily against the bridge.

"I thank you for this, Ralph Ashton," he said as he recovered his balance. "I will fight you when and where you please, but not to-night—not to-night."

"Yes; here and now!" Ralph Ashton cried, stamping his foot passionately. "Do you think I will give you another chance to play the part of assassin? The long account between us must be settled at once."

"As you will," Sir Roland said. "I have hated you all my life, and if the fates decree that I must fall, my last breath will invoke a curse on you."

"Of what avail are curses or blessings from your vile lips?" Ralph Ashton returned, as he drew his sword. "Your intended victims are safe; all your plans have ended in failure; and the sharer of your villainy—Jules Carleon—will fall to-night."

"You lie!" Sir Roland hissed.

"Nay," Ralph Ashton replied, "I speak but the truth. He is aware of your last venture—oh! Heaven, that you could sink so low as lo slay a defenceless man—and he is on your track. But another is close upon his heels, and he dies to-night."

"Another!" Sir Roland exclaimed. "I do not understand."

"His name is Lorrimer."

"I know him not."

"It is but an assumed name," Ralph replied. "He is better known as Harry Banks."

At this moment the moon shone out bright and clear, and its light fell full upon Sir Roland's distorted features.

Rage, fear, and every vile passion were depicted there.

"Harry Banks!" he hissed. "I give you the lie back in your teeth. He is playing his fool's part somewhere in the country, and is long-forgotten. My bitterest curse fall upon her— Daisy Leigh."

"So you have thought and hoped," Ralph Ashton replied, smiling; "but I have uttered no falsehood. But, come, draw your sword, for I swear that but one of us shall depart from hence.

"And thus I respond to your challenge," Sir Roland yelled; "and if the wound be not deeper and more effectual than the one I gave you before, I care not how soon I close my eyes upon the world."

The swords of the combatants met with such violence that sparks glinted from them.

Ralph Ashton was as cool as if he were taking or giving a fencing lesson, but Sir Roland was all impatience to end the fray.

Again and again he attempted to break through Ralph Ashton's guard, but each venture was attended by failure, and presently the baronet uttered a cry of pain.

"It was but a touch," Ralph said, lowering the point of his sword. "What! whine and cry like a child at the prick of a pin?"

Sir Roland, abandoning all discretion, rushed forward and lunged so furiously that he lost his balance, and Ralph's sword passed through his body.

"Ah!" the baronet gasped, "I am a dead man."

"One word," Ralph Ashton said, as their eyes met. "Let me hear you utter a word of repentance. Say 'Heaven forgive me!' and I shall be satisfied."

Sir Roland made no reply.

His eyes closed slowly, his arms fell helplessly to his sides, and he sank upon the ground, and after a few convulsive movements lay still.

"He brought his fate upon his own head," Ralph Ashton said, as he wiped his sword and flung the blood-stained cambric over the bridge. "Ugh! I would have spared him had it been possible to do so."

He turned sadly away, and huge clouds obscured the light of the moon as if to shut out the scene.

CHAPTER LXXX.
JACOB BUTLER GOES THROUGH MORE WOES.

THE hackney-coach which contained Jacob Butler and the two constables suddenly came to a standstill.

"Here we are," said Catchpole, thrusting his head out of the window. "Now then, driver, jump down and help us to carry a bundle of madness upstairs."

"I should like to know how much I am to have for this 'ere job," the coachman said, as he descended slowly from the box-seat. "It strikes me that there's more in this than appears on the surface."

"Look here," Grabham growled, as he alighted and rang the bell, "just you attend to your own business. We are constables of the law, and if we are so minded we need not pay you anything."

"Oh! that's the game, is it?" said the coachman. "Well, do your dirty work yourselves, for I'll be hanged if I take any hand in it."

Jacob Butler was still very weak, but a new hope grew into his heart as he listened to the altercation.

The coachman might be inclined to take his part, or better still, if the row went on, he might be able to escape.

Such an opportunity presently occurred. Catchpole, anxious to take his colleague's part, rushed out of one door of the coach, while Jacob, gathering all his remaining strength, flew out of the other.

So quickly was this done that neither the coachman nor the constables had the slightest notion that Jacob Butler had decamped, and they continued to snarl and jangle at each other.

"If you don't do as you are told," Catchpole said, "I'll see that you get seven years."

"Seven years of what?"

"Of transportation," Catchpole returned; "and it is just possible that I could pile it up so that you got a taste of the cat-o'-nine-tails into the bargain."

This so roused the coachman's ire that as he alighted in the roadway, he shook a fist about the size of a shoulder of mutton under Catchpole's nose.

"I'll cat-o'-nine-tails you!" he said.

"Grabham," Catchpole squeaked, "come here! Don't you see that he's going to hit me?"

At that moment the hostilities were interrupted by the door being thrown open by a long, lean, half-starved looking man.

"Is the doctor at home?" Grabham demanded.

"He is," was the reply. "My master is at breakfast, and I wish I was. Lor'! how hungry I am."

"Joles," said Grabham, grinning. "It's my opinion that you were born hungry, and will die so. I wonder what amount of wittles[117] would satisfy you?"

"I never went into that," Joles replied. "All I wish is that I could get enough."

He laid his hand tenderly upon his waistcoat, and groaned dismally.

"Well," he added, "what do you want? Since you come in a coach I suppose you are here on some important business."

---

[117] Victuals, or food.

"We are," Grabham replied, in a solemn voice that befitted the occasion. "We want the doctor to examine the mind of a poor chap."

"Where's the poor chap?" Joles demanded.

"A fainting in the coach," Grabham replied.

"Then all I can say that he has fainted himself under the seat," said Joles.

"Eh! what?" Catchpole and Grabham cried in a breath.

They made a dash towards the coach window and stood there aghast and overwhelmed with astonishment.

"Dash and jigger it!" Catchpole gasped. "Where is he?"

"Where is he?" Grabham repeated. "If you weren't a born fool you could see that he has got clear away and is chuckling in his sleeve by this time."

"Well," said Catchpole, rubbing his nose until it felt red hot, "I'm no more to blame than you. A nice journey we have had for nothing."

As if to relieve his feelings he seized the coachman by the shoulders and bumped his head against the door-post.

Nature had kindly furnished the man with a thick skull, but there is a limit to human endurance in all cases, and the afflicted one suddenly retaliated by hitting Catchpole a staggering blow between the eyes.

This was about the last thing the constable expected.

He who strikes an officer strikes at the law and braves the sword of justice, but the hackney-coachman neither thought nor cared for these things.

Before Catchpole had recovered from the effects of one blow he received another, which produced a pleasing vision of shooting stars, and then he sat down as if a cannon-ball had suddenly taken him in the waistcoat.

Grabham and Joles stood aghast and inactive at these proceedings, and it was not until Catchpole recovered his breath sufficiently to shriek for help that his brother officer drew his staff and attacked the coachman.

But Grabham had reckoned without his host.

He counted upon an easy victory and made a mistake.

Avoiding a blow from the staff, the hackney-coachman ducked his head and, running forward, caught Mr. Grabham in the abdomen and doubled him up like a hedge-hog.

Joles locked the door and bolted upstairs like a rocket.

"I'm a-dyin'!" Catchpole gasped.

"So am I," Grabham groaned. "I never felt so precious ill in my life."

"Well," observed the coachman, grinning, "you can die if you like, but I'll feel obliged if you'll put it off until after you have paid my fare."

"There's a warmint!" said Catchpole, as he staggered to his feet and leaned against a wall. "There's a double-dyed willin for you!"

"Oh!" said the coachman. "I don't mind you calling me names. Shell out—my fare is a crown—or I'll give you another dose of the same kind of physic."

As yet Mr. Grabham had not risen from the ground or made any effort to do so.

If he felt as queer as he looked he was certainly in a bad state.

"Catchpole," he said, panting for breath, "give him the money and let him go."

"But," Catchpole returned, "I haven't so much about me. Of course, I thought you would settle with him."

"Of course you thought I would do everything," Grabham snarled. "Settle! Dash it!

he has almost settled me."

"And I'll do it right off if you keep me here any longer," the coachman declared. "My money, you pair of cowards, or I'll take it out in kicks. Five times twelve makes sixty, so there'll be thirty a-piece for you."

"You'll find the money in my weskut-pocket," Grabham said, looking at Catchpole. "I'm too weak to fish it out. Get rid of the willin; we are sure to drop upon him some other time."

The coachman examined the crown piece, and tested it with his teeth before he put it in his pocket.

Having done so at last, he climbed leisurely upon the box-seat, and took the reins.

"Kim up!" he said to the bony quadruped supposed to be a horse.

The animal responded by trying to fall down, but, having been forcibly reminded that such things as whips had not been as yet proclaimed illegal, the brute trotted away.

Grabham and Catchpole continued to stare at each other.

"I s'pose it ain't any use seeing the doctor now?" Catchpole said.

"Not a bit, you born idiot!" Grabham returned. "We've nothing to do but to go and save up our wengeance. Lend me your arm, for I'm as weak as a half-drowned kitten."

Leaving them to totter away, we will follow the flying footsteps of the ill-fated Jacob Butler.

Well was it for him that in those days the neighbourhood had but one broad street running from Holborn into the Oxford-road—a route so well accustomed to the jolting of the hangman's cart.

The rest of the locality was composed of tortuous, narrow ways, evil-smelling courts and alleys, leading goodness only knew where, but each and every one the hotbed of ignorance, vice, and infamy.

Jacob ran on until his legs refused to go any further, and he took refuge in a dirty little beershop.

A greasy, ill-clad fellow, smoking a pipe scarcely blacker than his own dirty visage, was unfixing an obstinate shutter from the door.

The man swore roundly as Jacob jostled up against him.

"Oh! I beg your pardon, I am sure," he said, breathlessly; "but I am in a dreadful hurry to find a friend, who I thought I saw come in here. Did he?"

"Did who?" the man demanded.

"A gentleman in a white hat, with a green patch over his eye," said Jacob.

Of course he expected to find no such individual as he described, but he felt that it was necessary to say something to account for his unseemly haste.

The landlord of the beershop looked him up and down with supreme contempt.

"Do you think you can catch such an old bird with that sort of chaff?" he asked.

"I—I don't understand your meaning!" Jacob Butler stammered.

"Oh! no; of course not," said the man, emitting a volume of smoke from his mouth. "You'n precious innocent, ain't you? A man with a white hat and a green patch over one eye—ha! ha!"

Jacob Butler felt a little uneasy at the style in which the man treated him, but fearing that his ruthless pursuers might not be far away, he ventured to enter the inn.

"Not yet," said the landlord. "This is the Chequers, and you must give some account of yourself before you set a foot over the threshold."

"What," Jacob cried, in astonishment, "will you not serve me with refreshment? I have money to pay for it."

The greasy man laughed.

"I know which way the wind blows," he said. "The moment I set eyes on you racing down the street I said to myself, 'That cove's been and gone and prigged[118] something, and he's coming to the Chequers to dispose of it.' There, now, haven't I hit the right nail on the head?"

"No," Jacob replied; "whatever I maybe, I'm not a thief."

"Bless me! what a pity," said the landlord of the Chequers; "you are just the cut of one. However, I know that you are in some trouble or other, or you wouldn't be here."

"Well, I will own to that," Jacob Butler replied. "Only give me shelter, and I will pay you well out of my slender purse, and tell you the tale of my woes without a word of a lie."

"You'll be safe here, though the king's army were after you," the landlord said. "I, Ted Nickells, wasn't born and bred here without knowing my way about and how to baffle the two-legged traps. Follow me."

Gratefully enough Jacob Butler did so, and as soon as he and Ted Nickells were locked in a little room behind the bar, he told him the story of his wrongs.

Mr. Nickells did not appear to be much interested.

He smoked a great deal of bad tobacco and drank a large quantity of beer, which Jacob agreed, as a matter of course, to pay for, but he became more animated and genial when the fugitive took half-a-guinea and pressed it into his ready palm.

"Now that you really know how matters stand with me," Jacob said, "I should like to stay here for the rest of the day."

"And all night too, if you like," Nickells replied. "Hullo! Who's that knocking?"

Jacob Butler trembled from the top of his head down to his shoe-strings.

"Keep your teeth from chattering like marrowbones and cleavers," Nickells said, savagely. "I daresay it is only one of my friends, after all. I'll go and see. At any rate, you have nothing to fear."

"I—I am not afraid," Jacob gasped; "I caught a bad cold once, and these fits will come on me sometimes, in spite of myself."

Ted Nickells made no reply to this explanation, but, tying on an apron, he assumed a business-like air, and walked into the bar.

"What! Jem Basker?" Jacob Butler heard him cry out. "Welcome! Come into the parlour, there's only—"

Mr. Butler could not catch the rest of the words which were uttered in a low and subdued tone.

Presently Jacob Butler was regaled with the sight of the new-comer, and the more he took stock of him the less he liked of him.

"You may speak out," Nickells said. "This chap is in a bit of a hobble, and come what may he is not likely to peach. How is it that you have come to London without the boy?"

Jem Basker spat on the ground and jerked out a furious oath from his lips. "The boy is no longer with me," he said.

"Nonsense! bosh! But, stay," Ted Nickells added, "perhaps you have done the proper thing, and got your own price for him?"

---

[118] Stolen.

"I have received nothing but a blow that very nearly knocked the life out of me," Jem Basker replied. "Look here!"

He removed his hat and showed a livid scar running in almost a straight line across his forehead.

"Who did that?" Nickells demanded.

"Spring-Heeled Jack."

Jacob Butler had been sitting on the extreme edge of a bench.

On hearing Spring-Heeled Jack's name mentioned so unexpectedly his legs shot out, and he came down so heavily that every article in the room jumped and rattled.

"What's the matter with him?" Jem Basker demanded.

"Did you—did—did—did you say Spring-Heeled Jack?" Jacob rejoined, as he picked himself up slowly.

"Yes," Jem Basker replied, eyeing the speaker suspiciously. "Do you happen to know anything about him?"

"Oh! no," Joseph replied, hurriedly. "How should I? But I have heard of him, and the very thought of the man—if man he be—gives me a dreadful start."

"Man!" said Jem Basker contemptuously; "what man can fly from tree to tree like a bird? Mercy! I can see him now, hanging by his feet from a branch. Ugh!"

"Yes—yes!" said Ted Nickells, impatiently; "all these fairy tales are very pretty, but what of the boy?"

"I suppose Spring-Heeled Jack has got him," Basker replied. "At all events, when I came to myself, and more than half-dead then from loss of blood, the boy was gone."

"So," said Ted Nickells, "you really think to palm that story off on me?"

"May I—"

The landlord of the Chequers held up his hand.

"Oh! I have heard you swear to this and that," he interposed. "That kind of swearing goes for nothing. Look me in the face, Jem Basker."

He did so, and steadily.

"Enough," said Ted Nickells. "You have spoken the truth."

"Why should I do otherwise?" Basker demanded. "Was it not here that I brought the boy when—"

"Never mind when," said Ted Nickells, interrupting him. "We will keep so much to ourselves, if you don't mind. Have you been to the hall which begins with an M?"

Yes," Barker replied. "I disguised myself like an old man and went there; but the same story was told by a pampered overfed flunkey. 'Out upon all gipsies! Let the dogs on them! Shoot them down like vermin!'"

"Ah!" Nickells ejaculated, "then that fact alone almost proves that the boy has not found his way there."

"How should he," Basker demanded, "unless mere chance took him there?"

"Mere chance, as it is called, does wonderful things sometimes," Nickells observed, musingly. "Well, the matter stands thus. The boy has slipped through your fingers in an extraordinary way, and he must find his way back into them."

"Just so," Jem Basker assented, "and that is what I came to talk to you about. I—"

"Oh! I know what you are going to say before you speak. You are short of money?"

"You are a greater wizard than old Mother Corcoran, who used to be with Sir Roland

Ashton, and was a witch."

Jacob Butler opened his mouth and gave vent to a startled cry.

"There's those spasms again," he gasped. "They always take me unawares."

"I wish you would keep them to yourself for a while," Ted Nickells said, testily. "Your antics are enough to give a man the jumps."

"I'll walk into another room, if you like," said Jacob, who was cold all over with clammy perspiration.

"Do so," the landlord replied. "You will find the public kitchen at the end of the passage."

Jacob Butler walked, or rather tottered, out of the room.

"Is it possible?" he gasped, smiting his brow. "Can it be true? The old hag seems to be known by everybody. What does all this mean? Spring-Heeled Jack—a boy—Mrs. Corcoran. Ah! I begin to think that I had better stayed with Catchpole and Grabham, for if I am not mad now I shall be so soon."

"Where did you pick him up?" Jem Basker asked when he and the landlord were alone.

Ted Nickells explained, and gave a portion of Jacob's story briefly.

"He seems a likely sort of fellow, and may prove useful to us," Basker remarked. "There's something rather sneaky about him, and he would make a splendid spy. You must not be in a hurry to part with him, Nickells."

"You can't be too careful how you deal with a man like that," Ted Nickells replied. "He's all oil when he knows nothing and wants something, but he might turn to vinegar."

"I don't understand."

"Well," said Ted Nickells, "if we employed him to spy on other people, he might turn the tables, and spy on us."

"In that case," said Jem Basker, leaning across the table and speaking in a low tone of voice, "we should have to go to the expense of his funeral."

Ted Nickells laughed as if he had been listening to a good joke.

"I'll tell you what," said he; "there was something in our conversation that upset the fellow."

"So I thought."

"Then we must find it out," Ted Nickells rejoined. "I'll treat him well, and try to get on the right side of his affections."

"If it should transpire that he knows nothing about the Mildendale affair," Jem Basker said, "we can send him there with comparative safety."

"And what if he does?"

"Why, we must keep him under our thumbs, and take good care that he does not leave the Chequers until he has divulged all he knows."

"Right you are!" Ted Nickells returned. "Jem, my boy, your head is perfectly screwed on your shoulders. Who can tell but that this fellow coming here means a slice of luck for us?"

CHAPTER LXXXI.
WELL CAUGHT!

WE left Sir Roland lying upon the ground, prone, senseless, and to all appearances dead.

His sword lay at his side, and his hat close by.

One of the baronet's hands was pressed upon the wound he had received from Ralph

Ashton, but there were no signs of returning life.

He lay there with his face upturned to the lowering sky, and when dawn came the solemn light stole across his features in a grim and ghastly manner.

Slowly the band of light expanded in the eastern heavens, and just as the breeze rose, scattering the clouds in all directions, Mrs. Corcoran, leaning upon a ragged branch, and looking like a witch who had lost her way, hobbled towards the spot where Sir Roland Ashton lay.

"Has Bill Blarney deceived me?" she mumbled. "Has he given me the slip? No—no, he would not be such a fool as that when he knows that I have it in my power to set the bloodhounds on his track at any moment. Something must have happened."

Suddenly the old hag came to a standstill.

She dropped the gnarled branch and flung up her arms.

Then a cry of mingled terror and savage triumph burst from her lips.

"Sir Roland!" she shrieked, as she stood glaring down at the body. "Ho! ho! It is he sure enough! Ah! there is blood upon his coat. My curse upon the man who has robbed me of my revenge!"

She fell upon her knees, and placed her hand upon the regions of Sir Roland's heart.

"Yes—yes!" she cried; "I am too late. He is dead sure enough. Ha! what is that?"

The sound of horses' hoofs caught her keen ears.

Mrs. Corcoran rose to her feet and strained every nerve to listen.

"Should it be Bill Blarney," she said, "he will help me to secure the body. It will be some consolation to know that my hands performed the last offices for Sir Roland."

Suddenly she heard a whistle, and answered it with a shrill cry, and Bill Blarney presently appeared.

"I could not help keeping you waiting," he said. "The traps have been playing a game of hide and seek with me, and—"

"Look there!" Mrs. Corcoran interposed.

She pointed at Sir Roland's body, and Bill Blarney, flinging himself from the saddle, rushed to her side.

"Is this your work?" he demanded, furiously.

"My work!" Mrs Corcoran returned; "my work! Do you think that I should let him die so easily. It was my desire to see him poor, starving, dying, maimed, and then to triumph over his miseries until life could hold out no longer!"

Bill Blarney took one of Sir Roland's hands in his, and then let it fall.

"It appears to me," he said, "that this has been done in fair fight. See, there is his sword and he must have drawn it in self-defence."

"But is he dead?" Mrs. Corcoran gasped. "Tell me that he is not dead! There may—there must be some hope. The man who has led such a life as he has done does not die easily."

"At all events," Bill Blarney replied, "we had better remove the body. The light grows bolder and people will pass this way before long!" Raising Sir Roland's inanimate form in his arms, Bill Blarney placed it across the horse in as easy a posture as possible, and then, taking the rein led the horse away.

Mrs. Corcoran brought up the rear, mouthing, mumbling, and shaking her head, as if there were something novel and delicious in the scene.

"If he be not dead," she said, "I will nurse him. Ah! how tenderly I will nurse him."

"Hold your brimstone tongue!" Bill Blarney said, turning his head. "I have met a good many queer characters in my time, but never one like you. I thought I had a conscience like gun-metal, but I'll be hanged if the sound of your voice doesn't make my blood run cold."

"Thank 'ee, deary," said Mrs. Corcoran; "but don't flatter me."

A savage frown crossed Bill Blarney's face.

"Keep your dearies for that white-livered hound, Jacob Butler!" he said, with an oath. "If you give me any more of that kind of rubbish I'll find the means of silencing you."

"Keep your temper," Mrs. Corcoran returned. "Keep your temper, Bill Blarney. Old as I am I have no more fear of you that the stick I hold in my hand."

As she spoke she cracked her thumb at him, and the ruffian quailed before the glitter of her bead-like eyes.

"Well, well," he said, "I don't want to quarrel with you. Why should I?"

"Because it would not answer your purpose," the hag replied, chuckling. "We ought to understand each other perfectly. If we don't it is time we did."

"Your words imply a threat," Bill Blarney said, fiercely.

"No, not a threat, but a caution," the crone returned. "But get along—get along, for I am anxious to know whether there be a spark of life left in Sir Roland."

They went on at a quicker pace now, and avoiding the main roads, took to the lanes and byeways, and at last Bill Blarney suddenly stopped the horse.

An evil-looking house peeping from behind some trees as if it were ashamed of itself was just visible, and into this building Bill Blarney and Mrs. Corcoran bore Sir Roland Ashton.

They placed him upon a dirty, frowsy bed in a back room.

Bill Blarney tore Sir Roland's coat open and examined the wound.

"He bleeds still," he said. "Give me that piece of looking-glass?"

"What for?" Mrs. Corcoran demanded. "you want to admire yourself?"

"Do as I tell you," Bill Blarney hissed. "You are enough to send a man mad with rage.

Mrs. Corcoran made a horrible grimace as she obeyed Bill Blarney's order.

He brushed the piece of looking-glass carefully with his coat-sleeve, and then held it close to Roland's lips.

Suddenly Bill Blarney removed the glass and looked at it.

"See!" he cried; "there is breath upon it. Sir Roland lives."

"You are a most wonderful man, Bill Blarney," Mrs. Corcoran said, "and I feel that I should like to give you a kiss."

"Ugh!" said Bill Blarney, with a gasp of disgust. "Get out of my sight or I shall be tempted to do you a mischief."

*

Even as these things were transpiring, Jules Carleon, the Frenchman, was plodding along on foot.

He knitted his brows, and compressed his lips as he marched along.

"I was a fool to leave him," he said. "I never gave him credit for so much pluck. Little did I think that he would turn foot-pad, and how strange that I should be there to witness the scene!"

He stopped to look about him—now on the ground still sodden with rain-water, to see if he could find any traces of footsteps, and then across the meadows, which were occasionally illuminated by the light of the moon.

"Why did I not declare myself as he was robbing the body of the dead man?" he continued. "No! no! I was too clever to do that. Sir Roland might have paid the same kind attentions to me. And yet I have acted the part of a fool! I watched him return to the gaming-tables, I saw him stagger out again, a beggar, and then I might have confronted him with safety. It is a marvel how I lost him!"

Jules Carleon twisted his moustache savagely between his fingers.

"It was this way that he came," he added. "I marked his white face, and saw that he was determined to make another attempt to fill his empty purse."

As he finished speaking he stopped at the foot of a narrow bridge.

Jules Carleon's footsteps sounded hollow as he crossed to the other side.

Shading his eyes with his hands, he took a narrow survey of the country, and listened intently to every sound that came to his ears.

A faithful watch-dog was barking in the distance, the trees rustled and swayed gravely, as if whispering important secrets to each other, and the stream ran gurgling and murmuring on.

No other sounds disturbed the stillness of the early morning, and Jules Carleon shook his head dubiously.

"I am afraid that I have come on a fool's errand," he muttered between his set teeth.

"Can it be that Sir Roland saw me, and hastened to make good his flight? Bah! No! Hullo! What's that?"

The sound of a galloping horse had been borne suddenly to his ears.

Turning quickly, he saw a man splendidly mounted on a steed full of mettle.

"Halt, there!" the rider cried. "Jules Carleon, I call upon you to surrender!"

"In whose name?" Jules Carleon shouted.

"In the name of Spring-Heeled Jack," the man replied.

The Frenchman started to run. Terror lent wings to his heels, but something still more swift flew after him.

The man on horseback suddenly loosened a long rope from the saddle-bow, and, whirling it skilfully about his head, sent it whirling and writhing after the fugitive.

The looped end fell fairly over Jules Carleon's neck.

Then the rope tightened, and the Frenchman, uttering a yell of pain and terror, came to the ground with a crash.

CHAPTER LXXXII
LORD MILDENDALE RECEIVES A VISITOR.

WHEN Lord Mildendale had recovered from the effects of the strange and unaccountable vision presented to him on the terrace, he summoned his valet.

The man was a well-trained servant, an individual who never spoke unless spoken to, and one who had made up his mind to be surprised at nothing.

"Harmer," said his lordship, "has anything happened to disturb the household?"

"Nothing, my lord."

"You are quite sure?"

"Quite, my lord."

Lord Mildendale swept his hand across his brow, and, leaning back in his chair, closed his eyes.

"I am not well," he said, speaking with an effort. "Pour a little brandy into a glass and hand it to me."

Harmer hesitated.

"Why don't you do as I tell you?" Lord Mildendale demanded, sharply.

"Pardon me, my lord," the valet returned. "This is the first time that I have kept you, waiting for a moment, but—but, the doctor gave strict orders that you were to take nothing stronger than a little wine and water."

"Hang the doctor!" Lord Mildendale replied. "In future I will judge what is good for myself."

"Very good, my lord," the valet said, and passed the brandy.

Lord Mildendale conveyed the glass to his trembling lips, and then dashed it suddenly down upon the floor.

"No!" he said. "You are right, Harmer, and I am wrong. If I commence I shall go on until madness overtakes me again. Let me think. Has anybody called to-day?"

Harmer fidgeted about and pretended that he did not hear the question.

"I asked you whether anybody had called," Lord Mildendale said, sharply.

"No visitors, my lord."

"Visitors!" Lord Mildendale repeated. "Who worthy of that name have called upon me since? Harmer, you are keeping something from me—I read it in your face. Speak out, or fear my anger."

"Well, my lord," the valet replied, "a man did call at the servants' door; but, as he was of no consequence—merely a beggar, my lord—I thought you would not care to know."

"A beggar, and was he given alms?"

"No, my lord."

"And pray why not?"

"Because—because—"

"Well, because what?"

"Because he was a gipsy," the valet blurted out.

Lord Mildendale started to his feet.

"A gipsy!" he cried. "Why was I not told of this before? How is it that these vagabonds never appear only on this day, the day that brings back all the weary past? You have something more to tell me, Harmer?"

"I would have kept it from you," the valet replied, "for I know how these visits disturb your lordship's mind, The man who came here was apparently old and feeble, but—"

"Yes, yes—go on!" said Lord Mildendale. "Why do you falter and stammer? You drive me to desperation!"

"My lord," Harmer resumed, "I watched the man as he turned away, and suddenly all signs of age and feebleness left him. He stood erect, and, turning towards the hall, shook his fist."

"Ah!" gasped his lordship, "was it a spy in disguise, then?"

"Undoubtedly, my lord."

The nobleman sat silent for a few moments.

"I will go to bed now," he said, "and I shall not require your attendance any more to-night."

"Thank you, my lord."

His lordship sighed wearily as he left the room.

The moment the door had closed behind him the meek and staid demeanour of the valet changed.

Like the man he had described, he shook his fist.

"It is coming home to you now!" he hissed. "You treat your people worse than dogs, but the day of reckoning is at hand!"

Lord Mildendale retired to his sleeping apartment and examined it carefully.

He peeped behind the curtains, as if fearful that an assassin might start out from behind them.

His object, however, was not to go to bed.

Walking to the centre of the room, he stopped and folded his arms across his breast.

"So," he said, "I am to be denied a moment's peace. Those swarthy-skinned villains dog my footsteps and watch my house. I know what they mean—revenge! Ah! me, what is life to me, and why am I afraid to die?"

Suddenly he moved towards an old-fashioned bureau and touched a spring in its side. A secret door flew open.

Lord Mildendale sat down, and, taking a bundle of papers in his hand, smoothed them out carefully, and even with tenderness.

In one of the folded sheets was a lock of hair, as dark and glossy as a raven's wing.

His lordship's eyes grew moist as he gazed at it.

"Oh! my wife," he cried. "Oh! cruel—cruel Fate."

Then a strange and determined expression came over his face.

He put the letters away. He did not close the bureau, but opened another door, from which he took a small bottle, filled with a dark-coloured liquid.

"I have kept this," he said, holding it up to the light of the lamp, "in case that I might be driven to extremities. Ugh!"

He shuddered as his fingers closed upon the phial.

"Why should I hesitate?" he continued. "What else is left? Deserted, friendless, and alone, I am far more miserable than the rag-clad vagabond who whines for bread from door to door. Oh! horror to perish by a murderer's knife, and yet that is my promised doom. I know full well what the vision of to-night meant. It was my death omen."

Walking slowly but firmly to his dressing-table, he poured the liquid into a crystal glass.

"I wonder," he said, as he stood gazing at the reflection of his haggard face in the mirror, "if a single creature will mourn my death or shed a tear over my grave? No—no!"

He raised the glass, and tilted it slightly.

The death-dealing fluid touched his lips, where it stayed, for a hand of iron grasped his wrist.

Lord Mildendale turned cold, and it seemed to him that his heart had ceased to beat.

What new horror was this?

The hand upon his wrist was like ice.

Without the power to resist he gazed at it marking the blue veins and delicate hue of the skin; but his horror grew more intense, and he almost swooned as he saw that long, talon-like nails grew upon the fingers.

At last reaction set in.

Uttering a shriek of terror he tore himself free; and there, standing calmly before him, was the tall, ghostly white form, the horned head, the shaggy hair flowing over the broad muscular shoulders—the awful creature of his vision.

"Who are you?" Lord Mildendale gasped.

"I am called Spring-Heeled Jack," was the reply.

"Are you man or devil?"

"It is not for you to ask such a question," said Spring-Heeled Jack. "Let it suffice that I was sent to save you from a rash and foolish act."

As he spoke Spring-Heeled Jack dashed the glass containing the poison upon the floor, and trampled the atoms under his feet.

Lord Mildendale recoiled step by step from what he took to be an apparition from another world.

"Go!" he cried, wildly. "Torture me not."

"I bring you news," Spring-Heeled Jack said.

"From the region of torment?"

"Nay. News you will be glad to hear. Your son lives!"

Lord Mildendale started forward, but as he did so, Spring-Heeled Jack dashed something in his face, and the nobleman sank slowly upon the ground.

"Good!" said Spring-Heeled Jack. "Strange, indeed, that this man who owns this place knows but few of its secrets."

As he spoke he pressed his hand upon a panel in the wall.

A clicking sound followed, the panel revolved, and Spring-Heeled Jack vanished from the room.

CHAPTER LXXXIII.
SIR ROLAND IN THE HANDS OF HIS ENEMIES

IT was midnight.

A hundred clocks proclaimed the dismal hour.

Some jerked out the notes sharply, but the clock of St. Paul's boomed out each stroke slowly and sullenly, as if rejoicing in the murk and gloom that hung over the City of London.

Just at this time there came bumping and jolting along the Strand a huge, queer-looking vehicle.

At first sight it had the appearance of a hearse, and the sleepy watchmen stared at it stupidly, but made no attempt to approach it.

Those blink-eyed guardians over the public peace and safety were never in a hurry to run their heads into danger.

Indeed, all they ever did was to spring their rattles, wave their lanterns, and shout "Murder!"

The queer-looking thing upon wheels was nothing more terrible than a caravan, such as gipsies use when travelling from fair to fair.

A bony horse attached to it dragged its weary limbs over the uneven road, and it is more than probable that the poor animal would have fallen had not the constant application of a whip, wielded by a brutal man, reminded the beast that it would be as well to keep up.

Suddenly a little window opened, and Mrs. Corcoran thrust out her head.

"My lovey-dovey Billy Blarney," she said. "Wasn't it a good idea of mine?"

"What idea?" grumbled Bill Blarney, who was driving the worn-out quadruped.

"Why, hiring this conveyance. It holds Sir Roland nicely, doesn't it? Poor dear, he can lie down at full length, which he couldn't have done if we had hired a carriage."

"If he feels as easy as I do," said Bill Blarney, "his bones must be coming through his skin. I never had such a jolting and rocking in all my life."

"It will soon be over, my own," the hag returned. "Why have you made up your mind not to go to the Bull in Top Boots?"

"Because the boys would object."

"Object?"

"Yes. Sir Roland would be welcome enough if he had a pocketful of money," the ruffian replied; "but as he hasn't they would kick him into the street, and leave him to die in the gutter."

"Would they, now?" Mrs. Corcoran remarked. "How very unkind of them to be sure! Well, where are we going?"

"To the Chequers."

"Where's that?"

"A house in Smithfield just off Cloth Fair."

"Near our old quarters?"

"Yes," Bill Blarney replied; "but don't bother me with questions just now, or this blessed horse will go down on his knees."

"All right, my diddy-doddy."

Bill Blarney turned round with such a threatening gesture that Mrs. Corcoran withdrew her head precipitately.

"I'd give a few years out of my life to have the pleasure of choking her," Bill Blarney said, brutally. "Bah! the very sight of the old witch turns my heart."

The caravan rolled and jolted on until Blarney brought it to a standstill at the door of the Chequers.

Ted Nickells came running out.

"Why, Bill!" he said, starting at the sight of the ruffian, "who on earth would have thought of seeing you?"

"What, did you think I was dead?"

"The wicked live long," Ted Nickells replied, grinning. "You are a stranger indeed!"

"Am I welcome now?"

"Of course," the landlord replied. "But, I say, what is the meaning of this box on wheels? what is inside?"

"An old hag and a wounded man," Bill Blarney replied, in a whisper.

"Well," said Ted Nickells, "I'll ask no more questions, because I know what a strange fellow you are. Do you require any help?"

"Yes; to get Sir Roland out."

"Not the Sir Roland Ashton I have heard so much about?"

"The same."

Nickells put two fingers into his mouth and whistled shrilly.

"This is a surprise," he said. "Hullo! here is the old lady. Bless me! what a nice old party to take a drive with. Well, well, Bill Blarney. you always were a good judge of beauty."

Mrs. Corcoran put her head on one side and looked waggishly at Mr. Nickells.

"You do not mean what you say," she said. "Ah! men were ever deceivers."

Bill Blarney growled out something under his breath to the effect that there would be no deception in him if he could get Mrs. Corcoran's throat between his fingers.

"Come—come," said he, "we waste time. Let us have Sir Roland out."

The wretched baronet only moaned as he was taken into the house.

They carried him upstairs and placed him on a couch.

"This is a bad case," Ted Nickells said.

"A bad case!" Mrs. Corcoran repeated. "Oh—oh! he is worth a dozen dead men yet. You should have seen him a few days ago. He is quite cheerful now. Aren't you, Sir Roland?"

The miserable, pain-stricken man turned a pleading look upon the hag.

"What have you brought me here for?" he asked, in a voice that was scarcely audible.

"To make you well, deary," Mrs. Corcoran replied.

"Let me die!" Sir Roland groaned. "I shall be much better out of the world. What have I to live for?"

"Lots of things," Mrs. Corcoran returned, encouragingly. "Die! Heyday! I don't intend you to die for many a long day."

"You torture me—you persecute me," Sir Roland said. "You have brought me here out of no kind motive. Why not do your work at once? I am wounded and helpless. Kill me, if you will, but do not increase my pain by taunts and jeers!"

"Hear him!" Mrs. Corcoran said, turning to Ted Nickells. "We found him dead to all appearances, we take him to a nice country house, and supply him with all sorts of nice things, we bring him here at an enormous expense for a change, and this—this is his gratitude."

Sir Roland Ashton rolled his head from side to side, as if the bodily pain and mental torture he suffered were too great to bear.

Even Nickells, hardened as he was to all sorts of sights, could not help feeling a pang of pity for the unhappy man.

"Let him be," he said to Mrs. Corcoran. "You can do no good by worrying him."

"Quite right," said Mrs. Corcoran, courtesying—"you are quite right, my dear sir. I am Sir Roland's nurse, and when he gets well I hope that he will have no occasion to find fault with my treatment. Ha! ha! ho! ho!"

"Get her out of the room," Nickells whispered to Bill Blarney. "She will kill the man."

"It is all very well to say get her out of the room," Bill Blarney returned, "but to get her to do it is quite another thing."

"Does she drink?"

"Like a fish."

"Then I'll give her a dose which will quiet her," Ted Nickells said.

The landlord of the Chequers proved as good as his word.

He went below, and presently returned with a decanter and three glasses.

Putting one into Mrs. Corcoran's hand, he filled it up with brandy.

"Good stuff. this!" said Mrs. Corcoran, smacking her skinny lips.

"Yes," Nickells replied; "and the best of it is the liquor never paid a penny duty. Have another nip."

Mrs. Corcoran did not say No, nor did she object to a third, and presently her cat-like eyes began to blink and grow dim.

Then her head took to nodding, and finally she fell asleep and snored like a litter of pigs.

"Now, then, we can talk with freedom," Nickells said. "I have much to tell you, but I will begin with what has happened lately."

"Fire away," said Bill Blarney. "I am all attention."

"Jem Basker is here."

"Jem Basker! What Jem Basker? The outcast gipsy?"

"Yes."

"Why, it was he who—"

Ted Nickells held up his hand.

"Don't talk so loud," he said. "You remember the old adage that walls have ears?"

"I stand corrected," Blarney replied, softening his voice. "So Basker is here, and I suppose he has brought the boy with him?"

"Nothing of the kind."

"Why not?"

"Because it happens that something or somebody named Spring-Heeled Jack took the boy from Jem Basker."

Bill Blarney uttered an exclamation of surprise and struck himself a heavy blow on the chest.

"Spring-Heeled Jack!" he gasped.

"Yes. Do you know him?"

"I should think I did," Bill Blarney replied. "Why, man alive, if I have had one adventure with that flying demon, I have had a dozen."

"Who is he?" Ted Nickells asked.

"Sir Roland knows," Blarney replied, "or, at least, he says that he has more than a suspicion; but he will not impart the secret."

"Then he must be forced to do so."

"Leave that part of the business to Mrs. Corcoran," said Blarney, laughing. "If she can't screw the truth out of him nobody can."

"You think so?"

"I am sure of it."

"Well, then, we will leave him to her tender mercy," Nickells replied, grinning. "I have told you that Jem Basker is here, but I have said nothing about the other fellow."

"What other fellow?"

"Oh! a soft sort of cove, with frightened eyes, and who almost goes into fits at his own shadow."

"I suppose he has a name, and uses it sometimes?" Bill Blarney said. "What does he call himself?"

"Jacob Butler."

Bill Blarney burst into such a loud roar of laughter that Mrs. Corcoran woke up and started to her feet.

"What a noise!" she gasped. "I was just dreaming a pretty dream—that I saw you in the hangman's cart on your way to Tyburn. What were you laughing at?"

"At one of Ted Nickells' jokes," Blarney replied, cautiously, and winking at the same time at the landlord of the Chequers.

"May I hear it?" Mrs. Corcoran asked, glancing suspiciously from one to the other.

"Well, no," Nickells replied—"that is, you wouldn't care to hear it. It was about a man who came here and borrowed another man's property."

"Oh! that's nothing," said Mrs. Corcoran "I should imagine that happens very often."

"Just so," said Ted Nickells.

Bill Blarney was now more anxious than ever to consult with Ted Nickells.

"We will run downstairs while you look after Sir Roland," he said, glancing at Mrs. Corcoran,

"Very well," she replied; "but I know you want to talk secrets."

As soon as they were below stairs Bill Blarney clutched Nickells by the arm.

"That old witch must not know that Jacob Butler is here," he said. "Keep him close, but keep him out of my sight."

"You seem to be very anxious about this man?"

"I am," Bill Blarney replied; "and I have particular reasons for being so."

Suddenly the door upstairs opened, and the sweet voice of Mrs. Corcoran was heard.

"My lovey-dovey Billy!" she screeched, "Sir Roland has told me something good, and I want you to share it."

The conversation between the hag and the ruffian was carried on in whispers, but it resulted in Bill Blarney making a hasty exit from the Chequers and riding a horse, lent him by Ted Nickells, at full speed towards the village of Hoddeston.

"If Sir. Roland has not lied, or is not mad, a bold stroke means a fortune. Courage! Never say die! Here goes to live like a man or die like a mouse

END OF BOOK I

www.ingramcontent.com/pod-product-compliance
Lightning Source LLC
Chambersburg PA
CBHW062311200726

48292CB00006BA/1960